MORE
Deadly
THAN
THE MALE

MORE
Deadly
THAN
THE MALE

MASTERPIECES FROM
THE QUEENS OF HORROR

Edited by

GRAEME DAVIS

PEGASUS BOOKS
NEW YORK LONDON

MORE DEADLY THAN THE MALE

Pegasus Books Ltd.
148 W 37th Street, 13th Floor
New York, NY 10018

Compilation copyright © 2019 by Graeme Davis

Introduction © 2019 by Graeme Davis

First Pegasus Books cloth edition February 2019

Interior design by Maria Fernandez

Library of Congress Cataloging-in-Publication Data is available.

ISBN: 978-1-64313-011-8

10 9 8 7 6 5 4 3 2 1

Printed in the United States of America
Distributed by W. W. Norton & Company

Dedicated to my wife, my love, and my best friend, Jamie Paige Davis, who proves to me every day that women are amazing. I love you.

CONTENTS

INTRODUCTION *by Graeme Davis*   IX

THE TRANSFORMATION *by Mary Wollstonecraft Shelley*   1

THE DARK LADY *by Mrs. S. C. Hall*   19

MORTON HALL *by Elizabeth Gaskell*   31

A GHOST STORY *by Ada Trevanion*   69

AN ENGINEER'S STORY *by Amelia B. Edwards*   81

LOST IN A PYRAMID, OR THE MUMMY'S CURSE *by Louisa May Alcott*   101

TOM TOOTHACRE'S GHOST STORY *by Harriet Beecher Stowe*   113

KENTUCKY'S GHOST *by Elizabeth Stuart Phelps*   121

AT CHRIGHTON ABBEY *by Mary Elizabeth Braddon*   139

THE FATE OF MADAME CABANEL *by Eliza Lynn Linton*   171

FOREWARNED, FOREARMED *by Mrs. J. H. Riddell*   187

THE PORTRAIT *by Margaret Oliphant*   205

THE SHRINE OF DEATH *by Lady Dilke*   243

THE BECKSIDE BOGGLE *by Alice Rea*   249

THE HIDDEN DOOR *by Vernon Lee*   265

UNEXPLAINED *by Mary Louisa Molesworth*   291

LET LOOSE *by Mary Cholmondely*   339

THE CAVE OF THE ECHOES *by Helena Blavatsky*   357

THE YELLOW WALL PAPER *by Charlotte Perkins Gilman*   369

THE MASS FOR THE DEAD *by Edith Nesbit*   387

THE TYBURN GHOST *by The Countess of Munster*   397

THE DUCHESS AT PRAYER *by Edith Wharton*   405

THE VACANT LOT *by Mary E. Wilkins-Freeman*   427

AN UNSCIENTIFIC STORY *by Louise J. Strong*   443

A DISSATISFIED SOUL *by Annie Trumbull Slosson*   457

THE READJUSTMENT *by Mary Austin*   475

ACKNOWLEDGMENTS   483

INTRODUCTION

by Graeme Davis

In the seventeenth and eighteenth centuries, so-called "conduct books" advised parents—especially fathers—on how to instruct their children—especially daughters—in the ways of genteel civility. In these books, and elsewhere, a great deal of ink was devoted to the corrupting influence of the popular novel. Novels—indeed, all forms of popular fiction—supposedly stirred the emotions to an unhealthy pitch, instilling false expectations of life and false values in the reader, and over-indulgence in sensational reading was a sure step on the road to ruin.

And yet, women were not only reading Gothic and other sensational fiction: they were writing it as well. Clara Reeve—a clergyman's daughter, no less—published a Gothic novel titled *The Champion of Virtue* (later retitled *The Old English Baron*) in 1777, in imitation of Hugh Walpole's seminal *The Castle of Otranto*. Ann Radcliffe's two-volume novel *A Sicilian Romance* introduced the brooding "Byronic hero," modeled on the scandalous poet: this archetype is the direct ancestor of Edward Cullen and Christian Grey. Radcliffe went on to create the four-volume classic *The Mysteries of Udolfo*, and her work is said to have inspired later writers from Fyodor Dostoyevsky to Edgar Allan Poe and the Marquis de Sade. Her father was a respectable London haberdasher who moved to fashionable Bath to run a china shop.

To today's readers, though, one name stands above all: Mary Wollstonecraft Shelley, the author of *Frankenstein*. Although she stood on the shoulders of Reeve, Radcliffe, and other pioneering women, hers is the first work to have achieved true immortality. It certainly did not hurt that the story was conceived during a thunderstorm as part of a storytelling contest involving her husband, the Romantic poet Percy Bysshe Shelley, Lord Byron, and Byron's physician John Polidori, whose own entry became the first-ever vampire novel.

If the idea of women reading novels made men uncomfortable, then the thought of women writing novels was even more insupportable. Many female writers, like the Brontë sisters, decided to publish under male pseudonyms—Currier, Ellis, and Acton Bell in their cases—while others went by their initials, just as J. K. Rowling did two centuries later. Others still refused to bow to social pressure and published boldly under their own names.

However, according to British author and journalist Hephzibah Anderson, it was not until the 1970s that scholars and critics began to appreciate how an author's gender affected the horror fiction they wrote. In Charlotte Perkins Gillman's "The Yellow Wall Paper," for example, Anderson sees the author's postpartum depression elevated to near-psychotic levels by the restrictive, paternalistic confinement she suffered. Elsewhere there are hints of marital resentments transformed into bloody tales of murder and vengeful ghosts haunting the perpetrators of those crimes great and small that were part and parcel of a woman's existence in those times—and many of which still remain disturbingly commonplace today.

Not all horror stories written by women contain these subtexts, of course, and not all female ghosts are avengers freed by death from the constraints of society. It is as invidious and patronizing to define these writers solely by their gender as it would be to do so based on race, class, or any other factor. However, it is noticeable that many female writers excel at writing a more thoughtful, psychological form of horror tale, with little or none of the gore and sadism that can be found in the work of some male authors.

Violet Paget (who wrote as Vernon Lee) used the supernatural with such a light touch that it is not always easy to distinguish her horror tales from her social commentary.

Other writers embraced the supernatural with both hands. Mary Shelley could handle supernatural horror as deftly as the science fiction of *Frankenstein*. In "The Beckside Boggle," Alice Rea brings a common piece of English folklore to hair-raising life, while Helene Blavatsky, best known as the founder of the spiritualist Theosophical Society, tells a very serviceable ghost story in "The Cave of the Echoes."

Perhaps most interesting, though, are the unexpected tales by authors who became so famous for their work in other genres that their forays into the horror genre are all but forgotten. Louisa May Alcott and Harriet Beecher Stowe are certainly not remembered for their horror tales, while only horror connoisseurs remember Edith Nesbit for anything other than *The Railway Children*. Edith Wharton's great novel *The Age of Innocence* won her the Pulitzer Prize and she was nominated three times for the Nobel Prize for Literature, yet her horror stories are known only to a comparative few.

Wharton is not alone. Many of the authors in this collection wrote across a range of genres, and here, perhaps, is the greatest contrast with their male counterparts. Writers like Poe, Lovecraft, and M. R. James tended to stay within their genre, assiduously feeding the audiences who brought them fame and fortune; on the other hand, many of the ladies whose work graces these pages wrote whatever they pleased, crossing boundaries and blending genres as each story required. If they refused to be confined by social ideas of feminine gentility, they were equally reluctant to embrace the literary restrictions of genre and market. They just wrote damned good stories.

THE TRANSFORMATION

by Mary Wollstonecraft Shelley

1830

The daughter of the feminist philosopher Mary Wollstonecraft and the political philosopher, novelist, and proto-anarchist William Godwin, Mary is best known as the author of Frankenstein *and as the wife of the Romantic poet Percy Bysshe Shelley, a friend of Lord Byron. It is hard to imagine a background and career further from the ideals of feminine gentility.*

Mary never knew her mother, who died less than a month after her birth. She had a strained relationship with her father's second wife, a neighbor named Mary Jane Clairmont, whom he married four years later, but she received a broad and unconventional education based around her father's political theories.

Godwin's published works promoting justice and attacking political institutions won him many admirers, and among them was the poet Shelley. He was married when Mary met him in 1814, but they began an affair, which resulted in Mary becoming pregnant and the pair facing ostracism and poverty.

In 1816, Mary and Shelley famously traveled to Italy with Byron and his personal physician, John Polidori. It was on this trip that the idea for Frankenstein *was born. They married later that year, after the suicide of Shelley's first wife.*

Mary was a prolific writer. In addition to Frankenstein, *she wrote the post-apocalyptic tale* The Last Man *(1826), the historical novel* The Fortunes of Perkin Warbeck *(1830), and several other novels as well as short stories, travelogues, and reviews. Gothic and weird themes characterized much of her short fiction: in "The Transformation," Shelley anticipates Anne Rice's* The Tale of the Body Thief *with a story of a dissolute youth tricked into exchanging bodies with a misshapen and blasphemous creature. The story is full of textbook Gothic elements: decadence, poverty, rebellion, and endangered virtue.*

"Forthwith this frame of mine was wrench'd
With a woful agony,
Which forced me to begin my tale,
And then it set me free.

"Since then, at an uncertain hour,
That agony returns;
And till my ghastly tale is told
This heart within me burns."

—*Coleridge's Ancient Mariner*

I have heard it said, that, when any strange, supernatural, and necromantic adventure has occurred to a human being, that being, however desirous he may be to conceal the same, he feels at certain periods torn up as it were by an intellectual earthquake, and is forced to bare the inner depths of his spirit to another. I am a witness of the truth of this. I have dearly sworn to myself never to reveal to human ears the horrors to which I once, in excess of fiendly* pride, delivered myself over. The holy man who heard my confession, and reconciled me to the Church, is dead. None knows that once—

Why should it not be thus? Why tell a tale of impious tempting of Providence, and soul-subduing humiliation? Why? answer me, ye who are wise in the secrets of human nature! I only know that so it is; and in spite of strong resolve,—of a pride that too much masters me—of shame, and even of fear, so to render myself odious to my species,—I must speak.

Genoa! my birthplace—proud city! looking upon the blue Mediterranean—dost thou remember me in my boyhood, when thy cliffs and promontories, thy bright sky and gay vineyards, were my world? Happy time! when to the young heart the narrow-bounded universe, which leaves, by its very limitation, free scope to the imagination, enchains our physical energies, and, sole period in our lives, innocence and enjoyment are united. Yet, who can look back to childhood, and not remember its sorrows and its harrowing fears? I was born with the most imperious, haughty, tameless spirit. I quailed before my father only; and he, generous and noble, but capricious and tyrannical, at once fostered and checked the wild impetuosity of my character, making obedience necessary, but inspiring no respect for the motives which guided his commands. To be a man, free, independent; or, in better words, insolent and domineering, was the hope and prayer of my rebel heart.

My father had one friend, a wealthy Genoese noble, who in a political tumult was suddenly sentenced to banishment, and his property confiscated. The Marchese Torella went into exile alone. Like my father, he was a widower: he had one child, the almost infant Juliet, who was left under my father's guardianship. I should certainly have been unkind to the lovely girl, but that I was forced by my position to become her protector. A variety of childish incidents all tended to one point,—to make Juliet see in me a rock of defence; I in her, one who must perish through the soft sensibility of her nature too rudely visited, but for my guardian care. We grew up together. The opening rose in May was not more sweet than this dear girl. An irradiation of beauty was spread over her face. Her form, her

---

* i.e., fiendish.

3

step, her voice—my heart weeps even now, to think of all of relying, gentle, loving, and pure, that she enshrined. When I was eleven and Juliet eight years of age, a cousin of mine, much older than either—he seemed to us a man—took great notice of my playmate; he called her his bride, and asked her to marry him. She refused, and he insisted, drawing her unwillingly towards him. With the countenance and emotions of a maniac I threw myself on him—I strove to draw his sword—I clung to his neck with the ferocious resolve to strangle him: he was obliged to call for assistance to disengage himself from me. On that night I led Juliet to the chapel of our house: I made her touch the sacred relics—I harrowed her child's heart, and profaned her child's lips with an oath, that she would be mine, and mine only.

Well, those days passed away. Torella returned in a few years, and became wealthier and more prosperous than ever. When I was seventeen, my father died; he had been magnificent to prodigality; Torella rejoiced that my minority would afford an opportunity for repairing my fortunes. Juliet and I had been affianced beside my father's deathbed—Torella was to be a second parent to me.

I desired to see the world, and I was indulged. I went to Florence, to Rome, to Naples; thence I passed to Toulon, and at length reached what had long been the bourne* of my wishes, Paris. There was wild work in Paris then. The poor king, Charles the Sixth, now sane, now mad, now a monarch, now an abject slave, was the very mockery of humanity. The queen, the dauphin, the Duke of Burgundy, alternately friends and foes,—now meeting in prodigal feasts, now shedding blood in rivalry,—were blind to the miserable state of their country, and the dangers that impended over it, and gave themselves wholly up to dissolute enjoyment or savage strife. My character still followed me. I was arrogant and self-willed; I loved display, and above all, I threw off all control. My young friends were eager to foster passions which furnished them with pleasures. I was deemed handsome—I was master of every knightly accomplishment. I was disconnected with any political party. I grew a favourite with all: my presumption and arrogance

---

* An archaic word for a destination, among other things. "The undiscovered country from whose *bourn* no traveler returns." —Hamlet

4

was pardoned in one so young: I became a spoiled child. Who could control me? not the letters and advice of Torella—only strong necessity visiting me in the abhorred shape of an empty purse. But there were means to refill this void. Acre after acre, estate after estate, I sold. My dress, my jewels, my horses and their caparisons, were almost unrivalled in gorgeous Paris, while the lands of my inheritance passed into possession of others.

The Duke of Orleans was waylaid and murdered by the Duke of Burgundy. Fear and terror possessed all Paris. The dauphin and the queen shut themselves up; every pleasure was suspended. I grew weary of this state of things, and my heart yearned for my boyhood's haunts. I was nearly a beggar, yet still I would go there, claim my bride, and rebuild my fortunes. A few happy ventures as a merchant would make me rich again. Nevertheless, I would not return in humble guise. My last act was to dispose of my remaining estate near Albaro for half its worth, for ready money. Then I despatched all kinds of artificers, arras, furniture of regal splendour, to fit up the last relic of my inheritance, my palace in Genoa. I lingered a little longer yet, ashamed at the part of the prodigal returned, which I feared I should play. I sent my horses. One matchless Spanish jennet* I despatched to my promised bride: its caparisons flamed with jewels and cloth of gold. In every part I caused to be entwined the initials of Juliet and her Guido. My present found favour in hers and in her father's eyes.

Still to return a proclaimed spendthrift, the mark of impertinent wonder, perhaps of scorn, and to encounter singly the reproaches or taunts of my fellow-citizens, was no alluring prospect. As a shield between me and censure, I invited some few of the most reckless of my comrades to accompany me: thus I went armed against the world, hiding a rankling feeling, half fear and half penitence, by bravado.

I arrived in Genoa. I trod the pavement of my ancestral palace. My proud step was no interpreter of my heart, for I deeply felt that, though surrounded by every luxury, I was a beggar. The first step I took in claiming Juliet must widely declare me such. I read contempt or pity in the looks of all. I fancied that rich and poor, young and old, all regarded me with derision. Torella came not near me. No wonder that my second father should

---

* A type of light horse.

expect a son's deference from me in waiting first on him. But, galled and stung by a sense of my follies and demerit, I strove to throw the blame on others. We kept nightly orgies in Palazzo Carega. To sleepless, riotous nights followed listless, supine mornings. At the Ave Maria we showed our dainty persons in the streets, scoffing at the sober citizens, casting insolent glances on the shrinking women. Juliet was not among them—no, no; if she had been there, shame would have driven me away, if love had not brought me to her feet.

I grew tired of this. Suddenly I paid the Marchese a visit. He was at his villa, one among the many which deck the suburb of San Pietro d'Arena. It was the month of May, the blossoms of the fruit-trees were fading among thick, green foliage; the vines were shooting forth; the ground strewed with the fallen olive blooms; the firefly was in the myrtle hedge; heaven and earth wore a mantle of surpassing beauty. Torella welcomed me kindly, though seriously; and even his shade of displeasure soon wore away. Some resemblance to my father—some look and tone of youthful ingenuousness, softened the good old man's heart. He sent for his daughter—he presented me to her as her betrothed. The chamber became hallowed by a holy light as she entered. Hers was that cherub look, those large, soft eyes, full dimpled cheeks, and mouth of infantine sweetness, that expresses the rare union of happiness and love. Admiration first possessed me; she is mine! was the second proud emotion, and my lips curled with haughty triumph. I had not been the *enfant gâté** of the beauties of France not to have learnt the art of pleasing the soft heart of woman. If towards men I was overbearing, the deference I paid to them was the more in contrast. I commenced my courtship by the display of a thousand gallantries to Juliet, who, vowed to me from infancy, had never admitted the devotion of others; and who, though accustomed to expressions of admiration, was uninitiated in the language of lovers.

For a few days all went well. Torella never alluded to my extravagance; he treated me as a favourite son. But the time came, as we discussed the preliminaries to my union with his daughter, when this fair face of things should be overcast. A contract had been drawn up in my father's lifetime.

---

* French: a spoiled child.

I had rendered this, in fact, void by having squandered the whole of the wealth which was to have been shared by Juliet and myself. Torella, in consequence, chose to consider this bond as cancelled, and proposed another, in which, though the wealth he bestowed was immeasurably increased, there were so many restrictions as to the mode of spending it, that I, who saw independence only in free career being given to my own imperious will, taunted him as taking advantage of my situation, and refused utterly to subscribe to his conditions. The old man mildly strove to recall me to reason. Roused pride became the tyrant of my thought: I listened with indignation—I repelled him with disdain.

"Juliet, thou art mine! Did we not interchange vows in our innocent childhood? Are we not one in the sight of God? and shall thy cold-hearted, cold-blooded father divide us? Be generous, my love, be just; take not away a gift, last treasure of thy Guido—retract not thy vows—let us defy the world, and, setting at nought the calculations of age, find in our mutual affection a refuge from every ill."

Fiend I must have been with such sophistry to endeavour to poison that sanctuary of holy thought and tender love. Juliet shrank from me affrighted. Her father was the best and kindest of men, and she strove to show me how, in obeying him, every good would follow. He would receive my tardy submission with warm affection, and generous pardon would follow my repentance;—profitless words for a young and gentle daughter to use to a man accustomed to make his will law, and to feel in his own heart a despot so terrible and stern that he could yield obedience to nought save his own imperious desires! My resentment grew with resistance; my wild companions were ready to add fuel to the flame. We laid a plan to carry off Juliet. At first it appeared to be crowned with success. Midway, on our return, we were overtaken by the agonized father and his attendants. A conflict ensued. Before the city guard came to decide the victory in favour of our antagonists, two of Torella's servitors were dangerously wounded.

This portion of my history weighs most heavily with me. Changed man as I am, I abhor myself in the recollection. May none who hear this tale ever have felt as I. A horse driven to fury by a rider armed with barbed spurs was not more a slave than I to the violent tyranny of my temper. A fiend possessed my soul, irritating it to madness. I felt the voice of conscience within me; but if I yielded to it for a brief interval, it was only to be a moment after torn, as by a whirlwind, away—borne along on the stream of desperate rage—the plaything of the storms engendered by pride. I was imprisoned, and, at the instance of Torella, set free. Again I returned to carry off both him and his child to France, which hapless country, then preyed on by freebooters and gangs of lawless soldiery, offered a grateful refuge to a criminal like me. Our plots were discovered. I was sentenced to banishment; and, as my debts were already enormous, my remaining property was put in the hands of commissioners for their payment. Torella again offered his mediation, requiring only my promise not to renew my abortive attempts on himself and his daughter. I spurned his offers, and fancied that I triumphed when I was thrust out from Genoa, a solitary and penniless exile. My companions were gone: they had been dismissed the city some weeks before, and were already in France. I was alone—friendless, with neither sword at my side, nor ducat in my purse.

I wandered along the sea-shore, a whirlwind of passion possessing and tearing my soul. It was as if a live coal had been set burning in my breast. At first I meditated on what I should do. I would join a band of freebooters. Revenge!—the word seemed balm to me; I hugged it, caressed it, till, like a serpent, it stung me. Then again I would abjure and despise Genoa, that little corner of the world. I would return to Paris, where so many of my friends swarmed; where my services would be eagerly accepted; where I would carve out fortune with my sword, and make my paltry birthplace and the false Torella rue the day when they drove me, a new Coriolanus, from her walls. I would return to Paris—thus on foot—a beggar—and present myself in my poverty to those I had formerly entertained sumptuously? There was gall in the mere thought of it.

The reality of things began to dawn upon my mind, bringing despair in its train. For several months I had been a prisoner: the evils of my dungeon had whipped my soul to madness, but they had subdued my corporeal frame. I was weak and wan. Torella had used a thousand artifices to administer to my comfort; I had detected and scorned them all, and I reaped the harvest of my obduracy. What was to be done? Should I crouch before my foe, and sue for forgiveness?—Die rather ten thousand deaths!—Never should they obtain that victory! Hate—I swore eternal hate!

Hate from whom?—to whom?—From a wandering outcast—to a mighty noble! I and my feelings were nothing to them: already had they forgotten one so unworthy. And Juliet!—her angel face and sylph-like form gleamed among the clouds of my despair with vain beauty; for I had lost her—the glory and flower of the world! Another will call her his!—that smile of paradise will bless another!

Even now my heart fails within me when I recur to this rout of grim-visaged ideas. Now subdued almost to tears, now raving in my agony, still I wandered along the rocky shore, which grew at each step wilder and more desolate. Hanging rocks and hoar precipices overlooked the tideless ocean; black caverns yawned; and for ever, among the seaworn recesses, murmured and dashed the unfruitful waters. Now my way was almost barred by an abrupt promontory, now rendered nearly impracticable by fragments fallen from the cliff. Evening was at hand, when, seaward, arose, as if on the waving of a wizard's wand, a murky web of clouds, blotting the late azure sky, and darkening and disturbing the till now placid deep. The clouds had strange, fantastic shapes, and they changed and mingled and seemed to be driven about by a mighty spell. The waves raised their white crests; the thunder first muttered, then roared from across the waste of waters, which took a deep purple dye, flecked with foam. The spot where I stood looked, on one side, to the widespread ocean; on the other, it was barred by a rugged promontory. Round this cape suddenly came, driven by the wind, a vessel. In vain the mariners tried to force a path for her to the open sea—the gale drove her on the rocks. It will perish!—all on board will perish! Would I were among them! And to my young heart the idea of death came for the first time blended with that of joy. It was an awful sight to behold that vessel struggling with her fate. Hardly could I discern the sailors, but I heard them. It was soon all over! A rock, just covered by the tossing waves, and so unperceived, lay in wait for its prey. A crash of thunder broke over my head at the moment that, with a frightful shock, the vessel dashed upon her unseen enemy. In a brief space of time she went to pieces. There I stood in safety; and there were my fellow-creatures battling, how hopelessly, with annihilation. Methought I saw them struggling—too truly did I hear their shrieks, conquering the barking surges in their shrill agony. The dark breakers threw hither and thither the fragments of the wreck: soon it disappeared. I had been fascinated to gaze till the end: at last I sank on my knees—I covered my face with my hands. I again looked up; something was floating on the billows towards the shore. It neared and neared. Was that a human form? It grew more and more distinct; and at last a mighty wave, lifting the whole freight, lodged it upon a rock. A human being bestriding a sea-chest!—a human being! Yet was it one? Surely never such had existed before—a misshapen dwarf, with squinting eyes, distorted features, and body deformed, till it became a horror to behold. My blood, lately warming towards a fellow-being so snatched from a watery tomb, froze in my heart. The dwarf got off his chest; he tossed his straight, struggling hair from his odious visage.

"By St. Beelzebub!" he exclaimed, "I have been well bested." He looked round and saw me. "Oh, by the fiend! here is another ally of the mighty One. To what saint did you offer prayers, friend—if not to mine? Yet I remember you not on board."

I shrank from the monster and his blasphemy. Again he questioned me, and I muttered some inaudible reply. He continued:—

"Your voice is drowned by this dissonant roar. What a noise the big ocean makes! Schoolboys bursting from their prison are not louder than these waves set free to play. They disturb me. I will no more of their ill-timed brawling. Silence, hoary One!—Winds, avaunt!—to your homes!—Clouds, fly to the antipodes, and leave our heaven clear!"

As he spoke, he stretched out his two long, lank arms, that looked like spider's claws, and seemed to embrace with them the expanse before him. Was it a miracle? The clouds became broken and fled; the azure sky first peeped out, and then was spread a calm field of blue above us; the stormy gale was exchanged to the softly breathing west; the sea grew calm; the waves dwindled to riplets.

"I like obedience even in these stupid elements," said the dwarf. "How much more in the tameless mind of man! It was a well-got-up storm, you must allow—and all of my own making."

It was tempting Providence to interchange talk with this magician. But *Power*, in all its shapes, is respected by man. Awe, curiosity, a clinging fascination, drew me towards him.

"Come, don't be frightened, friend," said the wretch: "I am good-humoured when pleased; and something does please me in your well-proportioned body and handsome face, though you look a little woe-begone. You have suffered a land—I, a sea wreck. Perhaps I can allay the tempest of your fortunes as I did my own. Shall we be friends?"—And he held out his hand; I could not touch it. "Well, then, companions—that will do as well. And now, while I rest after the buffeting I underwent just now, tell me why, young and gallant as you seem, you wander thus alone and downcast on this wild sea-shore."

The voice of the wretch was screeching and horrid, and his contortions as he spoke were frightful to behold. Yet he did gain a kind of influence over me, which I could not master, and I told him my tale. When it was ended, he laughed long and loud: the rocks echoed back the sound: hell seemed yelling around me.

"Oh, thou cousin of Lucifer!" said he; "so thou too hast fallen through thy pride; and, though bright as the son of Morning, thou art ready to give up thy good looks, thy bride, and thy well-being, rather than submit thee to the tyranny of good. I honour thy choice, by my soul!—So thou hast fled, and yield the day; and mean to starve on these rocks, and to let the birds peck out thy dead eyes, while thy enemy and thy betrothed rejoice in thy ruin. Thy pride is strangely akin to humility, methinks."

As he spoke, a thousand fanged thoughts stung me to the heart.

"What would you that I should do?" I cried.

"I!—Oh, nothing, but lie down and say your prayers before you die. But, were I you, I know the deed that should be done."

I drew near him. His supernatural powers made him an oracle in my eyes; yet a strange unearthly thrill quivered through my frame as I said, "Speak!—teach me—what act do you advise?"

"Revenge thyself, man!—humble thy enemies!—set thy foot on the old man's neck, and possess thyself of his daughter!"

"To the east and west I turn," cried I, "and see no means! Had I gold, much could I achieve; but, poor and single, I am powerless."

The dwarf had been seated on his chest as he listened to my story. Now he got off; he touched a spring; it flew open! What a mine of wealth—of blazing jewels, beaming gold, and pale silver—was displayed therein. A mad desire to possess this treasure was born within me.

"Doubtless," I said, "one so powerful as you could do all things."

"Nay," said the monster humbly, "I am less omnipotent than I seem. Some things I possess which you may covet; but I would give them all for a small share, or even for a loan of what is yours."

"My possessions are at your service," I replied bitterly—"my poverty, my exile, my disgrace—I make a free gift of them all."

"Good! I thank you. Add one other thing to your gift, and my treasure is yours."

"As nothing is my sole inheritance, what besides nothing would you have?"

"Your comely face and well-made limbs."

I shivered. Would this all-powerful monster murder me? I had no dagger. I forgot to pray—but I grew pale.

"I ask for a loan, not a gift," said the frightful thing: "lend me your body for three days—you shall have mine to cage your soul the while, and, in payment, my chest. What say you to the bargain?—Three short days."

We are told that it is dangerous to hold unlawful talk; and well do I prove the same. Tamely written down, it may seem incredible that I should lend any ear to this proposition; but, in spite of his unnatural ugliness, there was something fascinating in a being whose voice could govern earth, air, and sea. I felt a keen desire to comply; for with that chest I could command the worlds. My only hesitation resulted from a fear that he would not be true to his bargain. Then, I thought, I shall soon die here on these lonely sands, and the limbs he covets will be mine no more:—it is worth the chance. And, besides, I knew that, by all the rules of art-magic, there were formula and oaths which none of its practisers dared break. I hesitated to reply; and he went on, now displaying his wealth, now speaking of the petty price he demanded, till it seemed madness to refuse. Thus is it;—place our bark in the current of the stream, and down, over fall and cataract it is hurried; give up our conduct to the wild torrent of passion, and we are away, we know not whither.

He swore many an oath, and I adjured him by many a sacred name; till I saw this wonder of power, this ruler of the elements, shiver like an autumn leaf before my words; and as if the spirit spake unwillingly and perforce within him, at last, he, with broken voice, revealed the spell whereby he might be obliged, did he wish to play me false, to render up the unlawful spoil. Our warm life-blood must mingle to make and to mar the charm.

Enough of this unholy theme. I was persuaded—the thing was done. The morrow dawned upon me as I lay upon the shingles, and I knew not my own shadow as it fell from me. I felt myself changed to a shape of horror, and cursed my easy faith and blind credulity. The chest was there—there the gold and precious stones for which I had sold the frame of flesh which nature had given me. The sight a little stilled my emotions: three days would soon be gone.

They did pass. The dwarf had supplied me with a plenteous store of food. At first I could hardly walk, so strange and out of joint were all my limbs; and my voice—it was that of the fiend. But I kept silent, and turned my face to the sun, that I might not see my shadow, and counted the hours, and ruminated on my future conduct. To bring Torella to my feet—to possess my Juliet in spite of him—all this my wealth could easily achieve. During dark night I slept, and dreamt of the accomplishment of my desires. Two suns had set—the third dawned. I was agitated, fearful. Oh expectation, what a frightful thing art thou, when kindled more by fear than hope! How dost thou twist thyself round the heart, torturing its pulsations! How dost thou dart unknown pangs all through our feeble mechanism, now seeming to shiver us like broken glass, to nothingness—now giving us a fresh strength, which can *do* nothing, and so torments us by a sensation, such as the strong man must feel who cannot break his fetters, though they bend in his grasp. Slowly paced the bright, bright orb up the eastern sky; long it lingered in the zenith, and still more slowly wandered down the west: it touched the horizon's verge—it was lost! Its glories were on the summits of the cliff—they grew dun and grey. The evening star shone bright. He will soon be here.

He came not!—By the living heavens, he came not!—and night dragged out its weary length, and, in its decaying age, "day began to grizzle its dark hair;" and the sun rose again on the most miserable wretch that ever upbraided its light. Three days thus I passed. The jewels and the gold—oh, how I abhorred them!

Well, well—I will not blacken these pages with demoniac ravings. All too terrible were the thoughts, the raging tumult of ideas that filled my soul.

At the end of that time I slept; I had not before since the third sunset; and I dreamt that I was at Juliet's feet, and she smiled, and then she shrieked—for she saw my transformation—and again she smiled, for still her beautiful lover knelt before her. But it was not I—it was he, the fiend, arrayed in my limbs, speaking with my voice, winning her with my looks of love. I strove to warn her, but my tongue refused its office; I strove to tear him from her, but I was rooted to the ground—I awoke with the agony. There were the solitary hoar precipices—there the plashing sea, the quiet strand, and the blue sky over all. What did it mean? was my dream but a mirror of the truth? was he wooing and winning my betrothed? I would on the instant back to Genoa—but I was banished. I laughed—the dwarf's yell burst from my lips—*I* banished! Oh no! they had not exiled the foul limbs I wore; I might with these enter, without fear of incurring the threatened penalty of death, my own, my native city.

I began to walk towards Genoa. I was somewhat accustomed to my distorted limbs; none were ever so ill-adapted for a straightforward movement; it was with infinite difficulty that I proceeded. Then, too, I desired to avoid all the hamlets strewed here and there on the sea-beach, for I was unwilling to make a display of my hideousness. I was not quite sure that, if seen, the mere boys would not stone me to death as I passed, for a monster; some ungentle salutations I did receive from the few peasants or fishermen I chanced to meet. But it was dark night before I approached Genoa. The weather was so balmy and sweet that it struck me that the Marchese and his daughter would very probably have quitted the city for their country retreat. It was from Villa Torella that I had attempted to carry off Juliet; I had spent many an hour reconnoitring the spot, and knew each inch of ground in its vicinity. It was beautifully situated, embosomed in trees, on the margin of a stream. As I drew near, it became evident that my conjecture was right; nay, moreover, that the hours were being then devoted to feasting and merriment. For the house was lighted up; strains of soft and gay music were wafted towards me by the breeze. My heart sank within me. Such was the generous kindness of Torella's heart that I felt sure that he would not have indulged in public manifestations of rejoicing just after my unfortunate banishment, but for a cause I dared not dwell upon.

The country people were all alive and flocking about; it became necessary that I should conceal myself; and yet I longed to address some one, or to hear others discourse, or in any way to gain intelligence of what was really going on. At length, entering the walks that were in immediate vicinity to the mansion, I found one dark enough to veil my excessive frightfulness; and yet others as well as I were loitering in its shade. I soon gathered all I wanted to know—all that first made my very heart die with horror, and then boil with indignation. To-morrow Juliet was to be given to the penitent, reformed, beloved Guido—to-morrow my bride was to pledge her vows to a fiend from hell! And I did this!—my accursed pride—my demoniac violence and wicked self-idolatry had caused this act. For if I had acted as the wretch who had stolen my form had acted—if, with a mien at once yielding and dignified, I had presented myself to Torella, saying, I have done wrong, forgive me; I am unworthy of your angel-child, but permit me to claim her hereafter, when my altered conduct shall manifest that I abjure my vices, and endeavour to become in some sort worthy of her. I go to serve against the infidels; and when my zeal for religion and my true penitence for the past shall appear to you to cancel my crimes, permit me again to call myself your son. Thus had he spoken; and the penitent was welcomed even as the prodigal son of Scripture: the fatted calf was killed for him; and he, still pursuing the same path, displayed such open-hearted regret for his follies, so humble a concession of all his rights, and so ardent a resolve to reacquire them by a life of contrition and virtue, that he quickly conquered the kind old man; and full pardon, and the gift of his lovely child, followed in swift succession.

Oh, had an angel from Paradise whispered to me to act thus! But now, what would be the innocent Juliet's fate? Would God permit the foul union—or, some prodigy destroying it, link the dishonoured name of Carega with the worst of crimes? To-morrow at dawn they were to be married: there was but one way to prevent this—to meet mine enemy, and to enforce the ratification of our agreement. I felt that this could only be done by a mortal struggle. I had no sword—if indeed my distorted arms could wield a soldier's weapon—but I had a dagger, and in that lay my hope. There was no time for pondering or balancing nicely the question: I might die in the attempt; but besides the burning jealousy and despair of my own heart, honour, mere humanity, demanded that I should fall rather than not destroy the machinations of the fiend.

The guests departed—the lights began to disappear; it was evident that the inhabitants of the villa were seeking repose. I hid myself among the trees—the garden grew desert—the gates were closed—I wandered round and came under a window—ah! well did I know the same!—a soft twilight glimmered in the room—the curtains were half withdrawn. It was the temple of innocence and beauty. Its magnificence was tempered, as it were, by the slight disarrangements occasioned by its being dwelt in, and all the objects scattered around displayed the taste of her who hallowed it by her presence. I saw her enter with a quick light step—I saw her approach the window—she drew back the curtain yet further, and looked out into the night. Its breezy freshness played among her ringlets, and wafted them from the transparent marble of her brow. She clasped her hands, she raised her eyes to heaven. I heard her voice. Guido! she softly murmured—mine own Guido! and then, as if overcome by the fulness of her own heart, she sank on her knees;—her upraised eyes—her graceful attitude—the beaming thankfulness that lighted up her face—oh, these are tame words! Heart of mine, thou imagest ever, though thou canst not portray, the celestial beauty of that child of light and love.

I heard a step—a quick firm step along the shady avenue. Soon I saw a cavalier, richly dressed, young and, methought, graceful to look on, advance. I hid myself yet closer. The youth approached; he paused beneath the window. She arose, and again looking out she saw him, and said—I cannot, no, at this distant time I cannot record her terms of soft silver tenderness; to me they were spoken, but they were replied to by him.

"I will not go," he cried: "here where you have been, where your memory glides like some heaven-visiting ghost, I will pass the long hours till we meet, never, my Juliet, again, day or night, to part. But do thou, my love, retire; the cold morn and fitful breeze will make thy cheek pale, and fill with languor thy love-lighted eyes. Ah, sweetest! could I press one kiss upon them, I could, methinks, repose."

And then he approached still nearer, and methought he was about to clamber into her chamber. I had hesitated, not to terrify her; now I was no longer master of myself. I rushed forward—I threw myself on him—I tore him away—I cried, "O loathsome and foul-shaped wretch!"

I need not repeat epithets, all tending, as it appeared, to rail at a person I at present feel some partiality for. A shriek rose from Juliet's lips. I neither heard nor saw—I *felt* only mine enemy, whose throat I grasped, and my dagger's hilt; he struggled, but could not escape. At length hoarsely he breathed these words: "Do!—strike home! destroy this body—you will still live: may your life be long and merry!"

The descending dagger was arrested at the word, and he, feeling my hold relax, extricated himself and drew his sword, while the uproar in the house, and flying of torches from one room to the other, showed that soon we should be separated. In the midst of my frenzy there was much calculation:—fall I might, and so that he did not survive, I cared not for the death-blow I might deal against myself. While still, therefore, he thought I paused, and while I saw the villainous resolve to take advantage of my hesitation, in the sudden thrust he made at me, I threw myself on his sword, and at the same moment plunged my dagger, with a true, desperate aim, in his side. We fell together, rolling over each other, and the tide of blood that flowed from the gaping wound of each mingled on the grass. More I know not—I fainted.

Again I return to life: weak almost to death, I found myself stretched upon a bed—Juliet was kneeling beside it. Strange! my first broken request was for a mirror. I was so wan and ghastly, that my poor girl hesitated, as she told me afterwards; but, by the mass! I thought myself a right proper youth when I saw the dear reflection of my own well-known features. I confess it is a weakness, but I avow it, I do entertain a considerable affection for the countenance and limbs I behold, whenever I look at a glass; and have more mirrors in my house, and consult them oftener, than any beauty in Genoa. Before you too much condemn me, permit me to say that no one better knows than I the value of his own body; no one, probably, except myself, ever having had it stolen from him.

Incoherently I at first talked of the dwarf and his crimes, and reproached Juliet for her too easy admission of his love. She thought me raving, as well she might; and yet it was some time before I could prevail on myself to admit that the Guido whose penitence had won her back for me was myself;

and while I cursed bitterly the monstrous dwarf, and blest the well-directed blow that had deprived him of life, I suddenly checked myself when I heard her say, Amen! knowing that him whom she reviled was my very self. A little reflection taught me silence—a little practice enabled me to speak of that frightful night without any very excessive blunder. The wound I had given myself was no mockery of one—it was long before I recovered—and as the benevolent and generous Torella sat beside me, talking such wisdom as might win friends to repentance, and mine own dear Juliet hovered near me, administering to my wants, and cheering me by her smiles, the work of my bodily cure and mental reform went on together. I have never, indeed, wholly recovered my strength—my cheek is paler since—my person a little bent. Juliet sometimes ventures to allude bitterly to the malice that caused this change, but I kiss her on the moment, and tell her all is for the best. I am a fonder and more faithful husband, and true is this—but for that wound, never had I called her mine.

I did not revisit the sea-shore, nor seek for the fiend's treasure; yet, while I ponder on the past, I often think, and my confessor was not backward in favouring the idea, that it might be a good rather than an evil spirit, sent by my guardian angel, to show me the folly and misery of pride. So well at least did I learn this lesson, roughly taught as I was, that I am known now by all my friends and fellow-citizens by the name of Guido il Cortese.

THE DARK LADY

by Mrs. S. C. Hall

1850

Anna Maria Fielding was born in Dublin in 1800, and came to England with her mother at the age of fifteen. There, she met the poet Frances Arabella Rowden, who took an interest in her education. Several of Rowden's pupils went on to become well-known writers in their day, including Caroline Ponsonby, who would, as Lady Caroline Lamb, scandalize polite society with her very public affair with Lord Byron, as well as publishing poems that mimicked his style and creating a thinly disguised portrait of the couple in her Gothic novel Glenarvon.

Anna's life, on the other hand, was free of scandal. She married the Irish-born journalist Samuel Carter Hall in 1824, and her mother lived with them until her death. Later in life, Anna was very active in charity work, helping to found the Hospital for Consumption at Brompton (now the Royal Brompton Hospital), the Nightingale Fund (used to set up the world's first nursing school), and charities for the relief of retired and distressed governesses and gentlewomen. She was also active in the fields of temperance and women's rights, and at the age of sixty-eight she was granted a state pension from the British government's Civil List in recognition of her contributions to society.

Anna's early work consisted of "sketches of Irish character," a style that was popular with the magazines of the time. She also wrote stage plays and novels, usually with an Irish setting or theme. Her work was never popular in Ireland, though, as she failed to take either the Catholic or Protestant side, finding much to praise and blame in each.

"The Dark Lady" is a departure from much of her other work, not for its supernatural content—her novel Midsummer Eve, a Fairy Tale of Love *drew upon Irish fairy lore—but because it is set on the Continent. As will be seen from other tales in this collection, continental Europe—Switzerland and Italy in particular—were popular settings at the time, bringing the romance of the Grand Tour to readers whose means did not permit them to undertake it themselves. Here, an ill-tempered Count is reformed by an encounter with a family ghost.*

People find it easy enough to laugh at "spirit stories" in broad daylight, when the sunbeams dance upon the grass, and the deepest forest glades are spotted and checkered only by the tender shadows of leafy trees; when the rugged castle, that looked so mysterious and so stern in the looming night, seems suited for a lady's bower; when the rushing waterfall sparkles in diamond showers, and the hum of bee and song of bird tune the thoughts to hopes of life and happiness; people may laugh at ghosts then, if they like, but as for me, I never could merely smile at the records of those shadowy visitors. I have large faith in things supernatural, and cannot disbelieve solely on the ground that I lack such evidences as are supplied by the senses; for they, in truth, sustain by palpable proofs so few of the many marvels by which we are surrounded, that I would rather reject them altogether as witnesses, than abide the issue entirely as they suggest.

My great grandmother was a native of the canton of Berne; and at the advanced age of ninety, her memory of "the long ago" was as active as it could have been at fifteen: she looked as if she had just stepped out of a piece of tapestry belonging to a past age, but with warm sympathies for the present. Her English, when she became excited, was very curious—a mingling of French, certainly not Parisian, with here and there scraps of German done into English, literally—so that her observations were at times remarkable for their strength. "The mountains," she would say, "in her country, went high, high up, until they could look into the heavens, and *hear* God in the storm." She never thoroughly comprehended the real beauty of England; but spoke with contempt of the flatness of our island—calling our mountains "inequalities," nothing more—holding our agriculture "cheap," saying that the land tilled itself, leaving man nothing to do. She would sing the most amusing *patois* songs, and tell stories from morning till night, more especially spirit-stories; but the old lady would not tell a tale of that character a second time to an unbeliever: such things, she would say, "are not for make-laugh." One in particular, I remember, always excited great interest in her young listeners, from its mingling of the real and the romantic; but it can never be told as she told it; there was so much of the picturesque about the old lady—so much to admire in the curious carving of her ebony cane, in the beauty of her point lace, the size and weight of her long ugly earrings, the fashion of her solid silk gown, the singularity of her buckled shoes—her dark-brown wrinkled face, every wrinkle an expression,—her broad thoughtful brow, beneath which glittered her bright blue eyes—bright, even when her eyelashes were white with *years*. All these peculiarities gave impressive effect to her words.

"In my young time," she told us, "I spent many happy hours with Amelie de Rohean, in her uncle's castle. He was a fine man—much size, stern, and dark, and full of noise—a strong man, no fear—he had a great heart, and a big head.

"The castle was situated in the midst of the most stupendous Alpine scenery, and yet it was not solitary. There were other dwellings in sight;

some very near, but separated by a ravine, through which, at all seasons, a rapid river kept its foaming course. You do not know what torrents are in this country; your torrents are as babies—ours are giants. The one I speak of divided the valley; here and there a rock, round which it sported, or stormed, according to the season. In two of the denies these rocks were of great value; acting as piers for the support of bridges, the only means of communication with our opposite neighbours.

"'Monsieur,' as we always called the Count, was, as I have told you, a dark, stern, violent man. All men are wilful, my dear young ladies," she would say; "but Monsieur was the most wilful: all men are selfish, but he was the most selfish: all men are tyrants—" Here the old lady was invariably interrupted by her relatives, with, "Oh, good Granny!" and, "Oh fie, dear Granny!" and she would bridle up a little and fan herself; then continue—"Yes, my dears, each creature according to its nature—all men are tyrants; and I confess that I do think a Swiss, whose mountain inheritance is nearly coeval with the creation of the mountains, has a *right* to be tyrannical; I did not intend to blame him for that: I did not, because I had grown used to it. Amelie and I always stood up when he entered the room, and never sat down until we were desired. He never bestowed a loving word or a kind look upon either of us. We never spoke except when we were spoken to."

"But when you and Amelie were alone, dear Granny?"

"Oh, why, then we did chatter, I suppose; though then it was in moderation; for Monsieur's influence chilled us even when he was not present; and often she would say, 'It is so hard trying to love him, for he will not let me!' There is no such beauty in the world now as Amelie's. I can see her as she used to stand before the richly carved glass in the grave oak-panelled dressing-room; her luxuriant hair combed up from her full round brow; the discreet maidenly cap, covering the back of her head; her brocaded silk, (which she had inherited from her grandmother,) shaded round the bosom by the modest ruffle; her black velvet gorget and bracelets, showing off to perfection the pearly transparency of her skin. She was the loveliest of all creatures, and as good as she was lovely; it seems but as yesterday that we were together—but as yesterday! And yet I lived to see her an old woman; so they called her, but she never seemed old to me! My own dear Amelie!"

Ninety years had not dried up the sources of poor Granny's tears, nor chilled her heart; and she never spoke of Amelie without emotion. "Monsieur was very proud of his niece, because she was part of himself: she added to his consequence, she contributed to his enjoyments; she had grown necessary; she was the one sunbeam of his house."

"Not the *one* sunbeam surely, Granny!" one of us would exclaim; "you were a sunbeam then."

"I was nothing where Amelie was—nothing but her shadow! The bravest and best in the country would have rejoiced to be to her what I was—her chosen friend; and some would hare perilled their lives for one of the sweet smiles which played around her uncle, but never touched his heart. Monsieur never would suffer people to be happy except in his way. He had never married; and he declared Amelie never should. She had, he said, as much enjoyment as he had: she had a castle with a drawbridge; she had a forest for hunting; dogs and horses; servants and serfs; jewels, gold, and gorgeous dresses; a guitar and a harpsichord; a parrot—and a friend! And such an uncle! he believed there was not such another uncle in broad Europe! For many a long day Amelie laughed at this catalogue of advantages—that is, she laughed when her uncle left the room; she never laughed before him. In time, the laugh came not: but in its place, sighs and tears. Monsieur had a great deal to answer for. Amelie was not prevented from seeing the gentry when they came to visit in a formal way, and she met many hawking and hunting; but she never was permitted to invite any one to the castle, nor to accept an invitation. Monsieur fancied that by shutting her lips, he closed her heart; and boasted such was the advantage of his good training, that Amelie's mind was fortified against all weaknesses, for she had not the least dread of wandering about the ruined chapel of the castle, where he himself dared not go after dusk. This place was dedicated to the family ghost—the spirit, which for many years had it entirely at its own disposal. It was much attached to its quarters, seldom leaving them, except for the purpose of interfering when anything decidedly wrong was going forward in the castle. 'La Femme Noir' had been seen gliding along the unprotected parapet of the bridge, and standing on a pinnacle, before the late master's death; and many tales were told of her, which in this age of unbelief would not be credited."

"Granny, did you know why your friend ventured so fearlessly into the ghost's territories?" inquired my cousin.

"I am not come to that," was the reply; "and you are one saucy little maid to ask what I do not choose to tell. Amelie certainly entertained no fear of the spirit; 'La Femme Noir' could have had no angry feeling towards her, for my friend would wander in the ruins, taking no note of daylight, or moonlight, or even darkness. The peasants declared their young lady must have walked over crossed bones, or drunk water out of a raven's skull, or passed nine times round the spectre's glass on Midsummer eve. She must have done all this, if not more: there could be little doubt that the 'Femme Noir' had initiated her into certain mysteries; for they heard at times voices in low, whispering converse, and saw the shadows of two persons cross the old roofless chapel, when 'Mamselle' had passed the footbridge alone. Monsieur gloried in this fearlessness on the part of his gentle niece; and more than once, when he had revellers in the castle, he sent her forth at midnight to bring him a bough from a tree that only grew beside the altar of the old ehapel; and she did his bidding always as willingly, though not as rapidly, as he could desire.

"But certainly Amelie's courage brought no calmness. She became pale; her pillow was often moistened by her tears; her music was neglected; she took no pleasure in the chase; and her chamois not receiving its usual attention, went off into the mountains. She avoided me—her friend! who would have died for her; she left me alone; she made no reply to my prayers, and did not heed my entreaties. One morning, when her eyes were fixed upon a book she did not read, and I sat at my embroidery a little apart, watching the tears stray over her cheek until I was blinded by my own, I heard Monsieur's heavy tramp approaching through the long gallery; some boots creak—but the boots of Monsieur!—they growled!

"'Save me, oh save me!' she exclaimed wildly. Before I could reply, her uncle crashed open the door, and stood before us like an embodied thunderbolt. He held an open letter in his hand—his eyes glared—his nostrils were distended—he trembled so with rage, that the cabinets and old china shook again.

"'Do you,' he said, 'know Charles le Maitre?'

"Amelie replied, 'She did.'

"'How did you make acquaintance with the son of my deadliest foe?'

"There was no answer. The question was repeated. Amelie said she had met him, and at last confessed it was in the ruined portion of the castle! She threw herself at her uncle's feet—she clung to his knees: love taught her eloquence. She told him how deeply Charles regretted the long-standing feud; how earnest, and true, and good, he was. Bending low, until her tresses were heaped upon the floor, she confessed, modestly but firmly, that she loved this young man; that she would rather sacrifice the wealth of the whole world, than forget him.

"Monsieur seemed suffocating; he tore off his lace cravat, and scattered its fragments on the floor—still she clung to him. At last he flung her from him; he reproached her with the bread she had eaten, and heaped odium upon her mother's memory! But though Amelie's nature was tender and affectionate, the old spirit of the old race roused within her; the slight girl arose, and stood erect before the man of storms.

"'Did you think,' she said, 'because I bent to you that I am feeble? because I bore with you, have I no thoughts? You gave food to this frame, but you fed not my heart; you gave me nor love, nor tenderness, nor sympathy; you showed me to your friends, as you would your horse. If you had by kindness sown the seeds of love within my bosom; if you had been a father to me in tenderness, I would have been to you—a child. I never knew the time when I did not tremble at your footstep; but I will do so no more. I would gladly have loved you, trusted you, cherished you; but I feared to let you know I had a heart, lest you should tear and insult it. Oh, sir, those who expect love where they give none, and confidence where there is no trust, blast the fair time of youth, and lay up for themselves an unhonoured old age.'

The scene terminated by Monsieur's falling down in a fit, and Amelie's being conveyed fainting to her chamber.

"That night the castle was enveloped by storms; they came from all points of the compass—thunder, lightning, hail, and rain! The master lay in his stately bed, and was troubled; he could hardly believe that Amelie spoke the words he had heard: cold-hearted and selfish as he was, he was also a clear-seeing man, and it was their truth that struck him. But still his heart was hardened; he had commanded Amelie to be locked into her chamber, and her lover seized and imprisoned when he came to his usual tryste. Monsieur, I have said, lay in his stately bed, the lightning, at intervals, illumining his dark chamber. I had cast myself on the floor outside her door, but could not hear her weep, though I knew that she was overcome of sorrow. As I sat, my head resting against the lintel of the door, a form passed through the solid oak from her chamber, without the bolts being withdrawn. I saw it as plainly as I see your faces now, under the influence of various emotions; nothing opened, but it passed through—a shadowy form, dark and vapoury, but perfectly distinct. I knew it was 'La Femme Noir,' and I trembled, for she never came from caprice, but always for a purpose. I did not fear for Amelie, for 'La Femme Noir' never warred with the high-minded or virtuous. She passed slowly, more slowly than I am speaking, along the corridor, growing taller and taller as she went on, until she entered Monsieur's chamber by the door exactly opposite where I stood. She paused at the foot of the plumed bed, and the lightning, no longer fitful, by its broad flashes kept up a continual illumination. She stood for some time perfectly motionless, though in a loud tone the master demanded whence she came, and what she wanted. At last, during a pause in the storm, she told him that all the power he possessed should not pre-vent the union of Amelie and Charles. I heard her voice myself; it sounded like the night-wind among fir-trees—cold and shrill, chilling both ear and heart. I turned my eyes away while she spoke, and when I looked again, she was gone! The storm continued to increase in violence, and the master's rage kept pace with the war of elements. The servants were trembling with undefined terror; they feared they knew not what: the dogs added to their apprehension by howling fearfully, and then barking in the highest possible key; the master paced about his chamber, calling in vain on his domestics, stamping and swearing like a maniac. At last, amid flashes of lightning, he made his way to the head of the great staircase, and presently the clang of the alarm-bell mingled with the thunder and the roar of the mountain torrents: this hastened the servants to his presence, though they seemed hardly capable of understanding his words—he insisted on Charles being brought before him. We all trembled, for he was mad and livid with rage. The warden, in whose care the young man was, dared not enter the hall that echoed his loud words and heavy footsteps, for when he went to seek his prisoner, he found every bolt and bar withdrawn, and the iron door wide open: he was gone. Monsieur seemed to find relief by his energies being called into action: he ordered instant pursuit, and mounted his favourite charger, despite the storm, despite the fury of the elements. Although the great gates rocked, and the castle shook like an aspen-leaf, he set forth, his path illumined by the lightning: bold and brave as was his horse, he found it almost impossible to get it forward; he dug his spurs deep into the flanks of the noble animal, until the red blood mingled with the rain. At last, it rushed madly down the path to the bridge the young man must cross; and when they reached it, the master discerned the floating cloak of the pursued, a few yards in advance. Again the horse rebelled against his will, the lightning flashed in his eyes, and the torrent seemed a mass of red fire; no sound could be heard but of its roaring waters; the attendants clung as they advanced to the hand-rail of the bridge. The youth, unconscious of the *pursuit,* proceeded rapidly: and again roused, the horse plunged forward. On the instant, the form of 'La Femme Noir' passed with the blast that rushed down the ravine; the torrent followed in her track, and more than half the bridge was swept away for ever. As the master reined back the horse he had so urged forward, he saw the youth kneeling with outstretched arms on the opposite bank—kneeling in gratitude for his deliverance from this double peril. All were struck with the piety of the youth, and earnestly rejoiced at his deliverance; though they did not presume to say so, or look as if they thought it. I never saw so changed a person as the master when he reentered the castle gate: his cheek was blanched—his eye quelled; his fierce plume hung broken over his shoulder—his step was unequal, and in the voice of a feeble girl he said—'Bring me a cup of wine.' I was his cupbearer, and for the first time in his life he thanked me graciously, and in the warmth of his gratitude tapped my shoulder; the caress nearly hurled me across the hall. What passed in his retiring-room, I know not. Some said, the 'Femme Noir' visited him again: I cannot tell, I did not see her; I speak of what I saw, not of what I heard. The storm passed away with a clap of thunder, to which the former sounds were but as the rattling of pebbles beneath the swell of a summer wave. The next morning Monsieur sent for the Pasteur. The good man seemed terror-stricken as he entered the hall; but

Monsieur filled him a quart of gold coins out of a leathern bag, to repair his church, and that quickly; and grasping his hand as he departed, looked him steadily in the face. As he did so, large drops stood like beads upon his brow; his stern, coarse features were strangely moved while he gazed upon the calm, pale minister of peace and love. 'You,' he said, 'bid God bless the poorest peasant that passes you on the mountain; have you no blessing to give the master of Rohean?'

"'My son,' answered the good man, 'I give you the blessing I may give:—May God bless you, and may your heart be opened to give and to receive."

"'I know I can give,' replied the proud man; 'but what can I receive?'

"'Love,' he replied. 'All your wealth has not brought you happiness, because you are unloving and unloved!'

"The demon returned to his brow, but it did not remain there.

"'You shall give me lessons in this thing,' he said; and so the good man went his way.

"Amelie continued a close prisoner; but a change came over Monsieur. At first he shut himself up in his chamber, and no one was suffered to enter his presence; he took his food with his own hand from the only attendant who ventured to approach his door. He was heard walking up and down the room, day and night. When we were going to sleep, we heard his heavy tramp; at daybreak, there it was again: and those of the household, who awoke at intervals during the night, said it was unceasing.

"Monsieur could read. Ah, you may smile; but in those days, and in those mountains, such men as 'the master' did not trouble themselves or others with knowledge; but the master of Rohean read both Latin and Greek, and commanded THE BOOK he had never opened since his childhood to be brought him. It was taken out of its velvet case, and carried in forthwith; and we saw his shadow from without, like the shadow of a giant, bending over THE BOOK; and he read in it for some days; and we greatly hoped it would soften and change his nature—and though I cannot say much for the softening, it certainly effected a great change; he no longer stalked moodily along the corridors, and banged the doors, and swore at the servants; he the rather seemed possessed of a merry devil, roaring out an old song—

'Aux bastions de Geneve, nos cannons
Sont branquex;
S'il y a quelque attaque nous les feront ronfler,
Viva! les cannoniers!'

and then he would pause, and clang his hands together like a pair of cymbals, and laugh. And once, as I was passing along, he pounced out upon me, and whirled me round in a waltz, roaring at me when he let me down, to practice *that* and break my embroidery frame. He formed a band of horns and trumpets, and insisted on the goatherds and shepherds sounding reveilles in the mountains, and the village children beating drums: his only idea of joy and happiness was noise. He set all the canton to work to mend the bridge, paying the workmen double wages; and he, who never entered a church before, would go to see how the labourers were getting on nearly every day. He talked and laughed a great deal to himself; and in his gaiety of heart would set the mastiffs fighting, and make excursions from home—we knowing not where he went. At last, Amelie was summoned to his presence, and he shook her and shouted, then kissed her; and hoping she would be a good girl, told her he had provided a husband for her. Amelie wept and prayed; and the master capered and sung. At last she fainted; and taking advantage of her unconsciousness, he conveyed her to the chapel; and there beside the altar stood the bridegroom—no other than Charles Le Maitre.

"They lived many happy years together; and when Monsieur was in every respect a better, though still a strange, man, 'the Femme Noir' appeared again to him—once. She did so with a placid air, on a summer night, with her arm extended towards the heavens.

"The next day the muffled bell told the valley that the stormy, proud old master of Rohean had ceased to live."

MORTON HALL

by Elizabeth Gaskell

1853

Like Mary Shelley, Elizabeth Cleghorn Stevenson never knew her mother, who died when she was a little over a year old. Unlike Mary, though, her upbringing was quite conventional. Like an Austen heroine, she was shipped off to an aunt and grew up with no wealth of her own and no guarantee of a permanent home. She received a typical education for a young lady of the time, focused on the arts, classics, and etiquette. In her free time, she wandered in the woods and glades around her aunt's house, collecting wildflowers and watching the birds. At the age of twenty-one she married a local Unitarian minister by the name of William Gaskell: their first child was stillborn and the second died in infancy, but three other daughters survived.

Elizabeth's writing career seems to have begun in 1835, with a diary documenting the development of her daughter Marianne; she went on to explore parenthood and write about her other children. The following year, she and William co-authored a series of poems, "Sketches Among the Poor," which was published in Blackwood's Magazine *the following January. Her first solo work, "Clopton Hall," was published in 1840 in a collection titled* Visits to Remarkable Places *and attributed only to "A*

Lady." Over the next eight years, she published various short stories under the masculine pseudonym "Cotton Mather Mills"—a name no doubt inspired by her Unitarian faith.

"Morton Hall" is one of her less frequently anthologized stories. Less overtly Gothic than Mary Shelley's work, it nonetheless incorporates a number of tropes that were popular in the Gothic and sensational fiction of the day: the crumbling hall, the unsuitable marriage, and the curse or prophecy fulfilled at last. Many of these elements are also found, more famously, in The Hound of the Baskervilles, *which Conan Doyle began as a straightforward horror tale before deciding to introduce Sherlock Holmes, risen again by public demand after his apparent death eight years earlier in* The Final Problem.

"Morton Hall" was first published in Household Words, *a weekly magazine edited by Charles Dickens from 1850 to 1859.*

CHAPTER I

O ur old Hall is to be pulled down, and they are going to build streets on the site. I said to my sister, "Ethelinda! if they really pull down Morton Hall, it will be a worse piece of work than the Repeal of the Corn Laws." And, after some consideration, she replied, that if she must speak what was on her mind, she would own that she thought the Papists had something to do with it; that they had never forgiven the Morton who had been with Lord Monteagle when he discovered the Gunpowder Plot; for we knew that, somewhere in Rome, there was a book kept, and which had been kept for generations, giving an account of the secret private history of every English family of note, and registering the names of those to whom the Papists owed either grudges or gratitude.

We were silent for some time; but I am sure the same thought was in both our minds; our ancestor, a Sidebotham, had been a follower of the Morton of that day; it had always been said in the family that he had been with his master when he went with the Lord Monteagle, and found Guy Fawkes and his dark lantern under the Parliament House; and the question flashed across our minds, were the Sidebothams marked with a black mark in that terrible mysterious book which was kept under lock and key by the Pope and the Cardinals in Rome? It was terrible, yet, somehow, rather pleasant to think of. So many of the misfortunes which had happened to us through life, and which we had called 'mysterious dispensations,' but which some of our neighbours had attributed to our want of prudence and foresight, were accounted for at once, if we were objects of the deadly hatred of such a powerful order as the Jesuits, of whom we had lived in dread ever since we had read the *Female Jesuit*. Whether this last idea suggested what my sister said next I can't tell; we did know the female Jesuit's second cousin, so might be said to have literary connections, and from that the startling thought might spring up in my sister's mind, for, said she, "Biddy!" (my name is Bridget, and no one but my sister calls me Biddy) "suppose you write some account of Morton Hall; we have known much in our time of the Mortons, and it will be a shame if they pass away completely from men's memories while we can speak or write." I was pleased with the notion, I confess; but I felt ashamed to agree to it all at once, though even, as I objected for modesty's sake, it came into my mind how much I had heard of the old place in its former days, and how it was, perhaps, all I could now do for the Mortons, under whom our ancestors had lived as tenants for more than three hundred years. So at last I agreed; and, for fear of mistakes, I showed it to Mr. Swinton, our young curate, who has put it quite in order for me.

Morton Hall is situated about five miles from the centre of Drumble. It stands on the outskirts of a village, which, when the Hall was built, was probably as large as Drumble in those days; and even I can remember when there was a long piece of rather lonely road, with high hedges on either side, between Morton village and Drumble. Now, it is all street, and Morton seems but a suburb of the great town near. Our farm stood where Liverpool Street runs now; and people used to come snipe-shooting just where the Baptist chapel is built. Our farm must have been older than the Hall, for we had a date of 1460 on one of the cross-beams. My father was rather proud of this advantage, for the Hall had no date older than 1554; and I remember his affronting Mrs. Dawson, the house-keeper, by dwelling too much on this circumstance one evening when she came to drink tea with my mother, when Ethelinda and I were mere children. But my mother, seeing that Mrs. Dawson would never allow that any house in the parish could be older than the Hall, and that she was getting very warm, and almost insinuating that the Sidebothams had forged the date to disparage the squire's family, and set themselves up as having the older blood, asked Mrs. Dawson to tell us the story of old Sir John Morton before we went to bed. I slyly reminded my father that Jack, our man, was not always so careful as might be in housing the Alderney in good time in the autumn evenings. So he started up, and went off to see after Jack; and Mrs. Dawson and we drew nearer the fire to hear the story about Sir John.

Sir John Morton had lived some time about the Restoration. The Mortons had taken the right side; so when Oliver Cromwell came into power, he gave away their lands to one of his Puritan followers—a man who had been but a praying, canting, Scotch pedlar till the war broke out; and Sir John had to go and live with his royal master at Bruges. The upstart's name was Carr, who came to live at Morton Hall; and, I'm proud to say, we—I mean our ancestors—led him a pretty life. He had hard work to get any rent at all from the tenantry, who knew their duty better than to pay it to a Roundhead. If he took the law to them, the law officers fared so badly, that they were shy of coming out to Morton—all along that lonely road I told you of—again. Strange noises were heard about the Hall, which got the credit of being haunted; but, as those noises were never heard before or since that Richard Carr lived there, I leave you to guess if the evil spirits did not know well over whom they had power—over schismatic rebels, and no one else. They durst not trouble the Mortons, who were true and loyal, and were faithful followers of King Charles in word and deed. At last, Old Oliver died; and folks did say that, on that wild and stormy night, his voice was heard high up in the air, where you hear the flocks of wild geese skirl, crying out for his true follower Richard Carr to accompany him in the terrible chase the fiends were giving him before carrying him down to hell. Anyway, Richard

Carr died within a week—summoned by the dead or not, he went his way down to his master, and his master's master.

Then his daughter Alice came into possession. Her mother was somehow related to General Monk, who was beginning to come into power about that time. So when Charles the Second came back to his throne, and many of the sneaking Puritans had to quit their ill-gotten land, and turn to the right about, Alice Carr was still left at Morton Hall to queen it there. She was taller than most women, and a great beauty, I have heard. But, for all her beauty, she was a stern, hard woman. The tenants had known her to be hard in her father's lifetime, but now that she was the owner, and had the power, she was worse than ever. She hated the Stuarts worse than ever her father had done; had calves' head for dinner every thirtieth of January; and when the first twenty-ninth of May came round, and every mother's son in the village gilded his oak-leaves, and wore them in his hat, she closed the windows of the great hall with her own hands, and sat throughout the day in darkness and mourning. People did not like to go against her by force, because she was a young and beautiful woman. It was said the King got her cousin, the Duke of Albemarle, to ask her to court, just as courteously as if she had been the Queen of Sheba, and King Charles, Solomon, praying her to visit him in Jerusalem. But she would not go; not she! She lived a very lonely life, for now the King had got his own again, no servant but her nurse would stay with her in the Hall; and none of the tenants would pay her any money for all that her father had purchased the lands from the Parliament, and paid the price down in good red gold.

All this time, Sir John was somewhere in the Virginian plantations; and the ships sailed from thence only twice a year: but his royal master had sent for him home; and home he came, that second summer after the restoration. No one knew if Mistress Alice had heard of his landing in England or not; all the villagers and tenantry knew, and were not surprised, and turned out in their best dresses, and with great branches of oak,* to welcome him as he rode into the village one July morning, with many gay-looking gentlemen by his side, laughing, and talking, and making merry, and speaking gaily

---

* Following the Battle of Worcester (pron. "Wooster") in 1651, the future King Charles II hid in an oak tree to avoid the Roundheads; oak became a Royalist symbol thereafter.

and pleasantly to the village people. They came in on the opposite side to the Drumble Road; indeed, Drumble was nothing of a place then, as I have told you. Between the last cottage in the village and the gates to the old Hall, there was a shady part of the road, where the branches nearly met overhead, and made a green gloom. If you'll notice, when many people are talking merrily out of doors in sunlight, they will stop talking for an instant, when they come into the cool green shade, and either be silent for some little time, or else speak graver, and slower, and softer. And so old people say those gay gentlemen did; for several people followed to see Alice Carr's pride taken down. They used to tell how the cavaliers had to bow their plumed hats in passing under the unlopped and drooping boughs. I fancy Sir John expected that the lady would have rallied her friends, and got ready for a sort of battle to defend the entrance to the house; but she had no friends. She had no nearer relations than the Duke of Albemarle, and he was mad with her for having refused to come to court, and so save her estate, according to his advice.

Well, Sir John rode on in silence; the tramp of the many horses' feet, and the clumping sound of the clogs of the village people were all that was heard. Heavy as the great gate was, they swung it wide on its hinges, and up they rode to the Hall steps, where the lady stood, in her close, plain, Puritan dress, her cheeks one crimson flush, her great eyes flashing fire, and no one behind her, or with her, or near her, or to be seen, but the old trembling nurse, catching at her gown in pleading terror. Sir John was taken aback; he could not go out with swords and warlike weapons against a woman; his very preparations for forcing an entrance made him ridiculous in his own eyes, and, he well knew, in the eyes of his gay, scornful comrades too; so he turned him round about, and bade them stay where they were, while he rode close to the steps, and spoke to the young lady; and there they saw him, hat in hand, speaking to her; and she, lofty and unmoved, holding her own as if she had been a sovereign queen with an army at her back. What they said, no one heard; but he rode back, very grave and much changed in his look, though his grey eye showed more hawk-like than ever, as if seeing the way to his end, though as yet afar off. He was not one to be jested with before his face; so when he professed to have changed his mind, and not to wish to disturb so fair a lady in possession, he and his cavaliers rode back to the village inn, and roystered there all day, and feasted the tenantry, cutting down the branches that had incommoded them in their morning's ride, to make a bonfire of on the village green, in which they burnt a figure, which some called Old Noll,* and others Richard Carr: and it might do for either, folks said, for unless they had given it the name of a man, most people would have taken it for a forked log of wood. But the lady's nurse told the villagers afterwards that Mistress Alice went in from the sunny Hall steps into the chill house shadow, and sat her down and wept as her poor faithful servant had never seen her do before, and could not have imagined her proud young lady ever doing. All through that summer's day she cried; and if for very weariness she ceased for a time, and only sighed as if her heart was breaking, they heard through the upper windows—which were open because of the heat—the village bells ringing merrily through the trees, and bursts of choruses to gay cavalier songs, all in favour of the Stuarts. All the young lady said was once or twice, "Oh God! I am very friendless!"—and the old nurse knew it was true, and could not contradict her; and always thought, as she said long after, that such weary weeping showed there was some great sorrow at hand.

I suppose it was the dreariest sorrow that ever a proud woman had; but it came in the shape of a gay wedding. How, the village never knew. The gay gentlemen rode away from Morton the next day as lightly and carelessly as if they had attained their end, and Sir John had taken possession; and, by-and-by, the nurse came timorously out to market in the village, and Mistress Alice was met in the wood walks just as grand and as proud as ever in her ways, only a little more pale, and a little more sad. The truth was, as I have been told, that she and Sir John had each taken a fancy to each other in that parley they held on the Hall steps; she, in the deep, wild way in which she took the impressions of her whole life, deep down, as if they were burnt in. Sir John was a gallant-looking man, and had a kind of foreign grace and courtliness about him. The way he fancied her was very different—a man's way, they tell me. She was a beautiful woman to be tamed, and made to come to his beck and call; and perhaps he read in

---

* A nickname for Oliver Cromwell, derived from "Oliver" in the same way that "Ned" is derived from "Edward."

her softening eyes that she might be won, and so all legal troubles about the possession of the estate come to an end in an easy, pleasant manner. He came to stay with friends in the neighbourhood; he was met in her favourite walks, with his plumed hat in his hand, pleading with her, and she looking softer and far more lovely than ever; and lastly, the tenants were told of the marriage then nigh at hand.

After they were wedded, he stayed for a time with her at the Hall, and then off back to court. They do say that her obstinate refusal to go with him to London was the cause of their first quarrel; but such fierce, strong wills would quarrel the first day of their wedded life. She said that the court was no place for an honest woman; but surely Sir John knew best, and she might have trusted him to take care of her. However, he left her all alone; and at first she cried most bitterly, and then she took to her old pride, and was more haughty and gloomy than ever. By-and-by she found out hidden conventicles; and, as Sir John never stinted her of money, she gathered the remnants of the old Puritan party about her, and tried to comfort herself with long prayers, snuffled through the nose, for the absence of her husband, but it was of no use. Treat her as he would, she loved him still with a terrible love. Once, they say, she put on her waiting-maid's dress, and stole up to London to find out what kept him there; and something she saw or heard that changed her altogether, for she came back as if her heart was broken. They say that the only person she loved with all the wild strength of her heart, had proved false to her; and if so, what wonder! At the best of times she was but a gloomy creature, and it was a great honour for her father's daughter to be wedded to a Morton. She should not have expected too much.

After her despondency came her religion. Every old Puritan preacher in the country was welcome at Morton Hall. Surely that was enough to disgust Sir John. The Mortons had never cared to have much religion, but what they had, had been good of its kind hitherto. So, when Sir John came down wanting a gay greeting and a tender show of love, his lady exhorted him, and prayed over him, and quoted the last Puritan text she had heard at him; and he swore at her, and at her preachers; and made a deadly oath that none of them should find harbour or welcome in any house of his. She looked scornfully back at him, and said she had yet to learn in what county of England the house he spoke of was to be found; but in the house her father purchased, and she inherited, all who preached the Gospel should be welcome, let kings make what laws, and kings' minions swear what oaths they would. He said nothing to this—the worst sign for her; but he set his teeth at her; and in an hour's time he rode away back to the French witch that had beguiled him.

Before he went away from Morton he set his spies. He longed to catch his wife in his fierce clutch, and punish her for defying him. She had made him hate her with her Puritanical ways. He counted the days till the messenger came, splashed up to the top of his deep leather boots, to say that my lady had invited the canting Puritan preachers of the neighbourhood to a prayer-meeting, and a dinner, and a night's rest at her house. Sir John smiled as he gave the messenger five gold pieces for his pains; and straight took post-horses, and rode long days till he got to Morton; and only just in time; for it was the very day of the prayer-meeting. Dinners were then at one o'clock in the country. The great people in London might keep late hours, and dine at three in the afternoon or so; but the Mortons they always clung to the good old ways, and as the church bells were ringing twelve when Sir John came riding into the village, he knew he might slacken bridle; and, casting one glance at the smoke which came hurrying up as if from a newly-mended fire, just behind the wood, where he knew the Hall kitchen chimney stood, Sir John stopped at the smithy, and pretended to question the smith about his horse's shoes; but he took little heed of the answers, being more occupied by an old serving-man from the Hall, who had been loitering about the smithy half the morning, as folk thought afterwards to keep some appointment with Sir John. When their talk was ended, Sir John lifted himself straight in his saddle; cleared his throat, and spoke out aloud:—

"I grieve to hear your lady is so ill." The smith wondered at this, for all the village knew of the coming feast at the Hall; the spring-chickens had been bought up, and the cade-lambs* killed; for the preachers in those days, if they fasted they fasted, if they fought they fought, if they prayed they prayed, sometimes for three hours at a standing; and if they feasted they feasted, and knew what good eating was, believe me.

---

* Lambs whose mothers died in delivery, and which were reared by hand.

"My lady ill?" said the smith, as if he doubted the old prim serving-man's word. And the latter would have chopped in with an angry asseveration (he had been at Worcester and fought on the right side), but Sir John cut him short.

"My lady is very ill, good Master Fox. It touches her here," continued he, pointing to his head. "I am come down to take her to London, where the King's own physician shall prescribe for her." And he rode slowly up to the hall.

The lady was as well as ever she had been in her life, and happier than she had often been; for in a few minutes some of those whom she esteemed so highly would be about her, some of those who had known and valued her father—her dead father, to whom her sorrowful heart turned in its woe, as the only true lover and friend she had ever had on earth. Many of the preachers would have ridden far,—was all in order in their rooms, and on the table in the great dining parlour? She had got into restless hurried ways of late. She went round below, and then she mounted the great oak staircase to see if the tower bed-chamber was all in order for old Master Hilton, the oldest among the preachers. Meanwhile, the maidens below were carrying in mighty cold rounds of spiced beef, quarters of lamb, chicken pies, and all such provisions, when, suddenly, they knew not how, they found themselves each seized by strong arms, their aprons thrown over their heads, after the manner of a gag, and themselves borne out of the house on to the poultry green behind, where, with threats of what worse might befall them, they were sent with many a shameful word (Sir John could not always command his men, many of whom had been soldiers in the French wars) back into the village. They scudded away like frightened hares. My lady was strewing the white-headed preacher's room with the last year's lavender, and stirring up the sweet-pot on the dressing-table, when she heard a step on the echoing stairs. It was no measured tread of any Puritan; it was the clang of a man of war coming nearer and nearer, with loud rapid strides. She knew the step; her heart stopped beating, not for fear, but because she loved Sir John even yet; and she took a step forward to meet him, and then stood still and trembled, for the flattering false thought came before her that he might have come yet in some quick impulse of reviving love, and that his hasty step might be prompted by the passionate tenderness of a husband. But when he reached the door, she looked as calm and indifferent as ever.

"My lady," said he, "you are gathering your friends to some feast. May I know who are thus invited to revel in my house? Some graceless fellows, I see, from the store of meat and drink below—wine-bibbers and drunkards, I fear."

But, by the working glance of his eye, she saw that he knew all; and she spoke with a cold distinctness.

"Master Ephraim Dixon, Master Zerubbabel Hopkins, Master Help-me-or-I-perish Perkins, and some other godly ministers, come to spend the afternoon in my house."

He went to her, and in his rage he struck her. She put up no arm to save herself, but reddened a little with the pain, and then drawing her necker-chief on one side, she looked at the crimson mark on her white neck.

"It serves me right," she said. "I wedded one of my father's enemies; one of those who would have hunted the old man to death. I gave my father's enemy house and lands, when he came as a beggar to my door; I followed my wicked, wayward heart in this, instead of minding my dying father's words. Strike again, and avenge him yet more!"

But he would not, because she bade him. He unloosed his sash, and bound her arms tight,—tight together, and she never struggled or spoke. Then pushing her so that she was obliged to sit down on the bed side,—

"Sit there," he said, "and hear how I will welcome the old hypocrites you have dared to ask to my house—my house and my ancestors' house, long before your father—a canting pedlar—hawked his goods about, and cheated honest men."

And, opening the chamber window right above those Hall steps where she had awaited him in her maiden beauty scarce three short years ago, he greeted the company of preachers as they rode up to the Hall with such terrible hideous language (my lady had provoked him past all bearing, you see), that the old men turned round aghast, and made the best of their way back to their own places.

Meanwhile, Sir John's serving-men below had obeyed their master's orders. They had gone through the house, closing every window, every shutter, and every door, but leaving all else just as it was—the cold meats on the table, the hot meats on the spit, the silver flagons on the side-board, all just as if it were ready for a feast; and then Sir John's head-servant, he that I spoke of before, came up and told his master all was ready.

"Is the horse and the pillion all ready? Then you and I must be my lady's tire-women;" and as it seemed to her in mockery, but in reality with a deep purpose, they dressed the helpless woman in her riding things all awry, and strange and disorderly, Sir John carried her down stairs; and he and his man bound her on the pillion; and Sir John mounted before. The man shut and locked the great house-door, and the echoes of the clang went through the empty Hall with an ominous sound. "Throw the key," said Sir John, "deep into the mere yonder. My lady may go seek it if she lists, when next I set her arms at liberty. Till then I know whose house Morton Hall shall be called."

"Sir John! It shall be called the Devil's House, and you shall be his steward."

But the poor lady had better have held her tongue; for Sir John only laughed, and told her to rave on. As he passed through the village, with his serving-men riding behind, the tenantry came out and stood at their doors, and pitied him for having a mad wife, and praised him for his care of her, and of the chance he gave her of amendment by taking her up to be seen by the King's physician. But, somehow, the Hall got an ugly name; the roast and boiled meats, the ducks, the chickens had time to drop into dust, before any human being now dared to enter in; or, indeed, had any right to enter in, for Sir John never came back to Morton; and as for my lady, some said she was dead, and some said she was mad, and shut up in London, and some said Sir John had taken her to a convent abroad.

"And what did become of her?" asked we, creeping up to Mrs. Dawson.

"Nay, how should I know?"

"But what do you think?" we asked pertinaciously.

"I cannot tell. I have heard that after Sir John was killed at the battle of the Boyne she got loose, and came wandering back to Morton, to her old nurse's house; but, indeed, she was mad then, out and out, and I've no doubt Sir John had seen it coming on. She used to have visions and dream dreams: and some thought her a prophetess, and some thought her fairly crazy. What she said about the Mortons was awful. She doomed them to die out of the land, and their house to be razed to the ground, while pedlars and huxters, such as her own people, her father, had been, should dwell where the knightly Mortons had once lived. One winter's night she strayed away, and the next morning they found the poor crazy woman frozen to death in Drumble meeting-house yard; and the Mr. Morton who had succeeded to Sir John had her decently buried where she was found, by the side of her father's grave."

We were silent for a time. "And when was the old Hall opened, Mrs. Dawson, please?"

"Oh! when the Mr. Morton, our Squire Morton's grandfather, came into possession. He was a distant cousin of Sir John's, a much quieter kind of man. He had all the old rooms opened wide, and aired, and fumigated; and the strange fragments of musty food were collected and burnt in the yard; but somehow that old dining-parlour had always a charnel-house smell, and no one ever liked making merry in it—thinking of the grey old preachers, whose ghosts might be even then scenting the meats afar off, and trooping unbidden to a feast, that was not that of which they were baulked. I was glad for one when the squire's father built another dining-room; and no servant in the house will go an errand into the old dining-parlour after dark, I can assure ye."

"I wonder if the way the last Mr. Morton had to sell his land to the people at Drumble had anything to do with old Lady Morton's prophecy," said my mother, musingly.

"Not at all," said Mrs. Dawson, sharply. "My lady was crazy, and her words not to be minded. I should like to see the cotton-spinners of Drumble offer to purchase land from the squire. Besides, there's a strict entail now. They can't purchase the land if they would. A set of trading pedlars, indeed!"

I remember Ethelinda and I looked at each other at this word "pedlars;" which was the very word she had put into Sir John's mouth when taunting his wife with her father's low birth and calling. We thought, "We shall see."

Alas! we have seen.

Soon after that evening our good old friend Mrs. Dawson died. I remember it well, because Ethelinda and I were put into mourning for the first time in our lives. A dear little brother of ours had died only the year before, and then my father and mother had decided that we were too young; that there was no necessity for their incurring the expense of black frocks. We mourned for the little delicate darling in our hearts, I know; and to this day I often wonder what it would have been to have had a brother. But when Mrs. Dawson died it became a sort of duty we owed to the squire's family to go into black, and very proud and pleased Ethelinda and I were with our new frocks. I remember dreaming Mrs. Dawson was alive again, and crying, because I thought my new frock would be taken away from me. But all this has nothing to do with Morton Hall.

When I first became aware of the greatness of the squire's station in life, his family consisted of himself, his wife (a frail, delicate lady), his only son, "little master," as Mrs. Dawson was allowed to call him, "the young squire," as we in the village always termed him. His name was John Marmaduke. He was always called John; and after Mrs. Dawson's story of the old Sir John, I used to wish he might not bear that ill-omened name. He used to ride through the village in his bright scarlet coat, his long fair curling hair falling over his lace collar, and his broad black hat and feather shading his merry blue eyes, Ethelinda and I thought then, and I always shall think, there never was such a boy. He had a fine high spirit, too, of his own, and once horsewhipped a groom twice as big as himself who had thwarted him. To see him and Miss Phillis go tearing through the village on their pretty Arabian horses, laughing as they met the west wind, and their long golden curls flying behind them, you would have thought them brother and sister, rather than nephew and aunt; for Miss Phillis was the squire's sister, much younger than himself; indeed, at the time I speak of, I don't think she could have been above seventeen, and the young squire, her nephew, was nearly ten. I remember Mrs. Dawson sending for my mother and me up to the Hall that we might see Miss Phillis dressed ready to go with her brother to a ball given at some great lord's house to Prince William of Gloucester, nephew to good old George the Third.

When Mrs. Elizabeth, Mrs. Morton's maid, saw us at tea in Mrs. Dawson's room, she asked Ethelinda and me if we would not like to come into Miss Phillis's dressing-room, and watch her dress; and then she said, if we would promise to keep from touching anything, she would make interest for us to go. We would have promised to stand on our heads, and would have tried to do so too, to earn such a privilege. So in we went, and stood together, hand-in-hand, up in a corner out of the way, feeling very red, and shy, and hot, till Miss Phillis put us at our ease by playing all manner of comical tricks, just to make us laugh, which at last we did outright, in spite of all our endeavours to be grave, lest Mrs. Elizabeth should complain of us to my mother. I recollect the scent of the *maréchale* powder with which Miss Phillis's hair was just sprinkled; and how she shook her head, like a young colt, to work the hair loose which Mrs. Elizabeth was straining up over a cushion. Then Mrs. Elizabeth would try a little of Mrs. Morton's rouge; and Miss Phillis would wash it off with a wet towel, saying that she liked her own paleness better than any performer's colour; and when Mrs. Elizabeth wanted just to touch her cheeks once more, she hid herself behind the great arm-chair, peeping out, with her sweet, merry face, first at one side and then at another, till we all heard the squire's voice at the door, asking her, if she was dressed, to come and show herself to madam, her sister-in-law; for, as I said, Mrs. Morton was a great invalid, and unable to go out to any grand parties like this. We were all silent in an instant; and even Mrs. Elizabeth thought no more of the rouge, but how to get Miss Phillis's beautiful blue dress on quick enough. She had cherry-coloured knots in her hair, and her breast-knots were of the same ribbon. Her gown was open in front, to a quilted white silk skirt. We felt very shy of her as she stood there fully dressed—she looked so much grander than anything we had ever seen; and it was like a relief when Mrs. Elizabeth told us to go down to Mrs. Dawson's parlour, where my mother was sitting all this time.

Just as we were telling how merry and comical Miss Phillis had been, in came a footman. "Mrs. Dawson," said he, "the squire bids me ask you to go with Mrs. Sidebotham into the west parlour, to have a look at Miss Morton before she goes." We went, too, clinging to my mother. Miss Phillis looked rather shy as we came in, and stood just by the door. I think we all must have shown her that we had never seen anything so beautiful as she was in our lives before; for she went very scarlet at our fixed gaze of admiration, and, to relieve herself, she began to play all manner of antics—whirling round, and making cheeses with her rich silk petticoat; unfurling her fan (a present from madam, to complete her dress), and peeping first on one side and then on the other, just as she had done upstairs; and then catching hold of her nephew, and insisting that he should dance a minuet with her until the carriage came; which proposal made him very angry, as it was an insult to his manhood (at nine years old) to suppose he could dance. "It was all very well for girls to make fools of themselves," he said, "but it did not do for men." And Ethelinda and I thought we had never heard so fine a speech before. But the carriage came before we had half feasted our eyes enough; and the squire came from his wife's room to order the little master to bed, and hand his sister to the carriage.

I remember a good deal of talk about royal dukes and unequal marriages that night. I believe Miss Phillis did dance with Prince William; and I have often heard that she bore away the bell at the ball, and that no one came near her for beauty and pretty, merry ways. In a day or two after I saw her scampering through the village, looking just as she did before she had danced with a royal duke. We all thought she would marry some one great, and used to look out for the lord who was to take her away. But poor madam died, and there was no one but Miss Phillis to comfort her brother, for the young squire was gone away to some great school down south; and Miss Phillis grew grave, and reined in her pony to keep by the squire's side, when he rode out on his steady old mare in his lazy, careless way.

We did not hear so much of the doings at the Hall now Mrs. Dawson was dead; so I cannot tell how it was; but, by-and-by, there was a talk of bills that were once paid weekly, being now allowed to run to quarter-day; and then, instead of being settled every quarter-day, they were put off to Christmas; and many said they had hard enough work to get their money then. A buzz went through the village that the young squire played high at college, and that he made away with more money than his father could afford. But when he came down to Morton, he was as handsome as ever; and I, for one, never believed evil of him; though I'll allow others might cheat him, and he never suspect it. His aunt was as fond of him as ever; and he of her. Many is the time I have seen them out walking together, sometimes sad enough, sometimes merry as ever. By-and-by, my father heard of sales of small pieces of land, not included in the entail; and, at last, things got so bad, that the very crops were sold yet green upon the ground, for any price folks would give, so that there was but ready money paid. The squire at length gave way entirely, and never left the house; and the young master in London; and poor Miss Phillis used to go about trying to see after the workmen and labourers, and save what she could. By this time she would be above thirty; Ethelinda and I were nineteen and twenty-one when my mother died, and that was some years before this. Well, at last the squire died; they do say of a broken heart at his son's extravagance; and, though the lawyers kept it very close, it began to be rumoured that Miss Phillis's fortune had gone too. Any way, the creditors came down on the estate like wolves. It was entailed, and it could not be sold; but they put it into the hands of a lawyer, who was to get what he could out of it, and have no pity for the poor young squire, who had not a roof for his head. Miss Phillis went to live by herself in a little cottage in the village, at the end of the property, which the lawyer allowed her to have because he could not let it to any one, it was so tumble-down and old. We never knew what she lived on, poor lady; but she said she was well in health, which was all we durst ask about. She came to see my father just before he died, and he seemed made bold with the feeling that he was a dying man; so he asked, what I had longed to know for many a year, where was the young squire? He had never been seen in Morton since his father's funeral. Miss Phillis said he was gone abroad; but in what part he was then, she herself hardly knew; only she had a feeling that, sooner or later, he would come back to the old place; where she should strive to keep a home for him whenever he was tired of wandering about, and trying to make his fortune.

"Trying to make his fortune still?" asked my father, his questioning eyes saying more than his words. Miss Phillis shook her head, with a sad meaning in her face; and we understood it all. He was at some French gaming-table, if he was not at an English one.

Miss Phillis was right. It might be a year after my father's death when he came back, looking old and grey and worn. He came to our door just after we had barred it one winter's evening. Ethelinda and I still lived at the farm, trying to keep it up, and make it pay; but it was hard work. We heard a step coming up the straight pebble walk; and then it stopped right at our door, under the very porch, and we heard a man's breathing, quick and short.

"Shall I open the door?" said I.

"No, wait!" said Ethelinda; for we lived alone, and there was no cottage near us. We held our breaths. There came a knock.

"Who's there?" I cried.

"Where does Miss Morton live—Miss Phillis?"

We were not sure if we would answer him; for she, like us, lived alone.

"Who's there?" again said I.

"Your master," he answered, proud and angry. "My name is John Morton. Where does Miss Phillis live?"

We had the door unbarred in a trice, and begged him to come in; to pardon our rudeness. We would have given him of our best, as was his due from us; but he only listened to the directions we gave him to his aunt's, and took no notice of our apologies.

CHAPTER II

Up to this time we had felt it rather impertinent to tell each other of our individual silent wonder as to what Miss Phillis lived on; but I know in our hearts we each thought about it, with a kind of respectful pity for her fallen low estate. Miss Phillis—that we remembered like an angel for beauty, and like a little princess for the imperious sway she exercised, and which was such sweet compulsion that we had all felt proud to be her slaves—Miss Phillis was now a worn, plain woman, in homely dress, tending towards old age; and looking—(at that time I dared not have spoken so insolent a thought, not even to myself)—but she did look as if she had hardly the proper nourishing food she required. One day, I remember Mrs. Jones, the butcher's wife (she was a Drumble person) saying, in her saucy way, that she was not surprised to see Miss Morton so bloodless and pale, for she only treated herself to a Sunday's dinner of meat, and lived on slop and bread-and-butter all the rest of the week. Ethelinda put on her severe face—a look that I am afraid of to this day—and said, "Mrs. Jones, do you suppose Miss Morton can eat your half-starved meat? You do not know how choice and dainty she is, as becomes one born and bred like her. What was it we had to bring for her only last Saturday from the grand new butcher's, in Drumble, Biddy?"—(We took our eggs to market in Drumble every

Saturday, for the cotton-spinners would give us a higher price than the Morton people: the more fools they!)

I thought it rather cowardly of Ethelinda to put the story-telling on me; but she always thought a great deal of saving her soul; more than I did, I am afraid, for I made answer, as bold as a lion, "Two sweet breads, at a shilling a-piece; and a forequarter of house-lamb, at eighteen-pence a pound." So off went Mrs. Jones, in a huff, saying, "their meat was good enough for Mrs. Donkin, the great mill-owner's widow, and might serve a beggarly Morton any day." When we were alone, I said to Ethelinda, "I'm afraid we shall have to pay for our lies at the great day of account;" and Ethelinda answered, very sharply—(she's a good sister in the main)—"Speak for yourself, Biddy. I never said a word. I only asked questions. How could I help it if you told lies? I'm sure I wondered at you, how glib you spoke out what was not true." But I knew she was glad I told the lies, in her heart.

After the poor squire came to live with his aunt, Miss Phillis, we ventured to speak a bit to ourselves. We were sure they were pinched. They looked like it. He had a bad hacking cough at times; though he was so dignified and proud he would never cough when any one was near. I have seen him up before it was day, sweeping the dung off the roads, to try and get enough to manure the little plot of ground behind the cottage, which Miss Phillis had let alone, but which her nephew used to dig in and till; for, said he, one day, in his grand, slow way, "he was always fond of experiments in agriculture." Ethelinda and I do believe that the two or three score of cabbages he raised were all they had to live on that winter, besides the bit of meal and tea they got at the village shop.

One Friday night I said to Ethelinda, "It is a shame to take these eggs to Drumble to sell, and never to offer one to the squire, on whose lands we were born." She answered, "I have thought so many a time; but how can we do it? I, for one, dare not offer them to the squire; and as for Miss Phillis, it would seem like impertinence." "I'll try at it," said I.

So that night I took some eggs—fresh yellow eggs from our own pheasant hen, the like of which there were not for twenty miles round—and I laid them softly after dusk on one of the little stone seats in the porch of Miss Phillis's cottage. But, alas! when we went to market at Drumble, early the next morning, there were my eggs all shattered and splashed, making an ugly yellow pool in the road just in front of the cottage. I had meant to have followed it up by a chicken or so; but I saw now that it would never do. Miss Phillis came now and then to call on us; she was a little more high and distant than she had been when a girl, and we felt we must keep our place. I suppose we had affronted the young squire, for he never came near our house.

Well, there came a hard winter, and provisions rose; and Ethelinda and I had much ado to make ends meet. If it had not been for my sister's good management, we should have been in debt, I know; but she proposed that we should go without dinner, and only have a breakfast and a tea, to which I agreed, you may be sure.

One baking day I had made some cakes for tea—potato-cakes we called them. They had a savoury, hot smell about them; and, to tempt Ethelinda, who was not quite well, I cooked a rasher of bacon. Just as we were sitting down, Miss Phillis knocked at our door. We let her in. God only knows how white and haggard she looked. The heat of our kitchen made her totter, and for a while she could not speak. But all the time she looked at the food on the table as if she feared to shut her eyes lest it should all vanish away. It was an eager stare like that of some animal, poor soul! "If I durst," said Ethelinda, wishing to ask her to share our meal, but being afraid to speak out. I did not speak, but handed her the good, hot, buttered cake; on which she seized, and putting it up to her lips as if to taste it, she fell back in her chair, crying.

We had never seen a Morton cry before; and it was something awful. We stood silent and aghast. She recovered herself, but did not taste the food; on the contrary, she covered it up with both her hands, as if afraid of losing it. "If you'll allow me," said she, in a stately kind of way, to make up for our having seen her crying, "I'll take it to my nephew." And she got up to go away; but she could hardly stand for very weakness, and had to sit down again; she smiled at us, and said she was a little dizzy, but it would soon go off; but as she smiled, the bloodless lips were drawn far back over her teeth, making her face seem somehow like a death's head. "Miss Morton," said I, "do honour us by taking tea with us this once. The squire, your father, once took a luncheon with my father, and we are proud of it to this day." I poured her out some tea, which she drank; the food she shrank away from as if the very sight of it turned her sick again. But when she rose to go, she looked at it with her sad, wolfish eyes, as if she could not leave it; and at last she broke into a low cry, and said, "Oh, Bridget, we are starving! We are starving for want of food! I can bear it; I don't mind; but he suffers—oh, how he suffers! Let me take him food for this one night."

We could hardly speak; our hearts were in our throats, and the tears ran down our cheeks like rain. We packed up a basket, and carried it to her very door, never venturing to speak a word, for we knew what it must have cost her to say that. When we left her at the cottage, we made her our usual deep courtesy, but she fell upon our necks, and kissed us. For several nights after she hovered round our house about dusk, but she would never come in again, and face us in candle or fire light, much less meet us by daylight. We took out food to her as regularly as might be, and gave it to her in silence, and with the deepest courtesies we could make, we felt so honoured. We had many plans now she had permitted us to know of her distress. We hoped she would allow us to go on serving her in some way as became us as Sidebothams. But one night she never came; we stayed out in the cold, bleak wind, looking into the dark for her thin, worn figure; all in vain. Late the next afternoon, the young squire lifted the latch, and stood right in the middle of our houseplace. The roof was low overhead, and made lower by the deep beams supporting the floor above; he stooped as he looked at us, and tried to form words, but no sound came out of his lips. I never saw such gaunt woe; no, never! At last he took me by the shoulder, and led me out of the house.

"Come with me!" he said, when we were in the open air, as if that gave him strength to speak audibly. I needed no second word. We entered Miss Phillis's cottage; a liberty I had never taken before. What little furniture was there, it was clear to be seen were cast-off fragments of the old splendour of Morton Hall. No fire. Grey wood ashes lay on the hearth. An old settee, once white and gold, now doubly shabby in its fall from its former estate. On it lay Miss Phillis, very pale; very still; her eyes shut.

"Tell me!" he gasped. "Is she dead? I think she is asleep; but she looks so strong—as if she might be—" He could not say the awful word again. I stooped, and felt no warmth; only a cold chill atmosphere seemed to surround her.

"She is dead!" I replied at length. "Oh, Miss Phillis! Miss Phillis!" and, like a fool, I began to cry. But he sat down without a tear, and looked vacantly at the empty hearth. I dared not cry any more when I saw him so stony sad. I did not know what to do. I could not leave him; and yet I had no excuse for staying. I went up to Miss Phillis, and softly arranged the grey ragged locks about her face.

"Ay!" said he. "She must be laid out, Who so fit to do it as you and your sister, children of good old Robert Sidebotham?"

"Oh, my master," I said, "this is no fit place for you. Let me fetch my sister to sit up with me all night; and honour us by sleeping at our poor little cottage."

I did not expect he would have done it; but after a few minutes' silence he agreed to my proposal. I hastened home, and told Ethelinda, and both of us crying, we heaped up the fire, and spread the table with food, and made up a bed in one corner of the floor. While I stood ready to go, I saw Ethelinda open the great chest in which we kept our treasures; and out she took a fine Holland shift that had been one of my mother's wedding shifts; and, seeing what she was after, I went upstairs and brought down a piece of rare old lace, a good deal darned to be sure, but still old Brussels point, bequeathed to me long ago by my god-mother, Mrs. Dawson. We huddled these things under our cloaks, locked the door behind us, and set out to do all we could now for poor Miss Phillis. We found the squire sitting just as we left him; I hardly knew if he understood me when I told him how to unlock our door, and gave him the key, though I spoke as distinctly as ever I could for the choking in my throat. At last he rose and went; and Ethelinda and I composed her poor thin limbs to decent rest, and wrapped her in the fine Holland shift; and then I plaited up my lace into a close cap to tie up the wasted features. When all was done we looked upon her from a little distance.

"A Morton to die of hunger!" said Ethelinda solemnly. "We should not have dared to think that such a thing was within the chances of life. Do you remember that evening, when you and I were little children, and she a merry young lady peeping at us from behind her fan?"

We did not cry any more; we felt very still and awestruck. After a while I said, "I wonder if, after all, the young squire did go to our house. He had a strange look about him. If I dared I would go and see." I opened the door; the night was black as pitch; the air very still. "I'll go," said I; and off I went, not meeting a creature, for it was long past eleven. I reached our house; the window was long and low, and the shutters were old and shrunk. I could peep between them well, and see all that was going on. He was there, sitting over the fire, never shedding a tear; but seeming as if he saw his past life in the embers. The food we had prepared was untouched. Once or twice, during my long watch (I was more than an hour away), he turned towards the food, and made as though he would have eaten it, and then shuddered back; but at last he seized it, and tore it with his teeth, and laughed and rejoiced over it like some starved animal. I could not keep from crying then. He gorged himself with great morsels; and when he could eat no more, it seemed as if his strength for suffering had come back. He threw himself on the bed, and such a passion of despair I never heard of, much less ever saw. I could not bear to witness it. The dead Miss Phillis lay calm and still. Her trials were over. I would go back and watch with Ethelinda.

When the pale grey morning dawn stole in, making us shiver and shake after our vigil, the squire returned. We were both mortal afraid of him, we knew not why. He looked quiet enough—the lines were worn deep before—no new traces were there. He stood and looked at his aunt for a minute or two. Then he went up into the loft above the room where we were; he brought a small paper parcel down; bade us keep on our watch yet a little time. First one and then the other of us went home to get some food. It was a bitter black frost; no one was out who could stop indoors; and those who were out cared not to stop to speak. Towards afternoon the air darkened, and a great snow-storm came on. We durst not be left only one alone; yet, at the cottage where Miss Phillis had lived, there was neither fire nor fuel. So we sat and shivered and shook till morning. The squire never came that night nor all next day.

"What must we do?" asked Ethelinda, broken down entirely. "I shall die if I stop here another night. We must tell the neighbours and get help for the watch."

"So we must," said I, very low and grieved. I went out and told the news at the nearest house, taking care, you may be sure, never to speak of the hunger and cold Miss Phillis must have endured in silence. It was bad enough to have them come in, and make their remarks on the poor bits of furniture; for no one had known their bitter straits even as much as Ethelinda and me, and we had been shocked at the bareness of the place. I did hear that one or two of the more ill-conditioned had said, it was not for nothing we had kept the death to ourselves for two nights; that, to judge from the lace on her cap, there must have been some pretty pickings. Ethelinda would have contradicted this, but I bade her let it alone; it would save the memory of the proud Mortons from the shame that poverty is thought to be; and as for us, why we could live it down. But, on the whole, people came forward kindly; money was not wanting to bury her well, if not grandly, as became her birth; and many a one was bidden to the funeral who might have looked after her a little more in her life-time. Among others was Squire Hargreaves from Bothwick Hall over the moors. He was some kind of far-away cousin to the Mortons'; so when he came he was asked to go chief mourner in Squire Morton's strange absence, which I should have wondered at the more if I had not thought him almost crazy when I watched his ways through the shutter that night. Squire Hargreaves started when they paid him the compliment of asking him to take the head of the coffin.

"Where is her nephew?" asked he.

"No one has seen him since eight o'clock last Thursday morning."

"But I saw him at noon on Thursday," said Squire Hargreaves, with a round oath. "He came over the moors to tell me of his aunt's death, and to ask me to give him a little money to bury her, on the pledge of his gold shirt-buttons. He said I was a cousin, and could pity a gentleman in such sore need; that the buttons were his mother's first gift to him; and that I was to keep them safe, for some day he would make his fortune, and come back to redeem them. He had not known his aunt was so ill, or he would have parted with these buttons sooner, though he held them as more precious than he could tell me. I gave him money; but I could not find in my heart to take the buttons. He bade me not tell of all this; but when a man is missing it is my duty to give all the clue I can."

And so their poverty was blazoned abroad! But folk forgot it all in the search for the squire on the moor-side. Two days they searched in vain; the third, upwards of a hundred men turned out, hand-in-hand, step to step, to leave no foot of ground unsearched. They found him stark and stiff, with Squire Hargreaves' money, and his mother's gold buttons, safe in his waistcoat pocket.

And we laid him down by the side of his poor aunt Phillis.

After the squire, John Marmaduke Morton, had been found dead in that sad way, on the dreary moors, the creditors seemed to lose all hold on the property; which indeed, during the seven years they had had it, they had drained as dry as a sucked orange. But for a long time no one seemed to know who rightly was the owner of Morton Hall and lands. The old house fell out of repair; the chimneys were full of starlings' nests; the flags in the terrace in front were hidden by the long grass; the panes in the windows were broken, no one knew how or why, for the children of the village got up a tale that the house was haunted. Ethelinda and I went sometimes in the summer mornings, and gathered some of the roses that were being strangled by the bindweed that spread over all; and we used to try and weed the old flower-garden a little; but we were no longer young, and the stooping made our backs ache. Still we always felt happier if we cleared but ever such a little space. Yet we did not go there willingly in the afternoons, and left the garden always long before the first slight shade of dusk.

We did not choose to ask the common people—many of them were weavers for the Drumble manufacturers, and no longer decent hedgers and ditchers—we did not choose to ask them, I say, who was squire now, or where he lived. But one day, a great London lawyer came to the Morton Arms, and made a pretty stir. He came on behalf of a General Morton, who was squire now, though he was far away in India. He had been written to, and they had proved him heir, though he was a very distant cousin, farther back than Sir John, I think. And now he had sent word they were to take money of his that was in England, and put the house in thorough repair; for that three maiden sisters of his, who lived in some town in the north, would come and live at Morton Hall till his return. So the lawyer sent for a Drumble builder, and gave him directions. We thought it would have been prettier if he had hired John Cobb, the Morton builder and joiner, he that had made the squire's coffin, and the squire's father's before that. Instead, came a troop of Drumble men, knocking and tumbling about in the Hall, and making their jests up and down all those stately rooms. Ethelinda and I never went near the place till they were gone, bag and baggage. And then what a change! The old casement windows, with their heavy leaded panes half overgrown with vines and roses, were taken away, and great staring sash windows were in their stead. New grates inside; all modern, newfangled, and smoking, instead of the brass dogs which held the mighty logs of wood in the old squire's time. The little square Turkey carpet under the dining-table, which had served Miss Phillis, was not good enough for these new Mortons; the dining-room was all carpeted over. We peeped into the old dining-parlour—that parlour where the dinner for the Puritan preachers had been laid out; the flag parlour, as it had been called of late years. But it had a damp, earthy smell, and was used as a lumber-room. We shut the door quicker than we had opened it. We came away disappointed. The Hall was no longer like our own honoured Morton Hall.

"After all, these three ladies are Mortons," said Ethelinda to me. "We must not forget that: we must go and pay our duty to them as soon as they have appeared in church."

Accordingly we went. But we had heard and seen a little of them before we paid our respects at the Hall. Their maid had been down in the village; their maid, as she was called now; but a maid-of-all-work she had been until now, as she very soon let out when we questioned her. However, we were never proud; and she was a good honest farmer's daughter out of Northumberland. What work she did make with the Queen's English! The folk in Lancashire are said to speak broad, but I could always understand our own kindly tongue; whereas, when Mrs. Turner told me her name, both Ethelinda and I could have sworn she said Donagh, and were afraid she was an Irishwoman. Her ladies were what you may call past the bloom of youth; Miss Sophronia—Miss Morton, properly—was just sixty; Miss Annabella, three years younger; and Miss Dorothy (or Baby, as they called her when they were by themselves), was two years younger still. Mrs. Turner was very confidential to us, partly because, I doubt not, she had heard of our old connection with the family, and partly because she was an arrant talker, and was glad of anybody who would listen to her. So we heard the very first week how each of the ladies had wished for the east bed-room—that which faced the north-east—which no one slept in in the old squire's days; but there were two steps leading up into it, and, said Miss Sophronia, she would never let a younger sister have a room more elevated than she had herself. She was the eldest, and she had a right to the steps. So she bolted herself in for two days, while she unpacked her clothes, and then came out, looking like a hen that has laid an egg, and defies any one to take that honour from her.

But her sisters were very deferential to her in general; that must be said. They never had more than two black feathers in their bonnets; while she had always three. Mrs. Turner said that once, when they thought Miss Annabella had been going to have an offer of marriage made her, Miss Sophronia had not objected to her wearing three that winter; but when it all ended in smoke, Miss Annabella had to pluck it out as became a younger sister. Poor Miss Annabella! She had been a beauty (Mrs. Turner said), and great things had been expected of her. Her brother, the general, and her mother had both spoilt her, rather than cross her unnecessarily, and so spoil her good looks; which old Mrs. Morton had always expected would make the fortune of the family. Her sisters were angry with her for not having married some great rich gentleman; though, as she used to say to Mrs. Turner, how could she help it? She was willing enough, but no rich gentleman came to ask her. We agreed that it really was not her fault; but her sisters thought it was; and now, that she had lost her beauty, they were always casting it up what they would have done if they had had her gifts. There were some Miss Burrells they had heard of, each of whom had married a lord; and these Miss Burrells had not been such great beauties. So Miss Sophronia used to work the question by the rule of three; and put it in this way—If Miss Burrell, with a tolerable pair of eyes, a snub nose, and a wide mouth, married a baron, what rank of peer ought our pretty Annabella to have espoused? And the worst was, Miss Annabella—who had never had any ambition—wanted to have married a poor curate in her youth; but was pulled up by her mother and sisters, reminding her of the duty she owed to her family. Miss Dorothy had done her best—Miss Morton always praised her for it. With not half the good looks of Miss Annabella, she had danced with an honourable at Harrogate three times running; and, even now, she persevered in trying; which was more than could be said of Miss Annabella, who was very broken-spirited.

I do believe Mrs. Turner told us all this before we had ever seen the ladies. We had let them know, through Mrs. Turner, of our wish to pay them our respects; so we ventured to go up to the front door, and rap modestly. We had reasoned about it before, and agreed that if we were going in our every-day clothes, to offer a little present of eggs, or to call on Mrs. Turner (as she had asked us to do), the back door would have been the appropriate entrance for us. But going, however humbly, to pay our respects, and offer our reverential welcome to the Miss Mortons, we took rank as their visitors, and should go to the front door. We were shown up the wide stairs, along the gallery, up two steps, into Miss Sophronia's room. She put away some papers hastily as we came in. We heard afterwards that she was writing a book, to be called *The Female Chesterfield; or, Letters from a Lady of Quality to her Niece.* And the little niece sat there in a high chair, with a flat board tied to her back, and her feet in stocks on the tail of the chair; so that she had nothing to do but listen to her aunt's letters; which were read aloud to her as they were written, in order to mark their effect on her manners. I was not sure whether Miss Sophronia liked our interruption; but I know little Miss Cordelia Mannisty did.

"Is the young lady crooked?" asked Ethelinda, during a pause in our conversation. I had noticed that my sister's eyes would rest on the child; although, by an effort, she sometimes succeeded in looking at something else occasionally.

"No! indeed, ma'am," said Miss Morton. "But she was born in India, and her backbone has never properly hardened. Besides, I and my two sisters each take charge of her for a week; and their systems of education—I might say non-education—differ so totally and entirely from my ideas, that when Miss Mannisty comes to me, I consider myself fortunate if I can undo the—hem!—that has been done during a fortnight's absence. Cordelia, my dear, repeat to these good ladies the geography lesson you learnt this morning."

Poor little Miss Mannisty began to tell us a great deal about some river in Yorkshire of which we had never heard, though I dare say we ought to, and then a great deal more about the towns that it passed by, and what they were famous for; and all I can remember—indeed, could understand at the time—was that Pomfret was famous for Pomfret cakes; which I knew before. But Ethelinda gasped for breath before it was done, she was so nearly choked up with astonishment; and when it was ended, she said,

"Pretty dear; it's wonderful!" Miss Morton looked a little displeased, and replied, "Not at all. Good little girls can learn anything they choose, even French verbs. Yes, Cordelia, they can. And to be good is better than to be pretty. We don't think about looks here. You may get down, child, and go into the garden; and take care you put your bonnet on, or you'll be all over freckles." We got up to take leave at the same time, and followed the little girl out of the room. Ethelinda fumbled in her pocket.

"Here's a sixpence, my dear, for you. Nay, I am sure you may take it from an old woman like me, to whom you've told over more geography than I ever thought there was out of the Bible." For Ethelinda always maintained that the long chapters in the Bible which were all names, were geography; and though I knew well enough they were not, yet I had forgotten what the right word was, so I let her alone; for one hard word did as well as another. Little miss looked as if she was not sure if she might take it; but I suppose we had two kindly old faces, for at last the smile came into her eyes—not to her mouth, she had lived too much with grave and quiet people for that—and, looking wistfully at us, she said,—

"Thank you. But won't you go and see aunt Annabella?" We said we should like to pay our respects to both her other aunts if we might take that liberty; and perhaps she would show us the way. But, at the door of a room, she stopped short, and said, sorrowfully, "I mayn't go in; it is not my week for being with aunt Annabella;" and then she went slowly and heavily towards the garden-door.

"That child is cowed by somebody," said I to Ethelinda.

"But she knows a deal of geography"—Ethelinda's speech was cut short by the opening of the door in answer to our knock. The once beautiful Miss Annabella Morton stood before us, and bade us enter. She was dressed in white, with a turned-up velvet hat, and two or three short drooping black feathers in it. I should not like to say she rouged, but she had a very pretty colour in her cheeks; that much can do neither good nor harm. At first she looked so unlike anybody I had ever seen, that I wondered what the child could have found to like in her; for like her she did, that was very clear. But, when Miss Annabella spoke, I came under the charm. Her voice was very sweet and plaintive, and suited well with the kind of things she said; all about charms of nature, and tears, and grief, and such sort of talk, which reminded me rather of poetry—very pretty to listen to, though I never could understand it as well as plain, comfortable prose. Still I hardly know why I liked Miss Annabella. I think I was sorry for her; though whether I should have been if she had not put it in my head, I don't know. The room looked very comfortable; a spinnet in a corner to amuse herself with, and a good sofa to lie down upon. By-and-by, we got her to talk of her little niece, and she, too, had her system of education. She said she hoped to develop the sensibilities and to cultivate the tastes. While with her, her darling niece read works of imagination, and acquired all that Miss Annabella could impart of the fine arts. We neither of us quite knew what she was hinting at, at the time; but afterwards, by dint of questioning little miss, and using our own eyes and ears, we found that she read aloud to her aunt while she lay on the sofa. *Santo Sebastiano; or, the Young Protector*, was what they were deep in at this time; and, as it was in five volumes and the heroine spoke broken English—which required to be read twice over to make it intelligible—it lasted them a long time. She also learned to play on the spinnet; not much, for I never heard above two tunes, one of which was God save the King, and the other was not. But I fancy the poor child was lectured by one aunt, and frightened by the other's sharp ways and numerous fancies. She might well be fond of her gentle, pensive (Miss Annabella told me she was pensive, so I know I am right in calling her so) aunt, with her soft voice, and her never-ending novels, and the sweet scents that hovered about the sleepy room.

No one tempted us towards Miss Dorothy's apartment when we left Miss Annabella; so we did not see the youngest Miss Morton this first day. We had each of us treasured up many little mysteries to be explained by our dictionary, Mrs. Turner.

"Who is little Miss Mannisty?" we asked in one breath, when we saw our friend from the Hall. And then we learnt that there had been a fourth—a younger Miss Morton, who was no beauty, and no wit, and no anything; so Miss Sophronia, her eldest sister, had allowed her to marry a Mr. Mannisty, and ever after spoke of her as "my poor sister Jane." She and her husband had gone out to India, and both had died there; and the general had made it a sort of condition with his sisters that they should take charge of the child, or else none of them liked children except Miss Annabella.

60

"Miss Annabella likes children," said I. "Then that's the reason children like her."

"I can't say she likes children; for we never have any in our house but Miss Cordelia; but her she does like dearly."

"Poor little miss!" said Ethelinda, "does she never get a game of play with other little girls?" And I am sure from that time Ethelinda considered her in a diseased state from this very circumstance, and that her knowledge of geography was one of the symptoms of the disorder; for she used often to say, "I wish she did not know so much geography! I'm sure it is not quite right."

Whether or not her geography was right, I don't know; but the child pined for companions. A very few days after we had called—and yet long enough to have passed her into Miss Annabella's week—I saw Miss Cordelia in a corner of the church green, playing, with awkward humility, along with some of the rough village girls, who were as expert at the game as she was unapt and slow. I hesitated a little, and at last I called to her.

"How do you, my dear?" I said. "How come you here, so far from home?"

She reddened, and then looked up at me with her large, serious eyes.

"Aunt Annabel sent me into the wood to meditate—and—and—it was very dull—and I heard these little girls playing and laughing—and I had my sixpence with me, and—it was not wrong, was it, ma'am?—I came to them, and told one of them I would give it to her if she would ask the others to let me play with them."

"But, my dear, they are—some of them—very rough little children, and not fit companions for a Morton."

"But I am a Mannisty, ma'am!" she pleaded, with so much entreaty in her ways, that if I had not known what naughty, bad girls some of them were, I could not have resisted her longing for companions of her own age. As it was, I was angry with them for having taken her sixpence; but, when she had told me which it was, and saw that I was going to reclaim it, she clung to me, and said,—

"Oh! don't, ma'am—you must not. I gave it to her quite of my own self."

So I turned away; for there was truth in what the child said. But to this day I have never told Ethelinda what became of her sixpence. I took Miss Cordelia home with me while I changed my dress to be fit to take her back to the Hall. And on the way, to make up for her disappointment, I began talking of my dear Miss Phillis, and her bright, pretty youth, I had never named her name since her death to any one but Ethelinda—and that only on Sundays and quiet times. And I could not have spoken of her to a grown-up person; but somehow to Miss Cordelia it came out quite natural. Not of her latter days, of course; but of her pony, and her little black King Charles's dogs, and all the living creatures that were glad in her presence when first I knew her. And nothing would satisfy the child but I must go into the Hall garden and show her where Miss Phillis's garden had been. We were deep in our talk, and she was stooping down to clear the plot from weeds, when I heard a sharp voice cry out, "Cordelia! Cordelia! Dirtying your frock with kneeling on the wet grass! It is not my week; but I shall tell your aunt Annabella of you."

And the window was shut down with a jerk. It was Miss Dorothy. And I felt almost as guilty as poor little Miss Cordelia; for I had heard from Mrs. Turner that we had given great offence to Miss Dorothy by not going to call on her in her room that day on which we had paid our respects to her sisters; and I had a sort of an idea that seeing Miss Cordelia with me was almost as much of a fault as the kneeling down on the wet grass. So I thought I would take the bull by the horns.

"Will you take me to your aunt Dorothy, my dear?" said I.

The little girl had no longing to go into her aunt Dorothy's room, as she had so evidently had at Miss Annabella's door. On the contrary, she pointed it out to me at a safe distance, and then went away in the measured step she was taught to use in that house; where such things as running, going upstairs two steps at a time, or jumping down three, were considered undignified and vulgar. Miss Dorothy's room was the least prepossessing of any. Somehow it had a north-east look about it, though it did face direct south; and as for Miss Dorothy herself, she was more like a "cousin Betty" than anything else; if you know what a cousin Betty is, and perhaps it is too old-fashioned a word to be understood by any one who has learnt the foreign languages: but when I was a girl, there used to be poor crazy women rambling about the country, one or two in a district. They never did any harm that I know of; they might have been born idiots, poor creatures! or crossed in love, who knows? But they roamed the country, and were well known at the farm-houses, where they often got food and shelter for as long a time as their restless minds would allow them to stay in any one place; and the farmer's wife would, maybe, rummage up a ribbon, or a feather, or a smart old breadth of silk, to please the harmless vanity of these poor crazy women; and they would go about so bedizened sometimes that, as we called them always "cousin Betty," we made it into a kind of proverb for any one dressed in a fly-away, showy style, and said they were like a cousin Betty. So now you know what I mean that Miss Dorothy was like. Her dress was white, like Miss Annabella's; but, instead of the black velvet hat her sister wore, she had on, even in the house, a small black silk bonnet. This sounds as if it should be less like a cousin Betty than a hat; but wait till I tell you how it was lined—with strips of red silk, broad near the face, narrow near the brim; for all the world like the rays of the rising sun, as they are painted on the public-house sign. And her face was like the sun; as round as an apple; and with rouge on, without any doubt: indeed, she told me once, a lady was not dressed unless she had put her rouge on. Mrs. Turner told us she studied reflections a great deal; not that she was a thinking woman in general, I should say; and that this rayed lining was the fruit of her study. She had her hair pulled together, so that her forehead was quite covered with it; and I won't deny that I rather wished myself at home, as I stood facing her in the doorway. She pretended she did not know who I was, and made me tell all about myself; and then it turned out she knew all about me, and she hoped I had recovered from my fatigue the other day.

"What fatigue?" asked I, immovably. Oh! she had understood I was very much tired after visiting her sisters; otherwise, of course, I should not have felt it too much to come on to her room. She kept hinting at me in so many ways, that I could have asked her gladly to slap my face and have done with it, only I wanted to make Miss Cordelia's peace with her for kneeling down and dirtying her frock. I did say what I could to make things straight; but I don't know if I did any good. Mrs. Turner told me how suspicious and jealous she was of everybody, and of Miss Annabella in particular, who had been set over her in her youth because of her beauty; but since it had faded, Miss Morton and Miss Dorothy had never ceased pecking at her; and Miss Dorothy worst of all. If it had not been for little Miss Cordelia's love, Miss Annabella might have wished to die; she did often wish she had had the small-pox as a baby. Miss Morton was stately and cold to her, as one who had not done her duty to her family, and was put in the corner for her bad behaviour. Miss Dorothy was continually talking at her, and particularly dwelling on the fact of her being the older sister. Now she was but two years older; and was still so pretty and gentle-looking, that I should have forgotten it continually but for Miss Dorothy.

The rules that were made for Miss Cordelia! She was to eat her meals standing, that was one thing! Another was, that she was to drink two cups of cold water before she had any pudding; and it just made the child loathe cold water. Then there were ever so many words she might not use; each aunt had her own set of words which were ungenteel or improper for some reason or another. Miss Dorothy would never let her say "red;" it was always to be pink, or crimson, or scarlet. Miss Cordelia used at one time to come to us, and tell us she had a "pain at her chest" so often, that Ethelinda and I began to be uneasy, and questioned Mrs. Turner to know if her mother had died of consumption; and many a good pot of currant jelly have I given her, and only made her pain at the chest worse; for—would you believe it?—Miss Morton told her never to say she had got a stomach-ache, for that it was not proper to say so, I had heard it called by a worse name still in my youth, and so had Ethelinda; and we sat and wondered to ourselves how it was that some kinds of pain were genteel and others were not. I said that old families, like the Mortons, generally thought it showed good blood to have their complaints as high in the body as they could—brain-fevers and headaches had a better sound, and did perhaps belong more to the aristocracy. I thought I had got the right view in saying this, when Ethelinda would put in that she had often heard of Lord Toffey having the gout and being lame, and that nonplussed me. If there is one thing I do dislike more than another, it is a person saying something on the other side when I am trying to make up my mind—how can I reason if I am to be disturbed by another person's arguments?

But though I tell all these peculiarities of the Miss Mortons, they were good women in the main: even Miss Dorothy had her times of kindness, and really did love her little niece, though she was always laying traps to catch her doing wrong. Miss Morton I got to respect, if I never liked her. They would ask us up to tea; and we would put on our best gowns; and taking the house-key in my pocket, we used to walk slowly through the village, wishing that people who had been living in our youth could have seen us now, going by invitation to drink tea with the family at the Hall—not in the housekeeper's room, but with the family, mind you. But since they began to weave in Morton, everybody seemed too busy to notice us; so we were fain to be content with reminding each other how we should never have believed it in our youth that we could have lived to this day. After tea, Miss Morton would set us to talk of the real old family, whom they had never known; and you may be sure we told of all their pomp and grandeur and stately ways: but Ethelinda and I never spoke of what was to ourselves like the memory of a sad, terrible dream. So they thought of the squire in his coach-and-four as high sheriff, and madam lying in her morning-room in her Genoa velvet wrapping-robe, all over peacock's eyes (it was a piece of velvet the squire brought back from Italy, when he had been on the grand tour), and Miss Phillis going to a ball at a great lord's house and dancing with a royal duke. The three ladies were never tired of listening to the tale of the splendour that had been going on here, while they and their mother had been starving in genteel poverty up in Northumberland; and as for Miss Cordelia, she sat on a stool at her aunt Annabella's knee, her hand in her aunt's, and listened, open-mouthed and unnoticed, to all we could say.

One day, the child came crying to our house. It was the old story; aunt Dorothy had been so unkind to aunt Annabella! The little girl said she would run away to India, and tell her uncle the general, and seemed in such a paroxysm of anger, and grief, and despair, that a sudden thought came over me. I thought I would try and teach her something of the deep sorrow that lies awaiting all at some part of their lives, and of the way in which it ought to be borne, by telling her of Miss Phillis's love and endurance for her wasteful, handsome nephew. So from little, I got to more, and I told her all; the child's great eyes filling slowly with tears, which brimmed over and came rolling down her cheeks unnoticed as I spoke. I scarcely needed to make her promise not to speak about all this to any one. She said, "I could not—no! not even to aunt Annabella." And to this day she never has named it again, not even to me; but she tried to make herself more patient, and more silently helpful in the strange household among whom she was cast.

By-and-by, Miss Morton grew pale, and grey, and worn, amid all her stiffness. Mrs. Turner whispered to us that for all her stern, unmoved looks, she was ill unto death; that she had been secretly to see the great doctor at Drumble; and he had told her she must set her house in order. Not even her sisters knew this; but it preyed upon Mrs. Turner's mind and she told us. Long after this, she kept up her week of discipline with Miss Cordelia; and walked in her straight, soldier-like way about the village, scolding people for having too large families, and burning too much coal, and eating too much butter. One morning she sent Mrs. Turner for her sisters; and, while she was away, she rummaged out an old locket made of the four Miss Mortons' hair when they were all children; and, threading the eye of the locket with a piece of brown ribbon, she tied it round Cordelia's neck, and kissing her, told her she had been a good girl, and had cured herself of stooping; that she must fear God and honour the king; and that now she might go and have a holiday. Even while the child looked at her in wonder at the unusual tenderness with which this was said, a grim spasm passed over her face, and Cordelia ran in affright to call Mrs. Turner. But when she came, and the other two sisters came, she was quite herself again. She had her sisters in her room alone when she wished them good-by; so no one knows what she said, or how she told them (who were thinking of her as in health) that the signs of near-approaching death, which the doctor had foretold, were upon her. One thing they both agreed in saying—and it was much that Miss Dorothy agreed in anything—that she bequeathed her sitting-room, up the two steps, to Miss Annabella as being next in age. Then they left her room crying, and went both together into Miss Annabella's room, sitting hand in hand (for the first time since childhood I should think), listening for the sound of the little hand-bell which was to be placed close by her, in case, in her agony, she required Mrs. Turner's presence. But it never rang. Noon became twilight. Miss Cordelia stole in from the garden with its long, black, green shadows, and strange eerie sounds of the night wind through the trees, and crept to the kitchen fire. At last Mrs. Turner knocked at Miss Morton's door, and hearing no reply, went in and found her cold and dead in her chair.

I suppose that some time or other we had told them of the funeral the old squire had; Miss Phillis's father, I mean. He had had a procession of tenantry half-a-mile long to follow him to the grave. Miss Dorothy sent for me to tell her what tenantry of her brother's could follow Miss Morton's coffin; but what with people working in mills, and land having passed away from the family, we could but muster up twenty people, men and women and all; and one or two were dirty enough to be paid for their loss of time.

Poor Miss Annabella did not wish to go into the room up two steps; nor yet dared she stay behind; for Miss Dorothy, in a kind of spite for not having had it bequeathed to her, kept telling Miss Annabella it was her duty to occupy it; that it was Miss Sophronia's dying wish, and that she should not wonder if Miss Sophronia were to haunt Miss Annabella, if she did not leave her warm room, full of ease and sweet scent, for the grim north-east chamber. We told Mrs. Turner we were afraid Miss Dorothy would lord it sadly over Miss Annabella, and she only shook her head; which, from so talkative a woman, meant a great deal. But, just as Miss Cordelia had begun to droop, the general came home, without any one knowing he was coming. Sharp and sudden was the word with him. He sent Miss Cordelia off to school; but not before she had had time to tell us that she loved her uncle dearly, in spite of his quick, hasty ways. He carried his sisters off to Cheltenham; and it was astonishing how young they made themselves look before they came back again. He was always here, there, and everywhere: and very civil to us into the bargain; leaving the key of the Hall with us whenever they went from home. Miss Dorothy was afraid of him, which was a blessing, for it kept her in order, and really I was rather sorry when she died; and, as for Miss Annabella, she fretted after her till she injured her health, and Miss Cordelia had to leave school to come and keep her company. Miss Cordelia was not pretty; she had too sad and grave a look for that; but she had winning ways, and was to have her uncle's fortune some day, so I expected to hear of her being soon snapped up. But the general said her husband was to take the name of Morton; and what did my young lady do but begin to care for one of the great mill-owners at Drumble, as if there were not all the lords and commons to choose from besides? Mrs. Turner was dead; and there was no one to tell us about it; but I could see Miss Cordelia growing thinner and paler every time they came back to Morton Hall; and I longed to tell her to pluck up a spirit, and he above a cotton-spinner. One day, not half a year before the general's death, she came to see us, and told us, blushing like a rose, that her uncle had given his consent; and so, although "he" had refused to take the name of Morton, and had wanted to marry her without a penny, and without her uncle's leave, it had all come right at last, and they were to be married at once; and their house was to be a kind of home for her aunt Annabella, who was getting tired of being perpetually on the ramble with the general.

"Dear old friends!" said our young lady, "you must like him. I am sure you will; he is so handsome, and brave, and good. Do you know, he says a relation of his ancestors lived at Morton Hall in the time of the Commonwealth."

"His ancestors," said Ethelinda. "Has he got ancestors? That's one good point about him, at any rate. I didn't know cotton-spinners had ancestors."

"What is his name?" asked I.

"Mr. Marmaduke Carr," said she, sounding each *r* with the old Northumberland burr, which was softened into a pretty pride and effort to give distinctness to each letter of the beloved name.

"Carr," said I, "Carr and Morton! Be it so! It was prophesied of old!" But she was too much absorbed in the thought of her own secret happiness to notice my poor sayings.

He was and is a good gentleman; and a real gentleman, too. They never lived at Morton Hall. Just as I was writing this, Ethelinda came in with two pieces of news. Never again say I am superstitious! There is no one living in Morton that knows the tradition of Sir John Morton and Alice Carr; yet the very first part of the Hall the Drumble builder has pulled down is the old stone dining-parlour where the great dinner for the preachers mouldered away—flesh from flesh, crumb from crumb! And the street they are going to build right through the rooms through which Alice Carr was dragged in her agony of despair at her husband's loathing hatred, is to be called Carr Street.

And Miss Cordelia has got a baby; a little girl; and writes in pencil two lines at the end of her husband's note, to say she means to call it Phillis.

Phillis Carr! I am glad he did not take the name of Morton. I like to keep the name of Phillis Morton in my memory very still and unspoken.

A GHOST STORY

by Ada Trevanion

1858

Little is known about Ada Trevanion. Online genealogy sources say she was born in 1829 at Bifrons House in Kent, and died in 1882. An obituary—in the Parsons Daily News *of Parsons, Kansas, of all places—says she was "the daughter of Henry Trevanion and of Byron's half-sister, Georgiana Augusta Leigh," which accords with the information from genealogy sites. In 1829, Bifrons House was home to Byron's estranged wife and their daughter Augusta (Ada), better known today as Ada Lovelace, the mother of computer programming. The* London Gazette *of May 8, 1866, mentions Georgiana's death and the passing of her estate to Ada: amusingly to American readers, the law firm handling the probate is named as Booty and Butts, of Gray's Inn in London.*

If the woman herself is something of a mystery, at least some of her work remains to us. She published a sizable collection of poetry, titled Poems, *in 1858:* The Saturday Review *for November 27 of that year called it "a good specimen of what mediocre poetry really is." Whatever that reviewer's opinion, Ada's poetry continued to be published in great quantity, in magazines such as* The Illustrated Magazine, *the* Ladies' Companion and Monthly Magazine, The New Monthly Bell Assemblée, The Ladies' Cabinet of Fashion, Music & Romance, *and* The Keepsake.

Her fiction is considerably more elusive. "Judge not, that ye be not Judged" appeared in the Ladies' Companion and Monthly Magazine, *1855, and "A Lover's Quarrel," in* The Home Circle, *1849: both appear to be conventional stories, aimed at the magazines' predominantly female readerships.*

"A Ghost Story" is also very feminine in nature, dealing with the relationship between a teacher and pupil at a girls' boarding school. Some feminist commentators have seen hints of a homoerotic side to this relationship, but that may be in the eye of the beholder: the text itself suggests a respectful friendship rather than romance, and a trust which leads the ghost to place responsibility for her family's future in the hands of the protagonist.

I will relate to you (said my friend Ruth Irvine), the whole history, from the beginning to the end:

Some years ago my father sent me to Woodford House—a ladies' school at Taunton, in Somersetshire, of which a Mrs. Wheeler was the principal. The school had fallen off, before I went, from fifty pupils to thirty; yet the establishment was in many respects a superior one, and the masters were very efficient.

Mrs. Wheeler and a parlour-boarder, with the two teachers, Madame Dubois and Miss Winter, and we thirty girls, composed the household. Miss Winter, the English teacher, slept in a small room adjoining ours, walked out with us, and never left us. She was about twenty-seven years of age, and had soft, thick, brown hair, and peculiar eyes, of which I find it difficult to give a description. They were of a greenish brown, and, with the least emotion, seemed to fill, as it were, with light, like the flashing brilliancy of moonshine upon water. At half-past six in the morning it was her duty to call us, and about seven we came down-stairs. We practised our scales, and looked over the lessons we had prepared the evening before, till half-past eight, when Mrs. Wheeler and Madame Dubois made their appearance; then prayers were read, and after that we had breakfast of coffee, and solid squares of bread and butter, which was very good the first part of the week. Breakfast over, Mrs. Wheeler took her seat at the head of the table, and the business commenced.

Mrs. Wheeler was a tall, stout person, with a loud voice, and a very authoritative manner. She paid assiduous attention to our deportment, and we were often assured that she was gradually falling a victim to the task of entreating us to hold up our heads.

Madame Dubois was a little old, shrivelled woman, with a very irascible temper. She wore a turban on her head, and kept cotton in her ears, and mumbled her language all to mash. At one o'clock Mrs. Wheeler shut up her desk, and sailed out of the room, while we proceeded up-stairs to dress for our walk. The dinner was ready on our return at three. This was a plain meal, soon over; and after it Miss Winter took Mrs. Wheeler's place at the long table, and presided over our studies until tea at seven. I thought this interval the pleasantest part of the day, for Miss Winter was clever, and took great pains where she saw intelligence, or a desire to learn. I was less with her, however, than many of the girls, because, as one of the elder pupils, I was expected by Mrs. Wheeler to practise on the piano for at least three hours daily. The study was a large, uncarpeted room, with a view of a spacious flower-garden. Some part of most fine spring and summer days was spent in this garden. I liked being there better than going for a walk, because we were not compelled to keep together. I used to take a book, and, when the weather was not too cold, I sat much near a fountain, under the shade of a laburnum-tree which hung over it. I wonder if the fountain and laburnum-tree are there still?

Woodford House was rather famous for mysterious inmates. There was Mrs. Sparkes, the parlour-boarder, who always took her breakfast in her room, and was rumoured to have come by sea from a distant part of the earth, where she and the late Captain Sparkes (her husband) had rolled in gold. It was understood that if she had her rights, she would be worth ten thousand a year. I am afraid she had them not, for I suspect her usual income amounted to little more than one hundred. She was very good-natured, and we all liked her; but our vague association of her with the sea, and storms, and coral reefs, occasioned the wildest legends to be circulated as her history. Then there was a fair pale girl, with bright curling hair, who, found out, or thought we found out, was the daughter of a Viscount, who did not like her. She was a very suggestive topic; as was a young Italian, who had in her possession a real dagger, which many of us believed she always carried about her. But I think all these were outshone, on the whole, by Miss Winter, who never talked about her relations, called at the post-office for her letters, in order that they might not be brought to the school; and, further, had a small oak wardrobe in her room, the key of which she wore around her neck. What a life she had with some of the girls! and how lonely she was, too! for she belonged neither to Mrs. Wheeler nor to us; and it was impossible to be on very friendly terms with Madame Dubois.

Poor Miss Winter! I never troubled her with impertinent questions—and perhaps she felt grateful to me for my forbearance; for my companions, one and all, declared that she "favoured Ruth Irvine." I was not popular among them, because I studied on half-holidays, and in the hour before bed-time, when we were left to our own devices. They tried to laugh me out of this; but they couldn't; so they hated me as school-girls only can hate, and revenged themselves by saying that "my father was poor, and I was, for this reason, anxious to make the most of my time while at Woodford House." This taunt was intended to inflict severe mortification, as a profound respect for wealth pervaded the school, which was, of course, derived from its head.

I suspect I over-studied at this period, for I became a martyr to excruciating headache, which prevented me from sleeping at night; and I had, besides, all kinds of awkward habits and nervous affections. Oh! Mrs. Wheeler's earnest endeavours to make me graceful; her despair of my elbows; her hopelessness in my shoulders, and her glare of indignation at my manner of entering a room!

I spent the summer vacation this year at Woodford House, for my father was abroad, and I had no relation kind enough to take pity on my home-less state, I was very dispirited; and my depression so much increased the low, nervous fever which was hanging about me, that I was compelled for some days, to keep my bed. Miss Winter nursed me of her own accord, and was like a sister to me. Now that the other girls were gone, she was quite communicative. I learnt that she was an orphan, and had a brother and three sisters, all younger than herself, who were used to consult her on every occasion of importance. I liked to hear about them much: I believed them to be wonders of talent and kindness. The brother was a clerk in some mercantile house in London: the sisters were being educated at a school for the daughters of military men. The affection which united her to this brother and these sisters seemed to me to be stronger than either death or life.

The teacher's holidays never began until long after ours; but in the summer vacation they were allowed to take pedestrian excursions; and Miss Winter would return from these to my sick chamber, laden with mosses and wildflowers. I used to feel it a great consolation, amidst the neglect and contempt of others, that she was attached to me. When the day for her departure came, she gave me "Coleridge's Rhymes of the Ancient Mariner;" and I was to keep it always, and never to forget her if I never saw her again. I do not think she spoke thus because she felt any foreboding of ill, for she was very happy in her quiet way; but she never allowed herself to look forward with much hope to the future. I got a letter from her, to say that she had arrived safely at her brother's lodging in the City, and was going to Dover, where her sisters were staying, and begging me not to fret for her sake. I tried to be cheerful, but time passed wearily without her. Every morning, at breakfast, I heard for the twentieth time of Miss Nash, who so appreciated the advantage of spending the vacation with such a person as Mrs. Wheeler, that she could scarcely be induced to leave Woodford House. *She* never complained that the piano in the back-parlour had several dumb notes, or that Rollin's "Ancient History" was not the most cheerful specimen of polite literature. It was uncharitable; but I couldn't help it—I hated Miss Nash. The latter part of the day was more agreeable: I was usually invited to tea and supper by Mrs. Sparkes, and was regaled in the front-parlour with seed-cake and rolls, likewise with currant-wine. I should have enjoyed these entertainments exceedingly, but I had written a poem in four cantos, in which the late Captain Sparkes figured as a pirate, and was shot for a voluminous catalogue of atrocities; and this secret lay like a load of lead on my mind, and prevented me from feeling at my ease with Mrs. Sparkes. It was after an evening spent with this lady, and in the absence of Mrs. Wheeler, who had gone to London to arrange about receiving a new pupil, that—*that it first happened.*

It was a still, sultry night; the moon very bright. I was lying in my narrow, white bed, with my hair disordered all over the pillow; not just falling asleep, by any means, but most persistently and obstinately broad awake, and with every sense so sharpened, that I could distinctly hear the flow of the fountain without, and the ticking of the clock in the hall far down below. I had left the door of my chamber open, on account of the heat. Suddenly, at midnight, when the house was profoundly silent, a draught of cold air seemed to blow right into the room; and almost immediately after, I heard the sound of a footfall upon the stairs. Sleep seemed many thousand miles farther off than ever, or I should have thought I was dreaming; for I could have declared the step was Miss Winter's; and yet I knew that she was not expected back for at least a fortnight. What could it mean? While I listened and wondered, the footsteps drew nearer and nearer, and then suddenly halted. I looked around, and beheld at the foot of the bed the form of my friend! She was attired in the plain dark dress which she usually wore; and I could see on the third finger of her left hand the sparkle of a ring, which was also familiar to me. Her face was very pale, and had, I thought, a strange, wistful expression. I noticed, too, that the bands of hair which shaded her forehead looked dark and dank, as if they had been immersed in water. I started up in bed, extending my arms, and exclaiming, "You here! When did you come? What has brought you back so soon?" But there was no answer, and she was gone the next moment. I was startled, almost terrified, by what I have described. I felt an indefinite fear that something was wrong with my friend. I arose, and passing through her chamber, which was unoccupied, went above and below, looking for her, and softly calling her by name: but every room I entered was empty and silent; and I presently returned to bed, bewildered and disappointed.

Towards morning I grew drowsy, and a little before my usual hour for rising I fell asleep. When I awoke the bright sunlight was shining in through the window. I heard the servants at their work below, and I was sure that it was very late. I was dressing hurriedly, when the door was softly opened. It was Mrs. Sparkes.

"I would not have you disturbed," she said; "for I heard you walking about last night. I thought, as it was holiday-time, you should sleep when you could."

"Oh, thank you," I replied, scarcely able to restrain my impatience. "Where is Miss Winter, Mrs. Sparkes?" She looked surprised at the question, but answered, without hesitation, "With her friends, no doubt! We need not expect her for this fortnight yet, you know."

"You are jesting," said I, half offended. "I know that she is returned. I saw her last night."

"You saw Miss Winter last night!"

"Yes," I answered; "she came into my bedroom."

"Impossible!" and Mrs. Sparkes burst out laughing—"unless she have the power of being in two places at once. You have been dreaming, Ruth."

"I could not dream," I said; "for I was broad awake. I am sure I saw Miss Winter. She stood at the foot of my bed, and looked at me; but she would not tell me when she came, or what had brought her back so soon."

Mrs. Sparkes still laughed. I said no more on the subject, for I thought there was some mystery, and she was trying to deceive me.

That day passed. I was little inclined to sleep, though I was very tired when night came. I kept thinking about Miss Winter, and wondering if she would come again. After I had been in bed a few hours I became terribly nervous—the slightest sound made my heart leap. Then the thought came into my head that I would get up, and go down-stairs. I slipped on a few things, and softly left my room. The house was so silent, and everything looked so dusky, that I felt frightened, and went on trembling more than before. There was a long passage in a line with the school-room, and there was a glass-door at one end of it, which opened upon the garden. I stood at this door several minutes, dreamily watching the silvery light which the moon threw upon the dark trees and the sleeping flowers without. While thus engaged I grew contented and serene. I had turned, to creep back to bed, when I heard, as I thought, some person trying the handle of the door behind me. The sound soon ceased; yet I almost believed the door was opened, for a rift of wind blew through the passage, which made me shudder. I stopped, and looked hurriedly back. The door was closely shut, and the bolt still fast; but standing in the moonlight, where I had lately stood, was the slight figure of Miss Winter! She was as white, and still, and speechless, as she had been on the preceding night; it almost seemed as if some dreadful misfortune had struck her dumb. I wished to speak to her, but there was something in her face which daunted me; and besides, the fever of anxiety I was in began to dry up my lips, as if they would never be able to shape any words again. But I moved quickly towards her, and bent forward to kiss her. To my surprise and terror her form vanished. A cry escaped me, which must have alarmed Mrs. Sparkes, for she came running down-stairs in her night-dress, looking pale and frightened. I told her what had happened, and very much in the same way that I have just been telling it now. There was an expression of uneasiness on her face as she listened. She said kindly, "Ruth, you are not well to-night—you are very feverish and excited. Go back to bed, and before to-morrow morning you will forget all about it."

I returned to bed; but I did not next morning forget what I had seen on the previous night; on the contrary, I was more positive than before. Mrs. Sparkes was disposed to think that I had seen Miss Winter in a dream on the first night, and that on the second, when broad awake, I had been unable to divest myself of the idea previously entertained. However, at my earnest and often repeated request, she promised she would pass the coming night with me in the girls' sleeping-room. All that day she was most kind and attentive. She could not have been more so if I had been seriously unwell. She put all exciting books out of my way, and asked me from time to time if my head ached. In the evening, after supper, she showed me some engravings which had belonged to her husband. I was very fond of pictures. We remained looking at them till a late hour, and then we went to bed. Tired as I was, I could not sleep. Mrs. Sparkes said she should stay awake also; but she soon became silent, and I knew by her breathing that she was sound asleep. She did not rest long. At midnight the room, which had been oppressively warm, grew suddenly cold and draughty; and again I heard Miss Winter's known step on the stairs. I laid hold of Mrs. Sparkes' arm, and shook her gently. She was sleeping heavily, and awoke slowly, as it seemed to me; but she sat up in bed, and listened to the approaching steps. I shall never forget her face at that moment. She seemed to be beside herself with terror, which she tried to hide, and uncertain what it would be the best for her to do; she caught my hand at last, and held it so tightly that she quite hurt me. The steps drew nigh, and halted, as they had done before. Mrs. Sparkes' gaze followed mine to the foot of the bed. The form of my friend was there. I can scarcely expect to be credited. I can state on my honour, what followed.

A night-lamp was burning in the room, for Mrs. Sparkes never slept in the dark. Its light showed me the pale still face of Miss Winter more clearly than I had seen it on the previous nights. The features were like those of a corse.* The eyes fixed direct on me, the long-familiar, grave, shining eyes. I see them now—I shall see them till I die! O how sad and earnest they looked! A full minute, or it seemed so, did he gaze in silence; then she said, in a low, urgent tone, still looking through me with her eyes, "Ruth, the oak wardrobe in the room which was mine, contains papers of importance—papers which will be wanted. Will you remember this!"

"I promise that I will," I replied. My voice was steady, though the cold drops stood on my brow. The restless, wistful look in her eyes changed, as I spoke, to a peaceful and happy expression. So, with a smile upon her face, she passed away. No sooner had Miss Winter's form disappeared than Mrs. Sparkes, who had been silent only because she was paralyzed with terror, began to scream aloud. She did more: she sprang out of bed, and rushed round the foot of it, out on the landing. When she could make the servants attend her, she told them that somebody was in the house; and all the women—a cook and two housemaids—went armed with poker, and shovels, and examined every room from cellar to attic. They found nothing, neither in the chimneys nor under the beds, nor in any closet or cupboard. And as the servants went back to bed, I heard them agree what a tiresome and wearying thing it was when ladies took fancies. Mrs. Sparkes wanted to leave the house the next day; but the thought of the ridicule to which she should expose herself, if the matter oozed out, induced her to summon up her courage, and remain where she was.

The morning after, Mrs. Wheeler returned. She and Mrs. Sparkes were talking together in the study for a long while. I could not help wondering what they were talking about, and so anxious did I feel that I could not

---

* An archaic form of "corpse."

settle to anything. At last the door opened, and Mrs. Sparkes came out. I heard her say, distinctly, "It is the most shocking thing I have ever heard. She was a pains-taking young person, and you will miss her sadly." At the sound of the opening of the door, with a sudden determination, I had rushed down-stairs, and was within a few steps of the study as Mrs. Sparkes came out.

Mrs. Wheeler was sitting at the table, with an open newspaper before her. She looked grave and shocked. After making some inquiries about my health, she said, "You will be sorry to hear Miss Winter will not return—an able teacher, and I believe you were much attached to her." She was going on; but I interrupted her with a wild cry—"Miss Winter is dead!" said I, and I swooned away.

It was noon when I woke, and saw Mrs. Sparkes bending over me, as I lay on my bed, and trying to restore me. I begged her to tell me everything, and she did so. My dear friend was indeed no more. The story of her death was, like all the sad stories I have ever heard told in real life very—very short. She had left the house where her sisters were lodging, late one evening; that was the last time they saw her alive. She had been found dead, lying along the rocks under the cliff. This was all that there really was to tell. There was nobody near her when she was found, and no evidence to show how she came there.

I cannot remember what happened for some days afterwards, for I was seriously ill, and kept my bed; and often in the long nights I would lie awake, thinking about my poor friend, and fancying that she would appear to me again. But she came no more.

Time passed on, and brought the last day of the vacation. I was sitting by myself in the study, Mrs. Wheeler and Mrs. Sparkes having both gone out, when a servant ushered in a strange gentleman, who, when I told him that Mrs. Wheeler was from home, immediately asked for Miss Irvine. On hearing that I was the person inquired for, he requested five minutes' conversation with me. I showed him into the back-parlour, and waited, rather surprised and nervous, to hear what he had to say. He was a young man, not more than twenty-one or twenty-two years of age, and had a very grave manner; and though I was certain that he was a stranger, yet there was something in his face which seemed not altogether unfamiliar to me.

He began by saying, "You were very fond of a teacher who was here, of the name of Winter. In her name, and for her sake, I thank you for the love and kindness you showed her."

"You knew Miss Winter, sir?" I asked, as calmly as I could.

"I am her brother," he replied.

There was silence between us, for the tears had sprung to my eyes at the mention of my dear lost friend's name; and, I believe, at heart he was crying too. At last he mastered his feelings, and by an effort resumed his former calm manner. "I have been for this last week seeking for some papers which my poor sister must have left behind her, and always seeking them in vain," he said. "If you could give me any clue as to where they may be, you would do a great kindness to my remaining sisters and myself."

He still spoke calmly; but there was a look in his eyes which showed me that he was suffering terrible anxiety. I hastened to relieve it, by saying, "I have reason to think that you will find the papers you are in want of in a small oak wardrobe which belonged to dear Miss Winter. If you please, I will show you where it stands." How his face lightened as he rose to follow me! his lips moving evidently with voiceless but thankful words on them.

We went up-stairs to the room that had been his sister's, where I pointed out the piece of furniture to which she had referred me on that dreadful night. And after using some considerable force, the lock yielded to his determined hand; and there, concealed under a false bottom, in one of the drawers, were the papers he sought for, with all the other things Miss Winter had most cherished—the letters which had passed between her father and mother before they were married; her mother's wedding-ring; her brother's picture; the first copy-books of her sisters' when they were learning to write; the little keepsakes which I at different times had given her. When my companion had taken all the letters and papers from the secret ledge, he turned to me, and said, "How much do you think these papers are worth to me, Miss Irvine?"

"Indeed, I can't tell," I replied; "but thank God you came hither to seek them, for I am so glad they are found."

"I thank you," he said. "I thank you, with all my heart."

We went down-stairs again, into the parlour; and then he told me how a kinsman of theirs, who was very rich, but nevertheless a great miser, had borrowed a large sum of money from their dead father, which he now refused to repay, and was even wicked enough to deny he had ever received; how they had gone to law about the matter; and how if the papers he had just found could not have been produced, he and his sisters would have been penniless; but as it was, they would recover the sum to which they were justly entitled, with interest for five years.

After this he begged my acceptance of a locket containing some of my dear Miss Winter's hair, and with her Christian name and the date of her death inscribed upon it; and bade me remember, if I should ever be friendless or in distress (which he prayed God I might never be), that he felt towards me as a brother.

I was quite overcome, and hid my face on the table. When I looked up again, he was gone.

A fresh surprise awaited me. The next day I met Mrs. Wheeler as she was going up-stairs. She said she was coming to bid me go into the parlour; and her manner was so gracious that I obeyed her without fear. My dear father was there. He was so shocked at my ill-looks that he resolved to remove me to the sea-side without loss of time. I begged to be taken to Dover. Yon will guess why. I sought out my poor friend's grave and made it as beautiful as I could with grass and flowers. There was no tombstone there then, but there is one now.

The tale I have told may seem very extraordinary; but it is, nevertheless, true in every particular. Most persons, who have visited Taunton for any length of time, will no doubt have had it narrated to them by Mrs. Sparkes or one of her friends.

AN ENGINEER'S STORY

by Amelia B. Edwards

1866

Amelia Ann Blandford Edwards was born in London in 1831. The daughter of a banker and former army officer, she was educated at home by her mother, and showed promise as a writer from an early age: she published her first poem at the age of seven, and her first short story at twelve. In her twenties, she became a popular novelist, known for the time and effort she spent on the settings and backgrounds of her stories. She once estimated that each one took her two years of research and writing.

The winter of 1873–4 was a turning point in her life: along with several friends, she visited Egypt, recording her travels in her 1877 best seller, A Thousand Miles Up the Nile. *She devoted much of her time thereafter to promoting the discovery and preservation of ancient monuments, co-founding the Egypt Exploration Fund and contributing to the* Encyclopedia Britannica *and the* Standard Dictionary. *In 1889–90, she embarked on a lecture tour of the United States, publishing her lectures in 1891 as* Pharaohs, Fellahs, and Explorers. *Such was her passion for Egypt that she stopped writing fiction entirely.*

Edwards never married. She died in April 1892, three months after her companion, Ellen Drew Braysher. The two were buried side by side—along with Braysher's daughter

Sarah, who had died in 1864—and in 2016, Historic England (officially the Historic Buildings and Monuments Commission for England) listed the grave as a historic monument, celebrating it as a landmark in English LGBT history.

Edwards wrote a number of ghost stories, many of which, like "The Phantom Coach" and "The Four-Fifteen Express," appear regularly in anthologies. Like the latter, "An Engineer's Tale" is a railway story: two young Englishmen go to Italy in search of work and excitement, and find themselves embroiled in love, murder, and—years later—a supernatural redemption.

H is name, sir, was Matthew Price; mine is Benjamin Hardy. We were born within a few days of each other; bred up in the same village; taught at the same school. I cannot remember the time when we were not close friends. Even as boys, we never knew what it was to quarrel. We had not a thought, we had not a possession, that was not in common. We would have stood by each other, fearlessly, to the death. It was such a friendship as one reads about sometimes in books: fast and firm as the great Tors upon our native moorlands, true as the sun in the heavens.

The name of our village was Chadleigh. Lifted high above the pasture flats which stretched away at our feet like a measureless green lake and melted into mist on the furthest horizon, it nestled, a tiny stone-built hamlet, in a sheltered hollow about midway between the plain and the plateau. Above us, rising ridge beyond ridge, slope beyond slope, spread the mountainous moor-country, bare and bleak for the most part, with here and there a patch of cultivated field or hardy plantation, and crowned highest of all with masses of huge grey crag, abrupt, isolated, hoary, and older than the deluge. These were the Tors—Druids' Tor, King's Tor,

Castle Tor, and the like; sacred places, as I have heard, in the ancient time, where crownings, burnings, human sacrifices, and all kinds of bloody heathen rites were performed. Bones, too, had been found there, and arrow-heads, and ornaments of gold and glass. I had a vague awe of the Tors in those boyish days, and would not have gone near them after dark for the heaviest bribe.

I have said that we were born in the same village. He was the son of a small farmer, named William Price, and the eldest of a family of seven; I was the only child of Ephraim Hardy, the Chadleigh blacksmith—a well-known man in those parts, whose memory is not forgotten to this day. Just so far as a farmer is supposed to be a bigger man than a blacksmith, Mat's father might be said to have a better standing than mine; but William Price with his small holding and his seven boys, was, in fact, as poor as many a day-labourer; whilst, the blacksmith, well-to-do, bustling, popular, and open-handed, was a person of some importance in the place. All this, however, had nothing to do with Mat and myself. It never occurred to either of us that his jacket was out at elbows, or that our mutual funds came altogether from my pocket. It was enough for us that we sat on the same school-bench, conned our tasks from the same primer, fought each other's battles, screened each other's faults, fished, nutted, played truant, robbed orchards and birds' nests together, and spent every half-hour, authorised or stolen, in each other's society. It was a happy time; but it could not go on for ever. My father, being prosperous, resolved to put me forward in the world. I must know more, and do better, than himself. The forge was not good enough, the little world of Chadleigh not wide enough, for me. Thus it happened that I was still swinging the satchel when Mat was whistling at the plough, and that at last, when my future course was shaped out, we were separated, as it then seemed to us, for life. For, blacksmith's son as I was, furnace and forge, in some form or other, pleased me best, and I chose to be a working engineer. So my father by-and-by apprenticed me to a Birmingham iron-master; and, having bidden farewell to Mat, and Chadleigh, and the grey old Tors in the shadow of which I had spent all the days of my life, I turned my face northward, and went over into "the Black Country."

I am not going to dwell on this part of my story. How I worked out the term of my apprenticeship; how, when I had served my full time and become a skilled workman, I took Mat from the plough and brought him over to the Black Country, sharing with him lodging, wages, experience—all, in short, that I had to give; how he, naturally quick to learn and brimful of quiet energy, worked his way up a step at a time, and came by-and-by to be a "first hand" in his own department; how, during all these years of change, and trial, and effort, the old boyish affection never wavered or weakened, but went on, growing with our growth and strengthening with our strength—are facts which I need do no more than outline in this place.

About this time—it will be remembered that I speak of the days when Mat and I were on the bright side of thirty—it happened that our firm contracted to supply six first-class locomotives to run on the new line, then in process of construction, between Turin and Genoa. It was the first Italian order we had taken. We had had dealings with France, Holland, Belgium, Germany; but never with Italy. The connection, therefore, was new and valuable—all the more valuable because our Transalpine neighbours had but lately begun to lay down the iron roads, and would be safe to need more of our good English work as they went on. So the Birmingham firm set themselves to the contract with a will, lengthened our working hours, increased our wages, took on fresh hands, and determined, if energy and promptitude could do it, to place themselves at the head of the Italian labour-market, and stay there. They deserved and achieved success. The six locomotives were not only turned out to time, but were shipped, despatched, and delivered with a promptitude that fairly amazed our Piedmontese consignee. I was not a little proud, you may be sure, when I found myself appointed to superintend the transport of the engines. Being allowed a couple of assistants, I contrived that Mat should be one of them; and thus we enjoyed together the first great holiday of our lives.

It was a wonderful change for two Birmingham operatives fresh from the Black Country. The fairy city, with its crescent background of Alps; the port crowded with strange shipping; the marvellous blue sky and the bluer sea; the painted houses on the quays; the quaint cathedral, faced with black and white marble; the street of jewellers, like an Arabian Nights' bazaar; the street of palaces, with its Moorish courtyards, its fountains and orange-trees; the women veiled like brides; the galley-slaves chained two and two; the processions of priests and friars; the everlasting clangour of bells; the babble of a strange tongue; the singular lightness and brightness of the climate—made, altogether, such a combination of wonders that we wandered about, the first day, in a kind of bewildered dream, like children at a fair. Before that week was ended, being tempted by the beauty of the place and the liberality of the pay, we had agreed to take service with the Turin and Genoa Railway Company, and to turn our backs upon Birmingham for ever.

Then began a new life—a life so active and healthy, so steeped in fresh air and sunshine, that we sometimes marvelled how we could have endured the gloom of the Black Country. We were constantly up and down the line: now at Genoa, now at Turin, taking trial trips with the locomotives, and placing our old experiences at the service of our new employers.

In the meanwhile we made Genoa our headquarters, and hired a couple of rooms over a small shop in a by-street sloping down to the quays. Such a busy little street—so steep and winding that no vehicles could pass through it, and so narrow that the sky looked like a mere strip of deep-blue ribbon overhead! Every house in it, however, was a shop, where the goods encroached on the footway, or were piled about the door, or hung like tapestry from the balconies; and all day long, from dawn to dusk, an incessant stream of passers-by poured up and down between the port and the upper quarter of the city.

Our landlady was the widow of a silver-worker, and lived by the sale of filigree ornaments, cheap jewellery, combs, fans, and toys in ivory and jet. She had an only daughter named Gianetta, who served in the shop, and was simply the most beautiful woman I ever beheld. Looking back across this weary chasm of years, and bringing her image before me (as I can and do) with all the vividness of life, I am unable, even now, to detect a flaw in her beauty. I do not attempt to describe her. I do not believe there is a poet living who could find the words to do it; but I once saw a picture that was somewhat like her (not half so lovely, but still like her), and, for aught I know, that picture is still hanging where I last looked at it—upon the walls of the Louvre. It represented a woman with brown eyes and golden hair, looking over her shoulder into a circular mirror held by a bearded man in the background. In this man, as I then understood, the artist had painted his own portrait; in her, the portrait of the woman he loved. No picture that I ever saw was half so beautiful, and yet it was not worthy to be named in the same breath with Gianetta Coneglia.

You may be certain the widow's shop did not want for customers. All Genoa knew how fair a face was to be seen behind that dingy little counter; and Gianetta, flirt as she was, had more lovers than she cared to remember, even by name. Gentle and simple, rich and poor, from the red-capped sailor buying his ear-rings or his amulet, to the nobleman carelessly purchasing half the filigrees in the window, she treated them all alike—encouraged them, laughed at them, led them on and turned them off at her pleasure. She had no more heart than a marble statue; as Mat and I discovered by-and-by, to our bitter cost.

I cannot tell to this day how it came about, or what first led me to suspect how things were going with us both; but long before the waning of that autumn a coldness had sprung up between my friend and myself. It was nothing that could have been put into words. It was nothing that either of us could have explained or justified, to save his life. We lodged together, ate together, worked together, exactly as before; we even took our long evening's walk together, when the day's labour was ended; and except, perhaps, that we were more silent than of old, no mere looker-on could have detected a shadow of change. Yet there it was, silent and subtle, widening the gulf between us every day.

It was not his fault. He was too true and gentle-hearted to have willingly brought about such a state of things between us. Neither do I believe—fiery as my nature is—that it was mine. It was all hers—hers from first to last—the sin, and the shame, and the sorrow.

If she had shown a fair and open preference for either of us, no real harm could have come of it. I would have put any constraint upon myself, and, Heaven knows! have borne any suffering, to see Mat really happy. I know that he would have done the same, and more if he could, for me. But Gianetta cared not one sou* for either. She never meant to choose between

---

* French: A small coin of low value. "Not a sou" was a common expression in English when this story was written.

us. It gratified her vanity to divide us; it amused her to play with us. It would pass my power to tell how, by a thousand imperceptible shades of coquetry—by the lingering of a glance, the substitution of a word, the flitting of a smile—she contrived to turn our heads, and torture our hearts, and lead us on to love her. She deceived us both. She buoyed us both up with hope; she maddened us with jealousy; she crushed us with despair. For my part, when I seemed to wake to a sudden sense of the ruin that was about our path and I saw how the truest friendship that ever bound two lives together was drifting on to wreck and ruin, I asked myself whether any woman in the world was worth what Mat had been to me and I to him. But this was not often. I was readier to shut my eyes upon the truth than to face it; and so lived on, wilfully, in a dream.

Thus the autumn passed away, and winter came—the strange, treacherous Genoese winter, green with olive and ilex, brilliant with sunshine, and bitter with storm. Still, rivals at heart and friends on the surface, Mat and I lingered on in our lodging in the Vicolo Balba. Still Gianetta held us with her fatal wiles and her still more fatal beauty. At length there came a day when I felt I could bear the horrible misery and suspense of it no longer. The sun, I vowed, should not go down before I knew my sentence. She must choose between us. She must either take me or let me go. I was reckless. I was desperate. I was determined to know the worst, or the best. If the worst, I would at once turn my back upon Genoa, upon her, upon all the pursuits and purposes of my past life, and begin the world anew. This I told her, passionately and sternly, standing before her in the little parlour at the back of the shop, one bleak December morning.

"If it's Mat whom you care for most," I said, "tell me so in one word, and I will never trouble you again. He is better worth your love. I am jealous and exacting; he is as trusting and unselfish as a woman. Speak, Gianetta; am I to bid you good-bye for ever and ever, or am I to write home to my mother in England, bidding her pray to God to bless the woman who has promised to be my wife?"

"You plead your friend's cause well," she replied, haughtily. "Matteo ought to be grateful. This is more than he ever did for you."

"Give me my answer, for pity's sake," I exclaimed, "and let me go!"

"You are free to go or stay, Signor *Inglese*," she replied. "I am not your jailor."

AMELIA B. EDWARDS

"Do you bid me leave you?"

"*Beata Madre!* Not I."

"Will you marry me, if I stay?"

She laughed aloud—such a merry, mocking, musical laugh, like a chime of silver bells!

"You ask too much," she said.

"Only what you have led me to hope these five or six months past!"

"That is just what Matteo says. How tiresome you both are!"

"O, Gianetta," I said, passionately, "be serious for one moment! I am a rough fellow, it is true—not half good enough or clever enough for you; but I love you with my whole heart, and an Emperor could do no more."

"I am glad of it," she replied; "I do not want you to love me less."

"Then you cannot wish to make me wretched! Will you promise me?"

"I promise nothing," said she, with another burst of laughter; "except that I will not marry Matteo!"

Except that she would not marry Matteo! Only that. Not a word of hope for myself. Nothing but my friend's condemnation. I might get comfort, and selfish triumph, and some sort of base assurance out of that, if I could. And so, to my shame, I did. I grasped at the vain encouragement, and, fool that I was! let her put me off again unanswered. From that day, I gave up all effort at self-control, and let myself drift blindly on—to destruction.

At length things became so bad between Mat and myself that it seemed as if an open rupture must be at hand. We avoided each other, scarcely exchanged a dozen sentences in a day, and fell away from all our old familiar habits. At this time—I shudder to remember it!—there were moments when I felt that I hated him.

Thus, with the trouble deepening and widening between us day by day, another month or five weeks went by; and February came; and, with February, the Carnival. They said in Genoa that it was a particularly dull carnival; and so it must have been; for, save a flag or two hung out in some of the principal streets, and a sort of *festa* look about the women, there were no special indications of the season. It was, I think, the second day when, having been on the line all the morning, I returned to Genoa at dusk, and, to my surprise, found Mat Price on the platform. He came up to me, and laid his hand on my arm.

"You are in late," he said. "I have been waiting for you three-quarters of an hour. Shall we dine together to-day?"

Impulsive as I am, this evidence of returning goodwill at once called up my better feelings.

"With all my heart, Mat," I replied; "shall we go to Gozzoli's?"

"No, no," he said, hurriedly. "Some quieter place—some place where we can talk. I have something to say to you."

I noticed now that he looked pale and agitated, and an uneasy sense of apprehension stole upon me. We decided on the "Pescatore," a little out-of-the-way trattoria, down near the Molo Vecchio. There, in a dingy salon, frequented chiefly by seamen, and redolent of tobacco, we ordered our simple dinner. Mat scarcely swallowed a morsel; but, calling presently for a bottle of Sicilian wine, drank eagerly.

"Well, Mat," I said, as the last dish was placed on the table, "what news have you?"

"Bad."

"I guessed that from your face."

"Bad for you—bad for me. Gianetta."

"What of Gianetta?"

He passed his hand nervously across his lips.

"Gianetta is false—worse than false," he said, in a hoarse voice. "She values an honest man's heart just as she values a flower for her hair—wears it for a day, then throws it aside for ever. She has cruelly wronged us both."

"In what way? Good Heavens, speak out!"

"In the worst way that a woman can wrong those who love her. She has sold herself to the Marchese Loredano."

The blood rushed to my head and face in a burning torrent. I could scarcely see, and dared not trust myself to speak.

"I saw her going towards the cathedral," he went on, hurriedly. "It was about three hours ago. I thought she might be going to confession, so I hung back and followed her at a distance. When she got inside, however, she went straight to the back of the pulpit, where this man was waiting for her. You remember him—an old man who used to haunt the shop a month or two back. Well, seeing how deep in conversation they were, and how they stood close under the pulpit with their backs towards the church, I fell into a passion of anger and went straight up the aisle, intending to say or do something: I scarcely knew what; but, at all events, to draw her arm through mine, and take her home. When I came within a few feet, however, and found only a big pillar between myself and them, I paused. They could not see me, nor I them; but I could hear their voices distinctly, and—and I listened."

"Well, and you heard—"

"The terms of a shameful bargain—beauty on the one side, gold on the other; so many thousand francs a year; a villa near Naples——Pah! It makes me sick to repeat it."

And, with a shudder, he poured out another glass of wine and drank it at a draught.

"After that," he said, presently, "I made no effort to bring her away. The whole thing was so cold-blooded, so deliberate, so shameful, that I felt I had only to wipe her out of my memory, and leave her to her fate. I stole out of the cathedral, and walked about here by the sea for ever so long, trying to get my thoughts straight. Then I remembered you, Ben; and the recollection of how this wanton had come between us and broken up our lives drove me wild. So I went up to the station and waited for you. I felt you ought to know it all; and—and I thought, perhaps, that we might go back to England together."

"The Marchese Loredano!"

It was all that I could say; all that I could think. As Mat had just said of himself, I felt "like one stunned."

"There is one other thing I may as well tell you," he added, reluctantly, "if only to show you how false a woman can be. We—we were to have been married next month."

"We? Who? What do you mean?"

"I mean that we were to have been married—Gianetta and I."

A sudden storm of rage, of scorn, of incredulity, swept over me at this, and seemed to carry my senses away.

"You!" I cried. "Gianetta marry you! I don't believe it."

"I wish I had not believed it," he replied, looking up as if puzzled by my vehemence. "But she promised me; and I thought, when she promised it, she meant it."

"She told me, weeks ago, that she would never be your wife!"

His colour rose, his brow darkened; but when his answer came, it was as calm as the last.

"Indeed!" he said. "Then it is only one baseness more. She told me that she had refused you; and that was why we kept our engagement secret."

"Tell the truth, Mat Price," I said, well-nigh beside myself with suspicion. "Confess that every word of this is false! Confess that Gianetta will not listen to you, and that you are afraid I may succeed where you have failed. As perhaps I shall—as perhaps I shall, after all!"

"Are you mad?" he exclaimed. "What do you mean?"

"That I believe it's just a trick to get me away to England—that I don't credit a syllable of your story. You're a liar, and I hate you!"

He rose, and, laying one hand on the back of his chair, looked me sternly in the face.

"If you were not Benjamin Hardy," he said, deliberately, "I would thrash you within an inch of your life."

The words had no sooner passed his lips than I sprang at him. I have never been able distinctly to remember what followed. A curse—a blow—a struggle—a moment of blind fury—a cry—a confusion of tongues—a circle of strange faces. Then I see Mat lying back in the arms of a bystander; myself trembling and bewildered—the knife dropping from my grasp; blood upon the floor; blood upon my hands; blood upon his shirt. And then I hear those dreadful words:

"O, Ben, you have murdered me!"

He did not die—at least, not there and then. He was carried to the nearest hospital, and lay for some weeks between life and death. His case, they said, was difficult and dangerous. The knife had gone in just below the collar-bone, and pierced down into the lungs. He was not allowed to speak or turn—scarcely to breathe with freedom. He might not even lift his head to drink. I sat by him day and night all through that sorrowful time. I gave up my situation on the railway; I quitted my lodging in the Vicolo Balba; I tried to forget that such a woman as Gianetta Coneglia had ever drawn breath. I lived only for Mat; and he tried to live more, I believe, for my sake than his own. Thus, in the bitter silent hours of pain and penitence, when no hand but mine approached his lips or smoothed his pillow, the old friendship came back with even more than its old trust and faithfulness. He forgave me, fully and freely; and I would thankfully have given my life for him.

At length there came one bright spring morning, when, dismissed as convalescent, he tottered out through the hospital gates, leaning on my arm, and feeble as an infant. He was not cured; neither, as I then learned to my horror and anguish, was it possible that he ever could be cured. He might live, with care, for some years; but the lungs were injured beyond hope of remedy, and a strong or healthy man he could never be again. These, spoken aside to me, were the parting words of the chief physician, who advised me to take him further south without delay.

I took him to a little coast-town called Rocca, some thirty miles beyond Genoa—a sheltered lonely place along the Riviera, where the sea was even bluer than the sky, and the cliffs were green with strange tropical plants, cacti, and aloes, and Egyptian palms. Here we lodged in the house of a small tradesman; and Mat, to use his own words, "set to work at getting well in good earnest." But, alas! it was a work which no earnestness could forward. Day after day he went down to the beach, and sat for hours drinking the sea air and watching the sails that came and went in the offing. By-and-by he could go no further than the garden of the house in which we lived. A little later, and he spent his days on a couch beside the open window, waiting patiently for the end. Ay, for the end! It had come to that. He was fading fast, waning with the waning summer, and conscious that the Reaper was at hand. His whole aim now was to soften the agony of my remorse, and prepare me for what must shortly come.

"I would not live longer, if I could," he said, lying on his couch one summer evening, and looking up to the stars. "If I had my choice at this moment, I would ask to go. I should like Gianetta to know that I forgave her."

"She shall know it," I said, trembling suddenly from head to foot.

He pressed my hand.

"And you'll write to father?"

"I will."

I had drawn a little back, that he might not see the tears raining down my cheeks; but he raised himself on his elbow, and looked round.

"Don't fret, Ben," he whispered; laid his head back wearily upon the pillow—and so died.

And this was the end of it. This was the end of all that made life life to me. I buried him there, in hearing of the wash of a strange sea on a strange shore. I stayed by the grave till the priest and the bystanders were gone. I saw the earth filled in to the last sod, and the gravedigger stamped it down with his feet. Then, and not till then, I felt that I had lost him for ever—the friend I had loved, and hated, and slain. Then, and not till then, I knew that all rest, and joy, and hope were over for me. From that moment my heart hardened within me, and my life was filled with loathing. Day and night, land and sea, labour and rest, food and sleep, were alike hateful to me. It was the curse of Cain, and that my brother had pardoned me made it lie none the lighter. Peace on earth was for me no more, and goodwill towards men was dead in my heart for ever. Remorse softens some natures; but it poisoned mine. I hated all mankind; but above all mankind I hated the woman who had come between us two, and ruined both our lives.

He had bidden me seek her out, and be the messenger of his forgiveness. I had sooner have gone down to the port of Genoa and taken upon me the serge cap and shotted chain* of any galley-slave at his toil in the public works; but for all that I did my best to obey him. I went back, alone and on foot. I went back, intending to say to her, "Gianetta Coneglia, he forgave you; but God never will." But she was gone. The little shop was let to a fresh occupant; and the neighbours only knew that mother and daughter had left the place quite suddenly, and that Gianetta was supposed to be under the "protection" of the Marchese Loredano. How I made inquiries here and there—how I heard that they had gone to Naples—and how, being restless and reckless of my time, I worked my passage in a French steamer, and followed her—how, having found the sumptuous villa that was now hers, I learned that she had left there some ten days and gone to Paris, where the Marchese was ambassador for the Two Sicilies—how, working my passage back again to Marseilles, and thence, in part by the river and in part by the rail, I made my way to Paris—how, day after day, I paced the streets and the parks, watched at the ambassador's gates, followed his carriage, and at last, after weeks of waiting, discovered her address—how,

---

* i.e., Ball and chain.

having written to request an interview, her servants spurned me from her door and flung my letter in my face—how, looking up at her windows, I then, instead of forgiving, solemnly cursed her with the bitterest curses my tongue could devise—and how, this done, I shook the dust of Paris from my feet, and became a wanderer upon the face of the earth, are facts which I have now no space to tell.

The next six or eight years of my life were shifting and unsettled enough. A morose and restless man, I took employment here and there, as opportunity offered, turning my hand to many things, and caring little what I earned, so long as the work was hard and the change incessant. First of all I engaged myself as chief engineer in one of the French steamers plying between Marseilles and Constantinople. At Constantinople I changed to one of the Austrian Lloyd's boats, and worked for some time to and from Alexandria, Jaffa, and those parts. After that, I fell in with a party of Mr. Layard's men at Cairo, and so went up the Nile and took a turn at the excavations of the mound of Nimroud. Then I became a working engineer on the new desert line between Alexandria and Suez; and by-and-by I worked my passage out to Bombay, and took service as an engine fitter on one of the great Indian railways. I stayed a long time in India; that is to say, I stayed nearly two years, which was a long time for me; and I might not even have left so soon, but for the war that was declared just then with Russia. That tempted me. For I loved danger and hardship as other men love safety and ease; and as for my life, I had sooner have parted from it than kept it, any day. So I came straight back to England; betook myself to Portsmouth, where my testimonials at once procured me the sort of berth I wanted. I went out to the Crimea in the engine-room of one of her Majesty's war steamers.

I served with the fleet, of course, while the war lasted; and when it was over, went wandering off again, rejoicing in my liberty. This time I went to Canada, and after working on a railway then in progress near the American frontier. I presently passed over into the States; journeyed from north to south; crossed the Rocky Mountains; tried a month or two of life in the gold country; and then, being seized with a sudden, aching, unaccountable longing to revisit that solitary grave so far away on the Italian coast, I turned my face once more towards Europe.

Poor little grave! I found it rank with weeds, the cross half shattered, the inscription half effaced. It was as if no one had loved him, or remembered him. I went back to the house in which we had lodged together. The same people were still living there, and made me kindly welcome. I stayed with them for some weeks. I weeded, and planted, and trimmed the grave with my own hands, and set up a fresh cross in pure white marble. It was the first season of rest that I had known since I laid him there; and when at last I shouldered my knapsack and set forth again to battle with the world, I promised myself that, God willing, I would creep back to Rocca, when my days drew near to ending, and be buried by his side.

From hence, being, perhaps, a little less inclined than formerly for very distant parts, and willing to keep within reach of that grave, I went no further than Mantua, where I engaged myself as an engine-driver on the line, then not long completed, between that city and Venice. Somehow, although I had been trained to the working engineering, I preferred in these days to earn my bread by driving. I liked the excitement of it, the sense of power, the rush of the air, the roar of the fire, the flitting of the landscape. Above all, I enjoyed to drive a night express. The worse the weather, the better it suited with my sullen temper. For I was as hard, and harder than ever. The years had done nothing to soften me. They had only confirmed all that was blackest and bitterest in my heart.

I continued pretty faithful to the Mantua line, and had been working on it steadily for more than seven months when that which I am now about to relate took place.

It was in the month of March. The weather had been unsettled for some days past, and the nights stormy; and at one point along the line, near Ponte di Brenta, the waters had risen and swept away some seventy yards of embankment. Since this accident, the trains had all been obliged to stop at a certain spot between Padua and Ponte di Brenta, and the passengers, with their luggage, had thence to be transported in all kinds of vehicles, by a circuitous country road, to the nearest station on the other side of the gap, where another train and engine awaited them. This, of course, caused great confusion and annoyance, put all our time-tables wrong, and subjected the public to a large amount of inconvenience. In the mean while an army of navvies* was drafted to the spot, and worked day and night to repair the damage. At this time I was driving two through trains each day; namely, one from Mantua to Venice in the early morning, and a return train from Venice to Mantua in the afternoon—a tolerably full days' work, covering about one hundred and ninety miles of ground, and occupying between ten and eleven hours. I was therefore not best pleased when, on the third or fourth day after the accident, I was informed that, in addition to my regular allowance of work, I should that evening be required to drive a special train to Venice. This special train, consisting of an engine, a single carriage, and a break-van, was to leave the Mantua platform at eleven; at Padua the passengers were to alight and find post-chaises waiting to convey them to Ponte di Brenta; at Ponte di Brenta another engine, carriage, and break-van were to be in readiness, I was charged to accompany them throughout.

"*Corpo di Bacco*," said the clerk who gave me my orders, "you need not look so black, man. You are certain of a handsome gratuity. Do you know who goes with you?"

"Not I."

"Not you, indeed! Why, it's the Duca Loredano, the Neapolitan ambassador."

"Loredano!" I stammered. "What Loredano? There was a Marchese—"

"*Certo.* He was the Marchese Loredano some years ago; but he has come into his dukedom since then."

"He must be a very old man by this time."

"Yes, he is old; but what of that? He is as hale, and bright, and stately as ever. You have seen him before?"

"Yes," I said, turning away; "I have seen him—years ago."

"You have heard of his marriage?"

I shook my head.

The clerk chuckled, rubbed his hands, and shrugged his shoulders.

"An extraordinary affair," he said. "Made a tremendous *esclandre*** at the time. He married his mistress—quite a common, vulgar girl—a

---

* A slang term of the time for laborers: from "navigation workers," who built the canals that preceded the railways in England.

** French: scandal.

Genoese—very handsome; but not received, of course. Nobody visits her."

"Married her!" I exclaimed. "Impossible."

"True, I assure you."

I put my hand to my head. I felt as if I had had a fall or a blow.

"Does she—does she go to-night?" I faltered.

"O dear, yes—goes everywhere with him—never lets him out of her sight. You'll see her—*la bella Duchessa!*"

With this my informant laughed, and rubbed his hands again, and went back to his office.

The day went by, I scarcely know how, except that my whole soul was in a tumult of rage and bitterness. I returned from my afternoon's work about 7.25, and at 10.30 I was once again at the station. I had examined the engine; given instructions to the *Fochista*, or stoker, about the fire; seen to the supply of oil; and got all in readiness, when, just as I was about to compare my watch with the clock in the ticket-office, a hand was laid upon my arm, and a voice in my ear said:

"Are you the engine-driver who is going on with this special train?"

I had never seen the speaker before. He was a small, dark man, muffled up about the throat, with blue glasses, a large black beard, and his hat drawn low upon his eyes.

"You are a poor man, I suppose," he said, in a quick, eager whisper, "and, like other poor men, would not object to be better off. Would you like to earn a couple of thousand florins?"

"In what way?"

"Hush! You are to stop at Padua, are you not, and to go on again at Ponte di Brenta?"

I nodded.

"Suppose you did nothing of the kind. Suppose, instead of turning off the steam, you jump off the engine, and let the train run on?"

"Impossible. There are seventy yards of embankment gone, and—"

"*Basta!* I know that. Save yourself, and let the train run on. It would be nothing but an accident."

I turned hot and cold; I trembled; my heart beat fast, and my breath failed.

"Why do you tempt me?" I faltered.

"For Italy's sake," he whispered; "for liberty's sake. I know you are no Italian; but, for all that, you may be a friend. This Loredano is one of his country's bitterest enemies. Stay, here are the two thousand florins."

I thrust his hand back fiercely.

"No—no," I said. "No blood-money. If I do it, I do it neither for Italy nor for money; but for vengeance."

"For vengeance!" he repeated.

At this moment the signal was given for backing up to the platform. I sprang to my place upon the engine without another word. When I again looked towards the spot where he had been standing, the stranger was gone.

I saw them take their places—Duke and Duchess, secretary and priest, valet and maid. I saw the station-master bow them into the carriage, and stand, bareheaded, beside the door. I could not distinguish their faces; the platform was too dusk, and the glare from the engine fire too strong; but I recognised her stately figure, and the poise of her head. Had I not been told who she was, I should have known her by those traits alone. Then the guard's whistle shrilled out, and the station-master made his last bow; I turned the steam on; and we started.

My blood was on fire. I no longer trembled or hesitated. I felt as if every nerve was iron, and every pulse instinct with deadly purpose. She was in my power, and I would be avenged. She should die—she, for whom I had stained my soul with my friend's blood! She should die, in the plenitude of her wealth and her beauty, and no power upon earth should save her!

The stations flew past. I put on more steam; I bade the fireman heap in the coke, and stir the blazing mass. I would have outstripped the wind, had it been possible. Faster and faster—hedges and trees, bridges, and stations, flashing past—villages no sooner seen than gone—telegraph wires twisting, and dipping, and twining themselves in one, with the awful swiftness of our pace! Faster and faster, till the fireman at my side looks white and scared, and refuses to add more fuel to the furnace. Faster and faster, till the wind rushes in our faces and drives the breath back upon our lips.

I would have scorned to save myself. I meant to die with the rest. Mad as I was—and I believe from my very soul that I was utterly mad for the time—I felt a passing pang of pity for the old man and his suite. I would have spared the poor fellow at my side, too, if I could; but the pace at which we were going made escape impossible.

Vicenza was passed—a mere confused vision of lights. Pojana flew by. At Padua, but nine miles distant, our passengers were to alight. I saw the fireman's face turned upon me in remonstrance; I saw his lips move, though I could not hear a word; I saw his expression change suddenly from remonstrance to a deadly terror, and then—merciful Heaven! then, for the first time, I saw that he and I were no longer alone upon the engine.

There was a third man—a third man standing on my right hand, as the fireman was standing on my left—a tall, stalwart man, with short curling hair, and a flat Scotch cap upon his head. As I fell back in the first shock of surprise, he stepped nearer; took my place at the engine, and turned the steam off. I opened my lips to speak to him; he turned his head slowly, and looked me in the face.

Matthew Price!

I uttered one long wild cry, flung my arms wildly up above my head, and fell as if I had been smitten with an axe.

I am prepared for the objections that may be made to my story. I expect, as a matter of course, to be told that this was an optical illusion, or that I was suffering from pressure on the brain, or even that I laboured under an attack of temporary insanity. I have heard all these arguments before, and, if I may be forgiven for saying so, I have no desire to hear them again. My own mind has been made up upon this subject for many a year. All that I can say—all that I know is—that Matthew Price came back from the dead, to save my soul and the lives of those whom I, in my guilty rage, would have hurried to destruction. I believe this as I believe in the mercy of Heaven and the forgiveness of repentant sinners.

LOST IN A PYRAMID, OR THE MUMMY'S CURSE

by Louisa May Alcott

1869

The author of Little Women *was more versatile than most modern readers know. Her 1877 novel* A Modern Mephistopheles, *published anonymously at first, is a shocking tale of lust and deception, sexuality and drug use, written in "the lurid style" that Alcott described as her "natural ambition."* Work: A Story of Experience *(1873) is a semi-autobiographical exploration of women's changing roles before and after the American Civil War.* Hospital Sketches *told of her experiences as a volunteer nurse with the Union Army, while* Transcendental Wild Oats: A Chapter from an Unwritten Romance *(1873) is a satire on her family's participation in a utopian agrarian commune in the 1840s. Even so, one is still surprised to see her name on a horror tale.*

Between Napoleon's invasion of 1798–1801 and the discovery of Tutankhamun's tomb in 1922, Egyptomania swept Europe and North America, affecting art, architecture, and fashion in wave upon wave as each new and sensational discovery was reported. Mummies appeared in every museum worthy of the name, and no private collection was complete without one. Fashionable people flocked to "unwrapping parties" to witness a mummy being taken apart.

The curse of the Pharaohs had been a part of the popular imagination at least since 1699, when Louis Penicher wrote of a Polish traveler whose journey home from Alexandria with two mummies was dogged by bad weather and spectral visions, which only abated once the mummies were thrown overboard. Many writers, from Mark Twain to Tennessee Williams to H. P. Lovecraft, used the tombs of ancient Egypt and their mummified occupants in stories of intrigue and horror; Alcott's contribution to the mummy subgenre has been unjustly overlooked by all but die-hard horror aficionados.

I

"And what are these, Paul?" asked Evelyn, opening a tarnished gold box and examining its contents curiously.

"Seeds of some unknown Egyptian plant," replied Forsyth, with a sudden shadow on his dark face, as he looked down at the three scarlet grains lying in the white hand lifted to him.

"Where did you get them?" asked the girl.

"That is a weird story, which will only haunt you if I tell it," said Forsyth, with an absent expression that strongly excited the girl's curiosity.

"Please tell it, I like weird tales, and they never trouble me. Ah, do tell it; your stories are always so interesting," she cried, looking up with such a pretty blending of entreaty and command in her charming face, that refusal was impossible.

"You'll be sorry for it, and so shall I, perhaps; I warn you beforehand, that harm is foretold to the possessor of those mysterious seeds," said Forsyth, smiling, even while he knit his black brows, and regarded the blooming creature before him with a fond yet foreboding glance.

"Tell on, I'm not afraid of these pretty atoms," she answered, with an imperious nod.

"To hear is to obey. Let me read the facts, and then I will begin," returned Forsyth, pacing to and fro with the far-off look of one who turns the pages of the past.

Evelyn watched him a moment, and then returned to her work, or play, rather, for the task seemed well suited to the vivacious little creature, half-child, half-woman.

"While in Egypt," commenced Forsyth, slowly, "I went one day with my guide and Professor Niles, to explore the Cheops. Niles had a mania for antiquities of all sorts, and forgot time, danger and fatigue in the ardor of his pursuit. We rummaged up and down the narrow passages, half choked with dust and close air; reading inscriptions on the walls, stumbling over shattered mummy-cases, or coming face to face with some shriveled specimen perched like a hobgoblin on the little shelves where the dead used to be stowed away for ages. I was desperately tired after a few hours of it, and begged the professor to return. But he was bent on exploring certain places, and would not desist. We had but one guide, so I was forced to stay; but Jumal, my man, seeing how weary I was, proposed to us to rest in one of the larger passages, while he went to procure another guide for Niles. We consented, and assuring us that we were perfectly safe, if we did not quit the spot, Jumal left us, promising to return speedily. The professor sat down to take notes of his researches, and stretching my self on the soft sand, I fell asleep.

"I was roused by that indescribable thrill which instinctively warns us of danger, and springing up, I found myself alone. One torch burned faintly where Jumal had struck it, but Niles and the other light were gone. A dreadful sense of loneliness oppressed me for a moment; then I collected myself and looked well about me. A bit of paper was pinned to my hat, which lay near me, and on it, in the professor's writing were these words:

"'I've gone back a little to refresh my memory on certain points. Don't follow me till Jumal comes. I can find my way back to you, for I have a clue. Sleep well, and dream gloriously of the Pharaohs. N N.'

"I laughed at first over the old enthusiast, then felt anxious then restless, and finally resolved to follow him, for I discovered a strong cord fastened to a fallen stone, and knew that this was the clue he spoke of. Leaving a line for Jumal, I took my torch and retraced my steps, following the cord along the winding ways. I often shouted, but received no reply, and pressed on, hoping at each turn to see the old man poring over some musty relic of antiquity. Suddenly the cord ended, and lowering my torch, I saw that the footsteps had gone on.

"'Rash fellow, he'll lose himself, to a certainty,' I thought, really alarmed now.

"As I paused, a faint call reached me, and I answered it, waited, shouted again, and a still fainter echo replied.

"Niles was evidently going on, misled by the reverberations of the low passages. No time was to be lost, and, forgetting myself, I stuck my torch in the deep sand to guide me back to the clue, and ran down the straight path before me, whooping like a madman as I went. I did not mean to lose sight of the light, but in my eagerness to find Niles I turned from the main passage, and, guided by his voice, hastened on. His torch soon gladdened my eyes, and the clutch of his trembling hands told me what agony he had suffered.

"'Let us get out of this horrible place at once,' he said, wiping the great drops off his forehead.

"'Come, we're not far from the clue. I can soon reach it, and then we are safe'; but as I spoke, a chill passed over me, for a perfect labyrinth of narrow paths lay before us.

"Trying to guide myself by such land-marks as I had observed in my hasty passage, I followed the tracks in the sand till I fancied we must be near my light. No glimmer appeared, however, and kneeling down to examine the footprints nearer, I discovered, to my dismay, that I had been following the wrong ones, for among those marked by a deep boot-heel, were prints of bare feet; we had had no guide there, and Jumal wore sandals.

"Rising, I confronted Niles, with the one despairing word, 'Lost!' as I pointed from the treacherous sand to the fast-waning light.

"I thought the old man would be overwhelmed but, to my surprise, he grew quite calm and steady, thought a moment, and then went on, saying, quietly:

"'Other men have passed here before us; let us follow their steps, for, if I do not greatly err, they lead toward great passages, where one's way is easily found.'

"On we went, bravely, till a misstep threw the professor violently to the ground with a broken leg, and nearly extinguished the torch. It was a horrible predicament, and I gave up all hope as I sat beside the poor fellow, who lay exhausted with fatigue, remorse and pain, for I would not leave him.

"'Paul,' he said suddenly, 'if you will not go on, there is one more effort we can make. I remember hearing that a party lost as we are, saved themselves by building a fire. The smoke penetrated further than sound or light, and the guide's quick wit understood the unusual mist; he followed it, and rescued the party. Make a fire and trust to Jumal.'

"'A fire without wood?' I began; but he pointed to a shelf behind me, which had escaped me in the gloom; and on it I saw a slender mummy-case. I understood him, for these dry cases, which lie about in hundreds, are freely used as firewood. Reaching up, I pulled it down, believing it to be empty, but as it fell, it burst open, and out rolled a mummy. Accustomed as I was to such sights, it startled me a little, for danger had unstrung my nerves. Laying the little brown chrysalis aside, I smashed the case, lit the pile with my torch, and soon a light cloud of smoke drifted down the three passages which diverged from the cell-like place where we had paused.

"While busied with the fire, Niles, forgetful of pain and peril, had dragged the mummy nearer, and was examining it with the interest of a man whose ruling passion was strong even in death.

"'Come and help me unroll this. I have always longed to be the first to see and secure the curious treasures put away among the folds of these uncanny winding-sheets. This is a woman, and we may find something rare and precious here,' he said, beginning to unfold the outer coverings, from which a strange aromatic odor came.

"Reluctantly I obeyed, for to me there was something sacred in the bones of this unknown woman. But to beguile the time and amuse the poor fellow, I lent a hand, wondering as I worked, if this dark, ugly thing had ever been a lovely, soft-eyed Egyptian girl.

"From the fibrous folds of the wrappings dropped precious gums and spices, which half intoxicated us with their potent breath, antique coins, and a curious jewel or two, which Niles eagerly examined.

"All the bandages but one were cut off at last, and a small head laid bare, round which still hung great plaits of what had once been luxuriant hair. The shriveled hands were folded on the breast, and clasped in them lay that gold box."

"Ah!" cried Evelyn, dropping it from her rosy palm with a shudder.

"Nay; don't reject the poor little mummy's treasure. I never have quite forgiven myself for stealing it, or for burning her," said Forsyth, painting rapidly, as if the recollection of that experience lent energy to his hand.

"Burning her! Oh, Paul, what do you mean?" asked the girl, sitting up with a face full of excitement.

"I'll tell you. While busied with Madame la Momie, our fire had burned low, for the dry case went like tinder. A faint, far-off sound made our hearts leap, and Niles cried out: 'Pile on the wood; Jumal is tracking us; don't let the smoke fail now or we are lost!'

"'There is no more wood; the case was very small, and is all gone,' I answered, tearing off such of my garments as would burn readily, and piling them upon the embers.

"Niles did the same, but the light fabrics were quickly consumed, and made no smoke.

"'Burn that!' commanded the professor, pointing to the mummy.

"I hesitated a moment. Again came the faint echo of a horn. Life was dear to me. A few dry bones might save us, and I obeyed him in silence.

"A dull blaze sprung up, and a heavy smoke rose from the burning mummy, rolling in volumes through the low passages, and threatening to suffocate us with its fragrant mist. My brain grew dizzy, the light danced before my eyes, strange phantoms seemed to people the air, and, in the act of asking Niles why he gasped and looked so pale, I lost consciousness."

Evelyn drew a long breath, and put away the scented toys from her lap as if their odor oppressed her.

Forsyth's swarthy face was all aglow with the excitement of his story, and his black eyes glittered as he added, with a quick laugh:

"That's all; Jumal found and got us out, and we both forswore pyramids for the rest of our days."

"But the box: how came you to keep it?" asked Evelyn, eyeing it askance as it lay gleaming in a streak of sunshine.

"Oh, I brought it away as a souvenir, and Niles kept the other trinkets."

"But you said harm was foretold to the possessor of those scarlet seeds," persisted the girl, whose fancy was excited by the tale, and who fancied all was not told.

"Among his spoils, Niles found a bit of parchment, which he deciphered, and this inscription said that the mummy we had so ungallantly burned was that of a famous sorceress who bequeathed her curse to whoever should disturb her rest. Of course I don't believe that curse has anything to do with it, but it's a fact that Niles never prospered from that day. He says it's because he has never recovered from the fall and fright and I dare say it is so; but I sometimes wonder if I am to share the curse, for I've a vein of superstition in me, and that poor little mummy haunts my dreams still."

A long silence followed these words. Paul painted mechanically and Evelyn lay regarding him with a thoughtful face. But gloomy fancies were as foreign to her nature as shadows are to noonday, and presently she laughed a cheery laugh, saying as she took up the box again:

"Why don't you plant them, and see what wondrous flower they will bear?"

"I doubt if they would bear anything after lying in a mummy's hand for centuries," replied Forsyth, gravely.

"Let me plant them and try. You know wheat has sprouted and grown that was taken from a mummy's coffin; why should not these pretty seeds? I should so like to watch them grow; may I, Paul?"

"No, I'd rather leave that experiment untried. I have a queer feeling about the matter, and don't want to meddle myself or let anyone I love meddle with these seeds. They may be some horrible poison, or possess some evil power, for the sorceress evidently valued them, since she clutched them fast even in her tomb."

"Now, you are foolishly superstitious, and I laugh at you. Be generous; give me one seed, just to learn if it will grow. See I'll pay for it," and Evelyn, who now stood beside him, dropped a kiss on his forehead as she made her request, with the most engaging air.

But Forsyth would not yield. He smiled and returned the embrace with lover-like warmth, then flung the seeds into the fire, and gave her back the golden box, saying, tenderly:

"My darling, I'll fill it with diamonds or bonbons, if you please, but I will not let you play with that witch's spells. You've enough of your own, so forget the 'pretty seeds' and see what a Light of the Harem I've made of you."

Evelyn frowned, and smiled, and presently the lovers were out in the spring sunshine reveling in their own happy hopes, untroubled by one foreboding fear.

II

"I have a little surprise for you, love," said Forsyth, as he greeted his cousin three months later on the morning of his wedding day.

"And I have one for you," she answered, smiling faintly.

"How pale you are, and how thin you grow! All this bridal bustle is too much for you, Evelyn," he said, with fond anxiety, as he watched the strange pallor of her face, and pressed the wasted little hand in his.

"I am so tired," she said, and leaned her head wearily on her lover's breast. "Neither sleep, food, nor air gives me strength, and a curious mist seems to cloud my mind at times. Mamma says it is the heat, but I shiver even in the sun, while at night I burn with fever. Paul, dear, I'm glad you are going to take me away to lead a quiet, happy life with you, but I'm afraid it will be a very short one."

"My fanciful little wife! You are tired and nervous with all this worry, but a few weeks of rest in the country will give us back our blooming Eve again. Have you no curiosity to learn my surprise?" he asked, to change her thoughts.

. The vacant look stealing over the girl's face gave place to one of interest, but as she listened it seemed to require an effort to fix her mind on her lover's words.

"You remember the day we rummaged in the old cabinet?"

"Yes," and a smile touched her lips for a moment.

"And how you wanted to plant those queer red seeds I stole from the mummy?"

"I remember," and her eyes kindled with sudden fire.

"Well, I tossed them into the fire, as I thought, and gave you the box. But when I went back to cover up my picture, and found one of those seeds on the rug, a sudden fancy to gratify your whim led me to send it to Niles and ask him to plant and report on its progress. Today I hear from him for the first time, and he reports that the seed has grown marvelously, has budded, and that he intends to take the first flower, if it blooms in time, to a meeting of famous scientific men, after which he will send me its true name and the plant itself. From his description, it must be very curious, and I'm impatient to see it."

"You need not wait; I can show you the flower in its bloom," and Evelyn beckoned with the *mechante** smile so long a stranger to her lips.

Much amazed, Forsyth followed her to her own little boudoir, and there, standing in the sunshine, was the unknown plant. Almost rank in their luxuriance were the vivid green leaves on the slender purple stems, and rising from the midst, one ghostly-white flower, shaped like the head of a hooded snake, with scarlet stamens like forked tongues, and on the petals glittered spots like dew.

"A strange, uncanny flower! Has it any odor?" asked Forsyth, bending to examine it, and forgetting, in his interest, to ask how it came there.

"None, and that disappoints me, I am so fond of perfumes," answered the girl, caressing the green leaves which trembled at her touch, while the purple stems deepened their tint.

"Now tell me about it," said Forsyth, after standing silent for several minutes.

I had been before you, and secured one of the seeds, for two fell on the rug. I planted it under a glass in the richest soil I could find, watered it faithfully, and was amazed at the rapidity with which it grew when once it appeared above the earth. I told no-one, for I meant to surprise you with it; but this bud has been so long in blooming, I have had to wait. It is a good omen that it blossoms today, and as it is nearly white, I mean to wear it, for I've learned to love it, having been my pet for so long.

---

* French: mischievous.

I would not wear it, for, in spite of its innocent color, it is an evil-looking plant, with its adder's tongue and unnatural dew. Wait till Niles tells us what it is, then pet it if it is harmless.

"Perhaps my sorceress cherished it for some symbolic beauty—those old Egyptians were full of fancies. It was very sly of you to turn the tables on me in this way. But I forgive you, since in a few hours, I shall chain this mysterious hand forever. How cold it is! Come out into the garden and get some warmth and color for tonight, my love."

But when night came, no-one could reproach the girl with her pallor, for she glowed like a pomegranate-flower, her eyes were full of fire, her lips scarlet, and all her old vivacity seemed to have returned. A more brilliant bride never blushed under a misty veil, and when her lover saw her, he was absolutely startled by the almost unearthly beauty which transformed the pale, languid creature of the morning into this radiant woman.

They were married, and if love, many blessings, and all good gifts lavishly showered upon them could make them happy, then this young pair were truly blest. But even in the rapture of the moment that made her his, Forsyth observed how icy cold was the little hand he held, how feverish the deep color on the soft cheek he kissed, and what a strange fire burned in the tender eyes that looked so wistfully at him.

Blithe and beautiful as a spirit, the smiling bride played her part in all the festivities of that long evening, and when at last light, life and color began to fade, the loving eyes that watched her thought it but the natural weariness of the hour. As the last guest departed, Forsyth was met by a servant, who gave him a letter marked "Haste." Tearing it open, he read these lines, from a friend of the professor's:

"DEAR SIR—Poor Niles died suddenly two days ago, while at the Scientific Club, and his last words were: 'Tell Paul Forsyth to beware of the Mummy's Curse, for this fatal flower has killed me.' The circumstances of his death were so peculiar, that I add them as a sequel to this message. For several months, as he told us, he had been watching an unknown plant, and that evening he brought us the flower to examine. Other matters of interest absorbed us till a late hour, and the plant was forgotten. The professor wore it in his buttonhole—a strange white, serpent-headed blossom, with pale glittering spots, which slowly changed to a glittering scarlet, till the leaves looked as if sprinkled with blood. It was observed that instead of the pallor and feebleness which had recently come over him, that the professor was unusually animated, and seemed in an almost unnatural state of high spirits. Near the close of the meeting, in the midst of a lively discussion, he suddenly dropped, as if smitten with apoplexy. He was conveyed home insensible, and after one lucid interval, in which he gave me the message I have recorded above, he died in great agony, raving of mummies, pyramids, serpents, and some fatal curse which had fallen upon him.

"After his death, livid scarlet spots, like those on the flower, appeared upon his skin, and he shriveled like a withered leaf. At my desire, the mysterious plant was examined, and pronounced by the best authority one of the most deadly poisons known to the Egyptian sorceresses. The plant slowly absorbs the vitality of whoever cultivates it, and the blossom, worn for two or three hours, produces either madness or death."

Down dropped the paper from Forsyth's hand; he read no further, but hurried back into the room where he had left his young wife. As if worn out with fatigue, she had thrown herself upon a couch, and lay there motionless, her face half-hidden by the light folds of the veil, which had blown over it.

"Evelyn, my dearest! Wake up and answer me. Did you wear that strange flower today?" whispered Forsyth, putting the misty screen away.

There was no need for her to answer, for there, gleaming spectrally on her bosom, was the evil blossom, its white petals spotted now with flecks of scarlet, vivid as drops of newly spilt blood.

But the unhappy bridegroom scarcely saw it, for the face above it appalled him by its utter vacancy. Drawn and pallid, as if with some wasting malady, the young face, so lovely an hour ago, lay before him aged and blighted by the baleful influence of the plant which had drunk up her life. No recognition in the eyes, no word upon the lips, no motion of the hand—only the faint breath, the fluttering pulse, and wide-opened eyes, betrayed that she was alive.

Alas for the young wife! The superstitious fear at which she had smiled had proved true: the curse that had bided its time for ages was fulfilled at last, and her own hand wrecked her happiness for ever. Death in life was her doom, and for years Forsyth secluded himself to tend with pathetic devotion the pale ghost, who never, by word or look, could thank him for the love that outlived even such a fate as this.

TOM TOOTHACRE'S GHOST STORY

by Harriet Beecher Stowe

1869

Harriet Beecher Stowe was born in Litchfield, Connecticut, in 1811, one of thirteen children born to Calvinist preacher Lyman Beecher. Several of her brothers became noted preachers; her elder sister Catharine was a pioneering educator and champion of women's education; and her younger half-sister Isabella Beecher Hooker became a leading light of the American suffragist movement. Harriet enrolled in the Hartford Female Seminary run by her sister Catharine, where she received the type of comprehensive education normally reserved for boys.

Along with her father, a twenty-one-year-old Harriet moved to Cincinnati in 1832, where she quickly became involved in the booming city's literary scene. There she met and married Calvin Ellis Stowe, a widowed Biblical scholar at the seminary where her father taught. The two became active supporters of the Underground Railroad, sheltering fugitive slaves on their way to Canada: these experiences moved her to write her most famous work, Uncle Tom's Cabin.

She wrote on a number of topics: sketches of New England life; explorations of witchcraft and spiritualism; biographies of women from the Bible; and an account of Lady Byron's life and tempestuous marriage to the scandalous poet, which was denounced as indecent and cost her some popularity. Far from courting sensation, however, Stowe maintained that the book was written "in defence of a beloved, revered friend, whose memory stood forth in the eyes of the civilised world charged with most repulsive crimes, of which I certainly *knew her innocent."*

Stowe's ghost stories are lighter fare altogether: most of them turn out not to be supernatural at all, but rather the product of human credulousness and mischief. "The Ghost in the Old Mill" is the best-known, but in many ways "Tom Toothacre's Ghost Story" is the better tale. Part of the collection Sam Lawson's Oldtown Fireside Stories, *it is written in a strong New England dialect that makes it challenging for the modern reader, but it is a solid and satisfying ghost story that repays persistence.*

W hat is it about that old house in Sherbourne?" said Aunt Nabby to Sam Lawson, as he sat drooping over the coals of a great fire one October evening.

Aunt Lois was gone to Boston on a visit; and, the smart spice of her scepticism being absent, we felt the more freedom to start our story-teller on one of his legends.

Aunt Nabby sat trotting her knitting-needles on a blue-mixed yarn stocking. Grandmamma was knitting in unison at the other side of the fire. Grandfather sat studying "The Boston Courier." The wind outside was sighing in fitful wails, creaking the pantry-doors, occasionally puffing in a vicious gust down the broad throat of the chimney. It was a drizzly, sleety evening; and the wet lilac-bushes now and then rattled and splashed against the window as the wind moaned and whispered through them.

We boys had made preparation for a comfortable evening. We had enticed Sam to the chimney-corner, and drawn him a mug of cider. We had set down a row of apples to roast on the hearth, which even now were giving faint sighs and sputters as their plump sides burst in the genial heat. The big oak back-log simmered and bubbled, and distilled large drops down amid the ashes; and the great hickory forestick had just burned out into solid bright coals, faintly skimmed over with white ashes. The whole area of the big chimney was full of a sleepy warmth and brightness just calculated to call forth fancies and visions. It only wanted somebody now to set Sam off; and Aunt Nabby broached the ever-interesting subject of haunted houses.

"Wal, now, Miss Badger," said Sam, "I ben over there, and walked round that are house consid'able; and I talked with Granny Hokum and Aunt Polly, and they've putty much come to the conclusion that they'll hev to move out on't. Ye see these 'ere noises, they keep 'em awake nights; and Aunt Polly, she gets 'stericky; and Hannah Jane, she says, ef they stay in the house, *she* can't live with 'em no longer. And what can them lone women do without Hannah Jane? Why, Hannah Jane, she says these two months past she's seen a woman, regular, walking up and down the front hall between twelve and one o'clock at night; and it's jist the image and body of old Ma'am Tillotson, Parson Hokum's mother, that everybody know'd was a thunderin' kind o' woman, that kep' every thing in a muss while she was alive. What the old crittur's up to now there ain't no knowin'. Some folks seems to think it's a sign Granny Hokum's time's comin'. But Lordy massy! says she to me, says she, 'Why, Sam, I don't know nothin' what I've done, that Ma'am Tillotson should be set loose on me.' Anyway they've all got so narvy, that Jed Hokum has ben up from Needham, and is goin' to cart 'em all over to live with him. Jed, he's for hushin' on't up, 'cause he says it brings a bad name on the property.

"Wal, I talked with Jed about it; and says I to Jed, says I, 'Now, ef you'll take my advice, jist you give that are old house a regular overhaulin', and paint it over with tew coats o' paint, and that are'll clear 'em out, if any thing will. Ghosts is like bedbugs,—they can't stan' fresh paint,' says I. 'They allers clear out. I've seen it tried on a ship that got haunted.'"

"Why, Sam, do ships get haunted?"

"To be sure they do!—haunted the wust kind. Why, I could tell ye a story'd make your har rise on eend, only I'm 'fraid of frightening boys when they're jist going to bed."

"Oh! you can't frighten Horace," said my grandmother. "He will go and sit out there in the graveyard till nine o'clock nights, spite of all I tell him."

"Do tell, Sam!" we urged. "What was it about the ship?"

Sam lifted his mug of cider, deliberately turned it round and round in his hands, eyed it affectionately, took a long drink, and set it down in front of him on the hearth, and began:—

"Ye 'member I telled you how I went to sea down East, when I was a boy, 'long with Tom Toothacre. Wal, Tom, he reeled off a yarn one night that was 'bout the toughest I ever hed the pullin' on. And it come all straight, too, from Tom. 'Twa'n't none o' yer hearsay: 'twas what he seen with his own eyes. Now, there wa'n't no nonsense 'bout Tom, not a bit on't; and he wa'n't afeard o' the divil himse'f; and he ginally saw through things about as straight as things could be seen through. This 'ere happened when Tom was mate o' The Albatross, and they was a-runnin' up to the Banks for a fare o' fish. The Albatross was as handsome a craft as ever ye see; and Cap'n Sim Witherspoon, he was skipper—a rail nice likely man he was. I heard Tom tell this 'ere one night to the boys on The Brilliant, when they was all a-settin' round the stove in the cabin one foggy night that we was to anchor in Frenchman's Bay, and all kind o' lavin' off loose.

"Tom, he said they was having a famous run up to the Banks. There was a spankin' southerly, that blew 'em along like all natur'; and they was hevin' the best kind of a time, when this 'ere southerly brought a pesky fog down on 'em, and it grew thicker than hasty-puddin'.* Ye see, that are's the pester o' these 'ere southerlies: they's the biggest fog-breeders there is goin'. And so, putty soon, you couldn't see half ship's length afore you.

"Wal, they all was down to supper, except Dan Sawyer at the wheel, when there come sich a crash as if heaven and earth was a-splittin', and then a scrapin' and thump bumpin' under the ship, and gin 'em sich a h'ist that the pot o' beans went rollin', and brought up jam ag'in the bulk-head; and the fellers was keeled over,—men and pork and beans kinder permiscus.

---

* A kind of porridge made with grains (usually ground corn in the United States) in water or milk. Best known today for giving its name to the famous theatrical club at Harvard University.

"'The divil!' says Tom Toothacre, 'we've run down somebody. Look out, up there!'

"Dan, he shoved the helm hard down, and put her up to the wind, and sung out, 'Lordy massy! we've struck her right amidships!'

"'Struck what?' they all yelled, and tumbled up on deck.

"'Why, a little schooner,' says Dan. 'Didn't see her till we was right on her. She's gone down tack and sheet. Look! there's part o' the wreck a-floating off: don't ye see?'

"Wal, they didn't see, 'cause it was so thick you couldn't hardly see your hand afore your face. But they put about, and sent out a boat, and kind o' sarched round; but, Lordy massy! ye might as well looked for a drop of water in the Atlantic Ocean. Whoever they was, it was all done gone and over with 'em for this life, poor critturs!

"Tom says they felt confoundedly about it; but what could they do? Lordy massy! what can any on us do? There's places where folks jest lets go 'cause they hes to. Things ain't as they want 'em, and they can't alter 'em. Sailors ain't so rough as they look: they'z feelin' critturs, come to put things right to 'em. And there wasn't one on 'em who wouldn't'a' worked all night for a chance o' saving some o' them poor fellows. But there 'twas, and 'twa'n't no use trying.

"Wal, so they sailed on; and by 'm by the wind kind o' chopped round no'theast, and then come round east, and sot in for one of them regular east blows and drizzles that takes the starch out o' fellers more'n a regular storm. So they concluded they might as well put into a little bay there, and come to anchor.

"So they sot an anchor-watch, and all turned in.

"Wal, now comes the particular curus part o' Tom's story: and it more curus 'cause Tom was one that wouldn't'a' believed no other man that had told it. Tom was one o' your sort of philosophers. He was fer lookin' into things, and wa'n't in no hurry 'bout believin'; so that this 'un was more 'markable on account of it's bein' Tom that seen it than ef it had ben others.

"Tom says that night he hed a pesky toothache that sort o' kep' grumblin' and jumpin' so he couldn't go to sleep; and he lay in his bunk, a-turnin' this way and that, till long past twelve o'clock.

"Tom had a'thwart-ship bunk where he could see into every bunk on board, except Bob Coffin's; and Bob was on the anchor-watch. Wal, he lay there, tryin' to go to sleep, hearin' the men snorin' like bull-frogs in a swamp, and watchin' the lantern a-swingin' back and forward; and the sou'westers and pea-jackets were kinder throwin' their long shadders up and down as the vessel sort o' rolled and pitched,—for there was a heavy swell on,—and then he'd hear Bob Coffin tramp, tramp, trampin' overhead,—for Bob had a pretty heavy foot of his own,—and all sort o' mixed up together with Tom's toothache, so he couldn't get to sleep. Finally, Tom, he bit off a great chaw o' 'baccy, and got it well sot in his cheek, and kind o' turned over to lie on't, and ease the pain. Wal, he says he laid a spell, and dropped off in a sort o' doze, when he woke in sich a chill his teeth chattered, and the pain come on like a knife, and he bounced over, thinking the fire had gone out in the stove.

"Wal, sure enough, he see a man a-crouchin' over the stove, with his back to him, a-stretchin' out his hands to warm 'em. He had on a sou'wester and a pea-jacket, with a red tippet round his neck; and his clothes was drippin' as if he'd just come in from a rain.

"'What the divil!' says Tom. And he riz right up, and rubbed his eyes. 'Bill Bridges,' says he, 'what shine be you up to now?' For Bill was a master oneasy crittur, and allers a-gettin' up and walkin' nights; and Tom, he thought it was Bill. But in a minute he looked over, and there, sure enough, was Bill, fast asleep in his bunk, mouth wide open, snoring like a Jericho ram's-horn. Tom looked round, and counted every man in his bunk, and then says he, 'Who the devil is this? for there's Bob Coffin on deck, and the rest is all here.'

"Wal, Tom wa'n't a man to be put under too easy. He hed his thoughts about him allers; and the fust he thought in every pinch was what to do. So he sot considerin' a minute, sort o' winkin' his eyes to be sure he saw straight, when, sure enough, there come another man backin' down the companion-way.

"'Wal, there's Bob Coffin, anyhow,' says Tom to himself. But no, the other man, he turned: Tom see his face; and, sure as you live, it was the face of a dead corpse. Its eyes was sot, and it jest came as still across the cabin, and sot down by the stove, and kind o' shivered, and put out its hands as if it was gettin' warm.

"Tom said that there was a cold air round in the cabin, as if an iceberg was comin' near, and he felt cold chills running down his back; but he jumped out of his bunk, and took a step forward. 'Speak!' says he. 'Who be you? and what do you want?'

"They never spoke, nor looked up, but kept kind o' shivering and crouching over the stove.

"'Wal,' says Tom, 'I'll see who you be, anyhow.' And he walked right up to the last man that come in, and reached out to catch hold of his coat-collar; but his hand jest went through him like moonshine, and in a minute he all faded away; and when he turned round the other one was gone too. Tom stood there, looking this way and that; but there warn't nothing but the old stove, and the lantern swingin', and the men all snorin' round in their bunks. Tom, he sung out to Bob Coffin. 'Hullo, up there!' says he. But Bob never answered, and Tom, he went up, and found Bob down on his knees, his teeth a-chatterin' like a bag o' nails, trying to say his prayers; and all he could think of was, 'Now I lay me,' and he kep' going that over and over. Ye see, boys, Bob was a dreffle wicked, swearin' crittur, and hadn't said no prayers since he was tew years old, and it didn't come natural to him. Tom give a grip on his collar, and shook him. 'Hold yer yawp,' said he. 'What you howlin' about? What's up?'

"'Oh, Lordy massy!' says Bob, 'we're sent for,—all on us,—there's been two on 'em: both on 'em went right by me!'

"Wal, Tom, he hed his own thoughts; but he was bound to get to the bottom of things, anyway. Ef 'twas the devil, well and good—he wanted to know it. Tom jest wanted to hev the matter settled one way or t'other: so he got Bob sort o' stroked down, and made him tell what he saw.

"Bob, he stood to it that he was a-standin' right for'ard, a-leanin' on the windlass, and kind o' hummin' a tune, when he looked down, and see a sort o' queer light in the fog; and he went and took a look over the bows, when up came a man's head in a sort of sou'wester, and then a pair of hands, and catched at the bob-stay; and then the hull figger of a man riz right out o' the water, and clim up on the martingale till he could reach the jib-stay with his hands, and then he swung himself right up onto the bowsprit, and stepped aboard, and went past Bob, right aft, and down into the cabin. And he hadn't more'n got down, afore he turned round, and there was another comin' in over the bowsprit, and he went by him, and down below: so there was two on 'em, jest as Tom had seen in the cabin.

"Tom he studied on it a spell, and finally says he, 'Bob, let you and me keep this 'ere to ourselves, and see ef it'll come again. Ef it don't, well and good: ef it does—why, we'll see about it.'

"But Tom he told Cap'n Witherspoon, and the Cap'n he agreed to keep an eye out the next night. But there warn't nothing said to the rest o' the men.

"Wal, the next night they put Bill Bridges on the watch. The fog had lifted, and they had a fair wind, and was going on steady. The men all turned in, and went fast asleep, except Cap'n Witherspoon, Tom, and Bob Coffin. Wal, sure enough, 'twixt twelve and one o'clock, the same thing came over, only there war four men 'stead o' two. They come in jes' so over the bowsprit, and they looked neither to right nor left, but dim down stairs, and sot down, and crouched and shivered over the stove jist like the others. Wal, Bill Bridges, he came tearin' down like a wild-cat, frightened half out o' his wits, screechin' 'Lord, have mercy! we're all goin' to the devil!' And then they all vanished.

"'Now, Cap'n, what's to be done?' says Tom. 'Ef these 'ere fellows is to take passage, we can't do nothin' with the boys: that's clear.'

"Wal, so it turned out; for, come next night, there was six on 'em come in, and the story got round, and the boys was all on eend. There wa'n't no doin' nothin' with 'em. Ye see, it's allers jest so. Not but what dead folks is jest as 'spectable as they was afore they's dead. These might'a' been as good fellers as any aboard; but it's human natur'. The minute a feller's dead, why, you sort o' don't know 'bout him; and it's kind o' skeery hevin' on him round; and so 'twan't no wonder the boys didn't feel as if they could go on with the vy'ge, ef these 'ere fellers was all to take passage. Come to look, too, there war consid'able of a leak stove in the vessel; and the boys, they all stood to it, ef they went farther, that they'd all go to the bottom. For, ye see, once the story got a-goin', every one on 'em saw a new thing every night. One on 'em saw the bait-mill a-grindin', without no hands to grind it; and another saw fellers up aloft, workin' in the sails. Wal, the fact war, they jest had to put about,—run back to Castine.

"Wal, the owners, they hushed up things the best they could; and they put the vessel on the stocks, and worked her over, and put a new coat o' paint on her, and called her The Betsey Ann; and she went a good vy'ge to the Banks, and brought home the biggest fare o' fish that had been for a long time; and she's made good vy'ges ever since; and that jest proves what I've been a-saying,—that there's nothin' to drive out ghosts like fresh paint."

KENTUCKY'S GHOST

by Elizabeth Stuart Phelps

1869

Elizabeth Stuart Phelps Ward challenged many things in the years immediately after the Civil War. An early feminist, she advocated clothing reform for women, questioned traditional views of a woman's role in marriage and the family, and even took aim at traditional Christian views of the afterlife in her 1868 novel The Gates Ajar. *She married a man seventeen years her junior, urged women to burn their corsets, and wrote about female ministers, physicians, and artists. She herself became the first woman to present a lecture series at Boston University. Late in life, she also became a vocal opponent of vivisection.*

Her fifty-seven volumes of fiction, poetry, and essays reflected her beliefs, challenging the standard attitude that a woman's place was in the home. The poet John Greenleaf Whittier and the leading abolitionist Thomas Wentworth Higginson both admired her work. She was published in Harper's Monthly, The Atlantic Monthly, *and other magazines, as well as in book form. Her baptismal name was Mary Gray Phelps, after a close friend of her mother's, but she wrote under her mother's name of Elizabeth Stuart Phelps. Rather confusingly for present-day literary scholars, her mother wrote the celebrated* Kitty Brown *series—said to be the first book series specifi-cally for girls—under the pseudonym of H. Trusta.*

"Kentucky's Ghost" was first published in The Atlantic Monthly's *November 1868 issue, and reappeared in the 1869 collection* Men, Women, and Ghosts. *It is unexpected in two ways. First, it contains little or none of the social agendas that underpin most of Elizabeth Stuart Phelps's other work; and second, it is a tale of the sea, a literary subgenre that was—and remains—even more heavily male-dominated than all the others. In telling the tale of a mother's love, Phelps conveys the atmosphere and language of the sea as strongly as any male author—and gives us a very satisfying ghost story into the bargain.*

T rue? Every syllable.

That was a very fair yarn of yours, Tom Brown, very fair for a landsman, but I'll bet you a doughnut I can beat it; and all on the square, too, as I say,—which is more, if I don't mistake, than you could take oath to. Not to say that I never stretched my yarn a little on the fo'castle in my younger days, like the rest of 'em; but what with living under roofs so long past, and a call from the parson regular in strawberry time, and having to do the flogging consequent on the inakkeracies of statement follering on the growing up of six boys, a man learns to trim his words a little, Tom, and no mistake. It's very much as it is with the talk of the sea growing strange to you from hearing nothing but lubbers who don't know a mizzen-mast from a church-steeple.

It was somewhere about twenty years ago last October, if I recollect fair, that we were laying in for that particular trip to Madagascar. I've done that little voyage to Madagascar when the sea was like so much burning oil, and the sky like so much burning brass, and the fo'castle as nigh a hell as ever fo'castle was in a calm; I've done it when we came sneaking into port with nigh about every spar gone and pumps going night and day; and I've done it with a drunken captain on starvation rations,—duff that a dog on land wouldn't have touched and two teaspoonfuls of water to the day,—but someways or other, of all the times we headed for the East Shore I don't seem to remember any quite as distinct as this.

We cleared from Long Wharf in the ship Madonna,—which they tell me means, My Lady, and a pretty name it was; it was apt to give me that gentle kind of feeling when I spoke it, which is surprising when you consider what a dull old hull she was, never logging over ten knots, and uncertain at that. It may have been because of Moll's coming down once in a while in the days that we lay at dock, bringing the boy with her, and sitting up on deck in a little white apron, knitting. She was a very good-looking woman, was my wife, in those days, and I felt proud of her,—natural, with the lads looking on.

"Molly," I used to say, sometimes,—"Molly Madonna!"

"Nonsense!" says she, giving a clack to her needles,—pleased enough though, I warrant you, and turning a very pretty pink about the cheeks for a four-years' wife. Seeing as how she was always a lady to me, and a true one, and a gentle, though she wasn't much at manners or book-learning, and though I never gave her a silk gown in her life, she was quite content, you see, and so was I.

I used to speak my thought about the name sometimes, when the lads weren't particularly noisy, but they laughed at me mostly. I was rough enough and bad enough in those days; as rough as the rest, and as bad as the rest, I suppose, but yet I seemed to have my notions a little different from the others. "Jake's poetry," they called 'em.

We were loading for the East Shore trade, as I said, didn't I? There isn't much of the genuine, old-fashioned trade left in these days, except the whiskey branch, which will be brisk, I take it, till the Malagasy carry the prohibitory law by a large majority in both houses. We had a little whiskey in the hold, I remember, that trip, with a good stock of knives, red flannel, handsaws, nails, and cotton. We were hoping to be at home again within the year. We were well provisioned, and Dodd,—he was the cook,—Dodd made about as fair coffee as you're likely to find in the galley of a trader. As for our officers, when I say the less said of them the better, it ain't so much that I mean to be disrespectful as that I mean to put it tenderly. Officers in the merchant service, especially if it happens to be the African service, are brutal men quite as often as they ain't (at least, that's my experience; and when some of your great ship-owners argue the case with me,—as I'm free to say they have done before now,—I say, "That's *my* experience, sir," which is all I've got to say);—brutal men, and about as fit for their positions as if they'd been imported for the purpose a little indirect from Davy Jones's Locker. Though they do say that the flogging is pretty much done away with in these days, which makes a difference.

Sometimes on a sunshiny afternoon, when the muddy water showed a little muddier than usual, on account of the clouds being the color of silver, and all the air the color of gold, when the oily barrels were knocking about on the wharves, and the smells were strong from the fish-houses, and the men shouted and the mates swore, and our baby ran about deck a-play with everybody (he was a cunning little chap with red stockings and bare knees, and the lads took quite a shine to him), "Jake," his mother would say, with a little sigh,—low, so that the captain never heard,—"think if it was *him* gone away for a year in company the like of that!"

Then she would drop her shining needles, and call the little fellow back sharp, and catch him up into her arms.

Go into the keeping-room there, Tom, and ask her all about it. Bless you! she remembers those days at dock better than I do. She could tell you to this hour the color of my shirt, and how long my hair was, and what I ate, and how I looked, and what I said. I didn't generally swear so thick when she was about.

Well; we weighed, along the last of the month, in pretty good spirits. The Madonna was as stanch and seaworthy as any eight-hundred-tonner in the harbor, if she was clumsy; we turned in, some sixteen of us or thereabouts, into the fo'castle,—a jolly set, mostly old messmates, and well content with one another; and the breeze was stiff from the west, with a fair sky.

The night before we were off, Molly and I took a walk upon the wharves after supper. I carried the baby. A boy, sitting on some boxes, pulled my sleeve as we went by, and asked me, pointing to the Madonna, if I would tell him the name of the ship.

"Find out for yourself," said I, not over-pleased to be interrupted.

"Don't be cross to him," says Molly. The baby threw a kiss at the boy, and Molly smiled at him through the dark. I don't suppose I should ever have remembered the lubber from that day to this, except that I liked the looks of Molly smiling at him through the dark.

My wife and I said good-by the next morning in a little sheltered place among the lumber on the wharf; she was one of your women who never like to do their crying before folks.

She climbed on the pile of lumber and sat down, a little flushed and quivery, to watch us off. I remember seeing her there with the baby till we were well down the channel. I remember noticing the bay as it grew cleaner, and thinking that I would break off swearing; and I remember cursing Bob Smart like a pirate within an hour.

The breeze held steadier than we'd looked for, and we'd made a good offing and discharged the pilot by nightfall. Mr. Whitmarsh—he was the mate—was aft with the captain. The boys were singing a little; the smell of the coffee was coming up, hot and home-like, from the galley. I was up in the maintop, I forget what for, when all at once there came a cry and a shout; and, when I touched deck, I saw a crowd around the fore-hatch.

"What's all this noise for?" says Mr. Whitmarsh, coming up and scowling.

"A stow-away, sir! A boy stowed away!" said Bob, catching the officer's tone quick enough. Bob always tested the wind well, when a storm was brewing. He jerked the poor fellow out of the hold, and pushed him along to the mate's feet.

I say "poor fellow," and you'd never wonder why if you'd seen as much of stowing away as I have.

I'd as lief see a son of mine in a Carolina slave-gang as to see him lead the life of a stow-away. What with the officers from feeling that they've been taken in, and the men, who catch their cue from their superiors, and the spite of the lawful boy who hired in the proper way, he don't have what you may call a tender time.

This chap was a little fellow, slight for his years, which might have been fifteen, I take it. He was palish, with a jerk of thin hair on his forehead. He was hungry, and homesick, and frightened. He looked about on all our faces, and then he cowered a little, and lay still just as Bob had thrown him.

"We—ell," says Whitmarsh, very slow, "if you don't repent your bargain before you go ashore, my fine fellow,—me, if I'm mate of the Madonna! and take that for your pains!"

Upon that he kicks the poor little lubber from quarter-deck to bowsprit, or nearly, and goes down to his supper. The men laugh a little, then they whistle a little, then they finish their song quite gay and well acquainted, with the coffee steaming away in the galley. Nobody has a word for the boy,—bless you, no!

I'll venture he wouldn't have had a mouthful that night if it had not been for me; and I can't say as I should have bothered myself about him, if it had not come across me sudden, while he sat there rubbing his eyes quite violent, with his face to the west'ard (the sun was setting reddish), that I had seen the lad before; then I remembered walking on the wharves, and him on the box, and Molly saying softly that I was cross to him.

Seeing that my wife had smiled at him, and my baby thrown a kiss at him, it went against me, you see, not to look after the little rascal a bit that night.

"But you've got no business here, you know," said I; "nobody wants you."

"I wish I was ashore!" said he,—"I wish I was ashore!"

With that he begins to rub his eyes so very violent that I stopped. There was good stuff in him too; for he choked and winked at me, and did it all up, about the sun on the water and a cold in the head, as well as I could myself just about.

I don't know whether it was on account of being taken a little notice of that night, but the lad always kind of hung about me afterwards; chased me round with his eyes in a way he had, and did odd jobs for me without the asking.

One night before the first week was out, he hauled alongside of me on the windlass. I was trying a new pipe (and a very good one, too), so I didn't give him much notice for a while.

"You did this job up shrewd, Kent," said I, by and by; "how did you steer in?"—for it did not often happen that the Madonna got fairly out of port with a boy unbeknown in her hold.

"Watch was drunk; I crawled down ahind the whiskey. It was hot, you bet, and dark. I lay and thought how hungry I was," says he.

"Friends at home?" says I.

Upon that he gives me a nod, very short, and gets up and walks off whistling.

The first Sunday out that chap didn't know any more what to do with himself than a lobster just put on to boil. Sunday's cleaning day at sea, you know. The lads washed up, and sat round, little knots of them, mending their trousers. Bob got out his cards. Me and a few mates took it comfortable under the to'gallant fo'castle (I being on watch below), reeling off the stiffest yarns we had in tow. Kent looked on at euchre awhile, then listened to us awhile, then walked about uneasy.

By and by says Bob, "Look over there,—spry!" and there was Kent, sitting curled away in a heap under the stern of the long-boat. He had a book. Bob crawls behind and snatches it up, unbeknown, out of his hands; then he falls to laughing as if he would strangle, and gives the book a toss to me. It was a bit of Testament, black and old. There was writing on the yellow leaf, this way:—

"Kentucky Hodge,
from his Affecshunate mother
who prays, For you evry day, Amen,"

The boy turned first red, then white, and straightened up quite sudden, but he never said a word, only sat down again and let us laugh it out. I've lost my reckoning if he ever heard the last of it. He told me one day how he came by the name, but I forget exactly. Something about an old fellow—uncle, I believe—as died in Kentucky, and the name was moniment-like, you see. He used to seem cut up a bit about it at first, for the lads took to it famously; but he got used to it in a week or two, and, seeing as they meant him no unkindness, took it quite cheery.

One other thing I noticed was that he never had the book about after that. He fell into our ways next Sunday more easy.

They don't take the Bible just the way you would, Tom,—as a general thing, sailors don't; though I will say that I never saw the man at sea who didn't give it the credit of being an uncommon good yarn.

But I tell you, Tom Brown, I felt sorry for that boy. It's punishment bad enough for a little scamp like him leaving the honest shore, and folks to home that were a bit tender of him maybe, to rough it on a trader, learning how to slush down a back-stay, or tie reef-points with frozen fingers in a snow-squall.

But that's not the worst of it, by no means. If ever there was a cold-blooded, cruel man, with a wicked eye and a fist like a mallet, it was Job Whitmarsh, taken at his best. And I believe, of all the trips I've taken, him being mate of the Madonna, Kentucky found him at his worst. Bradley—that's the second mate—was none too gentle in his ways, you may be sure; but he never held a candle to Mr. Whitmarsh. He took a spite to the boy from the first, and he kept it on a steady strain to the last, right along, just about so.

I've seen him beat that boy till the blood ran down in little pools on deck; then send him up, all wet and red, to clear the to'sail halliards; and when, what with the pain and faintness, he dizzied a little, and clung to the ratlines, half blind, he would have him down and flog him till the cap'n interfered,—which would happen occasionally on a fair day when he had taken just enough to be good-natured. He used to rack his brains for the words he slung at the boy working quiet enough beside him. It was odd, now, the talk he would get off. Bob Smart couldn't any more come up to it than I could: we used to try sometimes, but we had to give in always. If curses had been a marketable article, Whitmarsh would have taken out his patent and made his fortune by inventing of them, new and ingenious. Then he used to kick the lad down the fo'castle ladder; he used to work him, sick or well, as he wouldn't have worked a dray-horse; he used to chase him all about deck at the rope's end; he used to mast-head him for hours on the stretch; he used to starve him out in the hold. It didn't come in my line to be over-tender, but I turned sick at heart, Tom, more times than one, looking on helpless, and me a great stout fellow.

I remember now—don't know as I've thought of it for twenty years—a thing McCallum said one night; McCallum was Scotch,—an old fellow with gray hair; told the best yarns on the fo'castle always.

"Mark my words, shipmates," says he, "when Job Whitmarsh's time comes to go as straight to hell as Judas, that boy will bring his summons. Dead or alive, that boy will bring his summons."

One day I recollect especial that the lad was sick with fever on him, and took to his hammock. Whitmarsh drove him on deck, and ordered him aloft. I was standing near by, trimming the spanker. Kentucky staggered for'ard a little and sat down. There was a rope's-end there, knotted three times. The mate struck him.

"I'm very weak, sir," says he.

He struck him again. He struck him twice more. The boy fell over a little, and lay where he fell.

I don't know what ailed me, but all of a sudden I seemed to be lying off Long Wharf, with the clouds the color of silver, and the air the color of gold, and Molly in a white apron with her shining needles, and the baby a-play in his red stockings about the deck.

"Think if it was him!" says she, or she seems to say,—"think if it was *him!*"

And the next I knew I'd let slip my tongue in a jiffy, and given it to the mate that furious and onrespectful as I'll wager Whitmarsh never got before. And the next I knew after that they had the irons on me.

"Sorry about that, eh?" said he, the day before they took 'em off.

"*No*, sir," says I. And I never was. Kentucky never forgot that. I had helped him occasional in the beginning,—learned him how to veer and haul a brace, let go or belay a sheet,—but let him alone generally speaking, and went about my own business. That week in irons I really believe the lad never forgot.

One time—it was on a Saturday night, and the mate had been oncommon furious that week—Kentucky turned on him, very pale and slow (I was up in the mizzen-top, and heard him quite distinct).

"Mr. Whitmarsh," says he,—"Mr. Whitmarsh,"—he draws his breath in,—"Mr. Whitmarsh,"—three times,—"you've got the power and you know it, and so do the gentlemen who put you here; and I'm only a stowaway boy, and things are all in a tangle, *but you'll be sorry yet for every time you've laid your hands on me!*"

He hadn't a pleasant look about the eyes either, when he said it.

Fact was, that first month on the Madonna had done the lad no good. He had a surly, sullen way with him, some'at like what I've seen about a chained dog. At the first, his talk had been clean as my baby's, and he would blush like any girl at Bob Smart's stories; but he got used to Bob, and pretty good, in time, at small swearing.

I don't think I should have noticed it so much if it had not been for seeming to see Molly, and the sun, and the knitting-needles, and the child upon the deck, and hearing of it over, "Think if it was *him!*" Sometimes on a Sunday night I used to think it was a pity. Not that I was any better than the rest, except so far as the married men are always steadier. Go through any crew the sea over, and it is the lads who have homes of their own and little children in 'em as keep the straightest.

Sometimes, too, I used to take a fancy that I could have listened to a word from a parson, or a good brisk psalm-tune, and taken it in very good part. A year is a long pull for twenty-five men to be becalmed with each other and the devil. I don't set up to be pious myself, but I'm not a fool, and I know that if we'd had so much as one officer aboard who feared God and kept his commandments, we should have been the better men for it. It's very much with religion as it is with cayenne pepper,—if it's there, you know it.

If you had your ships on the sea by the dozen, you'd bethink you of that? Bless you, Tom! if you were in Rome you'd do as the Romans do. You'd have your ledgers, and your children, and your churches and Sunday schools, and freed n——,˙ and 'lections, and what not, and never stop to think whether the lads that sailed your ships across the world had souls, or not,—and be a good sort of man too. That's the way of the world. Take it easy, Tom,—take it easy.

Well, things went along just about so with us till we neared the Cape. It's not a pretty place, the Cape, on a winter's voyage. I can't say as I ever was what you may call scar't after the first time rounding it, but it's not a pretty place.

I don't seem to remember much about Kent along there till there come a Friday at the first of December. It was a still day, with a little haze, like

---

˙ The n-word was widely used when this story was written. Despite—or perhaps, because of—the casual racism of those times, it was not considered especially offensive.

white sand sifted across a sunbeam on a kitchen table. The lad was quiet-like all day, chasing me about with his eyes.

"Sick?" says I.

"No," says he.

"Whitmarsh drunk?" says I.

"No," says he.

A little after dark I was lying on a coil of ropes, napping it. The boys were having the Bay of Biscay quite lively, and I waked up on the jump in the choruses. Kent came up while they were telling

"How she lay

On that day

In the *Bay* of BISCAY O!"

He was not singing. He sat down beside me, and first I thought I wouldn't trouble myself about him, and then I thought I would.

So I opens one eye at him encouraging. He crawls up a little closer to me. It was rather dark where we sat, with a great greenish shadow dropping from the mainsail. The wind was up a little, and the light at helm looked flickery and red.

"Jake," says he all at once, "where's your mother?"

"In—heaven!" says I, all taken aback; and if ever I came nigh what you might call a little disrespect to your mother, it was on that occasion, from being taken so aback.

"Oh!" said he. "Got any women-folks to home that miss you?" asks he, by and by.

Said I, "Shouldn't wonder."

After that he sits still a little with his elbows on his knees; then he speers at me sidewise awhile; then said he, "I s'pose *I've* got a mother to home. I ran away from her."

This, mind you, is the first time he has ever spoke about his folks since he came aboard.

"She was asleep down in the south chamber," says he. "I got out the window. There was one white shirt she'd made for meetin' and such. I've never worn it out here. I hadn't the heart. It has a collar and some cuffs, you know. She had a headache making of it. She's been follering me round all day, a sewing on that shirt. When I come in she would look up bright-like

131

and smiling. Father's dead. There ain't anybody but me. All day long she's been follering of me round."

So then he gets up, and joins the lads, and tries to sing a little; but he comes back very still and sits down. We could see the flickery light upon the boys' faces, and on the rigging, and on the cap'n, who was damning the bo'sen a little aft.

"Jake," says he, quite low, "look here. I've been thinking. Do you reckon there's a chap here—just one, perhaps—who's said his prayers since he came aboard?"

"*No!*" said I, quite short: for I'd have bet my head on it.

I can remember, as if it was this morning, just how the question sounded, and the answer. I can't seem to put it into words how it came all over me. The wind was turning brisk, and we'd just eased her with a few reefs; Bob Smart, out furling the flying jib, got soaked; me and the boy sitting silent, were spattered. I remember watching the curve of the great swells, mahogany color, with the tip of white, and thinking how like it was to a big creature hissing and foaming at the mouth, and thinking all at once something about Him holding of the sea in a balance, and not a word bespoke to beg his favor respectful since we weighed our anchor, and the cap'n yonder calling on Him just that minute to send the Madonna to the bottom, if the bo'sen hadn't disobeyed his orders about the squaring of the after-yards.

"From his Affecshunate mother who prays, For you evry day, Amen," whispers Kentucky, presently, very soft. "The book's tore up. Mr. Whitmarsh wadded his old gun with it. But I remember."

Then said he: "It's 'most bedtime to home. She's setting in a little rocking-chair,—a green one. There's a fire, and the dog. She sets all by herself."

Then he begins again: "She has to bring in her own wood now. There's a gray ribbon on her cap. When she goes to meetin' she wears a gray bunnet. She's drawed the curtains and the door is locked. But she thinks I'll be coming home sorry some day,—I'm sure she thinks I'll be coming home sorry."

Just then there comes the order, "Port watch ahoy! Tumble up there lively!" so I turns out, and the lad turns in, and the night settles down a little black, and my hands and head are full. Next day it blows a clean, all but a bank of gray, very thin and still,—about the size of that cloud you see through the side window, Tom,—which lay just abeam of us.

The sea, I thought, looked like a great purple pincushion, with a mast or two stuck in on the horizon for the pins. "Jake's poetry," the boys said that was.

By noon that little gray bank had grown up thick, like a wall. By sundown the cap'n let his liquor alone, and kept the deck. By night we were in chop-seas, with a very ugly wind.

"Steer small, there!" cries Whitmarsh, growing hot about the face,—for we made a terribly crooked wake, with a broad sheer, and the old hull strained heavily,—"steer small there, I tell you! Mind your eye now, McCallum, with your foresail! Furl the royals! Send down the royals! Cheerily, men! Where's that lubber Kent? Up with you, lively now!"

Kentucky sprang for'ard at the order, then stopped short. Anybody as knows a royal from an anchor wouldn't have blamed the lad. I'll take oath to't it's no play for an old tar, stout and full in size, sending down the royals in a gale like that; let alone a boy of fifteen year on his first voyage.

But the mate takes to swearing (it would have turned a parson faint to hear him), and Kent shoots away up,—the great mast swinging like a pendulum to and fro, and the reef-points snapping, and the blocks creaking, and the sails flapping to that extent as you wouldn't consider possible unless you'd been before the mast yourself. It reminded me of evil birds I've read of, that stun a man with their wings; strike *you* to the bottom, Tom, before you could say Jack Robinson.

Kent stuck bravely as far as the cross-trees. There he slipped and struggled and clung in the dark and noise awhile, then comes sliding down the back-stay.

"I'm not afraid, sir," says he; "but I cannot do it."

For answer Whitmarsh takes to the rope's-end. So Kentucky is up again, and slips and struggles and clings again, and then lays down again.

At this the men begin to grumble a little low.

"Will you kill the lad?" said I. I get a blow for my pains, that sends me off my feet none too easy; and when I rub the stars out of my eyes the boy is up again, and the mate behind him with the rope. Whitmarsh stopped when he'd gone far enough. The lad climbed on. Once he looked back. He never opened his lips; he just looked back. If I've seen him once since, in my thinking, I've seen him twenty times,—up in the shadow of the great gray wings, a looking back.

After that there was only a cry, and a splash, and the Madonna racing along with the gale twelve knots. If it had been the whole crew overboard, she could never have stopped for them that night.

"Well," said the cap'n, "you've done it now."

Whitmarsh turns his back.

By and by, when the wind fell, and the hurry was over, and I had the time to think a steady thought, being in the morning watch, I seemed to see the old lady in the gray bunnet setting by the fire. And the dog. And the green rocking-chair. And the front door, with the boy walking in on a sunny afternoon to take her by surprise.

Then I remember leaning over to look down, and wondering if the lad were thinking of it too, and what had happened to him now, these two hours back, and just about where he was, and how he liked his new quarters, and many other strange and curious things.

And while I sat there thinking, the Sunday-morning stars cut through the clouds, and the solemn Sunday-morning light began to break upon the sea.

We had a quiet run of it, after that, into port, where we lay about a couple of months or so, trading off for a fair stock of palm-oil, ivory, and hides. The days were hot and purple and still. We hadn't what you might call a blow, if I recollect accurate, till we rounded the Cape again, heading for home.

We were rounding that Cape again, heading for home, when that happened which you may believe me or not, as you take the notion, Tom; though why a man who can swallow Daniel and the lion's den, or take down t'other chap who lived three days comfortable into the inside of a whale, should make faces at what I've got to tell I can't see.

It was just about the spot that we lost the boy that we fell upon the worst gale of the trip. It struck us quite sudden. Whitmarsh was a little high. He wasn't apt to be drunk in a gale, if it gave him warning sufficient.

Well, you see, there must be somebody to furl the main-royal again, and he pitched onto McCallum. McCallum hadn't his beat for fighting out the royal in a blow.

So he piled away lively, up to the to'-sail yard. There, all of a sudden, he stopped. Next we knew he was down like heat-lightning.

His face had gone very white.

"What's to pay with *you*?" roared Whitmarsh.

Said McCallum, "*There's somebody up there, sir.*"

Screamed Whitmarsh, "You're gone an idiot!"

Said McCallum, very quiet and distinct: "There's somebody up there, sir. I saw him quite plain. He saw me. I called up. He called down. Says he, '*Don't you come up!*' and hang me if I'll stir a step for you or any other man to-night!"

I never saw the face of any man alive go the turn that mate's face went. If he wouldn't have relished knocking the Scotchman dead before his eyes, I've lost my guess. Can't say what he would have done to the old fellow, if there'd been any time to lose.

He'd the sense left to see there wasn't overmuch, so he orders out Bob Smart direct.

Bob goes up steady, with a quid in his cheek and a cool eye. Half-way amid to'-sail and to'-gallant he stops, and down he comes, spinning.

"Be drowned if there ain't!" said he. "He's sitting square upon the yard. I never see the boy Kentucky, if he isn't sitting on that yard. '*Don't you come up!*' he cries out,—'*don't you come up!*'"

"Bob's drunk, and McCallum's a fool!" said Jim Welch, standing by. So Welch wolunteers up, and takes Jaloffe with him. They were a couple of the coolest hands aboard,—Welch and Jaloffe. So up they goes, and down they comes like the rest, by the back-stays, by the run.

"He beckoned of me back!" says Welch. "He hollered not to come up! not to come up!"

After that there wasn't a man of us would stir aloft, not for love nor money.

Well, Whitmarsh he stamped, and he swore, and he knocked us about furious; but we sat and looked at one another's eyes, and never stirred. Something cold, like a frost-bite, seemed to crawl along from man to man, looking into one another's eyes.

"I'll shame ye all, then, for a set of cowardly lubbers!" cries the mate; and what with the anger and the drink he was as good as his word, and up the ratlines in a twinkle.

In a flash we were after him,—he was our officer, you see, and we felt ashamed,—me at the head, and the lads following after.

I got to the futtock shrouds, and there I stopped, for I saw him myself,— a palish boy, with a jerk of thin hair on his forehead; I'd have known him anywhere in this world or t'other. I saw him just as distinct as I see you, Tom Brown, sitting on that yard quite steady with the royal flapping like to flap him off.

I reckon I've had as much experience fore and aft, in the course of fifteen years aboard, as any man that ever tied a reef-point in a nor'easter; but I never saw a sight like that, not before nor since.

I won't say that I didn't wish myself well on deck; but I will say that I stuck to the shrouds, and looked on steady.

Whitmarsh, swearing that that royal should be furled, went on and went up.

It was after that I heard the voice. It came straight from the figure of the boy upon the upper yard.

But this time it says, *"Come up! Come up!"* And then, a little louder, *"Come up! Come up! Come up!"* So he goes up, and next I knew there was a cry,—and next a splash,—and then I saw the royal flapping from the empty yard, and the mate was gone, and the boy.

Job Whitmarsh was never seen again, alow or aloft, that night or ever after.

I was telling the tale to our parson this summer,—he's a fair-minded chap, the parson, in spite of a little natural leaning to strawberries, which I always take in very good part,—and he turned it about in his mind some time.

"If it was the boy," says he,—"and I can't say as I see any reason especial why it shouldn't have been,—I've been wondering what his spiritooal condition was. A soul in hell,"—the parson believes in hell, I take it, because he can't help himself; but he has that solemn, tender way of preaching it as makes you feel he wouldn't have so much as a chicken get there if he could help it,—"a lost soul," says the parson (I don't know as I get the words exact),—"a soul that has gone and been and got there of its own free will and choosing would be as like as not to haul another soul alongside if he could. Then again, if the mate's time had come, you see, and his chances were over, why, that's the will of the Lord, and it's hell for him whichever side of death he is, and nobody's fault but hisn; and the boy might be in the good place, and do the errand all the same. That's just about it, Brown," says he. "A man goes his own gait, and, if he won't go to heaven, he *won't,* and the good God himself can't help it. He throws the shining gates all open wide, and he never shut them on any poor fellow as would have entered in, and he never, never will."

Which I thought was sensible of the parson, and very prettily put.

There's Molly frying flapjacks now, and flapjacks won't wait for no man, you know, no more than time and tide, else I should have talked till midnight, very like, to tell the time we made on that trip home, and how green the harbor looked a sailing up, and of Molly and the baby coming down to meet me in a little boat that danced about (for we cast a little down the channel), and how she climbed up a laughing and a crying all to once, about my neck, and how the boy had grown, and how when he ran about the deck (the little shaver had his first pair of boots on that very afternoon) I bethought me of the other time, and of Molly's words, and of the lad we'd left behind us in the purple days.

Just as we were hauling up, I says to my wife: "Who's that old lady setting there upon the lumber, with a gray bunnet, and a gray ribbon on her cap?"

For there was an old lady there, and I saw the sun all about her, and all on the blazing yellow boards, and I grew a little dazed and dazzled.

"I don't know," said Molly, catching onto me a little close. "She comes there every day. They say she sits and watches for her lad as ran away."

So then I seemed to know, as well as ever I knew afterwards, who it was. And I thought of the dog. And the green rocking-chair. And the book that Whitmarsh wadded his old gun with. And the front-door, with the boy a walking in.

So we three went up the wharf,—Molly and the baby and me,—and sat down beside her on the yellow boards. I can't remember rightly what I said, but I remember her sitting silent in the sunshine till I had told her all there was to tell.

"*Don't* cry!" says Molly, when I got through,—which it was the more surprising of Molly, considering as she was doing the crying all to herself. The old lady never cried, you see. She sat with her eyes wide open under her gray bunnet, and her lips a moving. After a while I made it out what it was she said: "The only son—of his mother—and she—"

By and by she gets up, and goes her ways, and Molly and I walk home together, with our little boy between us.

AT CHRIGHTON ABBEY

by Mary Elizabeth Braddon

1871

Mary Elizabeth Braddon was born in London in 1835. Her parents separated when she was five years old, and her mother saw to it that young Mary received a private education. She dabbled with acting and actually supported herself and her mother for three years by playing minor roles on the London stage.

In 1860, she met the publisher John Maxwell. He was married with five children, but his wife was confined to an asylum in their native Ireland. In 1861, Mary moved in with him, acting as stepmother to his children until 1874, when Maxwell's wife died and the two were able to marry. They went on to have six children of their own.

Mary's first novel, Three Times Dead, *was published the same year she met Maxwell. She went on to write more than eighty novels, some of them with supernatural themes but a great many—including her best-known work,* Lady Audley's Secret *(1862)—in the popular "sensation fiction" style. A blend of melodrama, Gothic romance, and social realism, sensation novels focused on Victorian social anxieties—loss of identity and position, social disgrace, and social deceit—with sometimes lurid plots that revolved around bigamy, illegitimacy, forged documents, and secret marriages.*

Her best-known horror tale is the oft-anthologized vampire story "Good Lady Ducayne." A Christmas ghost story featuring a family curse, "At Chrighton Abbey" was first published in 1876, in a collection titled My Sister's Confession and Other Stories. *Like* Lady Audley's Secret, *it was attributed to the sexless "M. E. Braddon," although a "Miss" was added to the name in later editions of some of her works.*

T he Chrightons were very great people in that part of the country where my childhood and youth were spent. To speak of Squire Chrighton was to speak of a power in that remote western region of England. Chrighton Abbey had belonged to the family ever since the reign of Stephen, and there was a curious old wing and a cloistered quadrangle still remaining of the original edifice, and in excellent preservation. The rooms at this end of the house were low, and somewhat darksome and gloomy, it is true; but, though rarely used, they were perfectly habitable, and were of service on great occasions when the Abbey was crowded with guests.

The central portion of the Abbey had been rebuilt in the reign of Elizabeth, and was of noble and palatial proportions. The southern wing, and a long music-room with eight tall narrow windows added on to it, were as modern as the time of Anne. Altogether, the Abbey was a very splendid mansion, and one of the chief glories of our County.

All the land in Chrighton parish, and for a long way beyond its boundaries, belonged to the great Squire. The parish church was within the park walls, and the living in the Squire's gift—not a very valuable benefice, but a useful thing to bestow upon a younger son's younger son, once in a way, or sometimes on a tutor or dependent of the wealthy house.

I was a Chrighton, and my father, a distant cousin of the reigning Squire, had been rector of Chrighton parish. His death left me utterly unprovided for, and I was fain to go out into the bleak unknown world, and earn my living in a position of dependence—a dreadful thing for a Chrighton to be obliged to do.

Out of respect for the traditions and prejudices of my race, I made it my business to seek employment abroad, where the degradation of one Chrighton was not so likely to inflict shame upon the ancient house to which I belonged. Happily for myself, I had been carefully educated, and had industriously cultivated the usual modern accomplishments in the calm retirement of the Vicarage. I was so fortunate as to obtain a situation at Vienna, in a German family of high rank; and here I remained seven years, laying aside year by year a considerable portion of my liberal salary. When my pupils had grown up, my kind mistress procured me a still more profitable position at St. Petersburg, where I remained five more years, at the end of which time I yielded to a yearning that had been long growing upon me—an ardent desire to see my dear old country home once more.

I had no very near relations in England. My mother had died some years before my father; my only brother was far away, in the Indian Civil Service; sister I had none. But I was a Chrighton, and I loved the soil from which I had sprung. I was sure, moreover, of a warm welcome from friends who had loved and honoured my father and mother, and I was still further encouraged to treat myself to this holiday by the very cordial letters I had from time to time received from the Squire's wife, a noble warm-hearted woman, who fully approved the independent course I had taken, and who had ever shown herself my friend.

In all her letters for some time past Mrs. Chrighton begged that, whenever I felt myself justified in coming home, I would pay a long visit to the Abbey.

"I wish you could come at Christmas," she wrote, in the autumn of the year of which I am speaking. "We shall be very gay, and I expect all kinds of pleasant people at the Abbey. Edward is to be married early in the spring—much to his father's satisfaction, for the match is a good and appropriate one. His fiancée is to be among our guests. She is a very beautiful girl; perhaps I should say handsome rather than beautiful. Julia Tremaine, one of the Tremaines of Old Court, near Hayswell—a very old family, as I daresay you remember. She has several brothers and sisters, and will have little, perhaps nothing, from her father; but she has a considerable fortune left her by an aunt, and is thought quite an heiress in the county—not, of course, that this latter fact had any influence with Edward. He fell in love with her at an assize ball in his usual impulsive fashion, and proposed to her in something less than a fortnight. It is, I hope and believe, a thorough love-match on both sides."

After this followed a cordial repetition of the invitation to myself. I was to go straight to the Abbey when I went to England, and was to take up my abode there as long as ever I pleased.

This letter decided me. The wish to look on the dear scenes of my happy childhood had grown almost into a pain. I was free to take a holiday, without detriment to my prospects. So, early in December, regardless of the bleak dreary weather, I turned my face homewards, and made the long journey from St. Petersburg to London, under the kind escort of Major Manson, a Queen's Messenger, who was a friend of my late employer, the Baron Fruydorff, and whose courtesy had been enlisted for me by that gentleman.

I was three-and-thirty years of age. Youth was quite gone; beauty I had never possessed; and I was content to think of myself as a confirmed old maid, a quiet spectator of life's great drama, disturbed by no feverish desire for an active part in the play. I had a disposition to which this kind of passive existence is easy. There was no wasting fire in my veins. Simple duties, rare and simple pleasures, filled up my sum of life. The dear ones who had given a special charm and brightness to my existence were gone. Nothing could recall them, and without them actual happiness seemed impossible to me. Everything had a subdued and neutral tint; life at its best was calm and colourless, like a grey sunless day in early autumn, serene but joyless.

The old Abbey was in its glory when I arrived there, at about nine o'clock on a clear starlit night. A light frost whitened the broad sweep of grass that stretched away from the long stone terrace in front of the house to a semicircle of grand old oaks and beeches. From the music-room at the end of the southern wing, to the heavily framed gothic windows of the old rooms on the north, there shone one blaze of light. The scene reminded me of some weird palace in a German legend; and I half expected to see the lights fade out all in a moment, and the long stone façade wrapped in sudden darkness.

The old butler, whom I remembered from my very infancy, and who did not seem to have grown a day older during my twelve years' exile, came out of the dining-room as the footman opened the hall-door for me, and gave me cordial welcome, nay insisted upon helping to bring in my portmanteau with his own hands, an act of unusual condescension, the full force of which was felt by his subordinates.

"It's a real treat to see your pleasant face once more, Miss Sarah," said this faithful retainer, as he assisted me to take off my travelling-cloak, and took my dressing-bag from my hand. "You look a trifle older than when you used to live at the Vicarage twelve year ago, but you're looking uncommon well for all that; and, Lord love your heart, miss, how pleased they all will be to see you! Missus told me with her own lips about your coming. You'd like to take off your bonnet before you go to the drawing-room, I daresay. The house is full of company. Call Mrs. Marjorum, James, will you?"

The footman disappeared into the back regions, and presently reappeared with Mrs. Marjorum, a portly dame, who, like Truefold the butler, had been a fixture at the Abbey in the time of the present Squire's father. From her I received the same cordial greeting, and by her I was led off up staircases and along corridors, till I wondered where I was being taken.

We arrived at last at a very comfortable room—a square tapestried chamber, with a low ceiling supported by a great oaken beam. The room looked cheery enough, with a bright fire roaring in the wide chimney; but it had a somewhat ancient aspect, which the superstitiously inclined might have associated with possible ghosts.

I was fortunately of a matter-of-fact disposition, utterly sceptical upon the ghost subject; and the old-fashioned appearance of the room took my fancy.

"We are in King Stephen's wing, are we not, Mrs. Marjorum?" I asked; "this room seems quite strange to me. I doubt if I have ever been in it before."

"Very likely not, miss. Yes, this is the old wing. Your window looks out into the old stable-yard, where the kennel used to be in the time of our Squire's grandfather, when the Abbey was even a finer place than it is now,

I've heard say. We are so full of company this winter, you see, miss, that we are obliged to make use of all these rooms. You'll have no need to feel lonesome. There's Captain and Mrs. Cranwick in the next room to this, and the two Miss Newports in the blue room opposite."

"My dear good Marjorum, I like my quarters excessively; and I quite enjoy the idea of sleeping in a room that was extant in the time of Stephen, when the Abbey really was an abbey. I daresay some grave old monk has worn these boards with his devout knees."

The old woman stared dubiously, with the air of a person who had small sympathy with monkish times, and begged to be excused for leaving me, she had so much on her hands just now.

There was coffee to be sent in; and she doubted if the still-room maid would manage matters properly, if she, Mrs. Marjorum, were not at hand to see that things were right.

"You've only to ring your bell, miss, and Susan will attend to you. She's used to help waiting on our young ladies sometimes, and she's very handy. Missus has given particular orders that she should be always at your service."

"Mrs. Chrighton is very kind; but I assure you, Marjorum, I don't require the help of a maid once in a month. I am accustomed to do everything for myself. There, run along, Mrs. Marjorum, and see after your coffee; and I'll be down in the drawing-room in ten minutes. Are there many people there, by the bye?"

"A good many. There's Miss Tremaine, and her mamma and younger sister; of course you've heard all about the marriage—such a handsome young lady—rather too proud for my liking; but the Tremaines always were a proud family, and this one's an heiress. Mr. Edward is so fond of her—thinks the ground is scarcely good enough for her to walk upon, I do believe; and somehow I can't help wishing he'd chosen someone else—someone who would have thought more of him, and who would not take all his attentions in such a cool offhand way. But of course it isn't my business to say such things, and I wouldn't venture upon it to any one but you, Miss Sarah."

She told me that I would find dinner ready for me in the breakfast-room, and then bustled off, leaving me to my toilet.

This ceremony I performed as rapidly as I could, admiring the perfect comfort of my chamber as I dressed. Every modern appliance had been added to the sombre and ponderous furniture of an age gone by, and the combination produced a very pleasant effect. Perfume-bottles of ruby-coloured Bohemian glass, china brush-trays and ring-stands brightened the massive oak dressing-table; a low luxurious chintz-covered easy-chair of the Victorian era stood before the hearth; a dear little writing-table of polished maple was placed conveniently near it; and in the background the tapestried walls loomed duskily, as they had done hundreds of years before my time.

I had no leisure for dreamy musings on the past, however, provocative though the chamber might be of such thoughts. I arranged my hair in its usual simple fashion, and put on a dark-grey silk dress, trimmed with some fine old black lace that had been given to me by the Baroness—an unobtrusive demi-toilette, adapted to any occasion. I tied a massive gold cross, an ornament that had belonged to my dear mother, round my neck with a scarlet ribbon; and my costume was complete. One glance at the looking-glass convinced me that there was nothing dowdy in my appearance; and then I hurried along the corridor and down the staircase to the hall, where Truefold received me and conducted me to the breakfast-room, in which an excellent dinner awaited me.

I did not waste much time over this repast, although I had eaten nothing all day; for I was anxious to make my way to the drawing-room. Just as I had finished, the door opened, and Mrs. Chrighton sailed in, looking superb in a dark-green velvet dress richly trimmed with old point lace. She had been a beauty in her youth, and, as a matron, was still remarkably handsome. She had, above all, a charm of expression which to me was rarer and more delightful than her beauty of feature and complexion.

She put her arms round me, and kissed me affectionately.

"I have only this moment been told of your arrival, my dear Sarah," she said; "and I find you have been in the house half an hour. What must you have thought of me!"

"What can I think of you, except that you are all goodness, my dear Fanny? I did not expect you to leave your guests to receive me, and am really sorry that you have done so. I need no ceremony to convince me of your kindness."

"But, my dear child, it is not a question of ceremony. I have been looking forward so anxiously to your coming, and I should not have liked to see you for the first time before all those people.

"Give me another kiss, that's a darling. Welcome to Chrighton. Remember, Sarah, this house is always to be your home, whenever you have need of one."

"My dear kind cousin! And you are not ashamed of me, who have eaten the bread of strangers?"

"Ashamed of you! No, my love; I admire your industry and spirit. And now come to the drawing-room. The girls will be so pleased to see you."

"And I to see them. They were quite little things when I went away, romping in the hay-fields in their short white frocks; and now, I suppose, they are handsome young women."

"They are very nice-looking; not as handsome as their brother. Edward is really a magnificent young man. I do not think my maternal pride is guilty of any gross exaggeration when I say that."

"And Miss Tremaine?" I said. "I am very curious to see her."

I fancied a faint shadow came over my cousin's face as I mentioned this name.

"Miss Tremaine—yes—you cannot fail to admire her," she said, rather thoughtfully.

She drew my hand through her arm and led me to the drawing-room: a very large room, with a fireplace at each end, brilliantly lighted tonight, and containing about twenty people, scattered about in little groups, and all seeming to be talking and laughing merrily. Mrs. Chrighton took me straight to one of the fireplaces, beside which two girls were sitting on a low sofa, while a young man of something more than six feet high stood near them, with his arm resting on the broad marble slab of the mantelpiece. A glance told me that this young man with the dark eyes and crisp waving brown hair was Edward Chrighton. His likeness to his mother was in itself enough to tell me who he was; but I remembered the boyish face and bright eyes which had so often looked up to mine in the days when the heir of the Abbey was one of the most juvenile scholars at Eton.

The lady seated nearest Edward Chrighton attracted my chief attention; for I felt sure that this lady was Miss Tremaine. She was tall and slim, and carried her head and neck with a stately air, which struck me more than anything in that first glance. Yes, she was handsome, undeniably handsome; and my cousin had been right when she said I could not fail to admire her; but to me the dazzlingly fair face with its perfect features, the marked aquiline nose, the short upper lip expressive of unmitigated pride, the full cold blue eyes, pencilled brows, and aureole of pale golden hair, were the very reverse of sympathetic. That Miss Tremaine must needs be universally admired, it was impossible to doubt; but I could not understand how any man could fall in love with such a woman.

She was dressed in white muslin, and her only ornament was a superb diamond locket, heart-shaped, tied round her long white throat with a broad black ribbon. Her hair, of which she seemed to have a great quantity, was arranged in a massive coronet of plaits, which surmounted the small head as proudly as an imperial crown.

To this young lady Mrs. Chrighton introduced me.

"I have another cousin to present to you, Julia," she said smiling—"Miss Sarah Chrighton, just arrived from St. Petersburg."

"From St. Petersburg? What an awful journey! How do you do, Miss Chrighton? It was really very courageous of you to come so far. Did you travel alone?"

"No; I had a companion as far as London, and a very kind one. I came on to the Abbey by myself."

The young lady had given me her hand with rather a languid air, I thought. I saw the cold blue eyes surveying me curiously from head to foot, and it seemed to me as if I could read the condemnatory summing-up—"A frump, and a poor relation"—in Miss Tremaine's face.

I had not much time to think about her just now; for Edward Chrighton suddenly seized both my hands, and gave me so hearty and loving a welcome, that he almost brought the tears "up from my heart into my eyes."

Two pretty girls in blue crape came running forward from different parts of the room, and gaily saluted me as "Cousin Sarah"; and the three surrounded me in a little cluster, and assailed me with a string of questions—whether I remembered this, and whether I had forgotten that, the battle in the hayfield, the charity-school tea-party in the vicarage orchard, our picnics in Hawsley Combe, our botanical and entomological excursions on Chorwell-common, and all the simple pleasures of their childhood and my youth. While this catechism was going on, Miss

Tremaine watched us with a disdainful expression, which she evidently did not care to hide.

"I should not have thought you capable of such Arcadian simplicity, Mr. Chrighton," she said at last. "Pray continue your recollections. These juvenile experiences are most interesting."

"I don't expect you to be interested in them, Julia," Edward answered, with a tone that sounded rather too bitter for a lover. "I know what a contempt you have for trifling rustic pleasures. Were you ever a child yourself, I wonder, by the way? I don't believe you ever ran after a butterfly in your life."

Her speech put an end to our talk of the past, somehow. I saw that Edward was vexed, and that all the pleasant memories of his boyhood had fled before that cold scornful face. A young lady in pink, who had been sitting next Julia Tremaine, vacated the sofa, and Edward slipped into her place, and devoted himself for the rest of the evening to his betrothed. I glanced at his bright, expressive face now and then as he talked to her, and could not help wondering what charm he could discover in one who seemed to me so unworthy of him.

It was midnight when I went back to my room in the north wing, thoroughly happy in the cordial welcome that had been given me. I rose early next morning—for early rising had long been habitual to me—and, drawing back the damask-curtain that sheltered my window, looked out at the scene below.

I saw a stable-yard, a spacious quadrangle, surrounded by the closed doors of stables and dog-kennels: low massive buildings of grey stone, with the ivy creeping over them here and there, and with an ancient moss-grown look, that gave them a weird kind of interest in my eyes. This range of stabling must have been disused for a long time, I fancied. The stables now in use were a pile of handsome red-brick buildings at the other extremity of the house, to the rear of the music-room, and forming a striking feature in the back view of the Abbey.

I had often heard how the present Squire's grandfather had kept a pack of hounds, which had been sold immediately after his death; and I knew that my cousin, the present Mr. Chrighton, had been more than once requested to follow his ancestor's good example; for there were no hounds now within twenty miles of the Abbey, though it was a fine country for fox-hunting.

George Chrighton, however—the reigning lord of the Abbey—was not a hunting man. He had, indeed, a secret horror of the sport; for more than one scion of the house had perished untimely in the hunting-field. The family had not been altogether a lucky one, in spite of its wealth and prosperity. It was not often that the goodly heritage had descended to the eldest son. Death in some form or other—on too many occasions a violent death—had come between the heir and his inheritance. And when I pondered on the dark pages in the story of the house, I used to wonder whether my cousin Fanny was ever troubled by morbid forebodings about her only and fondly loved son. Was there a ghost at Chrighton—that spectral visitant without which the state and splendour of a grand old house seem scarcely complete? Yes, I had heard vague hints of some shadowy presence that had been seen on rare occasions within the precincts of the Abbey; but I had never been able to ascertain what shape it bore.

Those whom I questioned were prompt to assure me that they had seen nothing. They had heard stories of the past—foolish legends, most likely, not worth listening to. Once, when I had spoken of the subject to my cousin George, he told me angrily never again to let him hear any allusion to that folly from my lips.

That December passed merrily. The old house was full of really pleasant people, and the brief winter days were spent in one unbroken round of amusement and gaiety. To me the old familiar English country-house life was a perpetual delight—to feel myself amongst kindred an unceasing pleasure. I could not have believed myself capable of being so completely happy.

I saw a great deal of my cousin Edward, and I think he contrived to make Miss Tremaine understand that, to please him, she must be gracious to me. She certainly took some pains to make herself agreeable to me; and I discovered that, in spite of that proud disdainful temper, which she so rarely took the trouble to conceal, she was really anxious to gratify her lover.

Their courtship was not altogether a halcyon period. They had frequent quarrels, the details of which Edward's sisters Sophy and Agnes delighted to discuss with me. It was the struggle of two proud spirits for mastery; but my cousin Edward's pride was of the nobler kind—the lofty scorn of all things mean—a pride that does not ill-become a generous nature. To me he seemed all that was admirable, and I was never tired of hearing his mother praise him. I think my cousin Fanny knew this, and that she used to confide in me as fully as if I had been her sister.

"I daresay you can see I am not quite so fond as I should wish to be of Julia Tremaine," she said to me one day; "but I am very glad that my son is going to marry. My husband's has not been a fortunate family, you know, Sarah. The eldest sons have been wild and unlucky for generations past; and when Edward was a boy I used to have many a bitter hour, dreading what the future might bring forth. Thank God he has been, and is, all that I can wish. He has never given me an hour's anxiety by any act of his. Yet I am not the less glad of his marriage. The heirs of Chrighton who have come to an untimely end have all died unmarried. There was Hugh Chrighton, in the reign of George the Second, who was killed in a duel; John, who broke his back in the hunting-field thirty years later; Theodore, shot accidentally by a schoolfellow at Eton; Jasper, whose yacht went down in the Mediterranean forty years ago. An awful list, is it not, Sarah? I shall fret as if my son were safer somehow when he is married. It will seem as if he has escaped the ban that has fallen on so many of our house. He will have greater reason to be careful of his life when he is a married man."

I agreed with Mrs. Chrighton; but could not help wishing that Edward had chosen any other woman than the cold handsome Julia. I could not fancy his future life happy with such a mate.

Christmas came by and by—a real old English Christmas—frost and snow without, warmth and revelry within; skating on the great pond in the park, and sledging on the ice-bound high-roads, by day; private theatricals, charades, and amateur concerts, by night. I was surprised to find that Miss Tremaine refused to take any active part in these evening amusements. She preferred to sit among the elders as a spectator, and had the air and bearing of a princess for whose diversion all our entertainments had been planned. She seemed to think that she fulfilled her mission by sitting still and looking handsome. No desire to show-off appeared to enter her mind. Her intense pride left no room for vanity. Yet I knew that she could have distinguished herself as a musician if she had chosen to do so; for I had heard her sing and play in Mrs. Chrighton's morning-room, when only Edward, his sisters, and myself were present; and I knew that both as a vocalist and a pianist she excelled all our guests.

The two girls and I had many a happy morning and afternoon, going from cottage to cottage in a pony-carriage laden with Mrs. Chrighton's gifts to the poor of her parish. There was no public formal distribution of blanketing and coals, but the wants of all were amply provided for in a quiet friendly way. Agnes and Sophy, aided by an indefatigable maid, the Rector's daughter, and one or two other young ladies, had been at work for the last three months making smart warm frocks and useful under-garments for the children of the cottagers; so that on Christmas morning every child in the parish was arrayed in a complete set of new garments. Mrs. Chrighton had an admirable faculty of knowing precisely what was most wanted in every household; and our pony-carriage used to convey a varied collection of goods, every parcel directed in the firm free hand of the chatelaine of the Abbey.

Edward used sometimes to drive us on these expeditions, and I found that he was eminently popular among the poor of Chrighton parish. He had such an airy pleasant way of talking to them, a manner which set them at their ease at once. He never forgot their names or relationships, or wants or ailments; had a packet of exactly the kind of tobacco each man liked best always ready in his coat-pockets; and was full of jokes, which may not have been particularly witty, but which used to make the small low-roofed chambers ring with hearty laughter.

Miss Tremaine coolly declined any share in these pleasant duties.

"I don't like poor people," she said. "I daresay it sounds very dreadful, but it's just as well to confess my iniquity at once. I never can get on with them, or they with me. I am not *simpatica*, I suppose. And then I cannot endure their stifling rooms. The close faint odour of their houses gives me a fever. And again, what is the use of visiting them? It is only an inducement to them to become hypocrites. Surely it is better to arrange on a sheet of paper what it is just and fair for them to have—blankets, and coals, and groceries, and money, and wine, and so on—and let them receive the things from some trustworthy servant. In that case, there need be no cringing on one side, and no endurance in the other."

"But, you see, Julia, there are some kinds of people to whom that sort of thing is not a question of endurance," Edward answered, his face flushing indignantly. "People who like to share in the pleasure they give—who like to see the poor careworn faces lighted up with sudden joy—who like to make these sons of the soil feel that there is some friendly link between themselves and their masters—some point of union between the cottage and the great house. There is my mother, for instance: all these duties which you think so tiresome are to her an unfailing delight. There will be a change, I'm afraid, Julia, when you are mistress of the Abbey."

"You have not made me that yet," she answered; "and there is plenty of time for you to change your mind, if you do not think me suited for the position. I do not pretend to be like your mother. It is better that I should not affect any feminine virtues which I do not possess."

After this Edward insisted on driving our pony-carriage almost every day, leaving Miss Tremaine to find her own amusement; and I think this conversation was the beginning of an estrangement between them, which became more serious than any of their previous quarrels had been.

Miss Tremaine did not care for sledging, or skating, or billiard-playing. She had none of the "fast" tendencies which have become so common lately. She used to sit in one particular bow-window of the drawing-room all the morning, working a screen in berlin-wool and beads, assisted and attended by her younger sister Laura, who was a kind of slave to her—a very colourless young lady in mind, capable of no such thing as an original opinion, and in person a pale replica of her sister.

Had there been less company in the house, the breach between Edward Chrighton and his betrothed must have become notorious; but with a house so full of people, all bent on enjoying themselves, I doubt if it was noticed. On all public occasions my cousin showed himself attentive and apparently devoted to Miss Tremaine. It was only I and his sisters who knew the real state of affairs.

I was surprised, after the young lady's total repudiation of all benevolent sentiments, when she beckoned me aside one morning, and slipped a little purse of gold—twenty sovereigns—into my hand.

"I shall be very much obliged if you will distribute that among your cottagers today, Miss Chrighton," she said. "Of course I should like to give them something; it's only the trouble of talking to them that I shrink from; and you are just the person for an almoner. Don't mention my little commission to any one, please."

"Of course I may tell Edward," I said; for I was anxious that he should know his betrothed was not as hard-hearted as she had appeared.

"To him least of all," she answered eagerly. "You know that our ideas vary on that point, he would think I gave the money to please him. Not a word, pray, Miss Chrighton." I submitted, and distributed my sovereigns quietly, with the most careful exercise of my judgement.

So Christmas came and passed. It was the day after the great anniversary—a very quiet day for the guests and family at the Abbey, but a grand occasion for the servants, who were to have their annual ball in the evening—a ball to which all the humbler class of tenantry were invited. The frost had broken up suddenly, and it was a thorough wet day—a depressing kind of day for any one whose spirits are liable to be affected by the weather, as mine are. I felt out of spirits for the first time since my arrival at the Abbey.

No one else appeared to feel the same influence. The elder ladies sat in a wide semicircle round one of the fireplaces in the drawing-room; a group of merry girls and dashing young men chatted gaily before the other. From the billiard-room there came the frequent clash of balls, and cheery peals of stentorian laughter. I sat in one of the deep windows, half hidden by the curtains, reading a novel—one of a boxful that came from town every month.

If the picture within was bright and cheerful, the prospect was dreary enough without. The fairy forest of snow-wreathed trees, the white valleys and undulating banks of snow, had vanished, and the rain dripped slowly and sullenly upon a darksome expanse of sodden grass, and a dismal background of leafless timber. The merry sound of the sledge-bells no longer enlivened the air; all was silence and gloom.

Edward Chrighton was not amongst the billiard-players; he was pacing the drawing-room to and fro from end to end, with an air that was at once moody and restless.

"Thank heaven, the frost has broken up at last!" he exclaimed, stopping in front of the window where I sat.

He had spoken to himself, quite unaware of my close neighbourhood. Unpromising as his aspect was just then, I ventured to accost him.

"What bad taste, to prefer such weather as this to frost and snow!" I answered. "The park looked enchanting yesterday—a real scene from fairyland. And only look at it today!"

"O yes, of course, from an artistic point of view, the snow was better. The place does look something like the great dismal swamp today; but I am thinking of hunting, and that confounded frost made a day's sport impossible. We are in for a spell of mild weather now, I think."

"But you are not going to hunt, are you, Edward?"

"Indeed I am, my gentle cousin, in spite of that frightened look in your amiable countenance."

"I thought there were no hounds hereabouts."

"Nor are there; but there is as fine a pack as any in the country—the Daleborough hounds—five-and-twenty miles away."

"And you are going five-and-twenty miles for the sake of a day's run?"

"I would travel forty, fifty, a hundred miles for that same diversion. But I am not going for a single day this time; I am going over to Sir Francis Wycherly's place—young Frank Wycherly and I were sworn chums at Christchurch—for three or four days. I am due today, but I scarcely dared to travel by cross-country roads in such rain as this. However, if the floodgates of the sky are loosened for a new deluge, I must go tomorrow."

"What a headstrong young man!" I exclaimed. "And what will Miss Tremaine say to this desertion?" I asked in a lower voice.

"Miss Tremaine can say whatever she pleases. She had it in her power to make me forget the pleasures of the chase, if she had chosen, though we had been in the heart of the shires, and the welkin ringing with the baying of hounds."

"O, I begin to understand. This hunting engagement is not of long standing."

"No; I began to find myself bored here a few days ago, and wrote to Frank to offer myself for two or three days at Wycherly. I received a most cordial answer by return, and am booked till the end of this week."

"You have not forgotten the ball on the first?"

"O, no; to do that would be to vex my mother, and to offer a slight to our guests. I shall be here for the first, come what may."

Come what may! so lightly spoken. The time came when I had bitter occasion to remember those words.

"I'm afraid you will vex your mother by going at all," I said. "You know what a horror both she and your father have of hunting."

"A most un-country-gentleman-like aversion on my father's part. But he is a dear old book-worm, seldom happy out of his library. Yes, I admit they both have a dislike to hunting in the abstract; but they know I am a pretty good rider, and that it would need a bigger country than I shall find about Wycherly to floor me. You need not feel nervous, my dear Sarah; I am not going to give papa and mamma the smallest ground for uneasiness."

"You will take your own horses, I suppose?"

"That goes without saying. No man who has cattle of his own cares to mount another man's horses. I shall take Pepperbox and the Druid."

"Pepperbox has a queer temper, I have heard your sisters say."

"My sisters expect a horse to be a kind of overgrown baa-lamb. Everything splendid in horseflesh and womankind is prone to that slight defect, an ugly temper. There is Miss Tremaine, for instance."

"I shall take Miss Tremaine's part. I believe it is you who are in the wrong in the matter of this estrangement, Edward."

"Do you? Well, wrong or right, my cousin, until the fair Julia comes to me with sweet looks and gentle words, we can never be what we have been."

"You will return from your hunting expedition in a softer mood," I answered; "that is to say, if you persist in going. But I hope and believe you will change your mind."

"Such a change is not within the limits of possibility, Sarah. I am fixed as Fate."

He strolled away, humming some gay hunting-song as he went. I was alone with Mrs. Chrighton later in the afternoon, and she spoke to me about this intended visit to Wycherly.

"Edward has set his heart upon it evidently," she said regretfully, "and his father and I have always made a point of avoiding anything that could seem like domestic tyranny. Our dear boy is such a good son, that it would be very hard if we came between him and his pleasures. You know what a morbid horror my husband has of the dangers of the hunting-field, and perhaps I am almost as weak-minded. But in spite of this we have never interfered with Edward's enjoyment of a sport which he is passionately fond of; and hitherto, thank God! he has escaped without a scratch. Yet I have had many a bitter hour, I can assure you, my dear, when my son has been away in Leicestershire hunting four days a week."

"He rides well, I suppose."

"Superbly. He has a great reputation among the sportsmen of our neighbourhood. I daresay when he is master of the Abbey he will start a pack of hounds, and revive the old days of his great-grandfather, Meredith Chrighton."

"I fancy the hounds were kenneled in the stable-yard below my bedroom window in those days, were they not, Fanny?"

"Yes," Mrs. Chrighton answered gravely; and I wondered at the sudden shadow that fell upon her face.

I went up to my room earlier than usual that afternoon, and I had clear hour to spare before it would be time to dress for the seven o'clock dinner. This leisure hour I intended to devote to letter-writing; but on arriving in my room I found myself in a very idle frame of mind; and instead of opening my desk, I seated myself in the low easy-chair before the fire, and fell into a reverie.

How long I had been sitting there I scarcely know; I had been half meditating, half dozing, mixing broken snatches of thought with brief glimpses of dreaming, when I was startled into wakefulness by a sound that was strange to me.

It was a huntsman's horn—a few low plaintive notes on a huntsman's horn—notes which had a strange far-away sound, that was more unearthly than anything my ears had ever heard. I thought of the music in *Der Freischutz*; but the weirdest snatch of melody Weber ever wrote was not so ghastly a sound as these few simple notes conveyed to my ear.

I stood transfixed, listening to that awful music. It had grown dusk, my fire was almost out, and the room in shadow. As I listened, a light flashed suddenly on the wall before me. The light was as unearthly as the sound—a light that never shone from earth or sky.

I ran to the window; for this ghastly shimmer flashed through the window upon the opposite wall. The great gates of the stable-yard were open, and men in scarlet coats were riding in, a pack of hounds crowding in before them, obedient to the huntsman's whip. The whole scene was dimly visible by the declining light of the winter evening and the weird gleams of a lantern carried by one of the men. It was this lantern which had shone upon the tapestried wall. I saw the stable-doors opened one after another; gentlemen and grooms alighting from their horses; the dogs driven into their kennel; the helpers hurrying to and fro; and that strange wan lantern-light glimmering here and there in the gathering dusk. But there was no sound of horse's hoof or of human voices—not one yelp or cry from the hounds. Since those faint far-away sounds of the horn had died out in the distance, the ghastly silence had been unbroken.

I stood at my window quite calmly, and watched while the group of men and animals in the yard below noiselessly dispersed. There was nothing supernatural in the manner of their disappearance. The figures did not vanish or melt into empty air. One by one I saw the horses led into their separate quarters; one by one the redcoats strolled out of the gates, and the grooms departed, some one way, some another. The scene, but for its noiselessness, was natural enough; and had I been a stranger in the house, I might have fancied that those figures were real—those stables in full occupation.

But I knew that stable-yard and all its range of building to have been disused for more than half a century. Could I believe that, without an hour's warning, the long-deserted quadrangle could be filled—the empty stalls tenanted? Had some hunting-party from the neighbourhood sought shelter here, glad to escape the pitiless rain? That was not impossible, I thought. I was an utter unbeliever in all ghostly things—ready to credit any possibility rather than suppose that I had been looking upon shadows. And yet the noiselessness, the awful sound of that horn—the strange unearthly gleam of that lantern! Little superstitious as I might be, a cold sweat stood out upon my forehead, and I trembled in every limb.

For some minutes I stood by the window, statue-like, staring blankly into the empty quadrangle. Then I roused myself suddenly, and ran softly downstairs by a back staircase leading to the servants' quarters, determined to solve the mystery somehow or other. The way to Mrs. Marjorum's room was familiar to me from old experience, and it was thither that I bent my steps, determined to ask the housekeeper the meaning of what I had seen. I had a lurking conviction that it would be well for me not to mention that scene to any member of the family till I had taken counsel with some one who knew the secrets of Chrighton Abbey.

I heard the sound of merry voices and laughter as I passed the kitchen and servants' hall. Men and maids were all busy in the pleasant labour of decorating their rooms for the evening's festival. They were putting the last touches to garlands of holly and laurel, ivy and fir, as I passed the open doors; and in both rooms I saw tables laid for a substantial tea. The housekeeper's room was in a retired nook at the end of a long passage—a charming old room, panelled with dark oak, and full of capacious cupboards, which in my childhood I had looked upon as storehouses of inexhaustible treasures in the way of preserves and other confectionery. It was a shady old room, with a wide old-fashioned fire-place, cool in summer, when the hearth was adorned with a great jar of roses and lavender; and warm in winter, when the logs burnt merrily all day long.

I opened the door softly, and went in. Mrs. Marjorum was dozing in a high-backed arm-chair by the glowing hearth, dressed in her state gown of grey watered silk, and with a cap that was a perfect garden of roses. She opened her eyes as I approached her, and stared at me with a puzzled look for the first moment or so.

"Why, is that you, Miss Sarah?" she exclaimed; "and looking as pale as a ghost, I can see, even by this firelight! Let me just light a candle, and then I'll get you some *sal volatile*. Sit down in my armchair, miss; why, I declare you're all of a tremble!"

She put me into her easy-chair before I could resist, and lighted the two candles which stood ready upon her table, while I was trying to speak. My lips were dry, and it seemed at first as if my voice was gone.

"Never mind the *sal volatile*, Marjorum," I said at last. "I am not ill; I've been startled, that's all; and I've come to ask you for an explanation of the business that frightened me."

"What business, Miss Sarah?"

"You must have heard something of it yourself, surely. Didn't you hear a horn just now, a huntsman's horn?"

"A horn! Lord no, Miss Sarah. What ever could have put such a fancy in to your head?"

I saw that Mrs. Marjorum's ruddy cheeks had suddenly lost their colour, that she was now almost as pale as I could have been myself. "It was no fancy," I said; "I heard the sound, and saw the people. A hunting-party has just taken shelter in the north quadrangle. Dogs and horses, and gentlemen and servants."

"What were they like, Miss Sarah?" the housekeeper asked in a strange voice.

"I can hardly tell you that. I could see that they wore red coats; and I could scarcely see more than that. Yes, I did get a glimpse of one of the gentlemen by the light of the lantern. A tall man, with grey hair and whiskers, and a stoop in his shoulders. I noticed that he wore a short-waisted coat with a very high collar—a coat that looked a hundred years old."

"The old Squire!" muttered Mrs. Marjorum under her breath; and then turning to me, she said with a cheery resolute air, "You've been dreaming, Miss Sarah, that's just what it is. You've dropped off in your chair before the fire, and had a dream, that's it."

"No, Marjorum, it was no dream. The horn woke me, and I stood at my window and saw the dogs and huntsmen come in."

"Do you know, Miss Sarah, that the gates of the north quadrangle have been locked and barred for the last forty years, and that no one ever goes in there except through the house?"

"The gates may have been opened this evening to give shelter to strangers," I said.

"Not when the only keys that will open them hang yonder in my cupboard, miss," said the housekeeper, pointing to a corner of the room.

"But I tell you, Marjorum, these people came into the quadrangle; the horses and dogs are in the stables and kennels at this moment. I'll go and ask Mr. Chrighton, or my cousin Fanny, or Edward, all about it, since you won't tell me the truth."

I said this with a purpose, and it answered. Mrs. Marjorum caught me eagerly by the wrist.

"No, miss, don't do that; for pity's sake don't do that; don't breathe a word to missus or master."

"But why not?"

"Because you've seen that which always brings misfortune and sorrow to this house, Miss Sarah. You've seen the dead."

"What do you mean?" I gasped, awed in spite of myself.

"I daresay you've heard say that there's been something seen at times at the Abbey—many years apart, thank God; for it never came that trouble didn't come after it."

"Yes," I answered hurriedly; "but I could never get any one to tell me what it was that haunted this place."

"No, miss. Those that know have kept the secret. But you have seen it all tonight. There's no use in trying to hide it from you any longer. You have seen the old Squire, Meredith Chrighton, whose eldest son was killed by a fall in the hunting-field, brought home dead one December night, an hour after his father and the rest of the party had come safe home to the Abbey. The old gentleman had missed his son in the field, but had thought nothing of that, fancying that master John had had enough of the day's sport, and had turned his horse's head homewards. He was found by a labouring-man, poor lad, lying in a ditch with his back broken, and his horse beside him staked. The old Squire never held his head up after that day, and never rode to hounds again, though he was passionately fond of hunting. Dogs and horses were sold, and the north quadrangle has been empty from that day."

"How long is it since this kind of thing has been seen?"

"A long time, miss. I was a slip of a girl when it last happened. It was in the winter-time—this very night—the night Squire Meredith's son was killed; and the house was full of company, just as it is now. There was a wild young Oxford gentleman sleeping in your room at that time, and he saw the hunting-party come into the quadrangle; and what did he do but throw his window wide open, and give them the view-hallo as loud as ever he could. He had only arrived the day before, and knew nothing about the neighbourhood; so at dinner he began to ask where were his friends the sportsmen, and to hope he should be allowed to have a run with the Abbey hounds next day. It was in the time of our master's father; and his lady at the head of the table turned as white as a sheet when she heard this talk. She had good reason, poor soul. Before the week was out her husband was lying dead. He was struck with a fit of apoplexy, and never spoke or knew any one afterwards."

"An awful coincidence," I said; "but it may have been only a coincidence."

"I've heard other stories, miss—heard them from those that wouldn't deceive—all proving the same thing: that the appearance of the old Squire and his pack is a warning of death to this house."

"I cannot believe these things," I exclaimed; "I cannot believe them. Does Mr. Edward know anything about this?"

"No, miss. His father and mother have been most careful that it should be kept from him."

"I think he is too strong-minded to be much affected by the fact," I said.

"And you'll not say anything about what you've seen to my master or my mistress, will you, Miss Sarah?" pleaded the faithful old servant. "The knowledge of it would be sure to make them nervous and unhappy. And if evil is to come upon this house, it isn't in human power to prevent its coming."

"God forbid that there is any evil at hand!" I answered. "I am no believer in visions or omens. After all, I would sooner fancy that I was dreaming—dreaming with my eyes open as I stood at the window—than that I beheld the shadows of the dead."

Mrs. Marjorum sighed, and said nothing. I could see that she believed firmly in the phantom hunt.

I went back to my room to dress for dinner. However rationally I might try to think of what I had seen, its effect upon my mind and nerves was not the less powerful. I could think of nothing else; and a strange morbid dread of coming misery weighted me down like an actual burden.

There was a very cheerful party in the drawing-room when I went downstairs, and at dinner the talk and laughter were unceasing; but I could see that my cousin Fanny's face was a little graver than usual, and I had no doubt she was thinking of her son's intended visit to Wycherly.

At the thought of this a sudden terror flashed upon me. How if the shadows I had seen that evening were ominous of danger to him—to Edward, the heir and only son of the house? My heart grew cold as I thought of this, and yet in the next moment I despised myself for such weakness.

"It is natural enough for an old servant to believe in such things," I said to myself; "but for me—an educated woman of the world—preposterous folly."

And yet from that moment I began to puzzle myself in the endeavour to devise some means by which Edward's journey might be prevented. Of my own influence I knew that I was powerless to hinder his departure by so much as an hour; but I fancied that Julia Tremaine could persuade him to any sacrifice of his inclination, if she could only humble her pride so far as to entreat it. I determined to appeal to her in the course of the evening.

We were very merry all that evening. The servants and their guests danced in the great hall, while we sat in the gallery above, and in little groups upon the staircase, watching their diversions. I think this arrangement afforded excellent opportunities for flirtation, and that the younger members of our party made good use of their chances—with one exception: Edward Chrighton and his affianced contrived to keep far away from each other all the evening.

While all was going on noisily in the hall below, I managed to get Miss Tremaine apart from the others in the embrasure of a painted window on the stairs, where there was a wide oaken seat.

Seated here side by side, I described to her, under a promise of secrecy, the scene which I had witnessed that afternoon, and my conversation with Mrs. Marjorum.

"But, good gracious me, Miss Chrighton!" the young lady exclaimed, lifting her pencilled eyebrows with unconcealed disdain, "you don't mean to tell me that you believe in such nonsense—ghosts and omens, and old woman's folly like that!"

"I assure you, Miss Tremaine, it is most difficult for me to believe in the supernatural," I answered earnestly; "but that which I saw this evening was something more than human. The thought of it has made me very unhappy; and I cannot help connecting it somehow with my cousin Edward's visit to Wycherly. If I had the power to prevent his going, I would do it at any cost; but I have not. You alone have influence enough for that. For heaven's sake use it! do anything to hinder his hunting with the Daleborough hounds."

"You would have me humiliate myself by asking him to forgo his pleasure, and that after his conduct to me during the last week?"

"I confess that he has done much to offend you. But you love him, Miss Tremaine, though you are too proud to let your love be seen: I am certain that you do love him. For pity's sake speak to him; do not let him hazard his life, when a few words from you may prevent the danger."

"I don't believe he would give up this visit to please me," she answered; "and I shall certainly not put it in his power to humiliate me with a refusal. Besides, all this fear of yours is such utter nonsense. As if nobody had ever hunted before. My brothers hunt four times a week every winter, and not one of them has ever been the worse for it."

I did not give up the attempt lightly. I pleaded with this proud obstinate girl for a long time, as long as I could induce her to listen to me; but it was all in vain. She stuck to her text—no one should persuade her to degrade herself by asking a favour of Edward Chrighton. He had chosen to hold himself aloof from her, and she would show him that she could live without him. When she left Chrighton Abbey, they would part as strangers.

So the night closed, and at breakfast next morning I heard that Edward had started for Wycherly soon after daybreak. His absence made, for me at least, a sad blank in our circle. For one other also, I think; for Miss Tremaine's fair proud face was very pale, though she tried to seem gayer than usual, and exerted herself in quite an unaccustomed manner in her endeavour to be agreeable to everyone.

The days passed slowly for me after my cousin's departure. There was a weight upon my mind, a vague anxiety, which I struggled in vain to shake off. The house, full as it was of pleasant people, seemed to me to have become dull and dreary now that Edward was gone. The place where he had sat appeared always vacant to my eyes, though another filled it, and there was no gap on either side of the long dinner-table. Lighthearted young men still made the billiard-room resonant with their laughter; merry girls flirted as gaily as ever, undisturbed in the smallest degree by the absence of the heir of the house. Yet for me all was changed. A morbid fancy had taken complete possession of me. I found myself continually brooding over the housekeeper's words; those words which had told me that the shadows I had seen boded death and sorrow to the house of Chrighton.

My cousins, Sophy and Agnes, were no more concerned about their brother's welfare than were their guests. They were full of excitement about the New-Year's ball, which was to be a very grand affair. Every one of importance within fifty miles was to be present, every nook and corner of the Abbey would be filled with visitors coming from a great distance, while others were to be billeted upon the better class of tenantry round about. Altogether the organization of this affair was no small business; and Mrs. Chrighton's mornings were broken by discussions with the housekeeper, messages from the cook, interviews with the head-gardener on the subject of floral decorations, and other details, which all alike demanded the attention of the chatelaine herself. With these duties, and with the claims of her numerous guests, my cousin Fanny's time was so fully occupied, that she had little leisure to indulge in anxious feelings about her son, whatever secret uneasiness may have been lurking in her maternal heart. As for the master of the Abbey, he spent so much of his time in the library, where, under the pretext of business with his bailiff, he read Greek, that it was not easy for any one to discover what he did feel. Once, and once only, I heard him speak of his son, in a tone that betrayed an intense eagerness for his return.

The girls were to have new dresses from a French milliner in Wigmore Street; and as the great event drew near, bulky packages of millinery were continually arriving, and feminine consultations and expositions of finery were being held all day long in bedrooms and dressing-rooms with closed doors. Thus, with a mind always troubled by the same dark shapeless foreboding, I was perpetually being called upon to give an opinion about pink tulle and lilies of the valley, or maize silk and apple-blossoms.

New-Year's morning came at last, after an interval of abnormal length, as it seemed to me. It was a bright clear day, an almost spring-like sunshine lighting up the leafless landscape. The great dining-room was noisy with congratulations and good wishes as we assembled for breakfast on this first morning of a new year, after having seen the old one out cheerily the night before; but Edward had not yet returned, and I missed him sadly. Some touch of sympathy drew me to the side of Julia Tremaine on this particular morning. I had watched her very often during the last few days, and I had seen that her cheek grew paler every day. Today her eyes had the dull heavy look that betokens a sleepless night. Yes, I was sure that she was unhappy—that the proud relentless nature suffered bitterly.

"He must be home today," I said to her in a low voice, as she sat in stately silence before an untasted breakfast.

"Who must?" she answered, turning towards me with a cold distant look.

"My cousin Edward. You know he promised to be back in time for the ball."

"I know nothing of Mr. Chrighton's intended movements," she said in her haughtiest tone; "but of course it is only natural that he should be here tonight. He would scarcely care to insult half the county by his absence, however little he may value those now staying in his father's house."

"But you know that there is one here whom he does value better than any one else in the world, Miss Tremaine," I answered, anxious to soothe this proud girl.

"I know nothing of the kind. But why do you speak so solemnly about his return? He will come, of course. There is no reason he should not come."

She spoke in a rapid manner that was strange to her, and looked at me with a sharp enquiring glance, that touched me somehow, it was so unlike herself—it revealed to me so keen an anxiety.

"No, there is no reasonable cause for anything like uneasiness," I said; "but you remember what I told you the other night. That has preyed upon my mind, and it will be an unspeakable relief to me when I see my cousin safe at home."

"I am sorry that you should indulge in such weakness, Miss Chrighton."

That was all she said; but when I saw her in the drawing-room after breakfast, she had established herself in a window that commanded a view of the long winding drive leading to the front of the Abbey. From this point she could not fail to see anyone approaching the house. She sat there all day; everyone else was more or less busy with arrangements for the evening, or at any rate occupied with an appearance of business; but Julia Tremaine kept her place by the window, pleading a headache as an excuse for sitting still, with a book in her hand, all day, yet obstinately refusing to go to her room and lie down, when her mother entreated her to do so.

"You will be fit for nothing tonight, Julia," Mrs. Tremaine said, almost angrily; "you have been looking ill for ever so long, and today you are as pale as a ghost."

I knew that she was watching for him; and I pitied her with all my heart, as the day wore itself out, and he did not come.

We dined earlier than usual, played a game or two of billiards after dinner, made a tour of inspection through the bright rooms, lit with wax-candles only, and odorous with exotics; and then came a long interregnum devoted to the arts and mysteries of the toilet; while maids flitted to and fro laden with frilled muslin petticoats from the laundry, and a faint smell of singed hair pervaded the corridors. At ten o'clock the band were tuning their violins, and pretty girls and elegant-looking men were coming slowly down the broad oak staircase, as the roll of fast-coming wheels sounded louder without, and stentorian voices announced the best people in the county.

I have no need to dwell long upon the details of that evening's festival. It was very much like other balls—a brilliant success, a night of splendour and enchantment for those whose hearts were light and happy, and who could abandon themselves utterly to the pleasure of the moment; a far-away picture of fair faces and bright-hued dresses, a wearisome kaleidoscopic procession of form and colour for those whose minds were weighed down with the burden of a hidden care.

For me the music had no melody, the dazzling scene no charm. Hour after hour went by; supper was over, and the waltzers were enjoying those latest dances which always seem the most delightful, and yet Edward Chrighton had not appeared amongst us.

There had been innumerable enquiries about him, and Mrs. Chrighton had apologized for his absence as best she might. Poor soul, I well knew that his non-return was now a source of poignant anxiety to her, although she greeted all her guests with the same gracious smile, and was able to talk gaily and well upon every subject. Once, when she was sitting alone for a few minutes, watching the dancers, I saw the smile fade from her face, and a look of anguish come over it. I ventured to approach her at this moment, and never shall I forget the look which she turned towards me.

"My son, Sarah!" she said in a low voice—"something has happened to my son!"

I did my best to comfort her; but my own heart was growing heavier and heavier, and my attempt was a very poor one.

Julia Tremaine had danced a little at the beginning of the evening, to keep up appearances, I believe, in order that no one might suppose that she was distressed by her lover's absence; but after the first two or three dances she pronounced herself tired, and withdrew to a seat amongst the matrons. She was looking very lovely in spite of her extreme pallor, dressed in white tulle, a perfect cloud of airy puffings, and with a wreath of ivy-leaves and diamonds crowning her pale golden hair.

The night waned, the dancers were revolving in the last waltz, when I happened to look towards the doorway at the end of the room. I was startled by seeing a man standing there, with his hat in his hand, not in evening costume; a man with a pale anxious-looking face, peering cautiously into the room. My first thought was of evil; but in the next moment the man had disappeared, and I saw no more of him.

I lingered by my cousin Fanny's side till the rooms were empty. Even Sophy and Aggy had gone off to their own apartments, their airy dresses sadly dilapidated by a night's vigorous dancing. There were only Mr. and Mrs. Chrighton and myself in the long suite of rooms, where the flowers were drooping and the wax-lights dying out one by one in the silver sconces against the walls.

"I think the evening went off very well," Fanny said, looking rather anxiously at her husband, who was stretching himself and yawning with an air of intense relief.

"Yes, the affair went off well enough. But Edward has committed a terrible breach of manners by not being here. Upon my word, the young men of the present day think of nothing but their own pleasures. I suppose that something especially attractive was going on at Wycherly today, and he couldn't tear himself away."

"It is so unlike him to break his word," Mrs. Chrighton answered. "You are not alarmed, Frederick? You don't think that anything has happened—any accident?"

"What should happen? Ned is one of the best riders in the county. I don't think there's any fear of his coming to grief."

"He might be ill."

"Not he. He's a young Hercules. And if it were possible for him to be ill—which it is not—we should have had a message from Wycherly."

The words were scarcely spoken when Truefold the old butler stood by his master's side, with a solemn anxious face.

"There is a—a person who wishes to see you, sir," he said in a low voice, "alone."

Low as the words were, both Fanny and myself heard them. "Someone from Wycherly?" she exclaimed. "Let him come here." "But, madam, the person most particularly wished to see master alone. Shall I show him into the library, sir? The lights are not out there."

"Then it is someone from Wycherly," said my cousin, seizing my wrist with a hand that was icy cold. "Didn't I tell you so, Sarah? Something has happened to my son. Let the person come here, Truefold, here; I insist upon it."

The tone of command was quite strange in a wife who was always deferential to her husband, in a mistress who was ever gentle to her servants.

"Let it be so, Truefold," said Mr. Chrighton. "Whatever ill news has come to us we will hear together."

He put his arm round his wife's waist. Both were pale as marble, both stood in stony stillness waiting for the blow that was to fall upon them.

The stranger, the man I had seen in the doorway, came in. He was curate of Wycherly church, and chaplain to Sir Francis Wycherly; a grave middle-aged man. He told what he had to tell with all kindness, with all the usual forms of consolation which Christianity and an experience of sorrow could suggest. Vain words, wasted trouble. The blow must fall, and earthly consolation was unable to lighten it by a feather's weight.

There had been a steeplechase at Wycherly—an amateur affair with gentlemen riders—on that bright New-Year's-day, and Edward Chrighton had been persuaded to ride his favourite hunter Pepperbox. There would be plenty of time for him to return to Chrighton after the races. He had consented; and his horse was winning easily, when, at the last fence, a double one, with water beyond, Pepperbox baulked his leap, and went over head-foremost, flinging his rider over a hedge into a field close beside the course, where there was a heavy stone roller. Upon this stone roller Edward Chrighton had fallen, his head receiving the full force of the concussion. All was told. It was while the curate was relating the fatal catastrophe that I looked round suddenly, and saw Julia Tremaine standing a little way behind the speaker. She had heard all; she uttered no cry, she showed no signs of fainting, but stood calm and motionless, waiting for the end.

I know not how that night ended: there seemed an awful calm upon us all. A carriage was got ready, and Mr. and Mrs. Chrighton started for Wycherly to look upon their dead son. He had died while they were carrying him from the course to Sir Francis's house. I went with Julia Tremaine to her room, and sat with her while the winter morning dawned slowly upon us—a bitter dawning.

I have little more to tell. Life goes on, though hearts are broken. Upon Chrighton Abbey there came a dreary time of desolation. The master of the house lived in his library, shut from the outer world, buried almost as completely as a hermit in his cell. I have heard that Julia Tremaine was never known to smile after that day. She is still unmarried, and lives entirely at her father's country house; proud and reserved in her conduct to her equals, but a very angel of mercy and compassion amongst the poor of the neighbourhood. Yes; this haughty girl, who once declared herself unable to endure the hovels of the poor, is now a Sister of Charity in all but the robe. So does a great sorrow change the current of a woman's life.

I have seen my cousin Fanny many times since that awful New-Year's night; for I have always the same welcome at the Abbey. I have seen her calm and cheerful, doing her duty, smiling upon her daughter's children, the honoured mistress of a great household; but I know that the mainspring of life is broken, that for her there hath passed a glory from the earth, and that upon all the pleasures and joys of this world she looks with the solemn calm of one for whom all things are dark with the shadow of a great sorrow.

THE FATE OF
MADAME CABANEL

by *Eliza Lynn Linton*

1873

The daughter of a vicar and granddaughter of a bishop, Eliza Lynn's mother died when she was just five months old. After a childhood in which she was largely left to educate herself, she left her native Keswick, in England's scenic Lake District, at the age of twenty-three to become a writer in London. The same year, with the help of the then-popular poet Walter Savage Landor, she published her first novel, Azeth, the Egyptian.

Along with two other novels over the next six years, Azeth *enjoyed little success, but Eliza found work as a journalist for the* Morning Chronicle *and* Household Words. *She was the first salaried female journalist in Britain.*

In 1858, Eliza married William James Linton, a wood-engraver, painter, writer, and political reformer. Although he was London-born, he had a house in the Lake District, overlooking Coniston Water: Eliza moved in with him and his seven children from a previous marriage, but the couple separated amicably in 1867, and Eliza returned to London.

In addition to more than twenty novels, Eliza wrote a good deal of nonfiction, much of it—perhaps surprisingly—critical of early feminism. She also wrote some regional pieces, a memoir called My Literary Life *(1899), and the historical survey* Witch Stories *(1861).*

Eliza's fiction was often dramatic, but almost never supernatural. "The Fate of Madame Cabanel" includes vampirism among its themes, but Linton refuses to tell the reader whether or not anything supernatural is really going on: instead, the monsters are human, driven by ignorance, xenophobia and superstition to destroy a neighbor who—in a rational world, at least—is completely innocent.

Fans of Sherlock Holmes may note the similarities between this story and "The Adventure of the Sussex Vampire," published in 1924. While Doyle's tale concerns the triumph of science and rationalism over superstition—ironic given the writer's interest in spiritualism and belief in the Cottingley Fairy hoax—"The Fate of Madame Cabanel" reaches the opposite conclusion, its unfortunate subject doomed by mere accusation.

P rogress had not invaded, science had not enlightened, the little hamlet of Pieuvrot, in Brittany. They were a simple, ignorant, superstitious set who lived there, and the luxuries of civilization were known to them as little as its learning. They toiled hard all the week on the ungrateful soil that yielded them but a bare subsistence in return; they went regularly to mass in the little rock-set chapel on Sundays and saints' days; believed implicitly all that *Monsieur le curé* said to them, and many things which he did not say; and they took all the unknown, not as magnificent, but as diabolical.

The sole link between them and the outside world of mind and progress was Monsieur Jules Cabanel, the proprietor, *par excellence*, of the place;

maire, juge de paix, and all the public functionaries rolled into one. And he sometimes went to Paris whence he returned with a cargo of novelties that excited envy, admiration, or fear, according to the degree of intelligence in those who beheld them.

Monsieur Jules Cabanel was not the most charming man of his class in appearance, but he was generally held to be a good fellow at bottom. A short, thick-set, low-browed man, with blue-black hair cropped close like a mat, as was his blue-black beard, inclined to obesity and fond of good living, he had need have some virtues behind the bush to compensate for his want of personal charms. He was not bad, however; he was only common and unlovely.

Up to fifty years of age he had remained the unmarried prize of the surrounding country; but hitherto he had resisted all the overtures made by maternal fowlers, and had kept his liberty and his bachelorhood intact. Perhaps his handsome housekeeper, Adèle, had something to do with his persistent celibacy. They said she had, under their breath as it were, down at *la Veuve Prieur's*; but no one dared to so much as hint the like to herself. She was a proud, reserved kind of woman; and had strange notions of her own dignity which no one cared to disturb. So, whatever the underhand gossip of the place might be, neither she nor her master got wind of it.

Presently and quite suddenly, Jules Cabanel, who had been for a longer time than usual in Paris, came home with a wife. Adèle had only twenty-four hours' notice to prepare for this strange home-coming; and the task seemed heavy. But she got through it in her old way of silent determination; arranged the rooms as she knew her master would wish them to be arranged; and even supplemented the usual nice adornments by a voluntary bunch of flowers on the salon table.

"Strange flowers for a bride," said to herself little Jeannette, the goose-girl who was sometimes brought into the house to work, as she noticed heliotrope—called in France *la fleur des veuves*—scarlet poppies, a bunch of belladonna, another of aconite—scarcely, as even ignorant little Jeannette said, flowers of bridal welcome or bridal significance. Nevertheless, they stood where Adèle had placed them; and if Monsieur Cabanel meant anything by the passionate expression of disgust with which he ordered them out of his sight, madame seemed to understand nothing, as she smiled with that vague, half-deprecating look of a person who is assisting at a scene of which the true bearing is not understood.

Madame Cabanel was a foreigner, and an Englishwoman; young, pretty and fair as an angel. *"La beauté du diable,"* said the Pieuvrotines, with something between a sneer and a shudder; for the words meant with them more than they mean in ordinary use. Swarthy, ill-nourished, low of stature and meagre in frame as they were themselves, they could not understand the plump form, tall figure and fresh complexion of the Englishwoman. Unlike their own experience, it was therefore more likely to be evil than good. The feeling which had sprung up against her at first sight deepened when it was observed that, although she went to mass with praiseworthy punctuality, she did not know her missal and signed herself à travers. *La beauté du diable*, in faith!

"Pouf!" said Martin Briolic, the old gravedigger of the little cemetery; "with those red lips of hers, her rose cheeks and her plump shoulders, she looks like a vampire and as if she lived on blood."

He said this one evening down at *la Veuve Prieur's*; and he said it with an air of conviction that had its weight. For Martin Briolic was reputed the wisest man of the district; not even excepting *Monsieur le curé* who was wise in his own way, which was not Martin's—nor Monsieur Cabanel who was wise in his, which was neither Martin's nor the *curé's*. He knew all about the weather and the stars, the wild herbs that grew on the plains and the wild shy beasts that eat them; and he had the power of divination and could find where the hidden springs of water lay far down in the earth when he held the baguette in his hand. He knew too, where treasures could be had on Christmas Eve if only you were quick and brave enough to enter the cleft in the rock at the right moment and come out again before too late; and he had seen with his own eyes the White Ladies dancing in the moonlight; and the little imps, the *lutins*, playing their prankish gambols by the pit at the edge of the wood. And he had a shrewd suspicion as to who, among those black-hearted men of La Crèche-en-bois—the rival hamlet—was a *loup-garou*, if ever there was one on the face of the earth and no one had doubted that! He had other powers of a yet more mystic kind; so that Martin Briolic's bad word went for something, if, with the illogical injustice of ill-nature his good went for nothing.

Fanny Campbell, or, as she was now Madame Cabanel, would have excited no special attention in England, or indeed anywhere but at such dead-alive, ignorant, and consequently gossiping place as Pieuvrot. She had no romantic secret as her background; and what history she had was commonplace enough, if sorrowful too in its own way. She was simply an orphan and a governess; very young and very poor; whose employers had quarrelled with her and left her stranded in Paris, alone and almost moneyless; and who had married Monsieur Jules Cabanel as the best thing she could do for herself. Loving no one else, she was not difficult to be won by the first man who showed her kindness in her hour of trouble and destitution; and she accepted her middle-aged suitor, who was fitter to be her father than her husband, with a clear conscience and a determination to do her duty cheerfully and faithfully—all without considering herself as a martyr or an interesting victim sacrificed to the cruelty of circumstances. She did not know however, of the handsome housekeeper Adèle, nor of the housekeeper's little nephew—to whom her master was so kind that he allowed him to live at the *Maison Cabanel* and had him well taught by the *curé*. Perhaps if she had she would have thought twice before she put herself under the same roof with a woman who for a bridal bouquet offered her poppies, heliotrope and poison-flowers.

If one had to name the predominant characteristic of Madame Cabanel it would be easiness of temper. You saw it in the round, soft, indolent lines of her face and figure; in her mild blue eyes and placid, unvarying smile; which irritated the more petulant French temperament and especially disgusted Adèle. It seemed impossible to make madame angry or even to make her understand when she was insulted, the housekeeper used to say with profound disdain; and, to do the woman justice, she did not spare her endeavours to enlighten her. But madame accepted all Adèle's haughty reticence and defiant continuance of mistress-hood with unwearied sweetness; indeed, she expressed herself gratified that so much trouble was taken off her hands, and that Adèle so kindly took her duties on herself.

The consequences of this placid lazy life, where all her faculties were in a manner asleep, and where she was enjoying the reaction from her late years of privation and anxiety, was, as might be expected, an increase in physical beauty that made her freshness and good condition still more remarkable.

Her lips were redder, her cheeks rosier, her shoulders plumper than ever; but as she waxed, the health of the little hamlet waned, and not the oldest inhabitant remembered so sickly a season, or so many deaths. The master too, suffered slightly; the little Adolphe desperately.

This failure of general health in undrained hamlets is not uncommon in France or in England; neither is the steady and pitiable decline of French children; but Adèle treated it as something out of all the lines of normal experience; and, breaking through her habits of reticence spoke to every one quite fiercely of the strange sickliness that had fallen on Pieuvrot and the *Maison Cabanel*; and how she believed it was something more than common; while as to her little nephew, she could give neither a name nor find a remedy for the mysterious disease that had attacked him. There were strange things among them, she used to say, and Pieuvrot had never done well since the old times were changed. Jeannette used to notice how she would sit gazing at the English lady, with such a deadly look on her handsome face when she turned from the foreigner's fresh complexion and grand physique to the pale face of the stunted, meagre, fading child. It was a look, she said afterwards, that used to make her flesh get like ice and creep like worms.

One night Adèle, as if she could bear it no longer, dashed down to where old Martin Briolic lived, to ask him to tell her how it had all come about—and the remedy.

"Hold, Ma'am Adèle," said Martin, as he shuffled his greasy tarot cards and laid them out in triplets on the table; "there is more in this than one sees. One sees only a poor little child become suddenly sick; that may be, is it not so? and no harm done by man? God sends sickness to us all and makes my trade profitable to me. But the little Adolphe has not been touched by the Good God. I see the will of a wicked woman in this. Hem!" Here he shuffled the cards and laid them out with a kind of eager distraction of manner, his withered hands trembling and his mouth uttering words that Adèle could not catch. "Saint Joseph and all the saints protect us!" he cried; "the foreigner—the Englishwoman—she whom they call Madame Cabanel—no rightful madame she!—Ah, misery!"

"Speak, Father Martin! What do you mean!" cried Adèle, grasping his arm. Her black eyes were wild; her arched nostrils dilated; her lips, thin, sinuous, flexible, were pressed tight over her small square teeth.

"Tell me in plain words what you would say!"

"Broucolaque!" said Martin in a low voice.

"It is what I believed!" cried Adèle. "It is what I knew. Ah, my Adolphe! woe on the day when the master brought that fair-skinned devil home!"

"Those red lips don't come by nothing, Ma'am Adèle," cried Martin nodding his head. "Look at them—they glisten with blood! I said so from the beginning; and the cards, they said so too. I drew 'blood' and a 'bad fair woman' on the evening when the master brought her home, and I said to myself, 'Ha, ha, Martin! you are on the track, my boy—on the track. Martin!'—and, Ma'am Adèle, I have never left it! *Broucolaque!* That's what the cards say, Ma'am Adèle. Vampire. Watch and see; watch and see; and you'll find that the cards have spoken true."

"And when we have found, Martin?" said Adèle in a hoarse whisper.

The old man shuffled his cards again. "When we have found, Ma'am Adèle?" he said slowly. "You know the old pit out there by the forest?—the old pit where the *lutins* run in and out, and where the White Ladies wring the necks of those who come upon them in the moonlight? Perhaps the White Ladies will do as much for the English wife of Monsieur Cabanel; who knows?"

"They may," said Adèle, gloomily.

"Courage, brave woman!" said Martin. "They will."

The only really pretty place about Pieuvrot was the cemetery. To be sure there was the dark gloomy forest which was grand in its own mysterious way; and there was the broad wide plain where you might wander for a long summer's day and not come to the end of it; but these were scarcely places where a young woman would care to go by herself; and for the rest, the miserable little patches of cultivated ground, which the peasants had snatched from the surrounding waste and where they had raised poor crops, were not very lovely. So Madame Cabanel, who, for all the soft indolence that had invaded her, had the Englishwoman's inborn love for walking and fresh air, haunted the pretty little graveyard a good deal. She had no sentiment connected with it. Of all the dead who laid there in their narrow coffins, she knew none and cared for none; but she liked to see the pretty little flower-beds and the wreaths of immortelles, and the like; the distance too, from her own home was just enough for her;

and the view over the plain to the dark belt of forest and the mountains beyond, was fine.

The Pieuvrotines did not understand this. It was inexplicable to them that any one, not out of her mind, should go continually to the cemetery—not on the day of the dead and not to adorn the grave of one she loved—only to sit there and wander among the tombs, looking out on to the plain and the mountains beyond when she was tired.

"It was just like—" The speaker, one Lesouëf, had got so far as this, when he stopped for a word.

He said this down at *la Veuve Prieur's* where the hamlet collected nightly to discuss the day's small doings, and where the main theme, ever since she had come among them, three months ago now, had been Madame Cabanel and her foreign ways and her wicked ignorance of her mass-book and her wrong-doings of a mysterious kind generally, interspersed with jesting queries, banded from one to the other, of how Ma'am Adèle liked it?—and what would become of le petit Adolphe when the rightful heir appeared?—some adding that *monsieur* was a brave man to shut up two wild cats under the same roof together; and what would become of it in the end? Mischief of a surety.

"Wander about the tombs just like what, Jean Lesouëf?" said Martin Briolic. Rising, he added in a low but distinct voice, every word falling clear and clean: "I will tell you like what, Lesouëf—like a vampire! La femme Cabanel has red lips and red cheeks; and Ma'am Adèle's little nephew is perishing before your eyes. La femme Cabanel has red lips and red cheeks; and she sits for hours among the tombs. Can you read the riddle, my friends? For me it is as clear as the blessed sun."

"Ha, Father Martin, you have found the word—like a vampire!" said Lesouëf with a shudder.

"Like a vampire!" they all echoed with a groan.

"And I said vampire the first," said Martin Briolic. "Call to mind I said it from the first."

"Faith! and you did," they answered; "and you said true."

So now the unfriendly feeling that had met and accompanied the young Englishwoman ever since she came to Pieuvrot had drawn to a focus. The seed which Martin and Adèle had dropped so sedulously had at last taken root; and the Pieuvrotines would have been ready to accuse of atheism and immorality any one who had doubted their decision, and had declared that pretty Madame Cabanel was only a young woman with nothing special to do, a naturally fair complexion, superb health—and no vampire at all, sucking the blood of a living child or living among the tombs to make the newly buried her prey.

The little Adolphe grew paler and paler, thinner and thinner; the fierce summer sun told on the half-starved dwellers within those foul mud-huts surrounded by undrained marshes; and Monsieur Jules Cabanel's former solid health followed the law of the rest. The doctor, who lived at Crèche-en-bois, shook his head at the look of things; and said it was grave. When Adèle pressed him to tell her what was the matter with the child and with monsieur, he evaded the question; or gave her a word which she neither understood not could pronounce. The truth was, he was a credulous and intensely suspicious man; a viewy man who made theories and then gave himself to the task of finding them true. He had made the theory that Fanny was secretly poisoning both her husband and the child; and though he would not give Adèle a hint of this, he would not set her mind at rest by a definite answer that went on any other line.

As for Monsieur Cabanel, he was a man without imagination and without suspicion; a man to take life easily and not distress himself too much for the fear of wounding others; a selfish man but not a cruel one; a man whose own pleasure was his supreme law and who could not imagine, still less brook, opposition or the want of love and respect for himself. Still, he loved his wife as he had never loved a woman before. Coarsely moulded, common-natured as he was, he loved her with what strength and passion of poetry nature had given him; and if the quantity was small, the quality was sincere. But that quality was sorely tried when—now Adèle, now the doctor—hinted mysteriously, the one at diabolical influences, the other at underhand proceedings of which it behoved him to be careful, especially careful what he ate and drank and how it was prepared and by whom; Adèle adding hints about the perfidiousness of English women and the share which the devil had in fair hair and brilliant complexions. Love his young wife as he might, this constant dropping of poison was not without some effect. It told much for his steadfastness and loyalty that it should have had only so small effect.

One evening however, when Adèle, in an agony, was kneeling at his feet—madame had gone out for her usual walk—crying: "Why did you leave me for such as she is?—I, who loved you, who was faithful to you, and she, who walks among the graves, who sucks your blood and our child's—she who has only the devil's beauty for her portion and who loves you not?"—something seemed suddenly to touch him with electric force.

"Miserable fool that I was!" he said, resting his head on Adèle's shoulders and weeping. Her heart leapt with joy. Was her reign to be renewed? Was her rival to be dispossessed?

From that evening Monsieur Cabanel's manner changed to his young wife but she was too easy-tempered and unsuspicious to notice anything, or if she did, there was too little depth in her own love for him—it was so much a matter of untroubled friendliness only—that she did not fret but accepted the coldness and brusqueness that had crept into his manner as good-naturedly as she accepted all things. It would have been wiser if she had cried and made a scene and come to an open fracas with Monsieur Cabanel. They would have understood each other better; and Frenchmen like the excitement of a quarrel and a reconciliation.

Naturally kind-hearted, Madame Cabanel went much about the village, offering help of various kinds to the sick. But no one among them all, not the very poorest—indeed, the very poorest the least—received her civilly or accepted her aid. If she attempted to touch one of the dying children, the mother, shuddering, withdrew it hastily to her own arms; if she spoke to the adult sick, the wan eyes would look at her with a strange horror and the feeble voice would mutter words in a patois she could not understand. But always came the same word, "*broucolaque!*"

"How these people hate the English!" she used to think as she turned away, perhaps just a little depressed, but too phlegmatic to let herself be uncomfortable or troubled deeply.

It was the same at home. If she wanted to do any little act of kindness to the child, Adèle passionately refused her. Once she snatched him rudely from her arms, saying as she did so: "infamous *broucolaque!* before my very eyes?" And once, when Fanny was troubled about her husband and proposed to make him a cup of beef-tea *à l'Anglaise,* the doctor looked at her as if he would have looked through her; and Adèle upset the saucepan; saying insolently—but yet hot tears were in her eyes—"Is it not fast enough for you, madame? Not faster, unless you kill me first!"

To all of which Fanny replied nothing; thinking only that the doctor was very rude to stare so fixedly at her and that Adèle was horribly cross; and what an ill-tempered creature she was; and how unlike an English housekeeper!

But Monsieur Cabanel, when he was told of the little scene, called Fanny to him and said in a more caressing voice than he had used to her of late: "Thou wouldst not hurt me, little wife? it was love and kindness, not wrong, that thou wouldst do?"

"Wrong? What wrong could I do?" answered Fanny, opening her blue eyes wide. "What wrong should I do to my best and only friend?"

"And I am thy friend? thy lover? thy husband? Thou lovest me dear?" said Monsieur Cabanel.

"Dear Jules, who is so dear; who so near?" she said kissing him, while he said fervently: "God bless thee!"

The next day Monsieur Cabanel was called away on urgent business. He might be absent for two days, he said, but he would try to lessen the time; and the young wife was left alone in the midst of her enemies, without even such slight guard as his presence might prove.

Adèle was out. It was a dark, hot summer's night, and the little Adolphe had been more feverish and restless than usual all the day. Towards evening he grew worse; and though Jeannette, the goose-girl, had strict commands not to allow madame to touch him, she grew frightened at the condition of the boy; and when madame came into the small parlour to offer her assistance, Jeannette gladly abandoned a charge that was too heavy for her and let the lady take him from her arms.

Sitting there with the child in her lap, cooing to him, soothing him by a low, soft nursery song, the paroxysm of his pain seemed to her to pass and it was as if he slept. But in that paroxysm he had bitten both his lip and tongue; and the blood was now oozing from his mouth. He was a pretty boy; and his mortal sickness made him at this moment pathetically lovely. Fanny bent her head and kissed the pale still face;—and the blood that was on his lips was transferred to hers.

While she still bent over him—her woman's heart touched with a mysterious force and prevision of her own future motherhood—Adèle, followed by old Martin and some others of the village, rushed into the room.

"Behold her!" she cried, seizing Fanny by the arm and forcing her face upwards by the chin—"behold her in the act! Friends, look at my child—dead, dead in her arms; and she with his blood on her lips! Do you want more proofs? Vampire that she is, can you deny the evidence of your own senses?"

"No! no!" roared the crowd hoarsely. "She is a vampire—a creature cursed by God and the enemy of man; away with her to the pit. She must die as she has made others to die!"

"Die, as she has made my boy to die!" said Adèle; and more than one who had lost a relative or child during the epidemic echoed her words, "Die, as she has made mine to die!"

"What is the meaning of all this?" said Madame Cabanel, rising and facing the crowd with the true courage of an Englishwoman. "What harm have I done to any of you that you should come about me, in the absence of my husband, with these angry looks and insolent words?"

"What harm hast thou done?" cried old Martin, coming close to her. "Sorceress as thou art, thou hast bewitched our good master; and vampire as thou art, thou nourishest thyself on our blood! Have we not proof of that at this very moment? Look at thy mouth—cursed *broucolaque*; and here lies thy victim, who accuses thee in his death!"

Fanny laughed scornfully, "I cannot condescend to answer such folly," she said lifting her head. "Are you men or children?"

"We are men, madame," said Legros the miller; "and being men we must protect our weak ones. We have all had our doubts—and who more cause than I, with three little ones taken to heaven before their time?—and now we are convinced."

"Because I have nursed a dying child and done my best to soothe him!" said Madame Cabanel with unconscious pathos.

"No more words!" cried Adèle, dragging her by the arm from which she had never loosed her hold. "To the pit with her, my friends, if you would not see all your children die as mine has died—as our good Legros' have died!"

A kind of shudder shook the crowd; and a groan that sounded in itself a curse burst from them. "To the pit!" they cried. "Let the demons take their own!"

Quick as thought Adèle pinioned the strong white arms whose shape and beauty had so often maddened her with jealous pain; and before the poor girl could utter more than one cry Legros had placed his brawny hand over her mouth. Though this destruction of a monster was not the murder of a human being in his mind, or in the mind of any there, still they did not care to have their nerves disturbed by cries that sounded so human as Madame Cabanel's. Silent then, and gloomy, that dreadful cortege took its way to the forest, carrying its living load; gagged and helpless as if it had been a corpse among them. Save with Adèle and old Martin, it was not so much personal animosity as the instinctive self-defence of fear that animated them. They were executioners, not enemies; and the executioners of a more righteous law than that allowed by the national code. But one by one they all dropped off, till their numbers were reduced to six; of whom Legros was one, and Lesouëf, who had lost his only sister, was also one.

The pit was not more than an English mile from the Maison Cabanel. It was a dark and lonesome spot, where not the bravest man of all that assembly would have dared to go alone after nightfall, not even if the *curé* had been with him; but a multitude gives courage, said old Martin Briolic; and half a dozen stalwart men, led by such a woman as Adèle, were not afraid of even *lutins* or the White Ladies.

As swiftly as they could for the burden they bore, and all in utter silence, the cortege strode over the moor; one or two of them carrying rude torches; for the night was black and the way was not without its physical dangers. Nearer and nearer they came to the fatal bourn; and heavier grew the weight of their victim. She had long ceased to struggle; and now lay as if dead in the hands of her bearers. But no one spoke of this or of aught else. Not a word was exchanged between them; and more than one, even of those left, began to doubt whether they had done wisely, and whether they had not better have trusted to the law. Adèle and Martin alone remained firm to the task they had undertaken; and Legros too was sure; but he was weakly and humanly sorrowful for the thing he felt obliged to do. As for Adèle, the woman's jealousy, the mother's anguish and the terror of superstition, had all wrought in her so that she would not have raised a finger to have lightened her victim of one of her pains, or have found her a woman like herself and no vampire after all.

The way got darker; the distance between them and their place of execution shorter; and at last they reached the border of the pit where this fearful monster, this vampire—poor innocent Fanny Cabanel—was to be thrown. As they lowered her, the light of their torches fell on her face.

"*Grand Dieu!*" cried Legros, taking off his cap; "she is dead!"

"A vampire cannot die," said Adèle, "It is only an appearance. Ask Father Martin."

"A vampire cannot die unless the evil spirits take her, or she is buried with a stake thrust through her body," said Martin Briolic sententiously. "I don't like the look of it," said Legros; and so said some others. They had taken the bandage from the mouth of the poor girl; and as she lay in the flickering light, her blue eyes half open; and her pale face white with the whiteness of death, a little return of human feeling among them shook them as if the wind had passed over them.

Suddenly they heard the sound of horses' hoofs thundering across the plain. They counted two, four, six; and they were now only four unarmed men, with Martin and Adèle to make up the number. Between the vengeance of man and the power and malice of the wood-demons, their courage faded and their presence of mind deserted them. Legros rushed frantically into the vague darkness of the forest; Lesouëf followed him; the other two fled over the plain while the horsemen came nearer and nearer. Only Adèle held the torch high above her head, to show more clearly both herself in her swarthy passion and revenge and the dead body of her victim. She wanted no concealment; she had done her work, and she gloried in it. Then the horsemen came plunging to them—Jules Cabanel the first, followed by the doctor and four *gardes champêtres*.

"Wretches! murderers!" was all he said, as he flung himself from his horse and raised the pale face to his lips.

"Master," said Adèle; "she deserved to die. She is a vampire and she has killed our child."

"Fool!" cried Jules Cabanel, flinging off her hand. "Oh, my loved wife! thou who did no harm to man or beast, to be murdered now by men who are worse than beasts!"

"She was killing thee," said Adèle. "Ask *monsieur le docteur*. What ailed the master, *monsieur?*"

"Do not bring me into this infamy," said the doctor, looking up from the dead. "Whatever ailed *monsieur*, she ought not to be here. You have made yourself her judge and executioner, Adèle, and you must answer for it to the law."

"You say this too, master?" said Adèle.

"I say so too," returned Monsieur Cabanel. "To the law you must answer for the innocent life you have so cruelly taken—you and all the fools and murderers you have joined to you."

"And is there to be no vengeance for our child?"

"Would you revenge yourself on God, woman?" said Monsieur Cabanel sternly.

"And our past years of love, master?"

"Are memories of hate, Adèle," said Monsieur Cabanel, as he turned again to the pale face of his dead wife.

"Then my place is vacant," said Adèle, with a bitter cry. "Ah, my little Adolphe, it is well you went before!"

"Hold, Ma'am Adèle!" cried Martin.

But before a hand could be stretched out, with one bound, one shriek, she had flung herself into the pit where she had hoped to bury Madame Cabanel; and they heard her body strike the water at the bottom with a dull splash, as of something falling from a great distance.

"They can prove nothing against me, Jean," said old Martin to the *garde* who held him. "I neither bandaged her mouth nor carried her on my shoulders. I am the gravedigger of Pieuvrot, and, *ma foi,* you would all do badly, you poor creatures, when you die, without me! I shall have the honour of digging *madame's* grave, never doubt it; and, Jean," he whispered, "they may talk as they like, those rich aristos who know nothing. She is a vampire, and she shall have a *slatte* through her body yet! Who knows better than I? If we do not tie her down like this, she will come out of her grave and suck our blood; it is a way these vampires have."

"Silence there!" said the *garde* commanding the little escort. "To prison with the assassins; and keep their tongues from wagging."

"To prison with martyrs and the public benefactors," retorted old Martin. "So the world rewards its best!"

And in this faith he lived and died, as a *forçat* at Toulon, maintaining to the last that he had done the world a good service by ridding it of a monster who else would not have left one man in Pieuvrot to perpetuate his name and race. But Legros and also Lesouëf, his companion, doubted gravely of the righteousness of that act of theirs on that dark summer's night in the forest; and though they always maintained that they should not have been punished, because of their good motives, yet they grew in time to disbelieve old Martin Briolic and his wisdom, and to wish that they had let the law take its own course unhelped by them—reserving their strength for the grinding of the hamlet's flour and the mending of the hamlet's *sabots*—and the leading of a good life according to the teaching of *Monsieur le curé* and the exhortations of their own wives.

FOREWARNED, FOREARMED

by Mrs. J. H. Riddell

1874

Charlotte Eliza Lawson Cowan was born in Carrickfergus, Ireland, the youngest daughter of James Cowan, high sheriff of county Antrim. She and her mother moved to London five years after her father's death; her mother died the following year, and a year later Charlotte married Joseph Hadley Riddell, a civil engineer who had moved to London from his native Staffordshire.

Her first novel appeared in 1858 under the gender-neutral pseudonym of F. G. Trafford. Over the next forty years or so, she published forty novels, numerous stories, and a number of collections, using her married name of Mrs. J. H. Riddell from 1864. In the 1860s, she was the part-owner and editor of The St. James's Magazine, *a prominent London literary journal, and she also edited another magazine titled* Home.

Like most writers of her day, male and female, Charlotte did not restrict herself to a single genre. Several of her novels involved hauntings, though, and in 1882 she published a collection of supernatural tales under the title Weird Stories. *Some of her short stories, like "The Old House in Vauxhall Walk," "The Last of Squire Ennismore," and "Hertford O'Donnell's Warning" appear regularly in collections of horror fiction.*

"Forewarned, Forearmed" comes from an earlier publication, the three-volume miscellany Frank Sinclair's Wife and Other Stories, *which appeared in 1874. Perhaps because of the collection's wide-ranging nature, "Forewarned, Forearmed" is less often anthologized than many of Mrs. Riddell's other supernatural fiction. This is a pity, because it is an effective tale of a disputed inheritance, attempted murder, and a prophetic dream.*

It is a tale within a tale, beginning with a description of the narrator: this was a popular format at the time, but frowned on by most modern editors. Every paragraph of the narrated story begins with an open quotation mark, which the reader may find distracting at first—but Mrs. Riddell's writing soon carries the reader along and the initial distraction quickly fades.

T he story which I am about to tell is not a chapter out of my own life. The incidents which go to furnish it were enacted years before I was born; the performers in it died forty years ago, and have left nor son nor heir to inherit the memory.

I question whether the man live (the woman may, seeing women are more enduring than men) who could identify the names of the persons concerning whom I shall have hereafter to speak, but the facts happened, nevertheless.

Many a time I have heard them rehearsed, many a night I have sat on the hearthrug fascinated, listening to how Mr. Dwarris dreamt a dream, and many a night I have passed through the folding-doors that led from the outer to the lesser hall, and walked to bed along the corridors thinking tremblingly of the face which continually reappeared—of the journey in the coach and the post-chaise—all the particulars of which I purpose in due time to recount. Further, it is in my memory, that I was wont to place a pillow against my back in the night season, lest some vague enemy should enter my room and strike me under the fifth rib; and I went through much anguish when the Storm King was abroad, fancying I heard stealthy footsteps in the long gallery, and the sound of another person's breathing in the room beside my own.

But in spite of this, Mr. Dwarris' dream was one of the awful delights of my childhood; and when strangers gathered around the social hearth, and the conversation turned upon supernatural appearances, as it often did in those remote days in lonely country houses, it was always with a thrill of pleasure that I greeted the opening passages of this, the only inexplicable yet true story we possessed.

It was the fact of this possession, perhaps, which made the tale dear to me—other stories belonged to other people; it was their friends or their relatives who had seen ghosts, and been honoured with warnings, but Mr. Dwarris' dream was our property.

We owned it as we owned the old ash tree that grew on the lawn. Though Mr. Dwarris was dead and gone, though at the age of threescore years and ten he had departed from a world which had used him very kindly, and which he had enjoyed thoroughly, to another world that he only knew anything of by hearsay, that in fact he only believed in after the vague gentlemanly sceptical fashion which was considered the correct thing about the beginning of this century, still he had been a friend of our quiet and non-illustrious family.

In our primitive society he had been considered a man of fashion, a person whose opinions might safely be repeated, whose decisions were not to be lightly contradicted. He was kind enough in the days when postage was very high (would those days could come back again) to write long letters to his good friends who lived far away from Court, and craved for political and fashionable gossip—long letters filled with scraps of news and morsels of scandal, which furnished topics of conversation for many days and weeks, and made pleasant little breaks in the monotony of that country existence.

By my parents, and by the chosen friends who were invited to dinner when he honoured our poor house with his presence, he was looked up to as a learned and travelled man of the world.

He had read everything at a time when people did not read so much as is the case at present. He had not merely made the grand tour, but he had wintered frequently abroad, and the names of princesses, duchesses, and counts flowed as glibly off his tongue as those of the vicar and family doctor from the lips of less fortunate mortals.

The best china was produced, and the children kept well out of the way while he remained in the house.

The accessories of his toilette table were a fearful mystery to our servants, and the plan he had of leaving his vails under his bolster or the soap dish, a more inscrutable mystery still.

He did not smoke, and though that was a time when the reputation of hard drinking carried with it no stigma—quite the reverse indeed—he was temperate to a degree. While not utterly insensible to the charms of female beauty, he regarded the sex rather as a critical than a devoted admirer, and he was wont to consider any unusually handsome woman as practically thrown away on our society.

He used to talk much of the "West End," and, to sum up the matter, he spoke as one having authority.

Looking back at his pretensions from a point of observation which has not been attained without a considerable amount of acquaintance, pleasant and otherwise, with men of the same rank in life and standing in society, I am inclined to think that Mr. Dwarris was, to a certain extent, a humbug; that he was not such a great man as our neighbours imagined, and that the style in which he lived at home was much less luxurious than that in which my parents considered it necessary to indulge when he honoured us with a visit.

Further, I believe the time he spent with us, instead of proving irksome and uncongenial to his superior mind, were periods of the most thorough enjoyment. Looking over his letters—which still remain duly labelled and tied up—I can see the natural man breaking through the conventional. I can perceive how happy a change it was for him to leave a life passed amongst people, richer, better born, cleverer, more fashionable than himself, in order to stay with friends who looked up to him, and believed in their simplicity; it was an honour to receive so great a man.

I understand that he had no genius, that he had little talent, that he loved the world and the high places thereof, that he had no passion for anything whether in nature or art, but that he had acquired a superficial knowledge of most subjects, and that he affected a fondness for painting, music, sculpture, literature, because he considered rich fondness the mark of a refined mind, and because the men and the women with whom he associated were content to think so too.

But when he recalls with words of pleasure the journey he and my father made through the wilds of Connemara, when he speaks with tenderest affection of his old friend Woodville—(my maternal grandfather's name was Woodville)—when he sends a word of kindly remembrance to each of the servants, who have been always happy to see, and wait upon him, I feel that the gloss and the pretension of learning were but superficial, that the man had really a heart, which, under happier auspices, would have rendered him a more useful and beloved member of society, instead of an individual in whose acquaintance we merely felt a pride, who was, as I have before said, one of our cherished possessions.

He was never married; he had no near relatives so far as we ever knew, and he lived all alone in a large house in a large English town, which, for sufficient reasons, I shall call Callersfield.

In his early youth he had been engaged in business, but the death of a distant relative leaving him independent of his own exertions, he severed all connexion with trade, and went abroad to study whatever may be, in foreign parts, analogous to "Shakespeare and the musical glasses" in England.

To the end of his life—long after travelling became a much easier and safer matter than it was towards the close of the last century—he retained his fondness for continental wanderings, and my mother's cabinets and my father's hot-houses bore ample testimony to the length of his journeys and the strength of his friendship. Seeds of rare plants, and bulbs from almost every country in Europe, found their way to our remote home, whilst curiosities of all kinds were sent with the best wishes of "an old friend," to swell that useless olio of oddities that were at once the wonder and admiration of my juvenile imagination.

But at length all these good gifts came to an end. No more lava snuff-boxes and Pompeian vases; no more corals, or fans, or cameos, or inlaid boxes; no more gorgeous lilies or rare exotics; for news arrived one morning that the donor had started on his last journey, and gone to that land whence no presents can be delivered by coach, railway, or parcels company, to assuage the grief of bereaved relatives. He was dead, and in due time there arrived at our house two of the most singular articles (as the matter appears to me now), that were ever forwarded without accessories of any kind to set them off, to people who had really been on terms of closest intimacy with the deceased.

One was a plaster bust of Mr. Dwarris, the other a lithograph likeness of the same gentleman.

The intrinsic value of the two might in those days have been five shillings, but then, as his heirs delicately put it, they knew my parents would value these mementoes of their lamented friend far beyond any actual worth which they might possess.

Where, when the old home was broken up, and the household gods scattered, that bust vanished I can form no idea, but the lithograph is still in my possession; and as I look at it I feel my mother's statement to have been utterly true, namely, that Mr. Dwarris was not a man either to be deluded by his imagination, or to tell a falsehood wittingly.

Perhaps in the next world some explanation may have been vouchsafed to him about his dream, but on this side of the grave he always professed himself unable to give the slightest solution of it.

"I am not a man," he was wont to declare, "inclined to believe in the supernatural;" and indeed he was not, whether in nature or religion.

To be sure he was secretly disposed to credit that great superstition which many persons now openly profess—of an universe without a Creator, of a future without a Redeemer—but still this form of credulity proceeds rather from an imperfect development of the reason than from a disordered state of the imagination.

In the ordinary acceptation of the word he was not superstitious. He was hard headed and he was cold-blooded—essentially a man to be trusted implicitly when he said such and such a thing had happened within his own experience.

"I never could account for it in any way," he declared—"and if it had chanced to another person, I should have believed he had made some mistake in the matter. For this reason, I have always felt shy of repeating my dream—but I do not mind telling it to you to-night."

And then he proceeded to relate the story which thenceforth became our property—the most enduring gift he ever gave us.

This is the tale he told while the wind was howling outside, and the snow falling upon the earth, and the woodfire crackling and leaping as a fit accompaniment.

I did not hear him recite his adventures—but I have often sat and listened while the story was rehearsed to fresh auditors—almost in his own words.

"The first time that I went abroad," he began, "I made acquaintance with Sir Harry Hareleigh. How our acquaintance commenced is of no consequence—but it soon ripened into a close friendship, which was only broken by his death. His father and my father had been early friends also—but worldly reverses had long separated our family from that of the Hareleighs, and it was only by the merest chance I resumed my connection with it. Sir Harry was the youngest son—but his brothers having all died before their father, he came into his title early—though he did not at the same time succeed to any very great amount of property.

"A large but unentailed estate, owned by a bachelor Ralph Hareleigh, would, people imagined, ultimately come into his hands—but Sir Harry himself considered this doubtful—for there was a cousin of his own who longed for the broad acres, and spent much of his time at Dulling Court, which was the name of Mr. Ralph Hareleigh's seat.

"'No one,' Sir Harry declared, 'should ever be able to say he sat watching for dead men's shoes;' and so he spent all his time abroad—visiting picture galleries and studios, and mixing much among artists and patrons and lovers of art.

"It seemed to me in those days that he was wasting his existence, and that a man of his rank and abilities ought to have remained more in his own country, and associated more with those of his own standing in society—but whenever I ventured to hint this to him, he only answered that—

"'England had been a cruel stepdame to him, and that of his own free-will he would never spend a day in his native country again.'

"He had a villa near Florence, where he resided when he was not wandering over the earth; and there I spent many happy weeks in his society—before returning, as it was needful and expedient for me to do, to Callersfield.

"We had been separated for some years—during the whole of which time we corresponded regularly, when one night I dreamt a dream which is as vivid to me now as it was a quarter of a century ago.

"I know I was well in health at the time—that I was undisturbed in my mind—that especially my thoughts had not been straying after Sir Harry Hareleigh. I had heard from him about a month previously, and he said in his letter that he purposed wintering in Vienna, where it would be a great pleasure if I could join him. I had replied that I could not join him at Vienna, but that it was not impossible we might meet the following spring if he felt disposed to spend a couple of months with me in Spain, a country which I then desired to visit.

"I was, therefore, not expecting to see him for half a year, at all events—and had certainly no thought of his arrival in England, and yet when I went to bed on the night in question, this was what happened to me. I dreamt that towards the close of an autumn day I was sitting reading by the window of my library—you remember how my house is situated at the corner of two streets, and that there is a slight hill from the town up to it—you may recollect, also, perhaps, that the windows of my library face on this ascent, while the hall door opens into King Charles Street. Well, I was sitting reading as I have said, with the light growing dimmer and dimmer, and the printed characters getting more and more indistinct, when all at once my attention was aroused by the appearance of a hackney coach driven furiously up Martyr Hill.

"The man was flogging his horses unmercifully, and they cantered up the ascent at a wonderful pace. I rose and watched the vehicle turn the corner of King Charles Street, when of course it disappeared from my observation. I remained, however, standing at the window looking out on the gathering twilight, and but little curious concerning a loud double knock which resounded through the house. Next moment, however, the library door opened, and in walked Sir Harry Hareleigh.

"'I want you to do me a favour, Dwarris,' were almost his first words. 'Can you—will you—come with me on a journey? Your man will just have time to pack a few clothes up for you, and then we shall be able to catch the coach that leaves "The Maypole" at seven. I have this moment arrived from Italy, and will explain everything as we go along. Can you give me a crust of bread and a glass of wine?'

"I rang the bell and ordered in refreshments. While he was hastily swallowing his food, Sir Harry told me that Ralph Hareleigh was dead and had left him every acre of land he owned and every guinea of money he possessed. 'He heard, it appears,' added Sir Harry, 'that my cousin George had raised large sums of money on the strength of certainly being his heir, so he cut him out and left the whole to me, saddled with only one condition, namely, that I should marry within six months from the date of his death.'

"'And when do the six months expire?' I inquired.

"'There's the pull!' he answered. 'By some accident my lawyer's first letter never reached me; and if by good fortune it had not occurred to him to send one of his clerks with a second epistle, I should have been done out of my inheritance. There is only a bare month left for me to make all my arrangements.'

"'And where are you going now?' I asked.

"'To Dulling Court,' he returned, 'and we have not a moment to lose if we are to catch the mail.'

"Those were the days in which gentlemen travelled with their pistols ready for use, and you may be sure I did not forget mine. My valise was carried out to the hackney carriage; Sir Harry and I stepped into the vehicle, and before I had time to wonder at my friend's sudden appearance, we were at the 'Maypole,' and taking our places as inside passengers to Warweald, from whence our route lay across country to Dulling.

"When we had settled ourselves comfortably, put on our travelling-caps, and buttoned our great coats up to our throats, I looked out to see whether any other passengers were coming.

"As I did so, my eye fell on a man who stood back a little from the crowd that always surrounds a coach at starting time, and there was something about him which riveted my attention, though I could not have told why.

"He was an evil-looking man, dressed in decent but very common clothes, and he stood leaning up against the wall of the 'Maypole,' and, as it chanced, directly under the light of an oil-lamp.

"It was this circumstance which enabled me to get so good a view of his face, of his black hair and reddish whiskers, of his restless brown eyes, and dark complexion.

"The contrast between his complexion and his whiskers I remember struck me forcibly, as did also a certain discrepancy between his dress and his appearance.

"He did not stand exactly as a man of his apparent class would stand, and I noticed that he bit his nails nervously, a luxury I never observed an ordinary working man indulge in.

"Further, he stared not at what was going on, but persistently at the coach window until he discovered my scrutiny, when he turned on his heel and walked away down the street.

"Somehow I seemed to breathe more freely when once he was gone: but as the coach soon started I forgot all about him, until two or three stages after, happening to get out of the coach for a glass of brandy, I beheld the same man standing at a little distance and watching the coach as before.

"My first impulse was to go up and speak to him, but a moment's reflection showed me that I should only place myself in a ridiculous position by doing so. No doubt the man was merely a passenger like ourselves, and if he chose to lean up against the wall of the inn while the horses were being changed, it was clearly no business of mine.

"At the next stage, however, when I looked out for him he was nowhere to be seen, and I thought no more of the matter till on arriving at Warweald I chanced to put my head out of the window furthest from the inn, when by the light of one of the coach lamps I saw my gentleman drop down from the roof and walk away into the darkness. We went into the inn parlour whilst post horses were put to, and then I told Sir Harry what I had witnessed.

"'Very likely a Bow Street runner,' he said, 'keeping some poor wretch well in sight. I should not wonder if the old gentleman who snored so persistently for the last twenty miles, be a hardened criminal on whom your friend will clap handcuffs, the moment he gets the warrant to arrest him.'

"The explanation seemed so reasonable that I marvelled it had not occurred to me before, and then I suppose I went off into deeper sleep, for I have only a vague recollection of dreaming afterwards, how we travelled miles and miles in a post chaise, how we ploughed through heavy country lanes, how we passed through dark plantations, and how we stopped at last in front of an old-fashioned way-side house.

"It was a fine night when we arrived there, but the wind was high and drifted black clouds over the moon's face. We alighted at this point and I remember how the place was engraved on my memory.

"It was an old inn, with a large deep door-way, two high gables, and small latticed windows. There were tall trees in front of it, and from one of these the sign *'A Bleeding Heart'* depended, rocking moanfully to and fro in the breeze. There were only a few leaves left on the branches, but the wind caught up those which lay scattered on the ground, and whirled them through the air. Not a soul appeared as our chaise drove up to the door. The postilion, however, applied the butt end of his whip with such vigour to the door that a head was soon thrust from one of the windows, and a gruff voice demanded, 'what the devil we wanted.'

"Just as he was about to answer, moved by some sudden impulse, I turned suddenly round and beheld stealing away in the shadow, my friend with the dark complexion and the red whiskers.

"At this juncture I awoke—always at this juncture I awoke, for I dreamt the same dream over and over again, till I really grew afraid of going to bed at night.

"I used to wake up bathed in perspiration with a horror on me such as I have never felt in my waking moments. I could not get the man's face out of my mind—waking I was constantly thinking of it, sleeping I reproduced it in my dreams—and at length I became so nervous that I had determined to seek relief either in medical advice or change of scene—when one evening in the late autumn as I sat reading in my library—the identical coach I had beheld in my dream drove up Martyr Hill, and next moment Sir Harry and I grasped hands.

"Though I had the dream in my mind all the while, something with-held me from mentioning it to him. We had always laughed at warnings and such things as old woman's tales, and so I let him talk on just as he had talked to me in my dream, and he ate and drank, and we went down together to the 'Maypole' and took our seats in the coach.

"You may be sure I looked well up the street, and down the street, to see if there were any sign of my friend with the whiskers, but not a trace of him could I discern. Somewhat relieved by this I leaned back in my corner, and really in the interest of seeing and talking to my old companion again, I forgot all about my dream, until the arrival of another passenger caused me to shift my position a little, when I glanced out again, and there standing under the lamp—with his restless brown eyes, his dark complexion and his red whiskers—stood the person whom I had never before seen in the flesh, biting his nails industriously.

"'Just look out for a moment, Hareleigh,' I said drawing back from the window, 'there is a man standing under the lamp I want you to notice.'

"'I see no man,' answered Sir Harry, and when I looked out again neither did I.

"As in my dream, however, I had beheld the stranger at different stages of our journey, so I beheld him at different stages with my waking eyes.

"Standing at the hotel at Warweald, I spoke seriously to my companion concerning the mysterious passenger, when to my amazement he repeated the same words I had heard in my dream.

"'Now, Hareleigh,' I said, 'this is getting past a joke. You know I am not superstitious, or given to take fancies, and yet I tell you I have had a warning about that man and I feel confident he means mischief,' and then I told Sir Harry my dream, and described to him the inn upon our arrival at which I had invariably awakened.

"'There is no such inn anywhere on the road between here and Dulling,' he answered after a moment's silence, and then he turned towards the fire again and knit his brow, and there ensued a disagreeable pause.

"'If I have offended you,' I remarked at last.

"'My dear friend,' he replied in an earnest voice, 'I am not offended, I am only alarmed. When I left the continent I hoped that I had put the sea between myself and my enemy; but what you say makes me fear that I am being dogged to my death. I have narrowly escaped assassination twice within the last three months, and I know every movement of mine has been watched, that there have been spies upon me. Even on board the vessel by which I returned to England I was nearly pitched overboard; at the time I regarded it as an accident, but if your dream be true, that was, as this is, the result of a premeditated plan.'

"'Then let us remain here for the night,' I urged.

"'Impossible,' he answered. 'I must reach Dulling before to-morrow morning, or otherwise the only woman I ever wanted to marry or ever shall marry will have dropped out of my life a second time.'

"'And she,' I suggested.

"'Is the widow of Lord Warweald, and she leaves for India to-morrow with her brother the Honourable John Moffat.'

"'Then,' said I, 'you can have no difficulty in fulfilling the conditions of Mr. Ralph Hareleigh's will.'

"'Not if she agrees to marry me,' he answered.

"At that moment the chaise was announced, and we took our places in it.

"Over the country roads, along lonely lanes, we drove almost in silence.

"Somehow Sir Harry's statement and the memory of my own dream made me feel anxious and nervous. Who could this unknown enemy be? had my friend played fast and loose with some lovely Italian, and was this her nearest of kin dogging him to his death?

"Most certainly the man who stood under the lamp at Callersfield had no foreign blood in his veins; spite of his complexion, he was English, in figure, habit, and appearance.

"Could there be any dark secret in Sir Harry's life? I then asked myself. His reluctance to visit England, his reserve about the earlier part of his existence, almost inclined me to this belief; and I was just about settling in my own mind what this secret might probably be, when the postilion suddenly pulled up, and after an examination of his horses' feet informed us that one of them had cast a shoe, and that it was impossible the creature could travel the nine miles which still intervened between us and the next stage.

"'There is an inn, however,' added the boy, 'about a mile from here on the road to Rindon; and if you could make shift to stop there for the night, I will undertake to have you at Dulling Court by nine o'clock in the morning.'

"Hearing this, I looked in the moonlight at my friend, and Sir Harry looked hard at me.

"'It is to happen so,' he said, and flinging himself back in the chaise, fell into a fit of moody musing.

"Meanwhile, as the horses proceeded slowly along, I looked out of the window, and once I could have sworn I saw the shadow of a man flung across the road.

"When I opened the door, however, and jumped out, I could see nothing except the dark trees almost meeting overhead, and the denser undergrowth lying to right and left.

"It was a fine night when we arrived at our destination, just such a night as I had dreamed was to come—moonlight, but with heavy black clouds drifting across the sky.

"There was the inn, there swung the sign, the dead leaves swirled about us as we stood waiting while the post-boy hammered for admittance.

"It all came about as I had dreamt, save that I did not see waking as I had done in my sleep a stealing figure creeping away in the shadow of the house.

"I saw the figure afterwards, but not then.

"We ate in the house, but we did not drink—we made a feint of doing so; but we really poured away the liquor upon the hot ashes that lay underneath the hastily replenished fire, though I believe this caution to have been unnecessary.

"We selected our bed chambers, Sir Harry choosing one which looked out on what our host called the Wilderness, and I selecting another that commanded a view of the garden.

"There were no locks or bolts to the doors, but we determined to pull up such furniture as the rooms afforded, and erect barricades for our protection.

"I wanted to remain in the same apartment with my friend, but he would not hear of such an arrangement.

"'We shall only delay the end,' he said stubbornly, in answer to my entreaties, 'and I have an ounce of lead ready for any one who tries to meddle with me.' So we bade each other good night, and separated.

"I had not the slightest intention of going to bed, so I sat and read my favourite poet till, overpowered by fatigue, I dropped asleep in my chair.

"When I awoke it was with a start; the candle had burnt out, and the moonlight was streaming through the white blind into the room.

"Was it fancy, or did I hear some one actually try my door? I held my breath, and then I knew it was no fancy, for the latch snicked in the lock, then stealthy footsteps crept along the passage and down the stairs.

"In a moment my resolution was taken. Opening my window, I crept on to the sill, and closing the casement after me, dropped into the garden.

"Keeping close against the wall, I crept to the corner of the house, where I concealed myself behind an *arbor vitae*.

"A minute afterwards the man I was watching for came round the opposite corner, and stood for a second looking at the window of Sir Harry's room. There was a pear tree trained against the wall on this side of the house, and up it he climbed with more agility than I should have expected from his appearance.

"I had my pistol in my hand, and felt inclined to wing him while he was fighting with the crazy fastening, and trying to open the window without noise, but I refrained. I wanted to see the play out; I desired to see his game, and so the moment he was in the room I climbed the pear tree also, and raising my eyes just above the sill, and lifting the blind about an inch, looked in.

"Like myself, Hareleigh had not undressed, but he lay stretched on the bed with his right hand under his head, and his left flung across his body.

"He was fast asleep, his pistols lay on a chair beside him, and I could see he had so far followed my advice as to have dragged an ancient secretaire* across the door.

"By the moonlight I got a good view now of the individual who had for so long a time troubled my dreams. As he stealthily moved the pistols he turned his profile a little towards the window, and then I knew what I already suspected, viz., that the man who had travelled with us from Callersfield was identical with the man who now stood beside Sir Harry meaning to murder him.

"It was the dream in that hour which seemed the reality, and the reality the dream.

"For an instant he stooped over my friend, and then I saw him raise his hand to strike, but the same moment I took deliberate aim, and before the blow could fall, fired and shot him in the right shoulder.

"There was a shriek and an imprecation, a rush to the window, where we met, he trying to get out, I striving to get in.

"I grappled with him, but having no secure foothold the impetus of his body was too much for me, and we both fell to the ground together. The force of the fall stunned me, I suppose, for I remember nothing of what followed till I found myself lying on a sofa in the inn, with Hareleigh sitting beside me.

"'Don't talk! for God's sake don't talk!' he entreated. 'We shall be out of this in five minutes' time if you think you can bear the shaking. I have

---

* An archaic term for a writing desk.

made the landlord lend us another horse, and we shall be at Dulling in two hours' time. There you shall tell me all about it.'

"But there I never told him all about it. Before we reached our next stage I was far too ill to travel further, and for weeks I lay between life and death at the 'Green Man and Still,' Aldney.

"When I was strong enough to sit up with him, Harry and Lady Hareleigh came over from Dulling to see me, but it was months before I could bear to speak of the events of that night, and though I never dreamed my dream again, it left its traces on me for life.

"Till the day of his death, however, Sir Harry always regarded me as his preserver, and the warmest welcome to Dulling Court was given by his wife to one whom she honoured by calling her dearest friend.

"When Sir Harry died, he left me joint guardian with Lady Hareleigh of his children. So carefully worded a will, I never read—in the event of the death of his children without issue, he bequeathed Dulling Court to various charitable institutions.

"'A most singular disposition of his property,' I remarked to his lawyer.

"'Depend upon it, my dear sir, he had his reasons,' that individual replied.

"'And those—' I suggested.

"'I must regard as strictly private and confidential.'

"The most singular part of my narrative has yet to come," Mr. Dwarris continued after a pause.

"Many years after Sir Harry's death, it chanced I arrived at a friend's house on the evening before the nomination day of an election, which it was expected would be hotly contested.

"'Mr. Blair's wealth of course gives him a great advantage,' sighed my hostess, 'and we all do dislike him so cordially—I would give anything to see him lose.'

"Accustomed to such thoroughly feminine and logical sentiments, I attached little importance to the lady's remarks, and with only a very slight feeling of interest in the matter, next morning accompanied my friend to the county town where the nomination was to take place.

"We were rather late in starting, and before our arrival Mr. Blair had commenced his harangue to the crowd.

"He was talking loudly and gesticulating violently with his left hand when I first caught sight of him. He was telling the free and independent electors that they knew who he was, what he was, and why he supported such and such a political party.

"At intervals he was interrupted by cheers and hisses, but at the end of one of his most brilliant perorations, I who had been elbowing my way through the crowd, shouted out at the top of my voice—

"'How about the man you tried to murder at the "Bleeding Heart?"'

"For a moment there was a dead silence, then the mob took up my cry—

"'How about the man you tried to murder at the "Bleeding Heart?"'

"I saw him look round as if a ghost had spoken, then he fell suddenly back, and his friends carried him off the platform.

"My hostess had her wish, for his opponent walked over the course, and a few weeks afterwards I read in the papers—

"'Died—At Hollingford Hall, in his forty-sixth year, George Hareleigh Blair, Esq., nephew of the late Ralph Hareleigh, Esq., of Dulling Court.

"'He married a Miss Blair, I presume,' I said to my host.

"'Yes, for her money,' was the reply, 'she had two hundred thousand pounds.'

"'So the mystery of the Bleeding Heart was cleared up at last; but on this side the grave I do not expect to understand how I chanced to dream of a man I had never seen—of places I had never visited—of events of which I was not then cognizant—of conversations which had then still to take place."

THE PORTRAIT

by Margaret Oliphant

1885

Margaret Oliphant Wilson was born in Musselburgh, near Edinburgh. Her first novel, Passages in the Life of Mrs. Margaret Maitland, *was published in 1849 when she was twenty-one, and her second,* Caleb Field, *three years later, in 1851. That was the year when she met the publisher William Blackwood in Edinburgh and was invited to contribute to his prestigious* Blackwood's Magazine: *she would go on to write over a hundred articles for that magazine alone.*

In 1852 she married Frank Oliphant, a cousin on her mother's side (becoming Margaret Oliphant Wilson Oliphant) and moved to London. Her life was dogged by tragedy: three of her six children died in infancy, and in 1859 Frank died of tuberculosis in Rome, where they had moved for the sake of his health. Left without resources, Margaret moved back to England with her three surviving children and strove to support them with her writing. In 1864 her daughter Maggie died in Rome, and was buried in her father's grave. Margaret's brother returned from Canada after suffering financial ruin there, adding his support and that of his children to Margaret's burdens.

Her two remaining sons, Cyril and Francis, entered Eton and Margaret moved to Windsor to be closer to them. For more than thirty years, she kept writing, but when

Cyril died in 1890 and Francis in 1894, she lost interest in life and began a decline that resulted in her own death in 1897.

Mrs. Oliphant, as she was credited in most of her works, was a remarkably prolific writer. Her bibliography includes novels, histories, travelogues, and literary criticism as well as countless articles on a wide range of topics. Her horror stories include "The Open Door" and "The Library Window," both great favorites of anthologists, and several others that are less well known. One of these is "The Portrait." Part ghost story and part morality tale, it takes up a common Victorian theme—the uncomfortable relationship between profit and conscience—as a young man becomes the unwilling medium in a dispute between his businesslike father and his long-dead mother.

A t the period when the following incidents occurred I was living with my father at The Grove, a large old house in the immediate neighbourhood of a little town. This had been his home for a number of years; and I believe I was born in it. It was a kind of house which, notwithstanding all the red and white architecture, known at present by the name of Queen Anne, builders nowadays have forgotten how to build. It was straggling and irregular, with wide passages, wide staircases, broad landings; the rooms large but not very lofty; the arrangements leaving much to be desired, with no economy of space: a house belonging to a period when land was cheap, and, so far as that was concerned, there was no occasion to economise. Though it was so near the town, the clump of trees in which it was environed was a veritable grove. In the grounds in spring the primroses grew as thickly as in the forest. We had a few fields for the cows, and an excellent walled garden. The place is being pulled down at this moment to make room for more streets of mean little houses,—the kind of thing, and not a dull house of faded gentry, which perhaps the neighbourhood requires. The house was dull, and so were we, its last inhabitants; and the furniture was faded, even a little dingy,—nothing to brag of. I do not, however, intend to convey a suggestion that we were faded gentry, for that was not the case. My father, indeed, was rich, and had no need to spare any expense in making his life and his house bright if he pleased; but he did not please, and I had not been long enough at home to exercise any special influence of my own. It was the only home I had ever known; but except in my earliest childhood, and in my holidays as a schoolboy, I had in reality known but little of it. My mother had died at my birth, or shortly after, and I had grown up in the gravity and silence of a house without women. In my infancy, I believe, a sister of my father's had lived with us, and taken charge of the household and of me; but she, too, had died long, long ago, my mourning for her being one of the first things I could rec-ollect. And she had no successor. There was, indeed, a housekeeper and some maids,—the latter of whom I only saw disappearing at the end of a passage, or whisking out of a room when one of "the gentlemen" appeared. Mrs. Weir, indeed, I saw nearly every day; but a curtsey, a smile, a pair of nice round arms which she caressed while folding them across her ample waist, and a large white apron, were all I knew of her. This was the only female influence in the house. The drawing-room I was aware of only as a place of deadly good order, into which nobody ever entered. It had three long windows opening on the lawn, and communicated at the upper end, which was rounded like a great bay, with the conservatory. Sometimes I gazed into it as a child from without, wondering at the needlework on the chairs, the screens, the looking-glasses which never reflected any living face. My father did not like the room, which probably was not wonderful, though it never occurred to me in those early days to inquire why.

I may say here, though it will probably be disappointing to those who form a sentimental idea of the capabilities of children, that it did not occur to me either, in these early days, to make any inquiry about my mother. There was no room in life, as I knew it, for any such person; nothing sug-gested to my mind either the fact that she must have existed, or that there was need of her in the house. I accepted, as I believe most children do, the facts of existence, on the basis with which I had first made acquaintance with them, without question or remark. As a matter of fact, I was aware that it was rather dull at home; but neither by comparison with the books I read, nor by the communications received from my school-fellows, did this seem to me anything remarkable. And I was possibly somewhat dull too by nature, for I did not mind. I was fond of reading, and for that there was unbounded opportunity. I had a little ambition in respect to work, and that too could be prosecuted undisturbed. When I went to the university, my society lay almost entirely among men; but by that time and afterwards, matters had of course greatly changed with me, and though I recognised women as part of the economy of nature, and did not indeed by any means dislike or avoid them, yet the idea of connecting them at all with my own home never entered into my head. That continued to be as it had always been, when at intervals I descended upon the cool, grave, colourless place, in the midst of my traffic with the world: always very still, well-ordered, serious—the cooking very good, the comfort perfect—old Morphew, the butler, a little older (but very little older, perhaps on the whole less old, since in my childhood I had thought him a kind of Methuselah), and Mrs. Weir, less active, covering up her arms in sleeves, but folding and caressing them just as always. I remember looking in from the lawn through the windows upon that deadly-orderly drawingroom, with a humorous recollection of my childish admiration and wonder, and feeling that it must be kept so for ever and ever, and that to go into it would break some sort of amusing mock mystery, some pleasantly ridiculous spell.

But it was only at rare intervals that I went home. In the long vacation, as in my school holidays, my father often went abroad with me, so that we had gone over a great deal of the Continent together very pleasantly. He was old in proportion to the age of his son, being a man of sixty when I was twenty, but that did not disturb the pleasure of the relations between us. I don't know that they were ever very confidential. On my side there was but little to communicate, for I did not get into scrapes nor fall in love, the two predicaments which demand sympathy and confidences. And as for my father himself, I was never aware what there could be to communicate on his side. I knew his life exactly—what he did almost at every hour of the day; under what circumstances of the temperature he would ride and when walk; how often and with what guests he would indulge in the occasional break of a dinner-party, a serious pleasure,—perhaps, indeed, less a pleasure than a duty. All this I knew as well as he did, and also his views on public matters, his political opinions, which naturally were different from mine. What ground, then, remained for confidence? I did not know any. We were both of us of a reserved nature, not apt to enter into our religious feelings, for instance. There are many people who think reticence on such subjects a sign of the most reverential way of contemplating them. Of this I am far from being sure; but, at all events, it was the practice most congenial to my own mind.

And then I was for a long time absent, making my own way in the world. I did not make it very successfully. I accomplished the natural fate of an Englishman, and went out to the Colonies; then to India in a semidiplomatic position; but returned home after seven or eight years, invalided, in bad health and not much better spirits, tired and disappointed with my first trial of life. I had, as people say, "no occasion" to insist on making my way. My father was rich, and had never given me the slightest reason to believe that he did not intend me to be his heir. His allowance to me was not illiberal, and though he did not oppose the carrying out of my own plans, he by no means urged me to exertion. When I came home he received me very affectionately, and expressed his satisfaction in my return. "Of course," he said, "I am not glad that you are disappointed, Philip, or that your health is broken; but otherwise it is an ill wind, you know, that blows nobody good—and I am very glad to have you at home. I am growing an old man—"

"I don't see any difference, sir," said I; "everything here seems exactly the same as when I went away—"

He smiled, and shook his head. "It is true enough," he said, "after we have reached a certain age we seem to go on for a long time on a plane, and feel no great difference from year to year; but it is an inclined plane—and the longer we go on, the more sudden will be the fall at the end. But at all events it will be a great comfort to me to have you here."

"If I had known that," I said, "and that you wanted me, I should have come in any circumstances. As there are only two of us in the world—"

"Yes," he said, "there are only two of us in the world; but still I should not have sent for you, Phil, to interrupt your career."

"It is as well, then, that it has interrupted itself," I said, rather bitterly; for disappointment is hard to bear.

He patted me on the shoulder, and repeated, "It is an ill wind that blows nobody good," with a look of real pleasure which gave me a certain gratification too; for, after all, he was an old man, and the only one in all the world to whom I owed any duty. I had not been without dreams of warmer affections, but they had come to nothing—not tragically, but in the ordinary way. I might perhaps have had love which I did not want, but not that which I did want,—which was not a thing to make any unmanly moan about, but in the ordinary course of events. Such disappointments happen every day; indeed, they are more common than anything else, and sometimes it is apparent afterwards that it is better it was so.

However, here I was at thirty stranded—yet wanting for nothing, in a position to call forth rather envy than pity from the greater part of my contemporaries,—for I had an assured and comfortable existence, as much money as I wanted, and the prospect of an excellent fortune for the future. On the other band, my health was still low, and I had no occupation. The neighbourhood of the town was a drawback rather than an advantage. I felt myself tempted, instead of taking the long walk into the country which my doctor recommended, to take a much shorter one through the High Street, across the river, and back again, which was not a walk but a lounge. The country was silent and full of thoughts—thoughts not always very agreeable—whereas there were always the humours of the little urban population to glance at, the news to be heard, all those petty matters which so often make up life in a very impoverished version for the idle man. I did not like it, but I felt myself yielding to it, not having energy enough to make a stand The rector and the leading lawyer of the place asked me to dinner. I might have glided into the society, such as it was, bad I been disposed for that—everything about me began to close over me as if I had been fifty, and fully contented with my lot.

It was possibly my own want of occupation which made me observe with surprise, after a while, how much occupied my father was. He had expressed himself glad of my return; but now that I had returned, I saw very little of him. Most of his time was spent in his library, as had always been the case. But on the few visits I paid him there, I could not but perceive that the aspect of the library was much changed. It had acquired the look of a business-room, almost an office. There were large business-like books on the table, which I could not associate with anything he could naturally have to do; and his correspondence was very large. I thought he closed one of those books hurriedly as I came in, and pushed it away, as if he did not wish me to see it. This surprised me at the moment, without arousing any other feeling; but afterwards I remembered it with a clearer sense of what it meant. He was more absorbed altogether than I had been used to see him. He was visited by men, sometimes not of very prepossessing appearance. Surprise grew in my mind without any very distinct idea of the reason of it; and it was not till after a chance conversation with Morphew that my vague uneasiness began to take definite shape. It was begun without any special intention on my part. Morphew had informed me that master was very busy, on some occasion when I wanted to see him. And I was a little annoyed to be thus put off: "It appears to me that my father is always busy," I said, hastily. Morphew then began very oracularly to nod his head in assent.

"A deal too busy, sir, if you take my opinion," he said.

This startled me much, and I asked hurriedly, "What do you mean?" without reflecting that to ask for private information from a servant about my father's habits was as bad as investigating into a stranger's affairs. It did not strike me in the same light.

"Mr. Philip," said Morphew, "a thing 'as 'appened as 'appens more often than it ought to. Master has got awful keen about money in his old age."

"That's a new thing for him," I said.

"No, sir, begging your pardon, it ain't a new thing. He was once broke of it, and that wasn't easy done; but it's come back, if you'll excuse me saying so. And I don't know as he'll ever be broke of it again at his age."

I felt more disposed to be angry than disturbed by this. "You must be making some ridiculous mistake," I said, "And if you were not so old a friend as you are, Morphew, I should not have allowed my father to be so spoken of to me."

The old man gave me a half-astonished, half contemptuous look. "He's been my master a deal longer than he's been your father," he said, turning on his heel. The assumption was so comical that my anger could not stand in face of it. I went out, having been on my way to the door when this conversation occurred, and took my usual lounge about, which was not a satisfactory sort of amusement. Its vanity and emptiness appeared to be more evident than usual to-day. I met half-a-dozen people I knew, and had as many pieces of news confided to me. I went up and down the length of the High Street. I made a small purchase or two. And then I turned homeward—despising myself, yet finding no alternative within my reach. Would a long country walk have been more virtuous?—it would at least have been more wholesome—but that was all that could be said. My mind did not dwell on Morphew's communication. It seemed without sense or meaning to me; and after the excellent joke about his superior interest in his master to mine in my father, was dismissed lightly enough from my mind. I tried to invent some way of telling this to my father without letting him perceive that Morphew had been finding faults in him, or I listening; for it seemed a pity to lose so good a joke. However, as I returned home, something happened which put the joke entirely out of my head. It is curious when a new subject of trouble or anxiety has been suggested to the mind in an unexpected way, how often a second advertisement follows immediately after the first, and gives to that a potency which in itself it had not possessed.

I was approaching our own door, wondering whether my father had gone, and whether, on my return, I should find him at leisure—for I had several little things to say to him—when I noticed a poor woman lingering about the closed gates. She had a baby sleeping in her arms. It was a spring night, the stars shining in the twilight, and everything soft and dim; and the woman's figure was like a shadow, flitting about, now here, now there, on one side or another of the gate. She stopped when she saw me approaching, and hesitated for a moment, then seemed to take a sudden resolution. I watched her without knowing, with a prevision that she was going to address me, though with no sort of idea as to the subject of her address. She came up to me doubtfully, it seemed, yet certainly, as I felt, and when she was close to me, dropped a sort of hesitating curtsey, and said, "It's Mr. Philip?" in a low voice.

"What do you want with me?" I said.

Then she poured forth suddenly, without warning or preparation, her long speech—a flood of words which must have been all ready and waiting at the doors of her lips for utterance. "Oh, sir, I want to speak to you! I can't believe you'll be so hard, for you're young; and I can't believe he'll be so hard if so be as his own son, as I've always heard he had but one, 'll speak up for us. Oh, gentleman, it is easy for the likes of you, that, if you ain't comfortable in one room, can just walk into another; but if one room is all you have, and every bit of furniture you have taken out of it, and nothing but the four walls left—not so much as the cradle for the child, or a chair for your man to sit down upon when he comes from his work, or a saucepan to cook him his supper—"

"My good woman," I said, "who can have taken all that from you? surely nobody can be so cruel?"

"You say it's cruel!" she cried with a sort of triumph. "Oh, I knowed you would, or any true gentleman that don't hold with screwing poor folks. Just go and say that to him inside there, for the love of God. Tell him to think what he's doing, driving poor creatures to despair. Summer's coming, the Lord be praised, but yet it's bitter cold at night with your counterpane gone; and when you've been working hard all day, and nothing but four bare walls to come home to, and all your poor little sticks of furniture that you've saved up for, and got together one by one, all gone—and you no better than when you started, or rather worse, for then you was young. Oh, sir!" the woman's voice rose into a sort of passionate wail. And then she added, beseechingly, recovering herself—"Oh, speak for us—he'll not refuse his own son—"

"To whom am I to speak? who is it that has done this to you?" I said.

The woman hesitated again, looking keenly in my face—then repeated with a slight faltering, "It's Mr. Philip?" as if that made everything right.

"Yes; I am Philip Canning," I said; "but what have I to do with this? and to whom am I to speak?"

She began to whimper, crying and stopping herself. "Oh, please sir! it's Mr. Canning as owns all the house property about—it's him that our court and the lane and everything belongs to. And he's taken the bed from under us, and the baby's cradle, although it's said in the Bible as you're not to take poor folks's bed."

"My father!" I cried in spite of myself—"then it must be some agent, some one else in his name. You may be sure he knows nothing of it. Of course I shall speak to him at once."

"Oh, God bless you, sir," said the woman. But then she added, in a lower tone—"It's no agent. It's one as never knows trouble. It's him that lives in that grand house." But this was said under her breath, evidently not for me to hear.

Morphew's words flashed through my mind as she spoke. What was this? Did it afford an explanation of the much occupied hours, the big books, the strange visitors? I took the poor woman's name, and gave her something to procure a few comforts for the night, and went indoors disturbed and troubled. It was impossible to believe that my father himself would have acted thus; but he was not a man to brook interference, and I did not see how to introduce the subject, what to say. I could but hope that, at the moment of broaching it, words would be put into my mouth, which often happens in moments of necessity, one knows not how, even when one's theme is not so all-important as that for which such help has been promised. As usual, I did not see my father till dinner. I have said that our dinners were very good, luxurious in a simple way, everything excellent in its kind, well cooked, well served, the perfection of comfort without show—which is a combination very dear to the English heart. I said nothing till Morphew, with his solemn attention to everything that was going, had retired—and then it was with some strain of courage that I began.

"I was stopped outside the gate to-day by a curious sort of petitioner—a poor woman, who seems to be one of your tenants, sir, but whom your agent must have been rather too hard upon."

"My agent? who is that?" said my father, quietly.

"I don't know his name, and I doubt his competence. The poor creature seems to have had everything taken from her—her bed, her child's cradle."

"No doubt she was behind with her rent."

"Very likely, sir. She seemed very poor," said I.

"You take it coolly," said my father, with an upward glance, half-amused, not in the least shocked by my statement. "But when a man, or a woman either, takes a house, I suppose you will allow that they ought to pay rent for it."

"Certainly, sir," I replied, "when they have got anything to pay."

"I don't allow the reservation," he said. But he was not angry, which I had feared he would he.

"I think," I continued, "that your agent must be too severe. And this emboldens me to say something which has been in my mind for some time"—(these were the words, no doubt, which I had hoped would be put

214

into my mouth; they were the suggestion of the moment, and yet as I said them it was with the most complete conviction of their truth)—"and that is this: I am doing nothing; my time hangs heavy on my hands. Make me your agent. I will see for myself, and save you from such mistakes; and it will be an occupation—"

"Mistakes! What warrant have you for saying these are mistakes?" he said testily; then after a moment: "This is a strange proposal from you, Phil. Do you know what it is you are offering?—to be a collector of rents, going about from door to door, from week to week; to look after wretched little bits of repairs, drains, &c.; to get paid, which, after all, is the chief thing, and not to be taken in by tales of poverty."

"Not to let you be taken in by men without pity," I said.

He gave me a strange glance, which I did not very well understand, and said, abruptly, a thing which, so far as I remember, he had never in my life said before, "You've become a little like your mother, Phil—"

"My mother!" The reference was so unusual—nay, so unprecedented—that I was greatly startled. It seemed to me like the sudden introduction of a quite new element in the stagnant atmosphere, as well as a new party to our conversation. My father looked across the table, as if with some astonishment at my tone of surprise.

"Is that so very extraordinary?" he said.

"No; of course it is not extraordinary that I should resemble my mother. Only—I have heard very little of her—almost nothing!"

"That is true." He got up and placed himself before the fire, which was very low, as the night was not cold—had not been cold heretofore at least; but it seemed to me now that a little chill came into the dim and faded room. Perhaps it looked more dull from the suggestion of a something brighter, warmer, that might have been. "Talking of mistakes," he said, "perhaps that was one: to sever you entirely from her side of the house. But I did not care for the connection. You will understand how it is that I speak of it now when I tell you—" He stopped here, however, said nothing more for a minute or so, and then rang the bell. Morphew came, as he always did, very deliberately, so that some time elapsed in silence, during which my surprise grew. When the old man appeared at the door—"Have you put the lights in the drawing-room, as I told you?" my father said.

"Yes, sir; and opened the box, sir; and it's a—it's a speaking likeness." This the old man got out in a great hurry, as if afraid that his master would stop him. My father did so with a wave of his hand.

"That's enough. I asked no information. You can go now."

The door closed upon us, and there was again a pause. My subject had floated away altogether like a mist, though I had been so concerned about it. I tried to resume, but could not. Something seemed to arrest my very breathing: and yet in this dull respectable house of ours, where everything breathed good character and integrity, it was certain that there could be no shameful mystery to reveal. It was some time before my father spoke, not from any purpose that I could see, but apparently because his mind was busy with probably unaccustomed thoughts.

"You scarcely know the drawing-room, Phil," he said at last.

"Very little. I have never seen it used. I have a little awe of it, to tell the truth."

"That should not be. There is no reason for that. But a man by himself, as I have been for the greater part of my life, has no occasion for a drawing-room. I always, as a matter of preference, sat among my books; however, I ought to have thought of the impression on you."

"Oh, it is not important," I said; "the awe was childish. I have not thought of it since I came home."

"It never was anything very splendid at the best," said he. He lifted the lamp from the table with a sort of abstraction, not remarking even my offer to take it from him, and led the way. He was on the verge of seventy, and looked his age: but it was a vigorous age, with no symptoms of giving way. The circle of light from the lamp lit up his white hair, and keen blue eyes, and clear complexion; his forehead was like old ivory, his cheek warmly coloured: an old man, yet a man in full strength. He was taller than I was, and still almost as strong. As he stood for a moment with the lamp in his hand, he looked like a tower in his great height and bulk. I reflected as I looked at him that I knew him intimately, more intimately than any other creature in the world,—I was familiar with every detail of his outward life; could it be that in reality I did not know him at all?

The drawing-room was already lighted with a flickering array of candles upon the mantelpiece and along the walls, producing the pretty starry effect which candles give without very much light. As I had not the smallest idea what I was about to see, for Morphew's "speaking likeness" was very hurriedly said, and only half comprehensible in the bewilderment of my faculties, my first glance was at this very unusual illumination, for which I could assign no reason. The next showed me a large full-length portrait, still in the box in which apparently it had travelled, placed upright, supported against a table in the centre of the room. My father walked straight up to it, motioned to me to place a smaller table close to the picture on the left side, and put his lamp upon that. Then he waved his hand towards it, and stood aside that I might see.

It was a full-length portrait of a very young woman—I might say a girl, scarcely twenty—in a white dress, made in a very simple old fashion, though I was too little accustomed to female costume to be able to fix the date. It might have been a hundred years old, or twenty, for aught I knew. The face had an expression of youth, candour, and simplicity more than any face I had ever seen,—or so, at least, in my surprise, I thought. The eyes were a little wistful with something which was almost anxiety—which at least was not content—in them; a faint, almost imperceptible, curve in the lids. The complexion was of a dazzling fairness, the hair light, but the eyes dark, which gave individuality to the face. It would have been as lovely had the eyes been blue—probably more so—but their darkness gave a touch of character, a slight discord, which made the harmony finer. It was not, perhaps, beautiful in the highest sense of the word. The girl must have been too young, too slight, too little developed for actual beauty; but a face which so invited love and confidence I never saw. One smiled at it with instinctive affection. "What a sweet face!" I said. "What a lovely girl! Who is she? Is this one of the relations you were speaking of on the other side?"

My father made me no reply. He stood aside, looking at it as if he knew it too well to require to look,—as if the picture was already in his eyes. "Yes," he said, after an interval, with a long-drawn breath, "she was a lovely girl, as you say."

"Was?—then she is dead. What a pity!" I said; "what a pity! so young and so sweet!"

We stood gazing at her thus, in her beautiful stillness and calm—two men, the younger of us full grown and conscious of many experiences, the other an old man—before this impersonation of tender youth. At length he said, with a slight tremulousness in his voice, "Does nothing suggest to you who she is, Phil?"

I turned round to look at him with profound astonishment, but he turned away from my look. A sort of quiver passed over his face.

"That is your mother," he said, and walked suddenly away, leaving me there.

My mother!

I stood for a moment in a kind of consternation before the white-robed innocent creature, to me no more than a child; then a sudden laugh broke from me, without any will of mine: something ludicrous, as well as something awful, was in it. When the laugh was over, I found myself with tears in my eyes, gazing, holding my breath. The soft features seemed to melt, the lips to move, the anxiety in the eyes to become a personal inquiry. Ah, no, nothing of the kind; only because of the water in mine. My mother! oh, fair and gentle creature, scarcely woman—how could any man's voice call her by that name! I had little idea enough of what it meant,—had heard it laughed at, scoffed at, reverenced, but never had learned to place it even among the ideal powers of life. Yet, if it meant anything at all, what it meant was worth thinking of. What did she ask, looking at me with those eyes? what would she have said if "those lips had language"? If I had known her only as Cowper did—with a child's recollection—there might have been some thread, some faint but comprehensible link, between us; but now all that I felt was the curious incongruity. Poor child I I said to myself; so sweet a creature: poor little tender soul! as if she had been a little sister, a child of mine,—but my mother! I cannot tell how long I stood looking at her, studying the candid, sweet face, which surely had germs in it of everything that was good and beautiful; and sorry, with a profound regret, that she had died and never carried these promises to fulfilment. Poor girl! poor people who had loved her! These were my thoughts: with a curious vertigo and giddiness of my whole being in the sense of a mysterious relationship, which it was beyond my power to understand.

Presently my father came back: possibly because I had been a long time unconscious of the passage of the minutes, or perhaps because he was himself restless in the strange disturbance of his habitual calm. He came in and put his arm within mine, leaning his weight partially upon me, with an affectionate suggestion which went deeper than words. I pressed his arm to my side: it was more between us two grave Englishmen than any embracing.

"I cannot understand it," I said.

"No. I don't wonder at that; but if it is strange to you, Phil, think how much more strange to me! That is the partner of my life. I have never had another—or thought of another. That—girl! If we are to meet again, as I have always hoped we should meet again, what am I to say to her—I, an old man? Yes; I know what you mean. I am not an old man for my years; but my years are threescore and ten, and the play is nearly played out. How am I to meet that young creature? We used to say to each other that it was for ever, that we never could be but one, that it was for life and death. But what—what am I to say to her, Phil, when I meet her again, that—that angel? No, it is not her being an angel that troubles me; but she is so young! She is like my—my grand-daughter," he cried, with a burst of what was half sobs, half laughter; "and she is my wife,—and I am an old man—an old man! And so much has happened that she could not understand."

I was too much startled by this strange complaint to know what to say. It was not my own trouble, and I answered it in the conventional way.

"They are not as we are, sir," I said; "they look upon us with larger, other eyes than ours."

"Ah! you don't know what I mean," he said quickly; and in the interval he had subdued his emotion. "At first, after she died, it was my consolation to think that I should meet her again—that we never could be really parted. But, my God, how I have changed since then! I am another man—I am a different being. I was not very young even then—twenty years older than she was: but her youth renewed mine. I was not an unfit partner; she asked no better: and knew as much more than I did in some things—being so much nearer the source—as I did in others that were of the world. But I have gone a long way since then, Phil—a long way; and there she stands just where I left her."

I pressed his arm again. "Father," I said, which was a title I seldom used, "we are not to suppose that in a higher life the mind stands still." I did not feel myself qualified to discuss such topics, but something one must say.

"Worse, worse!" he replied; "then she too will be like me, a different being, and we shall meet as what? as strangers, as people who have lost sight of each other, with a long past between us—we who parted, my God! with—with—"

His voice broke and ended for a moment: then while, surprised and almost shocked by what he said, I cast about in my mind what to reply, he withdrew his arm suddenly from mine, and said in his usual tone, "Where shall we hang the picture, Phil? It must be here in this room. What do you think will be the best light?"

This sudden alteration took me still more by surprise, and gave me almost an additional shock; but it was evident that I must follow the changes of his mood, or at least the sudden repression of sentiment which he originated. We went into that simpler question with great seriousness, consulting which would be the best light. "You know I can scarcely advise," I said; "I have never been familiar with this room. I should like to put off, if you don't mind, till daylight."

"I think," he said, "that this would be the best place." It was on the other side of the fireplace, on the wall which faced the windows,—not the best light, I knew enough to be aware, for an oil-painting. When I said so, however, he answered me with a little impatience,—"It does not matter very much about the best light. There will be nobody to see it but you and me. I have my reasons—" There was a small table standing against the wall at this spot, on which he had his hand as he spoke. Upon it stood a little basket in very fine lace-like wickerwork. His hand must have trembled, for the table shook, and the basket fell, its contents turning out upon the carpet,—little bits of needlework, coloured silks, a small piece of knitting half done. He laughed as they rolled out at his feet, and tried to stoop to collect them, then tottered to a chair, and covered for a moment his face with his hands.

No need to ask what they were. No woman's work had been seen in the house since I could recollect it. I gathered them up reverently and put them back. I could see, ignorant as I was, that the bit of knitting was something for an infant. What could I do less than put it to my lips? It had been left in the doing—for me.

"Yes, I think this is the best place," my father said a minute after, in his usual tone. We placed it there that evening with our own hands. The picture was large, and in a heavy frame, but my father would let no one help me but himself. And then, with a superstition for which I never could give any reason even to myself, having removed the packings, we closed and locked the door, leaving the candles about the room, in their soft strange illumination lighting the first night of her return to her old place.

That night no more was said. My father went to his room early, which was not his habit. He had never, however, accustomed me to sit late with him in the library. I had a little study or smoking-room of my own, in which all my special treasures were, the collections of my travels and my favourite books—and where I always sat after prayers, a ceremonial which was regularly kept up in the house. I retired as usual this night to my room, and as usual read—but to-night somewhat vaguely, often pausing to think. When it was quite late, I went out by the glass door to the lawn, and walked round the house, with the intention of looking in at the drawing-room windows, as I had done when a child. But I had forgotten that these windows were all shuttered at night, and nothing but a faint penetration of the light within through the crevices bore witness to the instalment of the new dweller there.

In the morning my father was entirely himself again. He told me without emotion of the manner in which he had obtained the picture. It had belonged to my mother's family, and had fallen eventually into the bands of a cousin of hers, resident abroad—"A man whom I did not like, and who did not like me," my father said; "there was, or bad been, some rivalry, he thought: a mistake, but he was never aware of that. He refused all my requests to have a copy made. You may suppose, Phil, that I wished this very much. Had I succeeded, you would have been acquainted, at least, with your mother's appearance, and need not have sustained this shock. But he would not consent. It gave him, I think, a certain pleasure to think that he had the only picture. But now he is dead—and out of remorse, or with some other intention, has left it to me."

"That looks like kindness," said I.

"Yes; or something else. He might have thought that by so doing he was establishing a claim upon me," my father said: but he did not seem disposed to add any more. On whose behalf he meant to establish a claim I did not know, nor who the man was who had laid us under so great an obligation on his deathbed. He *had* established a claim on me at least: though, as he was dead, I could not see on whose behalf it was. And my father said nothing more. He seemed to dislike the subject. When I attempted to return to it, he had recourse to his letters or his newspapers. Evidently he had made up his mind to say no more.

Afterwards I went into the drawing-room to look at the picture once more. It seemed to me that the anxiety in her eyes was not so evident as I had thought it last night. The light possibly was more favourable. She stood just above the place where, I make no doubt, she had sat in life, where her little work-basket was—not very much above it. The picture was full-length, and we had hung it low, so that she might have been stepping into the room, and was little above my own level as I stood and looked at her again. Once more I smiled at the strange thought that this young creature, so young, almost childish, could be my mother; and once more my eyes grew wet looking at her. He was a benefactor, indeed, who had given her back to us. I said to myself, that if I could ever do anything for him or his, I would certainly do, for my—for this lovely young creature's sake.

And with this in my mind, and all the thoughts that came with it, I am obliged to confess that the other matter, which I had been so full of on the previous night, went entirely out of my head.

It is rarely, however, that such matters are allowed to slip out of one's mind. When I went out in the afternoon for my usual stroll—or rather when I returned from that stroll—I saw once more before me the woman with her baby whose story had filled me with dismay on the previous evening. She was waiting at the gate as before, and—"Oh, gentleman, but haven't you got some news to give me?" she said.

"My good woman—I—have been greatly occupied. I have had—no time to do anything." "Ah!" she said, with a little cry of disappointment, "my man said not to make too sure, and that the ways of the gentlefolks is hard to know."

"I cannot explain to you," I said, as gently as I could, "what it is that has made me forget you. It was an event that can only do you good in the end. Go home now, and see the man that took your things from you, and tell him to come to me. I promise you it shall all be put right."

The woman looked at me in astonishment, then burst forth, as it seemed, involuntarily,—"What! without asking no questions?" After this there came a storm of tears and blessings, from which I made haste to escape, but not without carrying that curious commentary on my rashness away with me— "Without asking no questions?" It might be foolish, perhaps: but after all how slight a matter. To make the poor creature comfortable at the cost of what—a box or two of cigars, perhaps, or some other trifle. And if it should be her own fault, or her husband's—what then? Had I been punished for all my faults, where should I have been now. And if the advantage should be only temporary, what then? To be relieved and comforted even for a day or two, was not that something to count in life? Thus I quenched the fiery dart of criticism which my *protegée* herself had thrown into the transaction, not without a certain sense of the humour of it. Its effect, however, was to make me less anxious to see my father, to repeat my proposal to him, and to call his attention to the cruelty performed in his name. This one case I had taken out of the category of wrongs to be righted, by assuming arbitrarily the position of Providence in my own person—for, of course, I had bound myself to pay the poor creature's rent as well as redeem her goods—and, whatever might happen to her in the future, had taken the past into my own hands. The man came presently to see me who, it seems, had acted as my father's agent in the matter. "I don't know, sir, how Mr. Canning will take it," he said. "He don't want none of those irregular, bad-paying ones in his property. He always says as to look over it and let the rent run on is making things worse in the end. His rule is, 'Never more than a month, Stevens:' that's what Mr. Canning says to me, sir. He says, 'More than that they can't pay. It's no use trying.' And it's a good rule; it's a very good rule. He won't hear none of their stories, sir. Bless you, you'd never get a penny of rent from them small houses if you listened to their tales. But if so be as you'll pay Mrs. Jordan's rent, it's none of my business how it's paid, so long as it's paid, and I'll send her back her things. But they'll just have to be took next time," he added, composedly. "Over and over: it's always the same story with them sort of poor folks—they're too poor for anything, that's the truth," the man said.

Morphew came back to my room after my visitor was gone. "Mr. Philip," he said, "you'll excuse me, sir, but if you're going to pay all the poor folk's rent as have distresses put in, you may just go into the court at once, for it's without end—"

"I am going to be the agent myself, Morphew, and manage for my father: and we'll soon put a stop to that," I said, more cheerfully than I felt.

"Manage for—master," he said, with a face of consternation. "You, Mr. Philip!"

"You seem to have a great contempt for me, Morphew."

He did not deny the fact. He said with excitement, "Master, sir—master don't let himself be put a stop to by any man. Master's—not one to be managed. Don't you quarrel with master, Mr. Philip, for the love of God." The old man was quite pale.

"Quarrel!" I said. "I have never quarrelled with my father, and I don't mean to begin now." Morphew dispelled his own excitement by making up the fire, which was dying in the grate. It was a very mild spring evening, and he made up a great blaze which would have suited December. This is one of many ways in which an old servant will relieve his mind. He muttered all the time as he threw on the coals and wood. "He'll not like it—we all know as he'll not like it. Master won't stand no meddling, Mr. Philip,"—this last he discharged at me like a flying arrow as he closed the door.

I soon found there was truth in what he said. My father was not angry; he was even half amused. "I don't think that plan of yours will hold water, Phil. I hear you have been paying rents and redeeming furniture—that's an expensive game, and a very profitless one. Of course, so long as you are a benevolent gentleman acting for your own pleasure, it makes no difference to me. I am quite content if I get my money, even out of your pockets—so long as it amuses you. But as my collector, you know, which you are good enough to propose to be—"

"Of course I should act under your orders," I said; "but at least you might be sure that I would not commit you to any—to any—" I paused for a word.

"Act of oppression," he said with a smile—"piece of cruelty, exaction— there are half-a dozen words—"

"Sir—" I cried.

"Stop, Phil, and let us understand each other. I hope I have always been a just man. I do my duty on my side, and I expect it from others. It is your benevolence that is cruel. I have calculated anxiously how much credit it is safe to allow; but I will allow no man, or woman either, to go beyond what he or she can make up. My law is fixed. Now you understand. My agents, as you call them, originate nothing—they execute only what I decide—"

"But then no circumstances are taken into account—no bad luck, no evil chances, no loss unexpected."

"There are no evil chances," he said, "there is no bad luck—they reap as they sow. No, I don't go among them to be cheated by their stories, and spend quite unnecessary emotion in sympathising with them. You will find it much better for you that I don't. I deal with them on a general rule, made, I assure you, not without a great deal of thought."

"And must it always be so?" I said. "Is there no way of ameliorating or bringing in a better state of things?"

"It seems not," he said; "we don't get 'no forrarder' in that direction so far as I can see." And then he turned the conversation to general matters.

I retired to my room greatly discouraged that night. In former ages—or so one is led to suppose—and in the lower primitive classes who still linger near the primeval type, action of any kind was, and is, easier than amid the complications of our higher civilisation. A bad man is a distinct entity, against whom you know more or less what steps to take. A tyrant, an oppressor, a bad landlord, a man who lets miserable tenements at a rack-rent (to come down to particulars), and exposes his wretched tenants to all those abominations of which we have heard so much—well! he is more or less a satisfactory opponent. There he is, and there is nothing to be said for him—down with him! and let there be an end of his wickedness. But when, on the contrary, you have before you a good man, a just man, who has considered deeply a question which you allow to be full of difficulty; who regrets, but cannot, being human, avert, the miseries which to some unhappy individuals follow from the very wisdom of his rule,—what can you do—what is to be done? Individual benevolence at haphazard may baulk him here and there, but what have you to put in the place of his well-considered scheme? Charity which makes paupers? or what else? I had not considered the question deeply, but it seemed to me that I now came to a blank wall, which my vague human sentiment of pity and scorn could find no way to breach. There must be wrong somewhere—but where? There must be some change for the better to be made—but how?

I was seated with a book before me on the table, with my head supported on my hands. My eyes were on the printed page, but I was not reading—my mind was full of these thoughts, my heart of great discouragement and despondency, a sense that I could do nothing, yet that there surely must and ought, if I but knew it, be something to do. The fire which Morphew had built up before dinner was dying out, the shaded lamp on my table left all the corners in a mysterious twilight. The house was perfectly still, no one moving: my father in the library, where, after the habit of many solitary years, he liked to be left alone, and I here in my retreat, preparing for the formation of similar habits. I thought all at once of the third member of the party, the new-comer, alone too in the room that had been hers; and there suddenly occurred to me a strong desire to take up my lamp and go to the drawing-room and visit her, to see whether her soft angelic face would give any inspiration. I restrained, however, this futile impulse—for what could the picture say?—and instead wondered what might have been had she lived, had she been there, warmly enthroned beside the warm domestic centre, the hearth which would have been a common sanctuary, the true home. In that case what might have been? Alas! the question was no more simple to answer than the other: she might have been there alone too, her husband's business, her son's thoughts, as far from her as now, when her silent representative held her old place in the silence and darkness. I had known it so, often enough. Love itself does not always give comprehension and sympathy. It might be that she was more to us there, in the sweet image of her undeveloped beauty, than she might have been had she lived and grown to maturity and fading, like the rest.

I cannot be certain whether my mind was still lingering on this not very cheerful reflection, or if it had been left behind, when the strange occurrence came of which I have now to tell: can I call it an occurrence? My eyes were on my book, when I thought I heard the sound of a door opening and shutting, but so far away and faint that if real at all it must have been in a far corner of the house. I did not move except to lift my eyes from the book, as one does instinctively the better to listen; when—But I cannot tell, nor have I ever been able to describe exactly what it was. My heart made all at once a sudden leap in my breast. I am aware that this language is figurative, and that the heart cannot leap: but it is a figure so entirely justified by sensation, that no one will have any difficulty in understanding what I mean. My heart leapt up and began beating wildly in my throat, in my ears, as if my whole being had received a sudden and intolerable shock. The sound went through my head like the dizzy sound of some strange mechanism, a thousand wheels and springs, circling, echoing, working in my brain. I felt the blood bound in my veins, my mouth became dry, my eyes hot, a sense of something insupportable took possession of me. I sprang to my feet, and then I sat down again. I cast a quick glance round me beyond the brief circle of the lamplight, but there was nothing there to account in any way for this sudden extraordinary rush of sensation—nor could I feel any meaning in it, any suggestion, any moral impression. I thought I must be going to be ill, and got out my watch and felt my pulse: it was beating furiously, about 125 throbs in a minute. I knew of no illness that could come on like this without warning, in a moment, and I tried to subdue myself, to say to myself that it was nothing, some flutter of the nerves, some physical disturbance. I laid myself down upon my sofa to try if rest would help me, and kept still—as long as the thumping and throbbing of this wild excited mechanism within, like a wild beast plunging and struggling, would let me. I am quite aware of the confusion of the metaphor—the reality was just so. It was like a mechanism deranged, going wildly with ever-increasing precipitation, like those horrible wheels that from time to time catch a help-less human being in them and tear him to pieces: but at the same time it was like a maddened living creature making the wildest efforts to get free.

When I could bear this no longer I got up and walked about my room; then having still a certain command of myself, though I could not master the com-motion within me, I deliberately took down an exciting book from the shelf, a book of breathless adventure which had always interested me, and tried with that to break the spell. After a few minutes, however, I flung the book aside; I was gradually losing all power over myself. What I should be moved to do,— to shout aloud, to struggle with I know not what; or if I was going mad altogether, and next moment must be a raving lunatic,—I could not tell. I kept looking round, expecting I don't know what: several times, with the corner of my eye I seemed to see a movement, as if some one was stealing out of sight; but when I looked straight, there was never anything but the plain outlines of the wall and carpet, the chairs standing in good order.

At last I snatched up the lamp in my hand and went out of the room. To look at the picture? which had been faintly showing in my imagination from time to time, the eyes, more anxious than ever, looking at me from out the silent air. But no; I passed the door of that room swiftly, moving, it seemed, without any volition of my own, and before I knew where I was going, went into my father's library with my lamp in my hand.

He was still sitting there at his writing-table; he looked up astonished to see me hurrying in with my light. "Phil!" he said, surprised. I remember that I shut the door behind me, and came up to him, and set down the lamp on his table. My sudden appearance alarmed him. "What is the matter?" he cried. "Philip, what have you been doing with yourself?"

I sat down on the nearest chair and gasped, gazing at him. The wild commotion ceased, the blood subsided into its natural channels, my heart resumed its place. I use such words as mortal weakness can to express the sensations I felt. I came to myself thus, gazing at him, confounded, at once by the extraordinary passion which I had gone through, and its sudden cessation. "The matter? "I cried; "I don't know what is the matter."

My father had pushed his spectacles up from his eyes. He appeared to me as faces appear in a fever, all glorified with light which is not in them—his eyes glowing, his white hair shining like silver; but his look was severe. "You are not a boy, that I should reprove you; but you ought to know better," he said.

Then I explained to him, so far as I was able, what had happened. Had happened? nothing had happened. He did not understand me—nor did I, now that it was over, understand myself; but he saw enough to make him aware that the disturbance in me was serious, and not caused by any folly of my own. He was very kind as soon as he had assured himself of this, and talked, taking pains to bring me back to unexciting subjects. He had a letter in his hand with a very deep border of black when I came in. I observed it, without taking any notice or associating it with anything I knew. He had many correspondents, and although we were excellent friends, we had never been on those confidential terms which warrant one man in asking another from whom a special letter has come. We were not so near to each other as this, though we were father and son. After a while I went back to my own room, and finished the evening in my usual way, without any return of the excitement which, now that it was over, looked to me like some extraordinary dream. What had it meant? had it meant anything? I said to myself that it must be purely physical, something gone temporarily amiss, which had righted itself. It was physical; the excitement did not affect my mind. I was independent of it all the time, a spectator of my own agitation—a clear proof that, whatever it was, it had affected my bodily organisation alone.

Next day I returned to the problem which I had not been able to solve. I found out my petitioner in the back street, and that she was happy in the recovery of her possessions, which to my eyes indeed did not seem very worthy either of lamentation or delight. Nor was her house the tidy house which injured virtue should have when restored to its humble rights. She was not injured virtue, it was clear. She made me a great many curtseys, and poured forth a number of blessings. Her "man" came in while I was there, and hoped in a gruff voice that God would reward me, and that the old gentleman'd let 'em alone. I did not like the looks of the man. It seemed to me that in the dark lane behind the house of a winter's night he would not be a pleasant person to find in one's way. Nor was this all: when I went out into the little street which it appeared was all, or almost all, my father's property, a number of groups formed in my way, and at least half-a-dozen applicants sidled up. "I've more claims nor Mary Jordan any day," said one; "I've lived on Squire Canning's property, one place and another, this twenty year." "And what do you say to me," said another; "I've six children to her two, bless you, sir, and ne'er a father to do for them." I believed in my father's rule before I got out of the street, and approved his wisdom in keeping himself free from personal contact with his tenants. Yet when I looked back upon the swarming thoroughfare, the mean little houses, the women at their doors all so open-mouthed, and eager to contend for my favour, my heart sank within me at the thought that out of their misery some portion of our wealth came—I don't care how small a portion: that I, young and strong, should be kept idle and in luxury, in some part through the money screwed out of their necessities, obtained sometimes by the sacrifice of everything they prized! Of course I know all the ordinary commonplaces of life as well as any one—that if you build a house with your hands or your money, and let it, the rent of it is your just due, and must be paid. But yet—

"Don't you think, sir," I said that evening at dinner, the subject being reintroduced by my father himself, "that we have some duty towards them when we draw so much from them?"

"Certainly," he said; "I take as much trouble about their drains as I do about my own."

"That is always something, I suppose."

"Something! it is a great deal—it is more than they get anywhere else. I keep them clean, as far as that's possible. I give them at least the means of keeping clean, and thus check disease, and prolong life—which is more, I assure you, than they've any right to expect."

I was not prepared with arguments as I ought to have been. That is all in the Gospel according to Adam Smith, which my father had been brought up in, but of which the tenets had begun to be less binding in my day. I wanted something more, or else something less; but my views were not so clear, nor my system so logical and well-built, as that upon which my father rested his conscience, and drew his percentage with a light heart.

Yet I thought there were signs in him of some perturbation. I met him one morning coming out of the room in which the portrait hung, as if he had gone to look at it stealthily. He was shaking his head, and saying "No, no," to himself, not perceiving me, and I stepped aside when I saw him so absorbed. For myself, I entered that room but little. I went outside, as I had so often done when I was a child, and looked through the windows into the still and now sacred place, which had always impressed me with a certain awe. Looked at so, the slight figure in its white dress seemed to be stepping down into the room from some slight visionary altitude, looking with that which had seemed to me at first anxiety, which I sometimes represented to myself now as a wistful curiosity, as if she were looking for the life which might have been hers. Where was the existence that had belonged to her, the sweet household place, the infant she had left? She would no more recognise the man who thus came to look at her as through a veil with a mystic reverence, than I could recognise her. I could never be her child to her, any more than she could be a mother to me.

Thus time passed on for several quiet days. There was nothing to make us give any special heed to the passage of time, life being very uneventful and its habits unvaried. My mind was very much preoccupied by my father's tenants. He had a great deal of property in the town which was so near us,—streets of small houses, the best-paying property (I was assured) of any. I was very anxious to come to some settled conclusion: on the one hand, not to let myself be carried away by sentiment; on the other, not to allow my strongly roused feelings to fall into the blank of routine, as his had done. I was seated one evening in my own sitting-room busy with this matter,—busy with calculations as to cost and profit, with an anxious desire to convince him, either that his profits were greater than justice allowed, or that they carried with them a more urgent duty than he had conceived.

It was night, but not late, not more than ten o'clock, the household still astir. Everything was quiet—not the solemnity of midnight silence, in which there is always something of mystery, but the soft-breathing quiet of the evening, full of the faint habitual sounds of a human dwelling, a consciousness of life about. And I was very busy with my figures, interested, feeling no room in my mind for any other thought. The singular experience which had startled me so much had passed over very quickly, and there had been no return. I had ceased to think of it: indeed I had never thought of it save for the moment, setting it down after it was over to a physical cause without much difficulty. At this time I was far too busy to have thoughts to spare for anything, or room for imagination: and when suddenly in a moment, without any warning, the first symptom returned, I started with it into determined resistance, resolute not to be fooled by any mock influence which could resolve itself into the action of nerves or ganglions. The first symptom, as before, was that my heart sprang up with a bound, as if a cannon had been fired at my ear. My whole being responded with a start. The pen fell out of my fingers, the figures went out of my head as if all faculty had departed: and yet I was conscious for a time at least of keeping my self-control. I was like the rider of a frightened horse, rendered almost wild by something which in the mystery of its voiceless being it has seen, something on the road which it will not pass, but wildly plunging, resisting every persuasion, turns from, with ever increasing passion. The rider himself after a time becomes infected with this inexplainable desperation of terror, and I suppose I must have done so: but for a time I kept the upper hand. I would not allow myself to spring up as I wished, as my impulse was, but sat there doggedly, clinging to my books, to my table, fixing myself on I did not mind what, to resist the flood of sensation, of emotion, which was sweeping through me, carrying me away. I tried to continue my calculations. I tried to stir myself up with recollections of the miserable sights I had seen, the poverty, the helplessness. I tried to work myself into indignation; but all through these efforts I felt the contagion growing upon me, my mind falling into sympathy with all those straining faculties of the body, startled, excited, driven wild by something I knew not what. It was not fear. I was like a ship at sea straining and plunging against wind and tide, but I was not afraid. I am obliged to use these metaphors, otherwise I could give no explanation of my condition, seized upon against my will, and torn from all those moorings of reason to which I clung with desperation—as long as I had the strength.

When I got up from my chair at last, the battle was lost, so far as my powers of self-control were concerned. I got up, or rather was dragged up, from my seat, clutching at these material things round me as with a last effort to hold my own. But that was no longer possible; I was overcome. I stood for a moment looking round me feebly, feeling myself begin to babble with stammering lips, which was the alternative of shrieking, and which I seemed to choose as a lesser evil. What I said was, "What am I to do?" and after a while, "What do you want me to do?" although throughout I saw no one, heard no voice, and had in reality not power enough in my dizzy and confused brain to know what I myself meant. I stood thus for a moment looking blankly round me for guidance, repeating the question, which seemed after a time to become almost mechanical. What do you want me to do? though I neither knew to whom I addressed it nor why I said it. Presently—whether in answer, whether in mere yielding of nature, I cannot tell—I became aware of a difference: not a lessening of the agitation, but a softening, as if my powers of resistance being exhausted, a gentler force, a more benignant influence, had room. I felt myself consent to whatever it was. My heart melted in the midst of the tumult; I seemed to give myself up, and move as if drawn by some one whose arm was in mine, as if softly swept along, not forcibly, but with an utter consent of all my faculties to do I knew not what, for love of I knew not whom. For love—that was how it seemed—not by force, as when I went before. But my steps took the same course: I went through the dim passages in an exaltation indescribable, and opened the door of my father's room. He was seated there at his table as usual, the light of the lamp falling on his white hair: he looked up with some surprise at the sound of the opening door. "Phil," he said, and, with a look of wondering apprehension on his face, watched my approach. I went straight up to him, and put my hand on his shoulder. "Phil, what is the matter? What do you want with me? What is it?" he said.

"Father, I can't tell you. I come not of myself. There must be something in it, though I don't know what it is. This is the second time I have been brought to you here."

"Are you going—?" he stopped himself. The exclamation had been begun with an angry intention. He stopped, looking at me with a scared look, as if perhaps it might be true.

"Do you mean mad? I don't think so. I have no delusions that I know of. Father, think—do you know any reason why I am brought here? for some cause there must be."

I stood with my hand upon the back of his chair. His table was covered with papers, among which were several letters with the broad black border which I had before observed. I noticed this now in my excitement without any distinct associations of thoughts, for that I was not capable of; but the black border caught my eye. And I was conscious that he, too, gave a hurried glance at them, and with one hand swept them away.

"Philip," he said, pushing back his chair, "you must be ill, my poor boy. Evidently we have not been treating you rightly: you have been more ill all through than I supposed. Let me persuade you to go to bed."

"I am perfectly well," I said. "Father, don't let us deceive one another. I am neither a man to go mad nor to see ghosts. What it is that has got the command over me I can't tell: but there is some cause for it. You are doing something or planning something with which I have a right to interfere."

He turned round squarely in his chair with a spark in his blue eyes. He was not a man to be meddled with. "I have yet to learn what can give my son a right to interfere. I am in possession of all my faculties, I hope."

"Father," I cried, "won't you listen to me? no one can say I have been undutiful or disrespectful. I am a man, with a right to speak my mind, and I have done so; but this is different. I am not here by my own will. Something that is stronger than I has brought me. There is something in your mind which disturbs—others. I don't know what I am saying. This is not what I meant to say: but you know the meaning better than I. Some one—who can speak to you only by me—speaks to you by me; and I know that you understand."

He gazed up at me, growing pale, and his under lip fell. I, for my part, felt that my message was delivered. My heart sank into a stillness so sudden that it made me faint. The light swam in my eyes: everything went round with me. I kept upright only by my hold upon the chair; and in the sense of utter weakness that followed, I dropped on my knees I think first, then on the nearest seat that presented itself and covering my face with my hands, had hard ado not to sob, in the sudden removal of that strange influence, the relaxation of the strain.

There was silence between us for some time; then he said, but with a voice slightly broken, "I don't understand you, Phil. You must have taken some fancy into your mind which my slower intelligence—Speak out what you want to say. What do you find fault with? Is it all—all that woman Jordan?"

He gave a short forced laugh as he broke off, and shook me almost roughly by the shoulder, saying, "Speak out! what—what do you want to say?"

"It seems, sir, that I have said everything." My voice trembled more than his, but not in the same way. "I have told you that I did not come by my own will—quite otherwise. I resisted as long as I could: now all is said. It is for you to judge whether it was worth the trouble or not."

He got up from his seat in a hurried way. "You would have me as—mad as yourself," he said, then sat down again as quickly. "Come, Phil: if it will please you, not to make a breach, the first breach, between us, you shall have your way. I consent to your looking into that matter about the poor tenants. Your mind shall not be upset about that, even though I don't enter into all your views."

"Thank you," I said; "but, father, that is not what it is."

"Then it is a piece of folly," he said, angrily. "I suppose you mean—but this is a matter in which I choose to judge for myself."

"You know what I mean," I said, as quietly as I could, "though I don't myself know; that proves there is good reason for it. Will you do one thing for me before I leave you? Come with me into the drawing-room—"

"What end," he said, with again the tremble in his voice, "is to be served by that?"

"I don't very well know; but to look at her, you and I together, will always do something for us, sir. As for breach, there can be no breach when we stand there."

He got up, trembling like an old man, which he was, but which he never looked like save at moments of emotion like this, and told me to take the light; then stopped when he had got half-way across the room. "This is a piece of theatrical sentimentality," he said. "No, Phil, I will not go. I will not bring her into any such—Put down the lamp, and if you will take my advice, go to bed."

"At least," I said, "I will trouble you no more, father, to-night. So long as you understand, there need be no more to say."

He gave me a very curt "good-night," and turned back to his papers—the letters with the black edge, either by my imagination or in reality, always keeping uppermost. I went to my own room for my lamp, and then alone proceeded to the silent shrine in which the portrait hung. I at least would look at her to-night. I don't know whether I asked myself, in so many words, if it were she who—or if it was any one—I knew nothing; but my heart was drawn with a softness—born, perhaps, of the great weakness in which I was left after that visitation—to her, to look at her, to see perhaps if there was any sympathy, any approval in her face. I set down my lamp on the table where her little work-basket still was: the light threw a gleam upward upon her,—she seemed more than ever to be stepping into the room, coming down towards me, coming back to her life. Ah no! her life was lost and vanished: all mine stood between her and the days she knew. She looked at me with eyes that did not change. The anxiety I had seen at first seemed now a wistful subdued question; but that difference was not in her look but in mine.

I need not linger on the intervening time. The doctor who attended us usually, came in next day "by accident," and we had a long conversation. On the
following day a very impressive yet genial gentleman from town lunched
with us—a friend of my father's, Dr. Something; but the introduction was
hurried, and I did not catch his name. He, too, had a long talk with me
afterwards—my father being called away to speak to some one on business.
Dr.—drew me out on the subject of the dwellings of the poor. He said he
heard I took great interest in this question, which had come so much to
the front at the present moment. He was interested in it too, and wanted
to know the view I took. I explained at considerable length that my view
did not concern the general subject, on which I had scarcely thought, so
much as the individual mode of management of my father's estate. He was
a most patient and intelligent listener, agreeing with me on some points,
differing in others; and his visit was very pleasant. I had no idea until after
of its special object: though a certain puzzled look and slight shake of the
head when my father returned, might have thrown some light upon it. The
report of the medical experts in my case must, however, have been quite
satisfactory, for I heard nothing more of them. It was, I think, a fortnight
later when the next and last of these strange experiences came.

This time it was morning, about noon,—a wet and rather dismal spring
day. The halfspread leaves seemed to tap at the window, with an appeal
to be taken in; the primroses, that showed golden upon the grass at the
roots of the trees, just beyond the smooth-shorn grass of the lawn, were
all drooped and sodden among their sheltering leaves. The very growth
seemed dreary—the sense of spring in the air making the feeling of winter
a grievance, instead of the natural effect which it had conveyed a few
months before. I had been writing letters, and was cheerful enough, going
back among the associates of my old life, with, perhaps, a little longing
for its freedom and independence, but at the same time a not ungrateful
consciousness that for the moment my present tranquillity might be best.

This was my condition—a not unpleasant one—when suddenly the now
well-known symptoms of the visitation to which I had become subject
suddenly seized upon me,—the leap of the heart; the sudden, causeless,
overwhelming physical excitement, which I could neither ignore nor allay. I
was terrified beyond description, beyond reason, when I became conscious

that this was about to begin over again: what purpose did it answer, what good was in it? My father indeed understood the meaning of it, though I did not understand: but it was little agreeable to be thus made a helpless instrument without any will of mine, in an operation of which I knew nothing; and to enact the part of the oracle unwillingly, with suffering and such a strain as it took me days to get over. I resisted, not as before, but yet desperately, trying with better knowledge to keep down the growing passion. I hurried to my room and swallowed a dose of a sedative which had been given me to procure sleep on my first return from India. I saw Morphew in the hall, and called him to talk to him, and cheat myself, if possible, by that means. Morphew lingered, however, and, before he came, I was beyond conversation. I heard him speak, his voice coming vaguely through the turmoil which was already in my ears, but what he said I have never known. I stood staring, trying to recover my power of attention, with an aspect which ended by completely frightening the man. He cried out at last that he was sure I was ill, that he must bring me something; which words penetrated more or less into my maddened brain. It became impressed upon me that he was going to get some one—one of my father's doctors, perhaps—to prevent me from acting, to stop my interference,—and that if I waited a moment longer I might be too late. A vague idea seized me at the same time, of taking refuge with the portrait—going to its feet, throwing myself there, perhaps, till the paroxysm should be over. But it was not there that my footsteps were directed. I can remember making an effort to open the door of the drawing-room, and feeling myself swept past it, as if by a gale of wind. It was not there that I had to go. I knew very well where I had to go,—once more on my confused and voiceless mission to my father, who understood, although I could not understand.

Yet as it was daylight, and all was clear, I could not help noting one or two circumstances on my way. I saw some one sitting in the hall as if waiting—a woman, a girl, a black-shrouded figure, with a thick veil over her face: and asked myself who she was, and what she wanted there? This question, which had nothing to do with my present condition, somehow got into my mind, and was tossed up and down upon the tumultuous tide like a stray log on the breast of a fiercely rolling stream, now submerged, now coming uppermost, at the mercy of the waters. It did not stop me for a moment, as I hurried towards my father's room, but it got upon the current of my mind. I flung open my father's door, and closed it again after me, without seeing who was there or how he was engaged. The full clearness of the daylight did not identify him as the lamp did at night. He looked up at the sound of the door, with a glance of apprehension; and rising suddenly, interrupting some one who was standing speaking to him with much earnestness and even vehemence, came forward to meet me. "I cannot be disturbed at present," he said quickly; "I am busy." Then seeing the look in my face, which by this time he knew, he too changed colour. "Phil," he said, in a low, imperative voice, "wretched boy, go away—go away; don't let a stranger see you—"

"I can't go away," I said. "It is impossible. You know why I have come. I cannot, if I would. It is more powerful than I—"

"Go, sir," he said; "go at once—no more of this folly. I will not have you in this room. Go—go!"

I made no answer. I don't know that I could have done so. There had never been any struggle between us before; but I had no power to do one thing or another. The tumult within me was in full career. I heard indeed what he said, and was able to reply; but his words, too, were like straws tossed upon the tremendous stream. I saw now with my feverish eyes who the other person present was. It was a woman, dressed also in mourning similar to the one in the hall; but this a middle-aged woman, like a respectable servant. She had been crying, and in the pause caused by this encounter between my father and myself, dried her eyes with a handkerchief, which she rolled like a ball in her hand, evidently in strong emotion. She turned and looked at me as my father spoke to me, for a moment with a gleam of hope, then falling back into her former attitude.

My father returned to his seat. He was much agitated too, though doing all that was possible to conceal it. My inopportune arrival was evidently a great and unlooked-for vexation to him. He gave me the only look of passionate displeasure I have ever had from him, as he sat down again: but he said nothing more. "You must understand," he said, addressing the woman, "that I have said my last words on this subject. I don't choose to enter into it again in the presence of my son, who is not well enough to be made a party to any discussion. I am sorry that you should have had so much trouble in vain; but you were warned beforehand, and you have only yourself to blame. I acknowledge no claim, and nothing you can say will change my resolution. I must beg you to go away. All this is very painful and quite useless. I acknowledge no claim."

"Oh, sir," she cried, her eyes beginning once more to flow, her speech interrupted by little sobs. "Maybe I did wrong to speak of a claim. I'm not educated to argue with a gentleman. Maybe we have no claim. But if it's not by right, oh, Mr. Canning, won't you let your heart be touched by pity? She don't know what I'm saying, poor dear. She's not one to beg and pray for herself, as I'm doing for her. Oh, sir, she's so young! She's so lone in this world—not a friend to stand by her, nor a house to take her in! You are the nearest to her of any one that's left in this world. She hasn't a relation—not one so near as you—oh!" she cried, with a sudden thought, turning quickly round upon me, "this gentleman's your son! Now I think of it, it's not your relation she is, but his, through his mother! That's nearer, nearer! Oh, sir! you're young; your heart should be more tender. Here is my young lady that has no one in the world to look to her. Your own flesh and blood: your mother's cousin—your mother's—"

My father called to her to stop, with a voice of thunder. "Philip, leave us at once. It is not a matter to be discussed with you."

And then in a moment it became clear to me what it was. It had been with difficulty that I had kept myself still. My breast was labouring with the fever of an impulse poured into me, more than I could contain. And now for the first time I knew why. I hurried towards him, and took his hand, though he resisted, into mine. Mine were burning, but his like ice: their touch burnt me with its chill, like fire. "This is what it is?" I cried. "I had no knowledge before. I don't know now what is being asked of you. But, father—understand! You know, and I know now, that some one sends me—some one—who has a right to interfere."

He pushed me away with all his might "You are mad," he cried. "What right have you to think—? Oh, you are mad—mad! I have seen it coming on—"

The woman, the petitioner, had grown silent, watching this brief conflict with the terror and interest with which women watch a struggle between men. She started and fell back when she heard what he said, but did not take her eyes off me, following every movement I made. When I turned to go away, a cry of indescribable disappointment and remonstrance burst from her, and even my father raised himself up and stared at my withdrawal, astonished to find that he had overcome me so soon and easily. I paused for a moment, and looked back on them, seeing them large and vague through the mist of fever. "I am not going away," I said "I am going for another messenger—one you can't gainsay."

My father rose. He called out to me threateningly, "I will have nothing touched that is hers. Nothing that is hers shall be profaned—"

I waited to hear no more: I knew what I had to do. By what means it was conveyed to me I cannot tell; but the certainty of an influence which no one thought of calmed me in the midst of my fever. I went out into the hall, where I had seen the young stranger waiting. I went up to her and touched her on the shoulder. She rose at once, with a little movement of alarm, yet with docile and instant obedience, as if she had expected the summons. I made her take off her veil and her bonnet, scarcely looking at her, scarcely seeing her, knowing how it was: I took her soft, small, cool, yet trembling hand into mine; it was so soft and cool, not cold, it refreshed me with its tremulous touch. All through I moved and spoke like a man in a dream, swiftly, noiselessly, all the complications of waking life removed, without embarrassment, without reflection, without the loss of a moment. My father was still standing up, leaning a little forward as he had done when I withdrew, threatening, yet terror-stricken, not knowing what I might be about to do, when I returned with my companion. That was the one thing he had not thought of. He was entirely undefended, unprepared. He gave her one look, flung up his arms above his head, and uttered a distracted cry, so wild that it seemed the last outcry of nature—"Agnes!" then fell back like a sudden ruin, upon himself, into his chair.

I had no leisure to think how he was, or whether he could hear what I said. I had my message to deliver. "Father," I said, labouring with my panting breath, "it is for this that heaven has opened, and one whom I never saw, one whom I know not, has taken possession of me. Had we been less earthly we should have seen her—herself, and not merely her image. I have not even known what she meant. I have been as a fool without understanding. This is the third time I have come to you with her message, without knowing what to say. But now I have found it out. This is her message. I have found it out at last."

There was an awful pause—a pause in which no one moved or breathed. Then there came a broken voice out of my father's chair. He had not understood, though I think he heard what I said. He put out two feeble hands. "Phil—I think I am dying—has she—has she come for me?" he said.

We had to carry him to his bed. What struggles he had gone through before I cannot tell. He had stood fast, and had refused to be moved, and now he fell—like an old tower, like an old tree. The necessity there was for thinking of him saved me from the physical consequences which had prostrated me on a former occasion. I had no leisure now for any consciousness of how matters went with myself.

His delusion was not wonderful, but most natural. She was clothed in black from head to foot, instead of the white dress of the portrait. She had no knowledge of the conflict, of nothing but that she was called for, that her fate might depend on the next few minutes. In her eyes there was a pathetic question, a line of anxiety in the lids, an innocent appeal in the looks. And the face the same: the same lips, sensitive, ready to quiver; the same innocent, candid brow; the look of a common race, which is more subtle than mere resemblance. How I knew that it was so, I cannot tell, nor any man. It was the other—the elder—ah no! not elder; the ever young, the Agnes to whom age can never come—she who they say was the mother of a man who never saw her—it was she who led her kinswoman, her representative, into our hearts.

My father recovered after a few days: he had taken cold, it was said, the day before—and naturally, at seventy, a small matter is enough to upset the balance even of a strong man. He got quite well; but he was willing enough afterwards to leave the management of that ticklish kind of property which involves human wellbeing in my hands, who could move about more freely, and see with my own eyes how things were going on. He liked home better, and had more pleasure in his personal existence in the end of his life. Agnes is now my wife, as he had, of course, foreseen. It was not merely the disinclination to receive her father's daughter, or to take upon him a new responsibility, that had moved him, to do him justice. But both these motives had told strongly. I have never been told, and now will never be told, what his griefs against my mother's family, and specially against that cousin, had been; but that he had been very determined, deeply prejudiced, there can be no doubt. It turned out after, that the first occasion on which I had been mysteriously commissioned to him with a message which I did not understand, and which for that time he did not understand, was the evening of the day on which he had received the dead man's letter, appealing to him—to him, a man whom he had wronged—on behalf of the child who was about to be left friendless in the world. The second time, further letters, from the nurse who was the only guardian of the orphan, and the chaplain of the place where her father had died, taking it for granted that my father's house was her natural refuge—had been received. The third I have already described, and its results.

For a long time after, my mind was never without a lurking fear that the influence which had once taken possession of me might return again. Why should I have feared to be influenced—to be the messenger of a blessed creature, whose wishes could be nothing but heavenly? Who can say? Flesh and blood is not made for such encounters: they were more than I could bear. But nothing of the kind has ever occurred again.

Agnes had her peaceful domestic throne established under the picture. My father wished it to be so, and spent his evenings there in the warmth and light, instead of in the old library, in the narrow circle cleared by our lamp out of the darkness, as long as he lived. It is supposed by strangers that the picture on the wall is that of my wife; and I have always been glad that it should be so supposed. She who was my mother, who came back to me and became as my soul for three strange moments and no more, but with whom I can feel no credible relationship as she stands there, has retired for me into the tender regions of the unseen. She has passed once more into the secret company of those shadows, who can only become real in an atmosphere fitted to modify and harmonise all differences, and make all wonders possible the light of the perfect day.

THE SHRINE OF DEATH

by Lady Dilke

1886

Emilia Francis Strong—known as "Francis," with its masculine spelling, to family and friends—was educated at South Kensington Art School, and married Mark Pattison, the Rector of Lincoln College, Oxford, in 1861; after he died in 1884, she married the Liberal politician Sir Charles Dilke. Accordingly, she is credited as Francis Pattison, Mrs. Mark Pattison, or E. F. S. Pattison in her earlier publications, and as Lady Dilke or Emilia Dilke thereafter.

The bulk of her work was serious: she wrote about the trade union movement, art history, British and European politics, and women's issues. She contributed to London's respected Saturday Review *newspaper, and for some years she was the fine-art critic—and later art editor—for* The Academy, *a London-based review of literature, science, and art. She was also involved with the Women's Protective and Provident League (later the Women's Trade Union League) from near its inception in 1874, serving as its president for many years until her death.*

*Lady Dilke published two collections of supernatural stories in her lifetime—*The Shrine of Death and Other Stories *and* The Shrine of Love and Other Stories—*and* *a third, partial volume posthumously. Her stories are marked by a lyricism which contrasts with the rest of her writing: rather than evoking feelings of horror in the reader, they are dreamlike fables, more like dark fairy tales than the "spook stories" popular at the time. "The Shrine of Death," from the collection of the same name, is no exception: it may be short, but it is satisfying and disturbing in equal measure, full of powerful imagery that her rich language brings vividly to life.*

Ah! Life has many secrets!—These were the first words that fell on the ears of a little girl-baby, whose mother had just been brought to bed. As she grew up she pondered their meaning, and, before all things, she desired to know the secrets of life. Thus, longing and brooding, she grew apart from other children, and her dreams were ever of how the secrets of life should be revealed to her.

Now, when she was about fifteen years of age, a famous witch passed through the town in which she dwelt, and the child heard much talk of her, and people said that her knowledge of all things was great, and that even as the past lay open before her, so there was nothing in the future that could be hidden from her. Then the child thought to herself, "This woman, if by any means I get speech of her, can, if she will, tell me all the secrets of life."

Nor was it long after, that walking late in the evening with other and lesser children, along the ramparts on the east side of the town, she came to a corner of the wall which lay in deep shadow, and out of the shadow there sprang a large black dog, baying loudly, and the children were terrified, and fled, crying out, "It is the witch's dog!" and one, the least of all, fell in its terror, so the elder one tarried, and lifted it from the ground, and, as she comforted it—for it was shaken by its fall, and the dog continued baying—the witch herself came out of the shadow, and said, "Off with you, you little fools, and break my peace no more with your folly." And the little one ran for fear, but the elder girl stood still, and laying hold of the witch's mantle, she said, "Before I go, tell me, what are the secrets of life?" And the witch answered, "Marry Death, fair child, and you will know."

At the first, the saying of the witch fell like a stone in the girl's heart, but ere long her words, and the words which she had heard in the hour of her birth, filled all her thoughts, and when other girls jested or spoke of feasts and merriment, of happy love and all the joys of life, such talk seemed to her mere wind of idle tales, and the gossips who would have made a match for her schemed in vain, for she had but one desire, the desire to woo Death, and learn the secrets of life. Often now she would seek the ramparts in late evening, hoping that in the shadows she might once more find the witch, and learn from her the way to her desire; but she found her not.

Returning in the darkness, it so happened, after one of these fruitless journeys, that she passed under the walls of an ancient church, and looking up at the windows, she saw the flickering of a low, unsteady light upon the coloured panes, and she drew near to the door, and, seeing it ajar, she pushed it open and entered, and passing between the mighty columns of the nave, she stepped aside to the spot whence the light proceeded. Having done so, she found herself standing in front of a great tomb, in one side of which were brazen gates, and beyond the gates a long flight of marble steps leading down to a vast hall or chapel below; and above the gates, in a silver lamp, was a light burning, and as the chains by which the lamp was suspended moved slightly in the draught from the open door of the church, the light which burnt in it flickered, and all the shadows around shifted so that nothing seemed still, and this constant recurrence of change was like the dance of phantoms in the air. And the girl, seeing the blackness, thought of the corner on the ramparts where she had met the witch, and almost she expected to see her, and to hear her dog baying in the shadows.

When she drew nearer, she found that the walls were loaded with sculpture, and the niches along the sides were filled with statues of the wise men of all time; but at the corners were four women whose heads were bowed, and whose hands were bound in chains. Then, looking at them as they sat thus, discrowned but majestic, the soul of the girl was filled with sorrow, and she fell weeping, and, clasping her hands in her grief, she cast her eyes to heaven. As she did so, the lamp swayed a little forwards, and its rays touched with light a figure seated on the top of the monument. When the girl caught sight of this figure she ceased weeping, and when she had withdrawn a step or two backwards, so as to get a fuller view; she fell upon her knees, and a gleam of wondrous expectation shone out of her face; for, on the top of the tomb, robed and crowned, sat the image of Death, and a great gladness and awe filled her soul, for she thought, "If I may but be found worthy to enter his portals, all the secrets of life will be mine." And laying her hands on the gates, she sought to open them, but they were locked, so after a little while she went sadly away.

Each day, from this time forth, when twilight fell, the girl returned to the church, and would there remain kneeling for many hours before the shrine of Death, nor could she by any means be drawn away from her purpose. Her mind was fixed on her desire, so that she became insensible to all else; and the whole town mocked her, and her own people held her for mad. So then, at last, they took her before a priest, and the priest, when he had talked with her awhile, said, "Let her have her way. Let her pass a night within the shrine; on the morrow it may be that her wits will have returned to her."

So a day was set, and they robed her in white as a bride, and in great state, with youths bearing torches, and many maidens, whose hands were full of flowers, she was brought through the city at night fall to the church; and the gates of the shrine were opened, and as she passed within, the youths put out their torches and the maidens threw their roses on the steps beneath her feet. When the gates closed upon her, she stood still awhile upon the upper steps, and so she waited until the last footfall had ceased to echo in the church, and she knew herself to be alone in the long desired presence. Then, full of reverent longing and awe, she drew her veil about her, and as she did so, she found a red rose that had caught in it, and, striving to dislodge it, she brought it close to her face, and its perfume was very strong, and she saw, as in a vision, the rose garden of her mother's house, and the face of one who had wooed her there in the sun; but, even as she stood irresolute, the baying of a hound in the distant street fell on her ears, and she remembered the words of the witch, "Marry Death, fair child, if you would know the secrets of life," and casting the rose from her, she began to descend the steps.

As she went down, she heard, as it were, the light pattering of feet behind her; but turning, when she came to the foot, to look, she found that this sound was only the echoing fall from step to step of the flowers which her long robes had drawn after her, and she heeded them not, for she was now within the shrine, and looking to the right hand and to the left, she saw long rows of tombs, each one hewn in marble and covered with sculpture of wondrous beauty.

All this, though, she saw dimly; the plainest thing to view was the long black shadow of her own form, cast before her by the light from the lamp above, and as she looked beyond the uttermost rim of shadow, she became aware of an awful shape seated at a marble table whereon lay an open book. Looking on this dread shape, she trembled, for she knew that she was in the presence of Death. Then, seeing the book, her heart was uplifted within her, and stepping boldly forwards, she seated herself before it, and as she did so, it seemed to her that she heard a shiver from within the tombs.

Now, when she came near, Death had raised his finger, and he pointed to the writing on the open page, but, as she put her hands upon the book, the blood rushed back to her heart, for it was ice-cold, and again it seemed to her that something moved within the tombs. It was but for a minute, then her courage returned, and she fixed her eyes eagerly upon the lines before her and began to read, but the very letters were at first strange to her, and even when she knew them she could by no means frame them into words, or make any sentence out of them, so that, at the last, she looked up in her wonderment to seek aid. But he, the terrible one, before whom she sat, again lifted his finger, and as he pointed to the page, a weight as of lead forced down her eyes upon the book; and now the letters shifted strangely, and when she thought to have seized a word or a phrase it would suddenly begone, for, if the text shone out plain for an instant, the strange shadows, moving with the movements of the silver lamp, would blot it again as quickly from sight.

At this, distraction filled her mind, and she heard her own breathing like sobs in the darkness, and fear choked her; for ever, when she would have appealed for help, her eyes saw the same deadly menace, the same uplifted and threatening finger. Then, glancing to left and right, a new horror took possession of her, for the lids of the tombs were yawning wide, and whenever her thoughts turned to flight, their awful tenants peered at her from above the edges, and they made as though they would have stayed her.

Thus she sat till it was long past midnight, and her heart was sick within her, when again the distant baying of a hound reached her ears; but this sound, instead of giving her fresh courage, seemed to her but a bitter mockery, for she thought, "What shall the secrets of life profit me, if I must make my bed with Death?" And she became mad with anger, and she cursed the counsels of the witch, and in her desperation, like a creature caught in the toils, she sprang from her seat and made towards the steps by which she had come. Ere she could reach them, all the dreadful dwellers in the tombs were before her, and she, seeing the way to life was barred for ever, fell to the ground at their feet and gave up her spirit in a great agony. Then each terrible one returned to his place, and the book which lay open before Death closed with a noise as of thunder, and the light which burnt before his shrine went out, so that all was darkness.

In the morning, when that company which had brought her came back to the church, they wondered much to see the lamp extinguished, and, fetching a taper, some went down fearfully into the vault. There all was as it had ever been, only the girl lay face downwards amongst the withered roses, and when they lifted her up they saw that she was dead; but her eyes were wide with horror. And so another tomb was hewn in marble, and she was laid with the rest, and when men tell the tale of her strange bridal they say, "She had but the reward of her folly. God rest her soul!"

THE BECKSIDE BOGGLE

by Alice Rea

1886

Almost nothing is known about Alice Rea except that she published a three-volume novel titled The Dale Folk *in 1885, and a collection, of which this is the title story, in 1886. Her work is all set in England's Lake District, a scenic but remote region in the north-west of the country where superstitions persisted well into the twentieth century.*

To the modern reader, Rea's attempts to render the thick accent and dialect of this rural area may present some difficulties: a little persistence, though, and words begin to become comprehensible. "Mun" means "must," for example; "noo" means "now" and "hoose" means "house," as in Scots dialect; "coom" is "come," with the long "u" of northern English pronunciation spelled phonetically.

Beckside is a common name, "beck" being a northern English word for a small stream, similar to the Scottish "burn." "Boggle" is another dialect word, roughly equivalent to "bugaboo" and applied in local folklore to a wide range of imps and hobgoblins—or, as in this case, to a ghost.

Being close to the Scottish border, the Lake District saw its share of fighting during the wars and rebellions that lasted up until the final defeat of the Jacobite cause in

1745. Deserters and stragglers haunted the fells in those days, often surviving by theft and violence; the story's protagonist had good reason to fear her strange visitor.

B ut few of the ordinary lake country visitors will be aware of the existence of the small valley which is the scene of this story or tradition. It is a quiet, narrow little dale, situated at the foot of Scawfell, on the west side. Pedestrian tourists, crossing by the mountain track from Eskdale to Wastdale, leave it unnoticed. The black tarn at one side, and the giant fells around, with the treacherous bog beneath their feet, absorb their whole attention. But, to those who do know it, the little dale has an interest all its own.

A quiet hush pervades the place, different from the undisturbed silence of the wild fells above. There is an air of sadness in its solitude, and as you emerge from the narrow gorge, which forms its head, and follow the sheep track by the beckside, where trees and fields and signs of man appear, the riddle is solved. It is no unexplored nook of Nature's own keeping, but a once populous little dale, now forsaken and deserted. Here and there you stumble over heaps of stones—all that remains of what was once a cluster of rude cottages, inhabited, perhaps, in the days when the great peat-bog that surrounds the tarn above was a part of the vast forest of Eskdale and Wastdale.

Further still down the dale a few yards of double walling remain to remind us of the ancient packhorse road to Kendal.

Between these low walls, when our grandfathers were young, did the gallant bell-horses of nursery lore and their patient followers trot with their heavy packs, eager to rest their weary limbs in the hospitable stable of the

"Nanny Horns." Of this once busy house of entertainment for man and beast, one gable and a weed-grown garden alone remain.

Before we reach the ruins of the "Nanny Horns," however, we come to more hopeful signs of habitation. Here, by the beckside, stands a small farmhouse, with barn, cowhouse, and stable complete. A rude stone bridge spans the stream, and large trees wave solemnly overhead. But one look at the house, and the sense of desolation becomes stronger than before. The closed door, the blank stare of the window-frames, the grass-grown pavement, tell the same story of desertion.

But here it comes more closely to one's heart. The old dale folk still speak of the time when this home was alive and busy; we ourselves can almost remember when the smoke curled from its wide chimneys; and now it, too, belongs to the past.

Let us push open the creaking door and look around. Before us is a short passage, ending in a stone staircase; on the left we see a small ceiled room, evidently the old parlour or bedroom.

It is quite empty and covered with fallen plaster. To the right is the kitchen. The sun shines brightly through the two glassless windows. A wide, open fireplace occupies the greater part of the end of the room opposite the door. Facing the window are the entrances of the pantry and dairy. In one corner, clearly a fixture in the wall, there is an old oak cupboard—one shaky door hangs by a single hinge, and in it we may still see an old brass lock.

The most striking piece of furniture, however, if furniture we may name it, is a long freestone slab, or sconce, as dale folk call it, firmly fixed into the wall by the fireplace, which must have made a comfortable fireside couch in olden times, when a huge fire burned in the now empty grate, when the goodwife spun in the opposite corner, and the good-man carded wool in the armchair by her side.

Let us take our seat now upon the sconce, while I tell you the story of this last desertion, for around this slab of stone the whole tradition clings.

We need fear no interruption, for few of our neighbours would care to take our place, or, indeed, let a setting sun, such as we now see shining on the opposite fells, find them within a good quarter of a mile of this spot, for fear that their terror should suddenly take shape, and reveal to them the form of the Headless Woman of Beckside. There, the secret is out—the house is haunted.

Many years ago Beckside was inhabited by a man and his wife of the name of Southward—Joe and Ann Southward. They had been farm servants in their youth, and, being in the main sober, industrious folks, had each saved up a nice little sum of money; so when it just happened that they were both out of situation at the same time, they thought they could not do better than put their two little nest-eggs together. They therefore got married and settled down on this small farm. At this time neither of them was very young, and for several years they had no child; but at last Heaven blessed them with a son, and the whole course of their somewhat monotonous life was changed. I believe there was not to be found in any of the surrounding dales so happy a little family as theirs. They had few wants their farm could not supply, good health, and but one ambition—namely, to save as much money as ever they could to give their son a better start in life than they had had themselves. So they lived on as little as possible, and worked and hoarded until they had a very fair amount put away in an old teapot in the cupboard by the door. Upon the cupboard Joe put a strong lock—a very rare thing in a farm-house in those days—for he was sadly afraid of any harm or loss happening to his little store.

One autumn Joe Southward had to leave home for a whole day, and hardly expected to be back before the next morning, for he was going to Whitehaven on business. Such a thing had never happened before, although they had been married eight years.

"Thu mun cum back heam as seun as thu can, Joe," his wife said, as he mounted his horse, "and thu mun mind an' nut cau at ower mony public hooses on t' way back"—for though Joe was by no means in the habit of getting drunk, still he had been known to return home now and again from the Eskdale fair, or an occasional sale, just a little more excited than usual, and Ann feared lest in the unwonted dissipation of seeing Whitehaven—a place he had visited only once before, and of which he had told her grand tales—and in the excitement of spending a whole day, and perhaps a night, from home, he might be led on from one extravagance to another.

"Oh, aye, lass, ah'll coom heam as seun as iver ah can git, but thoo mun nut bide up for me efter nine be t' clock. If ah's nut heam be than, ah'll be stoppen feu t'neet at Santon or sum udder spot, maybe t' Crag."

"Varra weel," replied his wife, "ah'll nut waste t' cannel biden up for thee—good-bye. Hes te gitten thee monish gaily seaf? Ah wish thoo wad let me set a stitch in thee breeches pocket to keep folks' hands oot. Ah've heerd tell on a man 'at went t' Whitehebben yans, an' he had ivery thing 'at ever he had tean oot uv his pocket, an' he kent nowt aboot it whatever."

"Oh, aye, they're queerish-like folk thear, ah ken, but ah'll nut heve me pockets sowed up. Hoo does te think ah cud pay t' tolls, lass? Gie thee fadder a kiss, Joe, me lad. Noo mind thoo tak's care o' the sell, me lass. Cum up, Charlie," and he set off at a steady pace on his heavy brown horse over the little stone bridge and down the valley.

Ann, taking her child, a strong little fellow of fifteen months, in her arms, followed her husband as far as the bridge, and stood watching him till he was out of sight, and then, turning back, re-entered the kitchen. There was not much time for her to waste that day, for they had killed a sheep for their winter supply of meat, and Joe had cut it up the day before, ready for salting; so what with that and her ordinary work, and a good many extra things that generally fell to Joe's share, the afternoon was nearly over before she had time to think of her loneliness. But when she had finished cleaning her kitchen and made up the peat fire to boil her kettle she felt a great want of something she could not exactly tell what.

So long as she had been making plenty of noise herself she had never noticed the unusual quiet around her, but now, as she sat to rest for a moment or two in the armchair, not a sound was to be heard but the tick tock of the clock. Joe the younger was asleep. She longed intensely for something other than herself to break the silence.

Just as it was becoming insupportable a little bantam cock in the yard gave a shrill crow, and Ann heaved a great sigh of relief as she heard it.

"Dear, dear," she thought, "I dunna ken what's coom ore me, but I do feel lonesome-like someway. Folks 'ud say as I was feelin' t' want o' Joe, but him and me is nut o' that mak' to be sae daft-like. Not but what he's weel enough, an' when yar's lived wi' yan body for seven, going on eight, year, and scarce iver seed any udder body, you, maybe, do feel a bit queer

253

like when they gangs off. I mind when I was servant lass at Crag there was a girt black cat as allus followed me ivery spot where iver I was at, but it got catcht in t' trap yan day. I quite felt t' loss o' it for a bit. I was short o' summut for a day or two, and I's sure 'twas na for love on't, for it hed nowt to crack on in t' way o' leuks. It had lost hoaf on t' tail in t' trap afore, and its ears were maist riven off wi' feetin', yet I quite miste it loike. Now," she continued, rising, "I's just wesh me and lash me hair, then when I's had me sup o' milk and bread, and finished t' milking, I's melt down all that sheep fat and git a lock o' sieves* peeled ready for dipping. I mun mak a lock o' candles this back end."

By the time the cows were milked and Ann had had her sup of milk and bread (tea of course was not known in these parts in those days), and "lal Joe" had been put comfortably to sleep in his clumsy wooden cradle, the sun had nearly set, and Ann crossed the yard to the little bridge to see if there was any sign of her husband returning home.

The valley looked very beautiful, lit up by the last rays of the setting sun, which was dipping behind the shoulder of the Screes.

At the head of the dale Scawfell stood out bold and broad, bathed from base to summit in the glowing light, while the purple heather and golden bracken of the surrounding hills gave a warmth of colour to the scene which made it very lovely to behold.

Ann, however, regarded neither gold nor purple, light nor shade, but, turning her back to the king of the valley, Old Father Scawfell, gazed rather longingly (though she would on no account have owned to the feeling) along the rough fell road, which wound by the side of the beck towards the open country. There she stood, her fingers busily engaged knitting a blue wool stocking for her husband, and her eyes fixed upon the road, till the sun, entirely disappearing, left the valley in a hazy shade, and the light, gradually retreating up the fell-sides, robbed the brackens and heather of their glory as it bid them good-night.

Just as she was slowly leaving the bridge she happened to turn her eyes to the Screes side of the valley, and there she was sure she saw some one advancing towards her, yet not quite towards Beckside itself, for the person,

---

* rushes

whoever it might be, was coming along the old pack-horse road from Keswick, which crossed the dale half way between Beckside and Bakerstead, the next little farm, then without a tenant.

At the point where the old road passes the two houses, stood the "Nanny Horns," which was, even at the time I am telling you of, quite a ruin; but the garden belonging to it kept Ann supplied with gooseberries and rhubarb all the summer and spring.

It was when passing this ruin that the person disappeared. For some time Ann stood watching. Presently the figure emerged from the ruin and advanced quickly towards her. She could distinguish now that it was a woman, and that she seemed very tired. As soon as Ann perceived she was making direct for her house she went back and shut the door, for she did not at all like to have a stranger calling at that time of the evening when she was alone.

She had hardly turned from the door and crossed the kitchen towards the fireplace before she felt a shadow pass the window, and, turning suddenly round, she caught a glimpse of a muffled-up face peeping through. It was withdrawn immediately, and at the same moment there was a sharp tap at the door. Going to the window, she could see the woman knocking with a good stout stick. Ann opened the door and asked her what she wanted, rather sharply.

"If you please," said the woman, "can you give a poor body a night's lodgings? I's coom a lang way, and I's tired to death. I could na walk another mile to save me life, my feet are that cut wi' t' stones." And she showed her boots, all burst out and cut, and her swollen feet, which were seen through them.

"Weel, ye ma' coom in," Ann said at last, though with no very good grace. "I suppose there's na place else ye could gang til to neet. Where's ta coom fra? Tha's none fra these parts, I reckon."

"Na," she answered, seating herself on a bench that ran along by the table under the window. "Na, I's a Scotchwoman, and I coom fra Penrith. I's going to Ulverstone to see my son; he's got a gude bit o' wark there; I kent some folks in Borrowdale, so I came this way, but I did na ken it wad be sic a road as it is."

"It's a terrible bad road you've coomt, and ye leuk real tired out, but draw up to t' fire now ye is here," Ann said, feeling more kindly disposed when she heard the stranger had friends in Borrowdale, for her own people came from there. "Will ye net take yer shawl off, when ye're sae near t' fire?" she asked; for the woman had a small woollen shawl which she kept pinned over her head and the lower part of her face.

"Na, na, if ye'll excuse me," she answered, "I's got a bad pain in my teeth, and this warm shawl makes it a wee bit better."

"It's a nasty loike thing is teuthwark," said Ann: "I niver hed it mysel', but I mind my maister had a spell on't yance, and he were fairly druv hoaf daft wi' it."

"Your maister's not at home, maybe," the woman suggested, looking round the room.

Ann thought her eyes rested longer than they need have done on the cupboard, in the door of which the new lock showed rather conspicuously.

"Oh, yes," she answered, "he's been off t'day, but I should nut wonder if he be heam gaily seune."

Ann was very soon busy preparing the fat of the sheep they had killed for melting down to make candles and rushlights for their winter store.

First she brought in a very large three-legged pan and swung it upon the crook in the chimney, then a basket of peat and a good bundle of sticks, which she put down by the hearth, so that she might keep the fire well up under her pan without having to go out again in the dark. She next asked the woman if she would have a "sup o' poddidge" with her, for she meant to take hers while the fat was melting; but, to her surprise, the woman declined, alleging as a reason that her teeth ached so badly, anything hot would drive her wild.

She took a handful of oat-cake, however, and munched away at that as well as she could under her shawl.

It had now grown quite dark outside—indeed it was after eight o'clock, very nearly nine—but the kitchen looked bright and cheerful by the light of the fire.

"I canna offer ye a bed," Ann said to her visitor, as she poured out her milk porridge, "but ye mun choose whether ye had rayder sleep in t' barn or t' hayloft."

"Weel, since ye are sae kind," she answered, "wad ye mind if I slept here on this sconce? It will be nice and warm by the fire, and I'm that tired I's niver ken whether it be hard or soft."

"Aye, weel," said Ann, "thee can sleep thear if thee's a mind tul, but I's likely keep ye awake a bit. I wants to git all this fat melt down, all what's in t' pan and on this dish too; and, to tell t' truth, I don't think as Joe wad be sae weel pleased to see ony strange body sleeping here when he comes heam."

"Oh" she continued, "I'd sune get up and away into the barn if he came hame; but it's ower late for him to be coming now, is it not?" And she looked keenly over at Ann, who was standing stirring her porridge, to cool it, by the table.

"Ye mun feel lonesome when your guid-man is away. Does he often go off?"

"Noa," answered Ann, "we hev been married seven, gaan on eight, year, and he's niver been away a neet afore."

"Weel, he mun be a steady fellow; you'll be a fine saving couple. I should na wonder if you have a tidy bit of money laid by somewhere for that little chap?" pointing to the cradle where little Joe was sleeping soundly. "He's as fine a little laddie as iver I saw, and a good one too, or he'd wake up wi' our taking."

"That is he," replied Ann, her mother's heart warming at the praise of her son. "We wad like him to hev a better start in life than we hed oursels."

"Why you seem to have done varra weel," said the woman, "as far as I can see. I wad na mind changing places wi' ye," she added, with a disagreeable laugh and another look round the room. "You've a deal o' good furniture, and there's, maybe, summut worth having in that cupboard, that ye lock it up so close. I don't often see a cupboard wi' a lock like that in a farm kitchen."

"Don't ye?" said Ann, sharply, for she thought the woman was getting rather too familiar. "We locks our cupboards because we likes to keep our things to oursels. There's no knowing what mak o' folk may come tramping over t' fell." And she looked significantly at her visitor.

"Weel," the woman said, "if you've no objections I'll just lay me down and try to get a bit o' sleep; I mun be off sune in the morning."

"Well, then," said Ann, "I'll git the a lal lock o' hay to put under thee head." And she went out to the barn.

Hardly had she left the room, when the woman seized her half-empty basin and took a good drink of her porridge, and then replaced it as it was on the table.

"Theer," said Ann, as she returned with a good bundle of hay and spread it on the sconce, "that'll be a gay bit softer nar t' freestone."

She then went to the little parlour where she and her husband slept, and brought thence an old shawl, which she handed to the woman for a covering, saying, "Mak thysel as comfortable as thee can—ah 'ev gitten t' fat to leuk tul, and some seives to peel."

When Ann returned to her basin of porridge she thought it had gone down a good deal since she had left it, and looked towards the woman as though to ask her if she had taken some.

"Nea," she thought, "what wad she want supping my poddidge, when she wadn't have ony hersel? She'll get nea mair, howiver, an' it was her," she added, as she emptied the basin. "Now I'll just wesh these few things, and thin get to peeling my seives, but first I mun mak t' table straight gin Joe coom heam, though it's gitten ower late now, I fear. I wish he was heam. I don't more nor hoaf loike t' leuks o' this woman, she has sic a way wi' her o' leuking out o' t' corners of her eyes, and peeping all round loike; and she's a terrible girt body too, she mair nor hoaf a head higher ner I is, and ah's nut sa lal. She's seun fa'n asleep, she mun be tired."

So it seemed, for almost directly she had lain down she turned her face towards the pantry door, behind the sconce, drew her shawl more closely over her aching face, and was now breathing as regularly as a gigantic baby. And yet, as Ann moved quietly about, putting her things away, she had an uncomfortable feeling that the woman's sharp, cunning eyes were following her wherever she went. Once or twice she stopped and looked hard at her visitor, but she was as motionless as could be, and when she spoke to her she received not the slightest answer, but the breathing seemed, if anything, a little heavier. Once, indeed, when she had moved to the little table under the cupboard, she felt convinced the woman was not asleep, and turned suddenly round, for she felt sure she heard a slight rustle of the hay pillow. But no, except a sleepy sort of movement, as though she were covering her aching teeth more warmly from the draughts, the stranger lay as quietly as before.

"Dear, dear, I mun be gettin' silly. I wonder how lang that fat's gaun to be a-meltin'. When what's in is melt down a bit I'll full up t' pan wi' what's on t' dish."

As the clock in the corner pointed to nine, Ann thought of what her husband had said about not returning later than that hour, but still she felt as though she could not go to bed yet.

"He might happen to come." So she got some rushes, and sat down on her low chair to peel them, by the side of her child's cradle, opposite the sconce.

The house was almost as still as it had been in the morning, only that the ticking of the clock and the snoring of the sleeper (for the heavy breathing had passed into a regular snore) kept up a kind of monotonous duet, in which they seemed to be vainly attempting to keep time with each other; for first one took the lead and then the other, now they went on for a tick tock or two quite amicably, and then one would get the start, and the struggle for precedence would commence again.

It was sleepy work to sit peeling rushes and listening, and poor Ann grew more and more drowsy. She had had an unusually hard day's work, and it was now far past her ordinary bed-time, for the lazy hands of the clock had travelled from nine to half-past, and thence to ten. Ann's eyelids drooped lower and lower, the half-finished rush slipped out of her sleepy fingers, her head sank upon her chest, and there were three sleepers for the clock to keep time with.

Suddenly Ann started up; she had been roused by the fall of something, that rung like metal, to the ground. The fire was glowing low down on the hearth, but was still very hot.

"This willn't dea," she said to herself, rising, from her chair, and giving herself a shake, "I mun jest lig down on t' bed a bit. I'll nut take my things off. I wonder what o'clock it is, and how lang I've been asleep?"

She took a handful of sticks and threw them on to the fire to make a blaze by which she might see the time, and in a moment the kitchen was lighted up from one end to the other. The fingers of the clock stood at a little after twelve.

"Dear, dear!" thought Ann, "I hev slept a lang time," and she turned to the fire, for she felt chilly. Stooping by it she saw something bright on the floor near her. It was an open clasp knife; one of those long, sharp knives that are worn by the blue-jackets. It must have dropped from the hand or out of the dress of the woman on the sconce.

Instinctively Ann looked towards her; she was lying on her back, the light from the fire fell full upon her face, for the shawl had slipped off; and there, to Ann's horror, she saw it was not that of a woman at all, but of a powerful man. His mouth and chin were adorned with as much of a black bristly beard as would grow during a week's tramp over the fells, out of reach of a razor.

For a moment she stood as though paralyzed with fright, but not longer. He was fast asleep after his long walk; so far she had the advantage, and she was not the woman to let it slip. To catch up her child and run was her first impulse; but where to? The next inhabited house was a mile away, and the slightest noise, such as the opening of the clumsy old door, would wake the man. What should she do? She could not stand still and let herself be certainly robbed of all their hardly earned savings, and possibly murdered with her child. No! a thousand times! she would fight for it! But how? She looked at her child asleep in the cradle, then at the man.

There he lay, his mouth wide open, snoring loudly, one powerful hand closed upon the shawl she had lent him for a covering, while the skirts of his woman's attire hung to the ground.

What was to be done must be done at once.

She looked at the knife lying at her feet; it was sharp and strong; but she might miss her aim, and only wound him. Turning from it she gazed despairingly around the room till her eyes fell upon the pan of boiling fat. In a moment her resolve was taken. With a strength born of desperation, she lifted it off the crook and, without a sound, placed it close to the sconce. Then quietly and stealthily, as Jael crept round the sleeping Syrian captain,* the hardy daleswoman reached over to the table, and off it took a large tin dipper with a wooden handle, capable of holding from about five to six quarts. With compressed lips and clenched teeth she approached the sleeper, and, filling her dipper to the brim with the fat, poured it, boiling hot as it was, down his throat and over his face—one, two, three dippers full.

In vain were his struggles. When, at the first great shock he almost started up, she seized him by the throat with one hand, and pinned him down with the strength of a giantess, regardless of the scalding fat, which

* A reference to the story of Jael and Sisera from the Book of Judges in the Old Testament.

she continued to pour with the other hand, until the pan was well-nigh empty. Not a cry was heard, save the first half-choked scream of agony, but the struggling and writhing were fearful to behold. Still the woman held on. She had him in her power, lying on his back so far below her—and she was a powerful woman. Not a feature quivered, not a nerve relaxed till her work was done; the struggles and kicks became weaker, the writhing subsided into an occasional quiver, and that finally passed into perfect stillness. Not till then, when all was over, and the fight was ended, did her strength leave her. She withdrew her hand, the dipper fell from her now nerveless fingers, and she stood, the victor, indeed, but not triumphant, transfixed with horror at what she had dared to do, rooted to the spot, motionless as Lot's wife or the heap on the sconce.

The clock had it all its own way now; there was not another sound that dare break the silence after that one choked scream that had not even waked the baby in its cradle. How long she stood by that sconce, Ann never knew; but presently the clock struck one, and, as though it broke the spell that held her, Ann sank upon her chair by the fire; two, three, four o'clock struck, but still she sat on; five o'clock, and the grey dawn crept in at the windows; the fire had long since gone out. Still she sat.

At half-past five Joe Southward opened the door of his own farm-house and entered the kitchen.

"Weel, lass, I's heam at last," he said. But as his wife turned her pinched and ashy face towards him he too seemed overpowered by the spell of silence, though he knew not why. But the child, hearing his father's voice, set up a cry and shout. His mother flew to his cradle, lifted him into her uninjured arm, and rushed with him, folded tightly to her breast, out into the pure dim daylight, sobbing with great, long, heart-breaking sobs.

"Oh, my lal barn, I did it for thee—it was nut for mysel; thee mun niver, niver ken as thy mother did it; I did it for thee, my barn, my barn." And mother and child mingled their sobs and tears.

Meanwhile Joe had been looking about the kitchen, and now followed them out.

Bit by bit beneath the trees Joe heard the tale of horror, for Ann would not re-enter the house, but folded her child in her apron to shield him from the cold morning air.

At length her husband took him from her and carried him into their own bedroom.

"Now, Ann," he said, "we mun hide him, thu could deu nowt else, but we mun mind 'at neabody kens owt aboot it for t' sake o' t' barn."

So together, ere the day was fairly begun, they dragged the body up the stone stairs, laid it on the wool shelf, which is a kind of ledge between the top of the wall and the roof, in one of the bedrooms, and covered it with the rolled fleeces that were stored there, for they expected several neighbours that day to help in some farm work.

When the neighbours had left, and it was getting dark, Joe took his pick and spade to the ruins of the old public-house, and there he dug as deep a grave as was possible in the stony soil. In one corner of the ruin he found a bundle, done up in a handkerchief, containing the man's male attire, a considerable amount of money, and one or two little things of value which must have been stolen from other farms. After a long consultation they determined to bury these things with him, as they dared not make inquiries concerning them, for they feared lest the manner of his death should become known.

When all was dark and quiet, and "lal Joe" was fast asleep, Ann and her husband went up the stairs, and entered the little bedroom. Joe pulled away the fleeces, and together they dragged the body from the shelf on to the floor. It was a hideous sight. The fat had now solidified, and formed a hard, white mask, concealing yet indicating the features beneath. At sight of it Ann's face assumed the same ashy hue it had worn the night before; while Joe went about the work with the grim determination of a man upon whom had fallen one of the dirtiest bits of work the Fates could possibly have given. As it had fallen upon him, and what was to be done must be done, why according to his notion the sooner it was over the better. When they had stretched him out on the floor they folded the skirts of his dress about his legs, and then, taking a large corn-sack, carefully drew it over the whole, and stitched up the end.

Joe then went down a few stairs and dragged it upon his back like a sack of flour. It was a great weight, and many were the stops and stumbles before he reached the door of the kitchen, where he propped it up against the wall to take breath, while Ann placed the dip candle she had been holding to light him down in an old horn lantern. When she was ready Joe again hoisted his burden on his back, and stumbled along the passage; then very slowly they crossed the farm-yard, Ann going a little in advance with the lantern. It was a damp, dark night—not a star was to be seen; the branches of the old trees in front of the house, which were dimly visible as the light flickered for a moment across their broad trunks, moaned and creaked in the wind. All the familiar things surrounding them, as they made their way to the ruin, seemed to partake of their horror; even the merry little beck below the fold had changed its every-day chatter with the stones in its bed to a melancholy chant. Not a word did they speak to each other during the frequent pauses which had to be made for breath ere they reached the hole that Joe had dug. Once there, they soon lowered their burden into it, and threw in the bundle. Then, seizing his spade, Joe filled up the grave as fast as possible, only pausing now and then to stamp down the earth more firmly.

At length the last spadeful had been thrown in, the last stamp given, and a few loose stones piled up carelessly over the place, to hide any sign of recent digging. Then Joe broke the silence.

"Theer," he said, wiping his hot brow with his jacket sleeve, "that's done. He'll do naebody no harm now. Coom, lass, we'll ga heam, we've done a' we can," and drawing his wife's hand through his arm, as he had never done since the day of their wedding, they left the ruin, re-crossed the field beneath the trees, and entering their house, stood by the fire. Here at last Ann fairly gave way; she drew her hand from her husband's arm, and sank shivering upon her low rocking-chair.

"Oh," she said, "I carn't bide it, I canna bide to stop in t' hoose; it will be as if he was alius liggan theer. Thee mun niver gang away agaen, Joe," and the matter-of-fact, unimpressionable daleswoman clung to her husband like a child.

"Whist, lass," he said, soothingly, putting his brown hand upon her shoulder, "thee munna tak on seha, thee could nut heve done different. If thee hadn't been middlin' sharp wid him, he'd ha' seun doon for thee an' lal Joe wid his lang knife; thee munna set sic mich by it. We can do nae mair nor we hev done. Nobbut keep it til ourselves, and niver let on' at he iver coomed nar t' hoose."

Time passed on, Joe and Ann lived many long years in this house, for they feared that if they left, some new tenant might dig about the ruin.

Often, when the short autumn and winter afternoons drew to their close, Ann would leave her warm seat by the fire and cross the yard to speak to Joe in the barn, for she could bear to stay in the house alone no longer; and later on, at night, when she sat knitting while her husband was asleep in his armchair, if she raised her eyes from her work, she could fancy she saw the long, shapeless figure stretched out on the sconce, with the fat dropping on to the floor.

After their death, in some way a whisper of the tale began to float about from one farm kitchen to another. How it got out no one knew, but one thing I know, and that is, that when, after standing empty for a year or two, the house was let again, the farmer and his wife, on a certain night each year, used to see an indistinct figure, all muffled up about the head, enter the kitchen and stretch itself on the sconce, then in a few minutes a choked kind of scream would sound through the room, and the figure would disappear. The next night the same figure stepped from the wool niche, glided noiselessly down the stairs, and disappeared in the ruins of the "Nanny Horns."

THE HIDDEN DOOR

by Vernon Lee

1887

*Vernon Lee was a pseudonym of Violet Paget. The daughter of British expatriates,
she was born in France and spent most of her life "on the Continent," as the British
say, mostly in Italy.*

*A committed feminist and pacifist, she was known for adopting masculine dress and
had long-term relationships with three women: the poet Mary Robinson; the writer
and art theorist Clementina "Kit" Caroline Anstruther-Thomson; and the writer Amy
Levy. She also forged lasting relationships with the Italian artist Telemaco Signorini
and the scholar Mario Praz.*

*Although she is best known today for her weird fiction, she also wrote extensively on
Italian art and history, and was regarded as an authority on the Italian Renaissance.
Many of her tales of the uncanny are set in Italy, among the large and polyglot expa-
triate communities that had grown up in Florence, Venice, and Italy's other great cities.*

*While unusual in its English setting, "The Hidden Door" shares many of Lee's
favorite themes and motifs. She was particularly fascinated by the effects of guilt on
the over-wrought imagination, and its ability to plunge even a rational mind into*

superstitious dread. First published in Unwin's Annual *for 1887 and reprinted the same year in the American multi-author anthology* The Witching Time: Tales for the Year's End, *this is one of Lee's less well-known tales, but it is easily the equal of more commonly collected stories like "Amour Dure" and "The Legend of Madame Krasinska."*

I t seemed to Decimus Little that there could be no doubt left. His only wonder was whether any one else had been near making that discovery. As he sat in a deep window of the big drawing-room, the light of the candles falling yellow upon the shining white arms and shoulders, the shining white expanses of shirt-front, the lustrous silks and lustrous black cloth within doors; the great wave of moor and fell unfurling grayish-green in the pale-blue twilight without; as he sat there alone in the window, he wondered how it would be if any of these creatures assembled for the coming of age of the heir of Hotspur Hall could guess that he knew. His eyes mechanically followed the tall figure of his host, as his broad shoulders and gray beard appeared and reappeared in the crowd; they sought out the yellow ridge of curls of the son and heir, as his head rose and fell while talking to the ladies in the corner. What if either of them could guess? If old Sir Hugh Hotspur could guess that there was in the world another creature beside himself who knew the position of that secret door; if young Hotspur could guess that there existed close by another man who might, any day, penetrate into that secret chamber to which, at the close of these merry-making days, the youth must be solemnly admitted, to lose, during that fatal hour among unspeakable mysteries, all lightness of heart for ever?

Mr. Little was not at all surprised at the fact of having made this extraordinary discovery. Although in no way a conceited man, he was accustomed to think of himself as connected with extraordinary matters, and in some way destined for an extraordinary end. He was one of those men who, without ever having done, or even said, or perhaps even thought, anything especially remarkable, are yet remarkable men. Whenever he came into a room, he felt people's eyes upon him, and knew that they were asking, "Who is that young man?" And still Mr. Decimus Little did not consider himself handsome, nor did any one else consider him so, to his knowledge. From the matter-of-fact point of view, all one could say was that he was of middle height, more inclined to be fat than thin, with small not irregular features, hair varying between yellow and gray, a slight stoop, a somewhat defective sight, and a preference for clothes of ample cut and of neutral tints. But then the matter-of-fact eye just missed that something indefinable which constituted the remarkable character of Mr. Little's appearance. As it was with his person, so likewise was it with his history; there was more significance therein than could easily be defined. A distant relative, on the female side, of the illustrious border house of Hotspur, Mr. Little possessed a modest income and the education of a gentleman. He had never been to school, and had left college without taking his degree. He had begun reading for the law, and left off. He had tried writing for the magazines, but without success. He had at one time inclined to High-Church asceticism and the moralizing of Whitechapel; he had also been addicted to socialism, and spent six months learning to make a chest of drawers in a Birmingham co-operative workshop. He had begun writing a biography of Ninon de Lenclos, studying singing, and forming a collection of rare medals; and he was now considerably interested in Esoteric Buddhism and the Society for Psychical Research, although he felt by no means prepared to accept the new theosophy, nor to indorse the conclusions concerning thought transference. And finally, and quite lately, Mr. Decimus Little had also been in love, and had become engaged to a cousin of his, a young lady studying at Girton College; but he was not quite sure whether the engagement was absolutely binding on either side, or whether marriage would be certainly conducive to the happiness of both parties. For Mr. Decimus Little was gradually maturing a theory to the effect of his being a person with a double nature, reflective and idealistic on the one hand, and capable, on the other, of extraordinary impulses of lawlessness;

and it is notorious that such persons, and indeed, perhaps, all very complex and out-of-the-common personalities are not very fit for the marriage state. It was consonant with what Mr. Little often lamented as the excessive skepticism of his temper, that he should not have made up his mind about the hidden chamber at Hotspur Hall, and the strange stories concerning it. He had often discussed the matter, which, as he remarked, was a crucial one in all questions of the supernatural. He had triumphantly argued with a physiologist at his club that mere delusion could not be a sufficient explanation for so old and diffused a belief, as, indeed, mere delusion could not account for any belief of any kind. He had argued equally triumphantly with a clergyman in the train against the notion that the occupant of the secret chamber was the Evil One, and had added that the existence of evil spirits offered serious, very serious, difficulties to a thoughtful mind. And Mr. Little, being, as he often remarked, open to arguments and evidence on all points, had elaborated various explanations of the mystery of the hidden chamber, and had even attempted to sound the inhabitants of Hotspur Hall on the subject. But the servants had not understood his polished but rather shadowy Oxford English, or he had not understood their thick Northumbrian, and the members of the family had dropped the subject with a somewhat disconcerting sharpness of manner; and Mr. Little was the last man in the world to rudely invade the secrets of others, by experiments of towels hung out of windows, and such like; indeed, the person capable of such courses would have inspired him with horror.

And by an irony of fate—Mr. Little believed in the irony of fate, and was occasionally ironical himself—it had been given to him, to this skeptical and unobtrusive man, to discover that room hidden in the thickness of the Norman wall, and whose position had baffled so much ingenious, pertinacious, and impertinent inquiry.

There could no longer be any doubt about it; this door, revealed only by its hollow sound and its rusty iron bolt, against which Mr. Little had accidentally leaned that day when the shame of having intruded upon a flirtation (and a flirtation, too, between the heir of Hotspur and the heiress of his hereditary foes the Blenkinsops) had made him rush, like a mad creature, along unknown passages and up the winding staircase of the peel tower—this door, whitewashed to look like stone and hidden just under the highest battlements of Hotspur, could only be that of the mysterious chamber. It had flashed across Mr. Little's mind when first he had leaned, confused and panting, against the wall of the staircase, and the wall had yielded to his pressure and creaked perceptibly; and the certainty had grown with every subsequent examination of the spot, and of the exterior of the castle. People had hitherto wasted their ingenuity upon seeking a window in Hotspur Hall which should correspond with no ostensible room; accident had revealed to Mr. Little a room which corresponded with no window visible from without. It now seemed so simple that it was impossible to conceive how the secret could so long have been kept. The secret chamber was, could be, only in the oldest portion of the castle, in the peel tower, built for the protection of stock and goods from the Scottish raids; and it was, it could be, only under the very roof of the tower, taking air and light through some chimney or trap-door from the battlements above. There could be no doubt about it; and as Mr. Decimus Little sat in the window-seat of the great drawingroom at Hotspur, with on the one side the crowd of guests brilliant in the yellow candle-light, and the great darkwave of fell and moor rising into the blue twilight on the other, he thought how strange it was that of all these people there was only one, besides the master of Hotspur, who knew the position of the fatal room: only one besides the heir of Hotspur who might—who knows?—penetrate into its secrets, and that one person should be himself. Strange; and yet, somehow, it did not take him by surprise.

And, after all, what was the secret of that chamber? A monstrous creature, or race of creatures, hidden away by the unrightful heirs? An ancient ancestor, living on by diabolic arts throughout the centuries? A demon, a specter, some horror nameless because inconceivable to those who had not seen it, or perhaps some almost immaterial evil, some curse lurking in the very atmosphere of the place? It was notorious that the something, whatever it was, made it impossible for a Hotspur ever to marry a Blenkinsop; that the heir of Hotspur was introduced to this mystery on coming of age; and that no Hotspur, after coming of age, had ever been known to smile: these were well authenticated facts; but what mystery or horror upon earth or in hell could be sufficient cause for these well ascertained results, no one had ever discovered. Every explanation was futile and insufficient.

These were the thoughts which went on in Mr. Little's mind throughout that week of coming of age at Hotspur Hall. All day and all night—at least, as much of the night as he could account for—these questions kept going round and round in his mind, presenting now one surface, now another, but ever present and ever active. He walked about, ate his dinner, talked, danced automatically, knowing that he did it all, but as one knows what another person is doing, or what one is reading in a book, without any sense of its being one's self or its being real; nay, with a sense of being removed miles and miles from it all, living in a different time and place, to which this present is as the past and the distant. The secret chamber—its mystery; the door, the color of the wall, the shape of the iron bolt, the slant of the corkscrew steps—these were reality in the midst of all this unrealness. And withal a strange longing: to stand again before that door, to handle once more that rusty bolt; a wish like that for some song, or some beloved presence, the desire for that ineffable consciousness, that overwhelming sense of concentrated life and feeling, of being there, of realizing the thing. No one, reflected Mr. Little, can know what strange joys are reserved for strange natures; how certain creatures, too delicate and unreal for the every-day interests and pleasures of existence to penetrate through the soul atmosphere in which they wander, will vibrate, with almost agonized joy, live their full life on contact with certain mysteries. Every day Mr. Little would seek that winding staircase in the peel tower; at first with hesitation and shyness, stealing up almost ashamed of himself; then secretly and stealthily, but excited, resolute, like a man seeking the woman he loves, bent upon the joy of his life. Once a day at first, then twice, then thrice, counting the hours between the visits, longing to go back as soon as he had left, as a drunkard longs to drink again when he has just drunk. He would watch for the moment when the way was clear, steal along the corridors and up the winding stairs. Then, having reached close to the top of the staircase, near a trap-door in the ceiling which led on to the battlements of the tower, he would stop, and lean against the shelving turning wall opposite the door, or sit down on the steps, his eyes fixed on the tower wall, where a faint line and the rusty little bolt revealed the presence of the hidden chamber.

What he did it would be hard to say; indeed, he did nothing, he merely felt. There was nothing at all to see, in the material sense; and this piece of winding staircase was just like any other piece of winding staircase in the world: it was not anything external that he wanted, it was that ineffable something within himself. So at least Mr. Little imagined at first, frequently persuading himself that, to a nature like his, all baser satisfaction of curiosity was as nothing; telling himself that he did not care what was inside the room, that he did not even wish to know. Why, if by the pulling of that bolt he might see and know all, he would not pull it. And, saying this to himself, by way of proving it, he laid his fingers gently on the bolt. And in so doing he discovered the depth of his self-delusion. How different was this emotion when he felt—he actually felt—the bolt begin to slide in his hand, from what he had experienced before, while merely contemplating it! The blood seemed to rush through his veins, he felt almost faint. This was reality, this was possession. The mystery lay there, with the bolt, in the hollow of his hand; at any instant he might. . . . Mr. Little had no intention of drawing the bolt. He never reasoned about it, but he knew that that bolt never must, never should, be drawn by him. But in proportion to this knowledge was the entrancing excitement of feeling that the bolt might be drawn, that he grasped it in his fingers, that a little electric current through some of his nerves, a little twitch in some of his muscles, and the mystery would be disclosed.

It was the last of the seven days' revelry of the coming of age. All the other neighboring properties of the Hotspurs had been visited in turn; tenants had been made to dine and dance on one lawn after another; innumerable grouse had been massacred on the moors; endless sets of Venetian lanterns had been lighted, had caught fire, and tumbled on to people's heads; Sir Hugh's old port and Johannisberg, and the strange honey-beer, called Morocco, brewed for centuries at Hotspur, had flowed like water, or rather like the rain, which freely fell, but did not quench that northern ardor. There was to be a grand ball that night, and a grand display of fireworks. But Mr. Little's soul was not attuned to merriment, nor were the souls, as he suspected, of Sir Hugh Hotspur and his son. For, according to popular tradition, it was on this last night of the seven days' merry-making that the heir of Hotspur must be introduced into the hidden chamber.

Throughout lunch Mr. Little kept his eyes on the face of his host and his host's son. What might be passing in their mind? Was it hidden terror or a dare-devil desperation at the thought of what the night must bring? But neither Sir Hugh nor young Harry showed the slightest emotion; their faces, it seemed to Mr. Little, were imperturbable like stone.

Mr. Little waited till the family and guests were safely assembled on the tennis-lawn, then hastened along the corridor and up the steps of the peel tower. The afternoon, after all the rain, was hot and steamy, clearly foreboding a storm; and as Mr. Little groped his way up the tower steps, he felt his heart moving slackly and irregularly, and a clamminess spread over his face and hands; he had to stop several times in order to take breath. As usual, he seated himself on the topmost step, holding his knees with his arms, and looking at the piece of wall opposite, which concealed the mysterious door.

Mr. Little sat there a long time, while the tower stairs grew darker and darker, the faint line betraying the door grew invisible, and even the bolt was lost in the general darkness. To-night—the thought, nay, almost the sentence in which it was framed, went on like a bell in Mr. Little's mind—to-night they would creep up those stairs, they would stand before that door. Sir Hugh's hand would be upon that bolt: he saw it all so plainly, he felt every tingle and shudder that would pass through their bodies. Mr. Little rose and gently grasped the bolt; how easily it would move? Sir Hugh would not require the smallest effort. Or would it be young Harry Hotspur? No; it would doubtless be Sir Hugh. He would pause like that a moment, his hand on the bolt, whispering a few words of encouragement, perhaps a prayer. No; he would be silent. He would hold the bolt, little guessing how recently another hand had been upon it, little dreaming that, but a few hours before another member of the family of Hotspur (for Mr. Little always regarded himself in that light) had had it in his power to. . . .

The thought remained unfinished in Mr. Little's mind. With a cry he fell all of a heap upon the steps, a blinding light in his eyes, a deafening roar in his ears. He had opened the secret door.

He came slowly to his senses, and with life there returned an overwhelming, vague sense of horror. What he had done he did not know; but he knew he had done something terrible. He slid, it seemed to him that he almost trickled—for his limbs had turned to water—down the stairs. He ran, and yet seemed to be dragging himself, along the corridors and

out of one of the many ivy-grown doorways of the old border castle. To the
left hand of the gate, at a little distance, was the tennis-court; a long beam
of sun, yellow among the storm-clouds, fell upon the grass, burnishing it
into metallic green, and making the white, red, yellow, and blue of the
players' dresses stand out like colored enamel. Some of them shouted to
him, among others young Harry Hotspur; but Mr. Little rushed on, heed-
less of their shouts, scaling the banks of grass, breaking through the hedges,
scrambling up hillside after hillside, until he had got to the top of the fells,
where the short grayish-green grass began to be variegated with brown
patches of bog and lilac and black patches of heather, and cut in all directions by the low walls of loose black stones. He stopped and looked back.
But he started off again, as he saw in the distance below, among the ashes
and poplars of the narrow valley which furrowed those treeless undulations
of moorland, the chimney-stacks of Hotspur Hall, the battlements of the
square, black peel tower, reddened by the low light.

On he went, slower, indeed, but still onward, until every vestige of
Hotspur and of every other human habitation was out of sight, and the
chain of fells had closed round him, billow upon billow, under the fading
light. On he went, looking neither to the right nor to the left, save when he
was startled by the bubbling of a brook, spurting from the brown moor bog
on to the stony road; or by the bleating of the sheep who wandered, vague
white specks, upon the grayish grass of the hillside. The clouds accumulated
in gray masses, with an ominous yellow clearing in their midst, and across
the fells there came the sound of distant thunder. Presently a few heavy
drops began to fall; but Mr. Little did not heed them, but went quickly
on, among the bleating of the sheep and the cry of the curlews, along the
desolate road across the fells; rain-drop sueceeding rain-drop, till the hill-
tops were enveloped in a sheet of rain.

But Mr. Little did not turn back. He was dazed, vacant, quite unconscious of all save one thing: he had opened the hidden door at Hotspur Hall.

At length the road made a turn, began to descend, and in a dip of the
fells some light shone forth in the darkness and the mist. Mr. Little started,
and very near ran back: he had thought for a moment that these must
be the lights of Hotspur: but a second's reflection told him that Hotspur
must lie far behind, and presently, among the blinding rain which fell

in cold sheets, he found himself among some low black cottages. In the window of one of them was a light, and over the door, in the darkness, swung an inn sign. He knocked, and entered the inn kitchen, a trickle of water following him wherever he went, and, in the tone and with the look of a sleep-walker, said something about having been overtaken by a storm during a walk on the moors, and wanting a night's shelter. The innkeeper and his wife were evidently too pastoral-minded to reflect that gentlemen do not usually walk on the fells without a hat, and in blue silk socks and patent-leather shoes; and they heaped up the fire, by the side of which Mr. Little collapsed into an arm-chair, indifferent to the charms of bacon and beer and hot griddlecakes.

He tried to settle his ideas. Of what had passed he knew but this much for certain, that he had opened the secret door.

The following morning Mr. Little summoned up his courage, and, after a great argument with himself, turned his steps toward Hotspur Hall. The day was fresh and blowy; a delicate blue haze hung over the hills, out of which, larger and larger, emerged a brilliant blue sky. In the valley the towers of Hotspur and its tall chimneys rose among the trees. Soon Mr. Little could see the bright patches of geranium on the lawn. All this, he argued with himself, must have been a delusion, a result of over-psychological study and a thunder-storm upon a nervous and poetical temperament. He tried to remember what he had read about delusions in Carpenter's "Mental Physiology," and about that supposed robbery, or burglary, which Shelley believed himself to have witnessed. Mr. Little couldn't remember the details, but he was pleased it should have been Shelley. He felt quite foolish and almost happy as he passed through the rose garden, among the strawberry nets, and in at the by-entrance of Hotspur. He walked straight into the dining-room, where he knew the family was assembled at breakfast, jauntily, and one hand in his pocket. "Why, Little, where the deuce have you spent the night?" cried Sir Hugh Hotspur; and the question was echoed in various forms by the rest of the company. "Why, Little, have you been in the horse-pond?" cried young Harry, pointing to his guest's clothes, which, drenched the previous night, did indeed suggest some such immersion. Mr. Little did not answer; he felt himself grow cold and pale, and grasped a chair-back. In making this rude remark, the heir of Hotspur had burst into a peal of laughter.

Mr. Little understood; they had found the mysterious chamber empty, its horror fled; he had really opened that door; the heir of Hotspur could still laugh. He explained automatically how he had been caught by a storm on the fells, and been obliged to pass the night at a wayside inn; but the whole time, while he pretended to be eating his breakfast, his brain was on fire with a thought—

"Where had it gone—it, the something which he had let loose?"

That night Mr. Little slept, or rather, as our ancestors more correctly expressed it, lay, at Hotspur. For the word sleep was but a mockery. There was a second storm, and all night the wind howled in the trees, the drops fell from the eaves, and the room was illumined by fitful gleams of lightning. It seemed to Mr. Little that the evil spirit, or whatever else it might be, which had once been safely locked up in the hidden chamber, was now loose in the house. On reflection he could not doubt it: when he had fallen senseless on the stairs, something had passed out of the door; he had heard and felt the wind of its passage. It had issued from the room; it must now be somewhere else, at loose, free to wreak its will with every flash of lightning. Mr. Little expected that the solid masonry of Hotspur would catch fire and burn like a match; with every crash of thunder he expected that the great peel tower would come rattling on to the roof. He realized for the first time the tales of the companions of Ulysses opening the bag of the winds; of the Arabian fisherman breaking Solomon's seal on the flask which held the djinn; they no longer struck him as in the least ridiculous, these stories. He too had done alike. For, after all, was it not possible that there existed in Nature forces, beings, unknown to our ordinary every-day life? Did not all modern investigations point in that direction, and was it not possible, then, that by the mercy of Providence such a force or being, fatal to our weak humanity, might have been permitted to be inclosed within four walls—one family, or rather, one unhappy member of one family, being sacrificed for the good of mankind, and facing this terror alone, that the rest of his kind might not look upon that ineffable mystery? And now he, in the lawlessness of his skepticism, had stepped in and opened that sacred door. . . . He understood now why he had often felt that he was destined to commit some terrible crime.

Mr. Little sat up in bed, and as the lightning fitfully lit up the antique furniture of his room, he began mechanically to mutter some prayers of his childhood, and some Latin formulae of exorcism which he had learned at the time of his offering to do the article "Incubus" for the "Encyclopædia Britannica." What should he do? Confess to Sir Hugh Hotspur or to Sir Hugh's son? He felt terrified at the mere notion; but he understood that his terror was no mere vulgar fear of being reprimanded for a gross breach of hospitality and honor—that it was due to the sense that, having this terrible secret, he had no right to ruin therewith the lives of innocent men. The Hotspurs would know but too soon!

Meanwhile Mr. Little felt an imperative need to confess what he had done, to ask advice and assistance. He wished for once that he had been able to go over to Rome that time that Monsignor Tassel had tried to convert him, instead of being deterred by the oleographs* in Monsignor Tassel's chapel. What would he not give to kneel down in a confessional, and pour out the horrible secret through the perforated brass plate!

All of a sudden he jumped out of bed, struck a light, and dragged his portmanteau into the middle of the room. He had remembered Esmé St. John, and the fact that Esmé St. John, his former chum at Oxford, was working in the slums of Newcastle, not three hours hence. How could he ever, in the lawless hardness of his heart, have thought Esmé ridiculous, have actually tried to reason him out of his High Church asceticism? This was indeed the just retribution, the fall of the proud, that he should now seek shelter and peace in Esmé's spiritual arms, and bring to the man, nay, rather to the saint, at whom he had once scoffed, a story which he would himself have once ridiculed as the most childish piece of superstition. The mere thought of that act of humiliation did him good; and the terrors of the night seemed to diminish as Mr. Little stooped over his portmanteau and folded his clothes with neat but feverish hands. As soon as it was light, he stole out of the house, walked to the neighboring village, knocked up the half-idiotic girl who had charge of the post-office, and sent off a sixpenny telegram telling the Reverend Esmé St. John that he would join him at Newcastle that afternoon.

Mr. Little was rather surprised, and in truth rather dashed, when he met his old friend. He had spent the hours in the train framing his confession: a terrible tale to tell, yet which he felt a sudden disappointment at being

---

* A lithographic print textured to resemble an oil painting.

prevented from telling. Prevented he did feel. He found the Reverend Esmé St. John making a round among his parishioners; they had told him so at Mr. St. John's chapel, and he had realized vividly the whole scene; Esmé, emaciated, hollow-voiced, fresh from some death-bed, leaving the rest of his flock to follow the call of this pale creature, in whom he would scarcely recognize an old friend, and the very touch of whose band would tell him that things more terrible than death were at stake. But it was otherwise. After wandering about various black and grimy slums under the thick black Newcastle sky, and up various precipitous alleys and flights of steps strewed with egg-shells and herringheads, Mr. Little found his old friend in a back yard sheltered by the crumbling red roof of "The Musician's Rest" inn (where the first bars of "Auld Lang Syne" swung over the door). By his side was a fat, tattered, but extremely jovial red-haired woman washing in a tub, and opposite, an unkempt ragamuffin with his hands in his pockets, singing at the top of his little voice a comic song in Northumbrian dialect. Mr. Esmé St. John was leaning against the doorway, laughing with all his might; he was fat, bald, had a red face, and a very humorous eye—in fact, did not resemble in the least the hollowcheeked, flashing-eyed young fanatic of ten years before. He stretched out his broad hand to Mr. Little, and said: "Do listen to this song, it's about the Board School man—it's really too delicious, and the little chap sings it quite nicely!"

Mr. Little listened, not understanding a word, and thinking how little this man, laughing over a foolish song sung by a street-boy, guessed the terrible confession he was about to receive.

When the song was finished, the Reverend Esmé St. John took Little's arm, and began to overwhelm him with futile questions while leading him down the steep streets of Old Newcastle, until they got to the door of a large and gorgeous eating-house.

"You must be hungry," said Mr. St. John. "I've ordered dinner here for a treat, because my old house-keeper, although an excellent creature, does not rise above mutton chops and boiled potatoes, and one should do honor to an old friend."

Mr. Little shook his head. "I am not hungry," he answered, while his friend unfolded his napkin opposite him. He felt inclined to say, grimly, "When a man has let loose a mysterious unknown terror that has been locked up in Hotspur Hall for centuries, he doesn't feel inclined for roast mutton and Bass's beer."

But the place, the tables, plates, napkins, the smell of cooking, stopped him, and he felt stopped also by the face—the jovial, red face—of his old friend. This was not the Esmé to whom he had longed to unbosom himself. And he felt very irritated.

Mr. Little's irritation began to subside when he followed his friend to his lodgings.

"You asked for a bed, in your telegram," said the Reverend Esmé St. John, as they left the eating-rooms, "and I have had a bed put in a spare room of mine, just to show my hospitable intentions. But I shan't be the least bit offended if you prefer to go to the hotel, my dear fellow. You see, I think a clergyman, trying to reclaim the people of these slums, ought to live among his flock, and no better than they. But there is no reason why any one else should live in this crazy old barrack."

They walked, in the twilight, along some precipitous streets, lined with tinkers' dens and old-clothes shops, under the high-level bridge, over whose colossal span the square old castle stood out black against the sky.

Mr. Little crept through a battered wooden gateway, and picked his way among the puddles, the fallen beams, and the refuse heaps of a court-yard. A light appeared at a window.

"Here we are," said Esmé, and they followed an old, witch-like woman, herself following a thin, black cat, up some crazy, wooden stairs, and into a suite of low, large rooms. Mr. St. John held up a lantern. The room in which they stood was utterly dismantled, the very wainscoting torn out, the ceiling gaping in rent lath and plaster. In a corner stood a bed, a crazy chest of drawers, and washing apparatus, a table, and chair; and in the next room, where the old woman's light had preceded them, was a similar bed, a shelf of books, a large black cross nailed to the wall, and a wooden step for kneeling.

"That's my room," said the clergyman. "You may have it if you prefer. But here's a fireplace in this one, so you'd better keep it."

So saying, Mr. St. John applied a match to the faggots,* and the gaunt apartment was flooded with a red light.

---

* In British dialect of the time, this word referred to bundles of firewood.

"I must make some arrowroot for an old woman of mine," said the clergyman, producing a tin can and saucepan. "May I make it on your fire?"

Mr. Little watched him in silence, then suddenly said: "Esmé, I thought at first you were changed from old days, but I see you are still a saint. Alas! I fear it is I who have changed but too sadly;" and he sighed. "You are growing too fat," answered Mr. St. John good-humoredly, but quite missing the fact that this was the exordium of a confession. Then, to Mr. Little's annoyance, he asked him leave to carry the arrowroot to his old woman, who lived in a lane hard by. Mr. Little remained seated by the fire, while the housekeeper (since she must be dignified by such a title) unpacked his portmanteau. Yes, indeed, this was the man to whom he could make his confession, and this was the place—this dismantled, tumble-down old mansion, tenanted now only by a few poor bargees' families and by countless generations of rats. And Mr. Little put another piece of coal on, in preparation of the nightly conference he was about to have.

Presently Mr. St. John returned.

"Esmé," said Mr. Little, putting his hand on his friend's sleeve, "I wish to speak to you."

"About what?" asked Mr. St. John. "It's very late to begin talking."

"About myself," answered Mr. Little, gravely.

"Do you want anything else? Would you like some brandy and water, or another pillow? You may have mine—or an additional blanket?" asked his friend.

Mr. Little shook his head. "I have all I want in the way of material comforts."

"In that case," replied the clergyman, "I shall leave you at once. If, as you imply, you want spiritual comforts, you must wait till to-morrow, for I am perfectly worn out, and have to be up to-morrow at half-past four. I've been nursing a man from the chemical works these five nights. Goodnight!" and, taking his candle, Mr. St. John walked into his room, leaving his friend greatly disconcerted by this want of sympathy.

The following day Mr. Little accompanied his friend on one of his rounds. After visiting a number of squalid places, where Mr. Little would certainly have thought about measles and small-pox had he not been thinking about the mystery of Hotspur Hall, they returned to the row of houses, once fashionable mansions, with their fronts on the river, among which loomed, next to the black and crumbling former Town Hall, the shell of a family mansion in which they were lodged.

"This was once the fashionable part of Newcastle," said Mr. St. John. "An old lady of ninety once told me she could remember the time when this street used to be crowded with coaches and footmen and link boys of a winter's night. I want to show you my mission-room; I'm very proud of it."

They entered a black passage, close to an inexpressibly shabby public-house, and ascended a wide stone staircase, unswept for ages, as was attested by the cabbage-stalks and herring-heads which lay about in various stages of decomposition. On the first landing a rope was stretched, and a line of clothes, or rather rags, drying after the wash-tub, formed a picturesque screen before several open doors, whence issued squealing of babies, grind of sewing machines, and various unsavory odors. Mr. St. John unlocked a door and admitted his friend into a large hall, gracefully decorated with pastoral stucco moldings, but filled with church seats, and whose raised extremity, suggestive of the dais for an orchestra, was occupied by an altar duly appointed according to ritualistic notions. The place smelt considerably of stale tobacco and damp straw.

"These were the former assembly rooms," explained Mr. St. John; "and this, which is now my little chapel for the lowest scum of Newcastle slums, was once the ball-room. What would those ladies in hoops and powder think of the change, I wonder?"

Mr. Little saw his opportunity.

"This place must be haunted," he said. "By-the-way, Esmé, what are your views on the subject of ghosts and the supernatural? I should be very interested to know."

Mr. St. John had locked the door behind them. "Never mention the word ghost before me," he exclaimed, "it drives me perfectly wild to see all the tomfooling that has been going on of late about apparitions, haunted houses, secret chambers, and all that blasphemous rubbish. It is really a retribution of Heaven to see you agnostic wiseacres taking up such contemptible twaddle. I'm very sorry to hear that you have been in correspondence with those people, Little."

"But—" objected Mr. Little.

"No buts for me!" cried the Reverend Esmé St. John, hotly; "I can not conceive how any man of education and character can fiddle-faddle about idiotic superstitions which it is the duty of every Christian and every gentleman to pluck out of the minds of the vulgar."

It was clear that this was not the moment to begin a confession about the mysterious room at Hotspur.

"How surprised he will be," thought Mr. Little (and a vague sense of satisfaction mingled with the horror of the thought), "when he hears that I, even I, the skeptical, antinomian Little, have come in contact with mysteries more strange and awful than any ever examined into by any society for psychical research."

Despite his old friend's want of sympathy, Mr. Decimus Little continued to lodge with the Reverend Esmé St. John, in the grimy and crumbling old mansion by the Tyneside, following him about on his various errands of mercy. "A man situated like me," Mr. Little had said to himself, "a great sinner (if you like the pious formula of former ages), a character predestined to evil (if you prefer the more modern phraseology of determinism), does well to live in the shadow of a truly good man: his saintliness is a bulwark against evil spirits; or, at all events, the sight of perfect serenity and purity of mind must calm a deeply troubled spirit." Indeed, he more than once began to make this remark, in terms even more subtle, to his friend; but Mr. St. John, whether from fear of Mr. Little's dialectic power, which might shake some of his most cherished beliefs, or from some other reason, invariably turned a deaf ear to all such beginnings of confession.

But either the serenity of the ritualistic philanthropist was inadequate to calm a brain so over-excited or the evil spirits let loose by Mr. Little made short work of the bulwarks of Esmé's saintliness. The thought of that opened door began to haunt him like a nightmare: the effort at guessing what had been liberated when that door was opened wore out his energies. Was it a monster—a poor, loathsome, half-human thing, hiding, perhaps lying starving at this moment, in some corner of the castle: a thing without mind, or speech, or shape, but endowed with monstrous strength, starting forth in the night and throttling the unrightful owner or his young children with stupid glee? Or, more horrible almost, forcing by its presence that honorable and kindly old man into crime; tempting him, with the fear lest this hideousness should become known to the world, into spilling the blood of what seemed but a loathly reptile, but might be his third cousin, or his great-uncle? Mr. Little buried his face in his pillow at the thought. But it might be worse still—in that room might have been inclosed some ghastly mediaeval plague, some crumbling long-dead corpse, whose every particle was ready to take wing and spread forgotten diseases over the country. Or was it something less tangible, less conceivable—a ghost, a demon, some fearful supernatural evil?

Every rooming, when his tea was set down by the housekeeper upon the rickety table in his dismantled bedroom, Mr. Little would unfold, with trembling fingers, the local newspaper, half expecting that his eye would fall upon a notice headed "Hotspur Hall." And there were moments when he could scarce resist the impulse of rushing to the station, and buying a ticket for the village nearest Hotspur.

But a stop was put to such fears about a week after his arrival at Newcastle; alas! only to be succeeded by fears much more terrible. Returning home one day he saw a letter on his table; a presentiment told him it was about *that*. Yet he shook all over when he saw the address on the back of the envelope, "Hotspur Hall, Northumberland." He sank on to a chair, and was for some time unable to open the letter. It was from Sir Hugh—Sir Hugh writing to the guest, the cousin who had betrayed all the sacred laws of hospitality, to inform him of all the horrors in which his act had involved an innocent, honorable, and happy household. Mr. Little groaned, and held the letter unopened. Then suddenly be opened it, tore it open madly. It ran as follows:

> "MY DEAR Little:—I have been too busy of late to let you know that Edwardes discovered in your room here, two days after your sudden departure from Hotspur, a whole outfit which you had apparently forgotten. It consists of a shirt, a pair of check breeches, two white ties, a colored silk handkerchief, a sponge, and a razorstrop. Let us know where you wish all this to be sent. I write to relieve your mind on the subject, as you have doubtless missed these valuables. Lady Hotspur and Harry

unite in hoping that you are enjoying yourself, and that we may
see you soon again.

Yours, sincerely,
Hugh North Hotspur.

P. S.—I may tell you—but in strict confidence—a piece of news
that will doubtless give you pleasure. Our Hal is engaged since
the day before yesterday to the Honorable Cynthia Blenkinsop,
whom you admired the evening of the Yeomanry ball. The
wedding is for next May."

What did this mean? They did not suspect him, that was clear; and nothing
terrible had occurred, that was clear also. What then? Was it possible
that. . . . But Mr. Little's eyes rested on the postscript. Harry Hotspur
engaged to the Honorable Cynthia Blenkinsop: a marriage between the two
hereditary enemies, whose enmity dated from the time of Chevy Chase!*
And there returned to his mind the ancient Northumbrian prophecy (he
could not quite pronounce it in the original), that as long as the fell is green
and the moor is purple, as long as deer haunt the woods (they don't, thought
Mr. Little) and the seamew the rocks, as long as the secret door at the Hall
remains closed, so long will never a Hotspur wed a Blenkinsop.

The secret door had been opened, they knew it, and with its opening
the curse had been removed from the family. The heir might laugh, though
he had come of age (he had laughed at Mr. Little's wet clothes, if you
remember); he might marry a Miss Blenkinsop; the door had been opened,
and he had opened it!

Mr. Little jumped up from his chair and rushed to his friend's door.

"Esmé," he cried, "we'll dine at the Kafe" (that being the local pronunciation of the word Cafe) "to-night; and here's a sovereign for the poor woman
who broke her leg. . . . Harry Hotspur is going—" But he stopped himself,
and when the clergyman opened the door, astounded at these high spirits,

---

* Not the actor, but a battle that took place on the England-Scotland border in 1388. The
  "Chevy Chase" was a hunting preserve in the Cheviot Hills of Northumberland, where
  the battle was fought.

and asking why this sudden launching into festivities and lavish charities, he could only answer, "Only a letter I've had from Sir Hugh Hotspur. It seems—it seems I left quite a lot of things behind; a pair of check trowsers among others. Quite valuable, you know—quite valuable!"

But Mr. Little's happiness—nay, self-congratulation—came to a speedy end. That night, as he lay awake, owing to the unwonted luxury of coffee after dinner, a thought struck him. If the—the thing, the mystery, the whatever it was, had been liberated from the secret chamber, as was proved beyond doubt, not only by his consciousness of having opened the door, but by the news in Sir Hugh's letter; and if, at the same time, it had not manifested itself to the inhabitants of the Hall, as was likewise clearly the case from the cheerful tone in which the master of Hotspur wrote, why, then what had become of it? Mr. Little, who believed in the indestructibility of force, could not have imagined it to have come to an end; and, if still existing, it must be somewhere.

At this moment a sound—a moan, which made his blood run cold—issued from the darkness of the room. Mr. Little struck a light. The bare, dismantled room, with its wainscoted walls and torn lath ceiling, was empty, and its bareness admitted of no hiding-place anywhere.

"It is the wind in the chimney!" he said to himself, and extinguished his candle.

But the ghastly moan, this time ending in a sort of gurgling laugh, was repeated, and with it a horrible thought flashed across Mr. Little's mind: What if that mysterious something should attach itself to the man who had disturbed its long seclusion—if the Terror of Hotspur Hall should have fastened upon the rash creature who had let it loose!

And again there issued from the darkness of that dismantled room the moan, the gurgling laugh. In what shape would it reveal itself? Mr. Little, in the course of his studies, had read M. Maury's "Magie en Moyen Age"; a similar work by the Rev. Baring Gould; the valuable "Essay on Superstition in the Middle Ages," by Dr. Schindler, Royal Prussian Sanitary Councilor and Man-midwife at Greiffenberg; he had also once bought the works of Theophrastus Bombastes of Hohenheim, called "Paracelsus," but found them too boring to read. So that his mind was well stocked with alternatives among which a mediaeval mystery could select. His suspicions were one day aroused by a strange-looking man, dark and grimy, who got on to the Tyne steamer one evening at Wallsend, kept his hat over his face and his eyes fixed upon Mr. Little, and then dodged him up and down Newcastle to the very door of his house. "Who are you?" suddenly exclaimed Mr. Little, stopping short and facing him. He half expected the man to unmask—that is, to take off his hat, and, displaying the face of a corpse, to answer, like the mysterious stranger in Calderon's play, "I am thyself." But the man muttered something about its being very hard on a fellow; that since Mr. St. John had been good to the wife, he ought also to be good to the husband; that he had never touched a drop of liquor till after his marriage with that woman—he hadn't, etc. Mr. Little turned away in disgust. On another occasion, his suspicions were awakened by a large black dog, which insisted upon following him, and even walked into his room, but he proved to have his master's address on his collar, and was consequently sent home next morning. One day, again, as Mr. Little was leaning out of the lattice window, looking at the red roofs of Gateshead, the solitary black church on the green mound, surrounded by cinder-heaps and chemical refuse, above the Tyne, his eyes fell upon the gray mass of water which rolled slowly below him; and it seemed to him as if, suddenly, in the curl of a heavy-laden wave, he had seen a face, upturned eyes staring at him. "Pooh!" said Esmé St. John, whom slumming had made slightly cynical, "it's only some wretched creature who's drowned himself. They'll take him up at the next dead-house."

But Mr. Little shook his head: those eyes had looked at him.

Mr. Little had wondered whether he would be haunted: he soon began to be so, or very nearly. He scarcely ventured to enter his room alone, lest he should find waiting for him, he knew not what; or to approach his own bed, lest, on raising the sheet, he should find it already horribly occupied. Every knock made him start; and it was only by an effort that he could induce himself to cry "Come in!" to the old woman who brought him his hot water. But the day was serene compared with the night. He would lie awake for hours listening to the sullen lapping of the Tyne under the windows, to the scurrying of the rats round the walls, the creaking of broken woodwork in the wind, the rattling of the incessant trains over the high-level bridge close by: lie awake breathless, feeling a presence in the room, but never daring to open his eyes; feeling it coming nearer and nearer, and at the same time expanding, filling the place, choking him, yet never daring to look; until the horrible consciousness would die away as it had come, and there remain only the sickening terror it had brought, and the speculations, while listening to the strokes of the Gateshead clock, as to what the terror might be. Yet, was it something visible, definable, or was it merely a vague curse?

"Esmé," said Mr. Little one day, "do you consider—do you consider—that a man who knows his life to be under a curse; well, suppose something like insanity, you know: but not that—nothing really hereditary, merely a personal thing, a curse, a something making life quite unbearable to him and every one else—do you think that such a man would have a right to marry?"

Mr. St. John looked at him long and fixedly. "Such a man, in my humble opinion, ought to have a good course of iron, or phosphorus, or, best of all, of whipping, to take down his conceit; and he certainly oughtn't to get married, unless he knew for certain that the lady would administer some such treatment to him."

"You have grown very coarse, Esmé!" exclaimed Mr. Little, "I admit that you do a great deal of good to others, but I sometimes question whether a man of refinement by associating wholesale with laundresses and bargees does much good to himself."

"Very likely not," replied the clergyman, dryly. "Happily, some men aren't always thinking all day long whether they are doing good to themselves or not."

"He is right, all the same, he is right," said Mr. Little to himself.

Whatever the coarseness of fibre of Mr. St. John, and his lack of all power of sympathy and intuition, there was no denying that he had given expression to a very sound ethical view.

No; a man in the position of Decimus Little must not marry. He must not drag another life into the atmosphere of horror with which, in one second of lawlessness, he had surrounded himself. It was impossible to conceive a happy home with the mysterious horror of Hotspur Hall constantly in the background. No; he must never marry. But had he not foreseen this answer before putting the question to his friend? Nay, had he not always felt, long before setting his foot in Hotspur Hall, that some dark fate would come between him and happiness; that the joys of wife and children were not for a creature like him, unreal and lawless, marked for some strange and horrible destiny? All this had not been mere silly despondency, or, as his friend Esmé would have thought, morbid self-importance.

He determined to write to his cousin and break off at once. But how convey to this charming, buoyant, and decidedly positivistic and positive young student of Girton a fact so contrary to all her beliefs and tendencies, as that an unknown terror, inclosed for centuries in the secret chamber of a border castle, had suddenly, through his fault, shunted itself upon him? Mr. Little revolved the matter in his mind, and found a melancholy little pleasure in so doing. He determined at last upon merely telling the young lady that this marriage had become impossible, and hinting dimly to her that this was due to no diminution of affection, no want of duty on his part, but to a terrible and mysterious curse (*not insanity, nor consumption*—he would underline that) under which he was laboring, and which forbade his ever sharing a life which meant unspeakable horror.

Mr. Little sat for a long time before his writing-case, resting his chin on his hand, and jotting down half sentences at intervals.

Yes, he could see it all: the surprise and mystification of the dear girl, her tears of rage (he knew she would rage), her feeling of faintness and sickness, her sudden calling upon her bosom friend, Miss Hopper (the student of political economy, with the cropped hair and divided skirts)—he had always disliked Miss Hopper, an unwomanly young person—to shed light upon it. And even Miss Hopper, who, he knew, had once said she was surprised her Gwendolen could love any man, and least of all a little, gray-haired muff—even Miss Hopper would have to admit that her friend's unhappy lover was marvelously magnanimous. And then Gwendolen would write imploringly to know what had happened; nay, rather (he knew her well), she would come herself, arrive at Newcastle, drive to his house, and then there would be a grand explanation. Esmé St. John would be present, that would make everything proper, and Esmé would be so astounded; and Gwendolen would go on her knees to him and he on his knees to Gwendolen, and finally they would bid each other farewell, and Esmé would take her hand, and bid her kiss Decimus, and then lead her away to the nearest sisterhood, where she would immediately proceed to turn hospital nurse for the rest of her days, and wear a lock of Decimus's hair round her neck under a scapular.

Mr. Little covered his eyes with his bands, and began to cry. For the first time since opening that door he felt quite peaceable and pleased with himself.

He was startled by the entrance of Martha, Mr. St. John's old housekeeper.

"I beg your pardon, sir," she said, making a violent effort over a strong northern accent, "but would you mind my dusting a little?"

"Dust away," answered Mr. Little, sadly, implying that he, too, was dust and ashes.

In a room as scantily furnished as was Mr. Little's, the operation of dusting would, one might imagine, be necessarily a brief one; but Martha contrived to prolong it singularly. She was passing the duster for the fourth or fifth time over the lid of Mr. Little's portmanteau, when she suddenly turned round, and said—

"I beg your pardon, sir."

"I did not say anything," answered Mr. Little, gloomily.

"No, sir, no more you did, sir. But I was a-saying, sir, if as I might take the liberty, sir, as I see—but there was no prying, sir, I assure you, for I'm greatly averse to prying into folks' concerns, especially the gentry's, and it was all casual like, as we say. I was a-saying, sir, seeing how you received a letter from Sir Hugh Hotspur the other day; if you would just put in a word for me now as they've got a new butler, for it would indeed be a charity, let alone all the injustice, to get a body back into her rights, and a widow, too, as I've been these fifteen years, and with only a third cousin in the world."

"My good woman," interrupted Mr. Little, "explain yourself. I fail to comprehend a word."

"Well, then, sir," proceeded Martha, resuming the violent efforts to get the better of her Northumbrian accent, "you should know that I was once in a better place than this, as good a place as any of them have, . . . for I was laundress at Hotspur Hall, and a better laundress you never seed, sir, nor linen better kept than mine was. And then, as Heaven would have it, on account of the wickedness of men, I lost my place through no fault of mine, but merely all along of that room in the peel tower, the room as is lit from the top and as has no windows, as perhaps, sir, you know."

"Hush!" cried Mr. Little, with a gesture like that of a man fainting, "for mercy's sake, woman . . . explain . . . that room . . . the room on the topmost landing of the peel tower. . . ."

"Yes, sir, with a door as is hidden in the wall—secret like."

"You opened that door! You were sent away for opening that door! Answer me—for Heaven's sake, Martha, answer me!" and Mr. Little clutched the old lady's arm.

"Lor, sir! there was no harm meant. I did not mean to be prying into other folks' concerns, as I always says is best left alone. Although there is such as is always a-prying into everything—"

"You opened that door! Yes, or no!"

"Well, yes, sir, I did, as I was a-going to tell you, sir," cried Martha, terrified at Mr. Little's face, and trying to extricate her arm from his hand. "I beg your pardon, sir, as you're a-tearing of my sleeve."

Mr. Little let her go.

"That door—the last door in the peel tower, on the left; a door hidden in the wall; the door of a—room without a window; a room lit from the battlements above!"

"Yes, sir," answered Martha, beginning to quake all over; "exactly as you says, sir. The topmost door in the peel tower, on the left; a door hidden in the wall. It was all along of opening that, as you says, sir."

"Then, Martha," said Mr. Little, solemnly, sitting upright, and fixing his eyes on the old woman's, "you were sent away from Hotspur Hall for opening that door—the door of the secret chamber!"

"Well, sir, it may be called the secret chamber, for all as I know now, and the butler would have had me keep it a secret what I saw there, sure enough—all them bottles of wine as he had hidden away to sell to the 'Blue Bull' at Blenkinsop; but of my time there was no one as had a right to call it a secret room, seeing as it was the room as we used to put the drying lines in o' winter, when it was too damp to dry the clothes out of doors, as maybe it still is, on account of that draught from the skylight in the roof."

"Enough!" cried Mr. Little. "Woman, not one word more!"

Visitors at Hotspur Hall still continue to look for the secret room, to hang out towels from the windows, and pump the servants, all in vain. Young Harry Hotspur was never known to laugh quite as much as that time that Mr. Little appeared at breakfast in the clothes which he had worn that night on the fell; at least, he rarely laughed except when he chanced to see Mr. Little. As to the marriage question, and the difficulty of reconciling it to the prophecy that so long as the fell was green and the moor purple, and the deer haunted the woods and the seamew the rocks, as long as the secret chamber at Hotspur Hall remained undiscovered, so long would never a Hotspur wed a Blenkinsop, it might be interesting to examine into this incongruity in a serious psychological spirit. Such persons as are destitute of any taste for serious psychology merely answer to any objection of the kind, that the Honorable Cynthia Blenkinsop was possessed not merely of a charming person but of sixty thousand a year; and that a secret chamber inhabited by an unspecified horror, although a very delightful heirloom in an ancient family, is not sufficient capital in these days of ostentatious living and riotous luxury. As regards Mr. Decimus Little, he is at present in Turkey, on a trial trip with his cousin Gwendolen and her mother, which will decide whether or not he shall be married to her next January by the Reverend Esmé St. John.

UNEXPLAINED

by Mary Louisa Molesworth

1888

Mary Louisa Stewart was born in Rotterdam; her father was an English merchant who moved to Manchester and became prosperous enough to have her educated in Britain and Switzerland. At the age of twenty-two, she married a Major Molesworth, the nephew of an Irish Viscount. They were legally separated after eighteen years, but by then Mary had established herself as a popular writer, best known for her children's books: one critic dubbed her "the Jane Austen of the nursery." She kept her estranged husband's name, publishing as "Mrs. Molesworth" or occasionally as "M. L. S. Molesworth." Most of her children's stories have not aged well; they are too full of simplistic, saccharine moralism for modern tastes.

Her novels for adult readers appeared under the pseudonym "Ennis Graham." She published two collections of uncanny fiction: Four Ghost Stories (1888) and Uncanny Stories (1896), as well as a handful of ghost stories in her other collections.

"Unexplained" amounts almost to a novella, but it is one of her best. It was first published in 1888, in Four Ghost Stories.

PART I

"For facts are stubborn things." —SMOLLETT.

S ilberbach! What in the name of everything that is eccentric should you go there for? The most uninteresting, out-of-the-way, altogether unattractive little hole in all Germany? What can have put Silberbach in your head?"

"I really don't know," I answered, rather tired, to tell the truth, of the discussion. "There doesn't seem any particular reason why anybody ever should go to Silberbach, except that Goethe and the Duke of Weimar are supposed to have gone there to dance with the peasant maidens. I certainly don't see that that is any reason why *I* should go there. Still, on the other hand, I don't see that it is any reason why I should *not*? I only want to find some thoroughly country place where the children and I can do as we like for a fortnight or so. It is really too hot to stay in a town, even a little town like this."

"Yes, that is true," said my friend. "It is a pity you took up your quarters in the town. You might have taken a little villa outside, and then you would not have needed to go away at all."

"I wanted a rest from housekeeping, and our queer old inn is very comfortable," I said. "Besides, being here, would it not be a pity to go away without seeing anything of the far-famed Thuringian Forest?"

"Yes, certainly it would. I quite agree with you about everything except about Silberbach. *That* is what I cannot get over. You have not enough self-assertion, my dear. I am certain Silberbach is some freak of Herr von Walden's—most unpractical man. Why, I really am not at all sure that you will get anything to eat there."

"I am not afraid of *that* part of it," I replied philosophically. "With plenty of milk, fresh eggs, and bread and butter, we can always get on. And those I suppose we are sure to find."

"Milk and eggs—yes, I suppose so. Butter is doubtful once you leave the tourist track, and the bread will be the sour bread of the country."

"I don't mind that—nor do the children. But if the worst comes to the worst we need not stay at Silberbach—we can always get away."

"That is certainly true; if one can get there, one can, I suppose, always get away," answered Fräulein Ottilia with a smile, "though I confess it is a curious inducement to name for going *to* a place—that one can get away from it! However, we need not say any more about it. I see your heart is set on Silberbach, and I am quite sure I shall have the satisfaction of hearing you own I was right in trying to dissuade you from it, when you come back again," she added, rather maliciously.

"Perhaps so. But it is not *only* Silberbach we are going to. We shall see lots of other places. Herr von Walden has planned it all. The first three days we shall travel mostly on foot. I think it will be great fun. Nora and Reggie are enchanted. Of course I would not travel on foot alone with them; it would hardly be safe, I suppose?"

"Safe? oh yes, safe enough. The peasants are very quiet, civil people—honest and kindly, though generally desperately poor! But you would be *safe* enough anywhere in Thuringia. It is not like Alsace, where now and then one does meet with rather queer customers in the forests. So good-bye, then, my dear, for the next two or three weeks—and may you enjoy yourself."

"Especially at Silberbach?"

"*Even* at Silberbach—that is to say, even if I have to own you were right and I wrong. Yes, my dear, I am unselfish enough to hope you will return having found Silberbach an earthly paradise."

And waving her hand in adieu, kind Fräulein Ottilia stood at her garden-gate watching me make my way down the dusty road.

"She is a little prejudiced, I daresay," I thought to myself. "Prejudiced against Herr von Walden's choice, for I notice every one here has their pet places and their special aversions. I daresay we shall like Silberbach, and if not, we need not stay there after the Waldens leave us. Anyway, I shall be thankful to get out of this heat into the real country."

I was spending the summer in a part of Germany hitherto new ground to me. We had—the "we" meaning myself and my two younger children, Nora of twelve and Reggie of nine—settled down for the greater part of the time in a small town on the borders of the Thuringian Forest. Small, but not in its own estimation unimportant, for it was a "Residenz," with a fortress of sufficiently ancient date to be well worth visiting, even had the view from its ramparts been far less beautiful than it was. And had the little town possessed no attractions of its own, natural or artificial, the extreme cordiality and kindness of its most hospitable inhabitants would have left the pleasantest impression on my mind. I was sorry to leave my friends even for two or three weeks, but it was *too* hot! Nora was pale and Reggie's noble appetite gave signs of flagging. Besides—as I had said to Ottilia—it would be too absurd to have come so far and not see the lions of the neighbourhood.

So we were to start the next morning for an excursion in the so-called "Forest," in the company of Herr von Walden, his wife and son, and two young men, friends of the latter. We were to travel by rail over the first part of the ground, uninteresting enough, till we reached a point where we could make our way on foot through the woods for a considerable distance. Then, after spending the night in a village whose beautiful situation had tempted some enterprising speculator to build a good hotel, we proposed the next day to plunge still deeper into the real recesses of the forest, walking and driving by turns, in accordance with our inclination and the resources of the country in respect of *Einspänners*—the light carriage with the horse invariably yoked at one side of the pole instead of between shafts, in which one gets about more speedily and safely than might be imagined. And at the end of three or four days of this, weather permitting, agreeably nomad life, our friends the Waldens, obliged to return to their home in the town from which we started, were to leave my children and me for a fortnight's country air in this same village of Silberbach which Ottilia so vehemently objected to. I did not then, I do not now, know—and I am pretty sure he himself could not say—why our guide, Herr von Walden, had chosen

Silberbach from among the dozens of other villages which could quite as well—as events proved, indeed, infinitely better—have served our very simple purpose. It was a chance, as such things often are, but a chance which, as you will see, left its mark in a manner which can never be altogether effaced from my memory.

The programme was successfully carried out. The weather was magnificent. Nobody fell ill or footsore, or turned out unexpectedly bad-tempered. And it was hot enough, even in the forest shades, which we kept to as much as possible, to have excused some amount of irritability. But we were all sound and strong, and had entered into a tacit compact of making the best of things and enjoying ourselves as much as we could. Nora and Reggie perhaps, by the end of the second day, began to have doubts as to the delights of indefinitely continued walking excursions; and though they would not have owned to it, they were not, I think, sorry to hear that the greater part of the fourth day's travels was to be on wheels. But they were very well off. Lutz von Walden and his two friends—a young baron, rather the typical "German student" in appearance, though in reality as hearty and unsentimental as any John Bull of his age and rank—and George Norman, an English boy of seventeen or eighteen, "getting up" German for an army examination—were all three only too ready to carry my little boy on their backs on any sign of over-fatigue. And, indeed, more than one hint reached me that they would willingly have done the same by Nora, had the dignity of her twelve years allowed of such a thing. She scarcely looked her age at that time, but she was very conscious of having entered "on her teens," and the struggle between this new importance and her hitherto almost boyish tastes was amusing to watch. She was strong and healthy in the extreme, intelligent though not precocious, observant but rather matter-of-fact, with no undue development of the imagination, nothing that by any kind of misapprehension or exaggeration could have been called "morbid" about her. It was a legend in the family that the word "nerves" existed not for Nora: she did not know the meaning of *fear*, physical or moral. I could sometimes wish she had never learnt otherwise. But we must take the bad with the good, the shadow inseparable from the light. The first perception of things not dreamt of in her simple childish philosophy came to Nora as I would not have chosen it; but so, I must believe, it had to be.

"Where are we to sleep to-night, Herr von Walden, please?" asked Reggie from the heights of Lutz's broad shoulders, late that third afternoon, when we were all, not the children only, beginning to think that a rest even in the barest of inn parlours, and a dinner even of the most modest description, would be very welcome.

"Don't tease so, Reggie," said Nora. "I'm sure Herr von Walden has told you the name twenty times already."

"Yes, but I forget it," urged the child; and good-natured Herr von Walden, nowise loath to do so again, took up the tale of our projected doings and destinations.

"To-night, my dear child, we sleep at the pretty little town—yes, town I may almost call it—of Seeberg. It stands in what I may call an oasis of the forest, which stops abruptly, and begins again some miles beyond Seeberg. We should be there in another hour or so," he went on, consulting his watch. "I have, of course, written for rooms there, as I have done to all the places where we mean to halt. And so far I have not proved a bad courier, I flatter myself?"

He paused, and looked round him complacently.

"No, indeed," replied everybody. "The very contrary. We have got on capitally."

At which the beaming face of our commander-in-chief beamed still more graciously.

"And to-morrow," continued Reggie in his funny German, pounding away vigorously at Lutz's shoulders meanwhile, "what do we do to-morrow? We must have an *Einspänner*—is it not so? not that we are tired, but you said we had far to go."

"Yes, an *Einspänner* for the ladies—your amiable mother, Miss Nora, and my wife, and you, Reggie, will find a corner beside the driver. Myself and these young fellows," indicating the three friends by a wave of the hand, "will start from Seeberg betimes, giving you *rendez vous* at Ulrichsthal, where there are some famous ruins. And you must not forget," he added, turning to his wife and me, "to stop at Grünstein as you pass, and spend a quarter of an hour in the china manufactory there."

"Just what I wanted," said Frau von Walden. "I have a tea-service from there, and I am in hopes of matching it. I had a good many breakages last winter with a dreadfully careless servant, and there is a good deal to replace."

"I don't think I know the Grünstein china," I said. "Is it very pretty?"

"It is very like the blue-and-white that one sees so much of with us," said Frau von Walden. "That, the ordinary blue-and-white, is made at Blauenstein. But there is more variety of colours at Grünstein. They are rather more enterprising there, I fancy, and perhaps there is a finer quality of china clay, or whatever they call it, in that neighbourhood. I often wonder the Thuringian china is not more used in England, where you are so fond of novelties."

"And where nothing is so appreciated as what comes from a distance," said George Norman. "By Jove! isn't that a pretty picture!" he broke off suddenly, and we all stood still to admire.

It was the month of August; already the subdued evening lights were replacing the brilliant sunshine and blue sky of the glowing summer day. We were in the forest, through which at this part ran the main road which we were following to Seeberg. At one side of the road the ground descended abruptly to a considerable depth, and there in the defile far beneath us ran a stream, on one bank of which the trees had been for some distance cleared away, leaving a strip of pasture of the most vivid green imaginable. And just below where we stood, a goatherd, in what—thanks possibly to the enchant-ment of the distance—appeared a picturesque costume, was slowly making his way along, piping as he went, and his flock, of some fifteen or twenty goats of every colour and size, following him according to their own eccentric fashion, some scrambling on the bits of rock a little way up the ascending ground, others quietly browsing here and there on their way—the tinkling of their collar-bells reaching us with a far-away, silvery sound through the still softer and fainter notes of the pipe. There was something strangely fasci-nating about it all—something pathetic in the goatherd's music, simple, bar-baric even as it was, and in the distant, uncertain tinkling, which impressed us all, and for a moment or two no one spoke.

"What is it that it reminds me of?" said Lutz suddenly. "I seem to have seen and heard it all before."

"Yes, I know exactly how you mean," I replied. "It is like a dream;" and as I said so, I walked on again a little in advance of the others with Lutz and his rider. For I *thought* I saw a philosophical or metaphysical dissertation preparing in Herr von Walden's bent brows and general look of absorption, and somehow, just then, it would have spoilt it all. Lutz seemed instinctively to understand, for he too for a moment or so was silent, when suddenly a joyful cry arose.

"Seeberg!" exclaimed several voices; for the first sight of our temporary destination broke upon the view all at once, as is often the case in these more or less wooded districts. One travels for hours together as if in an enchanted land of changeless monotony; trees, trees everywhere and nothing but trees—one could fancy late in the afternoon that one was back at the early morning's starting-point—when suddenly the forest stops, sharply and completely, where the hand of man has decreed that it should, not by gradual degrees as when things have been left to the gentler management of nature and time.

So our satisfaction was the greater from not having known the goal of that day's journey to be so near. We began to allow to each other for the first time that we were "a *little* tired," and with far less hesitation that we were "*very* hungry." Still we were not a very dilapidated-looking party when the inhabitants of Seeberg turned out at doors and windows to inspect us. Reggie, of course, whom no consideration could induce to make his entry on Lutz's shoulders, looking the freshest of all, and eliciting many complimentary remarks from the matrons and maidens of the place as we passed.

Our quarters at Seeberg met with the approval of everybody. The supper was excellent, our rooms as clean and comfortable as could be wished.

"So far," I could not help saying to my friends, "I have seen no signs of the 'roughing it' for which you prepared me. I call this luxurious."

"Yes, this is very comfortable," said Herr von Walden. "At Silberbach, which we shall reach to-morrow evening, all will be much more homely."

"But that is what I like," I maintained stoutly. "I assure you I am not at all *difficile*, as the French say."

"Still," began Frau von Walden, "are you sure that you know what 'roughing it' means? One has such romantic, unpractical ideas till one really tries it. For me, I confess, there is something very depressing in being without all the hundred and one little comforts, not to say luxuries, that have become second nature to us, and yet I do not think I am a self-indulgent woman."

"Certainly not," I said, and with sincerity.

"If it were necessary," she went on, "I hope I should be quite ready to live in a cottage and make the best of it cheerfully. But when it is not necessary? Don't you think, my dear friend, it would perhaps be wiser for you to arrange to spend your two or three weeks *here*, and not go on to Silberbach? You might return here to-morrow from Ulrichsthal while we make our way home, by Silberbach, if my husband really wishes to see it."

I looked at her in some surprise. What possessed everybody to caution me so against Silberbach? Everybody, that is to say, except Herr von Walden himself. A spice of contradiction began to influence me. Perhaps the worthy Herr had himself been influenced in the same way more than he realised.

"I don't see why I should do so," I said. "We expect really to enjoy ourselves at Silberbach. You have no reason for advising me to give it up?"

"No, oh no—none in particular," she replied. "I have only a feeling that it is rather out of the way and lonely for you. Supposing, for instance, one of the children got ill there?"

"Oh, my dear, you are *too* fanciful," said her husband. "Why should the children get ill there more than anywhere else? If one thought of all these possibilities one would never stir from home."

"And you know my maid is ready to follow me as soon as I quite settle where we shall stay," I said. "I shall not be alone more than four-and-twenty hours. Of course it would have been nonsense to bring Lina with us; she would have been quite out of her element during our walking expeditions."

"And I have a very civil note from the inn at Silberbach, the 'Katze,'" said Herr von Walden, pulling a mass of heterogeneous-looking papers out of his pocket. "Where can it be? Not that it matters; he will have supper and beds ready for us to-morrow night. And then," he went on to me, "if you like it you can make some arrangement for the time you wish to stay, if not you can return here, or go on to any place that takes your fancy. We, my wife and I and these boys, *must* be home by Saturday afternoon, so we can only stay the one night at Silberbach," for this was Thursday.

And so it was settled.

The next day dawned as bright and cloudless as its predecessors. The gentlemen had started—I should be afraid to say how early—meaning to be overtaken by us at Ulrichsthal. Reggie had gone to bed with the firm intention of accompanying them, but as it was not easy to wake him and get him up in time to eat his breakfast, and be ready when the *Einspänner* came round to the door, my predictions that he would be too sleepy for so early a start proved true.

It was pleasant in the early morning—pleasanter than it would be later in the day. I noticed an unusual amount of blue haze on the distant mountain-tops, for the road along which we were driving was open on all sides for some distance, and the view was extensive.

"That betokens great heat, I suppose," I said, pointing out the appearance I observed to my companion.

"I suppose so. That bluish mist probably increases in hot and sultry weather," she said. "But it is always to be seen more or less in this country, and is, I believe, peculiar to some of the German hill and forest districts. I don't know what it comes from—whether it has to do with the immense number of pines in the forests, perhaps. Some one, I think, once told me that it indicates the presence of a great deal of electricity in the air, but I am far too ignorant to know if that is true or not."

"And I am far too ignorant to know what the effect would be if it were so," I said. "It is a very healthy country, is it not?"

"For strangers it certainly is. Doctors send their patients here from all parts of Germany. But the inhabitants themselves do not seem strong or healthy. One sees a good many deformed people, and they all look pale and thin—much less robust than the people of the Black Forest. But that may come from their poverty—the peasants of the Black Forest are pro-verbially well off."

A distant, very distant, peal of thunder was heard at this moment.

"I hope the weather is not going to break up *just* yet," I said. "Are there often bad thunderstorms here?"

"Yes; I think we do have a good many in this part of the world," she replied. "But I do not think there are any signs of one at present."

And then, still a little sleepy and tired from our unusual exertions of the last three days, we all three, Frau von Walden, Nora, and myself, sat very still for some time, though the sound of Reggie's voice persistently endeavouring to make the driver understand his inquiries, showed that he was as lively as ever.

He turned round after a while in triumph.

"Mamma, Frau von Walden," he exclaimed, "we are close to that place where they make the cups and saucers. Herr von Walden said we weren't to forget to go there—and you all *would* have forgotten, you see, if it hadn't been for me," he added complacently.

"Grünstein," said Frau von Walden. "Well, tell the driver to stop there, he can rest his horses for half an hour or so; and thank you for reminding us, Reggie, for I should have been sorry to lose the opportunity of matching my service."

The china manufactory was not of any very remarkable interest, at least not for those who had visited such places before. But the people were exceedingly civil, and evidently very pleased to have visitors; and while my friend was looking out the things she was specially in search of—a business which promised to take some little time—a good-natured sub-manager, or functionary of some kind, proposed to take the children to see the sheds where the first mixing and kneading took place, the moulding rooms, the painting rooms, the ovens—in short, the whole process. They accepted his offer with delight, and I wandered about the various pattern or show rooms, examining and admiring all that was to be seen, poking into corners where any specially pretty bit of china caught my eye. But there was no great variety in design or colour, though both were good of their kind, the Grünsteiners, like their rivals of Blauenstein, seeming content to follow in the steps of their fathers without seeking for new inspirations. Suddenly, however, all but hidden in a corner, far away back on a shelf, a flash of richer tints made me start forward eagerly. There was no one near to apply to at the moment, so I carefully drew out my treasure trove. It was a cup and saucer, evidently of the finest quality of china, though pretty similar in shape to the regular Grünstein ware, but in colouring infinitely richer—really beautiful, with an almost Oriental cleverness in the blending of the many shades, and yet decidedly more striking and uncommon than any of the modern Oriental with which of late years the facilities of trade with the East make us so familiar. I stood with the cup in my hand, turning it around and admiring it, when Frau von Walden and the woman who had been attending to her orders came forward to where I was.

"See here," I exclaimed; "here is a lovely cup! Now a service like that *would* be tempting! Have you more of it?" I inquired of the woman.

She shook her head.

"That is all that remains," she said. "We have never kept it in stock; it is far too expensive. Of course it can be made to order, though it would take some months, and cost a good deal."

"I wish I could order a service of it," I said; but when I heard how much it would probably cost it was my turn to shake my head. "No, I must consider about it," I decided; "but I really have never seen anything prettier. Can I buy this cup?"

The woman hesitated.

"It is the only one left," she said; "but I think—oh yes, I feel sure—we have the pattern among the painting designs. This cup belonged to, or rather was an extra one of, a tea-service made expressly for the Duchess of T——, on her marriage, now some years ago. And it is curious, we sold the other one—there were two too many—to a compatriot of yours (the gracious lady is English?) two or three years ago. He admired them so much, and felt sure his mother would send an order if he took it home to show her. A tall, handsome young man he was. I remember it so well; just about this time of the year, and hot, sultry weather like this. He was travelling on foot—for pleasure, no doubt—for he had quite the air of a *milord*. And he bought the cup, and took it with him. But he has never written! I made sure he would have done so."

"He did not leave his name or address?" I said; for the world is a small place: it was just possible I might have known him, and the little coincidence would have been curious.

"Oh no," said the woman. "But I have often wondered why he changed his mind. He seemed so sure about sending the order. It was not the price that made him hesitate; but he wished his lady mother to make out the list herself."

"Well, I confess the price *does* make *me* hesitate," I said, smiling. "However, if you will let me buy this cup, I have great hopes of proving a better customer than my faithless compatriot."

"I am sure he *meant* to send the order," said the woman. She spoke quite civilly, but I was not sure that she liked my calling him "faithless."

"It is evident," I said to Frau von Walden, "that the good-looking young Englishman made a great impression on her. I rather think she gave *him* the fellow cup for nothing."

But after all I had no reason to be jealous, for just then the woman returned, after consulting the manager, to tell me I might have the cup and saucer, and for a less sum than their real worth, seeing that I was taking it, in a sense, as a pattern.

Then she wrapped it up for me, carefully and in several papers, of which the outside one was bright blue; and, very proud of my acquisition, I followed Frau von Walden to the other side of the building containing the workrooms, where we found the two children full of interest about all they had seen.

I should here, perhaps, apologise for entering into so much and apparently trifling detail. But as will, I think, be seen when I have told all I have to tell, it would be difficult to give the main facts fairly, and so as to avoid all danger of any mistaken impression, without relating the whole of the surroundings. If I tried to condense, to pick out the salient points, to enter into no particulars but such as directly and unmistakably lead up to the central interest, I might unintentionally omit what those wiser than I would consider as bearing on it. So, like a patient adjured by his doctor, or a client urged by his lawyer, to tell the whole at the risk of long-windedness, I prefer to run that risk, while claiming my readers' forgiveness for so doing, rather than that of relating my story incompletely.

And what I would here beg to have specially observed is *that not one word about the young Englishman had been heard by Nora.* She was, in fact, in a distant part of the building at the time the saleswoman was telling us about him. And, furthermore, I am equally certain, and so is Frau von Walden, that neither she nor I, then or afterwards, mentioned the subject to, or in the presence of, the children. I did not show her the cup and saucer, as it would have been a pity to undo its careful wrappings. All she knew about it will be told in due course.

We had delayed longer than we intended at the china manufactory, and in consequence we were somewhat late at the meeting-place—Ulrichsthal.

The gentlemen had arrived there quite an hour before; so they had ordered luncheon, or dinner rather, at the inn, and thoroughly explored the ruins. But dinner discussed, and neither Frau von Walden nor I objecting to pipes, our cavaliers were amiably willing to show us all there was to be seen.

The ruins were those of an ancient monastery, one of the most ancient in Germany, I believe. They covered a very large piece of ground, and had they been in somewhat better preservation, they would have greatly impressed us; as it was they were undoubtedly, even to the unlearned in archæological lore, very interesting. The position of the monastery had been well and carefully chosen, for on one side it commanded a view of surpassing beauty over the valley through which we had travelled from Seeberg, while on the other arose still higher ground, richly wooded, for the irrepressible forest here, as it were, broke out again.

"It is a most lovely spot!" I said with some enthusiasm, as we sat in the shade of the ruined cloisters, the sunshine flecking the sward in eccentric patches as it made its way through what had evidently been richly-sculptured windows. "How one wishes it were possible to see it as it must have been—how many?—three or four hundred years ago, I suppose!"

Lutz grunted.

"What did you say, Lutz?" asked his mother.

"Nothing particular," he sighed. "I was only thinking of what I read in the guide-book, that the monastery was destroyed—partly by lightning, I believe, all the same—by order of the authorities, in consequence of the really awful wickedness of the monks who inhabited it. So I am not sure that it would have been a very nice place to visit at the time you speak of, gracious lady, begging your pardon."

"What a pity!" I said, with a little shudder. "I do not like to think of it. And I was going to say how beautiful it must be here in the moonlight! But now that you have disenchanted me, Lutz, I should not like it at all," and I arose as I spoke.

"Why not, mamma?" said Reggie curiously. I had not noticed that he and his sister were listening to us. "They're not here *now*—not those naughty monks."

"No, of course not," agreed practical Nora. "Mamma only means that it is a pity such a beautiful big house as this must have been *had* to be pulled down—such a waste when there are so many poor people in the world with miserable, little, stuffy houses, or none at all even! That was what you meant; wasn't it, mamma?"

"It is always a pity—the worst of pities—when people are wicked, wherever they are," I replied.

"But *all* monks are not bad," remarked Nora consolingly. "Think of the Great St. Bernard ones, with their dogs."

And on Reggie's inquiring mind demanding further particulars on the subject, she walked on with him somewhat in front of the rest of us, a happy little pair in the sunshine.

"Lutz," said his father, "you cannot be too careful what you say before children; they are often shocked or frightened by so little. Though yours are such healthy-minded little people," he added, turning to me, "it is not likely anything undesirable would make any impression on them."

I particularly remember this little incident.

It turned out a long walk to Silberbach, the longest we had yet attempted. Hitherto Herr von Walden had been on known ground, and thoroughly acquainted with the roads, the distances, and all necessary particulars; but it was the first time he had explored beyond Seeberg, and before we had accomplished more than half the journey, he began to feel a little alarm at the information given us by the travellers we came across at long intervals "coming from," not "going to St. Ives!" For the farther we went the greater seemed to be the distance we had to go!

"An hour or thereabouts," grew into "two," or even "three" hours; and at last, on a peculiarly stupid countryman assuring us we would scarcely reach our destination before nightfall, our conductor's patience broke down altogether.

"Idiots!" he exclaimed. "But I cannot stand this any longer. I will hasten on and see for myself; and if, as I expect, we are really not very far from Silberbach, it will be all the better for me to find out the 'Katze,' and see that everything is ready for your arrival."

Frau von Walden seemed a little inclined to protest, but I begged her not to do so, seeing that three able-bodied protectors still remained to us, and that it probably was really tiresome for a remarkably good and trained pedestrian like her husband to have to adapt his vigorous steps to ours. And comfort came from an unexpected quarter. The old peasant woman, strong and muscular as any English labourer, whom we had hired at Seeberg to carry our bags and shawls through the forest, overheard the discussion, and for the first time broke silence to assure "the gracious ladies" that Silberbach was at no great distance; in half an hour or so we should come upon the first of its houses.

"Though as for the 'Katze,'" she added, "that was farther off—at the other end of the village;" and she went on muttering something about "if she had known we were going to the 'Katze,'" which we did not understand, but which afterwards, "being translated," proved to mean that she would have stood out for more pay.

Sure enough, at the end of not more than three-quarters of an hour we came upon one or two outlying houses. Then the trees gradually here grew sparser, and soon ceased, except in occasional patches. It was growing dusk; but as we emerged from the wood we found that we were on a height, the forest road having been a steady, though almost imperceptible, ascent. Far below gleamed already some twinkling cottage lights, and the silvery reflection of a small piece of water.

"To be sure," said young von Trachenfels, "there is a lake at Silberbach. Here we are at last! But where is the 'Katze'?"

He might well ask. Never was there so tantalising a place as Silberbach. Instead of one compact, sensible village, it was more like three or four—nay, five or six—wretched hamlets, each at several minutes' distance from all the others. And the "Katze," of course, was at the farther end of the farthest off from where we stood of these miserable little ragged ends of village! Climbing is tiring work, but it seemed to me it would have been preferable to what lay before us,—a continual descent, by the ruggedest of hill-paths, of nearly two miles, stumbling along in the half light, tired, footsore past description, yet—to our everlasting credit be it recorded—laughing, or trying to laugh, determined at all costs to make the best of it.

"I have no feet left," said poor Frau von Walden. "I am only conscious of two red-hot balls attached somehow to my ankles. I daresay *they* will drop off soon."

How thankful we were at last to attain to what bore some faint resemblance to a village street! How we gazed on every side to discover anything like an inn! How we stared at each other in bewilderment when at last, from we could not see where, came the well-known voice of Herr von Walden, shouting to us to stop.

"It is here—*here*, I say. You are going too far."

"Here," judging by the direction whence came the words, seemed to be a piled-up mass of hay, of proportions, exaggerated perhaps by the uncertain light, truly enormous. Was our friend buried in the middle of it? Not so. By degrees we made out his sunburnt face, beaming as ever, from out of a window behind the hay—cartful or stack, we were not sure which; and by still further degrees we discovered that the hay was being unloaded before a little house which it had almost entirely hidden from view, and inside which it was being carried, apparently by the front door, for there was no other door to be seen; but as we stood in perplexity, Herr von Walden, whose face had disappeared, emerged in some mysterious way.

"You can come through the kitchen, ladies; or by the window, if you please." But though the boys and Nora were got, or got themselves, in through the window, Frau von Walden and I preferred the kitchen; and I remember nothing more till we found ourselves all assembled—the original eight as we had started—in a very low-roofed, sandy-floored, tobacco-impregnated sort of cabin which, it appeared, was the *salle-à-manger* of the renowned hostelry "zur Katze" of Silberbach!

Herr von Walden was vigorously mopping his face. It was very red, and naturally so, considering the weather and the want of ventilation peculiar to the "Katze"; but it struck me there was something slightly forced about the beamingness.

"So, so," he began; "all's well that ends well! But I must explain," and he mopped still more vigorously, "that—there has been a slight, in short, a little, mistake about the accommodation I wish to secure. The supper I have seen to, and it will be served directly. But as to the beds," and here he could not help laughing, "our worthy host has beds enough"—we found afterwards that every available mattress and pillow in the village had been levied—"but there is but one *bedroom*, or two, I may say." For the poor Herr had not lost his time since his arrival. Appalled by the want of resources, he had suggested the levy of beds, and had got the host to spread them on the floor of a granary for himself, the three young men, and Reggie; while his wife, Nora, and I were to occupy the one bedroom, which luckily contained two small beds and a sort of settee, such as one sees in old farmhouses all over the world.

So it was decided; and, after all, for one night, what did it matter? For one night? that was for me the question! The supper was really not bad; but the look, and still worse the smell, of the room where it was served, joined no doubt to our excessive fatigue, made it impossible for me to eat anything. My friends were sorry, and I felt ashamed of myself for being so easily knocked up or knocked down. How thoroughly I entered into Frau von Walden's honestly-expressed dislike to "roughing it"! Yet it was not only the uncivilised look of the place, nor the coarse food, nor the want of comfort that made me feel that one night of Silberbach would indeed be enough for me. A sort of depression, of fear almost, came over me when I pictured the two children and myself alone in that strange, out-of-the-world place, where it really seemed to me we might all three be made an end of without any one being the wiser of it! There was a general look of squalor and stolid depression about the people too: the landlord was a black-browed, surlily silent sort of man, his wife and the one maid-servant looked frightened and anxious, and the only voices to be heard were those of half-tipsy peasants drinking and quarrelling at the bar.

To say the least, it was not enlivening. Yet my pride was aroused. I did not like to own myself already beaten. After supper I sat apart, reflecting rather gloomily as to what I could or should do, while the young men and the children amused themselves with the one piece of luxury with which the poorest inn in Thuringia is sure to be provided. For, anomalous as it may seem, there was a piano, and by no means an altogether decrepit one, in the sandy-floored parlour!

Herr von Walden was smoking his pipe outside, the hay being by this time housed somewhere or other. His wife, who had been speaking to him, came in and sat down beside me.

"My dear," she said, "you must not be vexed with me for renewing the subject, but I cannot help it; I feel a responsibility. You must not, you really *must not*, think of staying here alone with those two children. It is not fit for you."

Oh, how I blessed her for breaking the ice! I could hardly help hugging her as I replied—diplomatically—

"You really think so?"

"Certainly I do; and so, though perhaps he won't say so as frankly—so does my husband. He says I am foolish and fanciful; but I confess to feeling a kind of dislike to the place that I cannot explain. Perhaps there is thunder in the air—that always affects my nerves—but I just feel that I *cannot* agree to your staying on here."

"Very well, I am quite willing to go back to Seeberg to-morrow," I replied meekly. "Of course we can't judge of the place by what we have seen of it to-night, but no doubt, as far as the inn is concerned, Seeberg is much nicer. I daresay we can see all we want by noon to-morrow, and get back to Seeberg in the afternoon."

Kind Frau von Walden kissed me rapturously on both cheeks.

"You don't *know*, my dear, the relief to my mind of hearing you say so! And now I think the best thing we can do is to go to bed. For we *must* start at six."

"So early!" I exclaimed, with a fresh feeling of dismay.

"Yes, indeed; and I must bid you good-bye to-night, for after all I am not to sleep in your room, which is much better, as I should have had to disturb you so early. My husband has found a tidy room next door in a cottage, and we shall do very well there."

What sort of a place she euphemistically described as "a tidy room" I never discovered. But it would have been useless to remonstrate, the kind creature was so afraid of incommoding us that she would have listened to no objections.

Herr von Walden came in just as we were about to wish each other good-night.

"So!" he said, with a tone of amiable indulgence, "so! And what do you think of Silberbach? My wife feels sure you will not like it after all."

"I think I shall see as much as I care to see of it in an hour or two to-morrow morning," I replied quietly. "And by the afternoon the children and I will go back to our comfortable quarters at Seeberg."

"Ah, indeed! Yes, I daresay it will be as well," he said airily, as if he had nothing at all to do with decoying us to the place. "Then good-night and pleasant dreams, and—"

"But," I interrupted, "I want to know *how* we are to get back to Seeberg. Can I get an *Einspänner* here?"

"To be sure, to be sure. You have only to speak to the landlord in the morning, and tell him at what hour you want it," he answered so confidently that I felt no sort of misgiving, and I turned with a smile to finish my good-nights.

The young men were standing close beside us. I shook hands with Trachenfels and Lutz, the latter of whom, though he replied as heartily as usual, looked, I thought, annoyed. George Norman followed me to the door of the room. In front of us was the ladder-like staircase leading to the upper regions.

"What a hole of a place!" said the boy. "I don't mind quite a cottage if it's clean and cheerful, but this place is so grim and squalid. I can't tell you how glad I am you're not going to stay on here alone. It really isn't fit for you."

"Well, you may be easy, as we shall only be here a few hours after you leave."

"Yes; so much the better. I wish I could have stayed, but I *must* be back at Kronberg to-morrow. Lutz could have stayed and seen you back to Seeberg, but his father won't let him. Herr von Walden is so queer once he takes an idea in his head—and he *won't* allow this place isn't all right."

"But I daresay there would be nothing to hurt us! Anyway, I will write to reassure you that we have not fallen into a nest of cut-throats or brigands," I said laughingly.

Certainly it never occurred to me or to my friends what *would* be the nature of the "experience" which would stamp Silberbach indelibly on our memory.

We must have been really very tired, for, quite contrary to our habit, the children and I slept late the next morning, undisturbed by the departure of our friends at the early hour arranged by them.

The sun was shining, and Silberbach, like every other place, appeared all the better for it. But the view from the window of our room was not encouraging. It looked out upon the village street—a rough, unkempt sort of track—and on its other side the ground rose abruptly to some height, but treeless and grassless. It seemed more like the remains of a quarry of some kind, for there was nothing to be seen but stones and broken pieces of rock.

"We must go out after our breakfast and look about us a little before we start," I said. "But how glad I shall be to get back to that bright, cheerful Seeberg!"

"Yes, indeed," said Nora. "I think this is the ugliest place I ever was at in my life." And she was not inclined to like it any better when Reggie, whom we sent down to reconnoitre, came back to report that we must have our breakfast in our own room.

"There are a lot of rough-looking men down there, smoking and drinking beer. You *couldn't* eat there," said the child.

But, after all, it was to be our last meal there, and we did not complain. The root coffee was not too unpalatable with plenty of good milk; the bread was sour and the butter dubious, as Ottilia had foretold, so we soaked the bread in the coffee, like French peasants.

"Mamma," said Nora gravely, "it makes me sorry for poor people. I daresay many never have anything nicer to eat than this."

"Not nicer than this!" I exclaimed. "Why, my dear child, thousands, not in Germany only, but in France and England, never taste anything as good."

The little girl opened her eyes. There are salutary lessons to be learnt from even the mildest experience of "roughing it."

Suddenly Nora's eyes fell on a little parcel in blue paper. It was lying on one of the shelves of the stove, which, as in most German rooms, stood out a little from the wall, and in its summer idleness was a convenient receptacle for odds and ends. This stove was a high one, of black-leaded iron; it stood between the door and the wall, on the same side as the door, and was the most conspicuous object in the room.

"Mamma," she exclaimed, "there is the parcel you brought away from the china place. What is it? I wish you would show it me."

I gave a little exclamation of annoyance.

"Frau von Walden has forgotten it," I said; for my friend, returning straight to Kronberg, had offered to take it home for me in her bag for fear of accidents. "It does not matter," I added, "I will pack it among our soft things. It is a very pretty cup and saucer, but I will show it to you at Kronberg, for it is so nicely wrapped up. Now I am going downstairs to order the *Einspänner*, and we can walk about for an hour or two."

The children came with me. I had some trouble in disinterring the landlord, but at last I found him, of course with a pipe in his mouth, hanging about the premises. He listened to me civilly enough, but when I waited for his reply as to whether the *Einspänner* would be ready about twelve o'clock, he calmly regarded me without speaking. I repeated my inquiry.

"At twelve?" he said calmly. "Yes, no doubt the gracious lady might as well fix twelve as any other hour, for there was no such thing as a horse, much less an *Einspänner*, to be had at Silberbach."

I stared at him in my turn.

"No horse, no carriage to be had! How do people ever get away from here then?" I said.

"They don't get away—that is to say, if they come at all, they go as they came, in the carriage that brought them; otherwise they neither come nor go. The lady came on foot: she can go on foot; otherwise she can stay."

There seemed something sinister in his words. A horrible, ridiculous feeling came over me that we were caught in a net, as it were, and doomed to stay at Silberbach for the rest of our lives. But I looked at the man. He was simply stolid and indifferent. I did not believe then, nor do I now, that he was anything worse than sulky and uncivilised. He did not even care to have us as his visitors: he had no wish to retain us nor to speed us on our way. Had we remained at the "Katze" from that day to this, I don't believe he would have ever inquired what we stayed for!

"I *cannot* walk back to Seeberg," I said half indignantly, "we are too tired; nor would it be safe through the forest alone with two children."

The landlord knocked some ashes off his pipe.

"There may be an ox-cart going that way next week," he observed.

"Next week!" I repeated. Then a sudden idea struck me. "Is there a post-office here?" I said.

Of course there was a post-office; where can one go in Germany where there is not a post and telegraph office?

"The telegraph officials must be sadly overworked here," I said to myself. But as far as mine host was concerned, I satisfied myself with obtaining the locality of the post-office, and with something like a ray of hope I turned to look for the children. They had been amusing themselves with the piano in the now empty room, but as I called to them, Reggie ran out with a very red face.

"I wish I were a man, mamma. Fancy! a peasant—one of those men who were drinking beer—came and put his arm around Nora as she was playing. *'Du spielst schön,'* he said, and I *do* believe he meant to kiss her, if I hadn't shaken my fist at him."

"Yes, indeed, mamma," said Nora, equally but more calmly indignant. "I certainly think the sooner we get away the better."

I had to tell them of my discomfiture, but ended with my new idea.

"If there is a post-office," I said, "the mail must stop there, and the mail takes passengers."

But, arrived at the neat little post-house—to reach which without a most tremendous round we had to climb up a really precipitous path, so called, over the stones and rocks in front of the inn—new dismay awaited us. The postmaster was a very old man, but of a very different type from our host. He was sorry to disappoint us, but the mail only stopped here for *letters*—all *passengers* must begin their journey at—I forget where—leagues off on the other side from Silberbach. We wanted to get away? He was not surprised. *What had we come for?* No one ever came here. Were we Americans! Staying at the "Katze"! Good heavens! "A rough place." "I should rather think so."

And this last piece of information fairly overcame him. He evidently felt he must come to the rescue of these poor Babes in the wood.

"Come up when the mail passes from Seeberg this evening at seven, and I will see what I can do with the conductor. If he *happens* to have no passengers to-morrow, he *may* stretch a point and take you in. No one will be the wiser."

"Oh, thanks, thanks," I cried. "Of course I will pay anything he likes to ask."

"No need for that. He is a *braver Mann*, and will not cheat you."

"We shall be here at seven, then. I would rather have started to walk than stayed here indefinitely."

"Not *to-day* anyway. We shall have a storm," he said, looking up to the sky. "Adieu. *Auf Wiedersehen!*"

"I wish we had not to stay another night here," I said. "Still, to-morrow morning will soon come."

We spent the day as best we could. There was literally nothing to see, nowhere to go, except back into the forest whence we had come. Nor dared we go far, for the day grew more and more sultry; the strange, ominous silence that precedes a storm came on, adding to our feelings of restlessness and depression. And by about two o'clock, having ventured out again after "dinner," we were driven in by the first great drops. Huddled together in our cheerless little room we watched the breaking loose of the storm demons. I am not affected by thunder and lightning, nor do I dread them. But what a storm that was! Thunder, lightning, howling wind, and rain like no rain I had ever seen before, all mingled together. An hour after it began, a cart, standing high and dry in the steep village street, was hidden by water to above the top of the wheels—a little more and it would have floated like a boat. But by about five, things calmed down; the few stupid-looking peasants came out of their houses, and gazed about them as if to see what damage had been done. Perhaps it was not much after all—they seemed to take it quietly enough; and by six all special signs of disturbance had disappeared—the torrents melted away as if by magic. Only a strange, heavy mist began to rise, enveloping everything, so that we could hardly believe the evening was yet so early. I looked at my watch.

"Half-past six. We must, mist or no mist, go up to the post-house. But I don't mind going alone, dears."

"No, no, mamma; I *must* go with you, to take care of you," said Reggie; "but Nora needn't."

"Perhaps it would be as well," said the little girl. "I have one or two buttons to sew on, and I *am* still rather tired."

And, knowing she was never timid about being left alone, thinking we should be absent half an hour at most, I agreed.

But the half hour lengthened into an hour, then into an hour and a half, before the weary mail made its appearance. The road through the forest must be all but impassable, our old friend told us. But oh, how tired Reggie and I were of waiting! though all the time never a thought of uneasiness with regard to *Nora* crossed my mind. And when the mail did come, delayed, as the postmaster had suspected, the good result of his negotiations made us forget all our troubles; for the conductor all but *promised* to take us the next morning, in consideration of a very reasonable extra payment. It was most unlikely he would have any, certainly not many passengers. We must be there, at the post-house, by nine o'clock, baggage and all, for he dared not wait a moment, and he would do his best.

Through the evening dusk, now fast replacing the scattered mist, Reggie and I, light of heart, stumbled down the rocky path.

"How pleased Nora will be! She will be wondering what has come over us," I said as the "Katze" came in view. "But what is that, Reggie, running up and down in front of the house? Is it a sheep, or a big white dog? or—or a child? Can it be Nora, and no cloak or hat? and so damp and chilly as it is? How can she be so foolish?"

And with a vague uneasiness I hurried on.

Yes, it was Nora. There was light enough to see her face. What had happened to my little girl? She was white—no, not white, ghastly. Her eyes looked glassy, and yet as if drawn into her head; her whole bright, fearless bearing was gone. She clutched me convulsively as if she would never again let me go. Her voice was so hoarse that I could scarcely distinguish what she said.

"Send Reggie in—he must not hear," were her first words—of rare unselfishness and presence of mind.

"Reggie," I said, "tell the maid to take candles up to our room, and take off your wet boots at once."

My children are obedient; he was off instantly.

Then Nora went on, still in a strained, painful whisper—

"Mamma, there has been a *man* in our room, and——"

"Did that peasant frighten you again, dear? Oh, I am so sorry I left you;" for my mind at once reverted to the man whom Reggie had shaken his fist at that morning.

"No, no; not that. I would not have minded. But, mamma, Reggie must never know it—he is so little, he could not bear it—mamma, it was *not* a man. It was—oh, mamma, I have seen a *ghost*!"

PART II

"A ghost," I repeated, holding the poor trembling little thing more closely. I think my first sensation was a sort of rage at whomever or whatever—ghost or living being—had frightened her so terribly. "Oh, Nora darling, it couldn't be a ghost. Tell me about it, and I will try to find out what it was. Or would you rather try to forget about it just now, and tell me afterwards? You are shivering so dreadfully. I *must* get you warm first of all."

"But let me tell you, mamma—I *must* tell you," she entreated piteously. "If you *could* explain it, I should be so glad, but I am afraid you can't," and again a shudder passed through her.

I saw it was better to let her tell it. I had by this time drawn her inside; a door in front stood open, and a bright fire caught my eyes. It was the kitchen, and the most inviting-looking room in the house. I peeped in—there was no one there, but from an inner room we heard the voice of the landlady hushing her baby to sleep.

"Come to the fire, Nora," I said. Just then Reggie came clattering down-stairs, followed by Lieschen, the taciturn "maid of the inn."

"She has taken a candle upstairs, mamma, but I've not taken off my boots, for there's a little calf, she says, in the stable, and she's going to show it me. May I go?"

"Yes, but don't stay long," I said, my opinion of the sombre Lieschen improving considerably; and when they were out of hearing, "Now, Nora dear, tell me what frightened you so."

"Mamma," she said, a little less white and shivering by now, but still with the strange strained look in her eyes that I could not bear to see, "it *couldn't* have been a real man. Listen, mamma. When you and Reggie went, I got out a needle and thread—out of your little bag—and first I mended a hole in my glove, and then I took off one of my boots—the buttoning-up-the-side ones, you know—to sew a button on. I soon finished it, and then, without putting my boot on, I sat there, looking out of the window and wondering if you and Reggie would soon be back. Then I thought perhaps I could see if you were coming, better from the window of the place outside our room, where the hay and bags of flour are." (I think I forgot to say that to get to our room we had to cross at the top of the stair a sort of landing, along one side of which, as Nora said, great bags of flour or grain and trusses of hay were ranged; this place had a window with a somewhat more extended view than that of our room.) "I went there, still without my boot, and I knelt in front of the window some time, looking up the rough path, and wishing you would come. But I was not the least dull or lonely. I was only a little tired. At last I got tired of watching there, and I thought I would come back to our room and look for something to do. The door was not closed, but I think I had half drawn it to as I came out. I pushed it open and went in, and then—I seemed to feel there was something that had not been there before, and I looked up; and just beside the stove—the door opens *against* the stove, you know, and so it had hidden it for a moment as it were—there, mamma, *stood a man*! I saw him as plainly as I see you. He was staring at the stove, afterwards I saw it must have been at your little blue paper parcel. He was a gentleman, mamma—quite young. I saw his coat; it was cut like George Norman's. I think he must have been an Englishman. His coat was dark, and bound with a little very narrow ribbon binding. I have seen coats like that. He had a dark blue neck-tie, his dress all looked neat and careful—like what all gentlemen are; I saw all that, mamma, before I clearly saw his face. He was tall and had fair hair—I saw that at once. But I was not frightened; just at first I did not even wonder how he *could* have got into the room—now I see he *couldn't* without my knowing. My first thought, it seems so silly," and Nora here smiled a little, "my first thought was, 'Oh, he will see I have no boot on,'"—which was very characteristic of the child, for Nora was a very "proper" little girl,—"and just as I thought that, *he* seemed to know I was there, for he slowly turned his head from the stove and looked at me, and then I saw his face. Oh, mamma!"

"Was there anything frightening about it?" I said.

"I don't know," the child went on. "It was not like any face I ever saw, and yet it does not *sound* strange. He had nice, rather wavy fair hair, and I think he must *have been* nice-looking. His eyes were blue, and he had a little fair moustache. But he was so *fearfully* pale, and a look over all that I can't describe. And his eyes when he looked at me *seemed not to see me,* and yet they turned on me. They looked dreadfully sad, and though they were so close to me, as if they were miles and miles away. Then his lips parted slightly, very slightly, as if he were going to speak. Mamma," Nora went on impressively, "they would have spoken if *I* had said the least word—I felt they would. But just then—and remember, mamma, it couldn't have been yet two seconds since I came in, I hadn't yet had *time* to get frightened—just then there came over me the most awful feeling. I *knew* it was not a real man, and I seemed to hear myself saying inside my mind, 'It is a ghost,' and while I seemed to be saying it—I had not moved my eyes—while I looked at him—"

"He disappeared?"

"No, mamma, he did not even disappear. He was just *no longer there*. I was staring at nothing! Then came a sort of wild fear. I turned and rushed downstairs, even without my boot, and all the way the horrible feeling was that even though he was no longer there he might still be coming after me. I should not have cared if there had been twenty tipsy peasants downstairs! But I found Lieschen. Of course I said nothing to her; I only asked her to come up with a light to help me to find my boot, and as soon as I had put it on I came outside, and ran up and down—it was a long time, I think—till you and Reggie came at last. Mamma, *can* you explain it?"

How I longed to be able to do so! But I would not deceive the child. Besides, it would have been useless.

"No, dear. As yet I cannot. But I will try to understand it. There are several ways it may be explained. Have you ever heard of optical delusions, Nora?"

"I am not sure. You must tell me;" and she looked at me so appealingly, and with such readiness to believe whatever I told her, that I felt I would give anything to restore her to her former happy fearlessness.

But just then Reggie came in from the stable.

"We must go upstairs," I said; "and Lieschen," turning to her, "bring up our supper at once. We are leaving very early to-morrow morning, and we will go early to bed."

"Oh, mamma," whispered Nora, "if only we had not to stay all night in that room!"

But there was no help for it, and she was thankful to hear of the success of our expedition to the post-office. During supper we, of course, on Reggie's account, said nothing of Nora's fright, but as soon as it was over, Reggie declaring himself very sleepy, we got him undressed and put to bed on the settee originally intended for Nora. He was asleep in five minutes, and then Nora and I did our utmost to arrive at the explanation we so longed for. We thoroughly examined the room; there was no other entrance, no cupboard of any kind even. I tried to imagine that some of our travelling cloaks or shawls hanging on the back of a chair might, in the uncertain light, have taken imaginary proportions; that the stove itself might have cast a shadow we had not before observed; I suggested everything, but in vain. Nothing shook Nora's conviction that she had seen something *not* to be explained.

"For the light was *not* uncertain just then," she maintained; "the mist had gone and it had not begun to get dark. And then I saw him *so* plainly! If it had been a fancy ghost it wouldn't have looked like that—it would have had a long white thing floating over it, and a face like a skeleton perhaps. But to see somebody just like a regular gentleman—I could never have *fancied* that!"

There was a good deal in what she said. I had to give up my suggestions, and I tried to give Nora some idea of what are called "optical delusions," though my own comprehension of the theory was of the vaguest. She listened, but I don't think my words had much weight. And at last I told her I thought she had better go to bed and try to sleep. I saw she shrank from the idea, but it had to be.

"We can't sit up all night, I suppose," she said, "but I wish we could. I am so dreadfully afraid of waking in the night, and—and—*seeing him there again.*"

"Would you like to sleep in my bed? though it is so tiny, I could make room and put you inside," I said.

Nora looked wistfully at the haven of refuge, but her good sense and considerateness for me came to the front.

"No," she said, "neither of us would sleep, and you would be *so* tired to-morrow. I will get into my own bed, and I *will* try to sleep, mamma."

"And listen, Nora; if you are the least frightened in the night, or if you can't sleep, call out to me without hesitation. I am sure to wake often, and I will speak to you from time to time."

That was the longest night of my life! The first part was not the worst. By what I really thought a fortunate chance it was a club night of some kind at Silberbach—a musical club, of course; and all the musically-gifted peasants of the countryside assembled in the sanded parlour of the "Katze." The noise was something indescribable, for though there may have been some good voices among them, they were drowned in the din. But though it prevented us from sleeping, it also fairly drove away all ghostly alarms. By twelve o'clock or thereabouts the party seemed to disperse, and all grew still. Then came some hours I can never forget. There was faint moonlight by fits and starts, and I not only found it impossible to sleep, I found it impossible to keep my eyes shut. Some irresistible fascination seemed to force them open, and obliged me ever and anon to turn in the direction of the stove, from which, however, before going to bed, I had removed the blue paper parcel. And each time I did so I said to myself, "Am I going to see that figure standing there as Nora saw it? Shall I remain sane if I do? Shall I scream out? Will it look at *me*, in turn, with its sad unearthly eyes? Will it speak? If it moves across the room and comes near me, or if I see it going towards Nora, or leaning over my Reggie sleeping there in his innocence, misdoubting of no fateful presence near, what, oh! what *shall* I do?"

For in my heart of hearts, though I would not own it to Nora, I felt convinced that what she had seen was no living human being—whence it had come, or *why*, I could not tell. But in the quiet of the night I had thought of what the woman at the china factory had told us, of the young Englishman who had bought the other cup, who had promised to write and never done so! What had become of him? "If," I said to myself, "if I had the slightest reason to doubt his being at this moment alive and well in his own country, as he pretty certainly is, I should really begin to think he had been robbed and murdered by our surly landlord, and that his spirit had appeared to us—the first compatriots who have passed this way since, most likely—to tell the story."

I really think I must have been a little light-headed some part of that night. My poor Nora, I am certain, never slept, but I can only hope her imagination was less wildly at work than mine. From time to time I spoke to her, and every time she was awake, for she always answered without hesitation.

"I am quite comfortable, dear mamma, and I don't think I am very frightened;" or else, "I have not slept much, but I have said my prayers a great many times, and all the hymns I could remember. Don't mind about me, mamma, and do try to sleep."

I watched the dawn slowly breaking. From where I lay I could see through the window the high mound of rough stones and fragments of rock that I have described. At its foot there was a low wall loosely constructed of these same unhewn blocks, and the shapes that evolved themselves out of this wall, beside which grew two or three stunted trees, were more grotesque and extraordinary than I could describe. They varied like the colours in a kaleidoscope with the wavering and increasing light. At one time it seemed to me that one of the trees was a gipsy woman enveloped in a cloak, extending her arm towards me threateningly; at another, two weird dogs seemed to be fighting together; but however fantastic and fearsome had been these strange effects of light and fancy mingled together, I should not have minded—I knew what they were; it was a relief to have anything to look at which could keep my eyes from constantly turning in the direction of that black iron stove.

I fell asleep at last, though not for long. When I woke it was bright morning—fresher and brighter, I felt, as I threw open the window, than the day before. With the greatest thankfulness that the night was over at last, as soon as I was dressed I began to put our little belongings together, and then turned to awake the children. Nora was sleeping quietly; it seemed a pity to arouse her, for it was not much past six, but I heard the people stirring about downstairs, and I had a feverish desire to get away; for though the daylight had dispersed much of the "eerie" impression of Nora's fright, there was a feeling of uneasiness, almost of insecurity, left in my mind since recalling the incident of the young man who had visited the china factory. How did I know but that some harm had really come to him in this very place? There was certainly nothing about the landlord to inspire confidence. At best it was a strange and unpleasant coincidence. The evening before I had half thought of inquiring of the landlord or his wife, or even of Lieschen, if any English had ever before stayed at the "Katze." If assured by them that we were the first, or at least the first "in their time," it would, I thought, help to assure Nora that the ghost had really been a delusion of some kind. But then, again, supposing the people of the inn hesitated to reply—supposing the landlord to be really in any way guilty, and my inquiries were to rouse his suspicions, would I not be risking dangerous enmity, besides strengthening the painful impression left on my own mind, and this corroboration of her own fear might be instinctively suspected by Nora, even if I told her nothing?

"No," I decided; "better leave it a mystery, in any case, till we are safely away from here." For, allowing that these people are perfectly innocent and harmless, their even telling me simply, like the woman at Grünstein, that such a person *had* been here, that he had fallen ill, possibly died here—I would rather not know it. It is certainly not probable that it was so; they would have been pretty sure to gossip about any occurrence of the kind, taciturn though they are. The wife would have talked of it to me—she is more genial than the others—for I had had a little kindly chat with her the day before, *à propos* of what every mother, of her class at least, is ready to talk about—the baby! A pretty baby too, though the last, she informed me with a sort of melancholy pride, of four she had "buried"—using the same expression in her rough German as a Lancashire factory hand or an Irish peasant woman—one after the other. Certainly Silberbach was not a cheerful or cheering spot. "No, no," I made up my mind, "I would rather at present know nothing, even if there is anything to know. I can the more honestly endeavour to remove the impression left on Nora."

The little girl was so easily awakened that I was half inclined to doubt if she had not been "shamming" out of filial devotion. She looked ill still, but infinitely better than the night before, and she so eagerly agreed with me in my wish to leave the house as soon as possible, that I felt sure it was the best thing to do. Reggie woke up rosy and beaming—evidently no ghosts had troubled *his* night's repose. There was something consoling and satisfactory in seeing him quite as happy and hearty as in his own English nursery. But though he had no uncanny reasons like us for disliking Silberbach, he was quite as cordial in his readiness to leave it. We got hold of Lieschen, and asked for our breakfast at once. As I had told the landlady the night before that we were leaving very early, our bill came up with the coffee. It was, I must say, moderate in the extreme—ten or twelve marks, if I remember rightly, for two nights' lodging and *almost* two days' board for three people. And such as it was, they had given us of their best. I felt a little twinge of conscience, when I said good-bye to the poor woman, for having harboured any doubts of the establishment. But when the gruff landlord, standing outside the door, smoking of course, nodded a surly "adieu" in return to our parting greeting, my feeling of unutterable thankfulness that we were not to spend another night under his roof regained the ascendant.

"Perhaps he is offended at my not having told him how I mean to get away, notwithstanding his stupidity about it," I said to myself, as we passed him. But no, there was no look of vindictiveness, of malice, of even annoyance on his dark face. Nay, more, I could almost have fancied there was the shadow of a smile as Reggie tugged at his Tam o' Shanter by way of a final salute. That landlord was really one of the most incomprehensible human beings it has ever been my fate to come across, in fact or fiction.

We had retained Lieschen to carry our modest baggage to the post-house, and having deposited it at the side of the road just where the coach stopped, she took her leave, apparently more than satisfied with the small sum of money I gave her, and civilly wishing us a pleasant journey. But though less gruff, she was quite as impassive as the landlord. She never asked where we were going, if we were likely ever to return again, and like her master, as I said, had we been staying there still, I do not believe she would ever have made an inquiry or expressed the slightest astonishment.

"There is really something very queer about Silberbach," I could not help saying to Nora, "both about the place and the people. They almost give one the feeling that they are half-witted, and yet they evidently are not. This last day or two I seem to have been living in a sort of dream or nightmare, and I shall not get over it altogether till we are fairly out of the place;" and though she said little, I felt sure the child understood me.

We were of course far, far too early for the post. The old man came out of his house, and seemed amused at our haste to be gone.

"I am afraid Silberbach has not taken your fancy," he said. "Well, no wonder. I think it is the dreariest place I ever saw."

"Then you do not belong to it? Have you not been here long?" I asked. He shook his head.

"Only a few months, and I hope to get removed soon," he said. So *he* could have told me nothing, evidently! "It is too lonely here. There is not a creature in the place who ever touches a book—they are all as dull and stupid as they can be. But then they are very poor, and they live on here from year's end to year's end, barely able to earn their daily bread. Poverty degrades—there is no doubt of it, whatever the wise men may say. A few generations of it makes men little better than—" He stopped.

"Than?" I asked.

"Than," the old philosopher of the post-house went on, "pardon the expression—than pigs."

There were two or three of the fraternity grubbing about at the side of the road; they may have suggested the comparison. I could hardly help smiling.

"But I have travelled a good deal in Germany," I said, "and I have never anywhere found the people so stupid and stolid and ungenial as here."

"Perhaps not," he said. "Still there are many places like this, only naturally they are not the places strangers visit. It is never so bad where there are a few country houses near, for nowadays it must be allowed it is seldom but that the gentry take some interest in the people."

"It is a pity no rich man takes a fancy to Silberbach," I said.

"That day will never come. The best thing would be for a railway to be cut through the place, but that, too, is not likely."

Then the old postmaster turned into his garden, inviting us civilly to wait there or in the office if we preferred. But we liked better to stay outside, for just above the post-house there was a rather tempting little wood, much prettier than anything to be seen on the other side of the village. And Nora and I sat there quietly on the stumps of some old trees, while Reggie found a pleasing distraction in alternately chasing and making friends with a party of ducks, which, for reasons best known to themselves, had deserted their native element and come for a stroll in the woods.

From where we sat we looked down on our late habitation; we could almost distinguish the landlord's slouching figure and poor Lieschen with a pail of water slung at each side as she came in from the well.

"What a life!" I could not help saying. "Day after day nothing but work. I suppose it is not to be wondered at if they grow dull and stolid, poor things." Then my thoughts reverted to what up here in the sunshine and the fresh morning air and with the pleasant excitement of going away I had a little forgotten—the strange experience of the evening before. It was difficult for me now to realise that I had been so affected by it. I felt *now* as if I wished I could see the poor ghost for myself, and learn if there was aught we could do to serve or satisfy him! For in the old orthodox ghost-stories there is always some reason for these eerie wanderers returning to the world they have left. But when I turned to Nora and saw her dear little face still white and drawn, and with an expression half-subdued, half-startled, that it had never worn before, I felt thankful that the unbidden visitor had attempted no communication.

"It might have sent her out of her mind," I thought. "Why, if he had anything to say, did he appear to her, poor child, and not to me?—though, after all, I am not at all sure that *I* should not have gone out of my mind in such a case."

Before long the post-horn made itself heard in the distance; we hurried down, our hearts beating with the fear of possible disappointment. It was all right, however, there were *no* passengers, and nodding adieu to our old friend, we joyfully mounted into our places, and were bowled away to Seeberg.

There and at other spots in its pretty neighbourhood we pleasantly enough spent two or three weeks. Nora by degrees recovered her roses and her good spirits. Still, her strange experience left its mark on her. She was never again quite the merry, thoughtless, utterly fearless child she had been. I tried, however, to take the good with the ill, remembering that thorough-going childhood cannot last for ever, that the shock possibly helped to soften and modify a nature that might have been too daring for perfect womanliness—still more, wanting perhaps in tenderness and sympathy for the weaknesses and tremors of feebler temperaments.

At Kronberg, on our return, we found that Herr von Walden was off on a tour to the Italian lakes, Lutz and young Trachenfels had returned to their studies at Heidelberg, George Norman had gone home to England. All the members of our little party were dispersed except Frau von Walden.

To her and to Ottilia I told the story, sitting together one afternoon over our coffee, when Nora was not with us. It impressed them both. Ottilia could not resist an "I told you so."

"I knew, I felt," she said, "that something disagreeable would happen to you there. I never will forget," she went on naïvely, "the dreary, dismal impression the place left on me the only time I was there—pouring rain and universal gloom and discomfort. We had to wait there a few hours to get one of the horses shod, once when I was driving with my father from Seeberg to Marsfeldt."

Frau von Walden and I could not help smiling at her. Still there was no smiling at my story, though both agreed that, viewed in the light of unexaggerated common sense, it was most improbable that there was any tragedy mixed up with the disappearance of the young man we had heard of at Grünstein.

"And indeed why we should speak of his 'disappearance' I don't know," said Frau von Walden. "He did not write to send the order he had spoken of—that was all. No doubt he is very happy at his own home. When you are back in England, my dear, you must try to find him out—perhaps by means of the cup. And then when Nora sees him, and finds he is not at all like the 'ghost,' it will make her the more ready to think it was really only some *very strange*, I must admit, kind of optical delusion."

"But Nora has never heard the Grünstein story, and is not to hear it," said Ottilia.

"And England is a wide place, small as it is in one sense," I said. "Still, if I *did* come across the young man, I half think I would tell Nora the whole, and by showing her how *my* imagination had dressed it up, I think I could perhaps lessen the effect on her of what she thought she saw. It would prove to her better than anything, the tricks that fancy may play us."

"And in the meantime, if you take my advice, you will allude to it as little as possible," said practical Ottilia. "Don't *seem* to avoid the subject, but manage to do so in reality."

"Shall you order the tea-service?" asked Frau von Walden.

"I hardly think so. I am out of conceit of it somehow," I said. "And it might remind Nora of the blue paper parcel. I think I shall give the cup and saucer to my sister."

And on my return to England I did so.

Two years later. A very different scene from quaint old Kronberg, or still more from the dreary "Katze" at Silberbach. We are in England now, though not at our own home. We are staying, my children and I—two older girls than little Nora, and Nora herself, though hardly now to be described as "little"— with my sister. Reggie is there too, but naturally not much heard of, for it is the summer holidays, and the weather is delightful. It is August again—a typical August afternoon—though a trifle too hot perhaps for some people.

"This time two years ago, mamma," said Margaret, my eldest daughter, "you were in Germany with Nora and Reggie. What a long summer that seemed! It is so much nicer to be all together."

"I should like to go to Kronberg and all those queer places," said Lily, the second girl; "especially to the place where Nora saw the ghost."

"I am quite sure you would not wish to *stay* there," I replied. "It is curious that you should speak of it just now. I was thinking of it this morning. It was just two years yesterday that it happened."

We were sitting at afternoon tea on the lawn outside the drawing-room window—my sister, her husband, Margaret, Lily, and I. Nora was with the schoolroom party inside.

"How queer!" said Lily.

"You don't think Nora has thought of it?" I asked.

"Oh no, I am sure she hasn't," said Margaret. "I think it has grown vague to her now. You know she spoke about it to us when she first came home. You had prepared us, you remember, mamma, and told us not to make too much of it. The first year after, she *did* think of it. She told me she was dreadfully frightened all that day for fear he should appear again. But since then I think she has gradually forgotten it."

"She is a very sensible child," said my sister. "And she is especially kind and sympathising with any of the little ones who seem timid. I found her sitting beside Charlie the other night for ever so long because he heard an owl hooting outside, and was frightened."

Just then a servant came out of the house, and said something to my brother-in-law. He got up at once.

"It is Mr. Grenfell," he said to his wife, "and a friend with him. Shall I bring them out here?"

"Yes, it would really be a pity to go into the house again—it is so nice out here," she replied. And her husband went to meet his guests.

He appeared again in a minute or two, stepping out through the low window of the drawing-room, accompanied by the two gentlemen.

Mr. Grenfell was a young man living in the neighbourhood, whom we had known from his boyhood; the stranger he introduced to us as Sir Robert Masters. He was a middle-aged man, with a quiet, gentle bearing and expression.

"You will have some tea?" said my sister, after the first few words of greeting had passed. Mr. Grenfell declined. His friend accepted.

"Go into the drawing-room, Lily, please, and ring for a cup and saucer," said her aunt, noting the deficiency. "There was an extra one, but some one has poured milk into the saucer. It surely can't have been you, Mark, for Tiny?" she went on, turning to her husband. "You *shouldn't* let a dog drink out of anything we drink out of ourselves."

My brother-in-law looked rather comically penitent; he did not attempt to deny the charge.

"Only, my dear, you must allow," he pleaded, "that we do not drink our tea out of the *saucers*."

On what trifling links hang sometimes important results! Had it not been for Mark's transgressing in the matter of Tiny's milk we should never have learnt the circumstances which give to this simple relation of facts—valueless in itself—such interest, speculative and suggestive only, I am aware, as it may be found to possess.

Lily, in the meantime, had disappeared. But more quickly than it would have taken her to ring the bell, and await the servant's response to the summons, she was back again, carrying something carefully in her hand.

"Aunt," she said, "is it not a good idea? As you have a tea-spoon—I don't suppose Tiny used the spoon, did he?—I thought, instead of ringing for another, I would bring out the ghost-cup for Sir Robert. It is only fair to use it for once, poor thing, and just as we have been speaking about it. Oh, I assure you it is not dusty," as my sister regarded it dubiously. "It was inside the cabinet."

"Still, all the same, a little hot water will do it no harm," said her aunt— "provided, that is to say, that Sir Robert has no objection to drink out of a cup with such a name attached to it?"

"On the contrary," replied he, "I shall think it an honour. But you will, I trust, explain the meaning of the name to me? It puzzles me more than if it were a piece of ancient china—a great-great-grandmother's cup, for instance. For I see it is not old, though it is very pretty, and, I suppose, uncommon?"

There was a slight tone of hesitation about the last word which struck me.

"I have no doubt my sister will be ready to tell you all there is to tell. It was she who gave me the cup," replied the lady of the house.

Then Sir Robert turned to me. Looking at him full in the face I saw that there was a thoughtful, far-seeing look in his eyes, which redeemed his whole appearance from the somewhat commonplace gentlemanliness which was all I had before observed about him.

"I am greatly interested in these subjects," he said. "It would be very kind of you to tell me the whole."

I did so, more rapidly and succinctly of course than I have done here. It is not easy to play the part of narrator, with five or six pairs of eyes fixed upon you, more especially when the owners of several of them have heard the story a good many times before, and are quick to observe the slightest discrepancy, however unintentional. "There is, you see, very little to tell," I said in conclusion, "only there is always a certain amount of impressiveness about any experience of the kind when related at first hand."

"Undoubtedly so," Sir Robert replied. "Thank you very much indeed for telling it me."

He spoke with perfect courtesy, but with a slight absence of manner, his eyes fixed rather dreamily on the cup in his hand. He seemed as if trying to recall or recollect something.

"There should be a sequel to that story," said Mr. Grenfell.

"That's what I say," said Margaret eagerly. "It will be too stupid if we never hear any more. But that is always the way with modern ghost stories—there is no sense or meaning in them. The ghosts appear to people who never knew them, who take no interest in them, as it were, and then they have nothing to say—there is no *dénouement*, it is all purposeless."

Sir Robert looked at her thoughtfully.

"There is a good deal in what you say," he replied. "But I think there is a good deal also to be deduced from the very fact you speak of, for it is a fact. I believe what you call the meaninglessness and purposelessness—the arbitrariness, one may say, of modern experiences of the kind are the surest proofs of their authenticity. Long ago people mixed up fact and fiction, their imaginations ran riot and on some very slight foundation—often, no doubt, genuine, though slight—they built up a very complete and thrilling 'ghost story.' Nowadays we consider and philosophise, we want to get to the root and reason of things, and we are more wary of exaggeration. The result is that the only genuine ghosts are most unsatisfactory beings;

they appear without purpose, and seem to be what, in fact, I believe they *almost* always are, irresponsible, purposeless will-o'-the-wisps. But from these I would separate the class of ghost stories the best attested and most impressive—those that have to do with the moment of death; any vision that appears just at or about that time has *generally* more meaning in it, I think you will find. Such ghosts appear for a reason, if no other than that of intense affection, which draws them near those from whom they are to be separated."

We listened attentively to this long explanation, though by no means fully understanding it.

"I have often heard," I said, "that the class of ghost stories you speak of are the only thoroughly authenticated ones, and I think one is naturally more inclined to believe in them than in any others. But I confess I do not in the least understand what you mean by speaking of *other* ghosts as 'will-o'-the-wisps.' You don't mean that though at the moment of death there is a real being—the soul, in fact, as distinct from the body, in which all but materialists believe—that this has no permanent existence, but melts away by degrees till it becomes an irresponsible, purposeless *nothing*—a will-o'-the-wisp in fact? I think I heard of some theory of the kind lately in a French book, but it shocked and repelled me so that I tried to forget it. Just as well, *better,* believe that we are nothing but our bodies, and that all is over when we die. Surely you don't mean what I say?"

"God forbid," said Sir Robert, with a fervency which startled while it reassured me. "It is my profound belief that not only we are something more than our bodies, but that our bodies are the merest outer dress of the real ourselves. It is also my profound belief that at death we—the real we—either enter at once into a state of rest temporarily, or, in some cases—for I do not believe in any cut-and-dry rule independently of *individual* considerations—are privileged at once to enter upon a sphere of nobler and purer labour," and here the speaker's eyes glowed with a light that was not of this world. "Is it then the least probable, is it not altogether discordant with our 'common sense'—a Divine gift which we may employ fearlessly—to suppose that these real 'selves,' freed from the weight of their discarded garments, would leave either their blissful repose, *or,* still less, their new activities, to come back to wander about, purposelessly and aimlessly, in this world, at best only perplexing and alarming such as may perceive them? Is it not contrary to all we find of the wisdom and *reasonableness* of such laws as we *do* know something about?"

"I have often thought so," I said, "and hitherto this has led me to be very sceptical about all ghost stories."

"But they are often true—so far as they go," he replied. "Our natures are much more complex than we ourselves understand or realise. I cannot now go at all thoroughly into the subject, but to give you a rough idea of my will-o'-the-wisp theory—can you not imagine a sort of shadow, or echo of ourselves, lingering about the scenes we have frequented on this earth, which under certain very rare conditions—the state of the atmosphere among others—may be perceptible to those still 'clothed upon' with this present body? To attempt a simile, I might suggest the perfume that lingers when the flowers are thrown away, the smoke that gradually dissolves after the lamp is extinguished! This is very, very loosely and roughly the *sort* of thing I mean by my 'will-o'-the-wisps.'"

"I don't like it at all," said Margaret, though she smiled a little. "I think I should be more frightened if I saw that kind of ghost—I mean if I thought it that kind—than by a good, honest, old-fashioned one, who knew what it was about and meant to come."

"But you have just said," he objected, "that they never do seem to know what they are about. Besides, why should you be frightened?—our fears, ourselves in fact—are the only thing we really need be frightened of—our weaknesses and ignorances and folly. There was great truth in that rather ghastly story of Calderra's, allegory though it is, about the man whose evil genius was himself; have you read it?"

We all shook our heads.

"It is ignorance that frightens us," he went on. "In this instance think of the appearances we are speaking of as almost of the nature of a photograph, or the reflection in a looking-glass. I daresay we should have been terrified by these, had we not grown used to them, did we not know what they are. Somebody said lately what appalling things we should think our own *shadows,* if we had suddenly for the first time become aware of them."

"I don't mind so much," said Margaret, "when you speak of ghosts as a sort of photograph. But —" she hesitated.

"Pray say what you are thinking."

"Just now when you said how incredible it was that *real souls* should return to this earth, you only spoke of good people, did you not?"

In his turn Sir Robert hesitated.

"It is difficult to draw a line even in thought between good and bad people," he said, "and, thank God, it is not for us to do so. 'To my Maker alone I stand or I fall.' There is evil in the best; there is, I would fain hope," but here his face grew grave and sad, "good in the worst. But even allowing that we could draw the line, is it likely that the bad, even those who have all but lost the last spark, who don't want to be good, is it likely that they, if, as we must believe, under Divine control, would be allowed to leave their new life of punishment—punishment in the sense of *correction*, mind you—to come back here, wasting their time, one may say, to frighten perfectly innocent people for no purpose? No, I think I am quite consistent. Only try to get rid of all *fears*—that is what we can all do. But really I should apologise for all this lecture;" and he was turning to me with a smile, when his eyes fell on the cup which he had replaced on the table.

"I cannot get over the impression that I have seen that cup—no, not that cup, but one just like it, before. Not long ago, I fancy," he said.

"Oh, you must let us know if you find out anything," we all exclaimed.

"I certainly shall do so," he said, and a few minutes afterwards he and Mr. Grenfell took their leave.

But I had time for a word or two with the latter out of hearing of the others.

"Who is Sir Robert Masters?" I asked. "Have you known him long? He is a very uncommon and impressive sort of man."

"Yes, I thought you would like him. I have not personally known him long, but he is an old friend of friends of ours. He is of good family, an old baronetcy, but he is not much known in fashionable society. He travels a great deal, or has done so rather, and people say he has 'peculiar ideas,' though that would not go against him in the world. Peculiar ideas, or the cant* of them, are rather the fashion it seems to me! But there is no cant

---

* Rhetoric, jargon, or slang. In this context, Mr. Grenfell is saying that Masters is an honest and straight-talking man.

UNEXPLAINED

about him. And whatever his ideas are," went on young Grenfell warmly, "he is one of the *best* men I ever knew. He has settled down for some years, and devotes his whole life to doing good, but so quietly and unostentatiously that no one knows how much he does, and others get the credit of it very often."

That was all I heard.

I have never seen Sir Robert again. Still I have by no means arrived yet at the end of my so-called ghost story.

The cup and saucer were carefully washed and replaced in the glass-doored cabinet. The summer gradually waned, and we all returned to our own home. It was at a considerable distance from my sister's, and we met each other principally in the summer time. So, though I did not forget Sir Robert Masters, or his somewhat strange conversation, amid the crowd of daily interests and pleasures, duties and cares, none of the incidents I have here recorded were much in my mind, and but that I had while still in Germany carefully noted the details of all bearing directly or indirectly on "Nora's ghost," as we had come to call it—though it was but rarely alluded to before the child herself—I should not now have been able to give them with circumstantiality.

Fully fifteen months after the visit to my sister, during which we had met Sir Robert, the whole was suddenly and unexpectedly recalled to my memory. Mark and Nora the elder—my sister, that is,—were in their turn staying with us, when one morning at breakfast the post brought for the latter an unusually bulky and important-looking letter. She opened it, glanced at an outer sheet enclosing several pages in a different handwriting, and passed it on to me.

"We must read the rest together," she said in a low voice, glancing at the children, who were at the table. "How interesting it will be!"

The sheet she had handed to me was a short note from Mr. Grenfell. It was dated from some place in Norway where he was fishing, and from whence he had addressed the whole packet to my sister's own home, not knowing of her absence.

"MY DEAR MRS. DAVENTRY"—it began. "The enclosed will have been a long time of reaching its real destination, for

333

it is, as you will see, really intended for your sister. No doubt
it will interest you too, as it has done me, though I am too
matter-of-fact and prosaic to enter into such things much. Still
it is curious. Please keep the letter; I am sure my friend intends
you to do so.

"Yours very truly,
"RALPH GRENFELL."

The manuscript enclosed was, of course, from Sir Robert himself. It
was in the form of a letter to young Grenfell; and after explaining that he
thought it better to write to him, not having my address, he plunged into
the real object of his communication.

"You will not," he said, "have forgotten the incident of the 'ghost-cup,'
in the summer of last year, and the curious story your friend was so good
as to tell us about it. You may remember—Mrs.—— will, I am sure, do
so—my strong impression that I had recently seen one like it. After I left
you I could not get this feeling out of my head. It is always irritating not to
be able, figuratively speaking, 'to lay your hand' on a recollection, and in
this instance I really wanted to get the clue, as it might lead to some sort
of 'explanation' of the little girl's strange experience. I cudgelled my brains,
but all to no purpose; I went over in memory all the houses at which I had
visited within a certain space of time; I made lists of all the people I knew
interested in 'china,' ancient or modern, and likely to possess specimens of
it. But all in vain. All I got for my pains was that people began to think I
was developing a new crotchet, or, as I heard one lady say to another, not
knowing I was within earshot, 'the poor man must be a little off his head,
though till now I have always denied it. But the revulsion from benevolent
schemes to china-collecting shows it only too plainly.' So I thought I had
better leave off cross-questioning my 'collecting' friends about porcelain
and faïence, German ware in particular. And after a while I thought no
more about it. Two months ago I had occasion to make a journey to the
north—the same journey and to stay at the same house where I have been
four or five times since I saw the 'ghost-cup.' But this was what happened
this time. There is a junction by which one must pass on this journey. I
generally manage to suit my trains so as to avoid waiting there, but this

is not always feasible. This time I found that an hour at the junction was inevitable. There is a very good refreshment room there, kept by very civil, decent people. They knew me by sight, and after I had had a cup of tea they proposed to me, as they have done before, to wait in their little parlour just off the public room. 'It would be quieter and more comfortable,' said either the mother or the daughter who manage the concern. I thanked them, and settled myself in an arm-chair with my book, when, looking up—there on the mantelpiece stood the fellow cup—the identical shape, pattern, and colour! It all flashed into my mind then. I had made this journey just before going into your neighbourhood last year, and had waited in this little parlour just as this time.

"'Where did you get that cup, Mrs. Smith?' I asked.

"There were two or three rather pretty bits of china about. The good woman was pleased at my noticing it.

"'Yes, sir. Isn't it pretty? I've rather a fancy for china. That cup was sent me by my niece. She said she'd picked it up somewhere—at a sale, I think. It's foreign, sir; isn't it?'

"'Yes, German. But can't you find out *where* your niece got it?' for at the word 'sale' my hopes fell.

"'I can ask her. I shall be writing to her this week,' she replied; and she promised to get any information she could for me within a fortnight, by which time I expected to pass that way again. I did so, and Mrs. Smith proved as good as her word. The niece had got the cup from a friend of hers, an auctioneer, and he, not she, had got it at a sale. But he was away from home—she could hear nothing more at present. She gave his address, however, and assurances that he was very good-natured and would gladly put the gentleman in the way of getting china like it, if it was to be got. He would be home by the middle of the month. It was now the middle of the month. The auctioneer's town was not above a couple of hours off my line. Perhaps you will all laugh at me when I tell you that I went those two hours out of my way, arriving at the town late that night and putting up at a queer old inn—worth going to see for itself—on purpose to find the man of the hammer. I found him. He was very civil, though rather mystified. He remembered the cup perfectly, but there was no chance of getting any like it where it came from!

"'And where was that?' I asked eagerly.

"'At a sale some miles from here, about four years ago,' he replied. 'It was the sale of the furniture and plate, and everything, in fact, of a widow lady. She had some pretty china, for she had a fancy for it. That cup was not of much value; it was quite modern. I bought it in for a trifle. I gave it to Miss Cross, and she sent it to her aunt, as you know. As for getting any like it—'

"But I interrupted him by assuring him I did not wish that, but that I had reasons for wanting some information about the person who, I believed, had bought the cup. 'Nothing to do any harm to any one,' I said; 'a matter of feeling. A similar cup had been bought by a person I was interested in, and I feared that person was dead.'

"The auctioneer's face cleared. He fancied he began to understand me.

"'I am afraid you are right, sir, if the person you mean was young Mr. Paulet, the lady's son. You may have met him on his travels? His death was very sad, I believe. It killed his mother, they say—she never looked up after; and as she had no near relative to follow her, everything was sold. I remember I was told all that, at the sale, and it seemed to me particularly sad, even though one comes across many sad things in our line of business.'

"'Do you remember the particulars of Mr. Paulet's death?' I asked.

"'Only that it happened suddenly—somewhere in foreign parts. I did not know the family till I was asked to take charge of the sale,' he replied.

"'Could you possibly get any details for me? I feel sure it is the same Mr. Paulet,' I said boldly.

"The auctioneer considered.

"'Perhaps I can. I rather think a former servant of theirs is still in the neighbourhood,' he replied.

"I thanked him and left him my address, to which he promised to write. I felt it was perhaps better not to pursue my inquiries further in person; it might lead to annoyance, or possibly to gossip about the dead, which I detest. I jotted down some particulars for the auctioneer's guidance, and went on my way. That was a fortnight ago. To-day I have his answer, which I transcribe:—

"'SIR—The servant I spoke of could not tell me very much, as she was not long in the late Mrs. Paulet's service. To hear more, she says, you must apply to the relations of the family. Young Mr. Paulet was tall and fair and very nice-looking. His mother and he were deeply attached to each other. He travelled a good deal and used to bring her home lots of pretty things. He met his death in some part of Germany where there are forests, for though it was thought at first he had died of heart disease, the doctors proved he had been struck by lightning, and his body was found in the forest, and the papers on him showed who he was. The body was sent home to be buried, and all that was found with it; a knapsack and its contents, among which was the cup I bought at the sale. His death was about the middle of August 18—. I shall be glad if this information is of any service.'

"This," continued Sir Robert's own letter, "is all I have been able to learn. There does not seem to have been the very slightest suspicion of foul play, nor do I think it the least likely there was any ground for such. Young Paulet probably died some way farther in the forest than Silber-bach, and it is even possible the surly landlord never heard of it. It *might* be worth while to inquire about it should your friends ever be there again. If I should be in the neighbourhood I certainly should do so; the whole coincidences are very striking."

Then followed apologies for the length of his letter which he had been betrayed into by his anxiety to tell all there was to tell. In return he asked Mr. Grenfell to obtain from me certain dates and particulars as he wished to note them down. It was the 18th of August on which "Nora's ghost" had appeared—just two years after the August of the poor young man's death!

There was also a postscript to Sir Robert's letter, in which he said, "I think, in Mrs.——'s place, I would say nothing to the little girl of what we have discovered."

And I have never done so.

This is all I have to tell. I offer no suggestions, no theories in expla-nation of the facts. Those who, like Sir Robert Masters, are able and desirous to treat such subjects scientifically or philosophically will doubtless form their own. I cannot say that I find *his* theory a perfectly satisfactory one, perhaps I do not sufficiently understand it, but I have tried to give it in his own words. Should this matter-of-fact relation of a curious experience meet his eyes, I am sure he will forgive my having brought him into it. Besides, it is not likely that he would be recognised; men, and women too, of "peculiar ideas," sincere investigators and honest searchers after truth, as well as their superficial plagiarists, being by no means rare in these days.

LET LOOSE

by Mary Cholmondely

1890

The daughter of a clergyman, Mary Cholmondely—a name the British pronounce Chumley—spent most of her first thirty years helping her sickly mother raise her seven siblings and assisting her father with parish work. Debilitated by asthma and thinking herself unlikely to marry (at the age of eighteen, she wrote in her journal "that is hardly likely, as I possess neither beauty nor charms"), she devoted herself to writing in addition to family life. She wrote Her Evil Genius *at the age of sixteen; it is now lost, and presumed destroyed. Her first novel, a detective story titled* The Danvers Jewels, *won her a small following, and was followed by* Sir Charles Danvers *and five more novels, as well as a memoir and some collections of stories.*

Mary's 1899 novel Red Pottage *caused a scandal when it was published. Despite—or perhaps, because of—her long devotion to her family and her father's parish, the book satirizes religious hypocrisy and narrow-minded country life; what caused it to be denounced from pulpits across England was its treatment of adultery, female sexuality, and gender roles—the last thing society expected from the daughter of a minister of the Church of England. The book became a sensation, and was even filmed in 1918, but it brought Mary little profit, as she had sold the copyright; she wrote at the time of the uneasiness that her sudden celebrity caused her.*

So far as is known, "Let Loose" was Mary's only foray into supernatural fiction. Published in the Temple Bar *magazine and later collected in* Moth and Rust *alongside more conventional tales, it is an effective ghost story—but in its day it was almost as controversial as* Red Pottage. *Mary was accused of plagiarizing the tale from a story by T. G. Loring titled "The Tomb of Sarah," which appeared in the* Pall Mall *magazine in December 1900. As a note in* Moth and Rust *shows, though, she was able to show that her story had been published first—but even so, Mary apologizes for any "unintentional plagiarism" that may have occurred.*

The dead abide with us! Though stark and cold
Earth seems to grip them, they are with us still.

Some years ago I took up architecture, and made a tour through Holland, studying the buildings of that interesting country. I was not then aware that it is not enough to take up art. Art must take you up, too. I never doubted but that my passing enthusiasm for her would be returned. When I discovered that she was a stern mistress, who did not immediately respond to my attentions, I naturally transferred them to another shrine. There are other things in the world besides art. I am now a landscape gardener.

But at the time of which I write I was engaged in a violent flirtation with architecture. I had one companion on this expedition, who has since become one of the leading architects of the day. He was a thin, determined-looking man with a screwed-up face and heavy jaw, slow of speech, and absorbed in his work to a degree which I quickly found tiresome. He was possessed of a certain quiet power of overcoming obstacles which I have rarely seen equalled. He has since become my brother-in-law, so I ought to know; for my parents did not like him much and opposed the marriage, and my sister did not like him at all, and refused him over and over again; but, nevertheless, he eventually married her.

I have thought since that one of his reasons for choosing me as his travelling companion on this occasion was because he was getting up steam for what he subsequently termed "an alliance with my family," but the idea never entered my head at the time. A more careless man as to dress I have rarely met, and yet, in all the heat of July in Holland, I noticed that he never appeared without a high, starched collar, which had not even fashion to commend it at that time.

I often chaffed him about his splendid collars, and asked him why he wore them, but without eliciting any response. One evening, as we were walking back to our lodgings in Middeburg, I attacked him for about the thirtieth time on the subject.

"Why on earth do you wear them?" I said.

"You have, I believe, asked me that question many times," he replied, in his slow, precise utterance; "but always on occasions when I was occupied. I am now at leisure, and I will tell you."

And he did.

I have put down what he said, as nearly in his own words as I can remember them.

Ten years ago, I was asked to read a paper on English Frescoes at the Institute of British Architects. I was determined to make the paper as good as I could, down to the slightest details, and I consulted many books on the subject, and studied every fresco I could find. My father, who had been an architect, had left me, at his death, all his papers and note-books on the subject of architecture. I searched them diligently, and found in one of them a slight unfinished sketch of nearly fifty years ago that specially interested me. Underneath was noted, in his clear, small hand—*Frescoed east wall of crypt. Parish Church. Wet Waste-on-the-Wolds, Yorkshire (via Pickering).*

The sketch had such a fascination for me that I decided to go there and see the fresco for myself. I had only a very vague idea as to where Wet Waste-on-the-Wolds was, but I was ambitious for the success of my paper; it was hot in London, and I set off on my long journey not without a certain degree of pleasure, with my dog Brian, a large nondescript brindled creature, as my only companion.

I reached Pickering, in Yorkshire, in the course of the afternoon, and then began a series of experiments on local lines which ended, after several hours, in my finding myself deposited at a little out-of-the-world station within nine or ten miles of Wet Waste. As no conveyance of any kind was to be had, I shouldered my portmanteau, and set out on a long white road that stretched away into the distance over the bare, treeless wold.* I must have walked for several hours, over a waste of moorland patched with heather, when a doctor passed me, and gave me a lift to within a mile of my destination. The mile was a long one, and it was quite dark by the time I saw the feeble glimmer of lights in front of me, and found that I had reached Wet Waste. I had considerable difficulty in getting any one to take me in; but at last I persuaded the owner of the public-house to give me a bed, and, quite tired out, I got into it as soon as possible, for fear he should change his mind, and fell asleep to the sound of a little stream below my window.

I was up early next morning, and inquired directly after breakfast the way to the clergyman's house, which I found was close at hand. At Wet Waste everything was close at hand. The whole village seemed composed of a straggling row of one-storeyed grey stone houses, the same colour as the stone walls that separated the few fields enclosed from the surrounding waste, and as the little bridges over the beck that ran down one side of the grey wide street. Everything was grey.

The church, the low tower of which I could see at a little distance, seemed to have been built of the same stone; so was the parsonage when I came up to it, accompanied on my way by a mob of rough, uncouth children, who eyed me and Brian with half-defiant curiosity.

The clergyman was at home, and after a short delay I was admitted. Leaving Brian in charge of my drawing materials, I followed the servant

---

* A local term for hill country.

into a low panelled room, in which, at a latticed window, a very old man was sitting. The morning light fell on his white head bent low over a litter of papers and books.

"Mr. er—?" he said, looking up slowly, with one finger keeping his place in a book.

"Blake."

"Blake," he repeated after me, and was silent.

I told him that I was an architect; that I had come to study a fresco in the crypt of his church, and asked for the keys.

"The crypt," he said, pushing up his spectacles and peering hard at me. "The crypt has been closed for thirty years. Ever since—" and he stopped short.

"I should be much obliged for the keys," I said again.

He shook his head.

"No," he said. "No one goes in there now."

"It is a pity," I remarked, "for I have come a long way with that one object;" and I told him about the paper I had been asked to read, and the trouble I was taking with it.

He became interested. "Ah!" he said, laying down his pen, and removing his finger from the page before him, "I can understand that. I also was young once, and fired with ambition. The lines have fallen to me in somewhat lonely places, and for forty years I have held the cure* of souls in this place, where, truly, I have seen but little of the world, though I myself may be not unknown in the paths of literature. Possibly you may have read a pamphlet, written by myself, on the Syrian version of the Three Authentic Epistles of Ignatius?"

"Sir," I said, "I am ashamed to confess that I have not time to read even the most celebrated books. My one object in life is my art. *Ars longa, vita brevis*, you know."

"You are right, my son," said the old man, evidently disappointed, but looking at me kindly.

"There are diversities of gifts, and if the Lord has entrusted you with a talent, look to it. Lay it not up in a napkin."

---

* A period word, meaning "care."

I said I would not do so if he would lend me the keys of the crypt. He seemed startled by my recurrence to the subject and looked undecided.

"Why not?" he murmured to himself. "The youth appears a good youth. And superstition! What is it but distrust in God!"

He got up slowly, and taking a large bunch of keys out of his pocket, opened with one of them an oak cupboard in the corner of the room.

"They should be here," he muttered, peering in; "but the dust of many years deceives the eye. See, my son, if among these parchments there be two keys; one of iron and very large, and the other steel, and of a long thin appearance."

I went eagerly to help him, and presently found in a back drawer two keys tied together, which he recognised at once.

"Those are they," he said. "The long one opens the first door at the bottom of the steps which go down against the outside wall of the church hard by the sword graven in the wall. The second opens (but it is hard of opening and of shutting) the iron door within the passage leading to the crypt itself. My son, is it necessary to your treatise that you should enter this crypt?"

I replied that it was absolutely necessary.

"Then take them," he said, "and in the evening you will bring them to me again."

I said I might want to go several days running, and asked if he would not allow me to keep them till I had finished my work; but on that point he was firm.

"Likewise," he added, "be careful that you lock the first door at the foot of the steps before you unlock the second, and lock the second also while you are within. Furthermore, when you come out lock the iron inner door as well as the wooden one."

I promised I would do so, and, after thanking him, hurried away, delighted at my success in obtaining the keys. Finding Brian and my sketching materials waiting for me in the porch, I eluded the vigilance of my escort of children by taking the narrow private path between the parsonage and the church which was close at hand, standing in a quadrangle of ancient yews.

The church itself was interesting, and I noticed that it must have arisen out of the ruins of a previous building, judging from the number of fragments of stone caps and arches, bearing traces of very early carving, now built into the walls. There were incised crosses, too, in some places, and one especially caught my attention, being flanked by a large sword. It was in trying to get a nearer look at this that I stumbled, and, looking down, saw at my feet a flight of narrow stone steps green with moss and mildew. Evidently this was the entrance to the crypt. I at once descended the steps, taking care of my footing, for they were damp and slippery in the extreme.

Brian accompanied me, as nothing would induce him to remain behind. By the time I had reached the bottom of the stairs, I found myself almost in darkness, and I had to strike a light before I could find the keyhole and the proper key to fit into it. The door, which was of wood, opened inwards fairly easily, although an accumulation of mould and rubbish on the ground outside showed it had not been used for many years. Having got through it, which was not altogether an easy matter, as nothing would induce it to open more than about eighteen inches, I carefully locked it behind me, although I should have preferred to leave it open, as there is to some minds an unpleasant feeling in being locked in anywhere, in case of a sudden exit seeming advisable.

I kept my candle alight with some difficulty, and after groping my way down a low and of course exceedingly dank passage, came to another door. A toad was squatting against it, who looked as if he had been sitting there about a hundred years. As I lowered the candle to the floor, he gazed at the light with unblinking eyes, and then retreated slowly into a crevice in the wall, leaving against the door a small cavity in the dry mud which had gradually silted up round his person. I noticed that this door was of iron, and had a long bolt, which, however, was broken.

Without delay, I fitted the second key into the lock, and pushing the door open after considerable difficulty, I felt the cold breath of the crypt upon my face. I must own I experienced a momentary regret at locking the second door again as soon as I was well inside, but I felt it my duty to do so. Then, leaving the key in the lock, I seized my candle and looked round. I was standing in a low vaulted chamber with groined roof, cut out of the solid rock. It was difficult to see where the crypt ended, as further light thrown on any point only showed other rough archways or openings, cut in the rock, which had probably served at one time for family vaults.

A peculiarity of the Wet Waste crypt, which I had not noticed in other places of that description, was the tasteful arrangement of skulls and bones which were packed about four feet high on either side. The skulls were symmetrically built up to within a few inches of the top of the low archway on my left, and the shin bones were arranged in the same manner on my right. *But the fresco!* I looked round for it in vain. Perceiving at the further end of the crypt a very low and very massive archway, the entrance to which was not filled up with bones, I passed under it, and found myself in a second smaller chamber. Holding my candle above my head, the first object its light fell upon was—the fresco, and at a glance I saw that it was unique. Setting down some of my things with a trembling hand on a rough stone shelf hard by, which had evidently been a credence table, I examined the work more closely. It was a reredos over what had probably been the altar at the time the priests were proscribed. The fresco belonged to the earliest part of the fifteenth century, and was so perfectly preserved that I could almost trace the limits of each day's work in the plaster, as the artist had dashed it on and smoothed it out with his trowel. The subject was the Ascension, gloriously treated. I can hardly describe my elation as I stood and looked at it, and reflected that this magnificent specimen of English fresco painting would be made known to the world by myself. Recollecting myself at last, I opened my sketching bag, and, lighting all the candles I had brought with me, set to work.

Brian walked about near me, and though I was not otherwise than glad of his company in my rather lonely position, I wished several times I had left him behind. He seemed restless, and even the sight of so many bones appeared to exercise no soothing effect upon him. At last, however, after repeated commands, he lay down, watchful but motionless, on the stone floor.

I must have worked for several hours, and I was pausing to rest my eyes and hands, when I noticed for the first time the intense stillness that surrounded me. No sound from *me* reached the outer world. The church clock which had clanged out so loud and ponderously as I went down the steps, had not since sent the faintest whisper of its iron tongue down to me below. All was silent as the grave. This *was* the grave. Those who had come here had indeed gone down into silence. I repeated the words to myself, or rather they repeated themselves to me.

Gone down into silence.

I was awakened from my reverie by a faint sound. I sat still and listened. Bats occasionally frequent vaults and underground places.

The sound continued, a faint, stealthy, rather unpleasant sound. I do not know what kinds of sounds bats make, whether pleasant or otherwise. Suddenly there was a noise as of something falling, a momentary pause—and then—an almost imperceptible but distant jangle as of a key.

I had left the key in the lock after I had turned it, and I now regretted having done so. I got up, took one of the candles, and went back into the larger crypt—for though I trust I am not so effeminate as to be rendered nervous by hearing a noise for which I cannot instantly account; still, on occasions of this kind, I must honestly say I should prefer that they did not occur. As I came towards the iron door, there was another distinct (I had almost said hurried) sound. The impression on my mind was one of great haste. When I reached the door, and held the candle near the lock to take out the key, I perceived that the other one, which hung by a short string to its fellow, was vibrating slightly. I should have preferred not to find it vibrating, as there seemed no occasion for such a course; but I put them both into my pocket, and turned to go back to my work. As I turned, I saw on the ground what had occasioned the louder noise I had heard, namely, a skull which had evidently just slipped from its place on the top of one of the walls of bones, and had rolled almost to my feet. There, disclosing a few more inches of the top of an archway behind, was the place from which it had been dislodged. I stooped to pick it up, but fearing to displace any more skulls by meddling with the pile, and not liking to gather up its scattered teeth, I let it lie, and went back to my work, in which I was soon so completely absorbed that I was only roused at last by my candles beginning to burn low and go out one after another.

Then, with a sigh of regret, for I had not nearly finished, I turned to go. Poor Brian, who had never quite reconciled himself to the place, was beside himself with delight. As I opened the iron door he pushed past me, and a moment later I heard him whining and scratching, and I had almost added, beating, against the wooden one. I locked the iron door, and hurried down the passage as quickly as I could, and almost before I had got the other one ajar there seemed to be a rush past me into the open air, and

Brian was bounding up the steps and out of sight. As I stopped to take out the key, I felt quite deserted and left behind. When I came out once more into the sunlight, there was a vague sensation all about me in the air of exultant freedom.

It was already late in the afternoon, and after I had sauntered back to the parsonage to give up the keys, I persuaded the people of the public-house to let me join in the family meal, which was spread out in the kitchen. The inhabitants of Wet Waste were primitive people, with the frank, unabashed manner that flourishes still in lonely places, especially in the wilds of Yorkshire; but I had no idea that in these days of penny posts and cheap newspapers such entire ignorance of the outer world could have existed in any corner, however remote, of Great Britain.

When I took one of the neighbour's children on my knee—a pretty little girl with the palest aureole of flaxen hair I had ever seen—and began to draw pictures for her of the birds and beasts of other countries, I was instantly surrounded by a crowd of children, and even grown-up people, while others came to their doorways and looked on from a distance, calling to each other in the strident unknown tongue which I have since discovered goes by the name of "Broad Yorkshire."

The following morning, as I came out of my room, I perceived that something was amiss in the village. A buzz of voices reached me as I passed the bar, and in the next house I could hear through the open window a high-pitched wail of lamentation.

The woman who brought me my breakfast was in tears, and in answer to my questions, told me that the neighbour's child, the little girl whom I had taken on my knee the evening before, had died in the night.

I felt sorry for the general grief that the little creature's death seemed to arouse, and the uncontrolled wailing of the poor mother took my appetite away.

I hurried off early to my work, calling on my way for the keys, and with Brian for my companion descended once more into the crypt, and drew and measured with an absorption that gave me no time that day to listen for sounds real or fancied. Brian, too, on this occasion seemed quite content, and slept peacefully beside me on the stone floor. When I had worked as long as I could, I put away my books with regret that even then I had not quite finished, as I had hoped to do. It would be necessary to come again for a short time on the morrow. When I returned the keys late that afternoon, the old clergyman met me at the door, and asked me to come in and have tea with him.

"And has the work prospered?" he asked, as we sat down in the long, low room, into which I had just been ushered, and where he seemed to live entirely.

I told him it had, and showed it to him.

"You have seen the original, of course?" I said.

"Once," he replied, gazing fixedly at it. He evidently did not care to be communicative, so I turned the conversation to the age of the church.

"All here is old," he said. "When I was young, forty years ago, and came here because I had no means of mine own, and was much moved to marry at that time, I felt oppressed that all was so old; and that this place was so far removed from the world, for which I had at times longings grievous to be borne; but I had chosen my lot, and with it I was forced to be content. My son, marry not in youth, for love, which truly in that season is a mighty power, turns away the heart from study, and young children break the back of ambition. Neither marry in middle life, when a woman is seen to be but a woman and her talk a weariness, so you will not be burdened with a wife in your old age."

I had my own views on the subject of marriage, for I am of opinion that a well-chosen companion of domestic tastes and docile and devoted temperament may be of material assistance to a professional man. But, my opinions once formulated, it is not of moment to me to discuss them with others, so I changed the subject, and asked if the neighbouring villages were as antiquated as Wet Waste. "Yes, all about here is old," he repeated. "The paved road leading to Dyke Fens is an ancient pack road, made even in the time of the Romans. Dyke Fens, which is very near here, a matter of but four or five miles, is likewise old, and forgotten by the world. The Reformation never reached it. It stopped here. And at Dyke Fens they still have a priest and a bell, and bow down before the saints. It is a damnable heresy, and weekly I expound it as such to my people, showing them true doctrines; and I have heard that this same priest has so far yielded himself to the Evil One that he has preached against me as withholding gospel truths from my flock; but I take no heed of it, neither of his pamphlet touching the Clementine Homilies, in which he vainly contradicts that which I have plainly set forth and proven beyond doubt, concerning the word Asaph."

The old man was fairly off on his favourite subject, and it was some time before I could get away. As it was, he followed me to the door, and I only escaped because the old clerk hobbled up at that moment, and claimed his attention.

The following morning I went for the keys for the third and last time. I had decided to leave early the next day. I was tired of Wet Waste, and a certain gloom seemed to my fancy to be gathering over the place. There was a sensation of trouble in the air, as if, although the day was bright and clear, a storm were coming.

This morning, to my astonishment, the keys were refused to me when I asked for them. I did not, however, take the refusal as final—I make it a rule never to take a refusal as final—and after a short delay I was shown into the room where, as usual, the clergyman was sitting, or rather, on this occasion, was walking up and down.

"My son," he said with vehemence, "I know wherefore you have come, but it is of no avail. I cannot lend the keys again."

I replied that, on the contrary, I hoped he would give them to me at once.

"It is impossible," he repeated. "I did wrong, exceeding wrong. I will never part with them again."

"Why not?"

He hesitated, and then said slowly:

"The old clerk, Abraham Kelly, died last night." He paused, and then went on: "The doctor has just been here to tell me of that which is a mystery to him. I do not wish the people of the place to know it, and only to me he has mentioned it, but he has discovered plainly on the throat of the old man, and also, but more faintly on the child's, marks as of strangulation. None but he has observed it, and he is at a loss how to account for it. I, alas! can account for it but in one way, but in one way!"

I did not see what all this had to do with the crypt, but to humour the old man, I asked what that way was.

"It is a long story, and, haply, to a stranger it may appear but foolishness, but I will even tell it; for I perceive that unless I furnish a reason for with-holding the keys, you will not cease to entreat me for them.

"I told you at first when you inquired of me concerning the crypt, that it had been closed these thirty years, and so it was. Thirty years ago a certain Sir Roger Despard departed this life, even the Lord of the manor of Wet Waste and Dyke Fens, the last of his family, which is now, thank the Lord, extinct. He was a man of a vile life, neither fearing God nor regarding man, nor having compassion on innocence, and the Lord appeared to have given him over to the tormentors even in this world, for he suffered many things of his vices, more especially from drunkenness, in which seasons, and they were many, he was as one possessed by seven devils, being an abomination to his household and a root of bitterness to all, both high and low.

"And, at last, the cup of his iniquity being full to the brim, he came to die, and I went to exhort him on his death-bed; for I heard that terror had come upon him, and that evil imaginations encompassed him so thick on every side, that few of them that were with him could abide in his presence. But when I saw him I perceived that there was no place of repentance left for him, and he scoffed at me and my superstition, even as he lay dying, and swore there was no God and no angel, and all were damned even as he was. And the next day, towards evening, the pains of death came upon him, and he raved the more exceedingly, inasmuch as he said he was being strangled by the Evil One. Now on his table was his hunting knife, and with his last strength he crept and laid hold upon it, no man withstanding him, and swore a great oath that if he went down to burn in hell, he would leave one of his hands behind on earth, and that it would never rest until it had drawn blood from the throat of another and strangled him, even as he himself was being strangled. And he cut off his own right hand at the wrist, and no man dared go near him to stop him, and the blood went through the floor, even down to the ceiling of the room below, and thereupon he died.

"And they called me in the night, and told me of his oath, and I counselled that no man should speak of it, and I took the dead hand, which none had ventured to touch, and I laid it beside him in his coffin; for I thought it better he should take it with him, so that he might have it, if haply some day after much tribulation he should perchance be moved to stretch forth his hands towards God. But the story got spread about, and the people were affrighted, so, when he came to be buried in the place of his fathers, he being the last of his family, and the crypt likewise full, I had it closed, and kept the keys myself, and suffered no man to enter therein any more; for truly he was a man of an evil life, and the devil is not yet wholly overcome, nor cast chained into the lake of fire. So in time the story died out, for in thirty years much is forgotten. And when you came and asked me for the keys, I was at the first minded to withhold them; but I thought it was a vain superstition, and I perceived that you do but ask a second time for what is first refused; so I let you have them, seeing it was not an idle curiosity, but a desire to improve the talent committed to you, that led you to require them."

The old man stopped, and I remained silent, wondering what would be the best way to get them just once more.

"Surely, sir," I said at last, "one so cultivated and deeply read as yourself cannot be biased by an idle superstition."

"I trust not," he replied, "and yet—it is a strange thing that since the crypt was opened two people have died, and the mark is plain upon the throat of the old man and visible on the young child. No blood was drawn, but the second time the grip was stronger than the first. The third time, perchance—"

"Superstition such as that," I said with authority, "is an entire want of faith in God. You once said so yourself."

I took a high moral tone which is often efficacious with conscientious, humble-minded people.

He agreed, and accused himself of not having faith as a grain of mustard seed; but even when I had got him so far as that, I had a severe struggle for the keys. It was only when I finally explained to him that if any malign influence *had* been let loose the first day, at any rate, it was out now for good or evil, and no further going or coming of mine could make any difference, that I finally gained my point. I was young, and he was old; and, being much shaken by what had occurred, he gave way at last, and I wrested the keys from him.

I will not deny that I went down the steps that day with a vague, indefinable repugnance, which was only accentuated by the closing of the two doors behind me. I remembered then, for the first time, the faint jangling of the key and other sounds which I had noticed the first day, and how one of the skulls had fallen. I went to the place where it still lay. I have already said these walls of skulls were built up so high as to be within a few inches of the top of the low archways that led into more distant portions of the vault. The displacement of the skull in question had left a small hole just large enough for me to put my hand through. I noticed for the first time, over the archway above it, a carved coat-of-arms, and the name, now almost obliterated, of Despard. This, no doubt, was the Despard vault. I could not resist moving a few more skulls and looking in, holding my candle as near the aperture as I could. The vault was full. Piled high, one upon another, were old coffins, and remnants of coffins, and strewn bones. I attribute my present determination to be cremated to the painful impression produced on me by this spectacle. The coffin nearest the archway alone was intact, save for a large crack across the lid. I could not get a ray from my candle to fall on the brass plates, but I felt no doubt this was the coffin of the wicked Sir Roger. I put back the skulls, including the one which had rolled down, and carefully finished my work. I was not there much more than an hour, but I was glad to get away.

If I could have left Wet Waste at once I should have done so, for I had a totally unreasonable longing to leave the place; but I found that only one train stopped during the day at the station from which I had come, and that it would not be possible to be in time for it that day.

Accordingly I submitted to the inevitable, and wandered about with Brian for the remainder of the afternoon and until late in the evening, sketching and smoking. The day was oppressively hot, and even after the sun had set across the burnt stretches of the wolds, it seemed to grow very little cooler. Not a breath stirred. In the evening, when I was tired of loitering in the lanes, I went up to my own room, and after contemplating afresh my finished study of the fresco, I suddenly set to work to write the part of my paper bearing upon it. As a rule, I write with difficulty, but that evening words came to me with winged speed, and with them a hovering impression that I must make haste, that I was much pressed for time. I wrote and wrote, until my candles guttered out and left me trying to finish by the moonlight, which, until I endeavoured to write by it, seemed as clear as day.

I had to put away my MS., and, feeling it was too early to go to bed, for the church clock was just counting out ten, I sat down by the open window and leaned out to try and catch a breath of air. It was a night of exceptional beauty; and as I looked out my nervous haste and hurry of mind were allayed. The moon, a perfect circle, was—if so poetic an expression be permissible—as it were, sailing across a calm sky. Every detail of the little village was as clearly illuminated by its beams as if it were broad day; so, also, was the adjacent church with its primeval yews, while even the wolds beyond were dimly indicated, as if through tracing paper.

I sat a long time leaning against the window-sill. The heat was still intense. I am not, as a rule, easily elated or readily cast down; but as I sat that light in the lonely village on the moors, with Brian's head against my knee, how, or why, I know not, a great depression gradually came upon me.

My mind went back to the crypt and the countless dead who had been laid there. The sight of the goal to which all human life, and strength, and beauty, travel in the end, had not affected me at the time, but now the very air about me seemed heavy with death.

What was the good, I asked myself, of working and toiling, and grinding down my heart and youth in the mill of long and strenuous effort, seeing that in the grave folly and talent, idleness and labour lie together, and are alike forgotten? Labour seemed to stretch before me till my heart ached to think of it, to stretch before me even to the end of life, and then came, as the recompense of my labour—the grave. Even if I succeeded, if, after wearing my life threadbare with toil, I succeeded, what remained to me in the end? The grave. A little sooner, while the hands and eyes were still strong to labour, or a little later, when all power and vision had been taken from them; sooner or later only—*the grave.*

I do not apologise for the excessively morbid tenor of these reflections, as I hold that they were caused by the lunar effects which I have endeavoured to transcribe. The moon in its various quarterings has always exerted a marked influence on what I may call the sub-dominant, namely, the poetic side of my nature.

I roused myself at last, when the moon came to look in upon me where I sat, and, leaving the window open, I pulled myself together and went to bed.

I fell asleep almost immediately, but I do not fancy I could have been asleep very long when I was wakened by Brian. He was growling in a low, muffled tone, as he sometimes did in his sleep, when his nose was buried in his rug. I called out to him to shut up; and as he did not do so, turned in bed to find my match box or something to throw at him. The moonlight was still in the room, and as I looked at him I saw him raise his head and evidently wake up. I admonished him, and was just on the point of falling asleep when he began to growl again in a low, savage manner that waked me most effectually. Presently he shook himself and got up, and began prowling about the room. I sat up in bed and called to him, but he paid no attention. Suddenly I saw him stop short in the moonlight; he showed his teeth, and crouched down, his eyes following something in the air. I looked at him in horror. Was he going mad? His eyes were glaring, and his head moved slightly as if he were following the rapid movements of an enemy. Then, with a furious snarl, he suddenly sprang from the ground, and rushed in great leaps across the room towards me, dashing himself against the furniture, his eyes rolling, snatching and tearing wildly in the air with his teeth. I saw he had gone mad. I leaped out of bed, and rushing at him, caught him by the throat. The moon had gone behind a cloud; but in the darkness I felt him turn upon me, felt him rise up, and his teeth close in my throat. I was being strangled. With all the strength of despair, I kept my grip of his neck, and, dragging him across the room, tried to crush in his head against the iron rail of my bedstead. It was my only chance. I felt the blood running down my neck. I was suffocating. After one moment of frightful struggle, I beat his head against the bar and heard his skull give way. I felt him give one strong shudder, a groan, and then I fainted away.

When I came to myself I was lying on the floor, surrounded by the people of the house, my reddened hands still clutching Brian's throat. Someone was holding a candle towards me, and the draught from the window made it flare and waver. I looked at Brian. He was stone dead. The blood from his battered head was trickling slowly over my hands. His great jaw was fixed in something that—in the uncertain light—I could not see.

They turned the light a little.

"Oh, God!" I shrieked. "There! Look! Look!"

"He's off his head," said some one, and I fainted again.

I was ill for about a fortnight without regaining consciousness, a waste of time of which even now I cannot think without poignant regret. When I did recover consciousness, I found I was being carefully nursed by the old clergyman and the people of the house. I have often heard the unkindness of the world in general inveighed against, but for my part I can honestly say that I have received many more kindnesses than I have time to repay. Country people especially are remarkably attentive to strangers in illness.

I could not rest until I had seen the doctor who attended me, and had received his assurance that I should be equal to reading my paper on the appointed day. This pressing anxiety removed, I told him of what I had seen before I fainted the second time. He listened attentively, and then assured me, in a manner that was intended to be soothing, that I was suffering from an hallucination, due, no doubt, to the shock of my dog's sudden madness.

"Did you see the dog after it was dead?" I asked.

He said he did. The whole jaw was covered with blood and foam; the teeth certainly seemed convulsively fixed, but the case being evidently one of extraordinarily virulent hydrophobia, owing to the intense heat, he had had the body buried immediately.

My companion stopped speaking as we reached our lodgings, and went upstairs. Then, lighting a candle, he slowly turned down his collar.

"You see I have the marks still," he said, "but I have no fear of dying of hydrophobia. I am told such peculiar scars could not have been made by the teeth of a dog. If you look closely you see the pressure of the five fingers. That is the reason why I wear high collars."

THE CAVE OF THE ECHOES

by Helena Blavatsky

1892

Helena Blavatsky is best known today as one of the founders of the Theosophical Society and the leading architect of its mystical religion, which blended Western esotericism with Hinduism and Buddhism. She was a controversial figure in her lifetime, alternately revered as an enlightened guru and reviled as a charlatan. Even more controversially, it has been claimed that her writings of secret masters and the Aryan race inspired some aspects of Nazi occultism after her death.

It is not widely known that, in addition to her extensive writings on Theosophy and other esoteric matters, Madame Blavatsky wrote supernatural fiction. Perhaps more remarkably, her horror fiction is completely independent of her esoteric researches, and does not promote Theosophical teachings. Some stories, such as "A Witch's Den" (1920), are clearly inspired by her extensive travels, but others are straightforward ghost and horror tales, typical of their time.

"The Cave of the Echoes" (subtitled "A Strange but True Story") is one such tale. The details of its Russian setting, which lend the tale such rich and authentic atmosphere, clearly owe much to Madame Blavatsky's extensive childhood travels around

the pre-revolutionary Russian Empire, but the tale itself is one of the classic ghost nar-
ratives, in which a murder victim reappears to accuse the guilty. It first appeared in
Nightmare Tales, *Madame Blavatsky's only collection of fiction, which was published*
in 1892 by the Theosophical Publishing Society.

This story is given from the narrative of an eye-witness, a
Russian gentleman, very pious, and fully trustworthy. Moreover,
the facts are copied from the police records of P——. The
eyewitness in question attributes it, of course, partly to divine
interference and partly to the Evil One.—H. P. B.

In one of the distant governments of the Russian empire, in a small
town on the borders of Siberia, a mysterious tragedy occurred
more than thirty years ago. About six *versts* from the little town of
P——, famous for the wild beauty of its scenery, and for the wealth of its
inhabitants—generally proprietors of mines and of iron foundries—stood an
aristocratic mansion. Its household consisted of the master, a rich old bachelor
and his brother, who was a widower and the father of two sons and three
daughters. It was known that the proprietor, Mr. Izvertzoff, had adopted his
brother's children, and, having formed an especial attachment for his eldest
nephew, Nicolas, he had made him the sole heir of his numerous estates.

Time rolled on. The uncle was getting old, the nephew was coming
of age. Days and years had passed in monotonous serenity, when, on the
hitherto clear horizon of the quiet family, appeared a cloud. On an unlucky
day one of the nieces took it into her head to study the zither. The instrument being of purely Teutonic origin, and no teacher of it residing in the
neighborhood, the indulgent uncle sent to St. Petersburg for both. After

diligent search only one Professor could be found willing to trust himself in such close proximity to Siberia. It was an old German artist, who, sharing his affections equally between his instrument and a pretty blonde daughter, would part with neither. And thus it came to pass that one fine morning the old Professor arrived at the mansion, with his music box under one arm and his fair Munchen leaning on the other.

From that day the little cloud began growing rapidly; for every vibration of the melodious instrument found a responsive echo in the old bachelor's heart. Music awakens love, they say, and the work begun by the zither was completed by Munchen's blue eyes. At the expiration of six months the niece had become an expert zither player, and the uncle was desperately in love.

One morning, gathering his adopted family around him, he embraced them all very tenderly, promised to remember them in his will, and wound up by declaring his unalterable resolution to marry the blue-eyed Munchen. After this he fell upon their necks and wept in silent rapture. The family, understanding that they were cheated out of the inheritance, also wept; but it was for another cause. Having thus wept, they consoled themselves and tried to rejoice, for the old gentleman was sincerely beloved by all. Not all of them rejoiced, though. Nicolas, who had himself been smitten to the heart by the pretty German, and who found himself defrauded at once of his belle and of his uncle's money, neither rejoiced nor consoled himself, but disappeared for a whole day.

Meanwhile, Mr. Izvertzoff had given orders to prepare his traveling carriage on the following day, and it was whispered that he was going to the chief town of the district, at some distance from his home, with the intention of altering his will. Though very wealthy, he had no superintendent on his estate, but kept his books himself. The same evening after supper, he was heard in his room, angrily scolding his servant, who had been in his service for over thirty years. This man, Ivan, was a native of northern Asia, from Kamschatka; he had been brought up by the family in the Christian religion, and was thought to be very much attached to his master. A few days later, when the first tragic circumstance I am about to relate had brought all the police force to the spot, it was remembered that on that night Ivan was drunk; that his master, who had a horror of this vice had paternally thrashed him, and turned him out of his room, and that Ivan had been seen reeling out of the door, and had been heard to mutter threats.

On the vast domain of Mr. Izvertzoff there was a curious cavern, which excited the curiosity of all who visited it. It exists to this day, and is well known to every inhabitant of P——. A pine forest, commencing a few feet from the garden gate, climbs in steep terraces up a long range of rocky hills, which it covers with a broad belt of impenetrable vegetation. The grotto leading into the cavern, which is known as the "Cave of the Echoes," is situated about half a mile from the site of the mansion, from which it appears as a small excavation in the hill-side, almost hidden by luxuriant plants, but not so completely as to prevent any person entering it from being readily seen from the terrace in front of the house. Entering the Grotto, the explorer finds at the rear a narrow cleft; having passed through which he emerges into a lofty cavern, feebly lighted through fissures in the vaulted roof, fifty feet from the ground. The cavern itself is immense, and would easily hold between two and three thousand people. A part of it, in the days of Mr. Izvertzoff, was paved with flagstones, and was often used in the summer as a ball-room by picnic parties. Of an irregular oval, it gradually narrows into a broad corridor, which runs for several miles underground, opening here and there into other chambers, as large and lofty as the ball-room, but, unlike this, impassable otherwise than in a boat, as they are always full of water. These natural basins have the reputation of being unfathomable.

On the margin of the first of these is a small platform, with several mossy rustic seats arranged on it, and it is from this spot that the phenomenal echoes, which give the cavern its name, are heard in all their weirdness. A word pronounced in a whisper, or even a sigh, is caught up by endless mocking voices, and instead of diminishing in volume, as honest echoes do, the sound grows louder and louder at every successive repetition, until at last it bursts forth like the repercussion of a pistol shot, and recedes in a plaintive wail down the corridor.

On the day in question, Mr. Izvertzoff had mentioned his intention of having a dancing party in this cave on his wedding day, which he had fixed for an early date. On the following morning, while preparing for his drive, he was seen by his family entering the grotto, accompanied only by his Siberian servant. Half-an-hour later, Ivan returned to the mansion for a snuff-box, which his master had forgotten in his room, and went back with it to the cave. An hour later the whole house was startled by his loud cries. Pale and dripping with water, Ivan rushed in like a madman, and declared that Mr. Izvertzoff was nowhere to be found in the cave. Thinking he had fallen into the lake, he had dived into the first basin in search of him and was nearly drowned himself.

The day passed in vain attempts to find the body. The police filled the house, and louder than the rest in his despair was Nicolas, the nephew, who had returned home only to meet the sad tidings.

A dark suspicion fell upon Ivan, the Siberian. He had been struck by his master the night before, and had been heard to swear revenge. He had accompanied him alone to the cave, and when his room was searched, a box full of rich family jewelry, known to have been carefully kept in Mr. Izvertzoff's apartment, was found under Ivan's bedding. Vainly did the serf call God to witness that the box had been given to him in charge by his master himself, just before they proceeded to the cave; that it was the latter's purpose to have the jewelry reset, as he intended it for a wedding present to his bride; and that he, Ivan, would willingly give his own life to recall that of his master, if he knew him to be dead. No heed was paid to him, however, and he was arrested and thrown into prison upon a charge of murder. There he was left, for under the Russian law a criminal cannot—at any rate, he could not in those days—be sentenced for a crime, however conclusive the circumstantial evidence, unless he confessed his guilt.

After a week had passed in useless search, the family arrayed themselves in deep mourning; and, as the will as originally drawn remained without a codicil, the whole of the property passed into the hands of the nephew. The old teacher and his daughter bore this sudden reverse of fortune with true Germanic phlegm, and prepared to depart. Taking again his zither under one arm, the old man was about to lead away his Munchen by the other, when the nephew stopped him by offering himself as the fair damsel's husband in the place of his departed uncle. The change was found to be an agreeable one, and, without much ado, the young people were married.

Ten years rolled away, and we meet the happy family once more at the beginning of 1859. The fair Munchen had grown fat and vulgar. From the day of the old man's disappearance, Nicolas had become morose and retired in his habits, and many wondered at the change in him, for now he was never seen to smile. It seemed as if his only aim in life were to find out his uncle's murderer, or rather to bring Ivan to confess his guilt. But the man still persisted that he was innocent.

An only son had been born to the young couple, and a strange child it was. Small, delicate, and ever ailing, his frail life seemed to hang by a thread. When his features were in repose, his resemblance to his uncle was so striking that the members of the family often shrank from him in terror. It was the pale shriveled face of a man of sixty upon the shoulders of a child nine years old. He was never seen either to laugh or to play, but, perched in his high chair, would gravely sit there, folding his arms in a way peculiar to the late Mr. Izvertzoff; and thus he would remain for hours, drowsy and motionless. His nurses were often seen furtively crossing themselves at night, upon approaching him, and not one of them would consent to sleep alone with him in the nursery. His father's behavior towards him was still more strange. He seemed to love him passionately, and at the same time to hate him bitterly. He seldom embraced or caressed the child, but, with livid cheek and staring eye, he would pass long hours watching him, as the child sat quietly in his corner, in his goblin-like, old-fashioned way.

The child had never left the estate, and few outside the family knew of his existence.

About the middle of July, a tall Hungarian traveler, preceded by a great reputation for eccentricity, wealth and mysterious powers, arrived at the town of P——from the North, where, it was said, he had resided for many years. He settled in the little town, in company with a Shaman or South Siberian magician, on whom he was said to make mesmeric experiments. He gave dinners and parties, and invariably exhibited his Shaman, of whom he felt very proud, for the amusement of his guests. One day the notables of

P——made an unexpected invasion of the domains of Nicolas Izvertzoff, and requested the loan of his cave for an evening entertainment. Nicolas consented with great reluctance, and only after still greater hesitancy was he prevailed upon to join the party.

The first cavern and the platform beside the bottomless lake glittered with lights. Hundreds of flickering candles and torches, stuck in the clefts of the rocks, illuminated the place and drove the shadows from the mossy nooks and corners, where they had crouched undisturbed for many years. The stalactites on the walls sparkled brightly, and the sleeping echoes were suddenly awakened by a joyous confusion of laughter and conversation. The Shaman, who was never lost sight of by his friend and patron, sat in a corner, entranced as usual. Crouched on a projecting rock, about midway between the entrance and the water, with his lemon-yellow, wrinkled face, flat nose, and thin beard, he looked more like an ugly stone idol than a human being. Many of the company pressed around him and received correct answers to their questions, the Hungarian cheerfully submitting his mesmerized "subject" to cross-examination.

Suddenly one of the party, a lady, remarked that it was in that very cave that old Mr. Izvertzoff had so unaccountably disappeared ten years before. The foreigner appeared interested, and desired to learn more of the circumstances, so Nicolas was sought amid the crowd and led before the eager group. He was the host and he found it impossible to refuse the demanded narrative. He repeated the sad tale in a trembling voice, with a pallid cheek, and tears were seen glittering in his feverish eyes. The company were greatly affected, and encomiums upon the behavior of the loving nephew in honoring the memory of his uncle and benefactor were freely circulating in whispers, when suddenly the voice of Nicolas became choked, his eyes started from their sockets, and with a suppressed groan, he staggered back. Every eye in the crowd followed with curiosity his haggard look, as it fell and remained riveted upon a weazened little face, that peeped from behind the back of the Hungarian.

"Where do you come from? Who brought you here, child?" gasped out Nicolas, as pale as death.

"I was in bed, papa; this man came to me, and brought me here in his arms," answered the boy simply, pointing to the Shaman, beside whom he stood upon the rock, and who, with his eyes closed, kept swaying himself to and fro like a living pendulum.

"That is very strange," remarked one of the guests, "for the man has never moved from his place."

"Good God! what an extraordinary resemblance!" muttered an old resident of the town, a friend of the lost man.

"You lie, child!" fiercely exclaimed the father. "Go to bed; this is no place for you."

"Come, come," interposed the Hungarian, with a strange expression on his face, and encircling with his arm the slender childish figure; "the little fellow has seen the double of my Shaman, which roams sometimes far away from his body, and has mistaken the phantom for the man himself. Let him remain with us for a while."

At these strange words the guests stared at each other in mute surprise, while some piously made the sign of the cross, spitting aside, presumably at the devil and all his works.

"By-the-bye," continued the Hungarian with a peculiar firmness of accent, and addressing the company rather than any one in particular; "why should we not try, with the help of my Shaman, to unravel the mystery hanging over the tragedy? Is the suspected party still lying in prison? What? he has not confessed up to now? This is surely very strange. But now we will learn the truth in a few minutes! Let all keep silent!"

He then approached the Tehuktchene, and immediately began his performance without so much as asking the consent of the master of the place. The latter stood rooted to the spot, as if petrified with horror, and unable to articulate a word. The suggestion met with general approbation, save from him; and the police inspector, Col. S——, especially approved of the idea.

"Ladies and gentlemen," said the mesmerizer in soft tones, "allow me for this once to proceed otherwise than in my general fashion. I will employ the method of native magic. It is more appropriate to this wild place, and far more effective as you will find, than our European method of mesmerization."

Without waiting for an answer, he drew from a bag that never left his person, first a small drum, and then two little phials—one full of fluid, the other empty. With the contents of the former he sprinkled the Shaman, who fell to trembling and nodding more violently than ever. The air was filled with the perfume of spicy odors, and the atmosphere itself seemed to become clearer. Then, to the horror of those present, he approached the Tibetan, and taking a miniature stiletto from his pocket, he plunged the sharp steel into the man's forearm, and drew blood from it, which he caught in the empty phial. When it was half filled, he pressed the orifice of the wound with his thumb, and stopped the flow of blood as easily as if he had corked a bottle, after which he sprinkled the blood over the little boy's head. He then suspended the drum from his neck, and, with two ivory drum-sticks, which were covered with magic signs and letters, he began beating a sort of *réveille*, to drum up the spirits, as he said.

The bystanders, half-shocked and half-terrified by these extraordinary proceedings, eagerly crowded round him, and for a few moments a dead silence reigned throughout the lofty cavern. Nicolas, with his face livid and corpse-like, stood speechless as before. The mesmerizer had placed himself between the Shaman and the platform, when he began slowly drumming. The first notes were muffled, and vibrated so softly in the air that they awakened no echo, but the Shaman quickened his pendulum-like motion and the child became restless. The drummer then began a slow chant, low, impressive and solemn.

As the unknown words issued from his lips, the flames of the candles and torches wavered and flickered, until they began dancing in rhythm with the chant. A cold wind came wheezing from the dark corridors beyond the water, leaving a plaintive echo in its trail. Then a sort of nebulous vapor, seeming to ooze from the rocky ground and walls, gathered about the Shaman and the boy. Around the latter the aura was silvery and transparent, but the cloud which enveloped the former was red and sinister. Approaching nearer to the platform the magician beat a louder roll upon the drum, and this time the echo caught it up with terrific effect! It reverberated near and far in incessant peals; one wail followed another, louder and louder, until the thundering roar seemed the chorus of a thousand demon voices rising from the fathomless depths of the lake. The water itself, whose surface, illuminated by many lights, had previously been smooth as a sheet of glass, became suddenly agitated, as if a powerful gust of wind had swept over its unruffled face.

Another chant, and a roll of the drum, and the mountain trembled to its foundation with the cannon-like peals which rolled through the dark and distant corridors. The Shaman's body rose two yards in the air, and nodding and swaying, sat, self-suspended like an apparition. But the transformation which now occurred in the boy chilled everyone, as they speechlessly watched the scene. The silvery cloud about the boy now seemed to lift him, too, into the air; but, unlike the Shaman, his feet never left the ground. The child began to grow, as though the work of years was miraculously accomplished in a few seconds. He became tall and large, and his senile features grew older with the ageing of his body. A few more seconds, and the youthful form had entirely disappeared. It was totally absorbed in another individuality, and to the horror of those present who had been familiar with his appearance, this individuality was that of old Mr. Izvertzoff, and on his temple was a large gaping wound, from which trickled great drops of blood.

This phantom moved towards Nicolas, till it stood directly in front of him, while he, with his hair standing erect, with the look of a madman gazed at his own son, transformed into his uncle. The sepulchral silence was broken by the Hungarian, who, addressing the child phantom, asked him in solemn voice:

"In the name of the great Master, of him who has all power, answer the truth, and nothing but the truth. Restless spirit, hast thou been lost by accident, or foully murdered?"

The specter's lips moved, but it was the echo which answered for them in lugubrious shouts: "Murdered! murdered!! mur-der-ed!!!"

"Where? How? By whom?" asked the conjuror.

The apparition pointed a finger at Nicolas and, without removing its gaze or lowering its arm, retreated backwards slowly towards the lake. At every step it took, the younger Izvertzoff, as if compelled by some irresistible fascination, advanced a step towards it, until the phantom reached the lake, and the next moment was seen gliding on its surface. It was a fearful, ghostly scene!

When he had come within two steps of the brink of the watery abyss, a violent convulsion ran through the frame of the guilty man. Flinging himself upon his knees, he clung to one of the rustic seats with a desperate clutch, and staring wildly, uttered a long piercing cry of agony. The phantom now remained motionless on the water, and bending its extended finger, slowly beckoned him to come. Crouched in abject terror, the wretched man shrieked until the cavern rang again and again: "I did not. . . . No, I did not murder you!"

Then came a splash, and now it was the boy who was in the dark water, struggling for his life, in the middle of the lake, with the same motionless stern apparition brooding over him.

"Papa! papa! Save me. . . . I am drowning!" . . . cried a piteous little voice amid the uproar of the mocking echoes.

"My boy!" shrieked Nicolas, in the accents of a maniac, springing to his feet. "My boy! Save him! Oh, save him! . . . Yes, I confess. . . . I am the murderer. . . . It is I who killed him!"

Another splash, and the phantom disappeared. With a cry of horror the company rushed towards the platform; but their feet were suddenly rooted to the ground, as they saw amid the swirling eddies a whitish shapeless mass holding the murderer and the boy in a tight embrace, and slowly sinking into the bottomless lake.

On the morning after these occurrences, when, after a sleepless night, some of the party visited the residence of the Hungarian gentleman, they found it closed and deserted. He and the Shaman had disappeared. Many are among the old inhabitants of P——who remember him; the Police Inspector, Col. S——, dying a few years ago in the full assurance that the noble traveler was the devil. To add to the general consternation the Izvertzoff mansion took fire on that same night and was completely destroyed. The Archbishop performed the ceremony of exorcism, but the locality is considered accursed to this day. The Government investigated the facts, and—ordered silence.

THE YELLOW WALL PAPER

by Charlotte Perkins Gilman

1892

Frederic Beecher Perkins abandoned his family soon after Charlotte's birth. Her mother was unable to support Charlotte and her brother Thomas alone, and they spent some time with Frederic's aunts, the author Harriet Beecher Stowe, the suffragist Elizabeth Beecher Hooker, and the educationalist Catharine Beecher.

Charlotte's formal education was erratic: a total of four years spent in seven different schools, ending when she was fifteen. Her teachers spoke highly of her natural intelligence, but were disappointed by her performance as a student. She much preferred to visit the public library and read at will: her favorite topics were ancient civilizations and "natural philosophy," a discipline that was to become modern physics. She enrolled in the Rhode Island School of Art and Design at the age of eighteen, and went on to make a living as a commercial artist and tutor.

Her first marriage, to the artist Charles Walter Stetson, lasted just four years and ended in divorce after ten. It was during this marriage, after a severe bout of postpartum psychosis, that she wrote "The Yellow Wall Paper," which was initially published under her married name of Charlotte Perkins Stetson: the name Gilman comes from her second, and much happier, marriage to her first cousin, Houghton Gilman. She was an active speaker on women's issues, ethics, labor, human rights, and social reform, and these themes informed much of her writing.

Beneath the description of encroaching madness, "The Yellow Wall Paper" also comments on the crushing lack of autonomy felt by many women of that time, which often came under the guise of masculine care and concern. Deprived of any form of stimulation in the name of a rest cure, the unnamed protagonist becomes obsessed with an ugly pattern on the wallpaper, and, with nothing else to fill her mind, gradually loses her grip on sanity. Despite its lack of any supernatural content, "The Yellow Wall Paper" is a horror story in every sense.

I t is very seldom that mere ordinary people like John and myself secure ancestral halls for the summer.

A colonial mansion, a hereditary estate, I would say a haunted house, and reach the height of romantic felicity—but that would be asking too much of fate!

Still I will proudly declare that there is something queer about it.

Else, why should it be let so cheaply? And why have stood so long untenanted?

John laughs at me, of course, but one expects that in marriage.

John is practical in the extreme. He has no patience with faith, an intense horror of superstition, and he scoffs openly at any talk of things not to be felt and seen and put down in figures.

John is a physician, and *perhaps*—(I would not say it to a living soul, of course, but this is dead paper and a great relief to my mind)—*perhaps* that is one reason I do not get well faster.

You see, he does not believe I am sick!

And what can one do?

If a physician of high standing, and one's own husband, assures friends and relatives that there is really nothing the matter with one but temporary nervous depression—a slight hysterical tendency—what is one to do?

My brother is also a physician, and also of high standing, and he says the same thing.

So I take phosphates or phosphites—whichever it is,—and tonics, and journeys, and air, and exercise, and am absolutely forbidden to "work" until I am well again.

Personally I disagree with their ideas.

Personally I believe that congenial work, with excitement and change, would do me good.

But what is one to do?

I did write for a while in spite of them; but it *does* exhaust me a good deal—having to be so sly about it, or else meet with heavy opposition.

I sometimes fancy that in my condition if I had less opposition and more society and stimulus—but John says the very worst thing I can do is to think about my condition, and I confess it always makes me feel bad.

So I will let it alone and talk about the house.

The most beautiful place! It is quite alone, standing well back from the road, quite three miles from the village. It makes me think of English places that you read about, for there are hedges and walls and gates that lock, and lots of separate little houses for the gardeners and people.

There is a *delicious* garden! I never saw such a garden—large and shady, full of box-bordered paths, and lined with long grape-covered arbors with seats under them.

There were greenhouses, too, but they are all broken now.

There was some legal trouble, I believe, something about the heirs and co-heirs; anyhow, the place has been empty for years.

That spoils my ghostliness, I am afraid; but I don't care—there is something strange about the house—I can feel it.

I even said so to John one moonlight evening, but he said what I felt was a *draught*, and shut the window.

I get unreasonably angry with John sometimes. I'm sure I never used to be so sensitive. I think it is due to this nervous condition.

But John says if I feel so I shall neglect proper self-control; so I take pains to control myself—before him, at least, and that makes me very tired.

I don't like our room a bit. I wanted one downstairs that opened on the piazza and had roses all over the window, and such pretty old-fashioned chintz hangings! but John would not hear of it.

He said there was only one window and not room for two beds, and no near room for him if he took another.

He is very careful and loving, and hardly lets me stir without special direction.

I have a schedule prescription for each hour in the day; he takes all care from me, and so I feel basely ungrateful not to value it more.

He said we came here solely on my account, that I was to have perfect rest and all the air I could get. "Your exercise depends on your strength, my dear," said he, "and your food somewhat on your appetite; but air you can absorb all the time." So we took the nursery, at the top of the house.

It is a big, airy room, the whole floor nearly, with windows that look all ways, and air and sunshine galore. It was nursery first and then playroom and gymnasium, I should judge; for the windows are barred for little children, and there are rings and things in the walls.

The paint and paper look as if a boys' school had used it. It is stripped off—the paper—in great patches all around the head of my bed, about as far as I can reach, and in a great place on the other side of the room low down. I never saw a worse paper in my life.

One of those sprawling flamboyant patterns committing every artistic sin.

It is dull enough to confuse the eye in following, pronounced enough to constantly irritate and provoke study, and when you follow the lame uncertain curves for a little distance they suddenly commit suicide—plunge off at outrageous angles, destroy themselves in unheard of contradictions.

The color is repellent, almost revolting; a smouldering, unclean yellow, strangely faded by the slow-turning sunlight.

It is a dull yet lurid orange in some places, a sickly sulphur tint in others.

No wonder the children hated it! I should hate it myself if I had to live in this room long.

There comes John, and I must put this away,—he hates to have me write a word.

We have been here two weeks, and I haven't felt like writing before, since that first day.

I am sitting by the window now, up in this atrocious nursery, and there is nothing to hinder my writing as much as I please, save lack of strength.

John is away all day, and even some nights when his cases are serious.

I am glad my case is not serious!

But these nervous troubles are dreadfully depressing.

John does not know how much I really suffer. He knows there is no *reason* to suffer, and that satisfies him.

Of course it is only nervousness. It does weigh on me so not to do my duty in any way!

I meant to be such a help to John, such a real rest and comfort, and here I am a comparative burden already!

Nobody would believe what an effort it is to do what little I am able—to dress and entertain, and order things.

It is fortunate Mary is so good with the baby. Such a dear baby!

And yet I *cannot* be with him, it makes me so nervous.

I suppose John never was nervous in his life. He laughs at me so about this wall-paper!

At first he meant to repaper the room, but afterwards he said that I was letting it get the better of me, and that nothing was worse for a nervous patient than to give way to such fancies.

He said that after the wall-paper was changed it would be the heavy bedstead, and then the barred windows, and then that gate at the head of the stairs, and so on.

"You know the place is doing you good," he said, "and really, dear, I don't care to renovate the house just for a three months' rental."

"Then do let us go downstairs," I said, "there are such pretty rooms there."

Then he took me in his arms and called me a blessed little goose, and said he would go down to the cellar, if I wished, and have it whitewashed into the bargain.

But he is right enough about the beds and windows and things.

It is an airy and comfortable room as any one need wish, and, of course, I would not be so silly as to make him uncomfortable just for a whim.

I'm really getting quite fond of the big room, all but that horrid paper.

Out of one window I can see the garden, those mysterious deep-shaded arbors, the riotous old-fashioned flowers, and bushes and gnarly trees.

Out of another I get a lovely view of the bay and a little private wharf belonging to the estate. There is a beautiful shaded lane that runs down there from the house. I always fancy I see people walking in these numerous paths and arbors, but John has cautioned me not to give way to fancy in the least. He says that with my imaginative power and habit of story-making, a nervous weakness like mine is sure to lead to all manner of excited fancies, and that I ought to use my will and good sense to check the tendency. So I try.

I think sometimes that if I were only well enough to write a little it would relieve the press of ideas and rest me.

But I find I get pretty tired when I try.

It is so discouraging not to have any advice and companionship about my work. When I get really well John says we will ask Cousin Henry and Julia down for a long visit; but he says he would as soon put fire-works in my pillow-case as to let me have those stimulating people about now.

I wish I could get well faster.

But I must not think about that. This paper looks to me as if it *knew* what a vicious influence it had!

There is a recurrent spot where the pattern lolls like a broken neck and two bulbous eyes stare at you upside-down.

I get positively angry with the impertinence of it and the everlastingness. Up and down and sideways they crawl, and those absurd, unblinking eyes are everywhere. There is one place where two breadths didn't match, and the eyes go all up and down the line, one a little higher than the other.

I never saw so much expression in an inanimate thing before, and we all know how much expression they have! I used to lie awake as a child and get more entertainment and terror out of blank walls and plain furniture than most children could find in a toy store.

I remember what a kindly wink the knobs of our big, old bureau used to have, and there was one chair that always seemed like a strong friend.

I used to feel that if any of the other things looked too fierce I could always hop into that chair and be safe.

The furniture in this room is no worse than inharmonious, however, for we had to bring it all from downstairs. I suppose when this was used as a playroom they had to take the nursery things out, and no wonder! I never saw such ravages as the children have made here.

The wall-paper, as I said before, is torn off in spots, and it sticketh closer than a brother—they must have had perseverance as well as hatred.

Then the floor is scratched and gouged and splintered, the plaster itself is dug out here and there, and this great heavy bed, which is all we found in the room, looks as if it had been through the wars.

But I don't mind it a bit—only the paper.

There comes John's sister. Such a dear girl as she is, and so careful of me! I must not let her find me writing.

She is a perfect and enthusiastic housekeeper, and hopes for no better profession. I verily believe she thinks it is the writing which made me sick!

But I can write when she is out, and see her a long way off from these windows.

There is one that commands the road, a lovely, shaded, winding road, and one that just looks off over the country. A lovely country, too, full of great elms and velvet meadows.

This wall-paper has a kind of sub-pattern in a different shade, a particularly irritating one, for you can only see it in certain lights, and not clearly then.

But in the places where it isn't faded and where the sun is just so—I can see a strange, provoking, formless sort of figure, that seems to skulk about behind that silly and conspicuous front design.

There's sister on the stairs!

Well, the Fourth of July is over! The people are gone and I am tired out. John thought it might do me good to see a little company, so we just had mother and Nellie and the children down for a week.

Of course I didn't do a thing. Jennie sees to everything now.

But it tired me all the same.

John says if I don't pick up faster he shall send me to Weir Mitchell in the fall.

But I don't want to go there at all. I had a friend who was in his hands once, and she says he is just like John and my brother, only more so!

Besides, it is such an undertaking to go so far.

I don't feel as if it was worth while to turn my hand over for anything, and I'm getting dreadfully fretful and querulous.

I cry at nothing, and cry most of the time.

Of course I don't when John is here, or anybody else, but when I am alone.

And I am alone a good deal just now. John is kept in town very often by serious cases, and Jennie is good and lets me alone when I want her to.

So I walk a little in the garden or down that lovely lane, sit on the porch under the roses, and lie down up here a good deal.

I'm getting really fond of the room in spite of the wall-paper. Perhaps *because* of the wall-paper.

It dwells in my mind so!

I lie here on this great immovable bed—it is nailed down, I believe—and follow that pattern about by the hour. It is as good as gymnastics, I assure you. I start, we'll say, at the bottom, down in the corner over there where it has not been touched, and I determine for the thousandth time that I *will* follow that pointless pattern to some sort of a conclusion.

I know a little of the principles of design, and I know this thing was not arranged on any laws of radiation, or alternation, or repetition, or symmetry, or anything else that I ever heard of.

It is repeated, of course, by the breadths, but not otherwise.

Looked at in one way each breadth stands alone, the bloated curves and flourishes—a kind of "debased Romanesque" with *delirium tremens*—go waddling up and down in isolated columns of fatuity.

But, on the other hand, they connect diagonally, and the sprawling outlines run off in great slanting waves of optic horror, like a lot of wallowing seaweeds in full chase.

The whole thing goes horizontally, too, at least it seems so, and I exhaust myself in trying to distinguish the order of its going in that direction.

They have used a horizontal breadth for a frieze, and that adds wonderfully to the confusion.

There is one end of the room where it is almost intact, and there, when the cross-lights fade and the low sun shines directly upon it, I can almost fancy radiation, after all,—the interminable grotesques seem to form around a common centre and rush off in headlong plunges of equal distraction.

It makes me tired to follow it. I will take a nap, I guess.

I don't know why I should write this.

I don't want to.

I don't feel able.

And I know John would think it absurd. But I *must* say what I feel and think in some way—it is such a relief!

But the effort is getting to be greater than the relief.

Half the time now I am awfully lazy, and lie down ever so much.

John says I mustn't lose my strength, and has me take cod-liver oil and lots of tonics and things, to say nothing of ale and wine and rare meat.

Dear John! He loves me very dearly, and hates to have me sick. I tried to have a real earnest reasonable talk with him the other day, and tell him how I wish he would let me go and make a visit to Cousin Henry and Julia.

But he said I wasn't able to go, nor able to stand it after I got there; and I did not make out a very good case for myself, for I was crying before I had finished.

It is getting to be a great effort for me to think straight. Just this nervous weakness, I suppose.

And dear John gathered me up in his arms, and just carried me upstairs and laid me on the bed, and sat by me and read to me till it tired my head.

He said I was his darling and his comfort and all he had, and that I must take care of myself for his sake, and keep well.

He says no one but myself can help me out of it, that I must use my will and self-control and not let my silly fancies run away with me.

There's one comfort, the baby is well and happy, and does not have to occupy this nursery with the horrid wall-paper.

If we had not used it, that blessed child would have! What a fortunate escape! Why, I wouldn't have a child of mine, an impressionable little thing, live in such a room for worlds.

I never thought of it before, but it is lucky that John kept me here, after all. I can stand it so much easier than a baby, you see.

Of course I never mention it to them any more—I am too wise,—but I keep watch of it all the same.

There are things in that paper that nobody knows but me, or ever will.

Behind that outside pattern the dim shapes get clearer every day.

It is always the same shape, only very numerous.

And it is like a woman stooping down and creeping about behind that pattern. I don't like it a bit. I wonder—I begin to think—I wish John would take me away from here!

It is so hard to talk with John about my case, because he is so wise, and because he loves me so.

But I tried it last night.

It was moonlight. The moon shines in all around, just as the sun does.

I hate to see it sometimes, it creeps so slowly, and always comes in by one window or another.

John was asleep and I hated to waken him, so I kept still and watched the moonlight on that undulating wall-paper till I felt creepy.

The faint figure behind seemed to shake the pattern, just as if she wanted to get out.

I got up softly and went to feel and see if the paper *did* move, and when I came back John was awake.

"What is it, little girl?" he said. "Don't go walking about like that—you'll get cold."

I thought it was a good time to talk, so I told him that I really was not gaining here, and that I wished he would take me away.

"Why darling!" said he, "our lease will be up in three weeks, and I can't see how to leave before.

"The repairs are not done at home, and I cannot possibly leave town just now. Of course if you were in any danger, I could and would, but you really are better, dear, whether you can see it or not. I am a doctor, dear, and I know. You are gaining flesh and color, your appetite is better. I feel really much easier about you."

"I don't weigh a bit more," said I, "nor as much; and my appetite may be better in the evening when you are here, but it is worse in the morning, when you are away!"

"Bless her little heart!" said he with a big hug, "she shall be as sick as she pleases! But now let's improve the shining hours by going to sleep, and talk about it in the morning!"

"And you won't go away?" I asked gloomily.

"Why, how can I, dear? It is only three weeks more and then we will take a nice little trip of a few days while Jennie is getting the house ready. Really, dear, you are better!"

"Better in body, perhaps"—I began, and stopped short, for he sat up straight and looked at me with such a stern, reproachful look that I could not say another word.

"My darling," said he, "I beg of you, for my sake and for our child's sake, as well as for your own, that you will never for one instant let that idea enter your mind! There is nothing so dangerous, so fascinating, to a temperament like yours. It is a false and foolish fancy. Can you not trust me as a physician when I tell you so?"

So of course I said no more on that score, and we went to sleep before long. He thought I was asleep first, but I wasn't,—I lay there for hours trying to decide whether that front pattern and the back pattern really did move together or separately.

On a pattern like this, by daylight, there is a lack of sequence, a defiance of law, that is a constant irritant to a normal mind.

The color is hideous enough, and unreliable enough, and infuriating enough, but the pattern is torturing.

You think you have mastered it, but just as you get well under way in following, it turns a back somersault, and there you are. It slaps you in the face, knocks you down, and tramples upon you. It is like a bad dream.

The outside pattern is a florid arabesque, reminding one of a fungus. If you can imagine a toadstool in joints, an interminable string of toadstools, budding and sprouting in endless convolutions,—why, that is something like it.

That is, sometimes!

There is one marked peculiarity about this paper, a thing nobody seems to notice but myself, and that is that it changes as the light changes.

When the sun shoots in through the east window—I always watch for that first long, straight ray—it changes so quickly that I never can quite believe it.

That is why I watch it always.

By moonlight—the moon shines in all night when there is a moon—I wouldn't know it was the same paper.

At night in any kind of light, in twilight, candlelight, lamplight, and worst of all by moonlight, it becomes bars! The outside pattern, I mean, and the woman behind it is as plain as can be.

I didn't realize for a long time what the thing was that showed behind,—that dim sub-pattern,—but now I am quite sure it is a woman.

By daylight she is subdued, quiet. I fancy it is the pattern that keeps her so still. It is so puzzling. It keeps me quiet by the hour.

I lie down ever so much now. John says it is good for me, and to sleep all I can.

Indeed, he started the habit by making me lie down for an hour after each meal.

It is a very bad habit, I am convinced, for, you see, I don't sleep.

And that cultivates deceit, for I don't tell them I'm awake,—oh, no!

The fact is, I am getting a little afraid of John.

He seems very queer sometimes, and even Jennie has an inexplicable look.

It strikes me occasionally, just as a scientific hypothesis, that perhaps it is the paper!

I have watched John when he did not know I was looking, and come into the room suddenly on the most innocent excuses, and I've caught him several times *looking at the paper!* And Jennie too. I caught Jennie with her hand on it once.

She didn't know I was in the room, and when I asked her in a quiet, a very quiet voice, with the most restrained manner possible, what she was doing with the paper she turned around as if she had been caught stealing, and looked quite angry—asked me why I should frighten her so!

Then she said that the paper stained everything it touched, that she had found yellow smooches on all my clothes and John's, and she wished we would be more careful!

Did not that sound innocent? But I know she was studying that pattern, and I am determined that nobody shall find it out but myself!

Life is very much more exciting now than it used to be. You see I have something more to expect, to look forward to, to watch. I really do eat better, and am more quiet than I was.

John is so pleased to see me improve! He laughed a little the other day, and said I seemed to be flourishing in spite of my wall-paper.

I turned it off with a laugh. I had no intention of telling him it was *because* of the wall-paper—he would make fun of me. He might even want to take me away.

I don't want to leave now until I have found it out. There is a week more, and I think that will be enough.

I'm feeling ever so much better! I don't sleep much at night, for it is so interesting to watch developments; but I sleep a good deal in the daytime.

In the daytime it is tiresome and perplexing.

There are always new shoots on the fungus, and new shades of yellow all over it. I cannot keep count of them, though I have tried conscientiously.

It is the strangest yellow, that wall-paper! It makes me think of all the yellow things I ever saw—not beautiful ones like buttercups, but old foul, bad yellow things.

But there is something else about that paper—the smell! I noticed it the moment we came into the room, but with so much air and sun it was not bad. Now we have had a week of fog and rain, and whether the windows are open or not the smell is here.

It creeps all over the house.

I find it hovering in the dining-room, skulking in the parlor, hiding in the hall, lying in wait for me on the stairs.

It gets into my hair.

Even when I go to ride, if I turn my head suddenly and surprise it—there is that smell!

Such a peculiar odor, too! I have spent hours in trying to analyze it, to find what it smelled like.

It is not bad—at first, and very gentle, but quite the subtlest, most enduring odor I ever met.

In this damp weather it is awful. I wake up in the night and find it hanging over me.

It used to disturb me at first. I thought seriously of burning the house—to reach the smell.

But now I am used to it. The only thing I can think of that it is like is the *color* of the paper!—a yellow smell.

There is a very funny mark on this wall, low down, near the mopboard. A streak that runs around the room. It goes behind every piece of furniture, except the bed, a long, straight, even *smooch*, as if it had been rubbed over and over.

I wonder how it was done and who did it, and what they did it for. Round and round and round—round and round and round—it makes me dizzy!

I really have discovered something at last.

Through watching so much at night, when it changes so, I have finally found out.

The front pattern *does* move—and no wonder! The woman behind shakes it!

Sometimes I think there are a great many women behind, and sometimes only one, and she crawls around fast, and her crawling shakes it all over.

Then in the very bright spots she keeps still, and in the very shady spots she just takes hold of the bars and shakes them hard.

And she is all the time trying to climb through. But nobody could climb through that pattern—it strangles so; I think that is why it has so many heads.

They get through, and then the pattern strangles them off and turns them upside-down, and makes their eyes white!

If those heads were covered or taken off it would not be half so bad.

I think that woman gets out in the daytime!

And I'll tell you why—privately—I've seen her!

I can see her out of every one of my windows!

It is the same woman, I know, for she is always creeping, and most women do not creep by daylight.

I see her in that long shaded lane, creeping up and down. I see her in those dark grape arbors, creeping all around the garden.

I see her on that long road under the trees, creeping along, and when a carriage comes she hides under the blackberry vines.

I don't blame her a bit. It must be very humiliating to be caught creeping by daylight!

I always lock the door when I creep by daylight. I can't do it at night, for I know John would suspect something at once.

And John is so queer, now, that I don't want to irritate him. I wish he would take another room! Besides, I don't want anybody to get that woman out at night but myself.

I often wonder if I could see her out of all the windows at once.

But, turn as fast as I can, I can only see out of one at one time.

And though I always see her, she *may* be able to creep faster than I can turn!

I have watched her sometimes away off in the open country, creeping as fast as a cloud shadow in a high wind.

If only that top pattern could be gotten off from the under one! I mean to try it, little by little.

I have found out another funny thing, but I shan't tell it this time! It does not do to trust people too much.

There are only two more days to get this paper off, and I believe John is beginning to notice. I don't like the look in his eyes.

And I heard him ask Jennie a lot of professional questions about me. She had a very good report to give.

She said I slept a good deal in the daytime.

John knows I don't sleep very well at night, for all I'm so quiet!

He asked me all sorts of questions, too, and pretended to be very loving and kind.

As if I couldn't see through him!

Still, I don't wonder he acts so, sleeping under this paper for three months.

It only interests me, but I feel sure John and Jennie are secretly affected by it.

Hurrah! This is the last day, but it is enough. John is to stay in town over night, and won't be out until this evening.

Jennie wanted to sleep with me—the sly thing! but I told her I should undoubtedly rest better for a night all alone.

That was clever, for really I wasn't alone a bit! As soon as it was moonlight and that poor thing began to crawl and shake the pattern, I got up and ran to help her.

I pulled and she shook, I shook and she pulled, and before morning we had peeled off yards of that paper.

A strip about as high as my head and half around the room.

And then when the sun came and that awful pattern began to laugh at me, I declared I would finish it to-day!

We go away to-morrow, and they are moving all my furniture down again to leave things as they were before.

Jennie looked at the wall in amazement, but I told her merrily that I did it out of pure spite at the vicious thing.

She laughed and said she wouldn't mind doing it herself, but I must not get tired.

How she betrayed herself that time!

But I am here, and no person touches this paper but me—not *alive!*

She tried to get me out of the room—it was too patent! But I said it was so quiet and empty and clean now that I believed I would lie down again and sleep all I could; and not to wake me even for dinner—I would call when I woke.

So now she is gone, and the servants are gone, and the things are gone, and there is nothing left but that great bedstead nailed down, with the canvas mattress we found on it.

We shall sleep downstairs to-night, and take the boat home to-morrow.

I quite enjoy the room, now it is bare again.

How those children did tear about here!

This bedstead is fairly gnawed!

But I must get to work.

I have locked the door and thrown the key down into the front path.

I don't want to go out, and I don't want to have anybody come in, till John comes.

I want to astonish him.

I've got a rope up here that even Jennie did not find. If that woman does get out, and tries to get away, I can tie her!

But I forgot I could not reach far without anything to stand on!

This bed will *not* move!

I tried to lift and push it until I was lame, and then I got so angry I bit off a little piece at one corner—but it hurt my teeth.

Then I peeled off all the paper I could reach standing on the floor. It sticks horribly and the pattern just enjoys it! All those strangled heads and bulbous eyes and waddling fungus growths just shriek with derision!

I am getting angry enough to do something desperate. To jump out of the window would be admirable exercise, but the bars are too strong even to try.

Besides I wouldn't do it. Of course not. I know well enough that a step like that is improper and might be misconstrued.

I don't like to *look* out of the windows even—there are so many of those creeping women, and they creep so fast.

I wonder if they all come out of that wall-paper as I did?

But I am securely fastened now by my well-hidden rope—you don't get *me* out in the road there!

I suppose I shall have to get back behind the pattern when it comes night, and that is hard!

It is so pleasant to be out in this great room and creep around as I please!

I don't want to go outside. I won't, even if Jennie asks me to.

For outside you have to creep on the ground, and everything is green instead of yellow.

But here I can creep smoothly on the floor, and my shoulder just fits in that long smooch around the wall, so I cannot lose my way.

Why there's John at the door!

It is no use, young man, you can't open it!

How he does call and pound!

Now he's crying for an axe.

It would be a shame to break down that beautiful door!

"John dear!" said I in the gentlest voice, "the key is down by the front steps, under a plantain leaf!"

That silenced him for a few moments.

Then he said—very quietly indeed, "Open the door, my darling!"

"I can't," said I. "The key is down by the front door under a plantain leaf!"

And then I said it again, several times, very gently and slowly, and said it so often that he had to go and see, and he got it of course, and came in. He stopped short by the door.

"What is the matter?" he cried. "For God's sake, what are you doing!"

I kept on creeping just the same, but I looked at him over my shoulder.

"I've got out at last," said I, "in spite of you and Jane. And I've pulled off most of the paper, so you can't put me back!"

Now why should that man have fainted? But he did, and right across my path by the wall, so that I had to creep over him every time!

THE MASS FOR THE DEAD

by Edith Nesbit

1893

Edith Nesbit is remembered mainly as the author of The Railway Children, *a children's favorite in her native Britain, which has been filmed several times. She wrote more than sixty books for children, and was one of the first children's authors to set stories in the real world rather than in the realms of fairy tale and fantasy. Noël Coward wrote "she had an economy of phrase, and an unparalleled talent for evoking hot summer days in the English countryside."*

In her childhood, Edith and her family traveled widely across England, France, Spain, and Germany, seeking a congenial climate for her sickly sister Mary. Returning to England, she met a bank clerk named Hubert Bland, whom she married, seven months pregnant, in 1880. The marriage was not a happy one: early on, Edith discovered another woman who was pregnant by Bland and believed herself to be his fiancée; later, Edith's good friend Alice Hoatson became pregnant with Bland's child, and Bland threatened Edith with abandonment if she did not permit Alice to live with them as housekeeper and adopt her child as her own. Thirteen years later, Alice had another child by Bland, and again Edith adopted the baby.

Bland and Edith had similar political views, and both were involved in the Fabian Society, a progressive, middle-class organization that was one of the ancestors of Britain's Labour Party. Edith spoke at the London School of Economics, and the two jointly edited the Fabian Society's journal Today. *In addition to children's stories, adult novels, nonfiction, and poetry, Edith published four collections of horror stories in her lifetime, mostly compiled from stories she had previously published in various magazines. Many of these tales, such as "Man-Size in Marble," are regularly included in anthologies of Victorian horror fiction. "The Mass for the Dead" was first published in* The Argosy *magazine's April 1892 issue; like the rest of her work, it was credited to the gender-neutral "E. Nesbit."*

I was awake—widely, cruelly awake. I had been awake all night; what sleep could there be for me when the woman I loved was to be married next morning—married, and not to me?

I went to my room early; the family party in the drawing-room maddened me. Grouped about the round table with the stamped plush cover, each was busy with work, or book, or newspaper, but not too busy to stab my heart through and through with their talk of the wedding.

Her people were near neighbours of mine, so why should her marriage not be canvassed in my home circle?

They did not mean to be cruel; they did not know that I loved her; but she knew it. I told her, but she knew it before that. She knew it from the moment when I came back from three years of musical study in Germany—came back and met her in the wood where we used to go nutting when we were children.

I looked into her eyes, and my whole soul trembled with thankfulness that I was living in a world that held her also. I turned and walked by her side, through the tangled green wood, and we talked of the long-ago days, and it was, "Have you forgotten?" and "Do you remember?" till we reached her garden gate. Then I said—

"Good-bye; no, *auf wiedersehn*, and in a very little time, I hope."

And she answered—

"Good-bye. By the way, you haven't congratulated me yet."

"Congratulated you?"

"Yes, did I not tell you I am to marry Mr. Benoliel next month?"

And she turned away, and went up the garden slowly.

I asked my people, and they said it was true. Kate, my dear playfellow, was to marry this Spaniard, rich, wilful, accustomed to win, polished in manners and base in life. Why was she to marry him?

"No one knows," said my father, "but her father is talked about in the city, and Benoliel, the Spaniard, is rich. Perhaps that's it."

That was it. She told me so when, after two weeks spent with her and near her, I implored her to break so vile a chain and to come to me, who loved her—whom she loved.

"You are quite right," she said calmly. We were sitting in the window-seat of the oak parlour in her father's desolate old house. "I do love you, and I shall marry Mr. Benoliel."

"Why?"

"Look around you and ask me why, if you can."

I looked around—on the shabby, bare room, with its faded hangings of sage-green moreen, its threadbare carpet, its patched, washed-out chintz chair-covers. I looked out through the square, latticed window at the ragged, unkempt lawn, at her own gown—of poor material, though she wore it as queens might desire to wear ermine—and I understood.

Kate is obstinate; it is her one fault; I knew how vain would be my entreaties, yet I offered them; how unavailing my arguments, yet they were set forth; how useless my love and my sorrow, yet I showed them to her.

"No," she answered, but she flung her arms round my neck as she spoke, and held me as one may hold one's best treasure. "No, no; you are poor, and he is rich. You wouldn't have me break my father's heart: he's so proud, and if he doesn't get some money next month, he will be ruined. I'm not deceiving any one. Mr. Benoliel knows I don't care for him; and if I marry him, he is going to advance my father a large sum of money. Oh, I assure you that everything has been talked over and settled. There is no going from it."

"Child! child!" I cried, "how calmly you speak of it! Don't you see that you are selling your soul and throwing mine away?"

"Father Fabian says I am doing right," she answered, unclasping her hands, but holding mine in them, and looking at me with those clear, grey eyes of hers. "Are we to be unselfish in everything else, and in love to think only of our own happiness? I love you, and I shall marry him. Would you rather the positions were reversed?"

"Yes," I said, "for then I would make you love me."

"Perhaps *he* will," she said bitterly. Even in that moment her mouth trembled with the ghost of a smile. She always loved to tease. She goes through more moods in a day than most other women in a year. Drowning the smile came tears, but she controlled them, and she said—

"Good-bye; you see I am right, don't you? Oh, Jasper, I wish I hadn't told you I loved you. It will only make you more unhappy."

"It makes my one happiness," I answered; "nothing can take that from me. And that happiness *he* will never have. Say again that you love me!"

"I love you! I love you! I love you!"

With further folly of tears and mad loving words we parted, and I bore my heartache away, leaving her to bear hers into her new life.

And now she was to be married to-morrow, and I could not sleep.

When the darkness became unbearable I lighted a candle, and then lay staring vacantly at the roses on the wall-paper, or following with my eyes the lines and curves of the heavy mahogany furniture.

The solidity of my surroundings oppressed me. In the dull light the wardrobe loomed like a hearse, and my violin case looked like a child's coffin.

I reached a book and read till my eyes ached and the letters danced a *pas fantastique* up and down the page.

I got up and had ten minutes with the dumbbells. I sponged my face and hands with cold water and tried again to sleep—vainly. I lay there, miserably wide awake.

I tried to say poetry, the half-forgotten tasks of my school days even, but through everything ran the refrain—

"Kate is to be married to-morrow, and not to me, not to me!"

I tried counting up to a thousand. I tried to imagine sheep in a lane, and to count them as they jumped through a gap in an imaginary hedge—all the time-honoured spells with which sleep is wooed—vainly.

Then the Waits came, and a torture to the nerves was superadded to the torture of the heart. After fifteen minutes of carols every fibre of me seemed vibrating in an agony of physical misery.

To banish the echo of "The Mistletoe Bough," I hummed softly to myself a melody of Palestrina's, and felt more awake than ever.

Then the thing happened which nothing will ever explain. As I lay there I heard, breaking through and gradually overpowering the air I was suggesting, a harmony which I had never heard before, beautiful beyond description, and as distinct and definite as any song man's ears have ever listened to.

My first half-formed thought was, "more Waits," but the music was choral music, true and sweet; with it mingled an organ's notes, and with every note the music grew in volume. It is absurd to suggest that I dreamed it, for, still hearing the music, I leaped out of bed and opened the window. The music grew fainter. There was no one to be seen in the snowy garden below. Shivering, I shut the window. The music grew more distinct, and I became aware that I was listening to a mass—a funeral mass, and one which I had never heard before. I lay in my bed and followed the whole course of the office.

The music ceased.

I was sitting up in bed, my candle alight, and myself as wide awake as ever, and more than ever possessed by the thought of *her*.

But with a difference. Before, I had only mourned the loss of her: now, my thoughts of her were mingled with an indescribable dread. The sense of death and decay that had come to me with that strange, beautiful music, coloured all my thoughts. I was filled with fancies of hushed houses, black garments, rooms where white flowers and white linen lay in a deathly stillness. I heard echoes of tears, and of dim-voiced bells tolling monotonously. I shivered, as it were on the brink of irreparable woe, and in its contemplation I watched the dull dawn slowly overcome the pale flame of my candle, now burnt down into its socket.

I felt that I must see Kate once again before she gave herself away. Before ten o'clock I was in the oak parlour. She came to me. As she entered the room, her pallor, her swollen eyelids and the misery in her eyes wrung my heart as even that night of agony had not done. I literally could not speak. I held out my hands.

Would she reproach me for coming to her again, for forcing upon her a second time the anguish of parting?

She did not. She laid her hands in mine, and said—

"I am thankful you have come; do you know, I think I am going mad? Don't let me go mad, Jasper."

The look in her eyes underlined her words.

I stammered something and kissed her hands. I was with her again, and joy fought again with grief.

"I must tell some one. If I am mad, don't lock me up. Take care of me, won't you?"

Would I not?

"Understand," she went on, "it was not a dream. I was wide awake, thinking of you. The Waits had not long gone, and I—I was looking at your likeness. I was not asleep."

I shivered as I held her fast.

"As Heaven sees us, I did not dream it. I heard a mass sung, and, Jasper, it was a mass for the dead. I followed the office. You are not a Catholic, but I thought—I feared—oh, I don't know what I thought. I am thankful there is nothing wrong with you."

I felt a sudden certainty, and complete sense of power possess me. Now, in this her moment of weakness, while she was so completely under the influence of a strong emotion, I could and would save her from Benoliel, and myself from life-long pain.

"Kate," I said, "I believe it is a warning. You shall not marry this man. You shall marry me, and none other."

She leaned her head against my shoulder; she seemed to have forgotten her father and all the reasons for her marriage with Benoliel.

"You don't think I'm mad? No? Then take care of me; take me away; I feel safe with you."

Thus all obstacles vanished in less time than the length of a lover's kiss. I dared not stop to consider the coincidence of supernatural warning—nor what it might mean. Face to face with crowned hope, I am proud to remember that common sense held her own. The room in which we were had a French window. I fetched her garden hat and a shawl from the hall, and we went out through the still, white garden. We did not meet a soul. When we reached my father's garden I took her in by the back way, to the summer-house, and left her, though I was half afraid to leave her, while I went into the house. I snatched my violin and cheque book, took all my spare money, scrawled a line to my father and rejoined her.

Still no one had seen us.

We walked to a station five miles away; and by the time Benoliel would reach the church, I was leaving Doctors' Commons with a special licence in my pocket. Two hours later Kate was my wife, and we were quietly and prosaically eating our wedding-breakfast in the dining-room of the Grand Hotel.

"And where shall we go?" I said.

"I don't know," she answered, smiling; "you have not much money, have you?"

"Oh dear me, yes. I'm not rich, but I'm not absolutely a church mouse."

"Could we go to Devonshire?" she asked, twisting her new ring round and round.

"Devonshire! Why, that is where——"

"Yes, I know: Benoliel arranged to go there. Jasper, I am afraid of Benoliel."

"Then why——"

"Foolish person," she answered. "Do you think that Benoliel will be likely to go to Devonshire *now*?"

We went to Devonshire—I had had a small legacy a few months earlier, and I did not permit money cares to trouble my new and beautiful happiness. My only fear was that she would be saddened by thoughts of her father; but I am thankful to remember that in those first days she, too, was happy—so happy that there seemed to be hardly room in her mind for any thought but of me. And every hour of every day I said to my soul—

"But for that portent, whatever it boded, she might have been not my wife but his."

The first four or five days of our marriage are flowers that memory keeps always fresh. Kate's face had recovered its wild-rose bloom, and she laughed and sang and jested and enjoyed all our little daily adventures with the fullest, freest-hearted gaiety. Then I committed the supreme imbecility of my life—one of those acts of folly on which one looks back all one's life with a half stamp of the foot, and the unanswerable question, "How on earth could I have been such a fool?"

We were sitting in a little sitting-room, hideous in intention, but redeemed by blazing fire and the fact that two were there, sitting hand-in-hand, gazing into the fire and talking of their future and of their love. There was nothing to trouble us; no one had discovered our whereabouts, and my wife's fear of Benoliel's revenge seemed to have dissolved before the flame of our happiness.

And as we sat there, peaceful and untroubled, the Imp of the Perverse jogged my elbow, as, alas! he does so often, and I was moved to tell my wife that I, too, had heard that unearthly midnight music—that her hearing of it was not, as she had grown to think, a mere nightmare—a strange dream—but something more strange, more significant. I told her how I had heard the mass for the dead, and all the tale of that night. She listened silently, and I thought her strangely indifferent. When I had finished, she took her hand from mine and covered her face.

"I believe it was a warning to us to flee temptation. We ought never to have married. Oh, my poor father!"

Her tone was one that I had never heard before. Its hopeless misery appalled me. And justly. For no arguments, no entreaties, no caresses, could win my wife back to the mood of an hour before.

She tried to be cheerful, but her gaiety was forced, and her laughter stung my heart.

She spoke no more about the music, and when I tried to reason with her about it she smiled a gloomy little smile, and said—

"I cannot be happy. I will not be happy. It is wrong. I have been very selfish and wicked. You think me very idiotic, I know, but I believe there is a curse on us. We shall never be happy again."

"Don't you love me any more?" I asked like a fool.

"Love you?" She only repeated my words, but I was satisfied on that score. But those were miserable days. We loved each other passionately, yet our hours were spent like those of lovers on the eve of parting. Long, long silences took the place of foolish little jokes and childish talk which happy lovers know. And more than once, waking in the night, I heard my wife sobbing, and feigned sleep, with the bitter knowledge that I had no power to comfort her. I knew that the thought of her father was with her always, and that her anxiety about him grew, day by day. I wore myself out in trying to think of some way to divert her thoughts from him. I could not, indeed, pay his debts, but I could have him to live with us, a much greater sacrifice; and having a good connection, both as a musician and composer, I did not doubt that I could support her and him in comfort.

But Kate had made up her mind that the disgrace of bankruptcy would break her father's heart; and my Kate is not easy to convince or persuade.

At Torquay it occurred to me that perhaps it would be well for her to see a priest. True, Father Fabian had counselled her to marry Benoliel, but I could hardly believe that most priests would advise a girl to marry a bad man, whom she did not love, for the sake of any worldly gain whatsoever.

She received the suggestion with favour, but without enthusiasm, and we sought out a Catholic church to make inquiries. As we opened the outer door of the church we heard music, and as we stood in the entrance and I laid my hand on the heavy inner door, my other hand was caught by Kate.

"Jasper," she whispered, "it is the same!"

Some person opening the door behind us compelled us to move forward. In another moment we stood in the dusky church—stood hand-in-hand in dim daylight, listening to the same music that each had heard in the lonely night on the eve of our wedding.

I put my arm round my wife and drew her back.

"Come away, my darling," I whispered; "it is a funeral service."

She turned her eyes on me. "I *must* understand, I must see who it is. I shall go mad if you take me away now. I cannot bear any more."

We walked up the aisle, and placed ourselves as near as possible to the spot where the coffin lay, covered with flowers and with tapers burning about it. And we heard that music again, every note of it the same that each had heard before. And when the service was over I whispered to the sacristan—

"Whose music was that?"

"Our organist's," he answered; "it is the first time they've had it. Fine, wasn't it?"

"Who is the—who was—who is being buried?"

"A foreign gentleman, sir; they do say as his lady as was to be gave him the slip on his wedding day, and he'd given her father thousands they say, if the truth was known."

"But what was he doing here?"

"Well, that's the curious part, sir. To show his independence, what does he do but go the same tour he'd planned for his wedding trip. And there was a railway accident, and him and every one in his carriage killed in a twinkling, so to speak. Lucky for the young lady she was off with somebody else."

The sacristan laughed softly to himself.

Kate's fingers gripped my arm.

"What was his name?" she asked.

I would not have asked: I did not wish to hear it.

"Benoliel," said the sacristan. "Curious name and curious tale. Every one's talking of it."

Every one had something else to talk of when it was found that Benoliel's pride, which had permitted him to buy a wife, had shrunk from reclaiming the purchase money when the purchase was lost to him. And to the man who had been willing to sell his daughter, the retention of her price seemed perfectly natural.

From the moment when she heard Benoliel's name on the sacristan's lips, all Kate's gaiety and happiness returned. She loved me, and she hated Benoliel. She was married to me, and he was dead; and his death was far more of a shock to me than to her. Women are curiously kind and curiously cruel. And she never could see why her father should not have kept the money. It is noteworthy that women, even the cleverest and the best of them, have no perception of what men mean by honour.

How do I account for the music? My good critic, my business is to tell my story—not to account for it.

And do I not pity Benoliel? Yes. I can afford, now, to pity most men, alive or dead.

THE TYBURN GHOST

by *The Countess of Munster*

1896

Wilhelmina FitzClarence's mother was an illegitimate daughter of King William IV of the United Kingdom (Queen Victoria's uncle and immediate predecessor), and Mina herself was born on the day of his accession to the throne. She traveled throughout Europe as a child, visiting the court of the "July monarchy" in France and that of the German Kingdom of Hanover, which had belonged to the British monarchs since the Elector of Hanover became King George I of Great Britain and Ireland after the death of his second cousin, Queen Anne.

Mina married her first cousin, the second Earl of Munster, and they had nine children together. William FitzClarence was another grandchild of William IV, his father being the king's illegitimate son by the same mistress as Mina's mother.

The couple lived quietly in the then-fashionable seaside town of Brighton. Mina took to writing late in life, publishing her first novel, Dorinda, *when she was close to sixty and drawing praise from no less a critic than Oscar Wilde. Her second novel,* A Scotch Earl, *was published two years later and was widely condemned for its unflattering portrait of a nobleman—which some critics regarded as dangerously close to Socialism—and for lacking "any merits of construction or style." She published two more books before her death, neither of them novels:* Ghostly Tales *(1896), a well-received collection of stories "written in a manner similar to accounts of true hauntings;" and her autobiography,* My Memories and Miscellanies *(1904).*

"The Tyburn Ghost" comes from Ghostly Tales. *This compact little ghost story lives up to the author's intention to mimic contemporary reports of alleged hauntings, both in the nature of the ghostly manifestation and the tone of the writing—so much so that the magazine* Lady's Realm *considered it, and the rest of her stories, to be based on fact.*

Tyburn is an evocative name to the British, and especially to Londoners. Close to the present-day site of Marble Arch, Tyburn was the site of a notorious gallows, the main execution site for London-area prisoners from the sixteenth through to the eighteenth centuries. It is the perfect spot for a haunted house built over an unmarked grave.

S ome years ago a lady and her three daughters, who generally resided in the country, had reason to visit the metropolis. After some trouble in the way of house-hunting, they settled in a lodging located in a small street in close proximity to the Marble Arch, Hyde Park.

It was summer-time, about the middle of July, and the heat being intense, the atmosphere (or the want of it!) in a small lodginghouse was very oppressive. Mrs. Dale, however, was not very sensitive to 'stuffiness'; besides which, had she been so, she was not well enough off to afford a more spacious dwelling. Indeed, had it not been for the landlady's obliging disposition, and readiness to accede to some alterations suggested by Mrs. Dale, in the arrangement of the apartment, the latter lady would have been forced to seek a *pied-a-terre* in a still less fashionable locality than even Dash-street.

But to make our story clear, we must describe the relative positions of the rooms in Dash-street, as well as what were the slight alterations suggested by Mrs. Dale, and carried out by the obliging Mrs. Parsons; who, knowing that the season was more than half over, felt it was better to put herself out a little, than not to let her rooms at all.

No. 5 Dash-street was a tenement of the most conventional furnished-apartment type; and the rooms hired by Mrs. Dale consisted of two small sitting-rooms on the drawing-room floor, with folding doors between them, and one tolerably good sized bed-room, on the upper storey, situated exactly above the front sitting-room. There was a large 'four-poster' in this upper bed-room, in which the two elder young ladies agreed to repose-together; and Mrs. Dale persuaded the landlady to allow another 'four-poster' to be placed in the back-sitting room for her convenience and that of her youngest daughter—they also electing to sleep therein together.

This was an economical arrangement, necessitating the use of only two beds instead of four (or at least of three), and, as lodging-house keepers charge according to the number of the beds used, the arrangement was a satisfactory one for Mrs. Dale.

Upon the appointed day, rather late in the evening, the Dale family arrived in Dash-street. Mrs. Dale had had some business to transact in the City; so, after a frugal supper, they began to think of retiring for the night. Mrs. Parsons, being a busy, hard-working woman, was nothing loth, and soon brought in the extra bed, toilet table, etc., and after bidding her lodgers a hearty good-night, left them to themselves.

Mrs. Dale had already thrown herself into the expectant arms of an inviting *fauteuil*, intent upon enjoying a free-and-easy yawn, when she suddenly noticed for the first time that there was a balcony outside the window which ran along the whole row of the Dash-street houses. Not being of an imaginative temperament, however, the only nocturnal danger which presented itself to the lady's innocently conventional mind, was—cats! Thereupon the following colloquy took place between her and her daughter Minny, who was to be her bed-fellow:

"Minny, mind you shut that window!" "By all means, mother!"

"And mind you lock it, too; for I am terrified at cats!"

Minny was a very dutiful daughter; but all the same she could not but think, in her 'inner consciousness', that if the window were shut, it would take a very uncommon cat to open it, even if it were not locked! She, however, silently and humbly obeyed orders, and, after much straining and struggling, managed to shut and lock the window, thus imprisoning within the stuffy little room the pleasing odour of the evening meal (which had consisted of pickled salmon and Welsh rare-bit!) and also effectually preventing the entrance of the least breath of fresh air!

"And now that we are comfortable," said Mrs. Dale, whose complexion was shining from a 'combination of heat and eat,' "we may as well go to bed!"

Accordingly, having kissed and dismissed her two daughters, who were to sleep upstairs, she and Minny commenced disrobing themselves in the back sitting-room.

"I think," said Mrs. Dale, after pondering a little, "that if we lock both the doors which open into the drawing-rooms from the staircase, we might safely sleep with the folding-doors open between the two rooms and so be cooler; and we shall get more air,"—(i.e., the atmosphere of the pickled salmon, etc.,)—"don't you think?"

"We will do so," said the obedient Minny, flinging open the folding-doors; she then kissed her mother affectionately, and got into bed.

Now the room was small, and the 'four-poster' was large; so it had been found necessary to place the latter almost in the centre of the former. There was just room for one chair between the bed and the wall on Minny's side, and only a little larger space, occupied by an ottoman and a small table, upon Mrs. Dale's side.

By this time Minny, who was the most active and efficient sister of the three, and upon whom the principal responsibilities of the family were laid, was very tired, and soon, very soon (after she had felt her mother lie down by her side) she fell fast asleep.

The ladies were lying back to back;—Minny's face being turned to the wall, and her mother's towards the ottoman, on the other side of the room.

Suddenly Minny was awakened by a sharp exclamation of seeming terror from her mother, and turning round she beheld the old lady sitting bolt upright in the bed; her teeth were chattering, her night-cap was awry, and she was shaking in every limb.

"What's the matter, mother?"

"I've—I've seen something!" she gasped.

"But, what? *What?*"

"An old hag!—with a villainous face, and hanging lips!"

"Oh! mother, don't you think it's fancy? You know you never sleep well in a strange bed!"

"It *wasn't* fancy!" answered the terrified woman; "she passed along there," pointing with a shaking hand along the wall, "and when she turned and saw me looking at her, she came close to me in a threatening way, and put her horrid putrid-looking face closer to mine. Faugh! I smelt Death! She also nodded viciously, and laughed at my fright, shewing black, slimy teeth! Then she pointed jeeringly with her brown skeleton finger close to my face, and curtsied very low;" and the perspiration poured off the poor old lady's face at the recollection.

"Dearest mother," said Minny tenderly, "you are over-tired and nervous! Come and sleep this side of the bed,—for no one can get at you here, between the bed and the wall!"

And the good daughter helped her mother over into her place, while she lay down in her mother's, feeling convinced that the old lady was suffering from the effects of—picked salmon!

Minny slept peacefully for some time, when suddenly she awoke, feeling curiously uneasy, and for some reason she dreaded to open her eyes! Then, after a second or two, she began to realise that something—someone—was very close to her; that in fact a face was almost touching hers; for she smelt a foetid breath, like to what (she fancied) must be the odour of the grave!

With an effort, she opened her eyes and beheld the figure of an old woman, who, as the terrified girl started into a sitting posture, retreated to the foot of the bed, seemingly prepared, however, to spring upon its occupant; for she clung to both the bed-posts with her brown, claw-like hands, both arms distended, and her head bent slightly forward; her small, lithe body meanwhile swaying to and fro, as though to give it the necessary impetus.

The hag's face was the wickedest Minny had ever seen, and was mottled and brown in colour, as though in a state of decomposition. She wore an old-fashioned mob-cap, trimmed with a wreath of roses (an incongruous head-dress for so ghastly a head!) and a malicious grin parted the charred and blackened lips. She was dressed in a brown silk *sacque*, embroidered all over with pink roses, and Minny fancied she heard the tapping of high-heeled shoes, as the detestable apparition seemingly changing its intention, relinquished the bed-posts and once more began to approach her,—curtseying ironically, as though enjoying the girl's terror!

But Minny, being religiously courageous, pulled herself together, and the sacred words seemed to spring solemnly to her lips: "In the name of the Father, the Son, and the Holy Ghost, I bid-thee be gone!"

A mingled expression of fear and malignant hatred appeared in the evil hag's face, as Minny slowly uttered these words; then the figure shrank, crouched against the wall, and finally disappeared.

Minny knew now that she had seen an evil spirit, and was also convinced that her adjuration had had effect, and that she should never be troubled again in the same way! Those sacred words would always (she felt) have power—complete power—over the devil and his angels! So, in peace she lay down and slept till morning.

She deemed it best to say nothing to her mother of what she had seen, and when the old lady, while dressing the next morning, reiterated her assertion that what she had seen was "not a dream, nor had it been night-mare,"—all that Minny answered was, "She hoped her mother would not relate her experiences to the two sisters who slept upstairs, as it was no use to frighten them." To this Mrs. Dale agreed.

The old lady felt nervous all the same for a night or two after the strange occurrence; but being troubled no more by the unpleasant nocturnal visitor, she became quite bold, and began to think that, after all, it might have been the fault of the pickled salmon, and that the Welsh rare-bit might also have had something to do with it! Having also a great deal of business to transact in the City, and the rooms being convenient, she decided to stay a fortnight longer in Dash-street.

One day, the second sister (Janet) asked for a private word with Minny, and told her that she (Janet) felt "very ill," and that both she and the other sister (Mary by name) fancied there must be "something unwholesome" in the bedroom in which they slept, as they had neither of them "felt well" since their *séjour* in Dash-street.

Minny looked anxiously at her sisters, and could not but acknowledge to herself that they both looked ill; and reproached herself for not having noticed it before. The fortnight was, however, nearly over, so she spoke to her mother, and it was settled that they should leave the very next day; but that they must send for the landlady and tell her so, as she was expecting them to stay a day or two longer.

Mrs. Parsons was much put out at the news, and asked the reason of so sudden a departure? Was there anything she could do? Or had she left anything undone? As she spoke she looked in a strangely suspicious manner at Mrs. Dale, and murmured, "she hoped if there was any reason of complaint that the ladies would tell her."

"Oh no, Mrs. Parsons," answered Mrs. Dale, "we have been most comfortable, but my daughters fancy there is a smell in their bedroom upstairs, and that consequently it is not quite wholesome. Can you account for this?"

"I hope the young ladies will tell me exactly from what they suffer? Is there anything else besides the smell?"

Minnie turned to Janet, who looked as though she could barely stand and gasped out: "Yes, I will tell the truth, and—Mary, come here and corroborate what I say! for I can bear it no longer! Mrs. Parsons, every night for the last week or more, between the hours of one and three, I and my sister are visited by a villainous old hag," and at the remembrance of what she had gone through, of distress and terror, Janet so nearly swooned that after a few minutes Mary was compelled to become spokeswoman.

"Yes!" she said, "what Janet says is true! but we kept silence, knowing it was an object to mother to remain here! The old hag," Mary continued, shuddering, "looks like—a Devil! and as though she had mouldered for years in her grave! Her lips look as though they were falling off—horrible!—horrible!"

"Enough!" said Mrs. Parsons, holding up her hand, "I know it all!—and this cursed house has been my ruin. I ought never to have stayed here; but what can a poor widow do! I got it cheap, as it had a bad name—and now, see!"

She then related that the house had been sold to her cheap by a relative,—who had warned her it was haunted by the old woman whom the Dale family had seen. She had never seen the ghost herself, and would not believe in it, but upon making anxious researches she had discovered that the house was built on the very site of Tyburn, and once when, for sanitary purposes, excavations had been made, a lot of charred bones had been unearthed,—thereby attesting to the truth of what she had been told.

After hearing her story Mrs. Dale felt sorry for the woman, and before leaving made her a small present in money—at the same time impressing upon her that it was scarcely fair or honourable for her, under the circumstances, to receive lodgers. She also offered to help her always in any small way she could;—and she felt glad afterwards to think she had done so; for not many months later, she read in the papers that No. 5, Dash-street, had been burnt to the ground, and that the poor landlady's body had been found among the ruins, bearing incontestable signs of the unfortunate woman having (mercifully) been suffocated.

Years later, as some workmen were digging on the same spot for fresh foundations, an old coffin was unearthed, and upon its being opened, it was found to contain fragments of a female skeleton,—a brown silk gown, in wonderful preservation, some human teeth, and a wreath of artificial roses!

THE DUCHESS AT PRAYER

by Edith Wharton

1900

Edith Newbold Jones was born into New York's upper crust. Her family was related to the Van Rensselaers, who helped found New Netherland, and their wealth is said by some to have inspired the common saying, "keeping up with the Joneses." Her privileged upbringing did not satisfy her, however. She had no interest in fashion, etiquette, and the other necessities of marrying well and making a good show in society. Instead, she supplemented the genteel education she received from tutors and governesses with extensive reading in her father's library.

To save the family from the embarrassment of having her name appear in print, her first published work—a translation of a German poem which she completed at age fifteen—was published under the name of A. E. Washburn, a friend of her father's and a supporter of women's education.

At twenty-three, she married Edward (Teddy) Robbins Wharton, a Boston sportsman and gentleman twelve years her senior. He shared her love of travel until struck down with acute depression in 1902, after which the couple was largely confined to their Massachusetts estate, which Edith designed herself. The marriage ended in divorce after twenty-eight years.

Edith moved to Paris after the divorce, remaining there throughout World War I and contributing to the French war effort and the support of Belgian refugees. Her articles on the war for Scribner's Magazine *were collected as* Fighting France: From Dunkerque to Belfort, *which became a best-seller in the United States. The French government awarded her the Legion of Honor for her wartime work. She returned to the United States only once, to receive an honorary doctorate from Yale University in 1923.*

The Age of Innocence, *Edith's twelfth novel, won the 1921 Pulitzer Prize for fiction. It remains her best known work, and fixed her image in most minds as a writer on the Gilded Age of the late eighteenth century. However, she also wrote poetry, non-fiction, and short stories, including several supernatural tales.*

"The Duchess at Prayer" is set in Italy, and was no doubt inspired by Edith's extensive travels there, both as a child and as a newly married adult. In this subtle tale, which may require more than one reading to fully appreciate, a bored and neglected wife is maneuvered into tragedy by her callous husband.

I

Have you ever questioned the long shuttered front of an old Italian house, that motionless mask, smooth, mute, equivocal as the face of a priest behind which buzz the secrets of the confessional? Other houses declare the activities they shelter; they are the clear expressive cuticle of a life flowing close to the surface; but the old palace in its narrow street, the villa on its cypress-hooded hill, are as impenetrable as death. The tall windows are like blind eyes, the great door is a shut mouth. Inside there may be sunshine, the scent of myrtles, and a pulse of life through all the arteries of the huge frame; or a mortal solitude, where bats lodge in the disjointed stones and the keys rust in unused doors. . . .

II

From the *loggia*, with its vanishing frescoes, I looked down an avenue barred by a ladder of cypress-shadows to the ducal escutcheon and mutilated vases of the gate. Flat noon lay on the gardens, on fountains, porticoes and grottoes. Below the terrace, where a chrome-colored lichen had sheeted the balustrade as with fine *laminae* of gold, vineyards stooped to the rich valley clasped in hills. The lower slopes were strewn with white villages like stars spangling a summer dusk; and beyond these, fold on fold of blue mountain, clear as gauze against the sky. The August air was lifeless, but it seemed light and vivifying after the atmosphere of the shrouded rooms through which I had been led. Their chill was on me and I hugged the sunshine.

"The Duchess's apartments are beyond," said the old man.

He was the oldest man I had ever seen; so sucked back into the past that he seemed more like a memory than a living being. The one trait linking him with the actual was the fixity with which his small saurian eye held the pocket that, as I entered, had yielded a *lira* to the gate-keeper's child. He went on, without removing his eye:

"For two hundred years nothing has been changed in the apartments of the Duchess."

"And no one lives here now?"

"No one, sir. The Duke, goes to Como for the summer season."

I had moved to the other end of the loggia. Below me, through hanging groves, white roofs and domes flashed like a smile.

"And that's Vicenza?"

"*Proprio!*" The old man extended fingers as lean as the hands fading from the walls behind us. "You see the palace roof over there, just to the left of the Basilica? The one with the row of statues like birds taking flight? That's the Duke's town palace, built by Palladio."

"And does the Duke come there?"

"Never. In winter he goes to Rome."

"And the palace and the villa are always closed?"

"As you see—always."

"How long has this been?"

"Since I can remember."

I looked into his eyes: they were like tarnished metal mirrors reflecting nothing. "That must be a long time," I said involuntarily.

"A long time," he assented.

I looked down on the gardens. An opulence of dahlias overran the box-borders, between cypresses that cut the sunshine like basalt shafts. Bees hung above the lavender; lizards sunned themselves on the benches and slipped through the cracks of the dry basins. Everywhere were vanishing traces of that fantastic horticulture of which our dull age has lost the art. Down the alleys maimed statues stretched their arms like rows of whining beggars; faun-eared terms grinned in the thickets, and above the laurustinus walls rose the mock ruin of a temple, falling into real ruin in the bright disintegrating air. The glare was blinding.

"Let us go in," I said.

The old man pushed open a heavy door, behind which the cold lurked like a knife.

"The Duchess's apartments," he said.

Overhead and around us the same evanescent frescoes, under foot the same *scagliola* volutes, unrolled themselves interminably. Ebony cabinets, with inlay of precious marbles in cunning perspective, alternated down the room with the tarnished efflorescence of gilt consoles supporting Chinese monsters; and from the chimney-panel a gentleman in the Spanish habit haughtily ignored us.

"Duke Ercole II," the old man explained, "by the Genoese Priest."

It was a narrow-browed face, sallow as a wax effigy, high-nosed and cautious-lidded, as though odeled by priestly hands; the lips weak and vain rather than cruel; a quibbling mouth that would have snapped at verbal errors like a lizard catching flies, but had never learned the shape of a round yes or no. One of the Duke's hands rested on the head of a dwarf, a simian creature with pearl ear-rings and fantastic dress; the other turned the pages of a folio propped on a skull.

"Beyond is the Duchess's bedroom," the old man reminded me.

Here the shutters admitted but two narrow shafts of light, gold bars deepening the subaqueous gloom. On a dais the bedstead, grim, nuptial, official, lifted its baldachin; a yellow Christ agonized between the curtains, and across the room a lady smiled at us from the chimney-breast.

The old man unbarred a shutter and the light touched her face. Such a face it was, with a flicker of laughter over it like the wind on a June meadow, and a singular tender pliancy of mien, as though one of Tiepolo's lenient goddesses had been busked into the stiff sheath of a seventeenth century dress!

"No one has slept here," said the old man, "since the Duchess Violante."

"And she was—?"

"The lady there—first Duchess of Duke Ercole II."

He drew a key from his pocket and unlocked a door at the farther end of the room. "The chapel," he said. "This is the Duchess's balcony." As I turned to follow him the Duchess tossed me a sidelong smile.

I stepped into a grated tribune above a chapel festooned with stucco. Pictures of bituminous saints mouldered between the pilasters; the artificial roses in the altar-vases were gray with dust and age, and under the cobwebby rosettes of the vaulting a bird's nest clung. Before the altar stood a row of tattered arm-chairs, and I drew back at sight of a figure kneeling near them.

"The Duchess," the old man whispered. "By the Cavaliere Bernini."

It was the image of a woman in furred robes and spreading fraise, her hand lifted, her face addressed to the tabernacle. There was a strangeness in the sight of that immovable presence locked in prayer before an abandoned shrine. Her face was hidden, and I wondered whether it were grief or gratitude that raised her hands and drew her eyes to the altar, where no living prayer joined her marble invocation. I followed my guide down the tribune steps, impatient to see what mystic version of such terrestrial graces the ingenious artist had found—the Cavaliere was master of such arts. The Duchess's attitude was one of transport, as though heavenly airs fluttered her laces and the love-locks escaping from her coif. I saw how admirably the sculptor had caught the poise of her head, the tender slope of the shoulder; then I crossed over and looked into her face—it was a frozen horror. Never have hate, revolt and agony so possessed a human countenance. . . .

The old man crossed himself and shuffled his feet on the marble.

"The Duchess Violante," he repeated.

"The same as in the picture?"

"Eh—the same."

"But the face—what does it mean?"

He shrugged his shoulders and turned deaf eyes on me. Then he shot a glance round the sepulchral place, clutched my sleeve and said, close to my ear: "It was not always so."

"What was not?"

"The face—so terrible."

"The Duchess's face?"

"The statue's. It changed after—"

"After?"

"It was put here."

"The statue's face *changed*—?"

He mistook my bewilderment for incredulity and his confidential finger dropped from my sleeve. "Eh, that's the story. I tell what I've heard. What do I know?" He resumed his senile shuffle across the marble. "This is a bad place to stay in—no one comes here. It's too cold. But the gentleman said, *I must see everything!*"

I let the *lire* sound. "So I must—and hear everything. This story, now—from whom did you have it?"

His hand stole back. "One that saw it, by God!"

"That saw it?"

"My grandmother, then. I'm a very old man."

"Your grandmother? Your grandmother was—?"

"The Duchess's serving girl, with respect to you."

"Your grandmother? Two hundred years ago?"

"Is it too long ago? That's as God pleases. I am a very old man and she was a very old woman when I was born. When she died she was as black as a miraculous Virgin and her breath whistled like the wind in a keyhole. She told me the story when I was a little boy. She told it to me out there in the garden, on a bench by the fish-pond, one summer night of the year she died. It must be true, for I can show you the very bench we sat on. . . ."

III

Noon lay heavier on the gardens; not our live humming warmth but the stale exhalation of dead summers. The very statues seemed to drowse like watchers by a death-bed. Lizards shot out of the cracked soil like flames and the bench in the laurustinus-niche was strewn with the blue varnished bodies of dead flies. Before us lay the fish-pond, a yellow marble slab above rotting secrets. The villa looked across it, composed as a dead face, with the cypresses flanking it for candles. . . .

IV

"Impossible, you say, that my mother's mother should have been the Duchess's maid? What do I know? It is so long since anything has happened here that the old things seem nearer, perhaps, than to those who live in cities. . . . But how else did she know about the statue then? Answer me that, sir! That she saw with her eyes, I can swear to, and never smiled again, so she told me, till they put her first child in her arms . . . for she was taken to wife by the steward's son, Antonio, the same who had carried the letters. . . . But where am I? Ah, well . . . she was a mere slip, you understand, my grandmother, when the Duchess died, a niece of the upper maid, Nencia, and suffered about the Duchess because of her pranks and the funny songs she knew. It's possible, you think, she may have heard from others what she afterward fancied she had seen herself? How that is, it's not for an unlettered man to say; though indeed I myself seem to have seen many of the things she told me. This is a strange place. No one comes here, nothing changes, and the old memories stand up as distinct as the statues in the garden. . . .

"It began the summer after they came back from the Brenta. Duke Ercole had married the lady from Venice, you must know; it was a gay city, then, I'm told, with laughter and music on the water, and the days slipped by like boats running with the tide. Well, to humor her he took her back the first autumn to the Brenta. Her father, it appears, had a grand palace there, with such gardens, bowling-alleys, grottoes and casinos as never were; gondolas bobbing at the water-gates, a stable full of gilt coaches, a theatre full of players, and kitchens and offices full of cooks and lackeys to serve up chocolate all day long to the fine ladies in masks and furbelows, with their pet dogs and their blackamoors and their *abates*. Eh! I know it all as if I'd been there, for Nencia, you see, my grandmother's aunt, travelled with the Duchess, and came back with her eyes round as platters, and not a word to say for the rest of the year to any of the lads who'd courted her here in Vicenza.

"What happened there I don't know—my grandmother could never get at the rights of it, for Nencia was mute as a fish where her lady was concerned—but when they came back to Vicenza the Duke ordered the villa set in order; and in the spring he brought the Duchess here and left her. She looked happy enough, my grandmother said, and seemed no object for pity. Perhaps, after all, it was better than being shut up in Vicenza, in the tall painted rooms where priests came and went as softly as cats prowling for birds, and the Duke was forever closeted in his library, talking with learned men. The Duke was a scholar; you noticed he was painted with a book? Well, those that can read 'em make out that they're full of wonderful things; as a man that's been to a fair across the mountains will always tell his people at home it was beyond anything *they'll* ever see. As for the Duchess, she was all for music, play-acting and young company. The Duke was a silent man, stepping quietly, with his eyes down, as though he'd just come from confession; when the Duchess's lap-dog yapped at his heels he danced like a man in a swarm of hornets; when the Duchess laughed he winced as if you'd drawn a diamond across a window-pane. And the Duchess was always laughing.

"When she first came to the villa she was very busy laying out the gardens, designing grottoes, planting groves and planning all manner of agreeable surprises in the way of water-jets that drenched you unexpectedly, and hermits in caves, and wild men that jumped at you out of thickets. She had a very pretty taste in such matters, but after a while she tired of it, and there being no one for her to talk to but her maids and the chaplain—a clumsy man deep in his books—why, she would have strolling players out from Vicenza, mountebanks and fortune-tellers from the market-place, travelling doctors and astrologers, and all manner of trained animals. Still it could be seen that the poor lady pined for company, and her waiting women, who loved her, were glad when the Cavaliere Ascanio, the Duke's cousin, came to live at the vineyard across the valley—you see the pinkish house over there in the mulberries, with a red roof and a pigeon-cote?

"The Cavaliere Ascanio was a cadet of one of the great Venetian houses, *pezzi grossi* of the Golden Book. He had been meant for the Church, I believe, but what! he set fighting above praying and cast in his lot with the captain of the Duke of Mantua's *bravi*, himself a Venetian of good standing, but a little at odds with the law. Well, the next I know, the Cavaliere was in Venice again, perhaps not in good odor on account of his connection with the gentleman I speak of. Some say he tried to carry off a nun from the convent of Santa Croce; how that may be I can't say; but my grandmother declared he had enemies there, and the end of it was that on some pretext or other the Ten banished him to Vicenza. There, of course, the Duke, being his kinsman, had to show him a civil face; and that was how he first came to the villa.

"He was a fine young man, beautiful as a Saint Sebastian, a rare musician, who sang his own songs to the lute in a way that used to make my grandmother's heart melt and run through her body like mulled wine. He had a good word for everybody, too, and was always dressed in the French fashion, and smelt as sweet as a bean-field; and every soul about the place welcomed the sight of him.

"Well, the Duchess, it seemed, welcomed it too; youth will have youth, and laughter turns to laughter; and the two matched each other like the candlesticks on an altar. The Duchess—you've seen her portrait—but to hear my grandmother, sir, it no more approached her than a weed comes up to a rose. The Cavaliere, indeed, as became a poet, paragoned her in his song to all the pagan goddesses of antiquity; and doubtless these were finer to look at than mere women; but so, it seemed, was she; for, to believe my grandmother, she made other women look no more than the big French fashion-doll that used to be shown on Ascension days in the Piazza. She was one, at any rate, that needed no outlandish finery to beautify her; whatever dress she wore became her as feathers fit the bird; and her hair didn't get its color by bleaching on the housetop. It glittered of itself like the threads in an Easter chasuble, and her skin was whiter than fine wheaten bread and her mouth as sweet as a ripe fig. . . .

"Well, sir, you could no more keep them apart than the bees and the lavender. They were always together, singing, bowling, playing cup and ball, walking in the gardens, visiting the aviaries and petting her grace's trick-dogs and monkeys. The Duchess was as gay as a foal, always playing pranks and laughing, tricking out her animals like comedians, disguising herself as a peasant or a nun (you should have seen her one day pass herself off to the chaplain as a mendicant sister), or teaching the lads and girls of the vineyards to dance and sing madrigals together. The Cavaliere had a singular ingenuity in planning such entertainments and the days were hardly long enough for their diversions. But toward the end of the summer the Duchess fell quiet and would hear only sad music, and the two sat much together in the gazebo at the end of the garden. It was there the Duke found them one day when he drove out from Vicenza in his gilt coach. He came but once or twice a year to the villa, and it was, as my grandmother said, just a part of her poor lady's ill-luck to be wearing that day the Venetian habit, which uncovered the shoulders in a way the Duke always scowled at, and her curls loose and powdered with gold. Well, the three drank chocolate in the gazebo, and what happened no one knew, except that the Duke, on taking leave, gave his cousin a seat in his carriage; but the Cavaliere never returned.

"Winter approaching, and the poor lady thus finding herself once more alone, it was surmised among her women that she must fall into a deeper depression of spirits. But far from this being the case, she displayed such cheerfulness and equanimity of humor that my grandmother, for one, was half-vexed with her for giving no more thought to the poor young man who, all this time, was eating his heart out in the house across the valley. It is true she quitted her gold-laced gowns and wore a veil over her head; but Nencia would have it she looked the lovelier for the change and so gave the Duke greater displeasure. Certain it is that the Duke drove out oftener to the villa, and though he found his lady always engaged in some innocent pursuit, such as embroidery or music, or playing games with her young women, yet he always went away with a sour look and a whispered word to the chaplain. Now as to the chaplain, my grandmother owned there had been a time when her grace had not handled him over-wisely. For, according to Nencia, it seems that his reverence, who seldom approached the Duchess, being buried in his library like a mouse in a cheese—well, one day he made bold to appeal to her for a sum of money, a large sum, Nencia said, to buy certain tall books, a chest full of them, that a foreign pedlar had brought him; whereupon the Duchess, who could never abide a book, breaks out at him with a laugh and a flash of her old spirit— 'Holy Mother of God, must I have more books about me? I was nearly smothered with them in the first year of my marriage;' and the chaplain turning red at the affront, she added: 'You may buy them and welcome, my good chaplain, if you can find the money; but as for me, I am yet seeking a way to pay for my turquoise necklace, and the statue of Daphne at the end of the bowling-green, and the Indian parrot that my black boy brought me last Michaelmas from the Bohemians—so you see I've no money to waste on trifles;' and as he backs out awkwardly she tosses at him over her shoulder: 'You should pray to Saint Blandina to open the Duke's pocket!' to which he returned, very quietly, 'Your excellency's suggestion is an admirable one, and I have already entreated that blessed martyr to open the Duke's understanding.'

"Thereat, Nencia said (who was standing by), the Duchess flushed wonderfully red and waved him out of the room; and then 'Quick!' she cried to my grandmother (who was too glad to run on such errands), 'Call me Antonio, the gardener's boy, to the box-garden; I've a word to say to him about the new clove-carnations. . . .'

"Now I may not have told you, sir, that in the crypt under the chapel there has stood, for more generations than a man can count, a stone coffin containing a thighbone of the blessed Saint Blandina of Lyons, a relic offered, I've been told, by some great Duke of France to one of our own dukes when they fought the Turk together; and the object, ever since, of particular veneration in this illustrious family. Now, since the Duchess had been left to herself, it was observed she affected a fervent devotion to this relic, praying often in the chapel and even causing the stone slab that covered the entrance to the crypt to be replaced by a wooden one, that she might at will descend and kneel by the coffin. This was a matter of edification to all the household and should have been peculiarly pleasing to the chaplain; but, with respect to you, he was the kind of man who brings a sour mouth to the eating of the sweetest apple.

"However that may be, the Duchess, when she dismissed him, was seen running to the garden, where she talked earnestly with the boy Antonio about the new clove-carnations; and the rest of the day she sat indoors and played sweetly on the virginal. Now Nencia always had it in mind that her grace had made a mistake in refusing that request of the chaplain's; but she said nothing, for to talk reason to the Duchess was of no more use than praying for rain in a drought.

"Winter came early that year, there was snow on the hills by All Souls, the wind stripped the gardens, and the lemon-trees were nipped in the lemon-house. The Duchess kept her room in this black season, sitting over the fire, embroidering, reading books of devotion (which was a thing she had never done) and praying frequently in the chapel. As for the chaplain, it was a place he never set foot in but to say mass in the morning, with the Duchess overhead in the tribune, and the servants aching with rheumatism on the marble floor. The chaplain himself hated the cold, and galloped through the mass like a man with witches after him. The rest of the day he spent in his library, over a brazier, with his eternal books. . . .

"You'll wonder, sir, if I'm ever to get to the gist of the story; and I've gone slowly, I own, for fear of what's coming. Well, the winter was long and hard. When it fell cold the Duke ceased to come out from Vicenza, and not a soul had the Duchess to speak to but her maid-servants and the gardeners about the place. Yet it was wonderful, my grandmother said, how she kept her brave colors and her spirits; only it was remarked that she prayed longer in the chapel, where a brazier was kept burning for her all day. When the young are denied their natural pleasures they turn often enough to religion; and it was a mercy, as my grandmother said, that she, who had scarce a live sinner to speak to, should take such comfort in a dead saint.

"My grandmother seldom saw her that winter, for though she showed a brave front to all she kept more and more to herself, choosing to have only Nencia about her and dismissing even her when she went to pray. For her devotion had that mark of true piety, that she wished it not to be observed; so that Nencia had strict orders, on the chaplain's approach, to warn her mistress if she happened to be in prayer.

"Well, the winter passed, and spring was well forward, when my grand-mother one evening had a bad fright. That it was her own fault I won't deny, for she'd been down the lime-walk with Antonio when her aunt fancied her to be stitching in her chamber; and seeing a sudden light in Nencia's window, she took fright lest her disobedience be found out, and ran up quickly through the laurel-grove to the house. Her way lay by the chapel, and as she crept past it, meaning to slip in through the scullery, and groping her way, for the dark had fallen and the moon was scarce up, she heard a crash close behind her, as though someone had dropped from a window of the chapel. The young fool's heart turned over, but she looked round as she ran, and there, sure enough, was a man scuttling across the terrace; and as he doubled the corner of the house my grandmother swore she caught the whisk of the chaplain's skirts. Now that was a strange thing, certainly; for why should the chaplain be getting out of the chapel window when he might have passed through the door? For you may have noticed, sir, there's a door leads from the chapel into the saloon on the ground floor; the only other way out being through the Duchess's tribune.

"Well, my grandmother turned the matter over, and next time she met Antonio in the lime-walk (which, by reason of her fright, was not for some days) she laid before him what had happened; but to her surprise he only laughed and said, 'You little simpleton, he wasn't getting out of the window, he was trying to look in'; and not another word could she get from him.

"So the season moved on to Easter, and news came the Duke had gone to Rome for that holy festivity. His comings and goings made no change at the villa, and yet there was no one there but felt easier to think his yellow face was on the far side of the Apennines, unless perhaps it was the chaplain.

"Well, it was one day in May that the Duchess, who had walked long with Nencia on the terrace, rejoicing at the sweetness of the prospect and the pleasant scent of the gilly-flowers in the stone vases, the Duchess toward midday withdrew to her rooms, giving orders that her dinner should be served in her bed-chamber. My grandmother helped to carry in the dishes, and observed, she said, the singular beauty of the Duchess, who in honor of the fine weather had put on a gown of shot-silver and hung her bare shoulders with pearls, so that she looked fit to dance at court with an emperor. She had ordered, too, a rare repast for a lady that heeded so little what she ate—jellies, game-pasties, fruits in syrup, spiced cakes and a flagon of Greek wine; and she nodded and clapped her hands as the women set it before her, saying again and again, 'I shall eat well to-day.'

"But presently another mood seized her; she turned from the table, called for her rosary, and said to Nencia: 'The fine weather has made me neglect my devotions. I must say a litany before I dine.'

"She ordered the women out and barred the door, as her custom was; and Nencia and my grandmother went down-stairs to work in the linen-room.

"Now the linen-room gives on the court-yard, and suddenly my grandmother saw a strange sight approaching. First up the avenue came the Duke's carriage (whom all thought to be in Rome), and after it, drawn by a long string of mules and oxen, a cart carrying what looked like a kneeling figure wrapped in death-clothes. The strangeness of it struck the girl dumb and the Duke's coach was at the door before she had the wit to cry out that it was coming. Nencia, when she saw it, went white and ran out of the room. My grandmother followed, scared by her face, and the two fled along the corridor to the chapel. On the way they met the chaplain, deep in a book, who asked in surprise where they were running, and when they said, to announce the Duke's arrival, he fell into such astonishment and asked them so many questions and uttered such ohs and ahs, that by the time he let them by the Duke was at their heels. Nencia reached the chapel-door first and cried out that the Duke was coming; and before she had a reply he was at her side, with the chaplain following.

"A moment later the door opened and there stood the Duchess. She held her rosary in one hand and had drawn a scarf over her shoulders; but they shone through it like the moon in a mist, and her countenance sparkled with beauty.

"The Duke took her hand with a bow. 'Madam,' he said, 'I could have had no greater happiness than thus to surprise you at your devotions.'

"'My own happiness,' she replied, 'would have been greater had your excellency prolonged it by giving me notice of your arrival.'

"'Had you expected me, Madam,' said he, 'your appearance could scarcely have been more fitted to the occasion. Few ladies of your youth and beauty array themselves to venerate a saint as they would to welcome a lover.'

"'Sir,' she answered, 'having never enjoyed the latter opportunity, I am constrained to make the most of the former.—What's that?' she cried, falling back, and the rosary dropped from her hand.

"There was a loud noise at the other end of the saloon, as of a heavy object being dragged down the passage; and presently a dozen men were seen haling across the threshold the shrouded thing from the oxcart. The Duke waved his hand toward it. 'That,' said he, 'Madam, is a tribute to your extraordinary piety. I have heard with peculiar satisfaction of your devotion to the blessed relics in this chapel, and to commemorate a zeal which neither the rigors of winter nor the sultriness of summer could abate I have ordered a sculptured image of you, marvellously executed by the Cavaliere Bernini, to be placed before the altar over the entrance to the crypt.'

"The Duchess, who had grown pale, nevertheless smiled playfully at this. 'As to commemorating my piety,' she said, 'I recognize there one of your excellency's pleasantries—'

"'A pleasantry?' the Duke interrupted; and he made a sign to the men, who had now reached the threshold of the chapel. In an instant the wrappings fell from the figure, and there knelt the Duchess to the life. A cry of wonder rose from all, but the Duchess herself stood whiter than the marble.

"'You will see,' says the Duke, 'this is no pleasantry, but a triumph of the incomparable Bernini's chisel. The likeness was done from your miniature portrait by the divine Elisabetta Sirani, which I sent to the master some six months ago, with what results all must admire.'

"'Six months!' cried the Duchess, and seemed about to fall; but his excellency caught her by the hand.

"'Nothing,' he said, 'could better please me than the excessive emotion you display, for true piety is ever modest, and your thanks could not take a form that better became you. And now,' says he to the men, 'let the image be put in place.'

"By this, life seemed to have returned to the Duchess, and she answered him with a deep reverence. 'That I should be overcome by so unexpected a grace, your excellency admits to be natural; but what honors you accord it is my privilege to accept, and I entreat only that in mercy to my modesty the image be placed in the remotest part of the chapel.'

"At that the Duke darkened. 'What! You would have this masterpiece of a renowned chisel, which, I disguise not, cost me the price of a good vineyard in gold pieces, you would have it thrust out of sight like the work of a village stonecutter?'

"'It is my semblance, not the sculptor's work, I desire to conceal.'

"'If you are fit for my house, Madam, you are fit for God's, and entitled to the place of honor in both. Bring the statue forward, you dawdlers!' he called out to the men.

"The Duchess fell back submissively. 'You are right, sir, as always; but I would at least have the image stand on the left of the altar, that, looking up, it may behold your excellency's seat in the tribune.'

"'A pretty thought, Madam, for which I thank you; but I design before long to put my companion image on the other side of the altar; and the wife's place, as you know, is at her husband's right hand.'

"'True, my lord—but, again, if my poor presentment is to have the unmerited honor of kneeling beside yours, why not place both before the altar, where it is our habit to pray in life?'

"'And where, Madam, should we kneel if they took our places? Besides,' says the Duke, still speaking very blandly, 'I have a more particular purpose in placing your image over the entrance to the crypt; for not only would I thereby mark your special devotion to the blessed saint who rests there, but, by sealing up the opening in the pavement, would assure the perpetual preservation of that holy martyr's bones, which hitherto have been too thoughtlessly exposed to sacrilegious attempts.'

"'What attempts, my lord?' cries the Duchess. 'No one enters this chapel without my leave.'

"'So I have understood, and can well believe from what I have learned of your piety; yet at night a malefactor might break in through a window, Madam, and your excellency not know it.'

"'I'm a light sleeper,' said the Duchess.

"The Duke looked at her gravely. 'Indeed?' said he. 'A bad sign at your age. I must see that you are provided with a sleeping-draught.'

"The Duchess's eyes filled. 'You would deprive me, then, of the consolation of visiting those venerable relics?'

"'I would have you keep eternal guard over them, knowing no one to whose care they may more fittingly be entrusted.'

"By this the image was brought close to the wooden slab that covered the entrance to the crypt, when the Duchess, springing forward, placed herself in the way.

"'Sir, let the statue be put in place to-morrow, and suffer me, to-night, to say a last prayer beside those holy bones.'

"The Duke stepped instantly to her side. 'Well thought, Madam; I will go down with you now, and we will pray together.'

"'Sir, your long absences have, alas! given me the habit of solitary devotion, and I confess that any presence is distracting.'

"'Madam, I accept your rebuke. Hitherto, it is true, the duties of my station have constrained me to long absences; but henceforward I remain with you while you live. Shall we go down into the crypt together?"

"'No; for I fear for your excellency's ague. The air there is excessively damp.'

"'The more reason you should no longer be exposed to it; and to prevent the intemperance of your zeal I will at once make the place inaccessible.'

"The Duchess at this fell on her knees on the slab, weeping excessively and lifting her hands to heaven.

"'Oh,' she cried, 'you are cruel, sir, to deprive me of access to the sacred relics that have enabled me to support with resignation the solitude to which your excellency's duties have condemned me; and if prayer and meditation give me any authority to pronounce on such matters, suffer me to warn you, sir, that I fear the blessed Saint Blandina will punish us for thus abandoning her venerable remains!'

"The Duke at this seemed to pause, for he was a pious man, and my grandmother thought she saw him exchange a glance with the chaplain; who, stepping timidly forward, with his eyes on the ground, said, 'There is indeed much wisdom in her excellency's words, but I would suggest, sir, that her pious wish might be met, and the saint more conspicuously honored, by transferring the relics from the crypt to a place beneath the altar.'

"'True!' cried the Duke, 'and it shall be done at once.'

"But thereat the Duchess rose to her feet with a terrible look.

"'No,' she cried, 'by the body of God! For it shall not be said that, after your excellency has chosen to deny every request I addressed to him, I owe his consent to the solicitation of another!'

"The chaplain turned red and the Duke yellow, and for a moment neither spoke.

"Then the Duke said, 'Here are words enough, Madam. Do you wish the relics brought up from the crypt?'

"'I wish nothing that I owe to another's intervention!'

"'Put the image in place then,' says the Duke furiously; and handed her grace to a chair.

"She sat there, my grandmother said, straight as an arrow, her hands locked, her head high, her eyes on the Duke, while the statue was dragged to its place; then she stood up and turned away. As she passed by Nencia, 'Call me Antonio,' she whispered; but before the words were out of her mouth the Duke stepped between them.

"'Madam,' says he, all smiles now, 'I have travelled straight from Rome to bring you the sooner this proof of my esteem. I lay last night at Monselice and have been on the road since daybreak. Will you not invite me to supper?'

"'Surely, my lord,' said the Duchess. 'It shall be laid in the dining-parlor within the hour.'

"'Why not in your chamber and at once, Madam? Since I believe it is your custom to sup there.'

"'In my chamber?' says the Duchess, in disorder.

"'Have you anything against it?' he asked.

"'Assuredly not, sir, if you will give me time to prepare myself.'

"'I will wait in your cabinet,' said the Duke.

"At that, said my grandmother, the Duchess gave one look, as the souls in hell may have looked when the gates closed on our Lord; then she called Nencia and passed to her chamber.

"What happened there my grandmother could never learn, but that the Duchess, in great haste, dressed herself with extraordinary splendor, powdering her hair with gold, painting her face and bosom, and covering herself with jewels till she shone like our Lady of Loreto; and hardly were these preparations complete when the Duke entered from the cabinet, followed by the servants carrying supper. Thereupon the Duchess dismissed Nencia, and what follows my grandmother learned from a pantry-lad who brought up the dishes and waited in the cabinet; for only the Duke's body-servant entered the bed-chamber.

"Well, according to this boy, sir, who was looking and listening with his whole body, as it were, because he had never before been suffered so near the Duchess, it appears that the noble couple sat down in great good humor, the Duchess playfully reproving her husband for his long absence, while the Duke swore that to look so beautiful was the best way of punishing him. In this tone the talk continued, with such gay sallies on the part of the Duchess, such tender advances on the Duke's, that the lad declared they were for all the world like a pair of lovers courting on a summer's night in the vineyard; and so it went till the servant brought in the mulled wine.

"'Ah,' the Duke was saying at that moment, 'this agreeable evening repays me for the many dull ones I have spent away from you; nor do I remember to have enjoyed such laughter since the afternoon last year when we drank chocolate in the gazebo with my cousin Ascanio. And that reminds me,' he said, 'is my cousin in good health?'

"'I have no reports of it,' says the Duchess. 'But your excellency should taste these figs stewed in malmsey—'

"'I am in the mood to taste whatever you offer,' said he; and as she helped him to the figs he added, 'If my enjoyment were not complete as it is, I could almost wish my cousin Ascanio were with us. The fellow is rare good company at supper. What do you say, Madam? I hear he's still in the country; shall we send for him to join us?'

"'Ah,' said the Duchess, with a sigh and a languishing look, 'I see your excellency wearies of me already.'

"'I, Madam? Ascanio is a capital good fellow, but to my mind his chief merit at this moment is his absence. It inclines me so tenderly to him that, by God, I could empty a glass to his good health.'

"With that the Duke caught up his goblet and signed to the servant to fill the Duchess's.

"'Here's to the cousin,' he cried, standing, 'who has the good taste to stay away when he's not wanted. I drink to his very long life—and you, Madam?'

"At this the Duchess, who had sat staring at him with a changed face, rose also and lifted her glass to her lips.

"'And I to his happy death,' says she in a wild voice; and as she spoke the empty goblet dropped from her hand and she fell face down on the floor.

"The Duke shouted to her women that she had swooned, and they came and lifted her to the bed. . . . She suffered horribly all night, Nencia said, twisting herself like a heretic at the stake, but without a word escaping her. The Duke watched by her, and toward daylight sent for the chaplain; but by this she was unconscious and, her teeth being locked, our Lord's body could not be passed through them.

"The Duke announced to his relations that his lady had died after partaking too freely of spiced wine and an omelet of carp's roe, at a supper she had prepared in honor of his return; and the next year he brought home a new Duchess, who gave him a son and five daughters. . . ."

V

The sky had turned to a steel gray, against which the villa stood out sallow and inscrutable. A wind strayed through the gardens, loosening here and there a yellow leaf from the sycamores; and the hills across the valley were purple as thunder-clouds.

"And the statue—?" I asked.

"Ah, the statue. Well, sir, this is what my grandmother told me, here on this very bench where we're sitting. The poor child, who worshipped the Duchess as a girl of her years will worship a beautiful kind mistress, spent a night of horror, you may fancy, shut out from her lady's room, hearing the cries that came from it, and seeing, as she crouched in her corner, the women rush to and fro with wild looks, the Duke's lean face in the door, and the chaplain skulking in the antechamber with his eyes on his breviary. No one minded her that night or the next morning; and toward dusk, when it became known the Duchess was no more, the poor girl felt the pious wish to say a prayer for her dead mistress. She crept to the chapel and stole in unobserved. The place was empty and dim, but as she advanced she heard a low moaning, and coming in front of the statue she saw that its face, the day before so sweet and smiling, had the look on it that you know—and the moaning seemed to come from its lips. My grandmother turned cold, but something, she said afterward, kept her from calling or shrieking out, and she turned and ran from the place. In the passage she fell in a swoon; and when she came to her senses, in her own chamber, she heard that the Duke had locked the chapel door and forbidden any to set foot there. . . . The place was never opened again till the Duke died, some ten years later; and then it was that the other servants, going in with the new heir, saw for the first time the horror that my grandmother had kept in her bosom. . . ."

"And the crypt?" I asked. "Has it never been opened?"

"Heaven forbid, sir!" cried the old man, crossing himself. "Was it not the Duchess's express wish that the relics should not be disturbed?"

THE VACANT LOT

by *Mary E. Wilkins-Freeman*

1903

Born in Randolph, Massachusetts, to strict Congregationalist parents, Mary Wilkins started writing children's stories as a teenager, to help support her family. When she was about fifteen, her family moved to Brattleboro, Vermont, and opened a dry-goods business; she attended the local high school and went on to Mount Holyoke College (then Mount Holyoke Female Seminary) and Glenwood Seminary. The family business failed when she was twenty, and the family moved back to Randolph; ten years later, with both her parents dead, Mary was obliged to support herself entirely through her writing.

In 1892, at the age of almost forty, she met Dr. Charles Manning Freeman, seven years her junior. After a long courtship, the two were married in 1902. Freeman was an alcoholic, drug addict, gambler, and womanizer, who was eventually admitted to the New Jersey State Hospital for the Insane in Trenton. Mary divorced him shortly afterward, and when he died, he left her one dollar; the rest went to his chauffeur.

Mary's strict New England Congregationalist upbringing shows through in much of her writing. "The Little Maid at the Door," for example, is a tale of the Salem witch trials, and several of her other stories are set in Congregationalist communities. She also wove a strong thread of domestic realism into many of her stories, and her female characters often challenge contemporary notions of a woman's role in society. "Luella Miller," one of her most popular tales, concerns a female vampire of sorts, who, far from being helpless, uses the appearance of feminine helplessness to literally drain the life out of others.

"The Vacant Lot" is a different kind of tale: a straightforward ghost story with something of affectionate pastiche in the way the characters are drawn. Even here, though, it is possible to see echoes of Mary's past: a family in the dry-goods business, moving from a smaller community to a city and then moving back again—not, in this case, because the business failed, but for an altogether darker reason.

When it became generally known in Townsend Centre that the Townsends were going to move to the city, there was great excitement and dismay. For the Townsends to move was about equivalent to the town's moving. The Townsend ancestors had founded the village a hundred years ago. The first Townsend had kept a wayside hostelry for man and beast, known as the "Sign of the Leopard." The sign-board, on which the leopard was painted a bright blue, was still extant, and prominently so, being nailed over the present Townsend's front door. This Townsend, by name David, kept the village store. There had been no tavern since the railroad was built through Townsend Centre in his father's day. Therefore the family, being ousted by the march of progress from their chosen employment, took up with a general country store as being the next thing to a country tavern, the principal difference consisting in the fact that all the guests were transients, never requiring bedchambers, securing their rest on the tops of sugar and flour barrels and codfish boxes, and their refreshment from stray nibblings at the stock in trade, to the profitless deplenishment of raisins and loaf sugar and crackers and cheese.

The flitting of the Townsends from the home of their ancestors was due to a sudden access of wealth from the death of a relative and the desire of Mrs. Townsend to secure better advantages for her son George, sixteen years old, in the way of education, and for her daughter Adrianna, ten years older, better matrimonial opportunities. However, this last inducement for leaving Townsend Centre was not openly stated, only ingeniously surmised by the neighbours.

"Sarah Townsend don't think there's anybody in Townsend Centre fit for her Adrianna to marry, and so she's goin' to take her to Boston to see if she can't pick up somebody there," they said. Then they wondered what Abel Lyons would do. He had been a humble suitor for Adrianna for years, but her mother had not approved, and Adrianna, who was dutiful, had repulsed him delicately and rather sadly. He was the only lover whom she had ever had, and she felt sorry and grateful; she was a plain, awkward girl, and had a patient recognition of the fact.

But her mother was ambitious, more so than her father, who was rather pugnaciously satisfied with what he had, and not easily disposed to change. However, he yielded to his wife and consented to sell out his business and purchase a house in Boston and move there.

David Townsend was curiously unlike the line of ancestors from whom he had come. He had either retrograded or advanced, as one might look at it. His moral character was certainly better, but he had not the fiery spirit and eager grasp at advantage which had distinguished them. Indeed, the old Townsends, though prominent and respected as men of property and influence, had reputations not above suspicions. There was more than one dark whisper regarding them handed down from mother to son in the village, and especially was this true of the first Townsend, he who built the tavern bearing the Sign of the Blue Leopard. His portrait, a hideous effort of contemporary art, hung in the garret of David Townsend's home. There was many a tale of wild roistering, if no worse, in that old roadhouse, and high stakes, and quarreling in cups, and blows, and money gotten in evil fashion, and the matter hushed up with a high hand for inquirers by the imperious Townsends who terrorized everybody. David Townsend terrorized nobody. He had gotten his little competence from his store by honest methods—the exchanging of sterling goods and true weights for country produce and country shillings. He was sober and reliable, with intense self-respect and a decided talent for the management of money. It was principally for this reason that he took great delight in his sudden wealth by legacy. He had thereby greater opportunities for the exercise of his native shrewdness in a bargain. This he evinced in his purchase of a house in Boston.

One day in spring the old Townsend house was shut up, the Blue Leopard was taken carefully down from his lair over the front door, the family chattels were loaded on the train, and the Townsends departed. It was a sad and eventful day for Townsend Centre. A man from Barre had rented the store—David had decided at the last not to sell—and the old familiars congregated in melancholy fashion and talked over the situation. An enormous pride over their departed townsman became evident. They paraded him, flaunting him like a banner in the eyes of the new man. "David is awful smart," they said; "there won't nobody get the better of him in the city if he has lived in Townsend Centre all his life. He's got his eyes open. Know what he paid for his house in Boston? Well, sir, that house cost twenty-five thousand dollars, and David he bought it for five. Yes, sir, he did."

"Must have been some out about it," remarked the new man, scowling over his counter. He was beginning to feel his disparaging situation.

"Not an out, sir. David he made sure on't. Catch him gettin' bit. Everythin' was in apple-pie order, hot an' cold water and all, and in one of the best locations of the city—real high-up street. David he said the rent in that street was never under a thousand. Yes, sir, David he got a bargain—five thousand dollars for a twenty-five-thousand-dollar house."

"Some out about it!" growled the new man over the counter.

However, as his fellow townsmen and allies stated, there seemed to be no doubt about the desirableness of the city house which David Townsend had purchased and the fact that he had secured it for an absurdly low price. The whole family were at first suspicious. It was ascertained that the house had cost a round sum only a few years ago; it was in perfect repair; nothing whatever was amiss with plumbing, furnace, anything. There was not even

a soap factory within smelling distance, as Mrs. Townsend had vaguely surmised. She was sure that she had heard of houses being undesirable for such
reasons, but there was no soap factory. They all sniffed and peeked; when
the first rainfall came they looked at the ceiling, confidently expecting to
see dark spots where the leaks had commenced, but there were none. They
were forced to confess that their suspicions were allayed, that the house
was perfect, even overshadowed with the mystery of a lower price than it
was worth. That, however, was an additional perfection in the opinion
of the Townsends, who had their share of New England thrift. They
had lived just one month in their new house, and were happy, although
at times somewhat lonely from missing the society of Townsend Centre,
when the trouble began. The Townsends, although they lived in a fine
house in a genteel, almost fashionable, part of the city, were true to their
antecedents and kept, as they had been accustomed, only one maid. She
was the daughter of a farmer on the outskirts of their native village, was
middle-aged, and had lived with them for the last ten years. One pleasant
Monday morning she rose early and did the family washing before breakfast, which had been prepared by Mrs. Townsend and Adrianna, as was
their habit on washing-days. The family were seated at the breakfast table
in their basement dining-room, and this maid, whose name was Cordelia,
was hanging out the clothes in the vacant lot. This vacant lot seemed a
valuable one, being on a corner. It was rather singular that it had not been
built upon. The Townsends had wondered at it and agreed that they would
have preferred their own house to be there. They had, however, utilized
it as far as possible with their innocent, rural disregard of property rights
in unoccupied land.

"We might just as well hang out our washing in that vacant lot," Mrs.
Townsend had told Cordelia the first Monday of their stay in the house.
"Our little yard ain't half big enough for all our clothes, and it is sunnier
there, too."

So Cordelia had hung out the wash there for four Mondays, and this
was the fifth. The breakfast was about half finished—they had reached
the buckwheat cakes—when this maid came rushing into the dining-room
and stood regarding them, speechless, with a countenance indicative of
the utmost horror. She was deadly pale. Her hands, sodden with soapsuds,

hung twitching at her sides in the folds of her calico gown; her very hair, which was light and sparse, seemed to bristle with fear. All the Townsends turned and looked at her. David and George rose with a half-defined idea of burglars.

"Cordelia Battles, what is the matter?" cried Mrs. Townsend. Adrianna gasped for breath and turned as white as the maid. "What is the matter?" repeated Mrs. Townsend, but the maid was unable to speak. Mrs. Townsend, who could be peremptory, sprang up, ran to the frightened woman and shook her violently. "Cordelia Battles, you speak," said she, "and not stand there staring that way, as if you were struck dumb! What is the matter with you?"

Then Cordelia spoke in a fainting voice.

"There's—somebody else—hanging out clothes—in the vacant lot," she gasped, and clutched at a chair for support.

"Who?" cried Mrs. Townsend, rousing to indignation, for already she had assumed a proprietorship in the vacant lot. "Is it the folks in the next house? I'd like to know what right they have! We are next to that vacant lot."

"I—dunno—who it is," gasped Cordelia. "Why, we've seen that girl next door go to mass every morning," said Mrs. Townsend. "She's got a fiery red head. Seems as if you might know her by this time, Cordelia."

"It ain't that girl," gasped Cordelia. Then she added in a horror-stricken voice, "I couldn't see who 'twas."

They all stared.

"Why couldn't you see?" demanded her mistress. "Are you struck blind?"

"No, ma'am."

"Then why couldn't you see?"

"All I could see was—" Cordelia hesitated, with an expression of the utmost horror.

"Go on," said Mrs. Townsend, impatiently.

"All I could see was the shadow of somebody, very slim, hanging out the clothes, and—"

"What?"

"I could see the shadows of the things flappin' on their line."

"You couldn't see the clothes?"

"Only the shadow on the ground."

"What kind of clothes were they?"

"Queer," replied Cordelia, with a shudder.

"If I didn't know you so well, I should think you had been drinking," said Mrs. Townsend. "Now, Cordelia Battles, I'm going out in that vacant lot and see myself what you're talking about."

"I can't go," gasped the woman.

With that Mrs. Townsend and all the others, except Adrianna, who remained to tremble with the maid, sallied forth into the vacant lot. They had to go out the area gate into the street to reach it. It was nothing unusual in the way of vacant lots. One large poplar tree, the relic of the old forest which had once flourished there, twinkled in one corner; for the rest, it was overgrown with coarse weeds and a few dusty flowers. The Townsends stood just inside the rude board fence which divided the lot from the street and stared with wonder and horror, for Cordelia had told the truth. They all saw what she had described—the shadow of an exceedingly slim woman moving along the ground with up-stretched arms, the shadows of strange, nondescript garments flapping from a shadowy line, but when they looked up for the substance of the shadows nothing was to be seen except the clear, blue October air.

"My goodness!" gasped Mrs. Townsend. Her face assumed a strange gathering of wrath in the midst of her terror. Suddenly she made a determined move forward, although her husband strove to hold her back.

"You let me be," said she. She moved forward. Then she recoiled and gave a loud shriek. "The wet sheet flapped in my face," she cried. "Take me away, take me away!" Then she fainted. Between them they got her back to the house. "It was awful," she moaned when she came to herself, with the family all around her where she lay on the dining-room floor. "Oh, David, what do you suppose it is?"

"Nothing at all," replied David Townsend stoutly. He was remarkable for courage and staunch belief in actualities. He was now denying to himself that he had seen anything unusual.

"Oh, there was," moaned his wife.

"I saw something," said George, in a sullen, boyish bass.

The maid sobbed convulsively and so did Adrianna for sympathy.

"We won't talk any about it," said David. "Here, Jane, you drink this hot tea—it will do you good; and Cordelia, you hang out the clothes in our own yard. George, you go and put up the line for her."

"The line is out there," said George, with a jerk of his shoulder.

"Are you afraid?"

"No, I ain't," replied the boy resentfully, and went out with a pale face.

After that Cordelia hung the Townsend wash in the yard of their own house, standing always with her back to the vacant lot. As for David Townsend, he spent a good deal of his time in the lot watching the shadows, but he came to no explanation, although he strove to satisfy himself with many.

"I guess the shadows come from the smoke from our chimneys, or else the poplar tree," he said.

"Why do the shadows come on Monday mornings, and no other?" demanded his wife.

David was silent.

Very soon new mysteries arose. One day Cordelia rang the dinner-bell at their usual dinner hour, the same as in Townsend Centre, high noon, and the family assembled. With amazement Adrianna looked at the dishes on the table.

"Why, that's queer!" she said.

"What's queer?" asked her mother.

Cordelia stopped short as she was about setting a tumbler of water beside a plate, and the water slopped over.

"Why," said Adrianna, her face paling, "I—thought there was boiled dinner. I—smelt cabbage cooking."

"I knew there would something else come up," gasped Cordelia, leaning hard on the back of Adrianna's chair.

"What do you mean?" asked Mrs. Townsend sharply, but her own face began to assume the shocked pallour which it was so easy nowadays for all their faces to assume at the merest suggestion of anything out of the common.

"I smelt cabbage cooking all the morning up in my room," Adrianna said faintly, "and here's codfish and potatoes for dinner."

The Townsends all looked at one another. David rose with an exclamation and rushed out of the room. The others waited tremblingly. When he came back his face was lowering.

"What did you—" Mrs. Townsend asked hesitatingly.

"There's some smell of cabbage out there," he admitted reluctantly. Then he looked at her with a challenge. "It comes from the next house," he said. "Blows over our house."

"Our house is higher."

"I don't care; you can never account for such things."

"Cordelia," said Mrs. Townsend, "you go over to the next house and you ask if they've got cabbage for dinner."

Cordelia switched out of the room, her mouth set hard. She came back promptly.

"Says they never have cabbage," she announced with gloomy triumph and a conclusive glance at Mr. Townsend. "Their girl was real sassy."

"Oh, father, let's move away; let's sell the house," cried Adrianna in a panic-stricken tone.

"If you think I'm going to sell a house that I got as cheap as this one because we smell cabbage in a vacant lot, you're mistaken," replied David firmly.

"It isn't the cabbage alone," said Mrs. Townsend.

"And a few shadows," added David. "I am tired of such nonsense. I thought you had more sense, Jane."

"One of the boys at school asked me if we lived in the house next to the vacant lot on Wells Street and whistled when I said 'Yes,'" remarked George.

"Let him whistle," said Mr. Townsend.

After a few hours the family, stimulated by Mr. Townsend's calm, common sense, agreed that it was exceedingly foolish to be disturbed by a mysterious odour of cabbage. They even laughed at themselves.

"I suppose we have got so nervous over those shadows hanging out clothes that we notice every little thing," conceded Mrs. Townsend.

"You will find out some day that that is no more to be regarded than the cabbage," said her husband.

"You can't account for that wet sheet hitting my face," said Mrs. Townsend, doubtfully.

"You imagined it."

"I *felt* it."

That afternoon things went on as usual in the household until nearly four o'clock. Adrianna went downtown to do some shopping. Mrs. Townsend sat sewing beside the bay window in her room, which was a front one in the third story. George had not got home. Mr. Townsend was writing a letter in the library. Cordelia was busy in the basement; the twilight, which was coming earlier and earlier every night, was beginning to gather, when suddenly there was a loud crash which shook the house from its foundations. Even the dishes on the sideboard rattled, and the glasses rang like bells. The pictures on the walls of Mrs. Townsend's room swung out from the walls. But that was not all: every looking-glass in the house cracked simultaneously—as nearly as they could judge—from top to bottom, then shivered into fragments over the floors. Mrs. Townsend was too frightened to scream. She sat huddled in her chair, gasping for breath, her eyes, rolling from side to side in incredulous terror, turned toward the street. She saw a great black group of people crossing it just in front of the vacant lot. There was something inexpressibly strange and gloomy about this moving group; there was an effect of sweeping, wavings and foldings of sable draperies and gleams of deadly white faces; then they passed. She twisted her head to see, and they disappeared in the vacant lot. Mr. Townsend came hurrying into the room; he was pale, and looked at once angry and alarmed.

"Did you fall?" he asked inconsequently, as if his wife, who was small, could have produced such a manifestation by a fall.

"Oh, David, what is it?" whispered Mrs. Townsend.

"Darned if I know!" said David.

"Don't swear. It's too awful. Oh, see the looking-glass, David!"

"I see it. The one over the library mantel is broken, too."

"Oh, it is a sign of death!"

Cordelia's feet were heard as she staggered on the stairs. She almost fell into the room. She reeled over to Mr. Townsend and clutched his arm. He cast a sidewise glance, half furious, half commiserating at her.

"Well, what is it all about?" he asked.

"I don't know. What is it? Oh, what is it? The looking-glass in the kitchen is broken. All over the floor. Oh, oh! What is it?"

"I don't know any more than you do. I didn't do it."

"Lookin'-glasses broken is a sign of death in the house," said Cordelia. "If it's me, I hope I'm ready; but I'd rather die than be so scared as I've been lately."

Mr. Townsend shook himself loose and eyed the two trembling women with gathering resolution.

"Now, look here, both of you," he said. "This is nonsense. You'll die sure enough of fright if you keep on this way. I was a fool myself to be startled. Everything it is is an earthquake."

"Oh, David!" gasped his wife, not much reassured.

"It is nothing but an earthquake," persisted Mr. Townsend. "It acted just like that. Things always are broken on the walls, and the middle of the room isn't affected. I've read about it."

Suddenly Mrs. Townsend gave a loud shriek and pointed.

"How do you account for that," she cried, "if it's an earthquake? Oh, oh, oh!"

She was on the verge of hysterics. Her husband held her firmly by the arm as his eyes followed the direction of her rigid pointing finger. Cordelia looked also, her eyes seeming converged to a bright point of fear. On the floor in front of the broken looking-glass lay a mass of black stuff in a grewsome long ridge.

"It's something you dropped there," almost shouted Mr. Townsend.

"It ain't. Oh!"

Mr. Townsend dropped his wife's arm and took one stride toward the object. It was a very long crape veil. He lifted it, and it floated out from his arm as if imbued with electricity.

"It's yours," he said to his wife.

"Oh, David, I never had one. You know, oh, you know I—shouldn't—unless you died. How came it there?"

"I'm darned if I know," said David, regarding it. He was deadly pale, but still resentful rather than afraid.

"Don't hold it; don't!"

"I'd like to know what in thunder all this means?" said David. He gave the thing an angry toss and it fell on the floor in exactly the same long heap as before.

Cordelia began to weep with racking sobs. Mrs. Townsend reached out and caught her husband's hand, clutching it hard with ice-cold fingers.

"What's got into this house, anyhow?" he growled.

"You'll have to sell it. Oh, David, we can't live here."

"As for my selling a house I paid only five thousand for when it's worth twenty-five, for any such nonsense as this, I won't!"

David gave one stride toward the black veil, but it rose from the floor and moved away before him across the room at exactly the same height as if suspended from a woman's head. He pursued it, clutching vainly, all around the room, then he swung himself on his heel with an exclamation and the thing fell to the floor again in the long heap. Then were heard hurrying feet on the stairs and Adrianna burst into the room. She ran straight to her father and clutched his arm; she tried to speak, but she chattered unintelligibly; her face was blue. Her father shook her violently.

"Adrianna, do have more sense!" he cried.

"Oh, David, how can you talk so?" sobbed her mother.

"I can't help it. I'm mad!" said he with emphasis. "What has got into this house and you all, anyhow?"

"What is it, Adrianna, poor child," asked her mother. "Only look what has happened here."

"It's an earthquake," said her father staunchly; "nothing to be afraid of."

"How do you account for *that*?" said Mrs. Townsend in an awful voice, pointing to the veil.

Adrianna did not look—she was too engrossed with her own terrors. She began to speak in a breathless voice.

"I—was—coming—by the vacant lot," she panted, "and—I—I—had my new hat in a paper bag and—a parcel of blue ribbon, and—I saw a crowd, an awful—oh! a whole crowd of people with white faces, as if—they were dressed all in black."

"Where are they now?"

"I don't know. Oh!" Adrianna sank gasping feebly into a chair.

"Get her some water, David," sobbed her mother.

David rushed with an impatient exclamation out of the room and returned with a glass of water which he held to his daughter's lips.

"Here, drink this!" he said roughly.

"Oh, David, how can you speak so?" sobbed his wife.

"I can't help it. I'm mad clean through," said David.

Then there was a hard bound upstairs, and George entered. He was very white, but he grinned at them with an appearance of unconcern.

"Hullo!" he said in a shaking voice, which he tried to control. "What on earth's to pay in that vacant lot now?"

"Well, what is it?" demanded his father.

"Oh, nothing, only—well, there are lights over it exactly as if there was a house there, just about where the windows would be. It looked as if you could walk right in, but when you look close there are those old dried-up weeds rattling away on the ground the same as ever. I looked at it and couldn't believe my eyes. A woman saw it, too. She came along just as I did. She gave one look, then she screeched and ran. I waited for some one else, but nobody came."

Mr. Townsend rushed out of the room.

"I daresay it'll be gone when he gets there," began George, then he stared round the room. "What's to pay here?" he cried.

"Oh, George, the whole house shook all at once, and all the looking-glasses broke," wailed his mother, and Adrianna and Cordelia joined.

George whistled with pale lips. Then Mr. Townsend entered.

"Well," asked George, "see anything?"

"I don't want to talk," said his father. "I've stood just about enough."

"We've got to sell out and go back to Townsend Centre," cried his wife in a wild voice. "Oh, David, say you'll go back."

"I won't go back for any such nonsense as this, and sell a twenty-five-thousand dollar house for five thousand," said he firmly.

But that very night his resolution was shaken. The whole family watched together in the dining-room. They were all afraid to go to bed—that is, all except possibly Mr. Townsend. Mrs. Townsend declared firmly that she for one would leave that awful house and go back to Townsend Centre whether he came or not, unless they all stayed together and watched, and Mr. Townsend yielded. They chose the dining-room for the reason that it was nearer the street should they wish to make their egress hurriedly, and they took up their station around the dining-table on which Cordelia had placed a luncheon.

"It looks exactly as if we were watching with a corpse," she said in a horror-stricken whisper.

"Hold your tongue if you can't talk sense," said Mr. Townsend.

The dining-room was very large, finished in oak, with a dark blue paper above the wainscotting. The old sign of the tavern, the Blue Leopard, hung over the mantel-shelf. Mr. Townsend had insisted on hanging it there. He had a curious pride in it. The family sat together until after midnight and nothing unusual happened. Mrs. Townsend began to nod; Mr. Townsend read the paper ostentatiously. Adrianna and Cordelia stared with roving eyes about the room, then at each other as if comparing notes on terror. George had a book which he studied furtively. All at once Adrianna gave a startled exclamation and Cordelia echoed her. George whistled faintly. Mrs. Townsend awoke with a start and Mr. Townsend's paper rattled to the floor.

"Look!" gasped Adrianna.

The sign of the Blue Leopard over the shelf glowed as if a lantern hung over it. The radiance was thrown from above. It grew brighter and brighter as they watched. The Blue Leopard seemed to crouch and spring with life. Then the door into the front hall opened—the outer door, which had been carefully locked. It squeaked and they all recognized it. They sat staring. Mr. Townsend was as transfixed as the rest. They heard the outer door shut, then the door into the room swung open and slowly that awful black group of people which they had seen in the afternoon entered. The Townsends with one accord rose and huddled together in a far corner; they all held to each other and stared. The people, their faces gleaming with a whiteness of death, their black robes waving and folding, crossed the room. They were a trifle above mortal height, or seemed so to the terrified eyes which saw them. They reached the mantel-shelf where the sign-board hung, then a black-draped long arm was seen to rise and make a motion, as if plying a knocker. Then the whole company passed out of sight, as if through the wall, and the room was as before. Mrs. Townsend was shaking in a nervous chill, Adrianna was almost fainting, Cordelia was in hysterics. David Townsend stood glaring in a curious way at the sign of the Blue Leopard. George stared at him with a look of horror. There was something in his father's face which made him forget everything else. At last he touched his arm timidly.

"Father," he whispered.

David turned and regarded him with a look of rage and fury, then his face cleared; he passed his hand over his forehead.

"Good Lord! What *did* come to me?" he muttered.

"You looked like that awful picture of old Tom Townsend in the garret in Townsend Centre, father," whimpered the boy, shuddering.

"Should think I might look like 'most any old cuss after such darned work as this," growled David, but his face was white. "Go and pour out some hot tea for your mother," he ordered the boy sharply. He himself shook Cordelia violently. "Stop such actions!" he shouted in her ears, and shook her again. "Ain't you a church member?" he demanded; "what be you afraid of? You ain't done nothin' wrong, have ye?"

Then Cordelia quoted Scripture in a burst of sobs and laughter.

"Behold, I was shapen in iniquity; and in sin did my mother conceive me," she cried out. "If I ain't done wrong, mebbe them that's come before me did, and when the Evil One and the Powers of Darkness is abroad I'm liable, I'm liable!" Then she laughed loud and long and shrill.

"If you don't hush up," said David, but still with that white terror and horror on his own face, "I'll bundle you out in that vacant lot whether or no. I mean it."

Then Cordelia was quiet, after one wild roll of her eyes at him. The colour was returning to Adrianna's cheeks; her mother was drinking hot tea in spasmodic gulps.

"It's after midnight," she gasped, "and I don't believe they'll come again to-night. Do you, David?"

"No, I don't," said David conclusively.

"Oh, David, we mustn't stay another night in this awful house."

"We won't. To-morrow we'll pack off bag and baggage to Townsend Centre, if it takes all the fire department to move us," said David.

Adrianna smiled in the midst of her terror. She thought of Abel Lyons.

The next day Mr. Townsend went to the real estate agent who had sold him the house.

"It's no use," he said, "I can't stand it. Sell the house for what you can get. I'll give it away rather than keep it."

Then he added a few strong words as to his opinion of parties who sold him such an establishment. But the agent pleaded innocent for the most part.

"I'll own I suspected something wrong when the owner, who pledged me to secrecy as to his name, told me to sell that place for what I could get, and did not limit me. I had never heard anything, but I began to suspect something was wrong. Then I made a few inquiries and found out that there was a rumour in the neighbourhood that there was something out of the usual about that vacant lot. I had wondered myself why it wasn't built upon. There was a story about it's being undertaken once, and the contract made, and the contractor dying; then another man took it and one of the workmen was killed on his way to dig the cellar, and the others struck. I didn't pay much attention to it. I never believed much in that sort of thing anyhow, and then, too, I couldn't find out that there had ever been anything wrong about the house itself, except as the people who had lived there were said to have seen and heard queer things in the vacant lot, so I thought you might be able to get along, especially as you didn't look like a man who was timid, and the house was such a bargain as I never handled before. But this you tell me is beyond belief."

"Do you know the names of the people who formerly owned the vacant lot?" asked Mr. Townsend.

"I don't know for certain," replied the agent, "for the original owners flourished long before your or my day, but I do know that the lot goes by the name of the old Gaston lot. What's the matter? Are you ill?"

"No; it is nothing," replied Mr. Townsend. "Get what you can for the house; perhaps another family might not be as troubled as we have been."

"I hope you are not going to leave the city?" said the agent, urbanely.

"I am going back to Townsend Centre as fast as steam can carry me after we get packed up and out of that cursed house," replied Mr. David Townsend.

He did not tell the agent nor any of his family what had caused him to start when told the name of the former owners of the lot. He remembered all at once the story of a ghastly murder which had taken place in the Blue Leopard. The victim's name was Gaston and the murderer had never been discovered.

AN UNSCIENTIFIC STORY

by Louise J. Strong

1903

For all its ability to chill a reader's blood, Frankenstein *is more science fiction than horror, and the same is true of this next tale. Once again, a scientist probing the nature of life has cause to regret his researches; but where Mary Shelley's classic tale is unrelieved Gothic horror and doom, Louise Strong's take on the theme is lighter of touch, and as apt to raise a wry smile as a shudder.*

The story first appeared in Cosmopolitan—*a magazine with a much more general readership in those days—in January 1903. Some have seen it as an allegory, reminding men that the creation of life is the domain of women, while to others it is an admonition of those men who would rather bury themselves in their work than deal with their wives, families, and social obligations.*

On a more superficial level, the story is reminiscent of Mickey Mouse's dilemma when he played "The Sorcerer's Apprentice" in Disney's classic movie Fantasia. *The professor's creations reproduce uncontrollably, ask inconvenient questions, and demand things of him that he would prefer not to give. To many fathers of that time—and afterward—children had many of the same disquieting properties.*

Louise Jackson Strong is little remembered today. She wrote short stories and novels, including Legs for the Chiefty, *a children's novel published in 1911, and* The Swoop of the Week, or, The Treasure at "Ma's Legacy." *According to the website of her great-grandson, artist George Asdel, she also composed music.*

H e sat, tense and rigid with excitement, expectancy, incredulity. Was it possible, after so many years of study, effort and failure? Could it be that at last success rewarded him? He hardly dared to breathe lest he should miss something of the wonderful spectacle. How long he had sat thus he did not know; he had not stirred for hours—or was it days?—except to adjust the light by means of the button under his hand.

His laboratory, at the foot of his garden, was lighted day and night in the inner room (his private workshop) with electricity, and no one was admitted but by especial privilege.

Some things he had accomplished for the good of mankind, more he hoped to accomplish, but most of all he had been searching for, and striving to create, the life-germ. He had spent many of his years and much of his great wealth in unsuccessful experiments. He had met ridicule and unbelief with Stoical indifference, upheld by the conviction that he would finally prove the truth of his theories. Over and over again, defeat and disappointment had dashed aside his hopes; over and over again, he had rallied and gone on with dogged persistence.

And now! He could not realize it yet! He leaned back, and clasped his hands over his closed eyes. Perhaps he had imagined it—his over-strained nerves having deceived him. Was it an optical illusion? It had happened before. There had been times when he felt that he had torn aside the veil, and grasped the secret, only to find that a few abortive movements were all that existed of his creation. In sudden haste he turned to the glass again.

A—h! He drew a long breath that was almost a shriek. It was not illusion of sight, no delusion of his mind. The creature—it was plainly a living creature—had grown, and taken shape, even in those few moments. It lived! It breathed! It moved! And his the power that had given it life! His breath came in gasps, his heart beat in great throbs, and his blood surged through his veins.

But soon his scientific sense asserted itself, and he carefully and minutely studied the prodigy. Its growth was phenomenal; the rapidity of its expansion was past belief. It took form, developed limbs, made repeated attempts at locomotion, and finally drew itself out of the glass receptacle of cunningly compounded liquid in which it had been created.

At that the learned professor leaped to his feet in a transport of exultation. The impossible had been achieved! Life! Life, so long the mystery and despair of man, had come at his bidding. He alone of all humanity held the secret in the hollow of his hand. He plunged about the room in a blind ecstasy of triumph. Tears ran unknown and unheeded down his cheeks. He tossed his arms aloft wildly, as if challenging Omnipotence itself. At that moment, he felt a very god! He could create worlds, and people them! A burning desire seized him to rush out, and proclaim the deed from the housetops, to the utter confounding of brother scientists and the theologians.

He dropped, panting, into his chair, and strove to collect and quiet his mind. Not yet the time to make known the incredible fact. He must wait until full development proved that it was indeed a living creation—with animal nature and desires.

It had lain, quivering, on the marble slab, breathing regularly and steadily, making aimless movements. The four limbs, that had seemed but swaying feelers, grew into long, thin arms and legs, with claw-like hands, and flat, six-toed feet. It lost its spherical shape; an uneven protuberance, in which was situated the breathing-orifice, expanded into a head with rudimentary features. He took his spatula, and turned it over. It responded to the touch with an effort to rise; the head wobbled weakly, and two slits opened in the dim face, from which looked out dull, fishy eyes. It grew!

Each moment found it larger, more developed; yet he could no more see the growth than he could see the movement of the hour-hand of his watch.

"It is probably of the simian order," he made memorandum. "Ape-like. Grows a strange caricature of humanity."

An aperture appeared in the oblong head, forming a lipless mouth below the lump of a nose; large ears stood out on either side.

The caricature-like resemblance to humanity increased as it grew older. It crawled a space, sat up, made many futile efforts and at last succeeded in standing. It took a few staggering steps. It made wheezy, puffing sounds in its motions, and drivelled idiotically. Finally it squatted down on its haunches, the knobby knees drawn up against the rotund paunch, the hands grasping the ankles.

"It grew!"

"The attitude of primitive man," the Professor muttered.

For long it crouched thus, increasing in size, and beginning to display a crude intelligence; looking about with eyes that evidently saw—noted things: the arc of light, the glistening glass and brass, and most of all, himself.

It had as yet made no manifestation that indicated desire; but soon a fly, alighting near it, was snatched up and thrust into its mouth with incredible quickness and an eager, sucking noise. At this expression of animalism, the Professor's hand shook so violently that he could scarcely record the movement.

Nervousness only! He would not admit to himself a feeling of startled misgiving. He was worn out. For days he scarcely tasted food, and he had dozed only at long intervals. A half-hour's sleep would refresh him, and the creature could not change much in that time, for its bodily development seemed nearly completed. His head dropped on his arms, and he slumbered profoundly.

He was awakened by a sense of suffocation and a gnawing at his neck; he started up with a cry, pushing off a clammy mass that lay heavy on the upturned side of his face. Merciful heaven! It was the beast attacking him; its teeth, which he had not before discovered, seeking his throat!

It lay where he had thrown it, its long tongue licking the shapeless mouth, its eyes hot with an awakened bloodthirstiness. In a wave of repulsion, he struck it savagely.

He was appalled at what he had done; he seemed to have committed a crime in striking it.

He went to the anteroom, where fresh food was left for him daily, and selected different sorts, questioning whether any would or could satisfy a creature which had been brought into existence in such a marvellous manner.

It met him, with alert expectancy, and ate, with a ravenous gluttony that was loathsome, of all that he put before it.

Apparently it possessed all the animal senses; all had been tested but hearing. He spoke a few words in an ordinary tone; it lifted its face, with an expression of inquiry.

He paced the room in perplexed thought. Could it possess mental faculties beyond those of an ordinary animal? He had not hoped to produce anything but a lower form of life. Never had he imagined a creature of his creating, with consciousness of its existence; that was a responsibility for which he was not prepared.

Exhausted in body and mind, he locked the creature in the inner room, and threw himself on the couch in his study for a night's rest.

The creature was standing when he entered, next morning, and, stepping toward him, it correctly repeated every word he had spoken the night before, as if reciting a lesson, showing an eager expectancy of approval.

"Good heavens!" ejaculated the Professor, reeling against the door.

"Good heavens!" it echoed, its small orbs sparkling.

He sprang toward it as if to force back this evidence of intelligent reason; it fled, keeping the table between them; brought to bay, it dropped on its knees, and put up beseeching hands, mumbling a prayer—a prayer from its own inner consciousness!

Aghast, terrified, he gazed at it, tremblingly assuring himself that many animals made imitative sounds—parrots readily learned human speech.

The curious creature had shown no bodily growth for several days; it had perhaps reached maturity, and would soon show signs of decay. Already a lump had appeared on its breast, which it picked at uneasily; he must not much longer delay exhibiting it. Yet he hesitated to do so until he was more certain concerning it.

He tested its power with a multitude of words that it not only easily repeated but retained perfectly, muttering them over, forming and reforming a number of proper sentences with various definitions, which it seemed to submit, in comparison, to some inner or waking intelligence.

Once, after long muttering, it came to him, with timid perplexity, and put the astonishing question: "What am I?" And when he answered not for amazement the poor creature wandered about, repeating the words. Like one rallying from long unconsciousness, it seemed seeking a dimly remembered clue to its identity.

Fear clutched him! Impossible! Oh, impossible that he had a human soul imprisoned in such hideous form! A soul that would, by and by, fully awake to the wrong he had done it! No! No! He spurned the thought as a wild fancy. But even so—he had done nothing unlawful. Man was free to use his intellect to the utmost. He had brought into existence a living creature, but he was not responsible farther than the body. To the Keeper of souls be the rest.

Possibly some long-disembodied spirit, grown wise in its freedom, animated the creature, and its full development would open a channel for such knowledge as the earth had never before known, and the world would ring with his name, and honour and fame be his! Again he exulted while making record of its mental unfoldment, which was as rapid as had been the development of its uncouth body, and with much the same distortion. It recognized him as its creator, did him reverence, and obeyed his commands.

The lump, which he had taken for a symptom of decay, assumed the appearance of a large scale, and dropped off. When he would have examined it more closely, the creature put a hand over it, looking up at him with a show of hostility and cunning, for the first time disregarding his command; and he would not enforce obedience.

He was confounded next morning to find that the scale had developed into a second creature! About it the first hovered with evident joy and pride, inviting his attention to it with the gushing babble of a child. He had not imagined it possessed the power of generation, but here was reproduction with an ease and rapidity beyond any creature of like size in existence.

The second one, fed and taught by the first, matured in body and mind more quickly; and they invented or discovered a speech of their own—a strange jargon (of which he could make nothing) by which they exchanged thoughts and conversed, and which he tried in vain to help them reduce to a written language, through which he might obtain the wisdom for which he hoped.

And reproduction went on; while he subjected them to many tests to determine their nature.

As they grew in age and numbers, they began to evince for him less reverence; and an animosity appeared, that burst out at times in a horrible flow of invectives—a mingling of their own strange speech and his.

When he did not comply with their desires, they wailed piteously—demanding: "Why?" "Why"—or hurled blasphemous defiance at him.

These things convinced him that they were a lower order of humanity, possessing souls; for no creature but man observed, with like or dislike, the bodily form in which its life was manifested. He was torn and racked with dread and a crushing sense of guilt and responsibility. It was as if he had started an avalanche that might overwhelm the world.

Already they had become a heavy burden to him. He was obliged to make nightly visits to the markets for food to satisfy their rapacity—food which he flung to them as to so many dogs, and which they pounced upon and fought over, with curses at each other's greed. Yet at a word of reproof from him, they banded solidly against him, each for all.

All complacency over his handiwork had vanished; never could he bring himself to exhibit to mortal eye these repulsive creatures. His only thought was the unanswerable question: what should he do with them? On this he brooded continually, reaching no conclusion because he could no more contemplate destroying creatures possessing human intelligence, however distorted and degraded, than he could have taken the life of a born idiot or one insane.

In his absorption he neglected to lock the door one day, and roused to find them swarming in his study. Besides the high skylight there was one large window, securely closed by a heavy inside shutter, above which was a long narrow opening admitting air. Some of them, clinging to shutter and casement, and uttering low, sharp cries, like wolves scenting their prey, had climbed to the opening, and were peering out with gloating eyes. They clawed and jibbered, with hot tongues lolling eagerly, the saliva dripping from their ugly mouths—hideous pictures of unsatiated animal appetite.

And what was it that so aroused their ghoulish lust? His little children playing on the lawn, their innocent voices rising like heavenly music in contrast to the hellish sounds within. A rippling laugh floated on the air, and the creatures' eagerness increased to a fury; with tooth and nail they strove to enlarge the opening, not heeding his horrified commands.

In a frenzy of rage, he snatched an iron rod, and swept them to the floor, driving them with blows and maledictions to their room. They fled before his wrath, but when he turned his back to lock the door, they flung themselves upon him, with desperate attempts to reach his throat.

After a sharp battle, he beat them off, and sent them huddling and whimpering to a corner. "Monsters! Monsters!" he cried, pale with the discovery. "Monsters, who would prey on human flesh! What a curse I have called forth! It is of the devil!"

"Devil; devil; yes, devil," one muttered, a leering and malicious knowledge gleaming in its oblique eyes.

In that moment he saw his duty—all hesitation vanished, and he made up his mind—they must be destroyed effectually, and he could not survive the destruction.

By that occult sense or power they possessed, which was beyond anything he had ever found in man, they divined his decision almost as soon as it was formed, and prostrated themselves with cries of mercy. They hastened to lay at his feet propitiatory offerings of their belongings: cards, pencils, picture-books—all that he had provided for their amusement and instruction—entreating him for life, the life that he himself had given them.

Their prayers and offerings rejected, the creatures became his open enemies. Intent on escaping from their prison, his every entrance was a battle with their persistent efforts to gain control of the door, the only outlet to the room.

They were not easily injured. No maiming nor bruises resulted from his hasty blows with the rod. Would it be possible to destroy them? Their bodily substance resembled clammy putty in appearance, with the consistency of rubber. He had never conquered his repugnance sufficiently to handle one. He could not experiment upon them, but the chemicals he meant to employ with the most powerful explosives, he trusted, would make the work of annihilation swift and thorough.

His preparations were delayed and hindered by their never-ending attempts to overcome him. The moment he became absorbed in his work, they crawled and crept with malignant insistence to a fresh attack. Once, in a movement of defence, he pricked the body of one with a sharpened tool, and he was almost suffocated by the fumes that arose from the yellow, viscid fluid that oozed from the wound.

Escaping from the affrighted, indignant uproar that followed, he stood at his study-window to recover from the dizzy sickness. "That alone would make them formidable enemies of mankind," he muttered.

"The slaughter of a few would put to flight an army. Turned loose, they are sufficient now in numbers, with all their hellish characteristics, to lay waste this teeming city. Wretched, impotent creator that I am! Could I but turn back the dial of time a few short weeks how happily I could take my place beside the most ignorant toiler, and meddle no more with the prerogative of the Almighty!"

In a few hours, the wound had healed, no trace of injury remaining; but they had learned new reason to fear him, and skulked about glowering, commenting upon him with shameless, insulting epithets.

He found a note from his wife in his mail, informing him of the arrival in the city of a noted scientist whose coming had been largely of his arranging, months before. There was much dissatisfaction expressed at his absence, and demands were made that he attend the forthcoming banquet.

"Of course, you will go," she wrote. "And, dear, do come in early enough to give a little time to your family. We have hardly seen you for weeks and weeks; and though I have obeyed the law, I so long to see you that I have been tempted to transgress, and boldly make my way to you. Baby, who was just beginning to totter about when you saw him last, runs easily now on his sturdy little legs, and he can say "papa" quite plainly. Do come, dear; a few hours with us will rest you."

Rest indeed! Heaven itself could seem no sweeter to the miserable man than this glimpse of his home. His dear wife, content to live the life Omnipotence had planned for her; his sweet children, daily and harmoniously unfolding new graces of mind and body like lovely flowers—not for him was it to see their perfected maturity, from which he had hoped so much. With a groan he dropped his head, and wept bitter tears—tears that meant the renunciation of his own forfeited life.

All was complete when the banquet-day arrived. He had but to press a small knob in the floor, and the mighty currents of electricity would flash around the room, setting in motion forces of such tremendous power and instantaneous action that the entire space would instantly be one flame, of an intensity that no conceivable matter could withstand.

He had taken extraordinary precautions to guard the works from the curiosity and cunning of the creatures, protecting the button that controlled the whole with a metallic cover, which was held closely to the floor by screws.

And now he looked upon the creatures, itemizing their hideousness, as if to prepare a paper descriptive of them for this gathering of scientific authorities. Pygmies, between three and four feet in height, immensely strong; long, thin, crooked limbs, in some of unequal length; squat, thick bodies; pointed heads, bald but for a tuft of hair at the crown; huge ears, that loosely flapped, dog-like; nose, little more than wide nostrils; mouth, a mere long slit, with protruding teeth; and eyes, ah! eyes that showed plainly far more than animal intelligence.

They were small, oblique, set closely together, of a beady black, their only lids being a whitish membrane that swept them at intervals—but they sparkled and glowed with passion, dimmed with tears, and widened with thought. Those eyes, more than a score of them, were fixed upon him now with entreaty, menace, fear, revolt, and, most of all, judgment burning in their depths. Even the smaller ones, of which there were many in various sizes, eyed him with resentment and hate, while scurrying, like frightened rats, from corner to corner as he moved about.

Let accident put him for a moment in their power, and the whole pack would be upon him, and tear him to shreds, as they would any human being. Yet so strange, so monstrous was this unprecedented creation, mingling of lowest animal ferocity and human mind and soul, that he had found it quite possible to teach them to read and write, and work mathematical problems, and they were perhaps capable of considerable education—but without one redeeming trait. Earth had no place for such.

Their taste for blood was appalling; of all the food he offered, they preferred raw meat, the more gory the better. He had provided a quantity to employ them while he was away, and left them snarling over it.

He tried to put all thought of them behind him as he locked the doors. For a few hours he would be free, rid of torment and anticipation. But a deep melancholy shadowed the happiness of his reunion with his family, and gloom sat with him at the banquet-table. He took no part in the festivities and discussions, and was so manifestly unfit to do so that none urged him. Only when the distinguished guest touched on the subject of the possibility—or impossibility, as he viewed it—of producing life chemically, did he rouse to interest.

"It can never be done," asserted the guest, "for the giving of the breath of life is the prerogative of the Omnipotent alone."

"Ah, but Professor Levison believes otherwise, and hopes some day to astonish us by exhibiting a creature which he has created, but whether beast or human we will have to wait for time to reveal!" one said, with light sarcasm.

"And in the impossibility to determine beforehand what the creation shall be lies my objection to man's assuming the responsibility, even if he could by any means attain to it. For who could say what a calamity might not be brought upon humanity in the shape of some detestable monstrosity, whose evil propensities would be beyond control? Science has a large field for research; one need not step aside to intrude where success, if possible, might mean widespread disaster."

The Professor shrank as from a blow, and the desire he had momentarily felt to exhibit his creation to the scoffers, and prove the reality of his assumption, died out in despair as he thought what an intolerable, devilish curse that creation was.

No, nothing remained but silence and annihilation. He wondered, vaguely, as to the state of himself and his creatures in that place beyond the seething crucible of fire through which they would shortly pass together.

His wife was alarmed at his worn face and the dull apathy with which he spoke of the meeting, to which he had formerly looked with such eagerness.

"Dear," she said, pleadingly, "you are wearing yourself out; drop everything, and rest. What will all the experiments and discoveries in the world matter to us if we have not you? Come, take a vacation, and let us go on our long-planned visit."

"I cannot now," he said, so decisively that she felt it useless to insist.

"At any rate, you can give yourself a few hours' rest. Do not go back to the laboratory tonight."

"Oh, but I must!" he exclaimed. Then, taking her in his arms, he added: "My dearest, I cannot stay now, but I am planning to take a long rest soon." This was for her comfort afterwards.

He gazed at his sleeping children with yearning tenderness, and took leave of her with a solemn finality of manner that increased her anxiety. "It is as if he never expected to see us again," she murmured, tearfully.

From his study he could hear the creatures leaping, laughing, wrangling, forgetful as children of the impending fate they so clearly realized in his presence. He pitied, but could not save, them.

And now the hour had come—all things waited the last act. But, like the condemned criminal taking leave of earth in a last lingering gaze, he longed for another farewell glimpse of the home he would enter no more.

Going to the anteroom he threw open the shutter, and leaned out. How quiet the night! With what divine precision all things ran their appointed course, held and guided by Omnipotence! He lifted his heart in a prayer for protection and blessing upon the silent house which contained his dear ones. How dear he had never known till this sad hour in—

What was it? Had the day of doom burst in all its terrible grandeur? The earth rocked with awful thunderings, the very heavens were blotted out with belching flame—then, suddenly, silence and darkness enveloped him.

He opened his eyes, and looked about with feeble efforts at thought. He was in his own bed, and surely that was his wife's dear face, bathed in happy tears, bending over him, asking: "Dear husband, are you better? Do you know me?"

He nodded, smiling faintly; then memory returned, and a stream of questions rushed from his lips.

"Hush! Hush!" She stopped him with her soft hand. "Be quiet. I will tell you all, for I know you will not rest otherwise. There was a fearful explosion at the laboratory, so fearful that it was heard across the city; the whole building seemed to burst out at once into flame, and—oh, my dearest!—we feared you were in it; but a kind providence must have sent you to the outer room, for you were blown through the hall-window, and you were rescued from the burning debris." She paused to control her emotion.

"How long?" he asked.

"Three weeks, and you have been in a raging fever till two days ago."

"Was all destroyed?" he breathed, anxiously.

"Yes dear; everything. Nothing was left but a few scraps of twisted metal. But we will not mind that when your precious life was spared. You can rebuild when you are entirely recovered."

"I belong to you and the children now," he murmured, in ambiguous answer, drawing her face down to his, feeling his stored life not his own.

It was clear to him what had happened. The creatures had loosened the screws of the cap covering the knob, and had themselves brought about their destruction. With a thankful sigh, he fell into a restful slumber.

A DISSATISFIED SOUL

by *Annie Trumbull Slosson*

1904

The ninth of ten children born to a Connecticut merchant and politician, Annie Trumbull (baptized Anna) attended the Hartford Female Seminary, one of the first major colleges for female students in the United States. In 1867, she married a New York lawyer named Edward Slosson; the couple had no children.

Several of her relatives were active in literary, scientific, and religious life, and at the time of her death, Annie was better known for her work in the field of entomology than for her fiction. Three species bear her name: Coelioxys slossoni, *a leaf-cutter bee;* Rhopalotria slossoni, *a weevil; and* Zethus slossonae, *a wasp.*

She wrote in the regionalist "local color" style that was popular in the late eighteenth and early twentieth centuries. Many of her short stories were published in The Atlantic Monthly *and* Harper's Bazaar, *and subsequently collected into book form. "A Dissatisfied Soul" was published in 1904, bound together with "A Prophetic Romancer," whose narrator meets her soul mate after discovering that they have both been struggling to compose the same story.*

"A Dissatisfied Soul" is a gentle sort of ghost story, about a friend who returns from the dead and, at first, carries on with her life as though nothing had happened. Her neighbors are full of questions that they do not quite know how to ask, but in the imperturbable Yankee fashion they accept things as they are. Even so, certain metaphysical problems cannot be ignored. While it is not the most terrifying tale in this collection, its gentle humanity and light touch upon profound issues make it quite satisfying.

I t was when Elder Lincoln was supplying the pulpit of the old Union Meeting-House in Franconia. He was a Congregationalist, but was always styled Elder, as was also any clergyman of any denomination; it was, and is now, considered there the fit and proper title for a minister. There were three places of worship in the village representing as many denominations, called colloquially by the residents the Congo, the Freewill, and the Second-Ad, these names being "short" for the Congregationalist, Freewill Baptist, and Second-Adventist churches.

The Congregationalists and Baptists held their services in the same house of worship, each taking its turn, yearly I think, in providing a clergyman. Elder Lincoln was the choice of the Congos at that time, a dear, simple-hearted old man whom we loved well.

We were sitting together, the good Elder and I, on the piazza of the little inn—it was when Uncle Eben kept it—and talking quietly of many things. I do not recall just how it came about, but I know that our conversation at last veered around to the subject of the soul's immortality, its condition immediately after it left the body, possible probation, and the intermediate state, technically so called. In the midst of this talk I saw an odd look upon the face of the Elder, a sort of whimsical smile, as if he were thinking of something not so grave as the topic of which we talked, and when he spoke, his words seemed strangely irrelevant. "Do you know," he asked, "who has taken the old mill-house on the Landaff road, the one, you know, where Captain Noyes lived?" I did not know; I had heard that somebody had lately moved into the old house, but had not heard the name of the new occupant.

"Well," said the Elder, still with that quaint smile upon his face, "before you form any definite opinions upon this subject of the intermediate state you should talk with the good woman who lives in that old house." He would not explain further, save to tell me that Mrs. Weaver of Bradford had taken the house, that she was an elderly woman, practically alone in the world, anxious to know her new neighbors and to make new friends.

It was largely owing to this hint that, soon after our Sunday evening talk, I came to know Mrs. Apollos Weaver, to gain her friendship and confidence, and to hear her strange story.

It was not told me all at one time, but intermittently as the summer days went by. Yet every word of the tale was spoken in the old mill-house, and I never pass that ancient brown dwelling, standing high above the road on its steep, grassy bank, with the two tall elms in front, the big lilac bush at the door, and the cinnamon rosebushes straggling down to the road, that I do not think of Mrs. Weaver and her story.

It was not in reply to any question of mine that she told it, for, notwithstanding Elder Lincoln's suggestion, I somehow shrank from asking her directly about her theological views and beliefs. I had received a telegram one day relating to a business matter, and as I sat with Mrs. Weaver at the open door of the mill-house, I spoke of it, and of the nervous dread the sight of one of those dull yellow envelopes always brought me.

"Yes," she said, "they're scary things, any way you take it; but sometimes the writing one is worse than getting one. I never shall forget, as long as I live, the time I tried and tried, till I thought I should go crazy trying, to put just the right words, and not more than ten of them, into a telegraph to John Nelson. Over and over I went with it, saying the words to myself, and trying to pick out something that would sort of break the news easy, and yet have him sense it without any mistake: 'Maria has come back, don't be scared, all well here.' No, the first part of that was too dreadful sudden.

'Don't be surprised to hear Maria is with us now!' Oh no, how could he help being surprised, and how could I help making him so?

"For you see, Maria was dead and buried, and had been for three whole weeks!

"John Nelson had stood by her dying bed at the very end; he'd been at the funeral, one of the mourners, being her own half-brother and her nighest relation. He was the last one of the family to view the remains, and had stayed behind with Mr. Weaver and one of the neighbors to see the grave filled up. So to hear she was staying with us now would be amazing enough to him, however I could break it or smooth it down. It was amazing to us, and is now to look back at, only we sort of got used to it after a spell, as you do to anything.

"Maria Bliven wasn't a near relation of ours, being only my first husband's sister,—I was Mrs. Bliven when I married Mr. Weaver, you know,—but she had lived with us off and on for years, and she'd been buried from our house. Mr. Weaver'd been real good about having her there, though lots of men wouldn't have been, she belonging, as you might say, to another dispensation, my first husband's relations. The fact was, she didn't stay to our house long enough at a time for anybody to get tired of her,—never stayed anywheres long enough for that. She was the fittiest, restlessest, changeablest person I ever saw or heard of; and never, never quite satisfied. A week in one place was enough, and more than enough, for Maria. She'd fidget and fuss and walk up and down, and twitch her feet and wiggle her fingers, and make you too nervous for anything, if she had to stay in one spot twenty-four hours, I was going to say. So always just as I was going to be afraid Mr. Weaver would get sick of seeing Maria around and having a distant relation like her at the table every meal, she'd come down some morning with her carpet-bag in her hand, and say she guessed she'd go over to Haverhill and spend a few days with Mrs. Deacon Colby, or she'd take the cars for Newbury or Fairlee to visit with the Bishops or Captain Sanborn's folks, and sometimes as far as Littleton to Jane Spooner's. Then Mr. Weaver and me, we'd have a nice quiet spell all to ourselves, and just when we were ready for a change and a mite of company and talk, Maria would come traipsing back. Something didn't suit her, and she wasn't satisfied, but she'd always have lots of news to tell, and we were glad to see her.

"Off and on, off and on, that was Maria all over, and more off than on. Why, the time she got her last sickness—the last one, I mean, before the time I'm telling you about—it was her getting so restless after she'd been staying three or four days with Aunt Ellen Bragg over to Piermont, and starting for home in a driving snowstorm. She got chilled through and through, took lung fever, and only lived about ten days.

"We did everything we could for her, had the best doctor in the neighborhood, and nursed her day and night. Mr. Weaver was real kind, she being only a distant relation, but nothing could raise her up, and she died. We had a real nice funeral, Elder Fuller attending it, and we buried her in our own lot next to Mr. Bliven. It seemed dreadful quiet, and so queer to think at this time she'd gone for good and all, and that she'd got to stay now where she was, and not keep coming back in her restless, changing kind of way whether she was satisfied or not. I really did miss her, and I believe Mr. Weaver did, too, though he wouldn't own it.

"And here she was, and here was I half crazy over making up a telegraph to tell John Nelson about it.

"She'd been gone just exactly three weeks to a day, she having died the 11th of March, and it being now the second day of April.

"I was sitting at the window about ten o'clock in the forenoon peeling potatoes for dinner. I'd brought them into the sitting-room because it had a better lookout and was lighter and pleasanter in the morning. It was an early spring that year, though it came out real wintry afterwards, and the grass was starting up, and the buds showing on the trees, and somehow I got thinking about Maria. She was always glad when it came round spring, and she could get about more and visit with folks, and I was thinking where she was, and how she could ever stand it with her changing ways, to stay put, as you might say. Just then I looked out from the window over towards the river and the bridge, and I saw a woman coming. The minute I saw her I says to myself, 'She walks something like Maria Bliven.' She was coming along pretty quick, though not exactly hurrying, and she had somehow a real Bliven way about her. She came straight on in the direction of our house, and the closer she came, the more she walked like Maria. I didn't think it was her, of course, but it gave me a queer feeling to see anybody that favored her so much. The window was open, and I got nearer and nearer to it, and at last stretched my head out and stared down the street, a potato in one hand and the knife in the other. The sun was warm when you were out in it, exercising, and I saw the woman untying her bonnet-strings and throwing them back. Dear me! that was a real Bliven trick. I'd seen Maria do it herself fifty times. She was getting pretty nigh now, and the first thing I knew she looked up at the house and nodded her head just as Maria used to when she came home from visiting. Then in a minute I saw her plain as day. It was Maria Bliven, sure enough; there was no mistaking her.

"I see by your face what you are thinking about; it's what strikes every soul I ever tell this to. You're wondering why I take this so cool, as if it wasn't anything so much out of the common.

"Well, first place, it all happened a good many years ago, and I've gone through a heap of things since then, good and bad both, enough to wear off some of the remembering. And again, somehow, I took it kind of cool even then. It appeared to come about so natural, just in the course of things, as you might say, and only what you might have expected from Maria with her fitty, unsatisfied ways. And then—well, you'll see it yourself as I go on—there was something about Maria and the way she took it, and seemed to expect us to take it, that kept us from getting excited or scared or so dreadful amazed.

"Why, what do you think was the first and only single remark I made as she came in at the door just as she had come in fifty times before after visiting a spell? I says, 'Why, good-morning, Maria, you've come back.' And she says, 'Good-morning, Lyddy; yes, I have.'

"That was all, outside, I mean, for I won't deny there was a swimmy feeling in my head and a choky feeling down my throat, and a sort of trembly feeling all over as I see Maria drop into a chair and push her bonnet-strings a mite further back. She sat there a few minutes, I don't recollect just how long, and I don't seem to remember what either one of us said. Appears to me Maria made some remark about its being warm weather for the beginning of April, and that I said 'twas so. Then sometimes I seem to remember that I asked her if she'd walked all the way or got a lift any part of it. But it don't hardly appear as if I could have said such a foolish thing as that, and anyways, I don't recollect what she answered. But I know she got up pretty soon and said she guessed she'd go up and take off her things, and she went.

"There was one potato dished up that day for dinner with the skin on, and it must have been the one I was holding when I first caught sight of Maria down the road. So that goes to show I was a good deal flustered and upset, after all. The first thing was to tell Mr. Weaver. He was in the barn, and out I went. I didn't stop to break the news then, but gave it to him whole, right out. 'Polios,' I says, all out of breath, 'Maria Bliven's come back. She's in her bedroom this minute, taking off her things.' I never can bring back to my mind what he said first. He took it kind of calm and cool, as he always took everything that ever happened since I first knew him. And in a minute he told me to go and telegraph to John Nelson. You see, besides John's being Maria's nearest relation, he had charge of the little property she'd left, and so 't was pretty important he should know right off that she hadn't left it for good.

"Now I've got back to where I begun about that telegraph. Well, I sent it, and John came over from Hanover next day. I can't go on in a very regular, straightahead way with this account now, but I'll tell what went on as things come into my head, or I'll answer any questions you want to ask as you appear so interested. Everything went on natural and in the old way after the first. Of course, folks found out pretty quick. Bradford's a small place now, and 'twas smaller then, and I don't suppose there was a man, woman, or child there that didn't know within twenty-four hours that Maria had come back. There was some talk naturally, but not as much as you'd think. Folks dropped in, and when they'd see her looking about as she did before she left, and we going on just the same, why, they got used to it themselves, and the talk most stopped.

"But though they thought she was the same as she used to be, I knew she wasn't. It's hard to put it into words to make you understand, but Maria hadn't been many hours in the house before I saw she was dreadful changed. First place, she didn't talk near so much. Before she left she was a great hand to tell about all her doings after she'd been on one of her visits. She'd go all over it to Mr. Weaver and me, and it was real interesting. But she never said one single word now about anything that had happened since we saw her last, where she'd been, what she'd done, or anything. She and me, we were together by ourselves a great deal, more than ever before, in fact, for somehow the neighbors didn't come in as much as they used to. Maria was always pleasant to them, but though they said she was just the same as ever, with nothing queer or alarming about her, I saw they didn't feel quite at home with her now, and didn't drop in so often. But sit together, she and me, hours at a time as we might, never one word of what I couldn't help hankering to know passed Maria's lips. Why didn't I ask her, you say? Well, I don't know. Seems to me now, as I think it all over, that I would do it if I could only have the chance again. You wouldn't hardly believe how I wish and wish now it's too late that I had asked her things I'm just longing to know about, now I'm growing old and need to look ahead a little, and particular now Mr. Weaver's gone, and I'm so hungry to know something about him, we having lived together most fifty years, you know. But there was something about Maria that kept me from asking. And sometimes I think there was something that kept her from telling. I feel sure she was on the point of making some statement sometimes, but she couldn't; the words wouldn't come; there didn't seem to be any way of putting the information into words she knew, or that was used in our part of the country, anyway. Dear me, what lots of times I've heard her begin something this way, 'When I first got there, I'—'Before I come back, I'—Oh, how I'd prick up my ears, and most stop breathing to hear! But she'd just stop, seem to be a-thinking about something way, way off, and never, never finish her remarks. Yes, I know you wonder I didn't question her about things. As I said before, I can't hardly explain why I didn't. But there was something about her looks and her ways, something that, spite of her being the old Maria Bliven I had lived in and out with so many years, somehow made her most like a stranger that I couldn't take liberties with.

"Mr. Weaver and me, of course, we talked about it when we were all by ourselves, mostly at night, when it was still and dark. It did seem real strange and out of the common someways. Neither one of us had ever had anything like it happen before to anybody we knew or heard of. Folks who'd died, generally—no, always, I guess, up to this time—died for good, and stayed dead. We were brought up Methodists; we were both professors, and knew our Bibles and the doctrines of the church pretty well. We knew about two futures for the soul—the joyful, happy one for the good and faithful, and the dreadful one for the wicked. And we'd always been learnt that to one of these localities the soul went the very minute, or second, it left the body. That there were folks that held different opinions, and thought there was a betwixt and between district where you stayed on the road, where even the good and faithful might rest and take breath before going into the wonderful glory prepared for them, and where the poor, mistaken, or ignorant, or careless souls would be allowed one more chance of choosing the right, we didn't know that. I never'd heard of that doctrine then, though a spell after that I hardly heard anything else.

"I don't know as I told you about Elder Janeway from down South somewhere coming on board with us one summer. He was writing a book called Probation and he had a way of reading out loud what he was writing in a preaching kind of way, so that you couldn't help hearing it all, even if you wanted to. And all day long, while I sat sewing or knitting, or went about my work, baking and ironing and all, I'd hear that solemn, rumbling voice of his going on about the 'place of departed spirits,' the Scripture proofs of there being such a place, what it was like, how long folks stayed there, and I don't know what all. That was just before I came down with the fever that I most died with, as I was telling you the other day, and they say this talk of the Elder's appeared to run in my mind when I was light-headed and wandering, and I'd get dreadful excited about it.

"But at the time I was telling about I hadn't heard this, so Mr. Weaver and I would talk it over and wonder and guess and suppose. 'Oh, Polios,' I whispered one night, 'you don't presume Maria is a—ghost?' 'No more than you be,' says Mr. Weaver, trying to whisper, but not doing it very well, his voice naturally being a bass one. 'Ghosts,' he says, 'are all in white, and go about in a creepy way, allowing there are any such things, which I don't.' 'But what else can she be, Polios,' I says, 'she having died and been buried, and now back again? Where's she, or her soul or spirit, been these three weeks, since that?'

"'Well, come to that, I don't know,' Mr. Weaver would say. And he didn't. No more did I.

"Where had she come from that morning when she appeared so unexpected as I sat peeling the potatoes? Not a single soul had seen her, as far as we could find out, before the very minute I catched sight of her at the turn of the road. Folks had been at their windows or doors, or in their yards all along that very road for miles back, and on the two different roads that come into the main one there were plenty of houses full of people, but nobody, not one of them, saw her go by. There was Almy Woolett, whose whole business in life was to know who passed her house, and what they did it for. She was at her front window every minute that forenoon, and it looked right out on the road, not fifteen foot back of where I first saw Maria, and she never saw her.

"Then, as to what clothes she came in, folks have asked me about that, and I can't give them a mite of satisfaction. For the life of me I can't remember what she had on before she went up to her room and took off her things. I'm certain sure she wasn't wearing what she went away in, for that was a shroud. In those days, you know, bodies was laid out in regular appropriate burying things, made for the occasion, instead of being dressed all up like living beings, as they do nowadays. And Maria didn't come back in that way, or I might have thought her a ghost sure enough. Sometimes I seem to recollect that she had on something sort of grayish, not black or white, but just about the color of those clouds out there, just over the mill, almost the color of nothing, you might say. But there, I ain't sure, it's so long ago. But I know she had on something I never'd seen her wear before, and she never wore again, for when she came downstairs she was dressed in her old blue gingham, with a white tie apron. I own up I did look about everywheres I could think of for the things she came in, but I couldn't find them high nor low. Nor a sign of them was there in her bedroom, in the closet or chest of drawers, or her little leather trunk, and I'm certain sure they wasn't anywheres in the house when I ransacked for them, and that wasn't two hours after Maria came back.

"It's only little specks of things I can tell you about that happened after this; anything, I mean, that had to do with her queer experience. I watched her close, and took notice of the least thing that seemed to bear on that. She complained a good deal of being lonesome, and when I recommended her going out more and visiting with the neighbors, she'd say so sorrowful and sad, 'There ain't anybody of my kind here, not a single one; I'm all alone in the world.' And, take it one way, she was.

"One day she and me were sitting together in the kitchen, and one of Billy Lane's boys came to the door to borrow some saleratus.* After he'd

---

* Sodium bicarbonate.

gone, I says to Maria, 'I told you, didn't I, that Billy Lane died last month? He died of lockjaw, and it came on so sudden and violent he wasn't able to tell how he hurt himself. They found a wound on his foot, but don't know how it came.' 'Oh,' says Maria, as quiet and natural as you please, 'he told me he stepped on a rusty nail down by the new fence.' I was just going to speak up quick, and ask how in the world he could have told her that, when he didn't die till a week after she did, when she started, put on one of her queer looks, and says, 'There, I forgot to shut my blinds, and it's real sunny,' and went upstairs.

"The first death that we had in Bradford after her coming back was little Susan Garret. We'd heard she was sick, but didn't know she was dangerous, and were dreadful surprised when Mr. Weaver came in to supper and told us she was dead. I felt sorry for Mrs. Garret, a widow with only one other child, and that a sickly boy, but I must say I was surprised to see how Maria took it to heart. She turned real white, kept twisting her hands together, and sort of moaning out, 'Oh, I wish I'd knowed she was going, I wish I'd knowed. If she'd only wait just a minute for me,' and crazy, nervy things like that. I had to get her upstairs and give her some camphor and make her lay down, she was so excited like. She didn't calm down right away, and when I heard her say sort of to herself, 'Oh, if I could only a seen her!' I says, 'Why, Maria, you can see her. We'll run right over there now. I guess they've laid the poor child out by this time, and they'll let us see the body.' Such a look as Maria gave me, real scornful, as you might say, as she says, 'That! See that! What good would it do to see that, I want to know.' Why, I tell you it made me feel for a minute as if a body was of no account at all, leastways in Maria's opinion. And yet she'd used hers to come back in anyways! 'Twas quite a spell before she cooled down, and she never explained why it worked her up so, and I'm sure I don't know. Whether it was because she thought little Susan had gone to the place she herself had come away from, and wished she had known in time to go back along with her just for company, or again, whether she felt bad because she hadn't had a chance to give the child some advice or directions that would have helped her along on the road that Maria knew and nobody else probably in all that county did know, why, I haven't an idea.

"I believe I told you a ways back that after she got home Maria all the time had a kind of look and way as if she'd done something she hadn't ought to done, or was somewhere she hadn't any business to be, somehow as if she belonged somewhere else.

"In the old days she wasn't ever satisfied long at a time in any place, but she was always pleased to get back, leastways for a spell. But from the minute she came this time she was troubled and worried. And that grew on her. She was always sort of listening and watching, as if she expected something to happen, starting at the least bit of noise, and jumping if anybody knocked or even came by the gate. She got dreadful white, and so poor she didn't weigh no more than a child, and such little trifling things worked her up. For instance, we had heard a spell before, Mr. Weaver and me, that Mr. Tewksbury over at South Newbury was dead, and we believed it, not knowing anything to the contrary. But one day Mr. Weaver came in and he says, 'Lyddy, you recollect we heard the other day that Silas Tewksbury was dead? Well, I met him just now coming over the bridge.' Maria was in the room, and first thing we knew she gave a kind of screech, and put her two hands together, and she says, 'Oh no, no, no, not another of us! I thought 't was only me. Oh, deary, deary me, that's what they meant. They said it wouldn't end with me; they begged me not to try; and now I've started it, and it won't never stop. They'll all come back, all, every single one of 'em,' and she cried and moaned till we were at our wits' ends what to do. It wasn't till she found out that Mr. Tewksbury hadn't ever died at all, but 't was his brother at White River Junction that was taken off, that she got quiet.

"So it went on, Maria sort of wearing out with worrying and grieving about something she couldn't seem to tell us about except by little hintings and such, and Mr. Weaver and me, we wondering and surmising and talking all alone nights in whispers. We didn't understand it, of course, but we'd made up our minds on one or two points, and agreed on them. Maria had never been to heaven, we felt sure of that. There were lots of reasons for that belief, but one is enough. Nobody, even the most discontented and changeablest being ever made, would leave that place of perfect rest and peace for this lonesome, dying, changing world, now would they? And as for the other locality, why, I just know certain, certain sure she'd never been there. That would have showed in her face, and her talk, and her ways. If it is one little mite like what I've always been learnt it is, one minute, one second spent there would alter you so dreadfully you'd never be recognized again by your nighest and dearest. And Maria was a good woman, a Christian woman. Her biggest fault was only her fretting and finding fault, and wanting to change about and find something better. Oh no, no; wherever Maria Bliven had come from that morning in April it wasn't from that place of punishment, we felt sure of that, Mr. Weaver and me. As I said once before, we hadn't heard then that there was any other place for the dead to go to. But from things Maria let drop, and the way she behaved, and our own thinking and studying over it, we began to come to this, that maybe there was a stopping-place on the road before it forked—to put it into this world's sort of talk—where folks could rest and straighten out their beliefs and learn what to expect, how to look at things, and try and be tried. Last summer I heard a new word, and it struck me hard. Mrs. Deacon Spinner told me her son had gone off to learn new ways of farming and gardening and such. She said they had places nowadays where they learnt boys all that and they called them 'Experiment Stations.' The minute I heard that I says to myself, 'That's the name! That's what the place where Maria came back from, and that Elder Janeway knew so much about, had ought to be called, an Experiment Station.' But at that time, in Maria's day, I'd never heard of this name no more than I had of Elder Janeway, and the place or state he was always writing and talking about. But, after all, I don't believe I care to go back on what ma and pa and all the good folks of old times held on those subjects. There wasn't any mincing matters those days; 'twas the very best or the very worst for everybody as soon as they departed this life, and no complaints made. I'm certain sure any of those ancestors of mine, particular on the Wells side—that was pa's, you know—would have taken the worst, and been cheerful about it, too, rather than have had the whole plan upset and a half-and-half place interduced. But then, if there ain't such a locality, where in the world did Maria come from that time? I tell you, it beats me.

"Now this very minute something comes into my head that I haven't told you about, that I don't believe I ever told anybody about; I don't know as I can tell it now. It is like a sound that comes to you from way, way off, that you think you catch, and then it's gone. It was just only a word Maria used two or three times after she came back, a dreadful, dreadful curious word. It wasn't like any word I ever heard spoke or read in a book; 'twasn't anything I can shape out in my mind to bring back now. First time I heard it she was sitting on the doorstep at night, all by herself. It was a nice night with no moon, but thousands of shining little stars, and the sky so sort of dark bluish and way, way off. Maria didn't know I was nigh, but I was, and I was peeking at her as she sat there. She looked up right overhead at the sky, and the shining and the blue, and then she spoke that word, that curious, singular word. I say she spoke it, and that I heard it, but somehow that don't make it plain what I mean. Seems if she only meant it, thought it, and I sort of catched it, felt it—oh, that sounds like crazy talk, I know, but I can't do any better. Somehow I knew without using my ears that she was saying or thinking a word, the strangest, meaningest, oh, the curiousest word! And once she said it in her sleep when I went into her room in the night, and another time as she sat by her own grave in the little burying-ground, and I had followed her there unbeknownst. I tell you, that wasn't any word they use in Vermont, or in the United States, or anywheres in this whole living world. It was a word Maria brought back, I'm certain sure from—well, wherever she'd been that time.

"Well, it was wearing to see Maria those days, growing poorer and poorer, and bleacheder and bleacheder, and failing up steady as the days went by. And one day just at dusk, when she and me were sitting by ourselves, I mustered up courage to speak out. 'Maria,' I says, 'you don't appear to be satisfied these times.'

"'Satisfied!' she says, 'course I ain't. Was I ever satisfied in all my born days? Wasn't that the trouble with me from the beginning? Ain't it that got me into all this dreadful trouble? Deary, deary me, if I'd only a stayed where'—She shut up quick and sudden, looking so mournful and sorry and wore out that I couldn't hold in another minute, and I burst out, 'Maria, if you feel that way about it, and I can see myself it's just killing you, why in the world don't you—go back again?' I was scared as soon as I'd said it, but Maria took it real quiet. 'Don't you suppose I've thought of that myself?' she says. 'I ain't thought of much else lately, I tell you. But as far's I know, and I know a lot more than you do about it, there ain't but just one way to there, and that,' she says, speaking kind of low and solemn, 'that is—the way—I went before. And I own up, Lyddy,' says she, 'I'm scaret o' that way, and I scursely dast to do it again.' 'But,' I says, getting bolder when I saw she wasn't offended at my speaking, 'you say yourself you ain't sure. Maybe there is some other way of getting back; there's that way—well, that way you came from there, you know.'

"'That's different,' says Maria. But I saw she was thinking and studying over something all the evening, and after she went to her bedroom she was walking about, up and down, up and down, the biggest part of the night. In the morning when it got to be nigh on to seven o'clock, and she not come down, I felt something had happened, and went up to her room. She wasn't there. The bed was made up, and everything fixed neat and nice, and she had gone away.

"'Oh, dear,' I says to Mr. Weaver, 'that poor thing has started off all alone, weak as she is, to find her way back.' 'Back where?' says Polios. Just as if I knew.

"But we both agreed on one point. We couldn't do anything. We felt to realize our own ignorance, and that this was a thing Maria must cipher out by herself, or with somebody that was way, way above us to help her. It was a dreadful long day, I tell you. I couldn't go about my work as if nothing had happened, and I couldn't get out of my head for one single minute that poor woman on her curious, lonesome travels. Would she find the road? I kept a-thinking to myself, and it was a hard, dark one like the one everybody else had to go on before they got to the afterwards-life, a valley full of shadows, according to Scripture, with a black, deep river to ford, a 'swelling flood,' as the hymn says?

"Well, the day went by somehow,—most days do, however slow they seem to drag along,—and the night came on. Though we didn't mean to meddle or interfere in this matter, Mr. Weaver and me, we had asked a few questions of folks who dropped in or went by that day. Maria had been seen by people all along the same road she had come home by that other time, and on both the roads that joined it. Two or three, seeing how beat out and white she looked, had offered her a ride, but whichever direction they were going she had always answered the same thing, that she wasn't going their way. It was nigh nine o'clock, and we were just shutting up the house for the night, when I heard steps outside and the gate screaked.

"I felt in a minute that it was Maria, and I opened the door as quick as I could. There she was trying to get up the steps, and looking just ready to drop and die right there and then. It took Polios and me both to get her in and upstairs. It wasn't any time for questions, but when Mr. Weaver had gone, and I was getting her to bed, I says, as I saw her white face with that dreadful look of disappointedness, 'You poor thing, you're all beat out.' 'Yes,' she whispers, her voice most gone she was so wore out, 'and I couldn't find the road. There ain't but one,—leastways to go there by,—and, that's the way I went first-off. I'd oughter known it. I'd oughter known it.'

"I couldn't bear to see her so sorrowful and troubled, and I said what I could to comfort her by using Scripture words and repeating the promises made there about that dark valley and the deep waters, and the help and company provided for the journey. But that mournful look never left her face, and she kept a-whispering, 'That's for once; not a word about the second time. Mebbe there ain't any provision for the second time.' And what could I say?

"I believe I haven't told you how much time the poor woman spent those days in the graveyard, sitting by her own grave. I can't get over that, even after all these years, that queer, uncommon sight of a person watching over their own burying place, weeding it and watering it as if their own nighest friend lay there. I don't see why, either. I don't even know whether her body was there. Folks don't have two, and she'd brought one back, and was in it now. And, as far as we could see, it was the very same body she wore when she died, and that we'd buried next to Mr. Bliven. Anyway, she appeared to like that place, and showed a lot of interest in taking care of it. There wasn't any headstone. We had ordered one, but it hadn't come home when she returned, and we had told Mr. Stevens to keep it a spell till we fixed what to do about it. I was glad it wasn't up. I can't think of anything that would be more trying than to see your own gravestone with your name and age and day you died, with a consoling verse, all cut out plain on it. I know, one time, I saw her putting a bunch of sweet-williams on that grave. She looked sort of ashamed when she saw I was watching her, and she says, a mite bashful, 'You know they was always her favorite posies.' 'Whose?' I asked, just to see what she'd say. But she was so busy fixing the sweet-williams she didn't take any notice.

"Maria failed up after this right along, and pretty soon she was that weak she couldn't get as far as the graveyard, hardly even down to the gate. And

I says to Mr. Weaver that she needn't worry about finding the way back to where she belonged, for she'd just go as she went the other time if she didn't flesh up and get a little ruggeder. One day, when I went into her room, she says to me, 'Lyddy, I want help, and mebbe I can get it in the old way we used to try. You fetch me the big Bible and let me open it without looking, and put my finger on a verse and then you read it out. Mebbe they'll take that way of telling me what to do, just mebbe.'

"I never approved of that kind of getting help, it always seemed like tempting Providence, but I felt I must do most anything that would help satisfy that poor woman, and I got the Bible. She opened it, her lean hands shaking, and she laid one of her bony fingers on a passage. I must say it took my breath away when I saw how appropriate it was, how pat it came in. 'Twas in Ezekiel, and it went this way: 'He shall not return by the gate whereby he came in.'

"Maria give a sort of cry and laid her head back against the pillow on the big chair she was sitting in. 'There, there,' she says, all shaking and weak, 'I most knew it afore, and now I'm certain sure. I've got to go—the—old—way.'

"And so she did. After all, I wasn't with her when she went, and it wasn't from our house she started. I got run down and pindling from taking care of her and studying how to help her out of her troubles. So Mr. Weaver wrote to John Nelson, and after a spell it was fixed that he should take Maria over to his house in Hanover, and he did. It was a hard journey for her, so weak as she was, and she didn't stand it very well. But she had one more journey to take, the one she'd been dreading so long, and trying to put off.

"It wasn't so dreadful hard, I guess, after all, for they said she fell asleep at the last like a baby. Just before she went, she says very quiet and calm, all the worry and fret gone out of her voice, she says to John and Harriet, who was standing by the bed, 'I'm dreadful tired, and I guess I'll drowse off a mite. And mebbe I'll be let to go in my sleep.' Then in a minute she says slow and sleepy, her eyes shut up, 'And if I do, wherever they carry me this time, I guess when I wake up I shall—be—satisfied,' and she dropped off.

"I guess she was, for she went for good that time and stayed. She was buried there in Hanover in John's lot. We all thought 't was best. It would have been awk'ard about the old grave, you know, whether to open it or not, and what to do about the coffin. So we thought 't was better to start all over again as if 'twas the first time, with everything brand-new, and nothing second-handed, and we did. But Maria Bliven's the only person I know that's got two graves. There's only one headstone, though, for we took the one we'd ordered before from Mr. Stevens, he altering the reading on it a little to suit the occasion. You see, the first time we'd had on it a line that was used a good deal on gravestones then, 'Gone forever.' That didn't turn out exactly appropriate, so we had it cut out, and this time we had on—Elder Fuller put it into our heads—that Scripture verse, a good deal like Maria's dying words, though I don't believe she knew she was quoting when she said it, 'I shall be satisfied.'"

"Well," said good Elder Lincoln one July day as we met on the Lisbon road, "have you heard Mrs. Weaver's account of Maria Bliven's unexpected return?"

The Elder had been at Streeter Pond fishing for pickerel, for he belonged to that class styled by dear old Jimmy Whitcher "tishin' ministers." He had not met with great success that day, but he had been all the morning in the open, and there was about him a breezy, woodsy, free look which seemed to dissipate shadows, doubts, and dreads. "Yes," I replied, "I have heard it all. What in the world do you make of it?"

"Well, I don't make anything of it," said the Elder. "There's no conspicuous moral to that story. Mrs. Weaver did not make the most of her opportunities, and we do not gain much new light from her account. Old Cephas Janeway, who wrote a ponderous work on Probation which nobody read, was largely responsible, I guess, for the feverish dream of the old woman. But to her it's all true, real, something that actually happened. And, do you know, somehow I almost believe it myself as I listen to the homely details, and it brings 'thoughts beyond the reaches of our souls.'"

He was silent a minute, then taking up his fishing basket, very light in weight that day, he raised the lid, looked with unseeing eyes at its contents, and said absently, "I can't help wishing I had met Maria after she came back. There is just one thing"—He did not complete the sentence, and I saw that his thoughts were far away. With a good-by word which I know he did not hear, I turned aside, leaving him there in the dusty road.

THE READJUSTMENT

by Mary Austin

1908

Mary Hunter Austin was born in Illinois and graduated from Blackburn College in 1888. That same year, her family moved to California and established a homestead in the San Joaquin Valley. In 1891, she married Stafford Wallace Austin—apparently no relation—in Bakersfield.

Mary studied Native American life in the Mojave Desert, and became an outspoken advocate for Native American and Spanish-American rights as well as an early feminist. She wrote novels, poetry, and plays, most notably The Arrow Maker, *which drew on her familiarity with Paiute life. Her tribute to the deserts of California,* The Land of Little Rain *(1903), also won acclaim.*

Forced out of the Owens Valley in California's Water Wars, Mary's husband moved to Death Valley, while she joined the arts colony of Carmel-by-the-Sea, whose members included Jack London, Ambrose Bierce, and Sinclair Lewis. She plunged into the colony's bohemian lifestyle, but her interest waned after she was disappointed by a 1915 production of The Arrow Maker *in Carmel's Forest Theater, and her visits to Carmel became shorter.*

In 1918, she visited Santa Fe, with its growing artistic community. She helped establish the Santa Fe Little Theatre (still operating today as the Santa Fe Playhouse) and the Spanish Colonial Arts Society, and co-authored Taos Pueblo *with the photographer Ansel Adams.*

Mary died in Santa Fe in 1934. Mount Mary Austin, in the Sierra Nevada near her longtime home in Independence, California, was named in her honor.

"The Readjustment" was published in the April 1908 issue of Harper's *Magazine. It is an unusual story, in which a disapproving spirit is treated to a few home truths by a down-to-earth neighbor.*

Emma Jossylin had been dead and buried three days. The sister who had come to the funeral had taken Emma's child away with her, and the house was swept and aired; then, when it seemed there was least occasion for it, Emma came back. The neighbor woman who had nursed her was the first to know it. It was about seven of the evening, in a mellow gloom: the neighbor woman was sitting on her own stoop with her arms wrapped in her apron, and all at once she found herself going along the street under an urgent sense that Emma needed her. She was half-way down the block before she recollected that this was impossible, for Mrs. Jossylin was dead and buried, but as soon as she came opposite the house she was aware of what had happened. It was all open to the summer air; except that it was a little neater, not otherwise than the rest of the street. It was quite dark; but the presence of Emma Jossylin streamed from it and betrayed it more than a candle. It streamed out steadily across the garden, and even as it reached her, mixed with the smell of the damp mignonette, the neighbor woman owned to herself that she had always known Emma would come back.

"A sight stranger if she wouldn't," thought the woman who had nursed her. "She wasn't ever one to throw off things easily."

Emma Jossylin had taken death, as she had taken everything in life, hard. She had met it with the same hard, bright, surface competency that she had presented to the squalor of the encompassing desertness, to the insuperable commonness of Sim Jossylin, to the affliction of her crippled child; and the intensity of her wordless struggle against it had caught the attention of the townspeople and held it in a shocked, curious awe. She was so long a-dying, lying there in the little low house, hearing the abhorred footsteps going about her house and the vulgar procedure of the community encroach upon her like the advances of the sand wastes on an unwatered field.

For Emma had always wanted things different, wanted them with a fury of intentness that implied offensiveness in things as they were. And the townspeople had taken offence, the more so because she was not to be surprised in any inaptitude for their own kind of success. Do what you could, you could never catch Emma Jossylin in a wrapper after three o'clock in the afternoon. And she would never talk about the child—in a country where so little ever happened that even trouble was a godsend if it gave you something to talk about. It was reported that she did not even talk to Sim. But there the common resentment got back at her. If she had thought to effect anything with Sim Jossylin against the benumbing spirit of the place, the evasive hopefulness, the large sense of leisure that ungirt the loins, if she still hoped somehow to get away with him to some place for which by her dress, by her manner, she seemed forever and unassailably fit, it was foregone that nothing would come of it. They knew Sim Jossylin better than that. Yet so vivid had been the force of her wordless dissatisfaction that when the fever took her and she went down like a pasteboard figure in the damp, the wonder was that nothing toppled with her. And as if she too had felt herself indispensable, Emma Jossylin had come back.

The neighbor woman crossed the street, and as she passed the far corner of the gate, Jossylin spoke to her. He had been standing, she did not know how long a time, behind the syringa bush, and moved even with her along the fence until they came to the gate. She could see in the dusk that before speaking he wet his lips with his tongue.

"She's in there," he said at last.

"Emma?"

He nodded. "I been sleeping at the store since—but I thought I'd be more comfortable—as soon as I opened the door, there she was."

"Did you see her?"

"No."

"How do you know, then?"

"Don't you know?"

The neighbor felt there was nothing to say to that.

"Come in," he whispered, huskily. They slipped by the rose tree and the wistaria and sat down on the porch at the side. A door swung inward behind them. They felt the Presence in the dusk beating like a pulse.

"What do you think she wants?" said Jossylin. "Do you reckon it's the boy?"

"Like enough."

"He's better off with his aunt. There was no one here to take care of him, like his mother wanted." He raised his voice unconsciously with a note of justification, addressing the room behind.

"I am sending fifty dollars a month," he said; "he can go with the best of them." He went on at length to explain all the advantage that was to come to the boy from living at Pasadena, and the neighbor woman bore him out in it.

"He was glad to go," urged Jossylin to the room. "He said it was what his mother would have wanted."

They were silent then a long time, while the Presence seemed to swell upon them and encroached upon the garden. Finally, "I gave Zeigler the order for the monument yesterday," Jossylin threw out, appeasingly. "It's to cost three hundred and fifty." The Presence stirred. The neighbor thought she could fairly see the controlled tolerance with which Emma Jossylin threw off the evidence of Sim's ineptitude.

They sat on helplessly without talking after that, until the woman's husband came to the fence and called her.

"Don't go," begged Jossylin.

"Hush!" she said. "Do you want all the town to know? You had naught but good from Emma living, and no call to expect harm from her now.

It's natural she should come back—if—if she was lonesome like—in—the place where she's gone to."

"Emma wouldn't come back to this place," Jossylin protested, "without she wanted something."

"Well, then, you've got to find out," said the neighbor woman.

All the next day she saw, whenever she passed the house, that Emma was still there. It was shut and barred, but the Presence lurked behind the folded blinds and fumbled at the doors. When it was night and the moths began in the columbine under the window, it went out and walked in the garden.

Jossylin was waiting at the gate when the neighbor woman came. He sweated with helplessness in the warm dusk, and the Presence brooded upon them like an apprehension that grows by being entertained.

"She wants something," he appealed, "but I can't make out what. Emma knows she is welcome to everything I've got. Everybody knows I've been a good provider."

The neighbor woman remembered suddenly the only time she had ever drawn close to Emma Jossylin touching the child. They had sat up with it together all one night in some childish ailment, and she had ventured a question: "What does his father think?" And Emma had turned her a white, hard face of surpassing dreariness. "I don't know," she admitted; "he never says."

"There's more than providing," suggested the neighbor woman.

"Yes. There's feeling . . . but she had enough to do to put up with me. I had no call to be troubling her with such." He left off to mop his forehead, and began again.

"Feelings," he said; "there's times a man gets so wore out with feelings, he doesn't have them any more."

He talked, and presently it grew clear to the woman that he was voiding all the stuff of his life, as if he had sickened on it and was now done. It was a little soul knowing itself and not good to see. What was singular was that the Presence left off walking in the garden, came and caught like a gossamer on the ivy tree, swayed by the breath of his broken sentences. He talked, and the neighbor woman saw him for once as he saw himself and Emma, snared and floundering in an inexplicable unhappiness. He had been disappointed too. She had never relished the man he was, and it made him ashamed. That was why he had never gone away, lest he should make her ashamed among her own kind. He was her husband; he could not help that, though he was sorry for it. But he could keep the offence where least was made of it. And there was a child—she had wanted a child, but even then he had blundered—begotten a cripple upon her. He blamed himself utterly, searched out the roots of his youth for the answer to that, until the neighbor woman flinched to hear him. But the Presence stayed.

He had never talked to his wife about the child. How should he? There was the fact—the advertisement of his incompetence. And she had never talked to him. That was the one blessed and unassailable memory, that she had spread silence like a balm over his hurt. In return for it he had never gone away. He had resisted her that he might save her from showing among her own kind how poor a man he was. With every word of this ran the fact of his love for her—as he had loved her with all the stripes of clean and uncleanness. He bared himself as a child without knowing; and the Presence stayed. The talk trailed off at last to the commonplaces of consolation between the retchings of his spirit. The Presence lessened and streamed toward them on the wind of the garden. When it touched them like the warm air of noon that lies sometimes in hollow places after nightfall, the neighbor woman rose and went away.

The next night she did not wait for him. When a rod outside the town—it was a very little one—the burrowing owls whoowhooed, she hung up her apron and went to talk with Emma Jossylin. The Presence was there, drawn in, lying close. She found the key between the wistaria and the first pillar of the porch; but as soon as she opened the door she felt the chill that might be expected by one intruding on Emma Jossylin in her own house.

"'The Lord is my shepherd!'" said the neighbor woman; it was the first religious phrase that occurred to her; then she said the whole of the psalm, and after that a hymn. She had come in through the door, and stood with her back to it and her hand upon the knob. Everything was just as Mrs. Jossylin had left it, with the waiting air of a room kept for company.

"Em," she said, boldly, when the chill had abated a little before the sacred words—"Em Jossylin, I've got something to say to you. And you've got to hear," she added with firmness as the white curtains stirred duskily at the window. "You wouldn't be talked to about your troubles when . . . you were here before, and we humored you. But now there is Sim to be thought of. I guess you heard what you came for last night, and got good of it. Maybe it would have been better if Sim had said things all along instead of hoarding them in his heart, but, anyway, he has said them now. And what I want to say is, if you was staying on with the hope of hearing it again, you'd be making a mistake. You was an uncommon woman, Emma Jossylin, and there didn't none of us understand you very well, nor do you justice, maybe; but Sim is only a common man, and I understand him because I'm that way myself. And if you think he'll be opening his heart to you every night, or be any different from what he's always been on account of what's happened, that's a mistake, too . . . and in a little while, if you stay, it will be as bad as it always was . . . men are like that . . . you'd better go now while there's understanding between you." She stood staring into the darkling room that seemed suddenly full of turbulence and denial. It seemed to beat upon her and take her breath, but she held on.

"You've got to go . . . Em . . . and I'm going to stay until you do," she said with finality; and then began again:

"'The Lord is nigh unto them that are of a broken heart,'" and repeated the passage to the end.

Then, as the Presence sank before it, "You better go, Emma," persuasively: and again, after an interval:

"'He shall deliver thee in six troubles.

"'Yea, in seven there shall no evil touch thee.'" The Presence gathered itself and was still; she could make out that it stood over against the opposite corner by the gilt easel with the crayon portrait of the child.

"'For thou shalt forget thy misery. Thou shalt remember it as waters that are past,'" concluded the neighbor woman, as she heard Jossylin on the gravel outside. What the Presence had wrought upon him in the night was visible in his altered mien. He looked, more than anything else, to be in need of sleep. He had eaten his sorrow, and that was the end of it—as it is with men.

"I came to see if there was anything I could do for you," said the woman, neighborly, with her hand upon the door.

"I don't know as there is," said he. "I'm much obliged, but I don't know as there is."

"You see," whispered the woman, over her shoulder, "not even to me." She felt the tug of her heart as the Presence swept past her. The neighbor went out after that and walked in the ragged street, past the schoolhouse, across the creek below the town, out by the fields, over the headgate, and back by the town again. It was full nine of the clock when she passed the Jossylin house. It looked, except for being a little neater, not other than the rest of the street. The door was open and the lamp was lit; she saw Jossylin black against it. He sat reading in a book like a man at ease in his own house.

ACKNOWLEDGMENTS

I would like to thank the following people, without whom this book would never have been possible:

Lawrence Ellsworth's *Big Book of Swashbuckling Adventure* was the inspiration behind this and my other anthologies. Philip Turner, my agent, gave me an invaluable education in crafting solid book proposals. I am indebted to both.

William Claiborne Hancock and the rest of the staff at Pegasus Books have been a dream to work with: enthusiastic about my ideas, patient with my changes when I found a better story for a particular slot or nitpicked over the wording of promotional text, and solicitous of my opinions on cover designs and other production matters. Particular thanks are due to Jessica Case, Sabrina Plomitallo-González, Maria Fernandez, Bowen Dunnan, and Katie McGuire for their ruthlessness in hunting down typos, their forbearance when some typos turn out to be matters of period style, and their knack for turning my drab computer files into books that are pleasing to the eye both inside and out, and a joy to hold in the hand.

Thanks, too, to Meg Sherman and Sari Martin at W. W. Norton for handling promotions and making sure I always have books to sign at book signings!

Linda Biagi of Biagi Literary Management has done great work helping to bring my books to foreign audiences.

Thanks are also due to:

Jamie Paige Davis, my wife, my love, my friend, and my fellow author, who somehow manages to keep putting up with me;

Hammer Films and Universal Pictures, whose films I devoured on my parents' black-and-white TV during my youth;

Tony Ackland and Pete Knifton, renowned fantasy artists, with whom I spent many happy evenings discussing horror, history, music, and everything under the sun in Nottingham's many hostelries;

And, of course, the ladies in this book, from Mary Shelley to Harriet Beecher Stowe, who could have bowed to society's pressure and been satisfied with invisibility. You did not, and we are all the richer for it.

ABOUT THE EDITOR

GRAEME DAVIS has worked as a writer and editor in the games industry since 1986. His work includes the '90s gothic classic *Vampire: The Masquerade* and Games Workshop's acclaimed fantasy-horror tabletop game *Warhammer Fantasy Roleplay*. He has also published a small (but hopefully, growing) amount of fantasy, horror, and adventure fiction, and edited the Pegasus Books anthology *Colonial Horrors*.

Born in England, Davis grew up surrounded by the crumbling castles and drafty mansions of the English Gothic, many of which he visited with his parents or on school outings. He developed a fondness for Universal and Hammer horror films that has stayed with him ever since, along with a taste for the authors on whose work those films were based: very loosely, in most cases. He studied archaeology at Durham University in the UK, where he spent far too much time playing *Dungeons & Dragons* and trying to write.

He lives in Colorado with his wife, Jamie Paige Davis, who is also an author.